TORMENTED DREAMS

by

Rita Moyes-Vandiver

ISBN: 1-4140-6911-1 (e-book)
ISBN: 1-4140-6910-3 (Paperback)

This book is printed on acid free paper.

1st Books - rev. 02/16/04

ACKNOWLEDGEMENTS

Thanks to the source of my inner voice for giving me the actual dream, without it there may not have been a story for you to enjoy.

Thanks to my cousin, who is in narcotic surveillance, for his expertise.
Thanks to Susan and Kim. Thanks to Randy and Rusty S., Pam and Jack, Chris and Donna for their computer help.
Many thanks to my "readers" who test marketed TORMENTED DREAMS for me prior to my decision to go public. Thanks to Marcia, Brenda, Vikki, DeeDee and Martina. Your help, enthusiasm, inspirations and personal critiques were invaluable. And to my writers group for all of your support.

Thanks to Tom Dusard, Chris Denny, and Lucy Davis at 1st Books and to John McMullen, author of ROMAN: UNPARALLED OUTRAGE, for all of their help.
Thanks to KIM WHITMORE-WEBER for the photo. She really took the time and care.
If I have left anyone out, I'm sorry, thanks to you.

DEDICATION

For Randy, who has always believed, and Katie and Zach, without their love and total support this book wouldn't have been completed in seven months. My heart is with yours. Also, for my mother who has always given me her honest opinion.

CHAPTER 1

"What do you think of this?" Charlie Osswell asked his best friend Patrick Wainscott, while holding up a rather dull looking blouse.

"You can't be serious. Becky will have your hide if you get that for her birthday."

"Well you know, I want to keep things simple for the time being. She knows that and is fine with it."

"But buddy, that's not saying keep things simple, that's saying goodbye."

"Maybe you're right. It is a bit frumpy. I guess I'll keep looking," Charlie said as he put the blouse back on the rack.

"Hey it's after four, I've got to get to the bookstore before it closes," Patrick said as they were walking out of the department store. The air was still stifling and hot when they stepped out of the store, almost hard to breathe.

"If you want to go ahead, I think I'll go into Remmington's for a second and see what they have. See you in a few," Charlie said as he slipped away into Remmington's Boutique.

Patrick found Charlie standing in line in the lingerie department. His height and his sandy blonde hair made it easy to spot him over the racks of clothes. His laughter filled the air as he asked the ladies around him what they thought about his choice of the skimpy see through number he had picked out for Becky.

"This is what you call simple?" Patrick asked walking up to the counter.

"This is simple. Not much to it. It's uncomplicated just like our relationship."

"If you say so. Somehow I think you're not seeing her for her intellectual aspect."

"Look Patrick." Charlie pointed to a poster in the window on the way out. "Mariah is having her annual birthday design show tomorrow. Do you think she'll be here?"

"Don't know Charlie, considering how she left and all. It's been six months since she's been gone you know."

"Yes, I remember and I hope you know what it has cost?"

"I know very well what it cost. Certain things a person regrets for a lifetime and there is not a damn thing you can do about it. We all live with our choices don't we?" Patrick said as they waited for traffic to pass before crossing the street. "Listen I'll catch you later. I've got to pick up a few more things before going home." He headed off toward his car.

Charlie realizing at the same moment that he had forgotten to get the gift receipt from the cashier, headed back into Mariah's boutique. How he missed just talking to her. He still considered her his best friend and hoped she still felt the same. They shared a lifetime of learning, as they were friends as children. With the receipt in hand, he heard someone come up behind him.

"Margo, here are the slips…" her voice trailing off. Charlie turned to face her.

"Mariah, is it really you?" he asked as he picked her up, swung her around and then suddenly set her gently back on the floor.

"Hello Charlie, how have you been? "I've missed you too." Mariah spoke so softly; Charlie had to practically strain to hear her.

"I'm sorry honey, I shouldn't have done that I guess," Charlie said referring to the swing.

"It's okay, Charlie. I'm fine. Everything is fine."

"Is that what I think it is? I mean I don't want to hurt your feelings or anything but have you gained weight or are you..?"

"It's okay, you can say it. I'm pregnant," Mariah said. "Lets go upstairs to my office and have a talk." She took his arm in hers. Charlie couldn't help but notice how beautiful she still was, now even more so. Her blonde mid-length locks cascading around her shoulders, her blue eyes were darker than usual, like sapphires. In spite of her pregnancy her slight build still held grace and elegance all wrapped up together. She carried herself differently and it wasn't due to the pregnancy either. This woman beside him was a different person than the one he knew six months ago. He wondered how far along in her pregnancy she was, but didn't dare ask.

Sitting in the office, Mariah offered him a cup of coffee and a stale donut. How many times had they shared a moment in this very same office? Its antique cherry furniture accented the white and gold damask curtains on the large window that overlooked the front of the boutique and down onto the street below.

"Nothing has changed in here," Charlie said. "But you shouldn't be eating this junk should you?"

"Don't worry, I'm not. I had a staff meeting this morning. It's left over." Sitting down on the sofa next to Charlie, Mariah took his hand and squeezed it. "Now my friend, tell me what is new with you." Looking into his shopping bag, she pulled out the nightie.

"Well I was never a good boy you know. I'd like you to meet Becky sometime. I met her a couple of months after you left."

"You don't waste any time do you? I would like to meet her, but I'm not planning to stay in town very long. Maybe a day or two at the most. I have business elsewhere I need to see to."

"What about lunch tomorrow?"

"I don't know.. you know with the show tomorrow afternoon and all I don't see how I can break away."

"Come on, you've got to eat. You're after all eating for two aren't you?"

"All right, all right. I'm not going to win this one. It'll have to be early.. say elevenish, down the block at the café? You must bring this Becky."

"Not a problem, she has the day off and she'll be delighted to meet you. I think the only store she ever shops is yours."

"Good I like this woman already." The phone rang startling her. "Yes Margo? Please put him through on line two. Thank you. Excuse me one minute Charlie."

Charlie waved at her but continued to stay put on the sofa. He pretended to be enthralled in a magazine but was actually listening to her conversation and wished suddenly he had paid attention in high school French class. He never had any use learning any other language than English. She spoke it so fluently. Where did she learn it and when? The only thing he understood was a name- Jean Paul, who is he and what is he to her? The new man in her life? The baby's father? A feeling of protectiveness came over him. He had to know the answers.

"Sorry for the call," Mariah said as she hung up the phone. Charlie didn't answer at first. He didn't know how to ask, hoping she'd give a hint of how to ask. "Charlie, did you hear me?"

"Oh yeah, it's okay. Business is business right?"

3

"Yes, Charlie it's all business. He was sending his best wishes for tomorrow's show. Why are you looking like that? What's bothering you?" She was referring to his frown.

"Did I say anything?"

"No you didn't but there's something you want to ask, so ask. We never stood on formality."

"All right, you know me too well. Who is this Jean Paul and what is he to you?"

"Are you jealous? He is a business partner. Does that satisfy you?" she responded as she walked across the room to gaze out the windows.

"I didn't mean to pry. Listen maybe I better go before you kick me out of here. We'll see you at the café, right?"

"Of course, I'm looking forward to meeting Becky. Before you leave can I ask a huge favor of you?"

"Sure sweetheart, what is it?"

"I'm assuming you and Patrick are still friends. Can you please not mention to him that I'm back in town? I want to do the show and get the hell out of dodge so to speak. Can you do that for me?"

"I don't know what to say. If he asks me, you want me to lie to him? Why don't you want him to know you're here? He saw the poster on the window. He knows how important the show has always been to you. Do you really think you can pull this one off?"

"This year's show is by invitation only. There'll be some press there too. By the way you'll need these." She handed two gold embossed invitations to him. "I'd rather not run into him under the circumstances. The last thing I need in my life right now is stress."

"Mariah, Patrick still cares for you. I think he knows what he threw away. What you and he had was special. You can't turn your back on that. He is truly sorry."

"The operative word is "was" and don't forget that." Charlie came around to the back of the desk and gently placed his hands on her shoulders. "Charlie don't give me that bull! He cares no more for me now as he did that night when he tossed me over. He'd have more compassion for a dog that was hit by a car than what he showed me.. for us that night. I can't forget that, I won't forget that!"

"I know it was a hard time. I was there for you remember? I won't say anything unless he directly asks. Is that okay with you?"

4

"If that's all I get I guess I'll have to settle for it."

"By the way dear, where are you staying?" Charlie asks as he kisses her on the cheek.

"Here, in the studio apartment of course."

"Call me. You have my cell if you need anything," Charlie said as he closed the door behind him. He had the feeling there was a lot more to this story than she was letting on and he would find out what it was. What was the real reason Mariah didn't want Patrick to know she was here? This was one time he wasn't sure he could keep her request. He would almost bet Patrick would know by the end of tomorrow if she were here or not.

The morning sun came beaming in through the window. It promised to be another hot day. How Mariah had started to hate the summer days in Southern California. Six months ago it didn't seem so bad but then again she wasn't pregnant either. The thought crossed her mind as she pulled the drapes to shut out the day a little while longer. She woke an hour later with a mixture of feelings, excitement for the show to begin and to be over at the same time. She was anxious because she had the feeling the day was not going to be routine. Mariah washed her face and put the coffee on. he wasn't supposed to drink it but she needed it to clear her thoughts first thing of a morning. What would she do if she did see Patrick? What would he do when he saw her? Mariah decided she couldn't nor wouldn't hide the baby. She had nothing to be ashamed of. This is 2004 after all and not the 1800's. The quicker the show was over, the quicker she could start preparing to go back home. Where ever home is she thought- her small cottage in Avondale, New England? At least she could relax on her own piece of coastline with the quiet beautiful solitude of the ocean lapping at her door. Then again there is her apartment she rents in New Orleans at Jean Paul's expense and suggestion of course since they had mutual business there. And there was always Jean Paul's estate in the south of France where she spent the past few months. He had invaluable connections all over the world. She would not sever those ties. If she was going to make a good living for her child, this was the only way. She had to concentrate on creating and promoting her designs.

The boutique was a final gift her father had given her before he passed away from cancer. He had never mentioned he was ill. Maybe he knew she couldn't have stood the news since her mother had passed on a year before. She had felt closer to her father than any other family member. Mariah had loved her mother but she always seemed more concern about her younger brother Sam. She hadn't seen Sam since their father's funeral. There was no telling where he was but she was sure he would surface when he needed to be bailed out of trouble. He never knew her unless it benefited him. Somehow Mariah felt her father knew Sam was mother's favorite so he seemed to always be there for her no matter what it took. She never understood how much he was there for her and how much she needed him until after he was gone. "Daddy always knew I wanted my own boutique so I could design and sell my own label. Heaven why am I thinking about these things? This is not the day to be getting mushy. I've got to keep a clear head. Too much to do, too much to do." Mariah suddenly realized she was talking out loud and wiped a tear from her cheek. She ate a light breakfast, took her medications and decided to put on the silky mid-length light rose satin dress with the sheer cream floral jacket. It was one of the first maternity designs she had done. Jean Paul had told her many times it was one of his favorites and how becoming she looked in it. She had to look her best today no matter what happened. Just as Mariah and Margo were going through the final preparations for the show the clock struck eleven.

"Oh my." Looking up to see the time. "I have a lunch date with Charlie and Becky at the café down the block," Mariah grabbed her jacket, purse and phone and headed out the front door. "You have my cell, call if need to. Thanks for your help," she said as she cleared the doorway.

Down the block Charlie and Becky had just been seated at a booth when Charlie's cell phone rang. "Hello, hi buddy, what's up?"

"What are you doing this afternoon?" Patrick asks.

"Ah, Becky and I have plans later. Why?"

"No reason. It's probably better I do this by myself anyway," Patrick hung up before Charlie could respond and just as Mariah walked up to the table.

"Hi, sorry I'm late. I lost track of time with the show and all. By the way you left these on my desk." She handed the invitations to Charlie. Becky took one and looked at it.

"Beautiful engraving. Why the invitations?" Becky asks.

"Decided to do something different and fun this year. It's a formal affair by the way, jacket, tie, dresses are required. There will be refreshments and finger foods so please come hungry, in case no one else shows up."

"I don't really think you have to worry about that hon., your shows are always captivating." Charlie squirmed in his seat when Becky kicked him under the table. "Ouch! Where are my manners? Rebecca Browning, please meet Mariah Remmington. Mariah please meet Rebecca."

"Rebecca, it is nice to meet you," Mariah extended her hand across the table.

"Please call me Becky. Rebecca sounds so stodgy for a twenty-three year old, don't you think? You don't think I'm too young for Charlie do you? I mean since he's thirty-two, you know what I mean?" Becky asked as she flipped her long black hair over her shoulders and flashed her big smile and green eyes toward Charlie.

"Oh by the way, happy birthday, Mariah. This isn't much but what do I get a woman who sells her own clothing designs in her own store?" Charlie hands her a card with a check in it.

"My yes, Mariah, happy birthday. I didn't know. How old are you?" Becky asks. This time it was Charlie's turn to do a kick under the table. Becky looked a little sheepish.

"I'm sorry Mariah, I didn't mean anything by that. I guess I'm just nervous meeting you and all."

"Becky it's okay. Please don't worry. If you don't mind talking about something other than birthdays I would appreciate it," Mariah replies just at the waiter came to get their orders. Food didn't appeal to Mariah at this moment, she felt nauseous all day but ordered a spinach salad and a very tall glass of ice water. That was the only thing she really wanted. Charlie kept the conversation going well. He was always good at social affairs and just to have around to listen and a shoulder to cry on every once in a while. Mariah's cell rang just as the food came.

"Sorry. Hello. They did what? No. No. That's not correct. I didn't order that. Everything was suppose to be gold and white, not lavender. I'm on my way, keep them there until I get there." Mariah hung up. "Sorry guys but I

7

do have to go. Some jerk screwed up my floral order," Mariah said as she got up.

"Mariah you haven't eaten, take your order with you," Becky suggested. Even Charlie had noticed she looked tired today.

"You'll need your strength," Charlie urged her.

"I'll get something later. I'm really not very hungry anyway. I'm so glad we got together today. Maybe we can talk after the show. I really want your opinion," Mariah leaned over and kissed Charlie.

"See ya later and she's lovely," she whispered in his ear. "Kim please put everyone's meal on the boutique's account," Mariah told the waitress as she headed out the door to her car parked outside.

"Is that her car?" Becky was stunned.

"She must have traded cars after she left. She had an old eighty-six Toyota before. I'm glad she's got something better, you know with the baby coming and all." Charlie couldn't help but wonder how she could afford a new white Mercedes S600. He knew the flagship's sticker price is over a hundred thousand and wondered if this Jean-Paul character had anything to do with it.

The boutique was closed to accommodate the show. Mariah had decorated the entire boutique in candles, gold and white Lilies and Roses. The chairs were facing the circular staircase presuming this is where the models would be appearing. On the far side of the room, some racks had been moved and in place was a buffet table loaded with various finger sandwiches, vegetable platters, pate, chilling Champaign and a huge three-tier cake decorated in the theme of gold and white of course.

By the time Patrick had arrived and realized it was a tie and invitation only affair, the show had already began. The doorman she hired insisted he show an invitation, since he had none and didn't notice Charlie or Becky sitting up front, all he could do was to stand outside looking in. Did she do the invitation bit just to keep him away? To prove some point to him? He was thinking about this when Margo came up and spoke with the doorman. They left together. Now was his time to get inside since the doors had not been secured. The doorman was probably not planning to be that long from his post. Patrick quietly slipped in, he glanced around for somewhere to sit so that he wouldn't be noticed. Just his luck, most of the racks had been rolled away. He did find a thick palm tree in the back corner so he slid beside it and found that he had a pretty good view of the staircase and the models. The designs were particularly intriguing this year with a new emphasis on maternity wear. She had never done that type of thing before. Why not he thought. It would be a moneymaker, that couldn't be denied. There were always going to be pregnancies. As the show was about to come to an end, Margo introduced Mariah. She descended the staircase dressed in a full white and gold off the shoulder empire waist chiffon mid-length gown. Her hair was pulled up in an elegant twist. How he wanted to put his fingers in it and pull it down.

"God, she is most beautiful thing that ever walked on this planet," he said to himself out loud but there was no one close by to hear him. He picked up there was something different about her but couldn't place it. If he could just find the opportunity to speak with her he would. He had to; he couldn't leave this afternoon without doing so.

The reception took forever. Slowly walking around the room and listening to the various conversations, it seemed the show was a success in every way. The designs were being ordered and bought right and left. Everyone was enjoying the food and drink. He was very happy things were going so well for Mariah but one thing bothered him. How could she afford all this "style"? She was far from being poor since the boutique was doing all right, but she wasn't exactly rich either. If she had said something to him about helping her to do this type of show when they were together he would have gladly helped her out financially. After another hour or so the crowd started to thin out. Still being careful not to be seen, he noticed Charlie and Becky speaking with Mariah. He made his way close enough to hear them.

"I'm so glad you could make it. How did you like the show?"

"Oh Mariah, it was gorgeous. The dresses were unbelievable. I can't wait to get the two I ordered," Becky said.

"Two? You didn't have to order one. That wasn't necessary."

"Yes it was and it is for me," Becky said laughing.

"Sweetheart you did a wonderful job. This has got to be one of the best shows you've given. Keep this up and this little one will not want for anything. I'm proud of you and how far you've come since six months ago."

Charlie leaned over and kissed her on the cheek and at the same time patted her stomach.

"Are you feeling okay?" Becky asks Mariah.

"Sure, why?"

"You look a little pale and very tired. Did you eat anything this afternoon?" Charlie was concerned at this point when he saw the Mariah's color drain out of her.

"No I guess I didn't. There was too much to do, please don't worry. We're fine. I just need to sit and relax a minute after everyone leaves." Charlie led Mariah to a chair and made her sit. Becky joined her. Charlie came back a few minutes later with a plate of food and bottled water. He handed them to Mariah.

"Here dear. Eat!"

"I will later."

"No now! If you won't do it for yourself do it for the baby." He pushed the food at her again.

"I'm not wasting away you know."

"Shut up and eat."

"I love you too, Charlie. Now, Becky, please get him home and keep him busy."

"I hope we get to see each other again before you leave town, Mariah. Thanks for a terrific afternoon. I know I've enjoyed it," Becky expressed.

Mariah hugged both of them in return. In a way she was glad to be back home if anything just to get to see Charlie again.

Patrick couldn't hear everything but he did catch a glimpse of Charlie patting her stomach. He wondered what that was all about. Margo handed a floral box to Mariah.

"These just came for you," she remarked. "I bet I know who they're from." Mariah opened the box and gasped. Patrick tried to get closer to hear. Mariah pulled out two-dozen white, long stem roses dipped in gold. The box fell to the floor.

"Who sent them?" Becky squealed with delight.

"I can't find the card. Wait a minute, here it is," Charlie replied as he bent to retrieve the box and search through the tissue paper. Before Mariah could take the card out of his hands Becky, grabbed it.

"The show was breathtaking. The closed circuit worked. Congratulations *mon amour*. Talk to you soon. Jean Paul." As Becky read she waved her hands in front of her like she was having a hot flash.

"Nothing going on, huh?" Charlie said low.

"I didn't ask for any remarks did I? Just go and live your own lives."

Mariah turned him around to face the door and nudged him while she laughed.

Patrick wasn't sure about all of the events that he witnessed but one thing was for sure he didn't like the roses. Who is this character? Did he hear the name right? Jean Paul? He was jealous and he knew it. He knew too that most of time his jealousy didn't benefit him. He'd have to watch it if he was to get Mariah back. That was the thing she really didn't like about him. Everyone was almost gone except for Margo. Mariah was standing with her back to him talking to her. Now was the time to make his move.

"Hello Mariah, happy birthday." Patrick was standing behind her. Mariah had a look of shear surprise on her face as she turned around to look on the man she had lived with and loved for the past five years. He hadn't changed much but then it had only been six months since she left. He still excited her but he must not know it, not now she thought, especially not now. Patrick is a man of medium but muscular build. He had obviously continued to work out in her absence. His black hair had grown a bit longer, waving just above his shirt collar with a strand or two falling on his forehead in a slight curl. He had grown a moustache. She discovered she liked the look on him. His blue eyes shined bright with excitement as he drew in his breath sharply with the sight of how beautiful she looked. There was something different about her.

"Patrick, what are you doing here? How did you get in?"

"I have my ways, my dear. Do you think I'd let this day go by without wishing you a happy birthday? By the way I want to congratulate you on a fabulous show. You really out did yourself this time. Everyone will expect same type of show next year. You've worked hard on your designs and it showed. I'm proud of you."

"Please Patrick, you're proud of me! What gives you the right to feel that way about me? If you don't mind I trust you can find your way out just like you did in. I have things to do." Mariah's anger flared at him with full force. He wasn't quite prepared for that. She turned her back on him but she felt his hand on her elbow. He wasn't going to make this easy. Damn him. She didn't feel like dealing with this right now. He had caught her off guard and that wasn't fair. He turned her around to face him.

"Mariah, I can't leave until we have had a chance to talk. Can we go upstairs to your office for privacy?"

"I said, I don't think we have anything to discuss," she said looking over her shoulder for the doorman.

"Mariah, do you want me to call the police?" Margo caught the anxious look Mariah gave toward the door and decided to step in to help. Patrick removed his hand from her arm.

"Ah, no Margo, not just yet. I can handle Mr. Wainscott." Mariah wanted to avoid a scene in front of Margo. She trusted Margo with the store but still didn't want all of her past aired publicly.

"Alright let's go upstairs." He nodded and escorted her up the stairs. He took notice of how careful she was being ascending them and gathering her gown so she wouldn't trip on it. Just as they reached the landing Margo rushed up behind them.

"Here you forgot these. They need water right away." She handed the boxed roses to Patrick. "You can carry these for her can't you?" She then disappeared calling over her shoulder to Mariah, "I'll lock up. See you in the morning."

"I'm getting a vase for the roses and changing into something more comfortable." Choosing an oversize tee shirt and baggy lightweight pants she then went into the bathroom splashed cold water on her face and then went to the kitchenette for the vase. She felt a little better but not much. She found Patrick at her office window holding a rose. She was waiting for the explosion she knew was coming. Nothing was said for a few minutes as she continued to place the roses in the vase. Then it came but it wasn't what she expected.

"YOU can handle me, huh?" he said with a sound of disbelief and a grin.

"Stop it! You know what I meant." Mariah looked over her shoulder catching his grin.

"Who is Jean Paul?"

Mariah starts to laugh; "Everyone seems to be asking me that lately. A friend if you must know. He has contacts in the industry."

"How well do you know him? Does he have a last name?"

"Did you come here to ask me about Jean Paul or did you have something else on your mind?" She swiftly changed the subject. She didn't want to reveal too much about Jean Paul. He did like his privacy.

"Okay, we won't discuss him any more. What I really want to say is that I don't like the way things ended between us. I am sorry. I was a fool to ever push you away. I will always regret what I did to you. Are you back to stay?"

"No and I really don't want to hear what you have to say."

"You're going to listen to me. I tried to find you. I even hired a private investigator. It was like you vanished off the face of the earth. Where did you go? Do you know what you put me through when I couldn't find you? I was sick with worry then I heard somewhere that your designs were being manufactured. Charlie and I knew you had to be okay and not floating somewhere in a river."

"That's sweet. Do you think I would even consider doing something like that? I don't think so! I can't believe that you hired a P.I." She was angry again. "What about what you put me through? You are the one that called it quits after five years. I gave you five years of my life! How dare you Patrick, I didn't so much even look at another man. I was so much in love with you; I would have done anything for you back then. You know why I walked out on you! It wasn't me in bed with ..what ever her name is; and in our bed too. You didn't even have the decency to hide your affair. Maybe I became too dependent on you. You didn't even give me any warning that you weren't happy with us. So don't talk to me about what you went through. I don't want to know. What about me? It was like you stabbed me with a knife and twisted it till there was nothing left. What was I suppose to do? Stand back and let you keep doing it, over and over again. Not me! You may burn me once but never again." Patrick walked over to her and tried to embrace her but she pulled away and placed her desk between them.

"I'm sorry. I'll say again and again if you want me to. I didn't mean to hurt you. I don't know what I was saying or doing that night. I was never unhappy with us, with you. I guess I thought I was being pressured somehow. We'd been through a lot this past year. I felt things were changing for us and didn't know what direction it was taking. I got scared, things were going out of my control, and so I took control. It wasn't the right thing to do. Maybe I just wanted to shake things up, I did that didn't I? I never meant to make you leave our home and never come back. If it means anything I never saw that woman again."

"True confessions, huh?"

"It is the truth. I've regretted loosing you every day for the past six months. Can you forgive me?"

"Now if that's all you have to say, you can leave now. You know the back door. I'm tired and want to go to bed."

"It's only seven. I thought maybe you would consider having dinner with me tonight? Come to think about it you don't look so good at the moment. Are you feeling all right? You're flushed." He noticed how deep red her lips looked and she had taken off her makeup when she was changing.

"Nothing for you to be concerned about, I assure you Patrick." He brushed his hand across her cheek.

"No fever, that's good." If he only knew what his touch did to her. How it seared through her skin.

"I think I need some water." She started to move past him.

"Sit, I'll get it." Many times he had been in the apartment. It felt like home to him and everything was still in its place. He handed the water to her. "Now what about dinner?"

"I said no."

"Tomorrow?"

"I won't be here."

"Where are you running to? Or is it you are just running away from me?" He was just inches from her face.

"Why would I do that?"

"You tell me. I don't believe you can just turn your back on the last five years. I don't believe you when you say you don't feel anything for me. You are a passionate woman. You put your heart into everything, no matter what it is."

"Not any more Patrick, things change. My priorities have changed. Too much has happened, too many changes and I'm one of those changes." Mariah says as she gets up and heads toward the door. He follows her, stops her by her elbow and stands face to face with her.

"Mariah, I still love you. More now than ever." As he embraces her, his one hand at the small of her back for support and the other tracing her jaw line ever so lightly. She was trying to make sure she kept at least a foot away from him but it was hard considering how tight he was trying to hold her against him.

"Patrick don't."

"I need you. Stay in town, come home." Before she could answer his mouth was on hers, kissing her as deeply as he could. His tongue felt hers.

The excitement that came to Mariah surprised her. How could he know she still loved him? She must not let it show. She must get out of his arms now. Her head was telling her the right thing to do but her heart desired only one thing, to go home, to their home. How she missed the ranch and Jezebel. She was becoming confused with every minute he was with her, so close he is, she thought. She had to keep to her plan. How could she believe anything he told her? Before Mariah could pull away from his embrace his hand came up to touch her breast. The fabric of her tee shirt seems to melt away under his touch.

She felt the heat of his hand as he tenderly caressed her but then he suddenly pulled her so close to him she couldn't stop him. His hand started down her side and stopped. Stepping back from her with wide eyes he asks.

"What the..?" Mariah slumps over in a faint. He catches her and carries her to the bed, suddenly realizing what her "changes are" he went to the bathroom to get a cold cloth. Just as he decides to call for an ambulance she wakes. He places the phone down and sits down next to her.

"I didn't think I had that kind of effect on you?"

"What happened?" She started to sit up.

"Don't, not yet. You fainted. This may not be the time to ask but are you pregnant?"

"You evidently have discovered that fact. Yes I am." Flabbergasted Patrick didn't know what to say for a minute or two. He walked over to the table and leaned on it keeping his back toward her.

"How? I mean whom? When? Are you married? I mean am I making a move on someone's wife?" He turned to face her. She was sitting up on the bed.

"No. I'm not married. I believe you know how it happens. That's all you need to know."

"By the look of things you must be at least half way through. Who is the father? I'll kill him if he took advantage of you."

"It wasn't like that.

"Is the father this Jean Paul person? I want to talk to him."

"Why? We're over remember? And no it's not Jean Paul's. Who the father of my child is, is not any of your concern. Understand that now once and for all!" Mariah says. "The father is not in my life."

"What kind of a man is he to walk away from you and his child?"

Patrick was so angry he couldn't look at her for a while. Was he angry with her for allowing herself to get pregnant, for having that kind of fling? Was he angry with himself for pushing her away like he did? Was he the real cause of this situation? He wasn't sure what the answers was to his feelings but he didn't like the questions. Now what to do? She had said there were a lot of changes, there sure was. Charlie. Charlie might know something, after all he was talking to her, he was patting her stomach. He knew! Charlie knew and didn't tell him she was in town or that she's pregnant. He was going to find out why. He was trying hard to gain his composure again.

"Are you okay? Do you need anything?"

"No, just some rest. Please go now. I just want to sleep. It's been a long day," Mariah said as she lay back down, turned to her left side and slipped into a deep sleep. Patrick sat on the bed beside her for a long time watching her. Wanting to hold her so much and to protect her and the child but didn't dare. He finally turned off the lights, went downstairs, reset the alarm and locked the back door of the boutique behind him.

CHAPTER 2

Becky answers the door. It was just his luck she was there. He would have to do something about that. What needed to be said was better off being said without extra ears.

"Hi Patrick. What brings you by?"

"Hey bud, come on in and get a load off." Charlie came through the front foyer on his way to the living room. "What can we do for you?" Patrick follows him and Becky into the room. It was a spacious room with just the necessary furniture in it. No clutter at all. The south wall was an entire window looking out into a neglected garden that surrounded an inground swimming pool.

"When are you going to do something about that ugly view?" Patrick laughed.

"I'm waiting on someone to take the task on. Gardening is not my thing. I can't grow anything and you know that."

"I've got plans to try it next spring," Becky chided in. "Look at the time! I'm so sorry guys but I must take my leave. I have a job to go to in the morning unlike both of you. Call me tomorrow," she addressed Charlie as she kissed him bye. "Bye Patrick, its nice seeing you again. I'll show myself out."

After hearing the front door shut Charlie asks, "So what's up?" thinking this probably has to do with Mariah.

"You knew she was in town. Why didn't you tell me?" Patrick asks.

"I only found out myself. Remember when I went back for the receipt? I ran into her then."

"Why didn't you call me?"

"She ask me not to," Charlie drew in a long breath as he said it.

"Why? I don't understand that."

"Come on buddy, with the history between you two. Maybe it's too painful for her."

"Maybe because she didn't want me to find out about the baby." The look on Charlie's face confirmed what he already knew.

"How did you find out?"

"I was at the show. We talked afterwards."

"And?"

"And do you know who she is involved with? Who the baby's father is?"

"No, I don't. I'm not sure how deeply involved she is with anyone at the moment. She hasn't spoken to me about anyone." There was no need to mention the phone call he over heard.

"Who is this Jean Paul?"

"Again, I don't know much about him except he's a business partner or something." Charlie knew he must have seen the roses.

"It's the something I'm afraid of. I'm pretty ticked off at you for not letting me know she's back." Patrick was pacing the floor.

"Man I told her if you came to ask I would be straight but she made me promise not to volunteer any information. She's one of my best friends, you're the other. I'm in a spot here you know. I've known her a lot longer than you, if I remind you and that is a friendship I don't want to throw away.

"You just love to remind me of that fact every chance you get don't you?"

"You know I don't do that. You're just sore at the moment. We all make mistakes, some of them are just worse than others."

"I didn't come here for a lecture. Who do you think you are? You don't have a clean record either." Patrick was feeling argumentative. Charlie was his best friend but he happens to be the closest on which to vent his frustration on.

Charlie could read his moods. He had been very moody in the past few months so he decided to let him sit in silence. Charlie turned on the television. He finally spoke.

"So how do you feel about the baby?"

"How would you feel, knowing the woman you love has been with another man and carrying his child. I'm mad as hell about it. I'd like to kill him." Patrick inhaled slowly, trying to control his temper.

"Pat, it wasn't like she betrayed you. That's probably the way she felt too."

"I know that. It's just not that simple is it. There's more here. But what?"

"Tell you what, come on." Charlie turned off the television, grabbed his keys off the coffee table. "Lets go get a drink. We'll try to figure out women over a cold one." As they headed out the door Patrick stopped. There was feeling of uneasiness in his body. He was still feeling angry over Charlie keeping secrets, over Mariah and the baby and not knowing whom this Jean Paul is. There was something else he couldn't put his finger on, it just kept nagging him. Just as they parked in front of the bar it hit Patrick. Something wasn't right with Mariah.

"Let's forget the drink. Don't ask me why but we need to get to Mariah now."

"Come on buddy, leave her be tonight. Talk to her in the morning. It's after ten already."

"I mean it Charlie, we've got to get over there now." Seeing his determination Charlie had no choice to follow his request.

"Okay, okay hold on." Charlie turned his truck around and headed back toward the boutique.

"See, she's here. There's her car."

"I don't see it."

"There in front of the store, the white Mercedes."

"Whoa! How can she afford the payments on that? It's new isn't it?" Patrick commented as they pulled up in front of the store. At the same time they both noticed an orangey-yellow glow from inside.

"The store is on fire!" Patrick jumps out of the truck reaching the front door before Charlie. Charlie had left his truck in the middle of the deserted street.

"I'll call 911."

"I can't get the alarm to go off. I need something heavy to break the window!" Patrick said looking around for something to throw.

"Wait, I've got a baseball bat in the truck."

"The place is starting to fill with smoke hurry! Mariah must still be upstairs."

It all came together at once, the glass breaking, the alarm screaming and the sounds of the sirens coming closer. In a second Patrick was up the stairs. Charlie went to the back of the store to see if he could do anything about the fire.

"Hello, anyone in here?" The firemen came running in with their hoses.

"Back here!" Charlie called. The smoke was getting thicker and thicker, it was hard to breath. He headed for the door there was nothing he could do.

"Get this man out of here. We'll take care of this. Anyone else in here?"

"Yes, two people upstairs. The woman is pregnant."

"Lets go men, get this fire out." The smoke was starting to fill the staircase well. The firemen met Patrick at the top of the stairs with Mariah in his arms unconscious. It was hard for Patrick to see, the smoke burning his lungs but he wasn't going to let go of her until she was safely outside. He told the firemen that Charlie was downstairs somewhere. One of them replied they had him out already. They cleared the front doors, Patrick tried to inhale the fresh air but it hurt too much. He was still holding Mariah close.

"Get a gurney!" one of the paramedics called as he took Mariah from Patrick's arms and placed her on the gurney.

"Help her!" was all he could say. Charlie sitting in the ambulance being treated for a burn on his arm got up and ran over to them.

"Is she alright?"

"I don't know, man. I found her unconscious."

"Dispatch, we have a late twenty to middle thirty year old woman," Patrick interrupted the EMT. "She's thirty."

"Correction, thirty year old. She appears to be approximately twenty-four weeks gestational. She is unconscious. Respiration is weak and rapid, pulse is weak," his words trailing off when he was handed Mariah's purse.

"Here Danny, we found this. There's insulin inside. Danny took the vial and the syringes out. He noticed a gold chain and tag outlined under Mariah's tee shirt. He pulls it out. "Oh wonderful," he says.

"What is that?' Patrick asks.

"Establish a I.V. Get her on the left side, get the pillow between her knees. More oxygen. Danny was telling his partner what to do then began to talk to dispatch again. He looked up at Patrick and Charlie standing over him. "You didn't know she is diabetic and has hypertension on top of that?"

"No," both guys said at once.

"Dispatch we're on our way. We may have a diabetic coma along with the fire trauma. Repeat please?"

Patrick's mind could not comprehend what Danny was saying at the moment. It was like everything was blocked out but he did see that they were giving her an injection. One of the other fireman was trying to get him to sit down so he could be examined. Charlie was trying to do the same. Suddenly everything seemed to snap back into place.

"Dispatch, we are on our way. ETA approximately five minutes."

"Please! I'm alright! I don't need this." Jerking away just in time to climb into the back of the ambulance before the door closed and drove away. "Is she going to be alright? Is the baby alright?" Patrick wanted answers.

"I'm sorry sir, I can't hear at the moment." The EMT was taking her vitals.

He sat back praying as hard as he could to please let Mariah and the child be okay. The child may not be his but suddenly it didn't matter as long as he had her. Her color wasn't good. She is so gray he thought to himself. What was taking them so long to get to the hospital? All he could do was to keep out of the way and watch the EMT work. How he hated the feeling of no control. He closed his eyes and had a flash back to the last time they rode in an ambulance together. He had come home from a run to the feed store and found Mariah sitting on the bathroom floor crying. When he went to help her up he discovered the blood. She had miscarried their child without either one of them knowing she was pregnant at the time. It was after that when things started changing for them. She had a hard time dealing with the loss and no matter what he did or said it didn't help. He prayed this would not be a repeat of that.

Charlie followed the ambulance to the hospital, there he found Patrick coming out of an exam room. "Are you okay?"

"Yea. They insisted on checking me out," he said while coughing. "I'm fine, just inhaled some smoke. They're giving me a prescription. Have you heard anything about Mariah yet?"

"No I just got here. I take it you haven't either?" Just then a tall slim woman with brown hair wearing a lab coat come out of the cubical toward them., she held a medical file in her hand,

"Is there someone here for Ms. Remmington?"

"I am," both Charlie and Patrick said together.

"Good, I'm Dr. Vivian Miles. Are you two relatives?"

21

"We're the closest she has. I'm Patrick Wainscott and this is Charlie Osswell."

"I need to get more information about the baby. Do you know her OB/GYN?"

"No. She just got back into town a day or so ago."

"So there's a good chance her doctor is out of town."

"She's been gone six months but where we're not sure. She hasn't told us."

"Okay, then we'll do an ultrasound to check things out there and see how far along she really is."

"How is Mariah? What's going on?" Patrick asks.

"She is in what we call a Diabetic Coma. She has developed a fever and we are working to get that down as well as stabilizing her blood sugar levels."

"This isn't related to the fire then?" Charlie asks.

"I don't think so. You two must be the ones who called in the fire. Thank God you came across it when you did, she and her child would not be here now if you hadn't pulled her out. She would never have heard the fire alarms in a coma."

"Can I see her?"

"Not yet Mr. Wainscott, we'll let you know when." Dr. Miles turned to leave.

"Wait Dr.! Is she and the baby going to be okay?" Charlie asked.

"We need to see what happens over the next few hours. It's a critical situation. The fact that she has high blood pressure doesn't help. Too many variables can happen. We're doing everything we can." Vivian touched his shoulder and left.

Neither one of them knew what to say so they stood there looking at each other. Both thinking the same thing, how could they lose her. They both love her each in their own way. This couldn't be happening. Not to Mariah, not to that unborn child. The only thing they could do was wait. After an hour or so Charlie decided to get some coffee since it looked like it was going to be a long night. Finally Mariah is wheeled out of the ER still unconscious.

"What's going on?" Charlie was the first to see her.

"We have a room for her now, 3012," the orderly says.

"I know you all are worried and she has a ways to go but the fever is starting to come down and her sugar levels are better."

"Does that mean she and the baby are going to make it?"

"Mr. Wainscott, it means things are better than what they were when she came in. Mariah still has a lot of work ahead of her. She has got to have the fight in her."

After Mariah had been settled in her room, Patrick sat beside her holding her hand. She still didn't look good to him. The only reassurance he had was the sound of the monitors hooked to Mariah and the baby. For the first time he realized he was hearing the baby's heart beat. It was a miracle but he still wanted to know who the baby's father was. The doctor had told them the ultrasound showed no signs of problems with the child, which was good news. She also told them she thought the child to be at the end of the second trimester. Patrick was falling asleep when Charlie stepped into the room. He had been in and out all night. Charlie was one person who couldn't sit still if he had to.

"Buddy, why don't you go stretch out in the waiting room for a few minutes. No one is out there. I'll stay with her."

"No man, I don't want to leave her. She needs to know I'm here for her."

"I'm sure she does Patrick. However we need to check her over now. If you both would please step out, we'll let you know when we are done." Deloris who is an R.N. has known both Charlie and Mariah since they were children. She met Patrick right after he moved to Crystal River, to escape the fast life of Los Angeles and started seeing Mariah. Deloris showed the men the door. They sat in the waiting room drinking coffee and dozing off and on.

It was about two o'clock in the morning when it began to rain. Someone told them the forecast warned of thunderstorms for the rest of the morning. Patrick thought it would match his mood that was brewing slow and steady.

"Pat, you left your top down on the car. Give me keys. I'll go home and put it up before everything gets soaked. You stay here in case she wakes up." Charlie knew his best friend took pride in his red 1968 Shelby Cobra.

He had a passion for the classics and had restored this one after finding it wrecked in a junkyard.

"Do you mind? I didn't even think about that." Patrick handed the keys over.

"Be back in a little while. Call me on the cell if anything happens."

Patrick snuck into Mariah's room every chance he got only to be told to leave the room by that old stodgy Deloris. He never really knew how to take her. She wouldn't let him stay with Mariah no matter how much he tried to flirt with her, which just about killed him considering how old and ugly she was. She did promise to come and get him if there were any changes. Knowing he couldn't win this battle he finally sat in the corner of the waiting room watching some old movie on TV until he fell asleep. He woke up to the sun shinning through the window, glancing at the clock striking six; he knew he had been asleep for three hours. No one had come to get him. What had happened in those three hours?

Stepping inside Mariah's room he saw Charlie sitting beside her bed. Looking up from reading a manuscript Charlie looked tired, too.

"Hi, feel better now that you got some sleep?"

Patrick ran his hands through his hair, "No. How is she?"

"Deloris said her vitals are getting stronger. The doctor should be in soon, then we'll know more."

"Did you get any rest?"

"Not much but I did get soaked trying to get your top up. I had trouble getting it to stay up. By the time I decided to give up and just move your car in my garage, and mine out I was soaked. It's pretty wet inside. I have some fans on it. Sorry."

"Don't worry about it. I'll just have it detailed somewhere. What's that you're reading?"

"It was delivered this morning with this note." Charlie handed the note to Patrick.

"Hey look at this. You've got a movie deal if you want it."

"It's a small role but the money isn't bad and I could use it right now. But the best thing is it isn't a long time commitment. They say I would only need to shoot a couple of weeks, three at tops."

"Where at?"

"Boston."

"Are you going to accept?"

"I don't know yet. I have until tomorrow to give my answer." Just then Dr. Miles steps in.

"Good morning gentlemen. How is our patient? Better than what you two look like. You both have been here all night?"

"Don't sweet talk us doc. Our hearts are only for her. Tell us some good news."

"Well Mr. Osswell, that much I can do. Her sugar levels are normal now. She is stable. Everything looks good so far. Hopefully she'll be waking soon from the coma. The signs are good so the best thing you two can do is to keep talking to her. Sometimes patients report they can hear everything around them when they are in a coma. I don't believe that she is that deep now." They spent the rest of the morning talking about anything and everything to Mariah, holding her hands, recalling the past memories they made together. Then suddenly ever so slightly Mariah's fingers moved while Charlie held her hand.

"Oh my word! She moved her fingers! Get the nurse."

"What's up guys?" The nurse asks as she came in. Deloris had left at seven and Patrick was glad of that.

"She moved. She's waking up right?" Charlie was so excited. Patrick was holding his breath. He knew that sometimes a person in a coma would have involuntary muscle spasms. He hoped he was wrong.

"Let me check her out. Mariah can you hear me? If you can squeeze my hand." No response. "Mariah, if you can hear me move your fingers."

Still no response. "Her vitals are back to normal. I don't know for sure what that was you felt but I am going to call the doctor and let her know. Keep working with her. I do believe she knows you are here." With that the nurse moved quietly out of the room.

Just then Charlie's cell rang. "Hello. Listen I've got to call you back in a minute. I can't use this phone here." He hung up. "I'll be back in a few. Got to take this, it's about the movie." Charlie headed out the door and Patrick was glad he was gone. This gave him a chance to be alone with her again.

"Mariah, come back to me. I need you in my life. I need your stubbornness. I need your passion for life. We were good for each other once. We can be good again if you just let us. I'll take care of you and the child. Mariah, damn it enough is enough! Come back to me!" Feeling very impatient, tired and anxious all rolled up into one huge emotion it all blurted out at once. He laid his head on the bed beside her still holding her hand and being careful not to disturb all the wires and IV connected to her. How could a person stand all of those contraptions? He wondered just as his eyes started to close he felt her move. When he looked up he couldn't believe his eyes. She was awake.

"Mariah. Oh my heaven! You're back. Thank God you're back." He leaned over and kissed her.

"Patrick? Where am I?" Mariah spoke softly and looking around the room.

"You gave us a scare. I found you last night unconscious. You're in Memorial Hospital."

"My baby? Is she alright?"

"Honey the baby is fine. It wasn't the baby. It was your blood sugar. It dropped too low. Did you forget to take your insulin or eat yesterday?" Then it dawned on him she said the baby was a girl. The thought had crossed his mind while he spent those long hours alone in her room last night, what if the child was his? The time span was right. Was he to have a daughter? He had to know if he was the father but how?

"I don't remember but are you sure my baby is okay?"

"Yes, that's what the doctor says."

Dr. Miles came into the room just at that moment. "Hello Mariah. I'm Dr. Vivian Miles. I'm on your case. How are you feeling? It is so good to see you awake."

"I'm confused, what happened?"

"That is what I want you to tell me. The confusion is part of the sugar problem, it will get better I promise. Do you think we can talk a little? Patrick, I need you to step out now so I can see to my patient." Patrick got up and kissed Mariah again.

"Honey, I'll be outside the door. I'm not leaving." Mariah couldn't believe her eyes. Patrick looked awful.

"You are one lucky woman to have two friends like those guys who brought you in last night," Vivian commented.

"What two guys?"

26

"Mr. Wainscott and Mr. Osswell, I think is his name. They came across the fire at the boutique and found you in a diabetic coma. If they hadn't you or your baby may not have been here today. You owe a lot to them. Patrick carried you out of the boutique."

"Wait a minute, I'm not understanding this. You said there was a fire at my store?"

"Yes, but I don't have all the details. I'm sure Patrick can help you with that. Now let's get on with our exam shall we?" The door was ajar enough that Patrick could hear a few things. He wasn't planning on telling Mariah about the fire just yet but now he would have to address the problem. He just hoped it wouldn't get her to upset. He stood there thinking how to handle that when he overheard the discussion about the baby. Dr. Miles was asking Mariah how far along she was and who her OB/GYN was.

"My doctor is Loren Rantoul. She practices in Southern France. My due date is December 26."

"I've heard of her. She lives in Marseille, doesn't she?" Mariah nodded her head. "She is one of the best OB's in the world. Specializes in high risk pregnancies doesn't she?" Again Mariah nodded her head.

"I've lost a child already and then with all my medical problems with this baby I felt I needed someone like her."

"I'll contact her office and let her know what is going on. See if I can get your file faxed here if that's okay."

"Sure. Is my daughter okay? I didn't hurt her did I?"

"So far my dear everything looks good. Remember though everything you do does affect that child. You cannot go without eating sensibly again and not taking your medication. No matter what is going on your first priority is that baby and yourself. Now if you like after I discharge you and for as long as you are in town I can continue to treat you and your baby. I am an OB/GYN as well. Will you be staying or going back to France to have the baby?"

Patrick's heart sank. He didn't hear what Mariah said. The south of France and this Jean Paul character, he had to have some answers. No wonder he couldn't find her. He was looking on the wrong continent. The P.I. couldn't come up with any leads that she left the country by plane. He didn't understand that and yet she said she was in France just now. He realized at that moment too, Mariah had confirmed the baby was due in December. It was no longer a theory. He had to be right, the baby had to be his.

Dr. Miles walked out of the room. "She wants to see you now. Mariah is very strong lady. I think she and her child will be just fine. I want to keep her here another day or so for observation. Go and talk to her but don't upset her right now. Answer her questions about the fire but play it down if you can. She does need to know." Patrick stepped in the door and drew in a deep breath.

"Hi sweetheart. The doc said you're going to be good as new in a few days. Promise me that you will never do this again," pulling the chair closer to the bed.

"Stop the bull. Tell me about the fire!"

"I was going to tell you when you were stronger. Okay, here is the deal. Charlie and I drove by your place last night, I had a feeling something was wrong. We saw the fire from the front windows. I broke it to get to you. While Charlie tried to put out the fire I found you upstairs unconscious. I was bringing you out when the emergency personnel showed up. That's pretty much it in a nut shell."

"How much damage was done? What started it?"

"The fire chief said one of the spot lights from the show was left plugged in and must have shorted out. Most of the damage is smoke but there were a few items near the back of the shop that burnt. We got there just after it started they said. Margo said all your new stuff is okay."

"Wait a minute you said you broke a window? What window?"

"I was afraid you would ask that, one of the front windows. It's okay, the police called Margo. She made sure it was boarded up last night. The glass is being replaced at my cost this morning. I'm sorry but I couldn't wait for the fire department to come. I had to get you out."

"Give me the phone. I need to call Margo."

"No you don't. You need to rest. Let me take care of this for you. Don't worry. I've been in touch with her. You can talk to her later but right now she is extremely busy. She's dealing with the insurance on the smoke damage to the store and clothes. Some of them are at the cleaners as we speak."

"What would I do without Margo?" Mariah's head was starting to hurt.

"Funny she said the same thing about you."

"OH!"

"What is it? Are you in pain? Why are you crying?" Patrick suddenly gets to his feet to summon the nurse.

"No everything is fine. The baby just kicked me. She kicked me hard. She kicked me hard." Mariah was smiling and crying at the same time.

"Can I feel? I mean do you mind?" Mariah takes his hand and places it on her stomach still crying. "I don't feel anything."

"Wait, give her a minute. There did you feel her?"

"Oh my word, I did feel her. What a kicker she is." Patrick was crying by this time too. He couldn't help it. It was such a wonderful feeling he couldn't explain except it felt like all the Christmas' in the world wrapped up in one.

After a few minutes of them sitting in silence basking in the joy of the moment Patrick tried to make his voice soft and loving before he spoke.

"Mariah, I have to ask you something. I don't want to upset you but I do need to have an answer. Am I that little girl's father? Is she ours?"

"Patrick, please don't do this. I can't tell you what you want to hear."

"Mariah, I know how far along you are. I did the math. That child could be ours unless you were unfaithful to me."

"How dare you say that to me! I was never unfaithful to you while we were together." She was getting uneasy.

"That's what I thought you'd say. So what you're saying without saying is that baby could be mine." He was still controlling his voice. His trick worked.

Before Mariah had a chance to respond the phone rang. Patrick answered it thinking it could be Margo. The operator said it was an international call.

"Just a minute." He really didn't want to hand the phone over but knew there was no other choice. "Here, its your friend."

Mariah took the phone and responded with a slight smile, *"Bonjour!"* It was Jean Paul. She spoke in French to him because Patrick was still in the room. Patrick understood enough French to know there was some talk about the boutique, her health and about the baby. A lot of references were being made about the baby and he didn't like it. He heard her tell Jean Paul

29

that she missed him and loved him. That hit hard in his gut. How could she say that? Maybe he just misunderstood, after all his French as not as fluent as hers. Neither was his Spanish he had to learn for a film once. He didn't know she knew another language but there she was speaking it like she had been born to it. What was he going to do about this guy? How could he get the truth out of Mariah about the baby?

"Here." She handed him the phone. He was so deep in thought that he didn't hear her.

"Here," Mariah said again.

"Sorry, I was thinking about something else."

"Patrick, I never said thanks. I do mean that." He had noticed her mood had softened since the phone call.

"Hey look at you beautiful! The nurses told me you were awake," Charlie said as he strode into the room. "Here these are for you," handing her some daisies.

"Thanks, put them in the water pitcher for me." Patrick's phone rang. He walks to the windows and stands with his back toward them. "Hello. What's up? They said what? No, that isn't right. Okay, I'll be there in a few minutes. Keep them there." He disconnects the line.

"Listen, I have got to go to the shop."

"Is there a problem?" Mariah asks.

"I don't think so but I'll handle it. Don't worry. The window will be fixed today I promise you." He leaned over and kissed her lightly. "I'll see you later. Love you."

"He really does love you. Why can't you ease up on him a little? He has been here all night. The man is running on pure caffeine at the moment."

"You know what he did. How can I forget that?"

"I know what he did. I'm not asking you to forget, just to forgive. He may be my best friend but we all are very capable of making mistakes. I think you still love him but you're afraid to tell him."

"Charlie, there's so much you don't know."

"Then my dear why don't you tell me what I don't know. I've got the rest of the day to give you."

"I can't."

"It's about the baby, isn't it? The night we were together. That night you two split up. It was six months ago. I've been thinking all day. You're six months along now, right? Could I be the father to your baby?"

The look on Mariah's face told him his answer. He could be. What they didn't know was Patrick was standing outside the door listening. He forgot his keys and only returned in time to hear Charlie's words and Mariah's silence. He was struck as if a lighting bolt had hit him. He was furious. The rage built up inside him. How could his best friend take advantage of his.. his what? Even though they hadn't made it legal he still felt like she was his wife all those years. Did he drive her into Charlie's arms, into his bed? It was just one night. It didn't mean that Charlie was the baby's father. He still had a chance to be everything to her and the child. They did have a healthy love life, even up to the last. That fact didn't help any. Patrick coughed before he entered the room.

"Sorry I forgot my keys."

"Everything okay buddy?" Charlie recognized the look on his face.

"No, not really. I need to talk to you outside. LIKE NOW!"

"Patrick, what's wrong? You're scaring me."

"Don't worry about anything. Come on BUDDY outside."

"I'll take care of this and be back soon. We need to talk." Charlie kisses her hand and leaves the room with Patrick.

"Okay what's up? You're in a foul mood. The coffee finally getting at you?"

"Not here in the lobby. Let's take this outside."

Charlie wondered how long Patrick was at the door. Could he have heard his conversation with Mariah about the paternity of the baby? If so, he had to be ready for anything.

Mariah couldn't do anything but lie there and cry. She had gotten things so messed up that there was no turning back now. Why did she go see Charlie that night? Because she needed her best friend that's why. She needed to feel loved that night, like she mattered to someone. He needed the same thing as it turned out. His grandmother had been buried that day. It was she who raised him. Charlie's parents died in a boating accident when he was eleven. He had stayed home to go to a ball game with friends that day. There was an explosion; she never really got the full story. Charlie didn't speak much of it and she never wanted to pry. It was always just enough that they became friends and he started looking out for her, keeping the bullies away from her in school. But she really messed up this time, she didn't want either one of them to know who her daughter's father is. Did she really think she could just blow into town, do the show and blow out without running in to one of them? Crystal River was not that big of a town to believe that was possible. Jean Paul warned her of this. Why didn't she listen to him? Why didn't she stay in France with him? He had accepted her for what she was, who she was and with no strings attached. He had accepted the baby too. So did his family, they all welcomed her into their home, their lives, with grace and love especially his mother. Her life in France had no worries, no baggage. The more Mariah cried the more her blood pressure rose. Deloris came in and gave her an injection to help her blood pressure to come down in spite of the pregnancy. It had started to climb into the danger zone for her and the baby. After a few minutes of talking Mariah was asleep. Deloris put the sign on the door "NO VISITORS" and turned off the lights.

Outside in the courtyard Charlie was the first to speak. "Okay buddy, why don't you tell me what this is all about?" Patrick stops pacing back and forth, his hands clenched. He had never seen him so filled with rage and fury. He was almost out of control and Charlie could guess why.

"Why don't you tell me?"

"Tell you what?" With that comment Patrick throws a punch and hits Charlie across the cheek knocking him to the ground unexpectedly. Charlie rubs his face and gets up.

"I hope that makes you feel better because it sure as hell doesn't help me." Charlie wanted to hit him back but held himself back. It wouldn't solve anything.

"Tell me about you and Mariah?"

"I'm not sure what you're talking about." Charlie being careful of what to say next, he didn't want to aggravate Patrick anymore than he was now. He didn't care about himself but he did care about what Mariah had to deal with. She had been through enough and it wasn't over yet.

"Don't play that game with me. Do you think I'm that stupid?" I know about the two of you."

"What do you think you know?"

"So help me! What did you do, get her drunk and take advantage of her? How long were you planning things? Have you always wanted her? You didn't waste any time moving in on her after she left me. Some friend you are. How long were things going on?"

"Patrick, it wasn't like that. It just happened the one time, the night you two broke up. Do you think I could take advantage of her? She happens to be my best friend, almost like a sister. I love her too much to hurt her like that. She came over to my house upset. Wanted to me to go have a drink with her but I was afraid she would get drunk and drive. So I convinced her to stay at the house, in one of the spare bedrooms since it was so late. I was feeling low, if you remember I buried my grandmother that day. I thought the company would be good for both of us. We talked a lot, then cried on each other's shoulders and I guess one thing lead to another. We absorbed each other's pain."

"OH PLEASE! Spare me the details."

"Patrick you know I love her like a sister."

"You love her too much, that's the problem now isn't it? Look at the shape of things. It means that child could be either yours or mine." Patrick hated the word as they came out of his mouth. He was so angry he couldn't look at Charlie but continued to pace.

"I know," is all Charlie could say. He rubbed his face; it still hurt from Patrick's punch.

Patrick's cell rang. "Leave me alone!" he screamed to the sky. A passer by looked at them but went on. "Hello. Oh Margo I forgot. Something came up but I'm on my way now." He hung up. "I'll deal with you later," he said to Charlie as he made his way to the parking lot.

"Pat, wait. You don't have the car here remember. I'll take you home to get it."

"No thanks, I'll get a taxi."

"Come on, you know how expensive they are and besides they take so long. My house is on the way to the boutique." They drove to Charlie's in silence. Charlie's face was still hurting but so were his feelings that his best friend could think that badly about him. He really didn't care what Patrick was feeling at the moment but he did on how all this was going to affect Mariah. He had to tell her what went down. At least she could be half way prepared for what was coming. He'd go back to the hospital before Patrick had the chance. After Patrick left the house, he gathered his mail and checked the messages. There was one from his manager regarding his decision on the movie. He had left the script at the hospital. Oh well, that would give him a legitimate reason to be there in case Patrick walked back in.

CHAPTER 3

"Hi, what's going on with Ms. Remmington? Why is her door posted?" Charlie was standing at the nurse's station.

"She needs her rest. She's doing better now but her blood pressure elevated. There will be no more visitors today. Doctor's orders."

"But she's okay, right?"

"She is now."

"I left my script in her room. Can I go and get it? I really need it tonight."

"I'm sorry you can't. Tell me where it is and I'll see if I can't find it for you."

"Do you mind? I think it's on the end table by the phone."

"Not more flowers. Let me guess who they are for, this time," one of the nurses says.

"That makes her ten bouquets of roses. Anymore we won't have a place to put them."

"Maybe she'll let us keep some out here. All I can say she is one lucky woman to have a man who loves her so much." Charlie overheard the conversation and couldn't help but ask, "Those are beautiful. Who are they for?"

"Why room 3012, Ms. Remmington of course. She's taken the prize for the most flowers delivered to one person in one afternoon, at least in this hospital."

"They're all from the same person? Who?"

"We're not suppose to look but after the third one we had to. Someone with the initials of J.P." J.P. could that be Jean Paul? It had to be. Could it be that Jean Paul is the wild card in all this? Is there more going on than Mariah says? Could he and Patrick totally have misread the situation and the baby's father is this Jean Paul? Charlie was so caught up in his thoughts that he didn't feel Becky's touch on his shoulder.

"Hi. I just heard about Mariah. I've tried reaching you but your phone is dead. How is she?"

"She's doing okay but it was touch and go there last night."

"Can we see her? Let her know I'm thinking about her and the baby?"

"Can't. No visitors the rest of the evening." The nurse handed Charlie his script. "Sorry it took me a minute to find it. Too many flowers and not enough space. The room smells like a funeral home." Deloris walks up behind the desk.

"Mary! One more remark like that will get you on report. It's a bad choice of words and I don't want to hear anything like that again. Do you understand me?" Mary walked off in a huff.

"You're just jealous you didn't get those roses. You don't have anyone that cares that much to give you any," one of the other nurses says to Mary behind her back.

"What are they talking about?" Becky asks with a question on her face.

"Mariah has been getting quite a few flowers from a J.P. person."

"You don't say." She squealed with delight. "It's got to be Jean Paul. I'd really like to meet him. Hey what happened to your face?"

"Don't ask. I ran into an object that wouldn't move." He turned back to Deloris. "Can I leave a note for Mariah?" He had to warn her but he couldn't do it in a note so instead he wrote he would see her early in the morning.

"I'll take this in to her right away, so when she wakes she'll see it." Deloris took the note and disappeared. That was all he could do at the moment so he took Becky by the arm and went home to explain as much as he could without saying anything about the possibility of the baby being his and his fight with Patrick.

The window repair took longer than expected but he saw to it until it was done and the shop was secure. The fire chief had showed up and interviewed him again. He had wanted to speak to Mariah but Patrick had convinced him to wait another day until she had a chance to get stronger. By the time things were done he was so tired he could hardly move. The events of the past twenty-four hours were catching up fast. He decided to go home, take a shower and fix something to eat. Afterwards he picked up the phone and called the hospital. He thought since it was so late he would say good night to Mariah over the phone. He became alarmed when the nurses station picked up the call.

"I'm sorry Mr. Wainscott, but Ms. Remmington is not allowed calls or visitors tonight. Doctor ordered complete quiet tonight."

"Why? What happened?"

"She had a little problem. I can't go into it with you but I can tell you she's stabilized and doing well now. We will have to see what the doctor says about visitors tomorrow. I'll tell her you called."

"Is the baby okay?"

"Yes sir, the baby is fine."

"Is her sugar okay?"

"Mr. Wainscott, please I'm not at liberty to speak."

"She got upset about something didn't she? Got her blood pressure up right?"

"Mr. Wainscott, talk to her or the doctor tomorrow. I have to get this line cleared."

"Wait! Call me if there are any more problems. You have my numbers."

"We'll do that. Now good night." With that the phone went dead.

Patrick was still upset with what he heard between Charlie and her but knew he had to get a check on his feelings before he saw her in the morning. As far as Charlie was concerned he didn't care if he saw or talk to him again. That was the last thought he had as he laid his head on the sofa.

Charlie woke early. He had sent Becky home about midnight. He hadn't felt like spending time with her last night. He just wanted to be alone. He knew Becky didn't understand but she didn't push too hard for an explanation. Thank heavens for that. He had made his decision about the movie so he had to deal with that, but first he had to deal with Mariah's situation. He drank his coffee, as he got dressed. He was going to be at the hospital before Patrick got there. Hopefully Patrick would be delayed he thought as he closed the front door behind him. He was relieved that the sign on Mariah's door was removed by the time he got there.

"Hi beautiful. How are you?"

"Charlie, are you okay? What happened to your face?"

"It's nothing. I just got clumsy and walked into a door in the middle of the night."

"You're a liar and you know it. You and Patrick fought didn't you? Why?"

"No I didn't fight with Patrick. What makes you think that?"

"Because how he was acting when you both left yesterday. What happened? I've never seen him so mad."

"Mariah, I don't want to upset you, but he knows about us." The look on Mariah's face was pure horror. "Honey, it's okay. He's not going to bother you. I'm sure of it."

"How Charlie? How did he find out?"

"Apparently he overheard us talking yesterday when he came back for his keys. He was on the other side of the door. He's mad at me, not you. He thinks I took advantage of you, got you drunk and the rest we all know."

"But it wasn't like that. We know that."

"I told him, but he didn't want to listen. He just has to have time to cool off. He loves you more than ever. That's why this is bugging him so much."

"I don't owe him any explanation. We were not together anymore."

"I know sweetheart, I know. Listen I just wanted you to know before he got here. There's something else I want to discuss. What are your plans when you get out of here?"

"I don't know. I need to see about some business out of town and from there I don't have any but now with the fire, I feel like I need to stay here until I get the shop back in order."

"That was my guess. You're going to need a place to stay. The apartment upstairs is not ready for you to stay in. The smoke won't be good for the baby you know."

"I guess I'll go to the Inn."

"You will not. I'm leaving town for three or four weeks to Boston. I've accepted a part that begins filming tomorrow. Here are my keys to the house. You use it for as long as you want. The kitchen is full of junk food and all that healthy stuff too. Barbara will be in to clean, as always so you don't have to do any of that. If there is anything you need just let her know and she'll get it for you."

"I can't do that."

"Why not? There is one thing you can do for me. Water my poor pathetic plants."

"I will need some place to stay. Okay I'll watch over your plants."

"Becky plans to stop in and see if she can do anything for you from time to time."

"That's sweet, but I'm a big girl. I can take care of myself you know."

"Yea, look where that got you, in here." Mariah just smiled back at Charlie. "Mariah, there is one more thing I need to ask you. Do you mind if I have a paternity test done?"

"You can't! I'm sorry but its too risky now. I don't need to know who my daughter's father is. It doesn't matter to me."

"But it matters to me. It will matter to Patrick in spite of what he may say. He will want to know if he is. There will always be that question nagging at him and to me too. You know that and in the end it may matter to you too."

"If I agree to this it will have to be done after the baby gets here. I'm going to have to think about it."

"Sure I can wait but I want you to know I will be here for you and the baby no matter if she is mine or not. I want a relationship with her. Is the position of Godfather taken?"

"Of course I want you to be a part of my child's life no matter what I decide to do. My feelings for you haven't changed."

Charlie was so relieved that the conversation went so well. Mariah stayed calm and she seemed to be in better spirits. Looking around the room for the first time since he entered, he couldn't believe his eyes. The nurses were right. The room was filled with roses, all colored roses.

"My goodness! Who sent all the flowers?" He was curious to find out if she would tell him anymore about Jean Paul.

"I was wondering if you would say anything. You might as well know, Jean Paul did. They're beautiful, aren't they?"

"I have to admit that. What does this guy do for a living to be able to afford all this?"

"You know what I told you. He is a business associate of mine."

"Honey, if you think he's all business, you had better think again. The writing is on the wall. Black and white, no smudges on this letter, he's staking his claim and letting the world know it. I am curious about one thing and I do have to ask. Is there any way he could be the baby's father?"

"Oh heaven no! You don't know as much as you think you do." Charlie noticed she suddenly looked flushed.

"Okay, I believe you but no matter what you say, Jean Paul means more than business to you and you to him."

Mariah lay there taking it all in for a second. Charlie was right and she knew it. Her attention was called back to what Charlie was saying.

"Mariah, did you hear me?"

"I'm sorry, what did you say?"

"I asked you if you decide to leave town, would you please let me know where you are at. I want to stay in touch. I was worried about you when you up and left without letting me know. I felt bad when you did that because of what happened between us."

"I'm sorry but I didn't feel like I could stay. Too much was happening too fast I needed time to myself."

"Will you let me know what you decide to do?"

"I promise this time I will."

"Good. Now here are my extra keys. Use the place like it's yours." Charlie placed the keys inside the drawer of the table. "Oh by the way I've moved my truck out of the garage, you can put that flagship of yours in. The remote will be on the kitchen table."

"You've seen my car?"

"Yea, its quite a gem and expensive, too. Don't get me wrong I'm so glad you got rid of that old rat trap but isn't the Mercedes a little pricey?"

"Don't beat a round the bush, what you really want to know is if it was a gift. Yes, Jean Paul bought the car. He knows I don't like flying so when I told him I was coming back here he insisted on getting something that would provide protection for me and the baby. At first I said no but when I thought about it, it just made sense. So I'm paying him back. Does that satisfy you?"

"Honey, I didn't mean to pry. I'm just concerned, that's all."

"Now about Jean Paul, he is the most dearest, caring man I've ever known, next to you that is."

"Yea but we feel about each other as family. Do you feel that way about him?" Mariah was quiet for a minute.

"No not like you and I feel about each other."

"Where does that leave Patrick? I know you still love him."

"I don't know. I guess I will always love him to some degree. He's my first love after all. I've spent the last five years of my life with him. We've been through a lot but times change Charlie and so have I. I've grown in the last six months." Mariah started laughing as she patted her stomach. Charlie grinned.

"Yes, my dear, so you have."

The nurse came in and told Mariah she had another visitor but only one person at a time was allowed. She and Charlie looked at each other. One guess it had to be Patrick.

"Are you up to seeing him?"

"I guess I have to be. It's either now or later so it should be now. Let's get it over with."

"Is there a problem I should be aware of?" the nurse asks overhearing Mariah's remark.

"I hope not. I think I can take care of Patrick without anyone's help."

"If anything starts to happen push the call button. I'll be in right a way."

"Honey, I better go. Got lots to do before I leave today. I'll call you and you have my cell if anything comes up."

"Thanks Charlie for everything. Have a safe trip. Love you."

"Love you, too, sweetheart. Enjoy the house." Charlie slipped out of the room without being seen by Patrick and that he was glad of.

Patrick entered the room holding a couple of balloons. "Hi, the nurse said you were up to visitors. How are you doing? What happened to you last night?" The look on Patrick's face when he saw the roses was pure surprise. "My word! I guess you really don't need these, do you?"

"Please Patrick, I do appreciate the balloons. Thank you." She took the balloons and tied them to the bed rail. She really wanted to keep things upbeat if possible. Patrick nodded and sat down beside her bed.

"So tell me what happened last night to put you in isolation?"

"I wasn't in isolation?"

"There weren't any calls or visitors allowed, pretty close to it."

"My blood pressure got a little high that's all. I just needed to rest."

"Everything okay now?"

"Yes, we're just fine, thank you."

"Anything else new?"

"No. I'm stuck here. I want to get to the shop and see what's going on."

"Don't worry about that. I've replaced the window. The insurance adjustor has been there already and has things underway with Margo. She sent this letter to you. It explains everything that's going on. She wanted to come but she felt it was best for her to stay there and take care of things.

41

The fire inspector will probably be stopping by to see you sometime today. He wanted to come yesterday, but I convinced him to give you a little more time."

"Why, does he think the fire was something more than an accident?"

"I don't think so. I think it's just a formality. That's all."

"So how are you?"

"I'm okay, my chest is better but I think the night's sleep did more good for me than the antibiotics."

"I'm sorry for the trouble."

"Don't be silly. You're going to make me mad if I hear that again. You're never any trouble." Mariah smiled at him. There was a moment of silence. Mariah trying hard to think of something to say that wasn't personal but couldn't come up with anything. She didn't want the subject of the baby coming up again.

"Are you working on anything?"

"No, I just finished a movie a couple of months ago. There's nothing definite in the works right now."

"Tell me about the movie."

"It's going to be released about Christmas time. I play a widower with triplets who are always getting in trouble."

"That doesn't sound like your usual story line."

"No, I thought I'd try something for fun this time." There was silence again. How she hated it.

"Do you still have Jezebel?"

"Of course I do. I wouldn't get rid of her even if she doesn't like me. She is your horse after all."

"Maybe if I have time before I leave I'd like to see her. I miss riding her."

"You don't have to ask. The ranch is your home. And what do you mean before you leave?"

"I can't stay here. I have other things that require my attention."

Patrick wasn't going to show his emotions about her leaving. Somehow he would have to make her want to stay, to come back to the ranch. He got up to look at some of the cards on the roses. They all read something different, MISSING YOU, GET WELL, THINKING OF YOU, DON'T WORRY ABOUT ANYTHING, LOVE ALWAYS and they were all signed the same way LOVE J.P. Patrick put the cards back in place. So this was all from Jean Paul he thought. What was he going to do about this situation? He was going to have to arrange a meeting with this guy as soon as he could find out whom he was. Mariah studied him very closely as he went through the cards. She was waiting for the questions.

"Who is this J.P.?"

"I told both you and Charlie he's a business associate and a friend. That's all I'm going to say."

"Why are you being so secretive? Why won't you talk about him? Is he married?"

"You are so far off track. He likes his privacy and I respect that," she was laughing.

"Mariah are you in a relationship with him? I need to know if that's the case."

"That's none of your business. All I'm going to say is he has helped me take my business to heights I've never dreamed I could achieve. He has connections that I can use and he knows that. He has helped me in ways I can't explain."

"He cares about you."

"Yes, he does."

"And you?"

"I'm not going to lie to you. I have grown very fond of him. He was there to pick up the pieces without asking for anything in return. He gave me the means of a fresh start in life. One I wouldn't have had if I stayed here in Crystal River. I owe him a lot, including my life as I know it today."

"So you feel obligated to him?"

"The only way I feel obligated to him is to do the best job I can to promote my designs so he doesn't lose the investment. Personally there is no feeling of obligation. I choose to be where I want to be."

"I have to ask. Do you have an intimate relationship with him?"

"Patrick! Again that isn't anyone's business including yours. Remember we were through when I walked in on you and that woman. As of that moment "we" didn't exist. What I chose to do after that is my business. Before you ask as I'm sure you will, I'll tell you what I told Charlie, Jean Paul is not my child's father. He wants to be, but he's not."

"Calm down. I didn't mean to get you upset. I just don't know where things stand between us. I can't read you anymore. The other night in your apartment when we kissed, all the feelings, all the passion was there like it had been all those years. You can't deny that." Mariah looked at him without saying anything. How could she, he was right and they both knew it.

"Since we are talking about this, I have to tell you I know about you and Charlie. I mean about the night we broke up. I have to be honest with you. I'm mad as hell about it. How could he do that to you?" There it had been said and he felt better for it.

"Who made you judge and jury? How can you stand there and say those things about your best friend? You have no right! Look at what you have done in the past. At least we were through when I made the choice to be with him. Do you hear me? I made the choice. It was just something that happened. He needed me and I needed him. We were both going through very personal situations at the time." Her anger flared like a thunderstorm. He was not prepared for that. She didn't seem to be easily angered in the past. He suddenly knew how much he must have hurt her and he was deeply sorry for that.

"Okay, I get the picture. Maybe I'm just mad at myself too, for pushing you out of my life. I will regret those actions every day of my life until I die. All I can do is try to make up for things now."

"There's nothing you can do for the past regrets, just like I can't do anything about my night with Charlie."

"I'm sorry. Please give me a chance, give us a chance. I know the baby is due in December. I know there is a possibility that is my child you're carrying. I pray it is. The child we couldn't have before. The child we wanted for so long. I'd like to have a paternity test done. I want you to know that even if the baby's not mine, if you would still give us a chance, that baby could be mine."

"I won't allow a test now. I already told Charlie I'm not sure I want one done. I couldn't stand it if something would go wrong by doing one now. If I agree I'll let you know."

"We need to know, what if something would happen and we need the information for an emergency."

"I said I would think about it."

"I mean what I said the baby could be mine even if the test is negative. We need to erase the doubt for all three of us. Why can't you just try to open up to me? Let us try to be a family again."

"I don't know Patrick. I don't know if I can go forward with you. I just know we can't and won't ever have what we had in the past. I can't promise you anything."

He knew what she said was true but she didn't close the doors all together. Maybe he still had a chance, now with Charlie leaving town for a few weeks, it would give him a chance to be alone with her. The next thing he would have to do is to find out about this Jean Paul.

After the fire chief had come by to question Mariah and tell her of his findings, he sat and talked with her for the rest of the day until she fell asleep. Then he decided to call the florist to see where the flowers came from. To his dismay they were wired from Marseille, France but there was no other details available to help him with the last name. That means Jean Paul was there. If he could just get his full name, then he would have something to go on to track this guy down and meet with him. He had to know what he was up against. Regardless what Mariah said, it was what she didn't say about her feelings toward Jean Paul that worried him. He was not going to lose her or the baby to Jean Paul if he could help it.

The next morning Dr. Miles came to release Mariah since she had been symptom free for 24 hours. Mariah understood her instructions and was ready to be out of the place in no time. She didn't want to have to wait on a ride from anyone. The nurse made a call for a taxi to take her to the boutique.

"What are you doing here?" Margo was surprised to see her.

"You know me, can't keep me down long."

"Shouldn't you be resting or something? Where's Patrick?"

"I don't know and don't care."

"Sorry."

"Let's get to work. Fill me in on what's going on."

Margo briefed her efficiently. It was clear that Margo had handled everything very well. They would have to have a sale to help bring back the patrons but that wouldn't be a big thing. Margo could handle the details. It didn't take very long to go through what was damaged and what wasn't. Mariah was satisfied. She was getting tired and wanted to lie down somewhere. She did have Charlie's keys. She would have to thank him again for the use of his house.

"Listen Margo, thanks for you help. I'm tired. If you need anything here is the number where I can be reached or you can call my cell but do call me if there is a problem. Do not call Patrick, do you understand?"

"Sure boss I do. The roses are going to brighten up the place a lot"

Mariah thought there was no need to haul them all over the place. She had enough to carry as it is. She picked up her car keys and left thankful that she had not met up with Patrick yet. She wondered how long it would take for him to realize she wasn't in the hospital. The drive to Charlie's took longer than usual. There was a three-car pile up on the freeway. She hoped the people involved were all right. Letting herself in she found the house in order just like Charlie said it would be. There was even a note from Barbara saying she would check in tomorrow to see if she needed anything. After taking what few clothes she had brought with her to the bedroom, she decided she needed to eat. A repeat of what happened was not what she wanted again. She found the fixing for a salad and grabbed a bottle of water from the refrigerator. After finishing off the salad she decided it was time to call Jean Paul and give him an update of the fire. She missed hearing his voice.

CHAPTER 4

It took about an hour to get an international call through. She put the phone on speaker, so she could move around the bedroom easily unpacking.

"Hi, it's me. I just wanted to give you the latest on the situation here."

"*Ma chérie*, where are you? I called the hospital and was told you were discharged. I was worried about you."

"I'm sorry I didn't mean to do that. I wanted to go to the boutique and see what was going on. We're okay." She stroked the baby as she said that thankful it was the truth. "I guess I was pretty stupid the other day, forgetting to take care of myself."

"I hope you learned from the experience."

"Now you sound like what my father would have said."

"I hope not *ma chérie*. I have no intentions on being your *père*. Your *père* would not like to kiss you like I would. It would be sinful. So where are you?"

"Quiet! Someone may be listening. I'm staying at Charlie's. You remember him? Anyway he's out of town for a few weeks so I'm baby-sitting the plants. The address is 5612 Old Hills Way and the phone is 222-314-6656."

"Do you need anything?"

"No, we have everything we need."

"How long are you staying there?"

"I don't know for sure. There wasn't a lot of fire damage but there was smoke damage. I want to be sure the boutique is up and running before I leave again. I'm anxious to get back to New Orleans and see what's up there. The other day before the show I got a call from Daphne. She said there was a problem getting a shipment in. It finally came in today when we were talking. That's never happened before."

"What origin was it?"

"I'm not sure but the trunk left Paris a day later than scheduled."

"That is odd. Let me know if anything else comes up. I'll do some checking here."

"Oh, about the roses, they are gorgeous. Thank you."

"Not as much as you are *ma chérie*. Now you haven't told me how things are going with Patrick? Is he leaving you alone?" That was all he had to say. The tears started to flow and she could do nothing to stop them.

"What is it? Please tell me why you are crying?"

"Oh Jean Paul, I should have listened to you. Everything is not what I wanted. Everything has blown up in my face. I was so stupid to land myself in the hospital. Charlie and Patrick suspect that each of them could be my daughter's father. They each want a paternity test. Patrick got mad and punched Charlie. They both want a relationship with the baby and Patrick wants me to forget everything that happened between us in the past. I just feel like I've screwed up everybody's life, that's all." It all blurted out so fast that Mariah couldn't stop herself.

"*Ma chérie*, you have done nothing. It is these other people that have screwed up as you put it. This Patrick did you wrong. This Charlie, well he was just there, these things happen. As you describe Charlie I think that regardless if *le bébé* is his or not, he just wants you to be happy. He cares and looks over you, *oui*? This Patrick I'm not so sure of by the way you describe him."

"You're right about Charlie. He will be a part of my life no matter what. Patrick says he regrets everything and that he has never stopped loving me."

"How does that make you feel?" Jean Paul really didn't want to hear the answer because he was afraid of what she might say. "Do you still love him?"

"I don't know."

"What will you do if *le bébé* happens to be his?"

"I don't know. I just want to get some space from here so I can think."

"*Ma chérie*, you know you and *le bébé* have a place here with me anytime you desire it. I would like it to be permanent. We have grown very close these past months. Our time is precious. I want you to seriously consider this but I won't push. When you are ready you will know it."

"I feel the same way Jean Paul. I will let you know what my plans are as soon as I know. I better go for now, I don't want to run up Charlie's bill. Until we talk again *mon cher*."

"*Au revoir, ma chérie*, till we talk again."

Mariah turned around to take the phone off the speaker and to her surprise found Patrick leaning against the doorway with his arms crossed.

"How long have you been standing there? Why didn't you ring the doorbell? How did you know where to find me?" She threw the questions out so fast that he didn't have time to respond.

"First of all, I went to the hospital. When you weren't there, I assumed you would go to the boutique. Margo couldn't deny anything because the roses are there. I saw your note on Charlie's address and phone on her desk. Your car was gone so I assumed you were here. Charlie left yet?"

"Yea, he's gone for a few weeks. I'm house sitting while the boutique is being cleaned up. I've decided to have some other things done since we're closed anyway. Staying there wouldn't be good for either one of us would it?" She stroked her baby lovingly. "Even though Charlie's gone that doesn't give you the right to walk in on me."

"I didn't. You didn't answer the doorbell. I got worried and came on in."

"Yea to eavesdrop on my private conversation. You ought to be put in jail for that!"

"I believe I have every right to hear what you two are saying about me, about us. I was the topic wasn't I?" Patrick took a few steps toward her, too close to her she thought.

"I've got to finish unpacking. Then I'm going to take a shower and go to bed. Dr's orders, you know." Patrick took the clothes out of her hands and hung them up.

"This Jean Paul doesn't have a good picture of me, does he?"

"It really doesn't matter." Mariah was heading downstairs to the living room. The bedroom was the last place she wanted to be with Patrick. Patrick followed.

"The hell it doesn't! It matters to me. I'm not the slump he thinks I am. If I have to fight a battle with him over you then I will. I am not going to lose you again without one. That much I can assure you."

Mariah was laughing as she sat on the sofa. "Would you listen to yourself? You must have every ounce of testosterone flowing in your body right now. I've tried to be honest with you since day one. You have to realize that I may not be able to give you what you want."

"Honest with me? What about not telling me about the baby? You call that honest?" Patrick sat down in the chair across from her.

"I didn't tell you because I couldn't tell you that you are the father. I didn't lie to you. We can change the subject now or you can leave. I'm not going to be bullied into talking about this anymore. I'm going to get something to drink since obviously I'm not going to be able to take a shower with you here."

"I'm not going anywhere at the moment. Sit, I'll get you something."

Patrick found some bottled water in the refrigerator. "I wasn't sure what you could have so I settled on the water." He handed it to her and she drank. Mariah turned on the television and searched the channels.

"You want to see anything?"

"Yea, now that you mention it. I'd like to see your car?"

"Why on earth do you want to do that? It's out there. I won't stop you."

"You want me to put it in the garage for you?"

"Sure, the keys are in it." He could look at the car all he wanted. The more time he spent outside with the car the less he would with her. She didn't trust her feelings. All she wanted at the moment was to be in his arms, but she couldn't and wouldn't let her feelings show. She had too much to lose this time. Her head was warning her and her heart was weak. She had left that life behind six months ago. She had a better life now for her and her child.

Fifteen minutes later Patrick came in and sat down on the sofa beside her. Why? Why did he have to sit so close? She thought to herself.

"Nice car. It's 2004 isn't it? That's the biggest one they make."

"Yes, she's a beauty isn't she?"

"I can say it beats that old Toyota you had. It's a lot safer, too, but I bet it cost you on the monthly payments and insurance." Patrick put the keys on the coffee table.

"The insurance isn't so bad and neither are the payments."

"Really?"

"Patrick, why don't you just ask me what you want and stop beating around the bush? Yes, Jean Paul, bought the car for me. Do you think I would buy that kind of car for myself? My stores are doing well but I'm reinvesting most of everything back into my product line. It costs money to make garments. There are employees and families to feed you know."

"So I take it this business partner of yours is loaded with the cash?"

"I don't see where that's relevant to anything."

"Hum." Patrick just looked at her. She wasn't going to make this easy. "You said your stores, plural. You have more than one, now?"

"Yes, I have one in New Orleans now. It's doing quite well."

"New Orleans, is that where you met this guy?"

"Patrick, will you stop! I don't want to discuss him with you."

"Just tell my about my adversary and I won't bother you again about him. It's only fair for a guy to know who his enemy is."

"He's not your enemy. The only thing I will tell you, yes I did meet him there. Now will you please shut up about Jean Paul? I really want to go to bed, so will you be so kind and leave?" She got up, went to the door and held it open. Patrick followed. She was looking tired.

"Only if you call me if you need anything tonight, otherwise I'll call you tomorrow morning. Promise me?"

"Yes, I promise. Now go home." She closed the door behind him, locked it and went upstairs. That was one promise that wouldn't be kept even if she did need something.

Sometime in the night she awakened startled with a nightmare. She was carrying her baby and running as fast she could and as far as she could. From what danger she didn't know. All she knew was she had to take her daughter and flee. It took along time for her to calm down. She got up, took her medications and went back to bed since it was still early morning. She woke to the sound of the phone ringing.

"Hello." Her voice sounded weak Patrick thought.

"Hi babe. Are you still sleeping?"

"I was. What time is it?

"Ten o'clock. Are you feeling okay?"

"I'm fine but I do need to get up and get moving."

"Listen, I've got to do some errands but after that would you like to go out to the marina with me and have a picnic?"

"Patrick, I don't know. Can't we just leave things be? At least we are talking, that's something to say. Besides I have a boutique to see to."

"Margo is handling things there. She can call us if she needs to."

"I'd rather not."

"I'm not taking no for an answer. I'll call you later when I get done. Besides you have to eat don't you? Think about what happened the last time you didn't." Before Mariah could refuse Patrick had hung up the phone.

Luckily the day wasn't so hot for late August. There's a gentle breeze blowing through Mariah's golden locks making it dance so ever slightly. The grass still held its thickness in spite of no rain, and the old oak tree they sat under offered plenty of cool shade. She was actually enjoying herself. She had always loved picnics.

"Do you want anything else to eat?"

"No, I couldn't. How did you know what my dietary requirements are?"

"Remember those errands I mentioned? I paid a visit to Dr. Miles and asked her."

"You did that, for this? What else did she tell you?"

"Nothing, why is there something you're not telling me?"

"What about me or the baby? No, you know as much as I do."

"You don't expect me to believe that do you?"

"Shut up, don't worry. All I want to do is sit here and watch the boats."

"Tell me about New Orleans. Where do you stay when you're there?"

"I have an apartment in Metairie." She didn't need to say much more she thought.

"Where's the store?"

"It's in the French Quarter. It's the most ideal place; there is a lot of traffic all day. It's where the tourists come; eventually they'll come in to browse. My sales are good so far."

"So your apartment is in a safer district?"

"There's some crime but nothing like in the French Quarter."

"Still it's expensive no matter where you live in that area."

"It's okay. I have a small one bedroom. I was going to install an efficiency in the store like I have here but someone talked me out of it. I'm glad I listened. Everyone in the complex is tight. We all look after each other. My best neighbors are the couple downstairs, Matt and Chris. They look after my things while I'm gone and when I'm there, they're constantly bringing me food. Matt is a chef and Chris is in computers."

"So are you comfortable there?"

"Why wouldn't I be? I have everything I need."

"Is Jean Paul financing the apartment?" Mariah thought it was best to ignore the question and continued to look out over the water. Patrick knew he had hit a nerve by the look on her face. It was probably Jean Paul who convinced her not to stay at the store, at least he showed some sense. The French Quarter isn't the best to be in after dark. This only proved to him that Jean Paul was deeper in her life than she let on. He would have to go slow and get little bits of information here and there.

"Wait here." Patrick got up and went to the car. He came back with a resting pillow. He placed it behind Mariah's back so she could lean up against the tree.

"You have thought of everything haven't you?" Mariah was glad to have the pillow since her back was starting to hurt. It felt good to lean against something soft. Patrick saw her actions and moved closer. He put his arms around her and leaned her slightly toward him. Oh he wasn't playing fair she thought. The next thing she knew he turned her face to him and kissed her fully on the lips. She started to push away but found herself kissing back. She couldn't do this! She had to stop at once. His arm was still supporting her. His other hand was touching her face, then her neck, then it traced down her shoulder to her breast. The touch was too much for her. She couldn't stand it. At that very moment she couldn't do anything but to give in to her desires. She could enjoy this one last embrace. Then his hand slipped on down.

"Patrick, stop!" Breaking away from him. "I can't. There's the baby and besides this isn't the time or place." Patrick pushing his hair from his face and exhaling deeply couldn't believe he had made another mistake in her eyes.

"I'm sorry honey, I don't know what happened. You are just so damn beautiful. I can't stand it. I want you like I've never wanted you before."

"I'm not beautiful. I'm as big as a house and going to get bigger before it's all over."

"Not in my eyes, sweetheart." He leans over and kisses again.

"I'd like to go home now. I think I've had enough sun and fun to last a few days. Now help me up." Patrick helps her to her feet and gathers up their belongings. He couldn't help but wonder if he had made another bad "move". She didn't seem mad but she didn't talk at all on the way back to Charlie's. It seems every time he took a step forward he wound up taking two back. He felt her resistance melt with the kiss but then her guard came back up. Somehow there had to be a way to lower it permanently to get across to her how much she really meant to him. He had the feeling that time was running out.

The next few days Mariah kept herself busy with the boutique. Patrick called and even stopped in the shop everyday to see her. She always had some excuse for not going to lunch or dinner with him. Once he even came in and bought a ruby pendant from the shop and gave it to her. Another time he brought her a baby gift, a little pink sweater and hat. He was still persistent, that had not changed any. Charlie had called once to see how she was getting along at the house. Barbara was keeping her promise to check in too. Then there was Becky. Becky had been over twice in the past week. With all the interruptions and well-meaning friends there was no way she could get any rest. There were days she just wanted to hide from the world and be alone. The weekend finally came and she was ready to take a break from the boutique and its needs. Things were coming along but not as fast as she hoped.

"Mariah here?" Patrick asks Margo as he approaches her hanging up clothes from the cleaners.

"Upstairs in the office."

"Thanks." Before she could realize whom she just spoke to he bounded up the stairs to the office.

"What are you doing up here?"

"This is my office or did you forget?"

"It still smells of smoke in here." Patrick makes himself comfortable on the sofa.

"I need some papers out of here." Mariah continues rummaging through the desk.

"Can I help?"

"No thank you. You wouldn't know what to look for. I need the shipment routing slips on some orders. Where did I put those? I have become so forgetful since the baby. They say it's normal and my mind will come back but I'm not so sure." Mariah pulled the routing slips out of a file designated for utility bills. "I would have never put them here. Why did I do that? So why are you here? I have work to do and don't have time to visit."

"Boy you don't even give a guy a chance do you? I came by to see if you wanted to come out to the ranch and see Jezebel later today?"

"Today? I can't today, too much to do."

"Honey, you can't push yourself like this. It can't be good for the baby. I know, tomorrow is Sunday. You can't do anything here. The contractors won't be here so there is no reason why you can't take the day off and come on out?"

Mariah knew he had her there. Maybe she could feign a headache, but then again she would like to see Jezebel. Patrick had bought her for Mariah as a birthday present. They had gone for a drive that day and wound up at a horse show. It was there she fell in love with the Tennessee Walkers, their beauty and grace. She was so taken with the breed that the next week Patrick surprised her with one. He preferred the stature of the Quarter horse. They were more durable and easier to ride in his opinion. But the Walker made her happy and she enjoyed taking care of the mare. The previous owners raised her from a colt. They had given her the name Jezebel due to her disposition around men. Very few of them she liked and she showed it through her wicked ways. Mariah and Jezebel seemed to bond almost instantly but bonding with Patrick was another thing. They found she would tolerate Jim, his part time stable man.

"Well, what do you say?" Patrick asks when Mariah didn't say anything.

"Oh, I guess tomorrow will be okay. I'll call before I come out." She did want to see the mare again but she didn't want Patrick to know how much.

"I can come in to town and pick you up. That way you won't get your car dirty on the gravel and I can spend more time with you." He flashed her a smile.

"Thank you anyway, but I'll drive myself. Since when am I concerned about a dirty car?" She thought the freedom of her car being there would make her feel better. If she would be uncomfortable with the situation she could just leave.

"Okay, I know it was a lame excuse but half an hour here or there that I can spend with you is more than what I've had lately."

"I said I would come now please I have business to tend to. Leave before I change my mind. I'm expecting a call very soon and I need to study these routing slips."

Getting up Patrick slips to the other side of her desk and puts his arms around her waist. He notices that Mariah's thin summer dress did nothing to conceal how much the baby had grown. He leans over and kisses her on the cheek. She is so engrossed in the paperwork that she hardly notices as he closes the door behind him.

It was well into early evening when she left to go back to Charlie's. Becky was sitting in the driveway when she pulled up.

"Hi, what brings you out here?"

"I was just going to write you a note. I was a bit lonely, you know with Charlie gone and all so I thought you might want to hang out for a few hours and watch this with me." Becky said holding up a 1939 video starring Clark Gable.

"I haven't seen that movie in ages. You know what? I was going to go to bed with a novel but this sounds better. Come on in."

"I'm glad you feel that way," she giggled.

"Do you want something to eat or drink? Why am I asking you? You've probably organized this kitchen. Help yourself. I'm going upstairs to change."

Becky had fixed herself a sandwich and a coke by the time Mariah came back down in shorts and a tee shirt. She then fixed her something to eat.

"I swear if I get any bigger nothing is going to fit." Becky had the tape rewinding as they got comfortable on the sofa.

"I don't think you have anything to worry about. You look good being pregnant."

"How do you know? You've never seen me otherwise."

"Yes I have. Patrick still has your pictures around the ranch. I asked Charlie who you were the first time I went over there. Man, he has a thing for you. Why aren't you two together anymore?"

"Too much to talk about and I would rather not. I don't want to hurt your feelings, but I don't want to think about him tonight."

"I'll tell you what. You are one lucky woman to have Patrick and this Jean Paul person after you. Why can't I be so lucky? But then again I have my hands full with Charlie. Why would I want another man? But then again if he was like your Jean Paul I might consider it." She laughed again.

"Becky, I don't want to talk about men tonight. Everyone has been bugging me about Jean Paul. It's getting old."

"I know what you mean. Right after Charlie and I started seeing each other, everyone was asking questions. There was a lot of press. Was it like that for you and Patrick?"

"Some but we ignored them."

"I guess its human nature to ask." There was a moment of silence. The movie began.

"Becky, what do you look for in a man? I mean how do you know what you want in that person and that you can trust him or not?"

"You're asking me that? I can't answer. Maybe it's just a feeling you get. Sure you can say I want this and that and check off all the good qualities but for every good there is the bad too. Everyone has those. Hopefully one side will out weigh the other and you'll see it before it becomes entangled with everything else a relationship has in it."

"Wow! All this from you, did you study psychology or something?"

"No let's just say life is a very good teacher. Is that it? Are you trying to decide between Patrick and Jean Paul?"

"No, heavens no. Patrick and I are through. There is nothing that can erase the past."

"Is that what you're looking for, a way to erase the past to see if there is a chance for you and Patrick or are you looking for a reason to be with Jean Paul?"

"Becky, Patrick and I had our time together, five years worth. It didn't work. I can't trust him anymore. It wouldn't be fair to my daughter to have her live in those circumstances. I won't do that to her. I need to make a secure life for her."

"Is Patrick the father?" Mariah should have felt offended by all that Becky was saying but for some reason she was not. She just knew she couldn't say anything to Becky about the possibility of who her daughter's father is. At this point she wasn't sure what Becky meant to Charlie but she wasn't going to mess things up for them. If Becky found out it would have to be through Charlie. She would have to be told if things started to develop farther between them.

"Look, here comes the part I like when Clark kisses her so dramatically," Becky remarked while she sipped her coke.

Mariah could only half way watch the movie; she kept hearing Becky's words. Was that what she was doing, trying to find a reason to stay? She had never expected that from her. She had underestimated Becky and that she wouldn't do again. Somehow she had a feeling that they would become friends.

It was after midnight when the movie was over and Becky went home so Mariah took advantage of the quiet and slept until two in the afternoon. The sound of the phone woke her up. Barbara was planning to come by with a few things to restock the cupboards and straighten up a little. Mariah had told her it wasn't necessary. The house wasn't dirty and she could get her own groceries, but she insisted. She said she had made a huge casserole and wanted to bring some over as well. Mariah mentioned she had plans to be gone that afternoon and to let herself in as usual. She thanked her for her efforts and thought Charlie had better not lose her. She just might have to hire her then. She went in to take a shower, it seemed to take her longer getting dressed and out the door than it had before.

Patrick was waiting impatiently for Mariah to call. He had worked hard to clean the house from top to bottom, all the laundry hidden in the machine and the dishes and bed were even done. He didn't know why exactly. Mariah knew how he was with the house, but this time everything had to be perfect. It was four o'clock. Where was she? Had she forgotten or did she just decide it was too much to come back home even for a short while? The thoughts passed through his mind just as his phone rang.

"Hello."

"Hi, it's me. Is it all right for me to come out now?"

"Baby, any time. Are you sure I can't come in to get you?"

"No, I'd rather have my car. See you in a few." She hung up.

The freeway was just as busy as ever but when she turned on to the gravel road leading up to the house she had to stop. Could she do this? The last time she was on this road, she was leaving for good. She hated leaving Jezebel but had decided if she ever got settled some place where she could have her she would send for her and pay Patrick back the money he spent to purchase her. Now here she was again on that same road. There were as many good memories in that house as there were bad. She had to concentrate on the good ones if she was to get through this visit. Pulling up to the garage, the house looked the same. It is an old brick two-story country house with a wrap around front porch. The flowerbeds were not tended to as well as she did, but they were passable. He had added a couple of rockers to the porch since she left, nice touch. Patrick saw her drive up and was coming out of the barn. She took a deep breath. This was not going to be easy. He is dressed in blue jeans and boots but had his shirt off. Every muscle Patrick possessed was tight and the sweat beaded down his chest. The heat of the day suddenly became overbearing to Mariah. She felt a little dizzy.

"Hi. You caught me putting some things away."

"Jim not here anymore? He usually does that."

"He wanted to cut his hours down, so he's just here every other day unless I'm working. Betty was ill for a while and they decided they wanted to spend some extra time together since they're both retired now."

"I hope it wasn't anything serious?"

"Jim said it was breast cancer but she's doing well and they think they have everything under control now. She just finished her chemotherapy last month."

"I'll have to call her before I leave. I hope the doctors are right for both of their sakes. Can I see Jezebel since we're out here?"

"She's ready. I told her you were coming by and you should have seen her ears perk up. It was like she knew you name," Patrick said walking into the stable with Mariah. He had one hand on her elbow to help steady her in case she should trip in a hole. She noticed but didn't object. As soon as she entered the doors Jezebel saw her and nickered a greeting.

"Hey girl, how are you? I've missed you so much. You look good." Mariah patting the mare's neck, then remembers she brought the horse some carrots. That was her favorite and had become a special treat from Mariah every day. The mare nudges her neck and takes the carrots happily.

"Do you still give her these?"

"Sometimes, but Jim has kept up the practice. He says it would be cruel to stop what she is used to. Funny, he said you would be back someday to see her."

"He knows how much I love her."

"He and Betty send their regards by the way. I told him you were coming out today."

"I wish I could ride her. Could you? I mean could you put her through her paces so I can watch her. Do you mind?"

"You really want me to do that?" I haven't been on her for quite some time. Jim exercises her for me. They get along better together than she does with me." Patrick saw the disappointment on her face. "Okay, I'll try but I can't guarantee it will be pretty." He leads the horse out to the paddock and saddles her. Mariah holds the reins and talks softly to her. The horse was excited that Mariah was there but also for the fact that she knew what Patrick was about to do. Outside in the ring Jezebel behaved at first, responding to Patrick's moves then all of a sudden she moves the opposite way catching Patrick off guard, then when she bucks he's thrown off.

"Patrick! Are you all right?" Mariah yells but is laughing at the same time.

"Yea. I told you she hasn't changed her opinion of me. The name fits her." Brushing the dirt off his body with the towel Mariah got off the fence. By this time the horse was nudging Mariah's neck and blowing horse kisses on her.

"She seems to be proud of what she did."

"Yea I'm sure she is. Let me take the tack off her. She can stay out here and work off some of that nastiness."

"Don't talk about her that way. She's a good girl. She just has a bad opinion of you. That's all."

"Why don't you go on in the house and take a load off. I'll be there in a jiff if this horse and I don't tangle again." Mariah thought that was a good idea since the heat was starting to bother her again.

The inside of the house was exactly as she had left it. Surprisingly enough it was very clean. That much she didn't expect to see. Sitting on the couch her eyes kept wandering upstairs. She had promised herself not to go upstairs, to be reminded of what happened in their bedroom but she couldn't keep that promise. She walked up the stairs. Patrick had turned the office upstairs into a gym. The room across the hall was theirs. She opened the door and to her amazement it was total different. The walls had been painted a soft green and hanging on them are portraits of derby winners intermingled in with prints of fox and hound hunts. It was all tastefully done with accents of pillows and bedspread in hunter green. But the one thing that surprised her more than anything was the bed. He had bought a new bedroom suite, one she had wanted for a long time. A four-poster cherry king size bed, complete with the highboy, dresser and mirror and two end tables. She couldn't believe her eyes. For a few minutes she had actually forgotten what had happened in this room a few months ago.

"You like?" Patrick was next to her ear. She hadn't heard him come upstairs. "I was hoping to show you this but wasn't sure I could?"

"Very much so but I'm sorry, I didn't mean to intrude on your space." She found herself sitting on the bed.

"Baby, this is your home and will always be. How many times do I have to tell you?" Patrick sat down on the Queen Anne chair across from the bed, because he was still dirty from the ride. She was grateful for that. "Listen do you mind if I take a shower? That horse of yours kicked mud at me. She hates me you know." He started to pull clothes from the closet. A shower, oh my, she thought. She had better leave while she could. "You hungry? I thought we could grill a couple of steaks if you like? They're ready to cook so it won't take them long and there is salad and fresh vegetables from the garden. You can eat steak, right?"

"Yes, I can, it's the carbohydrates I have to watch." Mariah was hungry and this was the diversion she needed right now. "I'll go down and get things going while you do the shower bit." She left the bedroom door open. Patrick watched her go downstairs while he pulled his jeans off. He had hoped she might want to stay with him but didn't want to push. She did seem to want to stay for dinner; this was turning out better than he had thought it would. With her driving he had thought she would come to see the horse then leave right away. Patrick chose cutoff shorts and the tee shirt that Mariah had given him on their vacation to the Smokey Mountains one summer long ago. Walking into the kitchen he found she had the radio on and was singing to it. How many times did he see her do that, it was too numerous to count. She found the vegetables and had started cleaning and chopping them to add to the salad.

"Well, look at you. All cleaned up. I can't believe you still have that old tee shirt."

"What are you talking about? It's me. I have it all broken in. Can I help with that?"

"No, I can handle this but you can do the steaks. I would rather not mess with the grill." Patrick put the steaks on, he was pretending to watch them cooking but was instead watching her through the kitchen window. Coming back in with the steaks he noticed she had the table set.

"I thought we could eat in here, I don't like the heat."

The conversation at dinner was a little awkward. They had passed the minutes with small talk until neither one could think of anything else to say. The silence sat in again, finally she had to ask. "Have you heard from Charlie yet?"

"No, I would think that you or Becky would hear from him before I would."

"Come on, Patrick. You can't still be mad at him? He is your best friend, please don't let me come between you two."

"I won't say that I'm not ticked off at him."

"You have to get over this. There is as much of a chance the baby is yours as well as his. If you need to blame someone then blame me. If I hadn't gone to see him, we would have never slept together. I should have left town that night instead of the next day like I did."

"If anyone is to blame in all this, it's me. Not you. Charlie should have had more restraint. It was only natural for you to go to see him. Let's face it what took place was because of what I did. I can't forgive myself for doing that to you."

"You're right you were the catalyst but I think we all need to look forward and not backwards. Today is what today is. We can't change the past but we can allow the future to take its course whatever way it does. I beg you not to let this situation break up your friendship. Get over it because if you can't I don't know if I'm going to be able to deal with all this. Neither my daughter nor I need this trash in our lives. I refuse to let her be involved in this mess. It's not her fault that life got in the way for us. Do you understand me?" Mariah started to clear the table.

"Leave them, I'll put them in the dishwasher later. Lets go into the living room. I know you make sense, just give me some time." They sat on the sofa together, he turned her to face him. Patrick was very close to her and holding both of her hands.

"I want you to know one thing. I don't care who the real father is, but if you would have me back we'll get married as soon as possible and give that little girl the family she deserves. I can be a father to her no matter what the DNA says." Mariah's face was blank, he couldn't read her thoughts.

"What do you say? Will you marry me?" Mariah couldn't believe her ears. A few months ago this is what she wanted but now?

"Patrick, I can't do it, not right now? It's not fair to all three of us to rush into anything. That is a decision that will affect everyone's future. I can't make that right now. I have too many raging hormones inside of me to be able to think clearly, besides there are outside factors. All I want to do is to get through one day at a time and get through this pregnancy. I don't want to hurt you but I can't. Please understand?"

"I don't. I know you still love me. It's not like I'm asking you to move to the moon, after all we've lived together for years. We know each other better than anyone else. Let's do it right this time. Every time we touch, kiss, I can feel what you want."

"I think you have things confused between love and desire. There is a difference."

"Not with you, my dear. Love and desire go hand in hand and you know it. The outside factor? Is it that Jean Paul character?"

"Look at the time! It's getting late. I need to be going." Mariah got up and found her purse and keys. "Thanks for letting me see Jezebel and for keeping her. I do love her. When I get a place where I can keep her, I'll let you know. Oh, thanks for the dinner, it was good." She headed out the door.

"Mariah, wait. I'm sorry if I made you uncomfortable, please stay?"

"I can't. Sorry" She got into her car and drove away just in time. The tears started to fall.

Patrick felt like screaming to the world again. Everything was going well until he brought up their failed relationship. He didn't know what else he could do to bring her back to him. Maybe he should turn his back on reviving their love but he couldn't turn his back on that baby. If she turned out to be his, it was a bond that even Mariah couldn't deny. He still had to convince her to have the paternity test. After he took Jezebel back to her stall: all of his bottled up feelings erupted. The tack room took the brunt of his raw emotions.

CHAPTER 5

Mariah had kept herself busy with the boutique. She had decided since it was to have a new look structurally, she would create a small office in the back for Margo to work out of. She needed a new look in clothes as well. Fall was around the corner. She needed to get a start on presenting her new fall designs and a few other designers as well. A fall sale would help bring back the shoppers as well as offering discounts on the summer stock. There had been three shipments of her stock from France that had been delayed without any explanation from anyone. Something was going on, but what?

Patrick called a couple of times in the past week to say hello and to bring back her watch that she had left at his house. She had taken it off when she was cleaning the vegetables so she wouldn't get it wet. He had wanted her to go to dinner a few times but she refused, saying she was too tired. She wasn't lying since the pregnancy was getting heavier to bear. Dr. Miles had told her during the last visit to start taking things easier and to get off her feet more. She thought her feet looked like they were going to explode from the swelling in them, which was staying constant. Her blood pressure was elevated a little but her sugar level was good. Patrick realized the physical changes in her and didn't press to spend a lot of extra time with her. He could only imagine what she felt like. He knew she was pushing herself too hard and needed to get as much rest as possible.

Mariah mentioned to him that Charlie called and said he would be back in a few days, but that she could continue to stay at his place since her apartment wasn't done yet. The house was certainly big enough for both. Patrick didn't like the thought of her being there but there wasn't anything he could do about it. What he didn't know was that Mariah didn't want to be there after Charlie's arrival. She had reserved a room at the Crystal River Suites and Inn. It wasn't exactly what she wanted to do since her hospital bills were starting to come in but had no choice since it would be a couple of weeks before her apartment would be ready. She wondered why Patrick had been so distant with her and had missed him. She almost picked up the phone several times just to hear his voice but then stopped herself. She was not ready to discuss marriage again.

The weekend was coming and she was glad. She could stay in bed all day. The contractors were taking Saturday off so there was no need for anyone to be at the shop. She had to just get through the rest of today. Four o'clock came and she was just about to call it a day when Becky came in.

"Hi. I was down the street and thought I'd stop by and see how the construction is coming. Looks pretty good."

"I'm glad you like it. I hope everyone else does too. I need to get it up and running soon. This down time is killing me."

"It will happen *mon amour*." That voice Mariah thought. It can't be him! Both women turned to face Jean Paul. It was instinct that Mariah flung her arms around his neck and kissed him. Jean Paul was just as happy to see her as she was he. He embraced her tightly and kissed her back. It was a long luscious kiss. "Look at you and *le bébé*. How we have grown!"

"Be careful! Never call a pregnant woman fat. What are you doing here?" Mariah's voice was full of joy and excitement.

"You will always have a figure of a goddess, pregnant or not. I couldn't get through on the telephone so I decided I needed to see you in person."

"You were in the neighborhood, huh?"

"I couldn't live another moment without touching you."

"I've missed you, too."

Becky cleared her throat. Mariah had forgotten that she was witnessing everything. Of all the people to know he was in town, Mariah would have not picked Becky to be it. There was nothing she could do about it now.

"Oh, I'm sorry, Jean Paul please meet my friend, Becky Browning. Ms. Becky Browning, meet my friend and business partner Jean Paul." Jean Paul tipped his head slightly and took Becky's hand as she extended it to shake but kissed it instead.

"Count DuMoiese at your service." Becky was so charmed at first that it didn't register he had said Count. Mariah felt a sudden panic attack coming. She didn't want to complicate things with the fact that he was a Count. Now it was sure to get out to both Patrick and Charlie that Jean Paul is a Count.

"It is very nice to meet you. I saw the drop-dead roses you sent to Mariah. They were beautiful." Jean Paul turned to Mariah.

"Were they dead when they arrived?" Both women couldn't help but laugh. Seeing his face Mariah hurriedly explained.

"No, Jean Paul, they were not dead. It's just an expression we have here."

"Good, I'm glad of that."

"Wait a minute, did you say you're a Count?"

"Why yes, I did."

"I've never met a Count before. I can't wait to tell my girlfriends that I've met you." Becky starts to head toward the doors. "Mariah, I'd keep this one," she calls out over her shoulder. "See ya soon. Bye." And with that Becky disappears.

"Can I do anything to help?" Margo overhearing some of the conversation came over.

"No Margo, everything here is just fine." Mariah's smile on her face proved it. "I want you to meet Count Jean Paul DuMoiese, my friend and partner in our Louisiana boutique. Count, please meet my store manager, Margo Williams. Without all her help, I couldn't do what I do." The Count tipped his head to her and kissed her hand, too, in one swift movement.

"I have heard so much about you, *Mademoiselle*. I am glad to be able to thank you for being a great help to Mariah."

"I'm just doing my job. I have a special interest in the shop as well as Mariah. She took a huge chance on hiring someone with no job experience after my marriage ended. Everything I know in this business I learned from her. So I feel that this shop is my responsibility too. I owe everything I have now to Mariah."

"Now that is dedication. Mariah you have made a good choice here."

"Jean Paul, not to change the subject but I'm sure you have come all this way for some reason. Shall we go upstairs and talk?"

"Of course. *Mademoiselle* Williams, would you please excuse us? There is some business I do need to discuss with Mariah." Margo nodded her head.

"You know what Mariah, it's after four, why don't you go on home. I'll close up. You and the Count would be more comfortable there than upstairs since most of the furniture has been sent out for cleaning. Go on now, get out of here. Get off your poor feet."

"*Ma chérie*, she speaks sense. Let us go home." Jean Paul had taken notice of her swollen ankles and feet when he first saw her. There wasn't anything about her that he didn't notice right away. He was just that way with people. There wasn't much he missed on first glance.

"Let me get my purse. Do you have a car? Is Claude with you?"

"Non, it is just Alec at the plane. I saw no need to bring along an escort, after all I want to spend time alone with you. I see him all the time and he's not very good looking in his night wear. Or any other time of the day actually to come to think about it, though he is very proficient in what he does."

"Stop that! That's not funny." Mariah playfully hit him on the shoulder.

"I rented a car from the airport. Claude is trying to find out why the shipments are going elsewhere as we speak. I will follow you if that is alright?"

Margo couldn't believe her ears or eyes. The Count was so terribly handsome, tall with dark brown hair that had started to gray at the temples as well as the tuft of hair that shown above his shirt collar. His tie wasn't as tight as she would have expected it to be for a man of his title. His eyes are the darkest she had ever seen, almost black it seemed. His stature was one of command and control. It all came together in a very distinguished looking package. It was no wonder Mariah hadn't said much about him, she wanted to keep him for herself and she didn't blame her. There was one problem that she knew she could help Mariah with. Whatever Mariah's desire was to keep this man a secret, whether it was the fact that he is a Count or the fact that she cared more deeply for this man than she admitted to or was it this man could be the baby's father, Margo didn't care at the moment. She had to make sure all the bases were covered correctly. Looking up Becky's phone number in the computer they kept for past purchases, she dialed and surprising enough she got through. She had asked Becky not to say anything about the Count. Mariah had enough stress in her life and feared it might cause problems for the baby if she spread the news around town. Becky thought for a minute and agreed, too. She didn't want anything to happen to the either one of them on account of her actions. She wouldn't even say anything to Charlie or Patrick. If they found out it would have to be of their own doing. She had become friends with Mariah and didn't want to jeopardize that.

As soon as they hit the front door Mariah told Jean Paul to make himself at home. She wanted to change into something more comfortable. At this stage of the pregnancy clothes bothered her. She went upstairs and chose a pale pink satin lounging shorts and top. It was in her new maternity line and wanted to get an honest reaction to it. She had stopped in the kitchen and got some sparkling water for both of them. She found Jean Paul on the sofa, his suite jacket and tie off and his shirt open to the third button exposing a bit of his well-defined chest and the mass of graying hair that curled there. So many times she had seen him relax like this, but this time she sensed he wasn't as relaxed as he looked.

"I hope this is all right? I don't have anything stronger to drink. Charlie doesn't drink much and with the baby I can't even have any wine."

Jean Paul turned from looking at the paper to her, the look on his face told her the outfit would be a smash on the sale rack.

"Do you like?"

"You don't need to ask *mon amour*. I thought you knew?"

"Silly, I mean the outfit. It's in my new maternity line."

"But of course. You have such a gift. Come, sit down beside me and let us talk." Mariah sits down and is immediately engulfed by his strong arms.

"I am curious to find out why you came all this distance. Is there something wrong?"

"Can a man not travel the globe to see someone he loves?"

"Jean Paul, I miss you too but there has to be another reason. So give it up and tell me."

"All right, I didn't want to get in to it this early in our visit but if you insist. I just came from the New Orleans shop. There have been several shipments that are being rerouted into Italy."

"Italy? I wasn't aware of that. Why Italy?"

"That is the question. The trunks are leaving Paris through the cargo planes as directed. So this means that the rerouting is being done between Pau and Paris and it is not long enough for anyone to notice the trunks are off schedule. I've also been checking out my own trunks. I've been hit on this a few times also."

"Why? I don't understand."

"I don't have an answer to that. The garments all seem to be in excellent condition when arriving at their destination with nothing missing. I have ordered an investigation into the problem through the plant and the warehouse but it may take several days to get answers."

"So we just wait?"

"It appears so. When I have any information I will let you know. I assure you I will stay on top of things for both of us."

"Do you think someone is trying to run us out of business?"

"I don't think so. There are swifter and more efficient means of doing that. Besides you are still a small enough operation that the people I could think of wanting to do this to me wouldn't even look at your shops. There would be no threat to them." Jean Paul seeing the worried look on her face decided it was time to change the subject. He didn't want her to worry about it all night. "Now how about something to eat. We must keep our strength up for *le bébé, oui?*" He got up and pulled Mariah to her feet. She felt his strength and was comforted by it. With his arm around her waist they walked into the kitchen.

"You know, *ma chérie*, I have missed you terribly. I really needed to see you. It has been too long."

"*Oui*, it has been too long."

"News on the home front, Guy sends his regards to you. He is talking like he wants to settle down finally and get involved in the family vineyard. Katelin has decided to sue for separation after she found out he has a mistress who is supposedly pregnant by him. He wants to prove to Katelin he has changed. I'm not so sure of what she'll do."

"I never would have thought he would ever have interest in the vineyard. He was always gone doing whatever it is he does. What are you going to do?"

"I haven't made up my mind yet. He has to prove to me he is worthy. I have offered him a job in the lower end of things. We shall see what he is all about."

"I do hope they can work things out. It's funny how sex can screw things up pretty fast."

"In some cases perhaps but not all. Let us eat, *oui?*"

All through the meal she knew he didn't take his eyes off her once. She felt safe, reassured and loved. They talked about their friends in France and her plans as to when she was coming back home to him. She explained she wanted to stop by the New Orleans shop first and didn't want to put a timetable on things just yet since the construction was going slower than planned. After the dishes were put away in the dishwasher, they retired to the living room. Sitting on the sofa, holding her in his arms Mariah found an old movie on the television. The phone rang. It was Becky, wanting to tell Mariah not to worry about anyone knowing the Count was in town, as she wasn't going to say a word. Mariah hung up with a sigh of relief.

"*Ma chérie* you haven't told me anything about what is going on here. What about this Charlie and Patrick fellow? Everything all right?"

"It is now, nothing is new. Charlie's coming home later tomorrow. He and Becky, you know, the woman you met in the store, anyway they are seeing each other. Patrick proposed to me a few days ago," she said the latter rather fast in hopes that he wouldn't catch it.

"What! What did you say?" Jean Paul raised his arm from around her and turned her to him. "What about my proposal to you? Have you forgotten?"

"How could I forget about yours? I said I couldn't. It's not fair to make a decision like that now. The baby will be here soon and I want my mind clear to concentrate on her." She felt his hard lean body relax a bit. "How can I really ever trust him again?"

"People have to earn trust, *ma chérie*."

"He and Charlie want paternity tests after the baby is here."

"How do you feel about that?"

"I don't know. Why can't things stay the way they are? She is MY daughter after all, that is what matters."

"Maybe not. The test results may need to be known sometime. I think you should think about it. It is a valid request, I would want to know and besides, she may want to know who her biological father is."

"But what am I suppose to do if Patrick turns out to be the father?"

"Time may tell. Let us worry about something else, shall we? I tire of this Patrick."

"What do you have in mind?"

"The clock is ticking too fast, taking with it our time together." He leans over, kisses her fully on the mouth a slow lingering kiss and holds her tightly.

"You never told me how long you are planning to stay?" she asked coming up for air. She felt warm and loved all at the same time. Her body was alive with the sense of him holding her.

"Just until tomorrow afternoon I'm afraid. I have business the day after that requires my time in Paris. There is something I want to ask you *ma chérie.* I had the distinct feeling that you were upset about my arrival? Why?"

"Oh no, Jean Paul. I could never be upset about being with you. That wasn't it at all. I was surprised. But I was even more surprised when you used your title."

"Why does my title bother you after all this time we've been together? I never knew it did."

"No, it's not your title.. it's just that I had not told anyone here who you really are. I can assure you that you or your title will never embarrass me so please don't even think that. I know you like your privacy. Patrick and Charlie had even deducted that you may be my baby's father, until the possibility of either one of them being the father came out. I just found it easier at first to let them believe what they wanted to. I was tired of the questions and pressure both of them were putting on me. I'm sorry I didn't mean to hurt your feelings. I'm very happy to be with you Count DuMoiese."

"It is all right. I'm not upset with you and I do understand why. It is too bad that I am not the baby's father. Think of it and the possibilities. I wish I were. Your life would be easier."

"But it is easier with you in it. You, I can trust and our relationship. It's very dear to me."

"You realize that the truth would have come out sooner or later about who I am. I do appreciate your concern about my privacy, but it is all right. This place, Crystal River is a small town compared to Paris. I think we can handle it, don't you?"

"Yes, together we can." After a few minutes Mariah turns back around to face Jean Paul. "Why is it we are so comfortable together? There isn't anything we can't discuss with each other, is there?"

"Perhaps we have found our place in life. What seems to be on your mind?"

"Do you think it is possible to love more than one person at a time? I mean love like a man and a woman?"

"*Oui.* I do. It has been known to happen. It is an odd feeling. Are you talking about this Patrick and Charlie fellow?" He held his breath.

"Oh no, not Charlie. I mean I love him like a brother. But lately I have come to realize I have some unresolved feelings toward Patrick." Those were not the words Jean Paul wanted to hear. "I just don't know what to do about them."

"But they are not strong enough for you to marry him?"

"No, they're not. I've discussed that all ready."

"You said two people? Who is the other man? I assume it is a man?" Grinning as he said it trying to put some humor into the heavy conversation. Mariah playfully hits him on the shoulder again.

"You are too silly. Don't you know it's you!"

"I was hoping you included me. You know I love you. I think I fell in love with you the moment I saw you standing on that sidewalk. So what you're saying is that you love both Patrick and myself?"

"*Oui*. Our love is different, it's easier, pure and honest, and it seems so natural. With Patrick it's so hard to be around him. I can't relax with him, not any more like I can with you."

"It is like that sometimes when love has gone astray. Sometimes circumstances get involved and you can never find what was before."

"You sound like you know first hand?"

"*Oui*. I, too, love two people." His words shocked her. He has always said he loves her.

"I don't understand?"

"I do love you, *ma chérie*, that will never change just as my love for Angelena continues."

"Angelena? You haven't really told me anything about her. I have wanted to ask you so many times about the woman in the portrait. All the staff would say she is your deceased wife and that she died young."

"Why didn't you just ask me?"

"I didn't know if I have the right to pry into that part of your life. You want to discuss her?"

"*Mon amour*, there is nothing in my life that is hidden from you. If you have questions then you have the right for answers. You have made me so wonderfully happy since we met. What can I tell you about Angelena? She was taken from me so very young. She was very beautiful just like you. She was Italian. We were married eight years. She cared about people so she dedicated her life to the service of others. Once she brought home a young lady, no more than fifteen maybe, who had run away. Her parents were abusive and addicted to something. Angelena met her sleeping on a park bench. She insisted we take her in and she helped the girl find a foster family who wanted to love her as their own. They adopted her and to this day that little wayward girl has a family of her own, a good head on her shoulders and a good job. She claims it is all because of what my Angelena had done."

"That's beautiful. Her portrait is so haunting as I recall. There seems to be sadness around her."

"*Oui*. You are very sensitive. The portrait was taken shortly after Jacques-Louis had died."

"Who is Jacques-Louis?"

"My son." Mariah was visually shaken at his words.

"It's all right, *mon amour*. I can see you want to ask why I have never spoken his name to you. I didn't want to upset you. It still upsets me to think my son didn't even have a chance to live. He died shortly after birth. The pregnancy ended early, too early- three months. You see my son was too little to survive. There was nothing the doctors could do in spite of their efforts. His lungs were not developed enough. Angelena never accepted his death totally. She blamed herself even though it wasn't the case. A couple of years later we tried again and it was then she was diagnosed with leukemia. I only had her another year. I have not loved another until you came along, but I still love her in my own way. There are times I feel that she brought us together. Certain things I watch you do or hear you say remind me of her."

"Do you believe in life after death?"

"Yes, I do. There is a greater power than what we know on this earth. The human soul lives on for eternity. I believe that our loved ones that have gone on to the next level still hold those of us left behind dear to them. They show their love to us in many ways. Some can have visitations to give us strength, some protect us and some offer us guidance. That day we met I was actually having lunch in a restaurant when I suddenly had the urge to leave. I can't explain it but I listened to the voice inside me and started walking not knowing where I was going. I think Angelena was urging me along. I just knew I had to go. I trusted that feeling. Then I saw you and my life changed. All the sadness I had inside was gone instantly. Death does not change how we feel about each other it just changes our physical status. I have seen it as so. We all will be reunited on the next level when it is our time. What do you believe?"

"You really do believe that don't you? I believe in God and in heaven but I'm not so sure about heavenly intervention. I thought we all had to walk our own paths?"

"We do, but sometimes we can ask for help and sometimes we get it in the most unexpected ways. Why are you crying?" Mariah wiped the silent tears from her cheek.

"I had no idea of the pain you went through. I'm so sorry."

"Shhh. Please don't cry. We must live for today and not look back so much. What was, is not what is. I have put to rest my sorrow. I still miss them but I have a wonderful future. I may be getting older but I'm a long way from being cold." After a few minutes Mariah's eyes brightened.

"Jean Paul, may I name my daughter Abigail Angelena?"

"You want to name *le bébé* after my mother and my wife? Are you sure?" Jean Paul was so touched, traces of wetness appeared around the corner of his eyes.

"*Oui*. Your mother was special to me too. We had some nice talks when I was visiting. She told me she hoped we could be together, that she saw a difference in you after we met. That I was good for you and she believed you were good for me. I really developed a fondness for her. She had a grand insight on life. Like mother like son. She accepted the baby and me like I was one of hers- very graceful and loving. And Angelena, I think, I would have liked her, too, but I am glad we met when we did. I really want to do this. Do I have your acceptance?"

"I think Abigail Angelena is a beautiful name. She will have two guardian angels watching over her."

"I'm glad. She will know her namesakes I promise."

They sat holding tightly to each other for quite some time watching the movie. Finally Mariah nods off to sleep against Jean Paul. He carries her upstairs and lies her in bed. She stirs a little. "Jean Paul don't go, stay with me."

"I am right here, *mon amour*. I will not go anywhere." He undresses quietly and slipped in bed beside her. How he wanted to show her how much she really means to him. But to make love to her all night long was out of the question due to her delicate condition. He would not do anything to hurt her or the baby. He had already lost too much so he settled on holding her as close as he could.

She woke with a start. That dream.. she had the same dream where she was carrying her baby away from something menacing but she didn't know what. She was crying in her sleep, saying no, no. Jean Paul woke from his sleep.

"Mariah? It is just a dream." Jean Paul woke her gently and held her tight against his chest. His heartbeat was comforting to Mariah.

"I don't know. I keep having this dream. I'm carrying my child and running away from something. It's always the same dream. I'm scared to death." She started to cry again.

"Shhh. It is all right, you are here with me. We are safe and so is *le bébé*. You have nothing to worry about." Jean Paul was rocking her slowly in his arms. Her sobs were quieting down.

"What if it is an omen? What if something is wrong with my child?"

"I doubt that. The doctor would have told you by now. Have you had the dream before I told you about Angelena and Jacques?"

"Yes. One other time, a few weeks ago."

"Angelena had some nightmares, too. The doctor told her sometimes in late pregnancies this is common. The fears of the birth manifest this way. Maybe you should speak to your doctor. Now lie back down, you need to rest. I shall be here to fight back all the goblins." Mariah felt better knowing he was there but still there was something she couldn't shake off.

"I'm glad you're here."

"I am too. Now sleep *ma chérie*."

Mariah felt all of his maleness next to her while his thick hair on his chest tickled her back. She wondered what it would be like to make love to him. She couldn't sleep.

"Jean Paul?"

"What?" His voice was huskier than normal.

"Make love to me." He couldn't believe his ears raising himself up on an elbow, he turned Mariah to him. This is what he had been wanting to hear for so long but knew she had to come to him in her own good time. He could not pressure her.

"*Ma chérie*, I have waited so long to hear you say those words to me but we can't. Not now, I want you so very much believe me. I don't want to do anything that may hurt you or little Abigail. We need to wait until she is born." They both sat up in bed and he took her in his arms.

"Attitudes have changed since years ago. You won't hurt me or Abigail."

"I can't take that chance. I love you both too much and I couldn't live with myself if something happened to either one of you."

"You do mean that don't you?" The feeling of his love swelled in her heart.

"With all my heart." He kissed her fully on the mouth. His tongue parted her lips lightly and slipped inside. She returned the kiss and explored his mouth. They had never kissed like this before, this passionate and with this urgency. He unbuttoned her satin top. The fabric felt cool and sensuous to him, it opened and fell unto the bed. His hands stroked her face, throat and each breast as he cupped them and teased them. And then he laid her down gently. The way he kissed her so completely she thought she would explode from desire. He kissed each ripple her skin made under his tongue until he found her breast. She moaned. His mouth traveled down her bulging stomach. With his hand underneath her satin shorts he gently coaxed them off, revealing there was not another layer of fabric to get in his way. The baby kicked just as he had done this and they both laughed. He started kissing her, drawing as much of her scent in as possible. Their tongues met again. His hands were stroking her legs, her inners thighs and came to rest in one spot. His fingers were teasing, stroking and caressing her while his tongue was traveling down her body once again. The desire was so great between them. She wanted him as much as he wanted her. By this time his tongue was tracing up her inner thigh and came to rest in that one delicate spot. His fingers moved ever so slightly to make room for his tongue. She made a little moan and gasp as she let go and fell into the blessed bliss. She shuddered. He took her to the depths of her desires so passionately and so caring that she couldn't remember ever feeling this way before. She was completely satisfied. He continued to tease her with his tongue as he stroked her. He didn't want to stop touching her. She was everything to him and for the first time she realized just how much. After a few moments he looked up at her and grinned. He was leaning over top of her, still holding her, stroking her.

"Will that do, *mon amour*, until we can correctly complete our task? Did this old Frenchman give you something to think about?"

"You are not by any means old. I am totally dissolved in your being. Words can not express what I feel at the moment." He knew the look on her face was one of complete peace and love. She pushed him down on his back.

"Now Count, let me show what American women can do." She was leaning over him this time and began to kiss him, her fingers traveling down his body, etching out every hard lean muscle he owned. This was a night for both to remember he thought as he got swept away in his own waves of passion.

He woke early as he was in a custom of doing. He slipped on his pants but neglected to put anything else on. He didn't want to spill anything on his shirt while he attempted to cook breakfast. He was so anxious to see Mariah that he went off without his luggage. He always kept fresh clothes and toiletries on his plane in case of emergencies so there wasn't a real need to pack. Once he got on the plane he would change and shave. He found the coffee and brewed a pot. He had no intentions of waking Mariah up just yet. He thought he could handle the range and cook up something simple like eggs and toast; as his kitchen staff usually prepared the meals. He was preparing a tray for her complete with one of the last roses in Charlie's poor pathetic garden when he thought he heard a noise. He went upstairs and found her still sleeping. He closed the bedroom door to block out any noise he would make while cooking breakfast. It wouldn't do to wake her up, after all they did have a long night. It still bothered him to think that this Patrick could still mean something to her, but what they shared last night was more than passion, it was true and real. And they both knew it.

Patrick hadn't heard from Mariah for a few days. He had received a call last night from his manager about having to redo some takes in the last film he did. Some idiot had edited too much out of one the crucial scenes. This meant he had to leave town for a few days but first he wanted to let Mariah know. He knew she probably would still be in bed but couldn't help it; as his plane was due to take off at eight-thirty.

To his surprise she already had company. He couldn't tell what the rental car was until he was walking up the driveway. To his astonishment it was a new Rolls Royce Silver Seraph. That had to cost a pretty penny to rent one of those, not too many companies had them in stock. Who does she know that could afford that? He was asking himself as he rung the doorbell. Through the side window of the door, Patrick could see an older man barely with any clothes on standing in front of the range, flipping something in a skillet and drinking coffee. The door was locked as he tried the knob. Jean Paul took the eggs out of the skillet, turned off the range and answered the door.

"*Oui*, may I help you?" There was no mistaking this must be the Jean Paul character Patrick thought. It had caught him off guard to see him here and dressed like that.

"I came to see Mariah. Where is she?" He didn't like the look of this guy. What was he doing running around with just his pants on and in someone else's home. He had to be in his late fifties in spite of looking like he spent twenty four/seven in the gym. He did wonder how much weight he lifted to keep that look. Patrick was muscular but not like him.

"I'm sorry *Monsieur* Wainscott, she is still asleep. She had a very long night. I was about to take her breakfast in a short while. Would you like something to eat or drink? Coffee maybe? I don't have much of an opportunity to practice my cooking but my coffee is drinkable as you say." Jean Paul motioned him to sit.

"No thank you. That's a nice Rolls out there."

"*Oui* it is. If I have to drive I prefer the smaller version next to my older Rolls. I have several cars at home for my staff and myself. I tend to collect them as a hobby."

"Several?" Patrick was surprised but also intrigued. "It was generous of you to buy Mariah a car. The old one she had was always breaking down but she wouldn't get rid of it."

"*Oui*, she did need a new one however she considers it to be a loan. Safety has no cost for her or *le bébé* in my eyes."

"How do you know who I am?" Patrick suddenly tired of small talk and wanted to get down to business. This was his chance he thought as he walked in to the kitchen where Jean Paul continued to finish the tray.

"I make it a point to know a lot about everything and everybody."

"So you must be Jean Paul? I'm sorry you have me at the disadvantage. I don't know your full name?"

"Ah, I am Count DuMoiese. So we finally meet *Monsieur* Wainscott. I think we have a lot in common, do we not? You may call me Count, there is no need to stand on full formalities is there?" He said with an air of authority. Patrick didn't like being talked to that way but said nothing for the moment.

"Count, Mariah has told me nothing about you. I'm not sure we have anything in common but her." It all made sense now; the Rolls, the Mercedes and her secrecy about him. How was he going to handle this one? It could only mean one thing and he didn't like it. The Count raised his eyebrow and looked at Patrick directly. He was sizing him up and Patrick knew it.

"I need to see Mariah, so if you excuse me." Patrick started up the stairs and Jean Paul stepped in front of him. There was no way he would allow this man to disturb the woman he loved and would protect her at all costs.

"*Monsieur* Wainscott, I said she is asleep. In her delicate condition she need not be disturbed at the moment. You do understand? Perhaps you can come back later and speak with her."

"What are you her bodyguard? Perhaps you do not understand. I cannot come back later. I have to speak to her now." His anger started to show through.

"*Monsieur* Wainscott, I assure you I am not her bodyguard unless she needs one of course. You see I care very deeply for *Mademoiselle* Remmington. I want only the best for her."

"So do I. In case you don't know we lived together for five years in every sense of being married."

"*Oui*, but not legally, correct? Perhaps it was better she found out about your roaming eyes before you were actually married. It was easier for her to get out of the relationship wasn't it?" Rage was starting to fill Patrick but he took control of it before it was too late.

"What Mariah and I have is none of your concern. But since we are discussing this I want to know what's between the two of you? What is your relationship? For heaven sakes, look at you! You are old enough to be her father." Patrick was practically in his face. He leaned against the kitchen cabinets with his arms crossed on his chest. Jean Paul refused to be brought down to his level so he took his coffee and sat down at the table.

"*Monsieur* Wainscott, as you so elegantly put it my personal relationship with her is none of your concern. We are business partners after all. There are things we have to discuss from time to time. And yes, I firmly believe the heavens did smile upon us the day we met. Now as far as my age, I could be your father, too, but I assure you it is not an issue between the *Mademoiselle* and myself. I am glad I am NOT her father. My age does not impair my functions for being a "hot-blooded" Frenchman. Do you have any more questions?" Jean Paul had a slight grin on his face that Patrick wanted to knock off but resisted.

"So you're implying that a personal relationship exists between you two?"

"Mariah has been a free agent now for some months. I don't have to fight you for her Wainscott." This time the Count left off the formalities. He was getting rather annoyed. "She is capable of making her own decisions."

"I'm very much aware of that. Let it be known I want our relationship back. Are you aware that the baby is mine?"

"*Le bébé* could be yours, or this Charlie's or possibly turn out to be mine in the end."

"Don't make me laugh. Yours?"

"Maybe not through DNA which I understand has been discussed but in every other way." Patrick was shaken to know the Count knew so much. He didn't expect that.

"Jean Paul? Everything okay? I heard voices?" Mariah descended the stairs. She rounded the corner into the kitchen and stopped short. "Patrick? What are you doing here?" Jean Paul met her in the kitchen and helped her to take a seat at the table. Patrick couldn't take his eyes off of her, how the satin lounging outfit clung to her and how the baby had grown in the past few days since he had seen her.

"*Mon amour*, please sit. I was going to bring you breakfast in bed but got delayed. My apologies for disturbing your sleep this way. I took the liberty of gathering your medications. I found them in the bathroom instead of your purse. Jean Paul sat down at the table beside Mariah. She took the medications out of his hands, her hands lingered for a second touching his. Patrick took notice he referenced he had been looking in her purse which was one thing Mariah never like him to do. She considered it her own space and personal property.

"Patrick?" Patrick had remembered that *mon amour* meant my love. He didn't hear what she was saying. "Patrick?"

"Huh? What? Oh I need to speak to you alone. I don't have much time." Patrick uncrosses his arms and sits at the table taking her hands in his.

"What is it then?" She glances at Jean Paul who raises an eyebrow and tilts his head slightly.

"I need to talk to you in private."

81

"Jean Paul, would you mind?"

"If you are sure, *mon amour*. I shall go and dress." Jean Paul turns to Patrick. "I am warning you, do not get her upset." He pointed a finger in Patrick's face and went upstairs. How dare him! Patrick wanted to strike him but with Mariah watching he didn't dare. It would mean that she would never speak to him again knowing her and her temper.

"Just who does he think he his? Are you sleeping together?"

"Patrick! That is none of your business." She had flashbacks of last night, her time with Jean Paul was precious. What did you come here for? You should have called first." She was anxious to get Patrick to leave.

"When did he get here and how long is he staying?"

"If you must know, he arrived last night and is staying until this afternoon. We have business to discuss."

"Yea, by the looks of things the two of you have discussed more than business. He's pretty intimate with you or does he go around half naked all the time? You know he's too old for you!"

"He is not! He's only fifty-six. And by the way I have seen you without your shirt on. So what's the difference?"

"Not in someone else's home."

"Stop it! He's dressed. If you had called all this could have been avoided. What is your point of coming over here anyway?

"I'm leaving town for a couple of days. There was a problem with my last fiim. I have to do some retakes. Here are my numbers. You can reach me if you need anything. Now with him being here, perhaps I can reschedule the takes."

"I'm sorry but you are NOT my keeper. I can associate with whom ever I want even if you are living in the same town. I think you had better leave town before I decided to pull the rug out from under the DNA test on your part. I don't need this jealousy. Do you understand me?" Mariah had gotten to her feet and was standing over top of him. Anger flashed in her eyes.

"So you've made a decision on the paternity test? Are you allowing it?"

"Yes for both you and Charlie but only after MY child comes. What I decide to do with the information will be my choice and only my choice."

"What is going on in here?" Jean Paul walked into the kitchen just in time to see her. She swayed a little on her feet. He took two steps and was beside her in a flash to steady her.

"I'm all right. I need my medicine." Jean Paul handed them to her and Patrick got her a glass of water.

"Sit down. Rest your head, *ma chérie*." Jean Paul stroking her hair looked directly at Patrick.

"What did you say to her?"

"Nothing Jean Paul, please calm down. Everyone calm down now! I just want some peace."

"I'm sorry Mariah, I'm sorry. I didn't mean for this to happen."

"It's everything, you and the pregnancy and everything that goes along with it. Thank you for consideration of letting me know you're leaving, now please just go."

"*Monsieur* Wainscott, have you said what you wanted? If so then it is time to leave so I can take care of Mariah and *le bébé*." Jean Paul went to the front door and held it open. "Please leave in a dignified manner or I will throw you out."

Patrick got up and glared at the Count. He didn't want to leave like this but thought it was for the best not getting Mariah upset any further. He noticed the Count had fully dressed in a suit that had to cost seven hundred or more. He had on a silk shirt and tie. His attire and manner reeked of money from his perfectly manicured hands to his leather loafers. He was going to have to pull out all the stops if he was in hopes of getting her back, not that she was after his money, he was sure that wasn't the case but she was letting Jean Paul close to her and her thoughts. This was a place that he wasn't allowed to go anymore. How could he fight this? He could make a good living for the three of them but couldn't compare with him. He had to think about his next move. What to do next?

On the way to the airport Patrick made a call. "Clark, its me. I need a favor. I need you to investigate someone by the name of Count Jean Paul DuMoiese. Why the hell would I know how to spell his last name? You're the detective. I want every bit of history on him. I want to know how he spends his time and who with. I want to know who and what he is. Do you understand me?"

"Man, I don't have time for this favor. I've got a big divorce case I'm working on right now. Get someone else or call me back in a couple of weeks."

"Clark, you don't get it do you buddy? I need this information yesterday! You have two days to get me all you can on this guy. I'll call you when I get back in town."

Patrick hangs up before Clark had a chance to refuse helping. Maybe he could find something out now that he knew who and where to look. It was time, he had no choice but to board the plane and leave Mariah alone with HIM even if it was just a few more hours until he would be gone. He still didn't like it.

CHAPTER 6

Mariah and Jean Paul had finished breakfast. She still had a raging headache so she took his advice to lie down for a little while longer. He cleared the dishes and straightened the kitchen. He then went upstairs to see how she was doing and found her fast asleep. Good. She needs to sleep, he thought to himself. As he was closing the door Mariah spoke.

"Jean Paul, please hold me." Her voice was much like a child's, so soft and innocent. He knew she was tormented on what path she should take for herself and the baby and he knew he was part of that torment and hated it. But he had come to love her and he was in it for the long haul no matter what path she decided. It wasn't going to change how he felt about her or the baby. He felt sure if she chose Patrick, it didn't work before and the possibility of it working now was slim. He would be there to pick up the pieces again. He didn't want to see her go through all the pain again but knew that this may be something she may have to do. And there was the business part of their relationship that would work in his favor, too. She needed him to be there for her and that was exactly what he was going to do. There had been no other woman for him since Angelena and he was not going to let her go so easily. He slipped off his jacket and shoes and lay beside her holding her. He held her so close to him that she could smell his scent, feel his strength and his love for her.

It was after one, when they woke. Mariah had slipped out of bed, washed her face and dressed. Her headache was better. Jean Paul was sitting up leaning against the headboard when she came out of the bathroom. She went to the dresser and started to put her earrings on.

"So you're up?" Mariah spoke softly.

"How do you feel?"

"My headache is better. What time did you say you have to leave?"

"Why? Are you tired of me already?"

"*Non*, not at all. You know I don't want you to go."

"It won't be that long until we can be together again."

"I was just wondering if we had time to get something to eat? I'm starved."

"I can think of several things to eat right now but it all would take too long. It must be savored and not rushed."

"Jean Paul would you get serious. I'm really hungry."

"Of course, *ma chérie*, we can get something at the airport café, can we not? Why don't you come with me now? Let me hire someone to help you with all this business here?"

"You're so sweet. I can't do that, besides I have Margo but I really need to do this myself. Do you understand?"

"*Oui*, but I don't like it."

Mariah sits down on the bed beside him and kisses him. He grabs her and pulls her down holding her on the bed underneath him and kisses her back.

She followed Jean Paul to the airport in her car. Just as they were entering the front doors, Charlie, not looking where he was going carrying his baggage, bumped into them. "Excuse me." He started to go around them without looking up. Jean Paul's arm went around Mariah protectively.

"Charlie! You're back." Mariah said as Jean Paul looks quickly at her.

"Mariah! That was you I bumped into? Are you okay? I'm so sorry. I didn't hurt you did I?"

"Don't be silly. We're fine." Mariah stroked her child.

"Oh my gosh, look at the size of that kid. That's got to be superman's baby." Charlie said jokingly.

"I love you too." Mariah retorted back. Jean Paul shifted his weight and Charlie suddenly noticed him.

"Oh, sorry. Where are my manners?" Jean Paul nodded his head slightly in response while Charlie extended his hand. Jean Paul shook it. "Hello, I'm Charles Osswell but everyone calls me Charlie. Mariah and I have been friends for years."

"*Monsieur* Osswell, I am.."

"Please let me." Mariah interrupted. "Charlie this is my friend and business partner Count Jean Paul DuMoiese. Count DuMoiese this is *Monsieur* Osswell." There was no need for Mariah to introduce him after Charlie heard the Count speak. He knew exactly who he was. Jean Paul had tipped his head toward Mariah with a grin when she used his title and Charlie noticed it. He also noticed how tight his arm was around Mariah's waist. This man was definitely staking his claim.

"Count it's very nice to meet you. Are you staying long?"

"*Non*, I regret that I am leaving actually." Jean Paul glanced at Mariah remembering their time together last night and smiled. She was smiling back at him.

"Oh, I'm sorry we don't have time to talk." He wondered if Patrick knew this guy was in town. Jean Paul's cell phone rang.

"*Bonjour. Oui. Je t'appellerai. Au revoir*." He placed the phone back into the inside pocket of his suit. "Please excuse that interruption. It seems my plane has been delayed at bit. Would *Monsieur* Osswell like a glass of wine with us in the café? Or do you not have the time?" Mariah looked questioning at him.

She had understood everything he had said including telling the pilot Alec, that he would call him. Obviously he wasn't ready to leave yet. There was nothing wrong with the plane. The delay was Charlie. What was he doing?

"Sure I have the time. I'd like that." Charlie replied. Walking toward the café Charlie hugged Mariah and told her it was good to see her. They chose a table by the runway windows.

"Just coffee for me." Charlie orders.

"I'd like a glass of your best Chablis, *s'il vous plait. Merci*," Jean Paul replies wondering just how good it would be. Mariah ordered something to eat. Jean Paul sipping his wine was watching Mariah and Charlie joking around. He wanted to get to know this Charlie, to assess if he was going to be a threat to his relationship with her. He had already believed he was not but had to make sure of it.

"Did Becky tell you I was coming in early?"

"No I haven't spoken to her since yesterday afternoon. Meeting you was a total surprise. Is she supposed to meet you?"

"No. I called her late last night, by that time it was too late for her to arrange a late lunch. Some big court case or something."

"If you need a ride I'll take you home. I need to get my things anyway."

"Why? Did the contractors finish?"

"Not yet, but I don't want to intrude on you and Becky's space."

"The house is plenty big enough for both of us."

"Yea, I know, but I can't."

"*Ma chérie*, what are your plans?"

"I've arranged a room at the Inn. I'll be there until they get my apartment done."

"You will not! There is no chance of that."

"Charlie this is what I'm going to do and I won't discuss it anymore. You and Becky need your space and I'm not going to be involved with that."

Jean Paul was listening intently to their conversation. He reached inside his suit to the hidden breast pocket. Charlie noticed the Count had pulled out a checkbook and was signing a check.

"*Ma chérie*, here take this. It will help with things at the moment." Jean Paul handed her a five thousand dollar check.

"No thank you. I don't need that but you're sweet to offer." She tore the check up and handed it back to Jean Paul but not before Charlie had the chance to see the amount. If he was surprised about the amount he didn't show it. "Here is my number at the Inn and of course you have my cell and the boutique." She handed the paper to Jean Paul who put it in his little black book he took out of the inside pocket of his jacket.

"So Count DuMoiese, I'm sorry that Becky and I didn't get a chance to take the two of you out to dinner."

"Please call me Count or Jean Paul if you prefer, if I may call you Charlie, is it?"

"Yes, it is." Mariah's eyes opened wide.

The Count never allowed the use of his first name unless it was with someone very close to him; his inside circle of friends, even most of the staff called him Count."

"This Becky? Is she someone special?"

"Well, maybe. I did miss her while I was gone."

"I think that's the start of things," Mariah replied grinning at him.

"So Jean Paul, where are you from?" Charlie thought that since the Count had chosen to ask such a personal question about Becky it gave him the right to return the same.

"I reside in Marseille. It is the second largest city and the oldest city in France. It is a beautiful place. You and this Becky should visit."

"That would be nice. Maybe we will sometime. What do you do? I mean outside of being a Count?" Mariah just about choked on her food.

"Are you all right, *ma chérie?*" Mariah nodded, she kept her eyes on Jean Paul. "I have a textile factory, but my passion is the vineyard and the winery. It has been in my family for ages. To grow something so beautiful as the grape and to create one of the finest wines in the world is an accomplishment. It took me years to get my label right. My forefather's have had their own label and I of course still produce them. Many men have tried to perfect the beverage but most cannot get that certain blend just right. You see under French laws wines are put into four categories- very cheap and low quality, reasonable quality and most of the time drinkable, good wines and then of course what my label falls under- the AOC or what you may call the top of the line- the elite of the industry. My vineyard is one of the largest in France. Then of course I have my business with Mariah." Charlie nodded his head as if in agreement. What did he really know about wine, nothing?"

"So.. do you have a lay over to get from here to France?" Charlie continued.

"*Non*, not at all. I don't travel commercial. I have my own plane. She is parked over there, the white one with black and gold on it." Jean Paul pointed to the holding lot on his right.

"Is that what I think it is? That's the best Boeing jet that's made. The surprise in Charlie's voice was evident. The plane was easy to spot since it was the largest on the lot.

"*Oui*, you know your planes, it is a J2. I ordered the interior to my specifications. Would you like to see inside?"

"Yes, I would." Mariah finished her meal just in time. She was not going to let them go by themselves. It would be hard telling what would happen.

The Count had called for the airport taxi, so she wouldn't have to walk the distance. They were boarding in a few minutes with Alec greeting them at the door. Jean Paul introduced him to Charlie. He then turned to Mariah.

"It is good to see you again *Mademioselle* Mariah. You are looking very well." Alec took her hand and kissed it.

"*Merci beaucoup*. You're just a charming as ever." Alec disappeared into the cockpit when the Count started the tour with Charlie.

There's seating for eight people in the cabin. Each seat is in fact a lounger so one could sleep very well if need be. In the same open area as the seats the small kitchen with a bar presented itself and with it a full bathroom just to the side of it. The Count's personal quarters were next. The Count held the door open for Charlie to enter. His room took up the rest of the plane. It was large enough for a king size bed and two dressers. In the corner stood an antique ladies vanity and mirror and chair set. The closet space was surprising for being on a plane. The bedroom had a full bath attached to it that included fixtures made of 24-carat gold. The interior of the plane was tastefully decorated with expensive upholstery and Berber carpet. The Count's quarters were much more elaborate with heavy corded drapes over the windows for privacy while the windows up front sported thinner drapes to keep the sun out but not to obstruct the view. Charlie couldn't believe his eyes. This plane was a moving apartment.

"Excuse me guys, but I have to use the facilities." Mariah disappears into the rear bathroom connecting off of the bedroom.

"Come Charlie, let us get a taste of my wine." Jean Paul showed Charlie to the front of the plane and poured him a glass. He wanted to get Charlie to himself for a minute. The wine impressed Charlie, it was one of the best he had tasted.

"This bird is impressive."

"*Merci.* Please sit. Since we have a moment alone I want to ask you something and I want the truth."

"What is it?" Charlie was suddenly on guard.

"I know that there is a possibility that you are *le bébé's* father. What are your intentions toward her and Mariah?"

"*Le bébé?* Oh, you mean the baby? I was wondering how much you knew. I assure you that I intend to be there for the baby and Mariah whether I am the father or not. We are all the family either one of us has so to speak. My intentions are what Mariah will let me be. It's up to her. We're not in love with each other but we do love each other, if you can understand that. She is very special to me. I want her to be happy. I just don't know for sure what it will take for her to be happy right now. And since we are talking about this I want you to know that I won't stand for anyone to hurt her again. She's has been through enough. Do you understand what I mean?"

"Do you feel that way toward *Monsieur* Wainscott too?"

"I do. He may be my best friend but enough is enough and I have told him so. He still loves her deeply, you know, but I won't stand by and let him hurt her either."

"I see. So you think I may hurt her in some way? I admire your courage but assure you that I will not let anything hurt her ever. I intend to make her very happy if she will let me. I do not believe that she has a life here in Crystal River any more than I do. There is too much heartbreak here for her."

Mariah overheard the last of the conversation. "Now boys, please don't talk about me behind my back. I can and will make my own decisions about my future and whom I am with." Jean Paul slipped between Mariah and Charlie and gave her a hug.

"It will be fun, *mon amour* to win your heart."

"You already have." Mariah flashed Jean Paul a grin as she said this. Charlie caught the drift of intimacy between them. Jean Paul's phone rang.

"*Oui*, I understand. *Merci*, Alec." He replaces the phone in the pocket of his jacket. "I am so sorry, *mon amour*, but it is time to leave if I'm going to make my other appointments." Charlie saw the look of disappointment on Mariah's face. There was a lot more to this than she wanted every one to believe. She couldn't deny it now.

"Excuse me, Charlie, but I would like to have a minute alone with Jean Paul, please?"

"Sure I'll just wait outside then. Jean Paul, it's nice to meet you. I enjoyed our talk." He shook hands with Jean Paul and walked down the stairs to the runway to wait for Mariah.

"I was hoping you would get rid of him, if not I would have." He took her in his arms and gave her a long kiss. His arms enveloped her and she gave in to her feelings. She kissed him back. She wanted to go with him but her head told her to settle things here first. She knew that was the best thing to do.

"Mariah, *Je t'aime*. I love you! You know there has never been another woman for me since Angelena passed on. You mean more to me than life itself."

"Jean Paul you have changed my life so much. I love you too." Jean Paul's cell rang again. He answered and told Alec that he would be just a minute more. He understood that they had clearance to take off.

"Please, *mon amour*, call me as soon as you get settled at the Inn. I'll worry about you until I can hold you in my arms again."

"We'll be just fine, don't worry about us." Mariah spoke softly in his ear as she gave him another kiss. He walked her down the stairs so she wouldn't trip. Charlie met her at the bottom, took her arm and led her away from the plane.

They stood by the terminal, waving as the jet took off. Mariah felt as if her world was dissolving and she couldn't stop it. Why? She still had her baby, she had a man who loved her tremendously and she had her business. And yet she had questions with no answers. What would her life be like if she had Patrick's heart, soul and mind like she had Jean Paul's? Their relationship didn't work then and it wouldn't now in spite of the baby, even if he was her father. Jean Paul would be a better father. He's more settled than Patrick and what Jean Paul could offer Abigail was beyond belief. Her thoughts filled her head so deeply that it took Charlie a couple of tries of getting her attention on the way home.

"Thanks for the ride home but you really don't need to move out."

"Sure I do and you know why. I can't possibly stay there now that you're back. I can't tear your friendship with Patrick apart any more or your relationship with Becky. I have decided to consent on the paternity test for both you and Patrick but only after the baby comes. Are you still planning not to say anything to Becky about the baby until we know for sure?"

"I don't see any reason to until later and I do thank you for the test."

"You know she wants to move in with you?"

"Yea, she's been talking about it but I haven't given her my answer yet."

"I'm not so sure not telling her is a wise move."

"I'll deal with it if I have to. Let me ask you something. Does Patrick know the Count was in town?"

"Yes. This morning he came by to say goodbye without calling first. He left for a day or so. It's a good thing too, I mean him leaving."

"What happened?"

"Well let us say he got an eyeful. Jean Paul was fixing breakfast for me in bed. We weren't exactly dressed for company."

"Oh, you're not telling me you two were..?"

"Heavens no! Jean Paul had his pants on but that was all."

"How did Patrick handle things?"

"Jean Paul said he was okay at first but then his containment left and he became demanding and jealous."

"And Jean Paul?"

"He took control of the situation and asked him to leave. I had a splitting headache and couldn't deal with him."

"I'm sorry he made a scene. I would talk to him but I don't think he wants to talk to me yet."

"I know I tried to get him to see reason on that but I don't think I got through either."

"Mariah don't worry about things. Given enough time he may come around."

"What if he doesn't?"

"Then we didn't have as strong a bond as I thought."

"But still.."

"I said don't worry about things. It will take care of itself. Now promise me you'll let this go?"

"I don't think I can. Look there's Becky."

Becky was in the driveway when they arrived. Charlie hugged her when she kissed him. Mariah went inside first and they followed. By that afternoon Mariah had her things packed. Charlie and Becky insisted on going to the Inn to help her with the luggage. It wasn't that she had that much but with the extra weight she was carrying with the baby, they didn't want her to hurt herself. After getting settled she called Margo to let her know the change in plans. They talked about Jean Paul and then hung up. Her phone rang immediately.

"Hello. Oh Jean Paul, I was going to call you later."

"I couldn't wait to hear your voice. I had to call. Are you alone?"

"Yes, why?"

"I want to know what you are not wearing *mon amour*?"

"Why Jean Paul, is this a dirty call?" She laughed as she said this.

"*Oui*, of course. I am a hot blooded man you know."

"How could I forget?"

"Are you okay? Did Charlie question you too much?"

"Not too bad. He knows about us. I couldn't hide anything from him?"

"That doesn't matter. It is better this way. Perhaps he can keep Patrick away from you if they talk."

"I'm not so sure of that Jean Paul. Now what about us? I miss you but I guess I will just have to dream about what happened last night over and over until we see each other again."

"Hopefully it won't be that long."

They spoke a while longer but Mariah was tired and wanted to go to bed. It was only five but she was so tired she climbed into bed without changing her clothes and slept until the next morning. By noon she was at the boutique. The workmen were making progress on the repairs. It would only be another day or two before she could be back in the apartment and that she was glad of that.

Patrick couldn't wait to get back home to find out what kind of information Clark had for him. He had to know about the Count now!

"Clark, it's me, do you have anything yet?"

"Man, it's early. I haven't had much time to work on this but so far here is what I've got. The Count is truly a Count by blood. He has family money and money he has made through his vineyard and winery, which carries his own label. Part of the vineyards were handed down to him and part is what he bought surrounding the original. Now it is one of the largest in southern France. He also owns a textile factory in Pau, France. There he has his own tailors to design a men's line. It seems that he found this one tailor and he liked his work so well that he set him up working solely for the Count designing a complete men's wardrobe. Then there is this business he entered into about six months ago.. it's in women's design. It seems that he bought interest in a boutique in New Orleans. The other partner is also a designer that goes by M. Remmington who happens to carry the same name of the boutique. My sources says he is manufacturing her line out of his factory. They say this designer is becoming quite well known throughout Europe and over here is some circles too. Hey didn't you used to live with a designer?" Clark continued and Patrick cut him off.

"Most of this I know already. How about something I don't know?"

"Well the Count has been married only once. His wife Angelena died twenty some years ago from Leukemia. They had one son who died shortly after birth. His mother's name is Abigail and she died recently at the age of eighty-five. His father's name is Louis and he has been dead for several years. The Count is the first born of two boys, which enabled him to take the title of Count. His younger brother Guy happens to be labeled as a playboy in the French society. He is married to Katelin and they have four children, fifteen to five. Katelin has recently left Guy due to his involvement with another young lady who is supposed to be pregnant by him."

"Enough about the family. What about him?"

"There isn't anything else Patrick. That's all there is. He's clean. Not a dirty morsel about him. Politically there is nothing against him either. He's thought of highly in that world too. Very strong in politics, he is what we call a lobbyist. He is always trying to improve some law or something to make the world better you know what I mean? Most recently he has been involved in helping to pass some pretty strict laws in France against drug running. He's a great deal of connections throughout Europe as well as other countries. Personally the Count is a private man and not much else is known."

"Keep working on it. If you come up with anything, call me right away. Understand?"

"Sure. Why is this man so important to you?"

"That's none of your concern." Patrick slammed the phone down. Damn it, he thought. What would he use out of all that to win back Mariah? There was nothing. She probably knew all of it anyway. Patrick had concluded his business early and caught the first flight back to Crystal River. He had to get home and see if the Count had left and what kind of damage repair he had to do.

It was well after six when he finally stepped off the plane. Mariah would be back at Charlie's by then and since it was fairly close to the airport he decided to stop before going home. He noticed her car wasn't in the drive but Charlie's truck was still out. She must of have put her car in the garage, he thought as he knocked. Charlie answered the door surprised.

"Hi buddy. Come on in." He opened it wide.

"I didn't know you were home. I'm looking for Mariah."

"I got back yesterday. She wouldn't stay. She's moved into the Inn until the apartment is done. I feel bad about her doing that but she insisted that under the circumstances and for the sake of all three of our friendships she thought it was for the best. Come on in and sit. Let's talk."

"I'm not sure we have anything to discuss."

"What about Mariah?" Patrick follows Charlie in to the living room and sits down.

"What about Mariah?"

"Look, I don't want our friendship to end like this. It doesn't have to. Mariah knows there are problems between us due to the baby. It's eating at her so much that all she wants to do is leave town as soon as the boutique gets done. If she does that I can bet she'll go directly back to Jean Paul without looking back at either one of us. I don't think you want to lose her again do you?"

"What do you mean? She is having my baby. There's a bond there that can't be broken."

"Patrick, you're a fool, man. That baby could be yours and most likely is. It's hard for me to believe that it's mine but it's possible I guess. I am not a threat to you. I'm going to tell you like I have told Mariah and Jean Paul that if the baby is mine, then I will be there for her and the child. I will be a father and support her and the child the best way Mariah will let me, however she is not looking to get married to me or anyone else at this point. I would do it but we are not in love with each other. We're family and we will always be family no matter what happens. I want this stress to stop for her. She needs it to stop. It's not good for either one of them. You have to get over what happened for her sake. Otherwise you'll drive her directly into the arms of Jean Paul permanently. She's just about there now."

"Its funny Mariah said almost the same thing to me. I know I only have myself to blame for all this, not you or Mariah. It's me that I'm kicking."

"Then if that is what you call it, you have to stop and concentrate on what is important now."

"You mentioned Jean Paul? How do you know so much about him?"

"I was coming back in town and bumped into them at the airport. We had a little chat, some with Mariah present and some without. Let's say they make a very cozy couple. I believe with what I saw they both have very real feelings for each other. He has a lot to offer her and the baby and he intends to do so. Make no bones about it."

"I got that impression too. I came over yesterday morning and found him half naked cooking breakfast. I knew something was going on. This guy acted like this was his place."

"And that Mariah was his too? That's the real sore spot isn't it?"

"Yea, she did nothing to stop him. He kept calling her my love and my dear all the time. Damn it, he's too old for her. He can't possibly keep her happy emotionally or physically."

"Listen to yourself. I disagree. Don't underestimate him. He may have some age but I bet there is nothing wrong with his vigor. He didn't look too old and flabby to me. Some women like older men. He even had Becky's head turned. She met him at the boutique the other day."

"She can't turn her back on what we had all those years. I even proposed to her while you were gone. I thought we were getting closer."

"And?"

"And nothing, she said it wouldn't be fair to the child or any one making a decision like that right now."

"Unless she is sure about things, she's right?"

"Then what am I to do? If this Count is so tight with her right now how can I stop that?"

"She still loves you, that much I know. Maybe do things her way, don't push so much. I think the first step has to be to show her that our friendship has weathered the storm then maybe she won't bolt as soon as she concludes her business here. We can do that by attending this awards dinner Becky had tickets for next week. Something to do about the lawyer of the year. Her firm has been nominated. You and Mariah can come as our guest. Maybe with all of us being together she'll start to get the picture."

"Maybe, but don't hold your breath. After the way I acted yesterday with HIM I'll be lucky to get her to speak to me next year."

Charlie walked him out to his car. Patrick extended his hand and Charlie shook it, he then pulled Patrick against him and embraced him.

"I'm glad we're talking."

"Me too."

"Now remember, don't push her but don't ignore her either."

Patrick got the room number from the front desk. He knocked at the door and no one answered. The door opened slightly so he came on in and found her sleeping. He sat down on the side of the bed and barely shook her.

"Mariah?" She stirred and opened her eyes.

"Patrick what are you doing here? How did you get in?"

"The door was open. You should be sure the locks are set. I was afraid you were having problems again when you didn't answer the door."

"I'm fine." Mariah started to sit up then remembered she wasn't clothed and pulled the covers closer to her. Clothes were not her favorite thing now days. Nothing seemed comfortable with the baby growing more and more every day.

"Patrick, do you mind turning around? I'd like to get dressed. What time is it anyway?"

"It's after eight and it's not like we haven't seen each other naked before."

Patrick walked over to the window to pull the drapes shut to provide her some privacy from eyes outside. She was on the third floor but you could never tell if some pervert was out there watching. He caught her reflections in the mirror just as she escaped into the bathroom. She came out in a simple cotton dress. The back of it was cut out and reached down to her waistline. It only had a pair of ribbons that laced across the back and at the waist where it was slightly gathered. She came out looking like a million dollars. Her golden hair was up in a French knot, which made her neck look longer than usual. He couldn't help but notice the huge diamond heart hanging at her throat and he wondered if the Count had given it to her. By the size of it he guessed it had to be so.

"My aren't you gorgeous. You did all that for me?"

"Don't be silly. Nothing fits right anymore. I'm going to get something to eat. I'm starved. These long afternoon naps aren't doing so much for my waistline. I'm hungry when I get up." Mariah was stroking the baby. Patrick noticed how much the baby had grown over the last couple of days.

"I think you must be eating for a football team. Is the baby okay?"

"She's fine." Mariah knew how big she was getting without someone constantly reminding her of it. She took her jacket and purse off the chair beside the bed. Patrick thought it would only take a small tug at those ribbons on her dress to free her of her bonds but didn't make a move.

"I'm leaving. Are you coming or not?"

"Oh sure. I just wanted to let you know I was back so if you needed anything to call."

"I guess you've talked with Charlie or else you wouldn't known where to find me. What happened?" Mariah asks as she locks the door behind them.

"Nothing. I've thought about what you said and you're right. I'm trying to put it all behind. It's not worth tearing down what took years to build. Charlie feels the same. I only have myself to blame."

"Is what you say true? I mean really true?"

"Yea. Charlie and I are talking again." Patrick noticed Mariah let out sigh of relief as they walked down the hall.

"Good. But one more thing, don't kick yourself too hard even if you do deserve it, okay."

Walking out the front door Patrick starts to turn to his left and stops as Mariah turns to her right toward where her car is parked and stops when Patrick starts to speak.

"Call me if you need anything. I'll talk to you soon." Patrick says with a wave of unhappiness starting to fall over him. All he wanted to do was to be with her, to hold her and never let go but Charlie was right, he can't push her anymore.

"Wait a minute. Have you eaten? I mean, if not, would you like to get something with me? I really hate eating out by myself anymore. I think everyone is watching to see how much the fat lady eats," she said with a grin. Patrick didn't think he had heard her correctly but when she stood there waiting for his reply, he realized he had.

"No, I haven't yet. I still have my bags in the car. Do you want to take my car or yours?"

"It doesn't matter. Is your car closer? I'm in the side lot."

"Mine's right around the corner. Watch your step! The sidewalk's raised here." Patrick takes her arm and heads to the car.

"That was very good. It's my treat though," Mariah remarked as she settled back from the table. "Thank you for coming tonight. I do appreciate it more than you know. But enough is enough Patrick. We've talked about almost everything under the sun tonight. And believe me when I say it's been nice not discussing anything heavy but I know there is one thing you want to discuss so bad it's eating you up inside. I'm probably asking for trouble but I trust we can discuss this in an adult and calm manner. So let's have it and get it over with." Mariah placed her napkin in her plate, scooted it away from her and folded her arms on the table in front of her like she was about to undertake an impossible task.

"I've enjoyed it too. It has been like old times, laughing and talking just like we used to. But I don't know what you mean? You obviously want to discuss something, what is it?" She knew him to well. He did want to discuss what he witnessed yesterday with Jean Paul and it was eating him alive not to do so but he had to play it cool.

"Oh please! You mean to tell me you are not one bit curious about Jean Paul? I expected you to grill me and yet here we sit two hours later and still no word about him from you. That's not in your character." Patrick shrugged his shoulders.

"What can I do about him? J.P. is in your life whether I like it or not. I know it's not all business, there is more to it than that whether you admit it or not. How can I fight that? I've told you how I feel about you and the baby. For heaven's sake I've even proposed to you, which still stands by the way. You said no, that this isn't the time to make that decision so what choice do I have but to accept your will. No, I don't like J.P. in the picture. I think he is too old for you and using you for some male ego thing.."

"Male ego thing?" She started to laugh.

"Yea, you know the old man can still get the young chick. J.P. sure is an example of that."

"Don't call him that! His name is Jean Paul, not J.P. and he's only fifty-six. I ask you to kindly call him by his proper name. I'm far from being some wide-eye school girl, I am thirty you know?" She was trying to hold her temper back.

"I know exactly how old you are. We've been together for the last five years remember. The guy probably had a heart attack the first time you and he were together all night."

"Patrick! I'm sorry I even brought this up. I thought you were old enough to be able to discuss this without your jealousy showing. Obviously, I was wrong. It's none of your business what Jean Paul and I do and I'm not going to sit here and discuss my sex life with you." Mariah's thought went back to their passionate night they shared at Charlie's. "I'll find my own way home, thank you." Mariah starts to get up but Patrick takes her hand and pulls her back down in the chair.

"No, I'm sorry. I really am. I thought I was handling things better. It was just a shock to see him half naked in the kitchen cooking you breakfast. You could have called me to let me know he was in town."

"Why? What good would that do? You still would find a reason to come by just to have a look at him. Jean Paul is a private person. What we have is total respect and admiration for each other."

"That is not all, my dear. I saw how you two looked at each other, how he hovered over you."

"He's just concerned about me."

"Mariah, he loves you, it's obvious, but I love you and the baby too. I may be the father of that little girl, if so, I have rights and I intend to use them if I have to. I know you still love me. Don't close the door on us, not yet. What do you feel for HIM? And where does all that leave us?" Mariah sat there not knowing how to answer his questions. She felt pressured into giving an answer. He was waiting.

"It's true I do have feelings for him but right now I just want to take one day at a time, that's all. He doesn't pressure me into anything. He accepts that I am capable of running my life. Jean Paul accepts me for who I am, the me now; not what I was six months ago." After a couple of minutes of silence and Patrick mulling things over, realizes he has to take another approach. Trying to totally bring back the past wasn't the move he needed to make.

"Okay. Then we'll take one day at a time. By the way there is an awards dinner at the Country Club next Wednesday night. Becky and Charlie are going and they have invited us. It's something about the attorney of the year thing. One of Becky's boss' has been nominated. So how about it?"

"I'll have to check my appointment book and let you know."

"Fine, you can do that." He knew she was putting him off. "Now let's have a dance." Patrick walks around the table and lifts her up gently and out onto the dance floor. He became very conscious of how much of her there was between them. It was hard to get close but when he did, the baby kicked him.

"For some reason our child know just when to kick doesn't she?" he laughed. Mariah smiled but was trapped in her thoughts about the events of tonight to pay attention to what he said. Patrick's sudden turn around about Charlie, his view about Jean Paul and the fact that he really didn't try to give her a hard time about "him" and his determination about loving her and the baby was all too much for her to comprehend at one time. Could he have really settled down? Could he be serious? He was right about one thing, she still loved him and always will.

After all, he was her first real love but she loves Jean Paul, too. What was she to do? She felt so confused Jean Paul is more stable. Was she looking for stability? Jean Paul loves her unconditionally and she him. Did she really need a man in her life? No was the answer and she knew that, but she didn't want to just throw everything away. She wanted a full life with everything it had to offer her. Patrick was very attentive to her needs all evening without mentioning Jean Paul again. It was like the Count wasn't in the picture as far as Patrick was concerned. She waited for the storm but it never came.

Patrick, on the other hand, was doing his best to control his feelings about Jean Paul. It would serve no purpose in verbally assaulting him to her and he understood that. He had to make this evening work in more ways than one. He had decided that in spite of her looking so appealing he would not make any advances toward her. Perhaps he needed to court her all over again. That is what he would do, start from scratch with their relationship but did he really have the time for all of that? That was the question he kept asking himself, the boutique would be done soon and then she would be gone.

"Thank you for a somewhat relaxing evening. But I'm tired, my feet hurt and I need to get some sleep so if you don't mind I think I'll go in by myself," Mariah says turning to him as she unlocks her hotel door.

"I wasn't planning on coming in actually. I have an early breakfast meeting in Los Angeles." Patrick opens the door and looks in to make sure everything is all right.

"Oh." Mariah a little surprised at his remark. She expected him to want to stay.

"Why do you always do that?"

"What"

"Look inside doors first?"

"It's a male thing. You can never be too careful. Hotels are not the safest places to be. Here's your key card. Good night sweetheart. Sleep well. Oh, let me know about the party, okay?" He barely kisses her on the forehead before he leaves. Mariah standing in the doorway watches him turn the corner of the hallway and disappears out of sight. She didn't have a chance to say good night.

Mariah had grown accustomed to arriving at the boutique later in the mornings but today it was past noon again. The workers had already left for the day but left word they needed something that had to be ordered to finish up the sprinkler system in her apartment. They wouldn't be back until it came in and that would be in a couple of days. It seemed it was always a couple of days. No one got in a hurry about completing a job anymore. If she ran her businesses that way she would be out of business. Her mood didn't improve with time. The word was out through the employees to stay clear of her today. No one had bothered her with any details except Margo. She was the only brave one to approach her the entire day.

"Mariah, I think you need to go back to the Inn and get some real rest. You've been pushing yourself too hard between here and the baby, you're over extended. I can handle things here."

"Will you please leave me alone? I'm just fine. The problem is that everyone seems too concerned about me and not enough concern is going into finishing this construction. I want my life back to normal again."

"Why are you so worried? This place will get done in time for the re-opening. We're ready for the sale now you know that. Everything is marked, cleaned and in place. The staff has worked very hard. There's something more to this mood than the construction, isn't it?"

"I know how hard everyone has helped. It's just.." Mariah started to cry. Margo poured her a glass of water and handed it to her then sat down in the leather chair in front of her desk.

"Now why don't you really tell me what's bothering you? It's not the store so could it be man trouble?"

"No! I mean, I don't know. Patrick and I went out for dinner last night. For the most part I had a good time and I think he did too. It was easy except for a few minutes when Jean Paul's name came up."

"And then what happened?"

"Nothing he told me how he felt about Jean Paul and then he let it go the rest of the evening."

"Isn't that a good thing?" When Mariah didn't answer she continued. "And after dinner what happened?"

"Nothing, he took me back to the Inn after I decided not to get my car and left."

"I wondered why your car was here but you weren't. You should have called me. I could have picked you up this morning," Margo said.

"I wanted to walk. It isn't that far and I need to exercise."

"Getting back to Patrick, isn't that what you want, for him to leave you alone?"

"He asked me to marry him the other day and I said no. I think I hurt his feelings."

"And you said no because you don't love him anymore?"

"I think I'll always love him to some degree." This was not news to Margo.

"What about the Count?" Is he pressuring you for more than a business relationship?"

"No, there's no pressure, but you see I have strong feelings for him too. I think I may be in love with him."

"And he shares those feelings. It was so obvious the other day when he was here. What do you want to do?"

"I don't know. I don't know. My relationship with the Count is everything a woman dreams of. It's so easy to be with him. Life is easy with him. But how can I love two men at the same time?"

"It happens more than you know."

"That's what Jean Paul said."

"You talked to him about you and Patrick?"

"Yes, of course, we don't have secrets. He has always understood things between Patrick and me. He knows I still have feelings for Patrick but he knows that I care deeply for him too. He asked me to marry him several months ago but I can't give him any more of an answer now as I can Patrick. What am I to do?"

"I was in a triangle once. I was much younger than you but it wasn't easy then either."

"You?"

"Yes me. It happened before I could stop things. I was engaged to Bill and there was this other one who attended college with me. Bill was from a well to do family and was an intern. His father was a doctor. Frank, the other one was studying art. He was a free spirit, didn't have money and didn't care about it but he always seemed to have what he needed to live on. I met him in the bookstore and a coffee date led to other things. I think it was the fact that Frank was unpredictable that attracted me to him."

"What happened in the end?"

"I lost them both. It took me a long time to realize that neither one of them was right for me. So please don't ask for my help in choosing."

"That makes me feel a whole lot better. How can things work out for Patrick and me when it didn't before?"

"But it was, wasn't it until the last year or so if I remember right?"

"There was stress especially after I lost the baby. That was probably the beginning of the end."

"Is that the reason you came back to Crystal River, to see Patrick?"

"Maybe unconsciously. I've asked myself the same question."

"What about the baby? Where does she fit in?"

"She's the best part of her father and me. She has everything to do with all this."

Margo still didn't know whom the father was but she wasn't going to pry. If Mariah wanted to confide in her about something as delicate as this then she would have to bring it up but she suspected the father was here in Crystal River, possibly even Patrick or else why would Mariah be having such a difficult time choosing whom she wanted to be with. In her opinion it would be the Count. "You're in a different place in your soul now. What you have to determine is whether Patrick has changed too. Perhaps you should move on to someone who shares the same place and time you are in now. No one can help you with this decision, not Patrick, the Count, or anyone else. You have to come to your own conclusions as what to do with your life. This I know from experience."

Mariah had stopped crying by now. She got up and was standing by the windows when she looked down and saw Patrick coming out of the shop across the street carrying a bag. He didn't even look up as he got in his Shelby. She remembered he always drove it a couple of times a week to keep the battery up, all the other times he would drive his BMW.

The phone rang and Margo answered for her.

CHAPTER 7

It was well after seven and getting dark as Mariah stepped through the front doors of the boutique and turned on the alarm system. Her mood wasn't much better so she told Margo to go on home when the store closed at five thirty. She had spent her time alone going over more shipping invoices to see if she could figure out what was going on. Daphne had called earlier and reported more trunks were being delayed, two days delayed. She had to get to the bottom of all this. The other department stores accepting her line weren't going to wait for their shipments. This could destroy her reputation if she couldn't deliver her goods as promised. The cool air felt good to her. She sighed out loud.

"You're not supposed to be working this late," Patrick spoke softly as he leaned against the store window with his arms crossed hiding a small wrapped package.

"WHAT THE! You scared me." Turning to see him right behind her. She didn't know why she didn't see him to begin with. "What are you doing here?" Mariah was glad it was dark and he couldn't see how puffy her eyes looked from crying all day.

"Waiting for you."

"Why didn't you come in?" Even though she was glad he didn't.

"I saw you were busy and didn't want to disturb you. Have you eaten?"

"No. I'm not hungry."

"Mariah, you know you have to eat. Let's get a bite somewhere. It can be carry out if you like?"

"I'm fine. I just need to go home and get off my feet. I'll get room service."

"Knowing you, you'll go back to the Inn, fall asleep without eating and be back in the hospital again. You're too tired."

"I promise that won't happen again. Now walk with me to my car and tell me why you're lurking around."

"I wasn't lurking. I was waiting for you to come out. I wanted to give this to you." He held the package out and she took it.

"What is this?"

"Open it and you'll find out." She opened the package and took out a glass angel. The streetlight offered just enough light to read the card-sometimes in life there are not enough angels around to stop a mistake from happening. Love Patrick.

"What's this for?"

"There's no reason. I saw it and thought of you. I was going to have it delivered to you but thought I would do it myself. I hope you don't mind?"

"Is there a hidden message in the note?"

"No why?"

"I wondered about the "mistake" you're referring to?"

"The many mistakes I have made with you. That's all."

"Oh," Mariah said as she placed the angel back in its box. "Thank you for the gift."

"You mean you're going to keep it?"

"Why shouldn't I? I do love it."

"I just thought you'd refuse it since you seem not to want me around."

"I never said that. All I said was to give me space."

"Same thing if you ask me but that's okay. We'll do it your way. You never gave me an answer if you're going with me to Becky's shindig. Have you decided yet?"

"I'm sorry I haven't had the chance to think about it. I'm not sure yet. Can I let you know the first of the week? I don't know if I'm going to have the energy." She placed the package on the front seat of her car and turned to face him.

"Look Patrick, if you don't mind I'm really very tired and I have a tremendous headache and if you don't mind.." Patrick catches her as she faints. He picks her up, closes the car door with his foot and carries her to his car across the street.

The emergency room nurse behind the desk told him Dr. Miles was currently with a patient in another cubical but that she would be out to speak to him shortly. They took Mariah away on a gurney. She was still out of it and that worried him. He knew he should call Charlie but for some reason he didn't. He had nothing to tell him about Mariah or the baby yet. It was a good hour before the doctor came out to see him.

"Patrick, Mariah is awake and stable. I think we're going to keep her for observation tonight. If everything goes okay then she can go home tomorrow."

"What's wrong with her?" Is it the baby?"

"No, I think the baby is fine. Her blood pressure is elevated at the moment. She's having a bit of nausea right now along with the headache."

"She said she had a headache before she passed out. You're sure this won't effect the baby?"

"That is why we're going to watch her tonight hopefully to keep that from happening. She won't tell me what has her so worked up. Do you know?"

"No. Is her sugar okay?"

"It's up a little. We are watching that, too."

"Can I see her?"

"She's in the third cubical to the right. We'll keep her here until we can get a room ready. Patrick, go slow with her. She's not in very good shape at the moment. Don't stay long." Patrick nodded and found her.

"Hi. What some people will do for a little attention." In the hospital lights he could tell she had been crying long and hard. It reminded him of when her father died. "What's up with you?"

"My blood pressure they say."

"Funny. That's not what I mean. Why is your pressure up?"

"I don't know. I guess everyone is right I've been working too hard." Mariah turned her face away from him. He was so close. She knew he could see how swollen her eyes looked; even her face and hands were swollen.

"Sweetheart, I can't help you if you won't talk to me. Please let me in."

"There's nothing to say. You can't help me with this."

"Let me try but you have to talk to me first."

"Did I break my angel?"

"It's okay. You put it in the front seat before you passed out. Don't you remember?"

"No."

Her poor hand looked so swollen with the I.V. stuck in it. He just wanted to hold her close but didn't dare, so he settled on holding her hand instead. He sat next to her bed in silence not knowing what to do or say to make things better. She closed her eyes but the tears wouldn't stop flowing until she slept.

His conscious got the better of him and slipped away to call Charlie. It wasn't long before Charlie and Becky showed up finding Patrick in the hallway.

"How is she?"

"Like I said, her blood pressure is up. They're getting ready to move her upstairs now."

"What caused it?" Becky inquired.

"Don't know and she's not talking." Patrick said with a shrug of his shoulders.

"Thanks for calling buddy. Is the baby okay?" Charlie expresses as he pats Patrick on the back.

"So far."

"How can she go on like this much longer?"

"I don't know Charlie, I don't know."

"Did anything happen between the two of you to cause this?"

"No. I haven't seen her for a day or so. I've taken your advice and backed off even if it has just about killed me to do so. It just happens that I was there tonight when she left the store. Who knows what would have happened if she had been driving?"

"Has anyone called Margo yet? She'll need to know what's going on," Becky asks.

"I didn't even think about her."

"Then I'll take care of it. Charlie, I need your phone. I'll be outside if you need me." Becky came back in a few minutes later. "Margo is taking care of everything. She says Mariah has been upset all day but she won't say what about. I know she knows something."

Mariah was being wheeled out of the emergency room on her way upstairs.

"Charlie, Becky, you're here?"

"Of course. We wouldn't be anywhere else." Charlie took her swollen hand and walked beside her bed while Patrick and Becky followed. It was after three a.m. when Charlie and Becky left the hospital. Patrick had decided to stay the night, so he conned Deloris into letting him stay in Mariah's room instead of the waiting room. She had given him a blanket and pillow. He settled in the recliner for the rest of the night dozing on and off.

"Patrick? Did you stay all night again?" Mariah said when she woke and found him sleeping. He stirred.

"Good morning, I think. So you beat me awake did you?"

"You didn't need to stay. I'm okay. I want you to go home and get some real rest. That chair doesn't look comfortable."

Patrick looked at the clock. It was half past seven. He got up, splashed cold water on his face from the sink in her room and found a paper towel to dry with. "I'm not going anywhere until we talk to the doctor so get used to it. I do think I'll find a coffee machine. Do you mind?"

"Go ahead. I'm not doing any sprints out of here." Patrick smiled and left the room. He wanted all of his senses intact and running by the time Dr. Miles came in. He wasn't gone but just a few minutes and when he entered the room; he found her crying again.

"What's wrong? What is it?" He set the coffee on the sink and went to her, worry covering his face. When she didn't answer he pressed. "Mariah, I have to ask. Has something happened between you and J.P.? Is that why you're crying?" It was the only thing he could think of that would upset her so much.

"What? NO. NO. It's not about him and please I have asked you not to call him that." Mariah was trying to brush the tears from her eyes.

"Then tell me what this is all about. If you don't stop they'll never let you out of here."

"Why are you still being so good to me? I have turned everyone's life upside down by coming back. I've given you a hard time. I can't give you any promises and you're still here. Why?"

"Why not? We've been through so much and we can get through this too. We just need time to get back on the right track."

"A lot has changed."

"You may think you love J.P. but I know you still love me. I still love you. Neither of us can stop the way we feel for each other."

"I don't think I love Jean Paul, I know I do." Patrick didn't like her answer.

"You can't deny that you don't have feelings for me. I know that little girl is mine. I'm so sure of it like I know my name. That in itself has us bonded together forever."

"I can't talk about this with you right now."

"Mariah, for heaven's sake if we don't talk nothing will get worked out."

Just then Dr. Vivian Miles came into the room. "Good morning Mariah. How are we doing today?" Mariah tried hiding the tears. "Well now, you're still upset I see. What's going on in here?" Patrick felt the doctor's look toward him was accusing him of upsetting her.

"Nothing that matters," Mariah said. What does she mean nothing that matters? Patrick thought, it mattered a hell of a lot to him.

"Patrick, if you don't mind I'd like to see my patient alone please."

Patrick nodded, "I'll be outside."

"Now that he's gone, how about telling me what is upsetting you?" Vivian asks while taking Mariah's blood pressure. "It's high normal for you but you won't be for long unless you get yourself under control." She pulled the chair up to the bed and sat down. "I'm waiting?"

"For what?"

"For you to tell me what the trouble is. I've got a few minutes before I have a meeting so start talking. I'm not going to let you out of here until I have some answers."

"You can't do that, can you?"

"Try me!"

"I don't know what to do."

"About what? The baby is fine. We've been lucky. I've talked to Dr. Rantoul this morning."

"About me? Why?" Mariah was concerned and surprised at the same time.

"She wanted me to give her updates about your progress. We both are very concerned about the progression of your condition. At the rate you're going you may end up with a premature baby."

"What do you mean? You said everything is okay with Abigail."

"Abigail? Is that the name you have chosen for the baby? I like it."

"Yes, Abigail Angelena. But what about her coming early?"

"Dr. Rantoul and I are concerned that if you can't keep your blood pressure down and the diabetes under control that we may have to deliver the baby early. You know you showed these problems early into the pregnancy, which is unusual. I know Dr. Rantoul has spoken to you about other complications when you have these underlying problems. Things like kidney and respiratory problems, seizures, strokes. Therefore you must help me and get everything under control now before I put you on complete bed rest until the end of this pregnancy."

"I can't do that. I need to get out of town as soon as I can."

"Why?"

"It's too hard being here. I should have stayed in New Orleans or France."

"Is that your plan, to go back to France?"

"Anywhere but here."

"I'm sorry Mariah but both Dr. Rantoul and I feel that is important that you do not travel until after the baby is born. It's too risky now." The doctor saw the look on Mariah's face. "I've got to ask, is the baby's father here? Is it Patrick? Is that the reason why it's so hard for you to be here?" Vivian's questions stunned her. Was she so transparent as that? Mariah broke down again and started crying.

Patrick could hear her sobs through the door. His heart was breaking listening to her cry. He wanted to go inside and stop whatever was going on but how could he? He couldn't stop it anymore than he could stop a runaway freight train and that is how he felt right now. He took a deep breath and went down the hall to the waiting room leaving word at the nurse's desk to see Dr. Miles before she left the floor.

"I can't leave town in a couple of weeks?"

"I wouldn't advise it. I'm afraid there'll be too much stress, the baby could come early. You don't want that do you?" Mariah had thoughts of what happened to Jacques-Louis. She couldn't bear the thought if she caused anything like that to happen to Abigail or to Jean Paul again.

"What if I flew on a private jet? It's a smooth ride."

"I'm sorry I still have to say no. I can't keep you here. I can only advise you but if I were you I would stay put. It's not that much longer." Mariah started to cry again. She told Vivian everything, including the question of paternity.

"Mariah, I'm not here to judge you and I can't tell you what to do with your life. It's a difficult situation. I'm not sure what I would do either if I was in your place but I can tell you that if anyone can handle this you can.

What I have seen and what Dr. Rantoul has told me about you; you can handle this. You can and are able to make whatever decisions you need to make for you and your child. Sometimes we need another shoulder to talk to, someone who is impartial. Why don't I have Sarah McKracken come and see you today?"

"Who is she?" Mariah asks between sobs.

"She's a friend of mine. She's a therapist. Maybe she can help you explore your feelings better than I can. Is it okay?"

"I don't need a therapist, do I?"

"Honey, I think that at some point in a person's life we all need a therapist. There's not a stigma attached now days like it was a few years ago. Everyone has one in his or her back pocket. That's why it's so hard to get an appointment anymore. Anyway my meeting is with her in a few minutes. Can I ask her to see you?" Mariah nodded. Maybe it would be a good idea to get a professional's opinion of things just this one time.

"Good. I'll talk to her. Listen I have to go but I'll check in on you later this morning."

"Then I'm not going home today?"

"Maybe later today but I can't promise anything. You need to promise me to get yourself calmed down. I'd like you to see Sarah first before I discharge you. Okay?" Vivian patted her hand. "We'll see about getting this I.V. out of you."

"Thank you for being a friend." Mariah's phone rang. Vivian answered.

"Hello. Room 3001. This is Dr. Miles, just a minute please." Vivian hands Mariah the receiver. "I believe it's your friend from overseas. He sounds sexy with that accent. I'll talk to you later." Vivian had a grin on her face. "Cheer up."

"*Bonjour*, Jean Paul."

"*Mon amour*, what has happened to you? I just saw you the other day and everything was fine. I called the Inn and they said they hadn't seen you since yesterday morning. So I called the boutique and Margo told me you were admitted."

"My blood pressure went up and I passed out. That's all. Now that they have me here they're not going to let me go."

"I want to talk to the doctor."

"She's already left. She and Dr. Rantoul have been talking."

114

"Is this serious?"

"They have concluded that I can't go anywhere until the baby comes. Jean Paul, what am I going to do?" Mariah tried very hard to keep the tears back. She didn't want him to know what caused her to be in the hospital to begin with. He would just worry and drop everything to be beside her again. He had his own life to take care of, things he felt he needed to accomplish.

"So you meant it when you said they were not going to let you go. Not even home to me? Does Rantoul agree?"

"Yes. They advised me not to fly even on your jet. They think the baby may come early due to all my health problems."

The Count sighed heavily. "Do you want me to talk to Rantoul? I will see her right away."

"No. I don't think Vivian would tell me that if it wasn't true. I trust her."

"I see. Well *mon amour*, we will have to make the best of things. Little Abigail deserves the best chance we can give her to be happy and healthy. I will come to you as much as I can."

"I can't ask you to do that? You have your business to attend to."

"We will see what we can work out. The most important thing for you to remember is that you are doing all this for Abigail. She is the one that matters now. *Oui*?"

"Yes, I know but I still wanted to go back to France. I didn't want the baby to be born here."

"I know but we can't help it now. We have no choice. *Excuse moi*, Claude just came in... Claude if you can wait in the outer office and let me finish this call *s'il vous plait*."

"It's okay Jean Paul, see what he needs. I think I'll be here until later today or possibly tomorrow yet. If I don't hear from you then I'll call you when I get out."

"Are you sure?"

"Very."

"*Je t'aime*. We will talk soon."

"I love you too. *Au revoir*." She felt better after talking to him. He always seems to be able to put things in perspective for her. The baby is what she needed to concentrate on.

Meanwhile Dr. Miles filled Patrick in to some degree. That she wasn't going to release Mariah until later today or tomorrow if her blood pressure went down and stayed down. Everything else she left out since she knew that part of Mariah's problems was Patrick.

She didn't want Patrick to put any more pressure on her patient and told him it was crucial that she had no more stress from now on for the sake of both mother and child. Patrick read between the lines and realized just how fragile things were. He went back to her room.

"Hi beautiful. I heard it might be a while before they spring you."

"Yea, the doctors are like leaches here. Once they get their hands on a person they don't let go."

"Sometimes they do know more than us. It is for the best you know? Do you want anything? A magazine, crossword puzzle, book?" She shook her head.

"What I want is for you to go home and get some rest. I don't need you to baby-sit me."

"Honey, is that how you feel about me being here? I'm not baby-sitting. I want to be with you but if you'll rest better with me gone, I'll do that and come back later."

"I need you to go by and lock my car up. I don't really want it sitting out on the street."

"Why don't you let me have your keys and I'll have Charlie go with me and we'll pick it up. I'll take it out to my place where it will be safe."

"You don't mind?"

"Not at all. This may be the only time I'll get to drive a new Mercedes."

"Please, you have more money than I do. You could buy one if you wanted. Hand me my purse." She dug for the keys and gave them to Patrick. He leaned over and kissed her before he left.

"No thanks, I'm happy with my Beamer and the Shelby. I'll see you later. I love you." He headed out the door.

Patrick couldn't find Charlie so he went back to the boutique and locked up the car, then drove home to find Jim working the horses. Patrick pulled his car up to the barn and got out.

"Hey Jim, how's things going?"

"Pretty well. I thought I'd come over and work a bit. I think I was getting on Betty's nerves."

"Listen since you're here how about going with me to pick up Mariah's car. I need to bring it back here."

"Sure thing boss."

"Don't call me that. You know I hate it." Jim took the reins off of the horse to let it run free in the arena and walked over to Patrick putting his arm around his shoulders.

"There are some things a man can never get used to. So what's up with Mariah?"

"She's in the hospital again."

"Why? Don't tell me it's the baby?"

"No. Her blood pressure's up. She passed out last night on me. Thank God I was there."

"He seems to be looking out after her all right. I mean you finding the fire and now this. Let me stable "Old Bucket" here and I'll be ready to go. If you don't mind we'll take my truck. I can stop by the feed store on the way back."

"Sure, your truck is fine. Some day I'll get one." Patrick walked over and leaned against the truck and started kicking the dirt around while waiting for him. He couldn't get the Count off his mind. How could he make Mariah believe that he was the only man for her and not the Count?

After retrieving the Mercedes he had plans to take a shower and sleep for an hour or so then go back to the hospital but before he went inside he placed the glass angel in his car to take back with him to the hospital.

Charlie and Becky checked in on Mariah only to find her sleeping. Margo did too. Mariah had slept for a couple of hours to wake and find notes from them on her bed table. She also found a vase of forget-me-nots from Jean Paul. He didn't waste any time getting them to her. She felt his love envelope her.

"Hello Mariah. I'm Dr. McKracken but please call me Sarah. Vivian asked me to stop in for a visit. Do you feel like talking?" Sarah turned out to be in her fifties but her hair was still flaming red.

"Sure why not." Sarah pulled the chair up to the bed and settled herself down.

"Vivian told me some about your situation but I want to hear it all from you. I want you to know that anything you tell me stays with me. It won't go anywhere else including to Vivian. I'm not here to judge you. I just want to help if I can. Why don't you start at the beginning. I have the time." Mariah retold the tale all over again. This time she was able to hold back some tears but not all. Sarah listened intently over two hours. They talked and even laughed at some things. There seemed to be a bond almost instantly between the two of them. Sarah had spent some time in the south of France and knew the land. She had heard of the Count but never met him, so few had unless they were in his inner circle.

Patrick showed up at the hospital with the angel and a vase of red roses in hand only to be told that Mariah was with Dr. Sarah McKracken. Upon inquiry of who she was he was told she was a therapist and no visitors were permitted until they were finished. He glanced at the clock above the nurse's station, it had been over two hours since he returned and had no choice but to go to the waiting room. Why was she seeing a therapist? Was she that upset? Was he to blame for all this? He was lost in his thoughts when the nurse came in to tell him Dr. McKracken had left.

"Hi, how are you?" he asked as he entered the room. "I thought these might cheer you up." Patrick presented her with the roses and the glass angel.

"You didn't have to do this." Referring to the roses as she drew in their scent. "And you brought my angel! Thank you. Why don't you put them on the window ledge? Maybe they won't get broken over there." Patrick did so and noticed the forget-me-nots. Glancing at the card he saw they were from Jean Paul. How did he know where she was and so fast but didn't say anything. He didn't want to upset her anymore. "What are you doing?"

"Making a list."

"A list of what?"

"Some things I have to work on." She refused to tell him what it was but he had the feeling it had to do with her talk with Dr. McKracken.

"I came by earlier but you were busy. Who's the new doctor?" Patrick sat down next to the window.

"Oh, she's a friend of Vivian's. She thought a visit from her might be nice since Sarah lived in southern France for a few years. We had a lot to talk about." She didn't know how much Patrick knew about Sarah but wasn't going to say anything else.

"I see. Did she help? I mean did you enjoy the visit, comparing your notes on France?" He quickly hid his question referring to the doctor's help. It was lame but he didn't know what else to say since she wasn't being completely honest with him. She wasn't telling what Sarah really was and he didn't want to push her.

"I guess." There was a moment of silence. Mariah caught the vague look of disbelief on Patrick's face. "France is an interesting country and we have a lot in common and know some of the same people." She tried to be convincing.

"Are you going to see her again?"

"Maybe, I like her. We may have lunch sometime now that I'm stuck in town for the duration."

"I don't understand?"

"I can't travel. Both of my doctors have ganged up on me."

"Both?"

"Yea, Vivian and Dr. Rantoul; they have decided that I'd be putting the baby at risk if I do."

"Is this serious? You're starting to worry me."

"I think it's a precaution but I don't like it just the same."

"You want to do the best for the baby don't you?"

"How can you ask that? Of course I do! I just want to go home that's all." Patrick wondered what home she meant- home to Jean Paul or home to New Orleans. He was sure she didn't mean his home, their home. He studied her in silence as she continued to make her list. Her spirits seemed better; at least she wasn't crying anymore which meant her blood pressure would hopefully drop.

"Any word as to when you'll be out of here?"

"Not yet. I'm ready to go now. If they would just get this I.V. out of me I'd leave now."

"You probably would but I'm going to see that you don't until the doctor says so."

119

"You think you can make me stay here?"

"I will if I have to camp out here until she says you're ready."

Deloris came in to check on Mariah. "It looks like you'll be staying tonight. The doctor wants to make sure you're pressure is stabilized before sending you out of here. If we can keep it down then it should be tomorrow."

"I don't like you very much," Mariah replied to Deloris. Patrick couldn't believe she had just said that to Deloris. Deloris caught his expression.

"Don't worry about it," she said to Patrick. "Now Mariah dear, you don't have to feel sorry for yourself. You'll get plenty of attention later. The doctor has ordered more blood work for this afternoon. By the way I still like you and always have." She patted Mariah's shoulder and left while Patrick busied himself with the television and Mariah continued to work on her list. They didn't speak for a while. He wasn't sure what to discuss.

Becky and Charlie came in holding hands. "Well, look at the two of you." Mariah remarked.

"You look better today. How are you doing?" Charlie bent over and kissed her on the forehead. Becky went to sit by Patrick.

"I'm better. I just feel so silly getting myself worked up like that."

"So what caused it?"

"I don't want to discuss it. I just want out of here."

"When is that going to happen?" Becky asks.

"Tomorrow. I'm ready to go now. I feel fine." Mariah responded unhappily.

"Tomorrow? I thought this was only for twenty-four hours?"

"Don't let her kid you. She was in rough shape this morning. Her pressure was still up. It's only been coming down for a couple of hours," Patrick interceded.

"Mariah is that right?" Charlie tilted his head to the side as he gazed at her.

"Are you going to believe him or me?"

"Right now, I think I'm going to believe him. I can always tell when you're lying and you are lying through your teeth."

"Then you can just leave. I don't want to see you if you're going to insult me!" Mariah was looking Charlie square in the face when she said this. Charlie couldn't tell if she was kidding or not, he quickly looked at Patrick and Becky. Patrick just shrugged his shoulders.

"Mariah! You know you don't mean that. What's up with you?" Charlie asks but before she could answer Becky goes over to the bed and takes her hand. She notices how swollen her hands and face are but doesn't say anything about them.

"Guess what? Charlie and I have decided to move in together. Isn't it great?"

Mariah glanced at Patrick and Charlie and smiled. "That's nice dear. I'm happy for you two. I'm glad someone can have a life."

"This isn't like you. I thought you'd be happy for us. I wanted to wait until you were on your feet again but Becky wanted to share the news with you."

"She is happy for us, aren't you Mariah?" Becky replied but not believing it herself.

"I'm sorry, I guess I'm just tired. I think I need to sleep, do you mind leaving?"

"Sure sweetheart. Come on Becky let's see her tomorrow."

"Mariah, I do hope you're feeling better. If there is anything I can do please let me know." Becky said as they started to leave. Patrick got up to walk them out.

"Charlie, wait a minute. I want to talk to you." Charlie stopped and looked at Mariah.

"Come on Becky, I'll walk you down the hall. Charlie don't get her pressure up," Patrick said as he gave a concerning look to Charlie. He then put his arm around Becky's shoulders and they left together. He had no idea what she was going to say to Charlie but wasn't sure he wanted to. Her mood was changing before they came but it had drastically changed when Becky made her announcement.

"What is it?" Charlie asks.

"How can you move in with her? Do you love her?"

"I think I do. My time away got me thinking about things. Why are you upset about this? I'm sorry she broke the news to you this way. I wanted to tell you myself. I'm still going to be here for you and the baby but you said you didn't want to marry me even if the baby is mine."

"This isn't about that. I don't want to marry you. How can you do this to her? Have you told her about the possibility of you being a father?"

"No, not yet." Charlie shook his head. "Is this what has you upset? I WILL tell her."

"When?"

"I don't know. This bit about cohabitating is just a trial period. You know to see if we want to take this any farther."

"Yes, I know, just like what Patrick and me did. See where that got us. Five years of nowhere. Don't do this to her unless you go in telling her the truth and all of the truth. If she backs out then she backs out but don't use her and then break her in the end. Let her know where things stand now. If you don't, I will. I promise you that."

"Mariah, calm down. Is this the reason why you're getting so worked up or is there more? I promise I will take care of things."

"There's more," Patrick said entering the room, just as he suspected she let Charlie have it about Becky.

"Where's Becky?" Charlie inquired.

"She's making a call in the waiting room so I'm sure we don't have much time."

"So what's the more? Is someone going to tell me?"

"Mariah's upset because she can't leave town now. The doctors said it's too risky for both of them."

"Why? What's happened?"

"There could be complications if she continues to have blood pressure problems."

"Mariah, I promised you I will tell Becky about everything but you have to promise to get a grip on things. We can work together on this. If you let us we can help you get through all this in the easiest way possible. You're not alone." Charlie was holding her hand. He too noticed how puffy she was and didn't like it. The tears started to fall again and Mariah couldn't stop them.

"Hear now, stop that!" Patrick handed her some tissues and slipped in between her and Charlie and held her. "Calm down, take some slow deep breaths."

Deloris came barreling through the door. "Honey, what's going on in here? Your monitor is going off like crazy at the nurse's station. You're going to have to calm down. I don't want to have to call the doctor. Gentlemen, I think Mariah has had enough company today. You both go home now.

She'll be here tomorrow." Deloris said after checking Mariah's pulse and blood pressure.

"You want me to stay the night?" Patrick addressed Mariah.

"No you don't. I'll take care of her tonight. You get your sleep, you need it by the way you look at the moment."

"Mariah?"

"Go home Patrick. It's okay."

"Call me if you need me. Do you understand?" Patrick told Deloris.

"Yes I do but we're not going to have to do that, now are we Mariah dear?" Deloris was patting her hand like a mother would. Mariah had stopped crying.

"Good night," Charlie said as Becky was coming back into the room. He turned her around and left.

"Good night baby. I love you. I'll be here early. Deloris you have my numbers." Patrick kissed Mariah and left. He caught up with Charlie and Becky and filled them in on the details and the therapist.

Charlie had dropped Becky off at her apartment after leaving the hospital. He was shaken about Mariah's attitude toward him and the fact that she and the baby may be at risk. He had told Becky that he was getting a migraine and wanted to be alone. She knew he was upset and wanted to stay with him but he finally was able to convince her otherwise. He promised they would get together after Becky got off work tomorrow for dinner. He had until tomorrow night to figure out how to tell Becky about the baby. Suddenly he realized how he really felt about her. Mariah was right she had to know if things were going in the direction he thought it was. He couldn't wait for the paternity test results like he planned. He also knew if he didn't tell her she would and she meant it.

Becky called him mid afternoon to tell him she would be working until six. Could they still have dinner? Charlie asked her to meet him at his place. He had some errands to do before that.

It was almost seven before she got to Charlie's. She hoped he was in a better mood than what he sounded like earlier that afternoon. Something was still bothering him but he wouldn't tell her. She wanted to talk to him about moving her things in. He did have plenty of room for some of her favorite pieces of furniture. She rang the doorbell since it was locked. Charlie never locked the door when he was home. His truck was in the driveway. She rang again.

"Come in Becky dear." He answered the door with a dishtowel in hand and an apron on. Becky was laughing as she came in.

"What is going on? I like the new you in that apron."

"Don't get used to it. I just thought instead of going out we'd stay in tonight. Sort of make up for last night." He walked into the kitchen as the timer was going off on the oven. Becky followed.

"What are we having? It smells good."

"Mr. Tai Chi Won's Special Chicken and vegetables."

"You've been cooking a long time, poor baby. And look we have hot rolls, too."

"There is one thing you have to know about me. I don't cook. I can hardly cook scrambled eggs without burning them. But I can set a mean looking table." He directed her to the dinning room. The table was beautiful including candles that was flickering in the darken room.

"Charlie you shouldn't have gone to all this trouble but I'm glad you did."

"Sit and enjoy." He disappeared back into the kitchen and brought out salads and a bottle of the Count's wine. He had to call around to several different stores to find one who carried his label. It had better be good for the price it had cost him.

Becky saw the wine and was intrigued. She held out her glass for Charlie to fill it.

"What is this all about?"

"Nothing I just wanted some peace and quiet tonight with you. Is that all right?"

"Of course, you know this salad is really good. I like this dressing. You know I was thinking about moving in. Do you mind if I bring some small pieces of furniture with me? You know my chair in the bedroom and my antique tables. I couldn't bear to put them in storage since they're so old. I'm afraid they would get damaged."

"That's fine whatever you want. You know there's room for whatever." Charlie had taken the salad plates in and brought out the main course.

"This wine is great. I didn't know the Count was into this?"

"It is good isn't it? It's one of his best labels they tell me."

"It taste expensive. Is it?"

"Plenty but I thought we'd try it anyway. Eat. Have I told you how pretty you look tonight?"

"Charlie, I'm in my work clothes. What's going on here?"

"What do you mean, we're having dinner and a great time together, right?"

"Tell me what's on your mind? You're not acting right. You're as nervous as a cat. Is something going on with Mariah?"

"Why do you say that?"

"I know how you feel about her. Is she in trouble again or is it the baby?"

"Becky I need to tell you something but I don't know how to do it without possibly upsetting you. Would you like some more wine?"

Becky sat back from the table and waited for the bomb to drop. Did he decide he didn't want to live with her after all? No that wasn't it he did say she could bring whatever she wanted over.

"No, I don't want any more wine. I want you to talk to me." Charlie couldn't look at her. He fidgeted with the plates. "Charlie talk to me."

"Okay, here it is. There's something you need to know, it happened before we met and it was just one time. You have to understand that." Becky turned her head to the side and frowned.

"Go on.."

"Do you remember me telling you why Mariah and Patrick split up?" Becky nodded yes. "She was upset and came to see me. My head wasn't on straight either since I buried my grandmother that same day. One thing lead to another and we took comfort in each other."

"So, that's natural since you two are practically family." Charlie drew in a deep breath.

"Becky we slept together. It was only the one time. It shouldn't have happened but it did. She left the next day. The baby could be mine but I doubt it. I still say Patrick has a better chance of that than I do." There it was out. The look on Becky's face was beyond comprehension. She felt like she had been kicked in the gut by an army. She didn't expect this. She was hurt.

"How long have you known?"

"I started to figure things out when she was in the hospital after the fire."

"And Patrick knows too? Charlie nodded. "Who else knows?"

"I don't think anyone."

"That's why Patrick punched you. He found out didn't he? I guess I ought to thank you for finally telling me, what after a month of you knowing. Why? Why didn't you tell me before this? I don't understand?"

"I didn't think there was a need to until we had the paternity test and I knew for sure. If I'm not the father then I wasn't going to tell you."

"Oh thank you that was so considerate of you. I can't believe you kept this from me. That all of you kept this from me, Mariah included. I thought she was my friend."

"She is. She is the one that made me decide to tell you. I couldn't keep this from you any longer since we're about to move in together. Becky I'm sorry I didn't tell you sooner. I'm sorry about all of it. What can I say?"

"Don't Charlie, don't say another word please. I don't want you to make a bigger fool out of me. Was everyone laughing at me behind my back all this time?"

"No Becky, no one was laughing. Mariah said if I didn't tell you she would. That's why she was so upset at the hospital when we told about our plans." Becky got up and picked up her purse.

"Wait please, where are you going?"

"Home to MY place. I need some time to think. I can't process this right now."

"You shouldn't be driving. Let me take you home you've been drinking."

"No I'm fine thank you. I'm VERY sober." She slammed the door behind her.

Charlie sat down on the floor in the foyer and held his head in his hands. This wasn't what he had hoped for. What could he have hoped for when he had been keeping something so important as this from her all this time? Now he had to wait. The ball was in her court. He had to wait and see if she would pick it up.

Mariah had gotten out of the hospital around noon that same day. Patrick had driven her back to the ranch, fixed some lunch and they sat on the back patio watching Jim work the horses. Jezebel seemed happy that she was there again and was putting extra effort into her prancing.

"She's gorgeous isn't she?" Mariah says with admiration of the horse.

"Yes, I would have to agree with that." Patrick was looking directly at Mariah.

"I'm talking about Jezebel. Whom are you talking about?"

"You of course."

"Don't make me laugh. I'm ugly, swollen and getting fatter by the second."

"Sweetheart you are far from being ugly, the rest is part of the baby which is a very beautiful thing. No man would disagree with that."

"The swelling isn't normal and you know it. But I can't control it."

"You listen to me. I know it bothers you and to be truthful it bothers me not really knowing what is going on with you and the baby but the swelling doesn't change who you are. It's only for a couple of months more." He took her hands in his and was rubbing them.

"I can't do anything right."

"This isn't like you. You're just tired. You've been on an emotional roller coaster for a long time now and it's just catching up with you. That's all." Patrick got up and walked behind her. He started to massage her neck and shoulders. Without thinking he let his hands drop toward her breast. Mariah got up right away. Instantly he regretted not controlling his actions.

"Excuse me I really need to call the boutique and check on things but first I need to use your facilities."

"It's your bathroom, too. Look I'm sorry, I didn't mean to do that. I just wasn't thinking."

Mariah nodded and went into the house. In a few minutes she returned with the portable phone.

"When are you going to get rid off that old hounds tooth coat?"

"What? Don't talk about my coat like that. It's finally broken in just the way I like it."

"It's tacky. Get yourself a new one."

"Where? No one in town carries them and I don't shop when I go to L.A. if I don't have to."

"You know you're right." There isn't a decent men's shop in town that has style." She paused for a minute thinking, "Mumm.."

"Ah oh..I know that look. What are you thinking?"

Mariah picks up the phone. "Susan.. is Margo there? Margo, its me. I'll be there in a little while. Listen stop whatever you are doing. Move the racks in the back of the show room. I want that space clear. I have a wonderful idea. And why I didn't think of this before I don't know. Is Danny still there? Good, put him on?"

"What are you doing?" Patrick asks while Mariah was waiting for Danny to get the phone..

"Danny! How are things coming there?

"Good, I think we'll be done with all the construction by tomorrow. Then we'll lay the carpet."

"How's the budget? Are we still okay with it?"

"We're right at the limit. Why?"

"You know those shelves we put up on that very back wall? I want some of those down and two dressing rooms installed with nice benches inside each one."

"You have three dressing rooms already."

"I know but I want these in the back of the boutique for a reason. Arrange them so that they are concealed around that little corner. I'm putting in a new line. Can you do this for me and how much more?"

"Sure. Three hundred more should do it. I can put a couple of men on it right away. Is there anything else?"

"When do you think it'll be finished?"

"Shouldn't take more than tomorrow. We can lay the carpet on Friday. Is that okay?"

"Fine. Design the rooms for the typical man, something that you would like."

"For a man? Are you putting in a men's line?"

"Sure am."

"Okay, that's what I'll do. We'll get on it right away."

"Thanks for everything." Mariah hung up. Patrick was staring at her with a grin.

"So you're putting in a men's line."

"Yep! I have a lot of planning to do and one very important phone call to make. I've got to go."

"Mariah, are you sure you're up to this? Aren't you supposed to take it easy?"

"This is therapy for me and believe it or not this is something on my list to do. I just didn't know it until this moment."

"What makes you think this is going to work? We already have two exclusive shops in town and then there is the other department stores."

"But think about it; everyone seems to carry the same type of stock. No one carries stock that has real style, something with a certain flair. My stock will be different than any one has seen around here. It's for the man with the discerning taste. It may not appeal to every man and I know that going into this but I want to see if I can do this. Let's say I'm going to shake this town up with some stiff competition."

"It sounds like this is going to be an expensive adventure. Who's line are you planning?" He thought he knew the answer already but had to ask.

"Jean Paul's of course. He has a wonderful hounds tooth jacket I know you would like."

"No thank you. I don't need another one." In truth he didn't want one that was designed by the Count as a constant reminder of him in his home.

"Got to go. I've got to make arrangements for the shipments. Thanks Patrick for the wonderful idea." She lightly squeezed his shoulder and headed for the gate to the driveway. Patrick couldn't stop her even if he wanted. She was gone.

Walking in the front doors of the boutique Mariah was greeted by all of her employees. She made sure she gave everyone a minute of her time; after all with out their hard work she wouldn't have anything. "Margo come up to the office in a few minutes. I need to call France first."

Mariah called directly to Jean Paul's cell phone. She was in luck it connected. "*Bonjour, mon amour*. Is this a bad time?"

"For you *ma chérie*, never. I was just thinking of you and wishing my arms was around you at this moment. Are you all right?"

"Yes, I'm at the boutique. I want to make a proposal."

"I have already done that haven't I?"

"Yes, you have but it's not that kind of proposal. I want to install your line in my boutique. Do you mind?"

"Isn't that going to be a lot of work for you? You should be taking it easy. Think of Abigail."

"I am thinking of Abigail. I promise it isn't going to be that bad on me. I have my staff here to help. I don't know why I didn't think about this before. Just think with both of our designs in one shop I can target the whole community. I fully plan to market your designs exactly like you require at home. We'll target the man with the discerning taste. Crystal River doesn't have a men's shop like what I plan to do. We'll give each man that comes in personal attention, from sales assistance to fitting to delivery of the garment. And we'll keep the files just like you require."

"Mariah, I am sure you can market the line without any problems but I am worried about you and the baby. Don't push yourself so hard. I want you both in my life forever."

Everything is fine. I need to do this. I want to do this. If I'm stuck in town then by heaven I am going to take this town by storm and shake it up a bit. So are you with me?"

"Of course, I am if you are sure. What do you want me to do?"

"Can I have Edmund or Tré for a few days to help train my staff on the line?"

"I don't see any problem with that. I'll talk to them and see who is free. When do you need them?"

"The construction is going to be done on Friday. I want the re-opening on next week, like Monday."

"That soon?"

"Yes why?"

"I'm not sure I can get the trunks to you by that time going commercial. Let me look at my schedule. Wait a minute. Why don't I send the jet with them? That way you will have them by Saturday."

"You wouldn't mind?"

"Not at all, if it will make you happy. I will get the details and call you later with arrival time on Saturday. Is that all right?"

"Sure that's fine. I really do appreciate it. Speaking of the trunks, have you been able to find anything else out?"

"Claude has spoken to the dock foreman. It seems the trunks leave the factory in excellent condition. They are sealed and weather tight and pass inspection before they are loaded on to the trucks. He says they have had a few replacement drivers due to illness. The foreman is checking identification on the drivers now and Claude has an appointment on Monday to interview the manager and the owner of the trucking firm. It seems that was the only day he could get the two of them together. They're coming to Pau for the meeting."

"Keep me posted. Wait a minute. Come on in Margo, have a seat." She motioned Margo to get herself a cup of coffee and sit down. "Is there anything else we need to discuss?" Getting back to Jean Paul.

"I know what I want to discuss but you can't with people listening, so *ma chérie* you have to be quiet for a change and listen."

"That is no fair."

"Shhh. Imagine yourself in my arms tonight, all night. Our naked bodies touching in all the right places and even those places that are not right to touch in, if you know what I mean. Imagine it to be even more heavenly than our night together if that is possible."

"Jean Paul please!"

"What you don't like?"

"*Non,* that is the problem I do like." Mariah saw Margo's note she handed to her. "Jean Paul wait a minute. I need to put you on the speaker system. Margo just handed me a note about some trunks."

"You had me worried there for a moment. I thought you wanted to share the dream with her."

"No way. It's all mine. Here you are on the speaker now." Mariah hung up the receiver. "What is it Margo?"

"I didn't want to tell you right away but since you two were talking about it now is the time. Daphne called this morning. There were two more trunks that were way laid. This time they were on the next flight into New Orleans but the silk lining had been cut. The garments are okay, a bit wrinkled but okay."

"Could the lining have pulled apart from the trunk with harsh handling?" Jean Paul asks.

"I asked that too. Daphne said no this was definitely cut. The slash was on the bottom. It was like someone was looking for something and was in a hurry."

"I will mention that to Claude. Thank you for the information."

"Is that all Margo?"

"That's all I have on that subject."

"What do you think of that Jean Paul?" Mariah was bewildered at why someone would do that type of act.

"I don't know for sure but we should get answers come Monday. I'm still being targeted on some of my deliveries too. Now do you have the speaker off yet?"

"Wait a minute. Margo why don't I call down when I get through with this?" Margo flashes a smile at Mariah and waves her hand in the air while mouthing ou la la. Mariah picks up a pencil off the desk and throws it at her just as the door closes behind Margo. She picks up the receiver and switches off the speaker. "Now I'm back. What do you have in mind?"

"To continue our discussion of what I'm going to do to you when I see you next."

"Be serious why don't you?"

"I am very serious, *mon amour*. I would like to come with the trunks but I have several meetings lined out in Paris next week. We are very close to changing some of those laws we spoke about. Hopefully by the end of next week life for the scum will be much harder."

"I do understand and what you are doing is so important but I do wish you were coming."

"I will soon, I promise. Now if I am to catch Tre' I had better call right away. Anything in particular you want us to send?"

"Nothing top of the line for right now, I want to see how the demand is before I take your best stock. I was thinking more of the middle to the upper price range.

"I will talk to Tré and see what he suggests then. I will call you soon. Are you still at the Inn?"

"Yes, until this weekend. Then I'll be at my apartment."

"Very well. Please take care of yourself and stay out of the hospital."

"I intend too."

"I miss you *mon amour*."

"I miss you too. *Au revoir*."

Mariah hung up the phone. She still had a smile on her face when Margo came back upstairs. "I see someone made you happy."

"He tries. Now here is my plan." She filled Margo in on all the details.

Margo had mentioned that Ben Thomas who was currently one of the handymen and stock room personal would be perfect for handling the men's line. There was no need to advertise for a new employee. He had demonstrated he had a sense of style, he carried himself well with the public and sometimes some of the regulars would ask his opinion on a color or a scarf. He and his wife Tracy were expecting their first child and they could use the extra money the position would bring. It was decided Margo would place a full ad in the paper announcing the re-opening sale on Monday and run through Wednesday. Everything had to be done and perfect by then.

At the staff meeting that afternoon the boutique was buzzing with excitement. The word got out that a new line was coming. Mariah had gathered everyone for an impromptu-catered dinner. She explained the concept of the line, that it would be a distinguished look and not every man would care for the more expensive items but hopefully they would carry enough of the lower price items that it would draw even those on a tight budget in. That the line was nothing like what Crystal River has in any other store but it had to be kept a secret until the Monday. She fully intended to surprise the town. She also interviewed Ben before the meeting and told him of Margo's recommendation. He had accepted the increased hours, work and responsibility without even thinking. He assured her he was up to it and would do a good job to see to the line's success as department manager. He understood the personal attention concept and the system of the files that would list each man's personal likes and dislike on clothing, sizes etc. That he could be called on to assist a shopper if need be if they couldn't come in to choose the clothing. There were several corporations in town that their executives could use this service. They were already doing some of this for a few of their special lady clients. The staff was overjoyed when she announced Ben's position. Everyone liked him and was afraid that he would have to leave the boutique to find better pay since the baby was on the way and Tracy had received notice of a temporary lay off at her factory. She also explained that they would host one of the designers of the line for a few days. He would handle the actual training of the staff so everyone could assist and answer questions if need be. There would be over time this weekend due to all the last minute arrangements. The trunks would be in Saturday so they didn't have a lot of time to get the new line up and running. Her staff didn't seem to mind and everyone was anxious to get back to work. Whatever it took they would do it. Mariah was always fair and compassionate to their needs and they understood how important this was for her. Mariah was more than a boss to them she was a friend who needed their support. They would make sure this line worked and with the holidays coming it would give them the boost they needed.

After Becky left Charlie picked up the phone and called Patrick. He wasn't sure Becky was going straight home and figured that Mariah may still be there since she wasn't at the Inn yet.

"Hi it's me. Is Mariah there?"

"No she left this afternoon and went back to the store. Why?"

"I just wanted to warn the both of you that Becky knows everything?"

"You told her? How did she take it?"

"Mad as hell, but I think it's directed at me. She's hurt because no one told her about it before now. I should have listened to Mariah but I thought I was handling it the best way possible."

"Do you think she's going to cause trouble with Mariah?"

"I don't think so. I stressed how things happened that.."

"I don't want to hear it again," Patrick interrupted. He still couldn't fully accept what had happened between Charlie and Mariah. If he was having trouble dealing with it even now after all these weeks how was Becky handling things. He felt sorry for her but wasn't going to get involved any more than he was. "I don't know what to tell you but I do think that someone needs to find Mariah before Becky does. If Becky confronts her without warning she may be asking for more than she bargained for. Mariah may just let her have it."

"I know. I'll try the Inn again. Maybe she'll be there by now."

"I'll try the boutique. I can't imagine that she would still be there but she ran off this afternoon with a hair brain idea of putting in a men's line in the store. She might still be there."

"Is she crazy? She's supposed to be taking it easy."

"I know but she's got the idea now and I'll be damn if she won't stop until she makes it happen one way or the other, if it doesn't kill her first."

"She's one stubborn woman," Charlie responded in disbelief of what Mariah had started in spite of the doctor's orders.

"That's not all. She's still having what I would call some pretty severe mood changes. She goes from one extreme to the next. This afternoon she was depressed and down on herself then the next she was excited and bouncing between the ground and the sky about her idea. I don't know if it's the pregnancy or what but it's hard to deal with, that's for sure. This isn't her."

"I know. She has always been outspoken but since the pregnancy she's worse."

"I think we need to make those calls. If you don't find her call me."

"Sure thing." Charlie hung up and tried the Inn, still no answer. Patrick called the boutique. The answering machine was on and Mariah's personal line upstairs wasn't being answered either. Where was she? He tried her cell phone. Thank heavens she picked up.

"Hello."

"You sound out of breath. What's up?"

"Just working. My re-opening is Monday. I have a lot of things to get done. So make it quick."

"That's a nice way to talk."

"I'm sorry but I am really busy. Everyone is still here."

"All the staff?"

"Patrick I don't have time to talk. What do you want?"

"This is important, give me a minute. Charlie is looking for you. He told Becky tonight about the baby and of course she's upset. He doesn't think she will confront you with anything but wanted to warn you anyway."

"Good I'm glad he told her. I'll handle things if she comes my way."

"Don't let her upset you."

"Everything will be fine. I wish everyone would stop worrying about me. I've got to get back to work. Anything else?"

"Just be careful please and good night. I love you."

"Mmm huh," Was all Mariah said not really listening to him as she moved some dresses and hung up the phone.

It was ten o'clock by the time Mariah placed the key card in her door at the Inn. She was dead tired but felt good and alive for a change. The tinge of excitement still lingered in her. Her phone was ringing as she stepped in the room. She threw her purse on the foot of the bed and grabbed the phone.

"Hello, Hello, I'm here don't hang up."

"*Bonjour.*"

"Jean Paul, oh I'm so glad you didn't hang up. I was just getting in."

"It's ten o'clock your time is it not? You haven't been working all this time?"

"Yes and I feel great so don't you say anything to me. I'm doing what I love. I need to do this."

"*Ma chérie*, I plan not to say anything except that I trust you not to overdo for *le bébé's* sake. The plane will be there Saturday around two. I'm not sure who will be accompanying the trunks but Tré and Edmund both are excited about this adventure of yours. They have already started putting the collection together for you. I told them your requirements and they understand. They are so thrilled to have this opportunity to help you."

"I've learned so much through them these past months. I should be doing something to repay them."

"I think you are. You are giving them a chance to show their work in your little world."

There was a knock on the door. Mariah answered the door while still talking to Jean Paul. "I still wish you were coming but I do understand. I miss you."

"I miss you, too, but I promise I will be there as soon as I can arrange things." Mariah motioned Charlie in the room and directed him to a chair but continued to talk to Jean Paul.

"I know you will. I'm sorry I truly don't mean to be a pain and demanding."

"*Mon amour*, you are neither. You just need me, that's all."

"You're right. I do need you. We need you."

"I have waited for you to say that to me, the feeling is the same for me."

Mariah smiled, her tears were falling. She turned her head so Charlie couldn't see her. He was preoccupied with the television but couldn't help hear her end of the conversation.

"Oh Jean Paul.."

"Please don't cry any more. It breaks my heart to hear such things and to know I can't be there to hold you, to make it better for you."

"You know me too well. I'm okay. I just wanted to be out of town by now."

"I know and soon you will be. You only have a couple of months left to go. You can get through this. You are one of the strongest women I know."

"You better not have known too many women." She laughed a little.

"*Mon amour* you have caught me. I have women stashed in my closets waiting for me to take them out of hiding. You know better than that."

"Just testing."

"Wait until I can get my hands on you." Static came over the phone line and then it went dead.

"Jean Paul?" Mariah realizing they lost the connection hung up.

"Sorry Charlie, but I had to take that call. It was business."

"Business huh? Sure didn't sound like it to me, but I wasn't listening you know."

"You were too and you know it. Maybe it wasn't all business but I am installing Jean Paul's line in the boutique. It's going to be fabulous and I'm getting one of the designers to come and train my staff next week. By the way I'm re-opening Monday."

"Patrick told me about the new line. Do you think you can handle this?"

"Why couldn't I? Besides I have my staff. Why are you here?" She wanted to change the subject before she heard slow down again from one more person.

"I wanted to tell you that Becky knows everything. I told her tonight at dinner."

"Patrick reached me a short while ago. She's pretty upset, huh?"

"Yea. I should have told her weeks ago. That seems to be what she's upset about, the fact that I didn't tell her. Not so much that I could be the baby's father. I think she understands the circumstances of that night and the fact that we weren't seeing each other helps but she said she feels like she was made a fool of and everyone was laughing behind her back at her. She just walked out and I haven't heard from her. I've tried to call a couple of times but she won't answer the phone."

"Give her time. Let her think things through tonight maybe even a couple of days, then call her if she hasn't called you first."

"She might never speak to me again. I didn't know how much I cared about her until she slammed the door behind her."

"She hasn't contacted me. As of eight thirty she didn't Patrick either."

"I had better be going. It's getting late and you look tired. I just wanted to warn you in case Becky contacts you. I don't think she'll do that but anyway I'm babbling. Are you okay?"

"Sure. We're great." Mariah rubbed Abigail and Abigail kicked in response. "See. She agrees with me." Charlie leans over and kisses her on the forehead.

"All right sweetheart, if you say so. Call me if you need anything. Okay?"

"Fine. Good night. Now go home. Charlie, you know you did the right thing don't you?"

"Yea, I hope so. Good night." Mariah closed the door behind him and locked it. She crawled into bed without changing her clothes and fell asleep almost instantly. The lights didn't even get turned off.

Danny was finishing up the new dressing rooms when Mariah walked in the store. They were exactly what she had in mind but there was one problem. Danny had received a call about the new carpet Mariah had ordered. The store didn't get it in like they promised so Mariah and Danny had to pick out something else from their stock.

"Good morning Margo." Patrick said in an uplifting voice.

"My, we are in a good mood this morning. You get lucky last night?"

"Margo Williams wash your mouth out. You know there's no one for me but Mariah. She here?"

"No, left a little while ago. Went with Danny to pick out the carpet."

"I thought that was done?"

"It was, some kind of mix up."

"So that's where the men's line is going to be, huh?" Patrick looked over the area. The wall that jutted out would provide a sense of privacy and their own space for the men.

"Yep. I guess it's going to be something by the way she talks about it. She has a good idea with it."

"Wouldn't know. Has Becky been in this morning?"

"Nope. Why?"

"Do me a favor. If she does, watch Mariah's back please. There may or may not be trouble. Mariah doesn't need to get her blood pressure up again."

"Of course I will but what's up?"

"I can't say but call me if you need to. Use my cell number and listen don't tell Mariah I stopped by. Okay."

"Sure if that's what you want." Margo wasn't sure if she would have told Mariah about his visit anyway. She still had the feeling that Patrick was behind a lot of Mariah's heartbreak now and in the past. But she could advise the rest of the staff to watch for trouble if Becky stopped in and intercede if need be. Mariah was after all their first concern.

"Did I wake you?" Becky asks as Charlie answers the phone, his voice thick with sleep.

"Huh?" The fog in his head cleared and he knew whom he's talking to. "Becky?"

"Good morning. I'm sorry I thought you would be up by now."

"It was four o'clock this morning before I could get to sleep. What time is it?"

"Nine."

"You don't sound too good. Are you sick?"

"No. Lets say you got more sleep than I did. Are you up to breakfast?"

"Sure. You want to come over here?"

"No. I have some errands to do later. Lets meet at the café, say at ten?"

"I'll be there."

"Good we need to talk." Becky hung up the phone. Charlie laid in bed a little while longer thinking this could the end of their relationship. He had to face it, this was all because of his stupid mistake of not being straight with Becky. The fact that Becky wanted to meet in a public place bothered him. There was no sense of putting it off he had to get up and get it over with.

Becky had parked her car half way between the café and Mariah's boutique. She needed the fresh air and the walk to get her mind in order before she met with Charlie. She had arrived early and taken a booth towards the back of the room. She was on her second cup of coffee when she spotted Charlie entering the door. Charlie saw her and tried to put his best smile on.

"Good morning. I'm so glad you called," he said as he sat down across the table from her. He took her hands in his. Becky didn't pull back as he expected her to.

"I didn't know what to order for you."

"That's okay, I'm not hungry."

"Coffee?" Becky poured him a cup from the pot she had ordered. Charlie took a sip. The strong brew was hot and it burned going down.

"So.. who begins?"

"I want you to know I'm still upset with what you did. Not about you and Mariah but the fact that you weren't truthful with me. I thought our relationship was built on truth and trust. Can I ever trust you again? Now I know how Mariah feels about Patrick and his unfaithfulness."

"Becky, that's a low blow. I wasn't unfaithful to you. Don't put me in the same category as Patrick. That's not fair."

"No it's not the same thing but it feels the same to me."

"So this is it?"

"Sit and be quiet. I'm not through with what I have to say." She took another drink of coffee before she continued. "How do you really feel about me?"

"I should have told you when Mariah wanted me to but I was afraid I would lose you. I didn't know just how much you meant to me until last night when you walked out. Becky I am sorry for hurting you. I want to see what we have together and I haven't changed my mind about moving in together." He leaned across the table trying to hold her hands but this time she withdrew and sat back away from him. Here it comes Charlie thought and sighed heavily.

"Well, it's like this in a nut shell. I expect certain things in a relationship. I didn't think I needed to spell it out but seeing how I was obviously wrong I'm going to. I need respect and honesty in any relationship. So I'm going to tell you how I honesty feel. I do love you. I'm not going to throw what we have away because of the situation we're in, but I am not going to put up with anymore of this. You will treat me with respect and give me the honesty I deserve or else I'm afraid we don't have a relationship worth having. I haven't kept anything from you and I wouldn't have something this important. Mariah was right to force you to tell me. I just wish you had done it on your own. These are my terms. Do you except? If you can't give me a hundred percent then I don't want you." Becky sat there unmoving while she spoke. Her voice was low but stern.

"Does this mean you still want to move in?"

"Only on my terms and that you take our relationship seriously. You have to know you want this too. I'm not doing this unless you're sure you can give me what I need. I don't want to be used then left behind."

"Becky, I promise I won't do that to you. Mariah said almost the same thing about us. She was concerned about you. I saw how she hurt when things went sour for them. I'm not like that. I've waited all this time to find a meaningful relationship. I haven't had anyone like you in my life before now. You somewhat remind me of my grandmother. You both have the same attitudes on a lot of issues. I never considered settling down until now. I will prove to you that I am serious and I do love you. There, I said it."

Becky leaned forward with her arms on the table. Charlie noticed her eyes were filling up. He once again took her hands and this time she let him. "We can try," is all she said. He then slipped around the table beside her and kissed her while he held her in his arms.

"Thank you darling for giving me another chance. You won't be sorry. Now what do you want me to bring over to the house and when?" It was an hour and half later when they finally left the café.

Charlie had business in Los Angeles that afternoon. Becky still had one more errand to do before she went in to work. She called in taking a half personal day but now with she and Charlie on a new road together she felt a lot better. She walked into Remmington's smiling.

Mariah was in the back office on the phone. Margo saw her come in and stopped her.

"Sorry, we're not open for business yet. Catch the sale Monday."

"Margo, if I didn't know any better I'd think you were trying to get rid of me."

"Now, why would I do that?"

"You tell me? Mariah here?"

"She's busy right now."

"I won't take to much time. I do need to see her though."

"You look pretty happy this morning but tired."

"I am Margo, I am."

Mariah stepped out of the tiny office on the main floor, carrying some invoices. "Margo I need you.. Becky.. How are you?"

"Better since I had breakfast with Charlie. Can I see you for a minute?"

"Okay. Have a seat in the office over there. Let me talk to Margo for a minute." Becky headed for the office.

"Do you want me to save you in a couple of minutes?" Margo asks.

"Why, because Becky's here to talk to me? I think I can handle things with her. You're acting like you know something I don't. What do you know?"

"Nothing except you don't need anymore trouble. I'm not supposed to tell you but Patrick came by and said to look out for her but didn't say why."

"He did, did he? I don't think she's looking for trouble. She's in a pretty good mood."

"None the less, I'm going to have my ears open for shouting."

"This is between Becky and I, not you. Take these invoices and warranties and file them UPSTAIRS please." She handed Margo the papers. Margo took them but had already made up her mind she would buzz Mariah in fifteen minutes to see if she needed help getting Becky to leave.

Stepping in the office and closing the door behind her, Mariah sits down behind the small desk. The room wasn't anymore than a walk-in closet made into an office. It was big enough for a small desk, an extra chair and file cabinet with a little room to spare.

"Now Becky what did you need to see me about?"

"Mariah, I want to be straight with you. I know about you, Charlie and the baby."

"Charlie told you. I'm glad he did."

"He did only because you forced him to. I know that."

"And.."

"And I don't blame you for this situation. I understand how and why things happened the way they did."

"Your talking about the night I spent with Charlie?"

"Yes. I didn't know him at that point so I can't condemn either one of you. I think I must have felt a little of what you felt- the betrayal when Charlie told me he was keeping the possibility of being the baby's father from me. I've been awake all night thinking about things. I do have to tell you I'm a little jealous of the fact that another woman other than myself may be carrying his baby but if it has to be then I'm glad it's you."

"I appreciate how you feel. How do things stand between you two?"

"We're still together. I've laid the law down and spelled things out in no uncertain terms what I expect from him and that I will not except anything else from this point on."

"What did he say?"

"He agreed. We're still moving in together this weekend."

"I'm glad things worked out. I am sorry it came down this way. I do love Charlie and don't want to hurt him but I felt he was wrong. I even thought about telling you myself but I thought the news should come from him first. Breaking the two of you up isn't in my game plan."

"Charlie asked me to marry him if the baby turns out to be his but I refused. He's the only family I have. I need him in that aspect but not as a father to my daughter." Maria continued watched her closely.

"I didn't know about the proposal but I'm not surprised either. He'd want to do the right thing."

"It may be right for him but not for us. I told him I wanted him to be a part of my child's life. She will need an uncle or godfather or whatever Charlie wants to be called. Is that okay with you?"

"Mariah, I wouldn't expect anything else. Since we're talking so candid you do understand that if this works out between Charlie and me that I will be a part of the baby's life too. Charlie already loves her and I will too. Is that all right with you?"

"She'll need an aunt. I hope our friendship didn't suffer. You know I made him tell you because of it."

"I know that and as far as I'm concerned our friendship has changed to some degree. It's deeper than what it was."

"I think so too," Mariah replied smiling. The phone buzzed and Mariah answered.

"Yes."

"Are you still alive in there?"

"Yes." Mariah was looking at Becky who seemed relaxed at this point.

"Do you need me to boot her out of here?"

"No. I can do that, thank you. I'll be out in a minute." Mariah hung up the phone. Becky got up and started for the door but stopped.

"Mariah, I'm glad we had this talk." Becky hugged her and left.

Margo approached Mariah leaning against the office doorway. "I take it everything is okay?"

"Sure is. What's the status out here?"

"We're done except for the carpet now. The guys went to get it as we speak."

"Good. Do you need me for anything right now?"

"Can't think why we should. You want to get out of here for a while?"

"I was thinking about it?" Margo took her purse out of the desk drawer and headed toward the front of the store. "I'll have the cell on if you need me."

Mariah drove away from the store. She thought about going back to the Inn for a nap since her energy seemed to be evaporating quickly but then decided to go to the beach. She hadn't been there since she had got back in town. She wanted to go to her spot, their spot and think. It was a habit she developed when anything bothered her. The beach was deserted and that pleased her. She walked along the surf barefooted. The sand felt warm to her feet even though the breeze was cool. Reaching the spot that she and Patrick always went to she sat down on the tree trunk and leaned against the rocks. She let her mind go blank, closed her eyes and listened to the sounds of the ocean. Sarah had told her to try doing something like this when she felt overly stressed. The ordeal with Becky was more taxing on her nerves than she had thought. She didn't know how long she had been sitting there with her eyes closed but suddenly she felt a touch on her shoulder. Startled she opened her eyes and tried to get up.

"I thought that was your car. Everything okay?"

"It's you. You scared me to death. What are you doing here?"

"I've been at the marina looking at a sailboat I might get. I noticed your car up there, so I came on down."

"You expect me to believe that? You probably followed me."

"Now why would I do that?"

"Why would you ask Margo to be a watchdog for Becky?"

"Oh you know." Patrick kicked the sand around his boot.

"She didn't want to tell me but I made her since she was bugging me so."

"Then I take it Becky showed up?"

"Yes and everything is fine. She decided to still give Charlie a chance but she's making him pay big time for not telling her right away."

"How were things left between you two?"

"Everything is fine. Becky's eyes are wide open you might say."

"Mm," Patrick sighed. "You want to walk or sit?"

"I got here first and I'm sitting. I just want to relax for a few minutes."

"Do you mind if I stay?"

"It's a free beach. I can't stop you." Patrick sat down on the tree trunk beside her.

"Do you come here often?"

"No. This is the first time since I've been back. It's beautiful here isn't it?"

"Yea. There usually aren't very many people on this side of the beach."

Mariah didn't respond. There was nothing to say. She wanted to soak in the warmth of the sand, the sun and the feel the mist of the ocean. Patrick sat leaning forward on the tree trunk and twirling his sunglasses between his fingers. He knew she didn't want to talk but after what seemed to be an extremely long period of silence he had to say something.

"Something bothering you?"

"Nope, not anymore," Patrick nodded his head.

"By the way you haven't said if you want to go to Becky's shindig with me on Wednesday night."

"I forgot about that. I do appreciate the invitation but I really don't have anything appropriate to wear being pregnant and all." Patrick started to laugh.

"Come on! You don't have anything to wear? Look at all the clothes you carry in the store, pregnant or not you do have your choice. What's the real reason?" He would ask her again before he gave up on her no. There was still a little time left.

"I do have the re-opening sale on Monday. Edmund or Tré will be coming in with the trunks on Saturday afternoon."

"Who are they?"

"They are the designers of "The Aristocrat Designer" line, you know the men's line?"

"Oh. I should have known it would carry a name like that. So you've talked to J.P. Is he coming too? I mean should I stay clear of you when he's here?"

"Please don't call him that. You know I don't like it and no he can't be here. He has business in Paris." Patrick leaned back against the rock but still didn't look directly at Mariah.

"Does that upset you?"

"Why are you asking so many questions? I have a lot to think about and do between now and Saturday. I don't need the fifth degree."

"I'm sorry I didn't mean to make it like that. You just seem down."

"I'm not. I'm tired and trying to recoup my energy."

"What about your sugar?"

"I was okay this morning."

"Have you eaten lunch?"

"Not yet I was going to get something on the way back. Danny and the crew were moving the new carpet in and I didn't want to be around when they laid it."

"Then go with me to the snack shop. You can buy if it makes you feel better. Come on." Patrick gets up, puts his sunglasses on and extends his hand to help her up. Mariah looked up at him. She hesitated but took his hand.

Patrick drove her back to her car after lunch. He had wanted her to go to the ranch with him but she wanted to get to the boutique since she had been gone a lot longer than she had planned. Sarah had told her she was going to have to come up with some plan to help her make the most important decision of her life. This she hadn't been able to do and she had an appointment tomorrow with her. Tomorrow was almost here. She said her thanks to Patrick and drove off. He again had the feeling that the distance was growing between them and that time was running out with her. It didn't really make sense to him since she was going to be in Crystal River another two months. He had eight weeks before the baby was born. What could he do in eight weeks to change her mind?

Mariah had worked the rest of the afternoon. She kept everyone hopping. As soon as Danny and his crew laid one section of carpet she had the racks and shelves in place in no time. The dressing rooms were done and with Margo's taste in fabric she had chosen for the benches they looked very masculine. It was exactly what she had in mind. There were just a few things to do tomorrow like hanging the wallpaper in the men's department and they would be done until the trunks came in.

"Margo I forgot to tell you I won't be in tomorrow morning until around eleven. I have a doctor's appointment and I don't know for sure how long it's going to take."

"Don't worry about it. I'll take care of whatever comes up."

"Thanks and I do mean that."

"I know you do, now go back to the Inn and get some rest." Margo handed Mariah her purse and jacket and gave her a slight push toward the door.

She sighed as she put her things in the closet by the door and latched it behind her. She had decided she would just do room service and relax in bed with a good movie before going to sleep. Then she noticed the light was left on in the kitchenette. She hadn't done that, maybe the maid had. Before she turned it off she noticed a note on the counter. "Dinner for two is served. Look in the refrigerator. Love Patrick." Intrigued she opened it and found a huge chef salad from one of her favorite restaurants. She called the desk and was informed that Patrick had stopped by with it and left the note. The bellhop had delivered it in the kitchen. Gratefully she ate it and curled up in bed.

CHAPTER 8

Mariah's session with Dr. Sarah McKracken was helpful as always but she did stress that somehow Mariah had to come up with a plan to explore her feelings more about Patrick and Jean Paul. She was pleased to find out Mariah had asserted herself upon Charlie to handle things with Becky. It took that much stress off her, so they were making progress.

By the time Mariah entered the boutique everything was done and everyone was waiting for her to get back to see the look on her face. Even Danny and his crew were still there. The boutique was ready and waiting for Jean Paul's line. But the best news of all was that her apartment upstairs was finally done and she could move back in. The new sprinkler system was installed, her furniture back in place just as she had it before the fire and a dozen roses on her desk with a card saying "We did it!" She turned around and saw all her employees standing behind her, smiling. She had expected the apartment to be done next week, not today. That meant she would only have to pay for the suite at the Inn she reserved for Tre' or Edmund and let her room go. She was ready to get back to something that was normal. She stepped over to the roses and one by one she handed each of her employees one and thanked them for standing by her and the boutique these past few months. She gave everyone the afternoon off but not before arranging a staff meeting the next day after the trunks get in. Everyone had to be briefed properly on the line and they didn't have a lot of time to learn it. All agreed to be there by the time the trunks came.

After everyone left she lay down on the bed and drifted off to sleep. The next thing she knew she was on the beach carrying a baby, she knew it was her daughter- Abigail, but didn't see her face. She was too busy running away from someone, her mother she thought. Running away from danger. All she knew was she had to get her daughter away from the danger. Her daughter had to be safe. Then a hand grabbed her shoulder. Mariah woke with a start and a scream. No one was there to hear her. It was all a dream but then the phone rang. Shaking she picked up the receiver almost afraid to answer it.

"Hello," Patrick said when she didn't speak.

"Patrick?"

"You sound horrible. What's happening?"

"Nothing. I was asleep."

"I'm at the front door. Let me in."

"What?" She was having difficulty comprehending what he had just said.

"I said I'm at the door. Turn off the alarm system and let me in."

Mariah didn't sound right to him. He didn't know what was going on but if she didn't let him in he would break the window again if he had to. "Mariah come on, deactivate the alarm system and let me in."

She came to her senses and realized what Patrick was asking her to do. She went to the control panel in her office. "Okay, it's off." She wasn't even half way down the stairs when he met her. "What's the problem?" She was confused as to why he wanted in so bad.

"You tell me? Sit down. You're shaking." He made her sit on the stairs. It was true she was shaking and she wanted to cry but didn't. All she could do was shake her head and stare blankly at Patrick. "Baby you need to tell me what's wrong. Is the baby okay?"

"It's not the baby. At least I don't think it is."

"What do you mean? Please Mariah talk to me. What is it? You're a white as a sheet."

"I was dreaming. It was just a nightmare I guess."

"Some nightmare. Can you tell me about it?"

"I don't want to talk about it. I'm thirsty. I want a drink." Mariah started to get up. Patrick helped her up and back into the apartment. She sat on the sofa in the office while Patrick got her some water. She took the afghan that was on the back of it and covered up. She was cold. This dream was so real this time. She knew that each time she had the dream it was more real than the previous one. Her reactions to it were getting stronger with each one.

"Here." He handed the glass to her. "Now tell me about it. Let's talk it out."

Mariah shook her head no and drank. Her hands were becoming steadier by this time and her head was clearing too. He sat down next to her and held her. She didn't try to move out of his arms.

"Baby, sometimes it helps to talk about things like this. Maybe we can figure out what it means. What affects you affects the baby. Talk to me, I'm not leaving until you do."

"All right. I was carrying the baby and running, running away from some danger only I couldn't run fast enough. Then someone grabbed me on the shoulder. That's when I woke up and I guess when you called." Patrick sighed and nodded his head.

"Okay. Well you were probably thinking about when we met on the beach the other day. Remember I touched your shoulder. And the running well I hate to admit it but maybe you were thinking about what drove you away from here; what I did to you. God I hope not."

Mariah got up and walked over to the windows still holding the afghan around her. She had stopped shaking by now but was still cold. She saw the traffic was heavy on the street below, which meant it must be the dinner hour already.

"What time is it?" She turned and glanced at the clock on the wall. "Oh crud!" Mariah threw off the afghan and picked up the phone book.

"What are you doing?" Patrick was perplexed by this time.

"I forgot to reserve a van for the trunks." She dialed a couple to numbers but received no answers. "Everything is closed now. What am I going to do? I need that van." Mariah sat behind her desk with her head in her hands. Patrick walked behind her and took the phone book from her hands and placed it back in the drawer it came from.

"There's no use trying to find someone open now. Let me do that for you tomorrow morning. I promise you I'll get on it first thing. You'll have a way to get those trunks here one-way or the other. I'll see to that."

"I can take care of this. I don't need your help."

"Yes you do and there's nothing you can do or say I'm doing this for you. You have enough to deal with."

"Are you sure you have time?"

"I've got nothing going tomorrow. How many trunks are coming?"

"Ten I think."

Patrick's raised an eyebrow as he repeated the number. "Ten. Isn't that a bit much to start with?"

"What do you know about marketing? Besides I don't want to use the plane any more than I have to, so I ordered more than I need right now. We can store the garments in the room across the hall.

"What ever you say. You're right I don't know much about marketing." He took her hands and pulled her up out of the chair. "I don't like the thought of you being here by yourself. Come home with me just for tonight." He ran his fingers down her cheek. There was his touch again. Up until this moment she had disassociated herself from his touch since the last time he affected her so much but he had caught her off guard again.

"No. I'm fine. Everything's fine. I'm going to stay here but I do need to go back to the Inn and get my things. I'm moving back in here. This is my home for the time being."

"I'm not going to be able to change your mind, am I?"

"No not at all."

"Then let me drive you to the Inn and get your things."

"I guess I'm not going to be able to say no to that, am I?"

"No not at all."

"Very funny." Patrick knew she was feeling better since she was being sarcastic.

"Get your umbrella. It's starting to rain out there."

Patrick and Mariah drove to the Inn and retrieved her belongings. She wouldn't have dinner with him but she did settle for a short drive along the coast. He would take any time he had with her even if it was just a few minutes here and there.

Saturday morning brought Patrick ready to pull his hair out. There wasn't any moving van around to be found. They all had been reserved for the weekend except the very large or the ones that were too small. He would have to go to Los Angeles to find one. That meant it would cost more to rent in the long run and he didn't want to see Mariah do so. As he got up from the kitchen table to get another cup of coffee the thought hit him to coordinate another type of effort.

"Hi Jim, it's me. Sorry to wake you but can I use your truck today?" He knew that on Saturdays Jim and Betty usually slept in a little later.

"Patrick? Uh, sure I'm not planning to do anything. Is there something you need over there?"

"No just your truck. Mariah has some trunks coming in at the airport and she doesn't have any way of getting them to the shop. If it's okay I'll swing by about ten and pick it up?"

"Sure. Can I help with anything else? What about the livestock?"

"Got that covered for today and I can't think of anything at the moment. I'm going to try to get Charlie to help out. Thanks."

"Anytime."

Patrick pressed the dial button and was connected to Charlie's place. Becky answered.

"Hi, sorry to wake you guys but can I talk to Charlie?" Becky woke Charlie.

"Man do you know what time it is?" Charlie glances at the alarm clock.

"Yea, its eight thirty. I've been up since five."

"What for? I know your crazy now."

"I have horses to feed remember? Besides Mariah needs a favor from you."

"Mariah? What's up?

"You know she's putting in a men's line at the shop. Well, the clothes are coming in this afternoon at two. She forgot to reserve a moving van to haul them from the airport back to the shop. Can you help with your truck?"

Charlie rose up on one elbow and looked at Becky. He was thankful that she was giving him another chance. They had plans to start moving her things in today but now with this?

"What is it? Is Mariah okay?" Becky was concerned when she heard her name mentioned.

"Mariah needs help getting some trunks moved from the airport this afternoon. Patrick is trying to find some trucks to do it. Can we do your things later today or tomorrow?"

"Is that all? Sure but I'm going to. Maybe there is something I can do to help, even if its putting things up at the store while you guys are gone." Charlie kisses her.

"Buddy, count us in. Listen call Ben and Tracy Thomas. He has a truck. What time do you need us?"

"The trunks will be arriving around two she said."

"We'll be at the boutique around noon if that's okay. Maybe she'll need us for something else. Becky wants to come to help with whatever."

"Is that wise you think?"

"I think so." He saw the look on Becky's face and covered with "I might have some rope in the garage." She relaxed and laid back on the bed. It took a second for Patrick to figure out what just happened.

"Oh, okay but I don't want anything to upset her today. She's stressed out over this in spite of what she says and those damn mood swings are something else."

"I know. See you later, right now I have to take care of something else." Charlie hung up the phone as he gazed at Becky with a smile on her face.

Patrick called Ben and Tracy and told them of the situation. Ben was going to be at the boutique by noon to see to any last minute details, so the truck part wasn't a problem. Tracy was going too just to be with him. Ben suggested that he would call a few other co-workers and alert them of the problem. If they didn't have pickups then maybe they would know someone who did. Patrick figured with ten trunks they would need at least four or five trucks depending on how big they were.

Ben called Patrick back an hour later and told him he was able to enlist three more husbands and their trucks. Susan, Ann and Kathy were all ready planning to be at the boutique to help with the unloading of the trunks and the stocking of the garments. The women didn't want to see Margo and their boss do all the work in her condition. They all knew what a difficult time she was having with the pregnancy. The more people they had the better. Patrick thanked Ben for his efforts and hung up. The problem should be solved he thought. Now to call Mariah.

"Hi sweetheart. How did you sleep?"

"Fine. I was just about to call you. What have you come up with on the truck situation?"

"It's taken care of. You have a ride for those trunks now."

"Where do I get the truck and how much do I need to cut the check for?"

"You don't get the truck and it's free."

"What? I don't understand, no wait a minute you're not paying for this."

"No I'm not. Let's just say I called in some favors."

"What have you done?" Mariah's tone was impatient.

"Relax will you. There wasn't a moving van available this weekend. I didn't want to see you have to go to Los Angeles for one so I made some calls. I've got Jim's truck and Charlie's." He neglected to tell her about Ben and the others as they all agreed they wanted to surprise her with their efforts.

"Oh my. It's going to take us forever to get all of them moved with just two trucks."

"I said relax. It's being handled. Trust me please. I'll come by the shop around noon okay?"

That didn't give Mariah much time to get ready. She felt horrible for the lack of sleep and she knew she looked the same way. There was no way she would let Edmund or Tré see her this way. That as all she needed for them to report back to Jean Paul about how she looked. She spent extra time on her makeup, and then she went to her closet and picked out a navy silk suit with a silver satin lapel and pockets accents. The neckline of the jacket was cut fairly low but not low enough to warrant a scarf underneath it. The skirt showed just enough thighs to intrigue a man but long enough not to show everything. She slowly put her panty hose on taking care that the seams were straight on her legs. She chose a pair of slip on navy flats. There was no way she could walk in heels. After dressing she looked at herself. She still looked drawn and tired. Nothing was going to help with that. After debating what to do with her hair she chose a French knot with bangs hanging down the left side of her face. This was the best she was going to do since she didn't have time to wash it. Perhaps if she tried to keep her enthusiasm up no one would notice how tired and swollen she was. She put on the diamond pendant and earrings that Jean Paul given her. Finally she was ready.

The day was already warm Patrick thought. He made sure the horses had plenty of water before he left since he figured he would be gone most of the day. He pulled off his stable boots at the back door and replaced them with his good pair and left.

Betty greeted Patrick at the door and asked if he wanted breakfast? Patrick refused but sat down at the table for a few minutes to chat. Jim had made up his mind that he was going to help with the trunks. There was no reason why he couldn't since they didn't have anything planned that day. Betty wanted to get together with the ladies from the church. Patrick accepted his help and waited for him to finish eating.

Charlie, Becky, Patrick and Jim all emerged at once on Mariah. She was downstairs moving some boxes out of the way when they walked in.

"The troops have arrived!" Charlie yelled out. Mariah turned to see them. Charlie and Becky came in first then behind them Jim and Patrick. Patrick took off his sunglasses and put them in his shirt pocket. He was dressed in a red tee shirt and jeans accentuating his tight body. His biceps were peaking out of the rolled up sleeves. She greeted them and hugged Jim. She was especially glad to see him. Patrick pulled her to the side and kissed her. "You look beautiful," he whispered in her ear even though she looked like she didn't get any sleep last night. She halfway smiled at him and joined the others. Patrick went to the boxes and inspected them; concerned she was lifting something heavy. Mariah caught what he was doing out of the corner of her eye.

"Before you say anything those were empty. I was just about to cut them up and get them out of here."

"Where's the cutter? I'll do that."

"This poor little pregnant woman can't even do that huh?" She replied to Patrick.

Patrick threw her a dirty look, one that Mariah caught. Becky and Charlie had their backs to them inspecting the new dressing rooms. But Jim caught the look. He went over to Mariah and put his arm around her neck and hugged her.

"That's right little missy. Pregnant folk's job is to sleep and eat and then eat and sleep some more, not use dangerous objects like box cutters, so just get used to it, eat and sleep that's what pregnant folk do. We men couldn't do what you do and that's a fact hey Charlie?" Jim saw Charlie and Becky coming back over to them. He hoped they would diffuse the tension.

"Now that's a fact for sure." Charlie agreed. Patrick watched them as he continued to break the boxes down. Mariah was grinning again. Jim did have a way with her. The phone rang. Mariah answered. She squealed with delight when she heard the voice on the other end. Patrick thought it had to be J.P.

"*Bonjour*, Edmund. Where are you? Have you landed?"

"*Non*, but it will be soon. We shall be there early, say around one thirty if that is all right with you. Alec has broken all speed limits in getting to you. He and Frederick sends their regards."

"Tell Alec and Frederick I said they had better not be reckless and I can't wait to see them too." She glances at the clock; it was twelve thirty by now. "We'll be there waiting."

156

"I can't wait to see you again."

"Me too." She hung up the phone. Between Tré and Edmund she was glad it was he coming. Edmund was less serious about life and always made her laugh. "We had better be going. They will be here in an hour. We'll need the extra time moving the trunks back here. Listen guys I do thank you for everything you're doing. What would I do without friends like you?" She was looking at Becky, Charlie and Jim who were standing together. She addressed Patrick this time. "And I'm sorry I'm so grumpy. I know you didn't have to arrange all this for me. I do appreciate it." All Patrick could do was to stand there wanting to take her in his arms and kiss her worries away but knew she wouldn't let him.

"Sweetheart all you have to do is ask. I'm there for you anytime."

"We've got to go. "She started fluttering around looking for her purse.

"Then let's go, what are we waiting for?" Jim said, "Patrick how are you going?"

Becky and Charlie headed out the door toward their truck and Jim toward his.

"Mariah?"

"I'm driving my car. Edmund's going to need a ride here."

"Then I'm going with you."

"Whatever you want Patrick. I don't feel like arguing with you."

"Good, then let me drive." She handed him the keys and they drove off.

"Did you get any sleep last night?"

"Some. I'm just nervous about today and the re-opening, that's all."

"Any more dreams?"

"No." Mariah shook her head and looked out the window.

"I was thinking that maybe you ought to talk to the doctor about it."

"Who? Dr. Miles? She's my OB/GYN, not a shrink." She wondered if Patrick was referring to Sarah McKracken and if he knew anything about her?

"To whomever could help get you answers as to why you're having the same dream."

"It's nothing. I'm sure of it." She continued to look out the car window. This is a subject that she didn't want to talk about anymore. "I'm not discussing this anymore."

"Okay." He didn't want her to figure out what he knew about Sarah and their continuous appointments. He was worried about her. She did look tired and her energy level seemed low. "Did you take your sugar today?"

"Yes. I'm fine. Will you please just drop it? I know I don't look the best right now but this is the best I can do."

"Sweetheart I'm not saying that. You always look good to me."

Mariah leaned her head on the back of the seat, adjusted the seat backwards a bit and closed her eyes. They still had a fifteen-minute ride and she hoped it would be long enough to psych herself up enough to put on a good front.

Patrick kept quiet the rest of the way but he was watching her. They pulled into a front parking spot at the airport. Charlie and Jim parked in the loading zones. Patrick looked around but didn't see anyone else. It was still a little early for them. He got out and went around the car, opened the door and helped Mariah out. They crossed the loading zones and headed into the terminal. She went to the windows; there was no sign of the Concord yet. She was too nervous to sit down. She had to get herself prepared. Becky saw her standing alone. Patrick was talking with Charlie and Jim in the corner.

"This is exciting isn't it?"

"Huh? Oh Becky, I want to thank you for understanding everything and I mean everything."

"Everything's going to work out the way it's meant to be. I feel it. Listen just tell me what you want me to do at the shop. I'm here to help you all day if you want me."

"When are you moving in at Charlie's?"

"Tomorrow or so. My things can wait. Your sale can't."

"That's so sweet of you to give up your plans for me and after the mess I caused for you and Charlie."

"Mariah, the "mess" as you put it was created by Charlie for not discussing any thing with me. As I said things between us are okay and Charlie and I have a new understanding as well."

"Hey, hey, hey, the gang's all here." Ben said as he and the extra help strolled through the door. Mariah recognized his voice and turned. Patrick glanced at Mariah. The look on her face was priceless. Ben and the others went over to her. She was starting to cry. "Are you guys here to help?" Ben nodded and hugged her.

"Do you think we're going to let you have all the fun? No way."

"I didn't ask you to work today, did I?"

"Nope and today is not a pay day for anyone. We all agreed we wouldn't accept anything from you. This is our gift to you and the baby."

"What do you mean "we"?"

"While we're here the wives are at the boutique ready and waiting to do their thing. By the way they put together a carry in meal to keep us going."

"Oh my, they're doing this for me?"

"Yep, for you and for the boutique. Your more than a boss to us you're a friend who needs our help."

"Thank you." Mariah hugged him.

"LOOK AT THAT PLANE!" Becky squealed.

They all turned toward the windows. It was Jean Paul's jet and it was show time for Mariah. She brushed the tears from her eyes, pulled her compact from her purse and checked her make up. Her lipstick still looked good but needed more blush. She checked her hair, which was still in good shape. The plane had come to a complete stop. She took a deep breath and smoothed her suit.

"I'm going down there. Anyone want to join me?"

"For sure. Come on Charlie." Becky beckoned for him. Charlie nodded toward Patrick to follow. Jim and the others waited inside the terminal.

By the time the four of them reached the outside gate the door was opening and out stepped Frederick the co-pilot, Edmund and Alec. The trio headed toward Mariah. Edmund was waving. Mariah gathered herself and in front of Patrick and Charlie's eyes she became another woman.

Upon reaching Mariah Edmund placed his file folder down on the ground and kneeled. "My dear, my eyes are blinded by the glow of your beauty. I must gaze upon you from this angle." Charlie and Patrick looked at each other.

"Edmund get up, you're embarrassing me." Mariah was almost laughing. Edmund got up and looked sheepishly at her. Frederick and Alec just shook their heads. Becky was engrossed in the scene.

"It is true. You are beautiful. Lady Godiva in all her glorious nudity has nothing on you. Look at the glow you have and the baby, she is growing well, *oui*?" Mariah blushed a little but let him take her hand and kiss it, then embrace her and kiss her on the cheek. He then stood back to look at her.

"Edmund, I am glad to see you too. How was the flight?"

"Never a bounce like always. They are the best as you know." Edmund looked at Alec and Frederick.

"*Mademoiselle*. It is so nice to see you again?" Alec spoke up. He kissed her hand.

"Alec, you're looking well. And Frederick how are you?" Mariah addressed them and hugged both of them. She was glad to see them again.

"*Mademoiselle*," Frederick greeted her and then kissed her hand.

Becky cleared her throat, which jolted Mariah in realizing that she wasn't alone. For a moment she had forgotten.

"Where are my manners? Rebecca Browning, I would like you to meet some very good friends of mine, *Monsieur* Edmund LaRue one of the designers of Jean Paul's line, *Monsieur* Alec Navarrié the pilot, and *Monsieur* Frederick Copaire, the co-pilot.

"Hello gentlemen, it's very nice to meet you," Becky replied and to her surprise Alec and Frederick each bowed and kissed her hand. Edmund on the other hand was more extravagant.

"*Mademoiselle* Becca. You don't mind me calling you Becca? It sounds more sophisticated than Rebecca, not to say there is anything wrong with Rebecca but with your beauty Becca suits you better like a tight leather glove." Charlie saw Becky blush.

"That..that's fine with me." Becky couldn't say much more because she was so entranced with the visitors. She also noticed Alec didn't take his eyes off her and so did Charlie. He wasn't sure what was going on just yet with Alec. Charlie stepped up.

"Mariah?"

"Oh, Charlie. I know I have lost my mind. Charlie Osswell, please meet.."

"I caught the names. Edmund, Alec, Frederick." Charlie shook everyone's hands.

"I have heard of you *Monsieur* Osswell. You are a special friend to Mariah, *oui*?" Edmund chirped in.

"Yes, you might say that."

Mariah glanced over her shoulder. Patrick was still standing behind her, he was sizing up the situation and the players involved. She motioned for him to step up, in which he did.

"Edmund, Alec, Frederick, I'd like you to meet.."

"*Monsieur* Patrick Wainscott. It is very nice to meet you," Edmund interrupted. Patrick was taken back and so was Mariah that Edmund knew who he was.

She knew Jean Paul must have spoken to him about Patrick. How else would he have known him? Mariah thought that if it surprised Patrick he hid it well. Must be the actor in him.

Patrick shook hands with everyone in spite of not liking the fact that obviously Jean Peal had warned Edmund about him. Was he suppose to be a watch dog for the Count he thought? He had to make an effort in front of Mariah to be civil at least. This deal was too important for her and he wouldn't do anything to mess things up if he could help it.

"Is this your first time in our country?" He couldn't think of anything else to say.

"*Non*, I have been here many times but this is the first time I've been to Southern California. My circle runs through New York mostly. That is where all the good designers are in my opinion except for you, you goddess of beauty." Edmund looked Mariah in the eyes when he said this. She grinned at him and shook her head. He could tell she wasn't feeling well but he wasn't going to let her know. She had taken such great pains to make herself look good and he knew it. The Count was right to be worried about her. The swelling in her face and hands alarmed him. He knew most women experience some swelling with a pregnancy but hers seemed to be more than that he thought. He would make sure she didn't over do with the addition of the line.

"That's some bird you have there?" Patrick addressed Alec and Frederick.

"Yes she is and she knows she's the best. The Count will not accept anything else but the best," Frederick replied very proudly while nodding his head. Patrick wondered why he said what he did.

"Would any of you like to see her before we start to unload? We do have to get clearance and start back very soon. The Count will need her tomorrow and she has to be detailed again."

"Alec, that would be very nice. I'm sure Patrick and Becky would like that," Mariah answered.

"*Monsieur* Osswell would you like to lead the way since you have seen her already?" Alec motioned for him to ascend the stairs. Becky followed. Patrick was going to wait for Mariah until he heard her speaking to Edmund about the trunks. There was a phone ringing somewhere when the group entered the plane. Alec excused himself and went through the cockpit doors. He came out a second later. "Frederick would you please show these good people our home away from home. I'll be there in a minute." He descended the stairs; spoke to Mariah and Edmund. She started up the stairs with Alec. Edmund followed. Patrick watched from the doorway.

Mariah passed him with a question on her face. "Go look at the plane. I know you haven't seen anything like this before." She went into the cockpit with Alec. He showed her what to do and came out closing the door behind him to give her some privacy.

"So *Monsieur* Wainscott let us see this wonder of modern technology."

Patrick let him show the plane. It is like an apartment away from home. All the décor was tastefully done but when he got to the bedroom it hit him. For some reason he didn't think there would be a bedroom on board. Has Mariah, the woman he loves, and the Count shared this bed? It was almost too real for him to think about. How many times he wondered? He couldn't stop the thoughts from entering his mind. Alec was busy answering questions from the others so he was able to slip away. There was a chair by the cockpit door so he took it but unfortunately he couldn't hear anything from inside. He picked up a magazine and pretended to look at it. Alec noticed he had left the group so he followed.

"Can I offer you something to drink? We have various wines from our vineyards of course, soft drinks and sparkling water." He stepped over to the bar and opened the refrigerator.

"No thank you. I'm fine."

Alec took a stool at the bar. He wasn't going to let Patrick be up front without supervision. Patrick knew this but didn't say anything. The Count must have warned him, too. It seemed to him that everyone considered him the bad boy so it was time to find out about these people. Frederick and the others were still in back.

"So Alec..do you mind me calling you that?"

"That is my name. May I call you Patrick or do you prefer Pat?"

"I usually go by my given name. How long have you been flying this thing?"

"Fifteen years now. I gained my appointment with the Count after I left the service."

"What service if you don't mind me asking?"

"Not at all, your American Air Force. You see I am American. My mother's family is from North Carolina and my father's family is from France. I was born in the states but shortly afterwards my parents moved to France and has been there all this time. I went to Yale actually."

"Impressive." Patrick wanted to know what was going on inside the cockpit. It seemed Mariah had been in there a long time but he knew it was only a few minutes.

"*Bonjour, mon amour*. How are you today?"

"Jean Paul I'm so glad to hear your voice. I would have called you tonight."

"I know but I couldn't wait. How is Edmund?"

"Still Edmund. You know him, as flamboyant as ever."

"Yes, I do know. I want to remind you that I will be in Paris tomorrow so if you need me call the cell; otherwise I will call you when I get a break from the meetings. I do not want you to over do. Let Edmund do the work, which is what I pay him for by the way."

"Don't worry about me please. I have some wonderful friends here. My staff surprised me today. I'll tell you about it when I see you. I promise I will do only what I can then I'll let someone else handle it, okay?"

"If you promise."

"By the way did you discuss Patrick with Edmund?"

"You caught me. Yes, I told him to look out for you and not to let Wainscott get in your way. I'm sorry but I felt it was needed." Mariah sighed.

"I thought so. I really don't need his help with Patrick. I can deal with him but thank you anyway. Listen, I had better let you go even though I could talk to you all day."

"I would like to do something other than talk to you all day. Just a reminder of our precious time together."

"How could I forget," she paused the continued. "I will give you a full report on how the line is doing next time we speak."

"That is not necessary and you know it. I just want to know about you. *Je t'aime.*"

"I love you, too." There was a crackle on the line then silence.

Mariah stepped out of the cockpit to find Patrick and Alec waiting. The others were coming up front by this time.

"Gentlemen?"

"*Mademoiselle*, can I get you something to drink?" Alec got up. Patrick wondered why he was addressing her in French since he was American.

"Sit back down." Mariah pushed him back on the bar stool and ran her hand across his cheek. "Haven't I told you before that I don't need you to pamper me like Jean Paul says?" She found herself a bottle of sparkling water and drank.

"Mariah, my goddess, I have forgotten to tell you the most fantastic news." Edmund saw the magazine that Patrick had in his lap. "Where did I put that paper?" He looked around.

Frederick found it on the end table and handed it to him. He in turn handed it to Mariah who sat down her water. The paper was written in French of course so everyone had to wait for her response. Her hand went to her mouth as she read.

"Oh my! I can't believe it!" Tears started to fall "Edmund is this for real?" Edmund nodded yes.

"What is it?" Patrick wasn't sure what was going on. Charlie and Becky looked at each other. Charlie placed his arm around Becky's waist. He didn't want to cause a scene so in his own way he was trying to tell Alec that Becky was taken since he was sure Alec was watching her for more reasons than one. Patrick got up and took the paper out of Mariah's hands. He couldn't read any of it.

"I can't believe it," Mariah spoke softer this time.

"It is true my dear you have been placed in the top ten designers in France." Edmund hugged and kissed her. "I am so proud of you." Alec and Frederick congratulated her.

"This is great! Congratulations." Becky and Charlie came up and hugged her.

"What place did you get?" Becky inquired.

"I got tenth but that's okay. I never thought I would get this far. Edmund, I owe all this to you and Tré. I've learned a lot from you two."

"My dear, you did this yourself. We just gave you some pointers that's all."

"Who was number one?" Becky had to ask.

"I don't know I didn't look. Let me see that." Patrick handed the paper to her, she read it and smiled. "Tré and Edmund always top the list."

"No, not always. There was one year we took second to *Madame* Ronalda. That however WAS six years ago," Edmund laughed.

"Congratulations, sweetheart. You deserve this." Patrick kissed her in front of everyone.

"This is going to make my sales sky high. Does Jean Paul know about this?"

"*Oui* he does. This is yesterday's paper. He wanted me to surprise you. That is why he didn't say anything to you. We have something else for you, too." Alec opened the refrigerator and brought out a vase with two-dozen long stemmed red roses arranged in it. He handed to Mariah. She was shaking and could hardly hold them.

"From Jean Paul?"

"*Oui*, one dozen from him and one dozen from Tré, Alec, Frederick and of course from *moi*." Edmund handed her a note scribbled in Jean Paul's hand. She read the note and placed it in her pocket without saying anything but smiled as she did so.

"They're beautiful. Thank you all."

"Their beauty fades next to you."

"I'm just speechless."

"I hate to break this lovely moment up but we do need to unload the trunks. We have to start back home soon." Alec mentioned.

"Of course, we must see to them soon so the fabric can breathe. Do we have baggage carts yet?"

"I called for them sometime ago. *Oui,* here they come now."

"Eight carts? How many trunks do we have?" Mariah inquired.

"We have put together fifteen for you."

"Fifteen!"

"*Oui*, we have a little of everything for you. Let us see to the task in front of us at the moment."

Everyone descended down the stairs with Patrick watching over Mariah when it was her turn to descend. Edmund carried the roses but handed them back to Mariah when they were on the ground. Patrick and Charlie started helping to move the trunks from the plane to the carts. So were Alec and Frederick. Edmund was directing the show as always but before he began he addressed Mariah and Becky once more.

"*Mesdemoiselles,* wait just a moment please." The ladies stopped and looked at him then at each other. Edmund pulled a small camera out of his duffle bag and took their picture.

"What a moment, two beautiful women who grace our presence. God has given us a true gift." Mariah knew how he went on about everything but Becky blushed a little. He and Alec made her feel special and she needed that right now.

Becky had been watching Alec as much as she dared too with Charlie hanging so close by. She was attracted to him perhaps because of the danger he possessed with Charlie being close by all the time. She had caught his slight smile he threw her way when possible however he didn't address her personally unless she initiated the conversation. She knew he was flirting with her subtlety and she was enjoying it. It would serve Charlie right to sweat a little over it she thought so she made it a point a few times to look directly at Alec when she knew Charlie was watching. Alec wasn't hard on the eyes at all. He had a rugged look from his dark complexion, dark hair, moustache and beard. His frame was medium but he was fit and no doubt be able to handle himself well in a fight. Charlie saw how they looked at each other but kept quiet for the time being. Alec came up to the two women and kissed their hands but spent what seemed to be an eternity kissing Becky's hand to her. Their eyes locked on each other. He said his goodbyes to the ladies and left. Edmund saw Becky's reaction to all of the attention as well.

Patrick and Charlie were passing by the women when they heard what Edmund said. Charlie softly asks Patrick, "Is he for real?"

Patrick struggled to get his end of the trunk up on the cart.

Edmund was within earshot of the two. "Gentlemen, if you Americans would treat your women with respect, love and admiration for the true gift they are to us then they wouldn't need men like us. Don't ever forget that a good woman can bring a man down to his knees and then crush him in a blink of an eye and not look back. There are a few of us on earth who knows how to treat a woman like a woman, the fine sculpture that she is." Edmund directed more trunks to other carts then continued. "A man can make love to a woman without being physical and I assure you the impression is everlasting for her." Patrick and Charlie looked at each other.

"What I want to know is, is he a he?" Patrick whispered to Charlie.

"I heard that, too. I assure you *Monsieur* Wainscott I have the same sexual desires as you do but the difference is that I do not have to prove I'm a man to anyone. The truth be known I enjoy making love to every woman I meet whether its physical or not, the excitement is still there."

Edmund looked Patrick square in the eyes and didn't alter his gaze for a few seconds. He then went on about his business. Patrick and Charlie looked at each other dumbfounded not knowing what to say. Edmund was rubbing Patrick the wrong way and Charlie was getting annoyed, too, but for Mariah's sake they held their tongues.

The last of the trunks were finally loaded into the pickup trucks and were headed toward the boutique when Mariah handed Edmund her keys to the Mercedes. Patrick was going to have to ride with someone else on the way back and he resented it. And for her to freely hand her car key over to him without hesitation was something she didn't do often.

"Thank you Edmund for doing this. I hope it didn't put you and Tré in a bind?"

"*Non*, my dear. Tré however was very sorry that he couldn't make it but with the Christmas show coming up and his wedding.."

"Wait a minute. Did you say wedding? Tré is getting married?"

"*Oui*, you did not know? New Year's Day to Martina. You remember her do you not?"

"She's the one with the purple hair right?"

"*Oui*, now it is her natural red she says and she's more refined than what she appeared to be originally. She said the purple was a mistake at the hairdresser but I still do not think I believe that. I think that she has a wild streak in her and that Tré will have his hands full after they are married. Maybe it will liven him up a bit."

"Edmund! He is your partner."

"*Oui*, he is one of closest friends as well but he can be a bit stodgy as you well know."

"I must send my regards to the happy couple. Turn in here and pull up anywhere."

She motioned to the right. Edmund pulled into the side parking lot and brought the car to a stop fairly close to the front of the shop. He helped her out. Together they walked into the boutique arm in arm. The convoy of trucks followed close behind. Mariah and Edmund were surprised to see the extent her employees went to with the carry in dinner. She was proud to know these friends. Susan noticed the guys coming with the trunks so she held the door for them. As soon as one was put down Edmund pulled the latches on it. Mariah and Edmund took out piece by piece and displayed it. She asked Ben to help them and to move the trunks. She thought the sooner he had the feel for the garments the better. Edmund was already in top form discussing each piece with her sales associates, answering questions and demonstrating coordination between the pieces. He also explained how they were going to market the line and what set this line apart from all others. Everyone seemed to be impressed by the line and its versatility. Mariah stayed out of the way so as not to disturb anyone. She knew all this so well that she started to mimic Edmund. She knew what he was going to say before he said it. As she hung up piece by piece she came across a tuxedo jacket with the shawl-style collar. The style was one of her favorites so she couldn't resist but put it on. It reminded her that Jean Paul preferred to wear this style of the jacket verses some of the other in the line, as well. He had several in his closet as she recalled. She went to the mirrors and turned around looking at herself. For a minute she could almost picture him standing there with her in the tux. She didn't hear Patrick come up behind her. She was smiling as she hugged herself.

"Looks good on you but you know what would look better than that?"

Mariah jumped at his whispered voice in her ear. "What? Is there something wrong with it in the back?" She took off the jacket.

"No sweetheart, I was referring to you wearing nothing underneath that."

"Stop that! Someone may hear you."

"And what if they do. What are you going to do?"

"Did you come here to help or to hinder. If it's to hinder then go home."

"Just wanted to let you know we have two more trunks to get from the plane. Charlie, Jim and I are going back for them."

"Fine, thank you. That reminds me I need to call Alec and Frederick again for helping me. Now where is that cordless?" She hung up the jacket and proceeded to look for the phone. Patrick left and she found the phone under the front cash register. She then called to Edmund for the number who in return gave it to her.

"*Bonjour* Alec, I wanted to thank you again for helping me do this. Frederick too, please tell him for me."

"*Bonjour Mademoiselle,* it is our pleasure. I am glad you called. I wanted to tell you that any time you need to use the plane all you have to do is call me. You have my number, *oui*?"

"Yes I do, but I can't just take the plane from Jean Paul like that?"

"I mean that, ANY TIME just call me and as soon as I can I will have the plane at your disposal. The order has been issued by the Count."

"*Merci.* I will remember should I need it. He does like to take care of me doesn't he?"

"And with good reason. Now was there anything else you wanted?"

"Oh, to tell you that the guys are on the way back to the plane for the other two trunks. They should be there fairly soon."

"Good, we do need to start back. The fueling and the service checks have just been completed so as soon as we deliver the trunks to them personally we will be on our way back home. We will see you again on Thursday I presume?"

"Yes, of course. What time will you be getting here?"

"The Count will call you with the details I heard him tell Edmund before we left."

"Fine. You both be careful and have a safe trip back. I will see you later this week. *Au revoir.*"

"*Au revoir.*"

With everyone's help the unpacking didn't take as long as they thought. They all agreed to have another staff meeting Sunday afternoon. Everyone would have time to think of more questions by that time.

It was after ten when they finished stocking. All the garments were in place and ready for the sale Monday morning. Mariah was tired and wanted to go to bed. She told everyone thank you again and made a note to call Jim.

Patrick had taken him home when they went back for the last two trunks however he still had Jim's truck. He would wait until morning to take it back since it was so late. All the others had left as soon as they could leaving just Mariah, Edmund and Patrick.

"Patrick, can you do me a favor? Would you mind terribly taking Edmund to the Inn for me?" Patrick looked at her.

"Sure." That wasn't what he wanted to say but he knew if he didn't help her out she would do it herself. She looked like she had been run over by a train. She needed to sleep.

"Just point me in the direction and I can find my way. It is late."

"You will not dear Edmund. I have a suite reserved for you under the boutique. I think you will find the Crystal Inn to your liking. It has a lot of personality."

"Thank you but I don't need a suite and I don't need the boutique to pay. I have an extremely generous expense account from the Count in which I almost never use so it is time that I do. Perhaps we can do so together?"

Mariah smiled. "Thank you Patrick for taking care of Edmund for me. If you will excuse me I think I'll go to bed. Edmund, I will see you tomorrow."

"Don't forget my dear heart but I don't rise until after eleven when I don't have to."

"I haven't forgotten. That's why I made the staff meeting at three. I knew you would be tired from today."

"Oh you are just so wonderfully thoughtful." Edmund kissed her but this time it was on the cheek. There was no need to be so formal when no one was watching and Patrick didn't count as far as he was concerned.

"I'm ready to go when you get through with things," Patrick said dryly.

Edmund hugged Mariah and grabbed his bag. He headed out the door with Patrick. This was Patrick's time to get more information on the Count but he had to be careful on how he did it. It was funny to see Edmund ride in Jim's pick up. He looked so out of place.

"Thank you for the ride. I know you are only doing it for Mariah."

"Did I say that?"

"You don't have to. I pick up a note of hostility from you." Patrick didn't say anything.

"Just so we understand each other. I don't think you like me and I don't think I like you either even though we don't know one thing about each other. Oh I take that back. You know of me through the Count, don't you?"

"I don't know you well enough to say I don't like you but I do have certain loyalties to the Count. What is it about me you don't like?"

Patrick wanted to list it all but held his tongue. He changed the subject. "So how long have you known the Count?"

"Several years now. You have a question to ask so why not just ask instead of beating around the tree as you Americans say?"

"The expression is "beating around the bush.""

"Whatever."

"I'm just making small talk."

"Mmm." Edmund didn't believe that but let his remark go. He wanted to see just where Patrick was taking this.

"I've met him you know."

"Is that so? I suppose you would meet him one way or the other?"

"What do you mean by that?"

"It is only natural that you two would meet because of Mariah. She is a fantastic sensuous woman. It would be hard for any man to get her out of his system."

"Listen, I really don't enjoy listening to you talk about her that way. She is more than that to me."

"And to the Count. I'm afraid it is your loss and the Count's gain. Their love and their souls have been entwined long before this lifetime. I believe they are soul mates."

"Do you really believe that stuff?" Patrick didn't like hearing his point of view.

"*Oui.* I do."

"So what is the Count really like?"

"It is not my place to say but I will tell you he is a very private person but one to be reckoned with. He doesn't take it well when someone he cares about gets hurt. He will not stand still and watch it either. So be warned."

"Oh, so is that it? The Count has told you to warn me?"

"*Non,* not at all. I am doing that. He will not let her go without a fight and I assure you he will not toss her aside like you did and she knows that. A woman needs to feel secure in a relationship and she has that with the Count. The kill will be swift." Referring to the Count's upper hand in his and Mariah's relationship verses one with Patrick, which was hopeless in Edmund's eyes. Patrick knew what he meant.

"I don't need some Frenchman to give me pointers in my relationship thank you." Patrick was just about to say more when they reached the Inn. He pulled up to the curb.

"Nice place. Thank you for the ride. No need to get out I can see to my own bag thank you." Edmund opened the truck door, got out and reached in the bed of the truck to retrieve his bag. Patrick thought he has got to be crazy to think that he would get his bag for him.

He was not in any mood to talk to anyone. The horses hadn't been out all day but he was to tired and to mad to see to them tonight. They would just have to wait till in the morning. He laid his keys on the kitchen bar, took off his boots at the door and grabbed himself a beer. It was almost midnight but he went in the living room turned on the television and settled in for the night. One beer lead to another. He couldn't get the picture of the Count standing half naked in Charlie's kitchen out of his mind and Edmunds words rang in his ears. How dare her to turn to that old man and to this new life of hers. How dare her not to include him. He wanted her just as much as the Count did and she knew it too. They had a history that was more than she and that titled stuffed shirt had. He had made up his mind right then that if the Count wanted a battle then he would give him the battle of his life. He wouldn't play Mr. nice guy anymore. The beer was taking its toll on his reasoning and senses as well. He didn't remember anything else until he woke up still on the couch with the television playing a blank screen. The time was five a.m. The horses were restless, no doubt they needed out of the stalls to stretch. Patrick started out the back door to see to them but stopped to put on his stable boots. It had rained sometime last night. He had one hell of a headache and his stomach ached. It took him a minute to remember why; he hadn't drunk that much for a long time. His resistance to the alcohol must be low.

The horses galloped around the outside ring glad to be out. Jezebel even went out without giving him any trouble. He checked their food and water and would do their stalls later after he felt better. Patrick was leaving the barn when he tripped on a bucket and fell face first in the mud. It was a good thing that no one was around to hear him swear. Inside the back door he stripped his muddy clothes, grabbed a beer out of the refrigerator and headed upstairs to the shower. The cold beer tingled his throat as it went down.

The water was hot and the steam helped his head some. He stood bracing himself against the wall with his hands in front of him and his legs apart. The water ran down his back. He thought he had heard the phone ring so he turned off the water and listened. There was no sound. He decided to get dressed and try some coffee. His whole body still ached. It had been a long time since he was hung over like this and it served as a reminder not to do it again. What need was there to get dressed right now? His plan was a pot of coffee and a bed for a while longer. He walked in the kitchen naked, put the coffee on and sat down at the table. His head on his arm.

Mariah couldn't sleep after waking up afraid again. She had that same dream. There was nothing different about it this time but the fear was worse than before. Her nerves was fried. She dressed in almond slacks and a peach colored peasant blouse. She found her penny loafers and slipped them on. Where were her keys? She couldn't stay there. There was nothing to do until three when the staff meeting would begin. She had tried to call Patrick just to talk, but he wasn't there.

She had wondered where he was so early but then realized that if he was with someone it wasn't her business anymore. She drove along the coastal highway. The sunrise on the ocean was the most beautiful thing she thought she had ever seen in her life. She walked along the beach then headed the opposite direction not really knowing where she was going. Suddenly she found herself across from Patrick's driveway. She sat in the car pondering whether to go up or not. She would like to see Jezebel again. What harm would she do if she did go on up? Patrick wasn't there. No one would know she was there. She could see her and leave before Patrick got home. Before she knew it she had turned her car on to the gravel driveway. There was no stopping now.

Jezebel saw her as she got out of the car and whinnied. The horses were out all ready. She went to the ring and loved the horse, some of the others came up looking for carrots. She was sorry she didn't have any to offer. It was time to go she thought. She turned to go back to the car being careful not to step in any more mud than needed. She noticed the kitchen door wasn't latched. That was highly unusual. She stepped inside the door and called out, no answer, she called again, still no answer. She went around the corner, smelled the coffee. Maybe Jim made the coffee seeing how the Shelby was gone and Jim's truck was parked outside. Then she saw him sitting at the table with his head down.

"Patrick. Patrick.. are you all right?" There was no answer and he didn't move. She went to him and touched him on the shoulder. He didn't move yet. She shook him a little harder, the tablecloth fell away from him. She saw that he was naked. She couldn't remember ever seeing him walk around the house naked before. She headed upstairs to get a robe or something when she saw all the beer bottles cluttering the living room. He was drunk and hung over. What caused this? He never drank that much in the past. She grabbed the robe and went down to the kitchen again. His hair was still wet so what was a little more water. She got a glass of water and poured it on Patrick's head. He jumped up dropping the robe to the floor that she had placed over him.

"What the hell?" His voice was thick and his head still buzzed. He opened his eyes and saw Mariah sitting across the table from him.

"Hi. You look terrible."

"What do you want?"

"That's a fine hello. Haven't you said I was always welcome here?" Mariah was laughing by this time. Patrick pushed his hair from his face. Then he realized she had caught him in the buff. What difference did it make? She had seen him many times like that. He needed coffee and wasn't going to ask her to get it for him. He got up and poured himself a cup. Mariah cleared her throat.

"Honey, you've seen me before. I don't care anymore."

"What does that mean?"

"Nothing except I'm pulling out all stops now and heaven help who ever gets in my way."

"You're in a mean mood. What made you drink like that? That's not you."

"You should know." He sat back down at the table and laced his coffee with a ton of sugar. Mariah wrinkled her nose at his action.

"You're going to wack out your sugar levels with all that. I think that's enough." She pulled the sugar bowl away from him. Their fingers touched. Mariah didn't pull away, she placed her hand over his but Patrick's body ached too much to respond. He grimaced when a pain shot through his back. He stiffened his back and sat up.

"What's wrong?" She was concerned.

"I think I must have hurt my back when I fell this morning." He took a drink of the hot brew. It was too sweet but he wasn't going to let her know it was almost undrinkable.

"You did what?" She was more concerned by now, was he that drunk that he couldn't even walk?"

"It's nothing. I went out to the stables and tripped and fell in the mud. I've got to get those holes fixed out there." Mariah was laughing. "Thanks for laughing at me. What brings you out here?"

"I couldn't sleep so I went to the beach and found myself here visiting Jezebel. The back door was ajar so I came in. I did knock first but you were out of it."

"You never gave me an answer on going to the dinner with me Wednesday night."

"Yes, I did. I can't go. Wednesday is the last day of the sale and with Edmund being here till Thursday I don't want to leave him alone that night."

"I think Becky has already bought the tickets for us. I guess I'll pay her back because if you don't go I'm not either."

"That's silly. If she can't take the tickets back then why don't you go ahead and go. Enjoy yourself."

"I won't enjoy anything unless you're there."

"Well, I'm not going. If you have to pay then let me know and I'll take care of my ticket."

Patrick put his head on the table again. It was beginning to throb. He was getting to old to drink like that. "You won't pay."

"I will and if she can't take the tickets back then you should go."

Patrick stretched his head and neck back on his shoulders. In spite of the coffee he still looked like hell.

"Seriously, what made you drink like that?"

"Can't a man relax in his own home anymore without answering the third degree?"

"I'm sorry if I'm overstepping. You're right. It's your business and not mine." She got up and put her coffee cup in the sink. "I think I'm going home. I'll talk to you when you're in a better mood."

He got up and caught her, as she was about to leave the kitchen. He backed her into a corner and pinned her there with both of his arms. She couldn't get past him.

"What are you doing?" Her voice was even and controlled. She knew he wouldn't hurt her but the adrenaline was starting to pump. Their bodies were touching.

"This." He kissed her fully on the mouth. His tongue traced her lips. The excitement was over whelming. He wanted her so much and he wanted to show her. At first she fought the kiss then gave in to it. She actually kissed him back and he felt her respond. This was what he was waiting for. He dropped his right hand and touched her face. She closed her eyes. His hands traced down her neck to the buttons of her blouse. She knew she needed to move but for some reason couldn't make her body do so. She still stood there with her back in the corner. He unbuttoned her blouse. He wanted to feel her and not the layers of fabric and satin that composed her camisole and bra. He slipped inside to her breast and started to caress her. She moaned, as she was tender from the pregnancy. His touch almost hurt. She felt him against her in all of his glory. She came to her senses.

"Patrick.. I don't, I can't.."

"You can't what?" He unsnapped the front closure of her bra freeing her breasts. He ran his hands over them teasing them and cupping them. His voice was soft, his eyes were partially closed and his breath was hot on her neck as he kissed her neck, bent down and started kissing her breast. Her breathing quickened even though she was trying to control her feelings. She couldn't let this go any farther. Her mind was yelling at her to stop things now before she was sorry. "Take a hot shower with me." His left hand loosened her waistband on her slacks and stroked her thigh toward the inside.

"I can't do this. I have to go." She tried to pull away from him she had even given him a slight shove to do so. He stood steady still caressing her and kissing her.

"Mariah, you mean more to me than anything else. I love you and I want to show you just how much."

"I have to go. We are not the same people we used to be."

"I know I'm labeled as the bad boy now remember? I'm just living up to the title." He laughed a little and looked up at her and grinned. She had her hands on his shoulders trying to get some space between them. She gave him a questioning look. "I have a title now just like the Count." He laughed a little more. Patrick shifted his weight just a tad so his hand could go deeper in her slacks, this was the moment she was waiting for. She pulled up on his arm and shoved him away from her at the same time. It gave her the space she wanted. She removed herself from the corner and pulled her clothing back in place.

"Is that why you got drunk last night because of Jean Paul?" He didn't answer. "I hope you realize that was a stupid reason to do so. Go take your shower and go back to bed. I'm leaving." She slammed the kitchen door behind her.

Mariah spent the rest of the day getting ready for the sale tomorrow. The staff meeting with Edmund was productive. After everyone had left leaving she and Edmund alone they went up to her apartment and relaxed over a cup of tea.

"I think you have chosen correctly with Benjamin. He does have an aptitude for style. He even put together the same pieces I was going to show him."

"It was all Margo's suggestion. She needs the credit."

"I will tell her tomorrow when I see her. Now how do you feel, my dear?"

"Fine why?"

"If you don't mind me saying but you do look a bit peaked."

"I'm tired that's all. I didn't sleep well last night. It's so hard to get comfortable now days."

"I can imagine it so. The baby is coming along fine?"

"Oh my, yes. She is doing just fine." She placed a pillow on the cherry coffee table and propped her feet on it. She stroked her stomach as she sat in silence. Edmund poured himself another cup of hot tea and sat down next to her.

"Come here my dear." He leaned her against his shoulder. "Are you worried about the opening?" He asked as he took a sip of tea.

"No, not really. I think it will go like all the other sales I've had." She shook her head against his shoulder. She was thankful for just being able to sit quietly. Her mind kept going back to that morning with Patrick. "Can I ask something?"

"Sure what is it?"

"Last night when Patrick took you to the Inn, what did you two talk about?"

"Nothing much. He tried to pump me for information concerning the Count but I didn't tell him what he wanted."

"What did you tell him?" She sat straight up.

"Only that he is a man of great character. A man who takes his business seriously and YOU are his business."

"Edmund, what else did you say?"

"Just the truth my dear that Jean Paul loves you very much and no one will stand in his way. That is all." Edmund took another sip.

Mariah sighed as she leaned back against him. So that was it. That was why Patrick had got drunk and was acting like he did. She was still on that emotional roller coaster and taking everyone on the ride with her. Sarah was right she had to come up with a game plan to end this. But the solution still wasn't any closer than before.

The boutique was all a buzz. Everyone was excited about reopening and there was a crowd already outside the front doors. Mariah glanced toward the men's section and saw Ben and Edmund talking. Edmund looked toward Mariah and she touched her watch. Edmund nodded his head toward her.

"My dear beauty, let us dazzle these good people."

"Right you are. Listen up everybody, I just want to thank you for all the hard work you've given this boutique and me. I love you all. It's show time." Mariah picked the keys out of the cash register and opened the doors. "Come on in. Welcome!"

The boutique was filled with activity immediately. There were even men coming in to investigate the new line. Edmund stood back to see how Ben would perform. He would be there if he was needed but Ben was eager to do it on his own. Mariah would occasionally stroll by to listen. Edmund would nod at her and smile. She noticed he stepped in when it was necessary but Ben was handling the position very nicely, even suggesting certain pieces. It was to her benefit that the banquet was in two days.

Crystal River was composed of many types of people just like any other town. It had its prominent types as well as the working class. She was in hopes the more prominent would grace her establishment in need of something more elaborate and refined for the banquet than what the town already had. She was proven correct throughout the morning when several attorneys bought tuxes. It turned out the banquet was a black tie event.

"Margo dear, I need something really sexy for a date. What do you have?" Margo turned around to see Amy Kincade.

"Well, well, look who just came in. How are you?" Margo answered.

"I'm fine but I really need something sensational. What does Mariah have?"

"Tell me what you need it for and I'll see."

"I have this banquet to attend Wednesday night."

"The one about the attorneys?"

"You've heard about it?"

"Several people have come in concerning it," Margo acknowledged.

"Then you know all about it. I want something really sexy you see I have a hot date. Oh I can't keep it quiet everyone is going to know it anyway. The most eligible bachelor in town has asked me to be his date. I'm going with Patrick Wainscott." Margo dropped the scissors she had in her hand. They fell on the desk with a clank. She glanced over Amy's shoulder to see Mariah standing there and the look on her face.

"Is something wrong Margo? Did you cut yourself?"

"No, no everything is fine, Amy," Margo replied as Mariah hugged Amy.

"Amy dear, how are you."

"Mariah you're here! I mean I didn't think you were in town any longer. I mean.."

"Margo did you cut yourself?" Mariah saw Margo holding her finger.

"No the scissors just slipped that's all." Margo nodded and wiped the cut off.

"Well now Amy, let's see what we can do for you. If you would want to start checking the racks I think your size is over there to the right."

"Mariah, can I speak to you a minute?" Margo stopped her.

"Amy go ahead dear and see if there is anything you like." She pointed Amy in the right direction. "Is there a problem Margo?"

"Yea there's a problem. Are you really going to sell her something knowing what she wants it for and for whom?"

"Margo, business is business. Her money is as good as the next."

"I know you heard what she said and it doesn't bother you that she's going with Patrick?"

"I had the chance to go and refused it. I told him to go with someone else if Becky couldn't return the tickets. I don't have anyone to blame but myself besides do I have to remind you that Patrick and I are no longer together and haven't been for months now. I have Jean Paul remember?"

"I don't mean to butt in but.."

"No butts about it. I'll take care of Amy and you continue as normal."

"Amy does anything appeal to you yet?"

"Mariah, I didn't know you were in town when I ran into Patrick yesterday at the grocery. We started talking and one thing led to another and somehow he asked me to go. If I had known you were here I wouldn't have accepted. I just got back in town two days ago."

"Amy, there's no need to explain. Here what about this number?" Mariah pulled out a slinky silver sequined halter style gown. With Amy being tall and slim it would look good on her. She would need to style her hair up for the full effect of the dress as it was distracting to the neckline. She was a model and would figure that out on her own and if she didn't oh well.

"That's it!" Amy did try to hold back her enthusiasm some. "Mariah I hope that with me going with Patrick won't cut me out of working for you when you need someone?"

"Amy that's business. I will still use you if you are available. That won't change. Now go and try this on." She pointed her to the dressing room. A few minutes later Amy came out smiling.

"This is it."

"Good, now lets see about the right jewelry and accessories to go with it. Let's go over here." Mariah pointed to the jewelry case. "Where were you anyway when I did my birthday show?"

"I was doing a job in Rome. I was afraid to turn it down since there may not be that many more opportunities for me."

"And why not? You're good at what you do?"

"Let's face it Mariah I'm almost thirty and will soon be washed up in this business. You know they always want younger flesh for the big jobs. The really good jobs will start to fade and I need to start thinking about what I want to do with the rest of my life. I'm at a loss on what direction." Mariah knew the feeling and could almost sympathize with her.

"Well that hasn't happened yet, hopefully it will be a few more years until it does."

"That's the real reason why this party is so important to me. Maybe I can make some good contacts."

Mariah thought contact is what she would make for sure. "Oh by the way Amy I don't want you to think I'm telling you what to do but I would do something with your hair. The roots are showing and I'm sure you don't want that, now do you?"

Amy looked at her short blonde hair, she didn't see any roots since she just had the color touched up when she got back in town but if Mariah says it was showing she needed to complain to her hairdresser and get it redone by Wednesday. Mariah had left her in the hands of Susan who sold her an expensive sapphire pendant, earring and bracelet set. She also bought new shoes and a purse to match as well. When Amy had left Margo and Susan approached Mariah standing alone at one of the cash registers.

"What's up ladies?" she asks.

"Just thought you might want to know how much she spent?" Susan replied.

"Ladies please that isn't very nice of you to tell but what is it?"

"A total of six hundred fifty seven dollars and thirty nine cents plus tax."

"Very good! You have done your job well. I think she will represent our little boutique very well, don't you?" Margo and Susan laughed.

Mariah smiled and walked away toward the men's department. "Hi how are things going over here?"

"We are doing very well. As you noticed I'm sure we have had a steady flow of customers in. Some are just browsing as we can expect but most are buying something. It seems the shirts are the favorite at the moment. Oh by the way we have sold four tuxedos so far the most expensive being the seven fifty style.

"That is great! I didn't think those would sell that fast. Shows how much I know."

"You know a lot, my dear. And everyone seems to like the idea of having a personal shopper available and the Count's idea of a file on each person's taste. No one has turned us down in filling out the questionnaire."

"I'm so glad this is working out for Jean Paul but I still have to wonder if the idea will pan out after the sale."

"Word of mouth has begun to spread. The flock will be in. I assure you."

"Oh my I can't believe it?"

"What is it my dear?" Edmund looked in the same direction as Mariah.

"That is old Mr. Martin Gray. He may not look like it but he's loaded with money. His house is the stone mansion on the hill. Remember you saw it coming in from the airport?"

"Ah yes, I do remember that one. I remember thinking it looks so cold."

"He's coming back here. Ben, please help Mr. Gray." Ben had walked up to Edmund and her by this time. He saw Martin walk in as well as everyone else in the store.

Martin Gray was at least eighty-five and hunched over due to several broken backs while he was brawling in the taverns in his younger days. He now walked with a cane. His white hair and beard was longer than she remembered seeing before she left town but his choice in clothes was the same, nothing matched. In spite of how he looked he always kept a sunny disposition. He didn't have any family left, his wife had died several years ago and his son was killed in the Vietnam War. He had told her once that he didn't have any reason to fix himself up anymore. He had almost given up on being anything other than a hermit. No one really saw him out except for the trips to the grocery and half the time he would have it delivered to his house. This was truly a first for him.

"Good afternoon Mr. Gray. How can we help you today?" Ben was more nervous than ever. If he could get this man to buy something than he could make a sale to anyone.

"Yes, young man. What is your name? I don't think I know you."

"I'm Ben. Can I show you some things or would you like to browse?"

"Well, Ben, I was at the post office and overheard that you all have a top notch men's line here. This town needs something like that so I thought I would pop over and see for myself."

"We are very proud of our line. Please let me show you."

"Fine. You know I need a new suit for my niece's wedding next month in Chicago. I haven't had a new suit for years. No need since my Martha died. I wasn't going to go but since she called me and asked me to come, she said it wouldn't feel right for me not to be there. I didn't know she felt that way about me. I want this old body to look as good as it can. I hope you do have a better line than the other stores in town. That is why I don't buy clothes anymore than I have to. The styles are the same everywhere, no taste, and no individuality I hear that this line originates out of France. Is that so?"

"Yes Mr. Gray it is. I would like you to meet one of the designers of the Aristocrat Designs. Mr. Martin Gray, please meet *Monsieur* Edmund LaRue."

"*Bonjour* Mr. Gray."

"*Bonjour Monsieur* LaRue."

"*Vous parlez français?*"

"*Oui, Monsieur* LaRue I do speak French but it is rusty. It has been a long time since I have used it so *pardonnez-moi*." Edmund nodded.

"Where did you learn our beautiful language?"

"I was stationed in France during World War II."

"Things have changed a lot since then. You probably would not know the country now."

"I expect not. Life has a way of doing that nasty little trick doesn't she? Now Ben, let me see what you have."

Ben and Edmund worked together, Ben handling the line and Edmund enjoyed conversing with Martin about his country. An hour later Mr. Martin Gray walked out of the boutique with Edmund in tow carrying his new suit of clothes. Edmund walked over to where Mariah and Margo were standing.

"My dear that was most enjoyable. He is a rather odd man but one with taste. One would never have guessed him to have such quality. He has told us that he will be in more often now that we have a line that is worth the money. That is why he hasn't been much on clothes, this town hasn't had anything worth his taste."

"That's remarkable. I can't believe we did it. The word will be out now that he actually bought something here." Margo was as happy as could be.

"Ben, please come here." Mariah called out as he stepped through the front door.

"Yes ma'am?"

"I want to congratulate you on a job well done with Mr. Gray." Mariah extended her hand to him and they shook.

It was mid-afternoon when Mariah came back down to the boutique. She had escaped for a long lunch at the insistence of Edmund and Margo. She had taken a nap while upstairs and felt refreshed. The boutique was still hopping with customers. As she reached the bottom of the stairs she spotted Edmund and Margo huddled together at the front cash register talking. Margo glanced up and saw Mariah coming their way.

"Am I interrupting anything?" Edmund moved a step away from Margo and smiled at Mariah then back to Margo.

"Of course not. Feel better?"

"Yes, I do. Thank you Margo. Any problems down here?"

"Not a thing. We've been busy. Speaking of that here I go again." Margo headed toward a customer.

"Edmund, I was thinking about something. What do you want to do for dinner tonight?"

"Dinner? My dear I'm sorry I didn't think you would feel like doing something tonight. I have made other arrangements already. Perhaps I can change it though."

"No, please don't do that for me. You go ahead and do whatever your plans are. By the way, what are your plans if you don't mind me asking?" She had the feeling it was concerning Margo.

"I have a date."

"You have a date all ready? With whom?"

"A very lovely lady but that is all I'm going to say."

"What you don't kiss and tell?"

"*Non*, not at all and by the way I haven't kissed yet."

"No, but you will."

"And I am a very good kisser, too. Seriously, are you sure you don't mind my plans?"

"Of course not I want you to enjoy yourself here. Go and have fun. I know Margo will."

"Margo? Okay what gave me away?"

"The way you were looking at her. I know that look very well."

"Well, that one was a dud," Margo said as she walked up to them. "Edmund, I think Ben was needing to see you for a minute."

"Well then I shall go and see what he requires. *Merci*."

"In truth I wanted to tell you something in private. Patrick has called a couple to times. He's been really insistent to speak with you. I've told him I would tell you he called and that you were upstairs and didn't want to be disturbed. Was that all right?"

Mariah sighed. "Yes thank you. I'm not ready to talk to him yet."

"Uh oh. What happened?"

"Let's say he rubbed me the wrong way and I am as mad as hell about it."

"I don't understand?"

"I know, but I do. I don't want to talk to him so I'm still busy. Head me up if you see him come in."

"Sure thing."

"And listen, you might tell the girls that I am busy in case they would answer the phone."

"Already done that."

"Margo what a friend you are. I love you." Mariah hugged Margo who returned it. "Oh by the way, I think you'll have a wonderful time tonight with Edmund."

"You know? Did he tell you?"

"Didn't have to. I wasn't born yesterday. I want details tomorrow."

CHAPTER 9

Margo had called and said she was going to be a few minutes late. She said she had a flat tire and her neighbor was changing it as she spoke. The thought had crossed Mariah's mind that Edmund wasn't there yet either but just as she hung up the phone she saw him walking through the front doors.

"Good morning, my dear. How do you feel this morning? You are as radiant as ever." Edmund kissed her on both cheeks.

"My you are pretty chipper this morning. Do I need to ask how your date was?"

"We had a beautiful time. Margo is a wonderful lady. I am surprised that she isn't taken yet." He saw the smile Mariah was directing toward his remark. "It isn't anything like you think. That's all I'm going to say. There is Ben now. I need to see him before we open. Ta ta." Edmund left Mariah standing there.

Margo was a half an hour late but Mariah didn't mind. She pretty much had the privilege to come and go depending on what needed to be done.

"Hi. Sorry for this but I woke up and found the tire flat as a pancake."

"I'm happy it happened that way and not while you were driving. So put you things down and come over here and tell me the details." Mariah sat herself on the stool.

"What do you mean?"

"You know what. I want to know about your date."

"It was nice. Your friend is very different than all the other men I know. If there were more like him this town would be more interesting. And that is all I'm going to say."

"He said the same thing. That's no fair. My love life is in the pits so give me something to go on till this baby gets here. Please."

"Sorry boss. I can't do that. Edmund is a gentleman through and through."

"Nothing juicy to tell me? Come on I know him remember?"

"Okay, he's a great kisser. I'll say that. We wanted to keep things simple since he won't be here long. There was no sense in complicating things."

"I see your point." Mariah glanced in the direction of the Edmund and Ben "Did Patrick call anymore yesterday?" Mariah continued.

"No, I didn't get any more calls. As far as I know he didn't try. Now what about you? Give it up."

"Let's say I walked in on him recovering from a drunk. He made major advances toward me and I don't know whom I am the maddest at… him for doing it or me for allowing it at first." Mariah walked away leaving Margo to wonder about things.

The day was just as busy as yesterday. Mariah kept herself occupied between paperwork and helping to do floor duty when needed so she didn't have much time to think about anything. By five thirty she was more than glad to leave the closing of the boutique to Margo. Mariah excused herself to go up stairs. Her feet were hurting. All she wanted to do was to get off them. No sooner did she sit down and kick off her shoes than there was a knock on the door. "Come in."

"My dear, I though I'd see if you needed anything?" Edmund was standing in the doorway. He had taken off his suit coat and untied his tie. It was hanging around his neck. The top two buttons on his shirt were unbuttoned too. In all, he looked like a schoolboy just coming in from classes all day ready to relax and have fun. Mariah had to laugh at the sight of him. "What is so funny?"

"You. I mean you look like I feel right now. Come in and sit down." Edmund sat on the sofa beside her and grinned as he put his arm around her.

"And how do you feel I may ask?"

"Tired and sloppy."

"Thank you for the compliment. We did have a rather good day I believe, *oui?*"

"I don't have the figures yet but I think we did just fine. I want to tell you my feet hurt." She kicked off her shoes. Edmund noticed that her ankles were even more swollen than before. He didn't think that was possible considering how they looked this morning. He noticed there was a small bottle of lotion on the end table. Before Mariah could stop him he reached over her legs and placed them in his lap. He picked up the bottle and warmed it in his hands then started rubbing the lotion into her feet.

"Oh Edmund, please don't stop. That feels so good. How did you know I need that touch?"

"Every woman needs that touch my dear," Edmund grinned as he replied.

Patrick stood outside the partially closed door listening. What was he about to walk into? One thing for sure that Frenchman was about to lose his ability to breath if he was making advances to Mariah. After all she was still his. Patrick opened the door after knocking only once and very quickly before hand. He stepped inside expecting to find….

"Patrick, what are you doing here?"

"I just got back in town, thought I'd stop by and see how the sale is going."

Patrick stood in the doorway his eyes on the scene on the sofa. Edmund was rubbing her feet and legs. He didn't lose his stroke at the sight of Patrick nor did he remove his hands from her. Patrick didn't like the cozy scene but knew better than to say anything just yet.

"You've been out of town? How nice," Edmund addressed Patrick.

"Huh? How nice was what?" Patrick's voice was in a bit of a huff. Mariah noticed it and before anyone else could say anything she butted in.

"Are you going to stand there all night? Come on in and sit down. If you will excuse me I think I'll get a drink." She started to remove her legs from Edmund's lap but he held her tight without it being obvious to anyone but them.

She glanced at him.

Patrick noticed Edmund's hands were stroking her calves and working just past her knees to where her skirt draped across her legs. That was high enough and he was about to say something when Edmund spoke up.

"My dear, you have had a very hard day perhaps *Monsieur* Wainscott will be more than happy to retrieve a drink for you."

"What? Oh sure. What do you want?"

"Ice water would be fine, thank you."

Patrick disappeared into the kitchenette. He heard Edmund say something but couldn't make it out.

"Thank you." Mariah took the glass from Patrick. "So what did you really come here for?"

"I told you I just came back in town and wanted to stop by. Is that a crime?"

"I'm sorry Patrick but I really don't have time to visit. I still have the restocking to do and the daily cash receipts to go through. Then Edmund and I are planning to go to dinner."

"I get it. You don't want to see me but I think we need to discuss something and it can't wait any longer."

Mariah pulled her legs from Edmund's lap. She got up and put the glass on the kitchen table and came back in. "Patrick, I don't think we have anything to discuss."

"There sweetheart, you are wrong." He came up beside her. "We need to talk alone please." He turned toward Edmund. Edmund got up.

"Mariah?"

"It's okay, Edmund. I'll see Mr. Wainscott and then we can be on our way."

"Very well, I shall be downstairs." Edmund left but he kept the door ajar so he could hear if there was a problem. He stood outside the door for a few minutes. When things were quiet he decided to go downstairs. He did want to see Margo before she left.

"Now Patrick, what did you really want?" She asked as he moved closer to her.

She intended to keep a distance between them but he moved in too fast and kissed her. The kiss caught her off guard and she jerked backwards.

"What was all that about?" Patrick asks. "You never complained about our kisses before."

"You know why I don't want you near me. What did you want to talk about that was so urgent that you made Edmund leave? That was very rude of you."

"I simply wanted to be alone with you. You seem mad at me. What have I done?"

"Do I have to spell it out to you or perhaps come to think about it I just might have to do that seeing how you were drunk the last time we saw each other."

"Oh that. You're sore that I was drunk. How did I know you would show up that early in the morning?"

"That's not it and you know it." She crossed in front him to the window and looked out to the street below.

"Then fill me in why don't you?"

190

"You dumb idiot. I'm mad at you for the advances you made on me and I'm mad at myself for letting you. You should never have done that?"

"Oh I see. If you want me to give you an apology then I'm sorry for what I did. But I wasn't half as drunk as you want to believe. By that time I was fully aware of all my senses and yours, too. I won't apologize about how you feel about yourself. You see, I believe, you still love me. Your actions proved that to me." He went up behind her and put his arms around her. She raised her elbows and removed his grip on her.

"Regardless of what you want to believe I stand firm with my view. I have a new life and new people in that life who are very dear to me."

"I haven't said anything about your new friends now have I? I've been talking about you and me, not them."

Edmund entered the room before Mariah could reply. "My dear, are you about ready to go to dinner? It is getting later by the minute. I trust that your business with *Monsieur* Wainscott is concluded?"

"Why yes, Edmund, we are finished here. Thank you, Patrick, for stopping by and discussing that issue with me. I trust you will think about what I said." Mariah slipped on her shoes and picked up her purse. She handed her keys to Edmund. Please, dear friend, if you would drive. I think I'm too tired mentally to do so."

"Very well, it would be my pleasure goddess."

Mariah and Edmund headed out the door. She stops and looks behind, Patrick was still standing there shaking his head back and forth with his arms across his muscular chest. His jaw was clenched and Mariah could see his jugular vein bulging in his neck. Good, she thought, he deserves to steam. "Patrick, I'm sorry but you must leave now so I can set the alarm system."

Mariah had just turned to start her descent on the staircase when she verbalized a low scream of pain. She doubled over and practically fell. Edmund who was quick enough to see what was happening reached for her and stopped the fall. Patrick was behind her in a second, scooped her up in his arms and carried her back inside her office. He gently placed her on the sofa. Edmund was right behind them. She was holding her abdomen.

"What's going on? Is it the baby?" Patrick wasn't wasting any time he was ready to call for an ambulance if need be. He sat down beside her on the sofa.

"Let me be for a minute." Mariah was waiting for the pain to come back but it didn't. "I think it's gone now."

"My dear, would you like some water maybe?" That was all Edmund could think of at the moment to say. He was very concerned seeing how she pushed herself all day and ignored everyone's wishes to take a break from the floor.

"No, it's okay, there isn't any pain now." She took Edmund's hand and squeezed it. "Thank you for catching me. I probably would have fallen if you hadn't."

"Thank God for small miracles." Edmund kissed her hand.

Patrick watched but didn't say anything. It was true if Edmund hadn't been on his toes and as quick as he was she would have fallen. He was just out of her reach to be able to have stopped her. He did owe Edmund a thank you at least.

"I want to thank you, too. You saved both of their lives." Edmund nodded and sat down in the chair at the end of the sofa. "I think we need to get you to the hospital to be checked out."

"Sorry, but I'm not going. I've seen enough of hospitals these past few weeks."

"Mariah you need to see if the baby is okay?" Patrick stated his case.

"See, the baby is just fine. She just kicked me and there is no pain."

"We need to be sure of it. If you won't go with me then I'll call an ambulance." He picked up the phone on the desk.

"Patrick, stop that! I'm not going and that is that."

"Wait Patrick, I have an idea," Edmund spoke up. Patrick was surprised when he áddressed him that way.

"Go on."

"Let us call the doctor. We will see what the doctor thinks and if it is best for Mariah to go in or not. Will that be all right with you, my dear?"

"Yes, but I'm not making an unnecessary trips to the hospital. I have Vivian's number on the roll-a-deck." Patrick found the number and dialed. Vivian would have to be paged and call them back.

Forty-five minutes later Mariah's phone rang. Patrick answered. Edmund and Patrick insisted that she remain on the sofa until the doctor gives her opinion of things.

"Hello. Oh Dr. Miles we were wondering if you had gotten our page. Yes, it's Mariah. She was in some sort of pain earlier. Okay, here she is." He handed Mariah the phone.

"Hi Vivian, I'm so sorry to bother you this time of the night but it was either call you or make a trip to the hospital according to Patrick. So here we are."

"Can you explain the pain to me?"

"It hit fast and hard but then went away."

"Was it a cramping like pain or was it sudden stabbing pain?"

"Now that you mention it, it was more of a cramp but only worse than what I have. I think it just scared me more than anything."

"Any bleeding or disorientation?"

"No."

"Are you able to move okay without any pain?"

"If they'll let me off of this sofa I'll see." She stood up and walked around. "I'm fine."

"And what about your blood pressure and sugar levels?"

"All about the same as the last time I saw you. Nothing major there."

"Good. What I think you had is what we call a Braxton Hicks contraction. It's where the uterus tightens to strengthen its muscles for labor. This is normal and hits in the third trimester. I want to play it safe though and see you in my office at seven thirty in the morning. I'm sorry it's going to be so early but I have a surgery scheduled at nine and the rest of the day is booked. Can you do it?"

"Sure, I don't see why not. I don't sleep much these days anyway."

"Good, oh by the way, don't drive yourself and I would feel better if you didn't stay by yourself tonight just in case it happens again and it's not the Braxton Hicks. I want you to go to bed now and stay there until the morning."

"Vivian, you are telling me everything?" Patrick and Edmund looked at each other when they heard her say this.

"Yes, I am I'm just being cautious that's all. Is Patrick around where I can speak to him?"

"You're not going to mention the night thing are you?"

"If you should go in labor you will need someone with you to help. I don't want to scare you but anything is a possibility. Remember our talk?"

"Yes, I do. I understand. Here wait a minute." She handed the phone to Patrick with a disgusted look on her face. He took it.

"Hello…yes I understand. She won't be. Okay I'll have her there in the morning. Thank you, doctor. I appreciate it." He hung up the phone.

"Now young lady off to bed with you immediately."

"I haven't been called a young lady for some time now and I'm not in the mood to be bossed at either. I will go to bed after Edmund and I have had dinner."

"You will not. The doctor said to go to bed and that is what you will do if I have to pick you up and put you there myself." Patrick advanced toward her.

"Is that correct my dear? Your doctor has put you on bed rest?"

"Yes, Edmund but just until I see her in the morning. She said it's probably nothing but practice contractions, which she says, are normal but if that's practice I want some good drugs when the time comes. I really wanted to have dinner with you and show you around town tonight." Mariah was pouting a little.

"Do not worry about that right now. We can still have dinner, *oui*? Why not have it catered in?"

"You wouldn't mind?"

"Of course not. It will be my treat. I do have this expense account to use. You will need to make the call since I do not know who caters."

"I know exactly what I want to eat. There is this place… Patrick what are you doing?" She could see he was getting in the closet in the apartment and pulling out a blanket.

"I'm just getting this for me before I forget. I don't want to disturb you if you're sleeping." Patrick came back in the office and put the blanket on the edge of the sofa.

"You're not staying here tonight?"

"You heard the doctor, she said someone needed to be here tonight."

"Someone will be, Edmund will stay won't you, dear friend?"

Edmund sighed, "Is that what the doctor told you, that you need someone to be here?"

"Yes, so what? It's just a precaution that's all. I promise. I really don't need anyone to stay. I can call 911 myself if I have to." She suddenly changed her train of thought.

"My dear, if I felt like I could help you in an emergency I would and will of course but I fear I may not be useful not knowing the town. Perhaps as much as I hate to admit it Patrick here may be the better choice of us two. I can stay however until you fall asleep if you like?" Edmund surprised Patrick again. Maybe he did have some sense after all.

"Okay, I know when I'm beat. Now let's get that food ordered in."

"Tell me what you two want and I'll get it taken care of." Patrick opened up the phone book.

"I trust your taste goddess even though you may want pickles and ice cream. I'll be back in just a minute." Edmund went downstairs.

"Where the hell is he going?"

"Patrick, I wish you would stop that. He is really a very dear man."

"Hum." This was all Patrick muttered as he placed their dinner order.

It was only a few minutes that Edmund had left. He returned carrying one of Mariah's designs. It was the last design she had done before she left France. She didn't even know that it was all ready being manufactured. The ivory nightgown he had handed to her had a soft chiffon bodice with a low v neckline while the rest of the gown was shear and gauzy. The robe was made of chiffon too and it had big puffy sleeves. Lots of ribbon peeked out of the sleeves and down in to the cuffs. Pearls adorned the bodice of the gown and robe.

"When did this come?" It was always a thrill for her to see the actual designs take a physical form.

"When I found out I was coming I told Rene at the plant to start production on it. I absolutely had to bring it to you. Go put it on."

"I can't do that. It needs to go on the rack but I haven't decided what to sell it for yet."

"*Non, non* my dear goddess. This one is for you and you alone. Is it not your size?"

"Yes, it is. How did you know what size I would be by this time?"

"I had a little help."

"Jean Paul?"

"*Oui*, he sends his regards to you with this." Patrick didn't like this talk. It was getting too personal about Mariah and Jean Paul. "Now go and put it on then get yourself to bed and let us pamper you and the baby."

195

"Edmund you are too good to me."

"Shh. Now go and do as the doctor says. We all want a healthy baby, *oui?*"

"All right I'm going. Thank you." She goes over to Edmund, hugs him and kisses him on the cheek, then disappears into the bathroom.

Patrick sits down and looks at his watch. "The food should be here in twenty minutes. Thank you for getting her to change her mind about dinner and you staying tonight."

"It is just a practical thing that I do. If she needs someone to stay then it should be someone who would have an advantage over what I could do for her. Since no one else is here except you then it should be you. But mind you do not take advantage of this situation. You will answer if you do."

"Is that a threat?"

"*Non,* no threat just a friendly warning. I have seen what wolves will do to protect their own." Patrick looked at him and was about to respond when..

"Now what are you two talking about? I can't leave you two alone for anything can I?"

Edmund and Patrick turned to look at her as she came out of the bathroom.

"Oh my word, you're gorgeous." Patrick drew in his breath so sharply that even Edmund looked at him.

"Thank you, Edmund, for doing this for me."

"Thank the Count, my dear."

"You said you asked Rene in production to make this up?"

"Yes, I did, but it was the Count's idea to bring you a special gift." Mariah smiled and crossed the room to the bed. She pulled the covers down and propped herself up with the pillows.

"There is everyone happy now? I'm starving! Where's the food?"

"Shouldn't be too long now. I'll go down in a few."

It was around ten thirty when Edmund left. He insisted on seeing himself back to the Inn in spite of Mariah's feelings on the subject. He told her not to worry about the boutique in the morning that he would be there early to see to things and of course she could rely on Margo as always. Mariah had dozed off shortly after Edmund had left so Patrick made himself a bed on the sofa. He forgot to get a pillow so he quietly opened the bedroom closet and retrieved one. He glanced at Mariah sleeping, a blanket had fallen off the bed so he picked it up and placed it on her. He had turned on the bathroom light and cracked the door so she could see if she needed to get up in the middle of the night but the door between her office and the apartment he left wide open. He wanted to be able to hear her if she needed him. He loved her so much, if only she would give them another chance. Maybe after the paternity test proved to her what he knew in his heart she would give in to her feelings toward him. She was a woman but in some ways she still seemed a child, the insecurity, the need to be loved. He handled all that without any problems but then he hurt her so badly with his one stupid act. It still wasn't totally clear as to why he did what he did. Could he ever regain her trust and love again. This child, their child, could be the bond he needed to make her see they were a family, past, present and future. These thoughts filled his head as he lay on the sofa. He prayed that everything was okay with the baby and finally slept.

Mariah woke in the middle of the night. As she came out of the bathroom she noticed someone on the sofa, confused and a little frightened she stepped in the office and turned on the light switch. She realized it was Patrick and it all came back to her. She quickly turned the light off thankful that he didn't wake up. She stood there in the doorway watching him sleep. She heard that snore he did when he was really tired. How many times had she watched him sleep in the five years they were together? Most of the time he slept the best on his left side. He looked awkward trying to do that on her sofa. It was chilly in the office so she pulled an extra blanket off the bed and covered him. It was then she noticed his clothes on the back of the chair. At first she was stunned to know he would be so comfortable in her office to sleep like that but then she remembered they had shared a few nights together in the apartment if she was working late and didn't want to drive all the way out to the ranch. Why wouldn't he be comfortable here? This was his place too at one time. Patrick woke up when he felt the blanket touch him and took her hand as she started to turn away.

"Come here," he said quietly.

"I'm sorry I woke you. I thought you might need another blanket since the furnace automatically cools down at night. I put the boutique on the energy saver plan." She tried to pull away but Patrick held her hand tight. "Good night. I hope you can get back to sleep."

"Wait a minute. Everything all right I mean no pains?" The blanket fell to the floor as he sat up. She couldn't help but notice he how much he had been working out. His chest and forearms definitely had a chiseled appearance even as slight as it was the look was there. Seeing him reminded her of Jean Paul who at fifty-six took pride in his body and lifted weights every day. Jean Paul's torso was more defined in her opinion. He did it not only for relaxation but for the cardiovascular benefits as well. She stood there just looking at Patrick while those thoughts took her to Jean Paul. "Mariah?"

"Huh, what?"

"Where did you go just now? Is everything all right?"

"Oh yes, the baby is fine. I'm going back to bed." She pulled her hand out of his and closed the bedroom door behind her. She tossed and turned for a while then reached over to turn on the light by the bed. She dialed the phone. Patrick couldn't get back to sleep either. When he saw the bedroom light was on he started to knock on the door but heard her speaking softly to someone. He couldn't be sure but he thought he had caught a few words in French. Not wanting to hear anymore he backed away and lay back down on the couch swallowing the tears away. Mariah couldn't get an answer to Jean Paul's cell phone so she decided to leave a message on his voice mail. She turned off the light, settled in bed and closed her eyes. This time her dream was of the two of them being safe and happy and playing with Abigail.

The morning came too fast. Mariah was up and ready to go by six a.m. She woke Patrick up even though she was sorry to drag him up so early. She knew he didn't sleep any better than she had.

"Well Vivian, what do you think happened last night?" Mariah asked as she sat up on the exam table.

"I still think you experienced some Braxton-Hicks. Like I said you're going to feel this periodically until you deliver. I see nothing to be concerned about at this moment but I want you to go down the hall with me so we can do an ultrasound. Get dressed and I'll meet you in the outer office."

Patrick was waiting in the reception area. He stood up when he saw Mariah enter the room and took her by the hand, searching her face for answers. "So?" he questioned.

"So far everything is fine."

"I'm sorry for the delay. I had a page to answer. Are you ready to see that baby of yours?" Vivian addressed Mariah.

"What are we doing?" He inquired.

"I'm having an ultrasound." Patrick started grinning. "You mean we're going to see what the baby looks like?"

"Well, that's not what I'm checking for but yes is your answer," Vivian replied as they were walking down the hall.

"Mariah, I have to ask you. Do you mind? I mean can I come in too? I promise I won't be in the way. It is okay doctor isn't it?" Patrick looked at Mariah then at Vivian then back to Mariah.

"That's up to Mariah, Patrick."

"Okay, I don't want to fight with you this morning. Come on in." Mariah held the door open behind her.

"Oh my gosh, that's the baby? She's beautiful! I can't believe this. It's so..so..look she's turning to us. Look! It looks like she's waving at us." Mariah noticed Patrick's eyes were filled with tears. He didn't realize he was holding her hand and trembling at the same time. She herself was holding back the tears of joy to see her baby so well.

"I still get a thrill every time I personally do an ultrasound. Children are truly a gift from God." Vivian let them view the baby a few seconds longer. "Now we're done here. Patrick would you please wait outside for us."

"Huh, sure. I'll be out there." He pointed to the hallway and left.

"What is it Vivian? Is there something wrong?" The concern was showing through Mariah's voice.

"No honey, nothing medically at the moment but I think you should know this baby is going to be a big one."

"Just how big?" Mariah was almost laughing with relief by this time.

"If I'm reading this right and I think I am, I'm estimating her to be about eight pounds. She still has another month yet to develop which is when she'll really pack on the weight."

"Are you serious?" Mariah stopped laughing. "You're joking with me right?"

Vivian shook her head no. Mariah stood up and adjusted her clothing.

"Vivian, do you think I'll have trouble delivering? Is that why you're mentioning this?"

"As you know your medical problems can contribute to the size of the baby. As far as trouble I can never say on that. You should be able to handle it but we'll watch how things develop. If we have to do a C-section then we will."

"Surgery?" Mariah frowned at the prospect. "I'll tell you what before we do that give me whatever pain killers you can and let me see what I can do."

"The recovery time is less if I have this baby naturally isn't it?"

"Yes, it is. Why does that matter just as long as we have a healthy baby."

"Don't get me wrong I want that, too, but I still want to leave town as soon as possible."

"Okay, Mariah, stop brooding. I can't stand this any longer. What did the doctor say to you when I left the ultrasound? You two were in there a while."

Mariah was watching the houses pass outside the car.

"The baby is normal."

"So that's good news isn't it? But tell me what's bothering you? Please don't keep this to yourself. This is my daughter and you know it."

"Don't get huffy with me. I remind you this could be yours but then again it could not be either. The thing for you to remember is this baby is MY daughter."

"Okay, I'm sorry, I just mean I want to be involved with all of this. If something is wrong I want you to tell me. Share your worry with me."

Mariah sighed, "It's just that the baby's going to be big."

"How big?" Patrick looked at her. She was looking straight ahead and she spoke without glancing at him.

"She'll be over eight pounds. This is becoming too real for me now."

"Over eight? Well lets think about this now, I'm sure there are a lot of babies born over eight pounds. Look at all the women in the hundred of years ago who delivered babies and then went back to work in the fields. They did it, so can you."

"Oh thank you very much, I don't want to work in the fields after delivering?"

"You know what I mean. I'm just trying to lighten things up. Seriously sweetheart I think you can handle this. What does the doctor say?"

"She's not predicting anything. She said she thought I could deliver naturally but she did mention a possible C-section. I don't want that."

"We can handle whatever needs to be done. Many women have C-sections and do well. You are not alone in this. I want to be with you when you deliver if you will let me."

"I don't know about that. What did I do with that piece of paper she gave me?" Mariah started to search her purse. Patrick notices the paper on the floorboard.

"Is that it?" He pointed to it.

"Thank you." She picks it up and stuffs it in her purse.

"What is it?"

"Just information on child birth classes. She feels it would benefit for me to start them as soon as possible."

"You'll need a coach. Consider me if you would?"

"Patrick, I'll have to think about it. I don't know. This may not be your baby you know?"

"Why do you keep reminding me of that? Yes I know, but the fact is I love you, will always love you, there is no one else for me but you and I promise I will treat this little girl like she is mine even if she isn't. I'm already in love with her, too."

He pulled in front of the boutique, opened her door and walked her inside. There he kissed her and left but not before Edmund took notice. He had to get back to the ranch to tend to the horse. Even though she didn't give him an answer to being her coach he was still elated after all she did give him a copy of the ultrasound picture, of his daughter. He knew she had a copy to give to Charlie but it didn't bother him too much. He felt even stronger now the baby would call him Daddy.

Mariah showed off the baby's picture to everyone who wanted to see. Edmund was of course thrilled and if he was upset about seeing Patrick kiss her he didn't show it. Margo had told her they had seen it. She made excuses and disappeared upstairs for a few minutes and called Charlie to see if he could stop by. She had something to give him and wanted to catch up on things with him and Becky.

By that evening when Susan locked the doors Mariah was more than ready to relax. The swelling in her feet was getting worse again and she wanted to get off of them. Edmund suggested that they have dinner but she was too tired to do so. She told him to ask Margo and promised they would have dinner tomorrow night no matter what since it would be the last night he would spend in Crystal River. Edmund knew she was wiped out and told her so. He understood and proceeded over to Margo who was smiling as he approached.

Sometime in the night she had that same dream, the one where she was carrying her baby and running away from something, then suddenly Jean Paul was there running after her and then there was Patrick. She had the feeling that she wasn't running from the men but from something else but she didn't know what. After that she couldn't get back to sleep. The phone rang, it was four in the morning.

"Hello."

"*Bonjour, mon amour.*"

"*Bonjour,* Jean Paul. I am so glad to hear from you. I tried to call you last night but couldn't get through. Are you okay?"

"Yes, of course. Why do you ask?"

"Nothing I just had this dream and you were in it and there was something very wrong in it."

"Did you tell your doctor about the dreams?"

"Yes, I did and she said sometimes it happens. Tell me what is going on with you?"

"After you tell me how you and *le bébé* are doing? I want to know everything." Mariah couldn't help it but everything poured out including Patrick and the ultrasound. She then discussed the re-opening of the shop and the sales on his line.

Jean Paul listened intently and said almost nothing until she was finished. "Well *mon amour,* I don't think you should be worrying about all of this right at the moment. The doctor will know what to do when the times comes for Abigail to see this world. You must do whatever she says, *oui*?"

"Yes, I will and you know that but.."

"There is no but about it, you will have a healthy baby and we will be together I promise."

"I miss you."

"I can not tell you what I feel when you say that."

"You say that like you're relieved, why?"

"You know I am not an insecure man but I don't like the time that Wainscott is spending with you. I wish it was me helping you go through all this."

"That's sweet. I wish it was you, too."

"Mariah, I have to ask this but has your feelings for Wainscott changed since we last saw each other?"

"What do you mean?"

"You were honest with me and told me that you still have feelings for him and that bothers the hell out of me. How did you put it that you loved two men at once-Wainscott and myself? Have you worked through all that yet?"

"Jean Paul, I'm not sure what to say. I don't want to hurt you. You know how I feel about you, about us but for some reason I'm still having trouble closing the door on him. Sarah says probably the reason why is because of the baby. Maybe deep down I'm willing to believe that Abigail is his and not Charlie's. She says I'm going to have to come up with a way to resolve my feelings."

"I'm right beside you with whatever you choose. I love you and that will not change. You and Abigail are my life now. Didn't I ask you to marry me, *oui*?"

"Yes, you did. Do you know what you just said? You told me you loved me in English instead of saying, *Je t'aime*. I think I prefer the French way. It's more you."

"I think you're correct. It sounds like something Wainscott would say."

Mariah and Jean Paul laughed. "Jean Paul that isn't nice and you know it."

"The devil got in me, *pardon*."

"Seriously I'm glad we have what we have. You've been my saving grace from the moment I laid eyes on you."

"Mariah you are a lot stronger than you think. I have told you that before. You could handle all this by yourself if you had to including Abigail's birth."

"I wonder?"

"You know I'm right. You are a much stronger woman now than when we met seven months ago. Not that you were weak but you were like a robot that had been disassembled. It was you that put the pieces back together and with a bond much stronger than before."

"I thank you for the vote of confidence. I love you, too."

"You know we have spoken for over an hour now. I have to let you get some sleep. *Pardon*."

"It's okay. I don't sleep much anymore. I will tell Edmund what time the plane will be here tomorrow. I wish you were coming but I understand why you need to be in Paris yet. What you are doing is so important and I'm so proud of you."

"I'm just doing what needs to be done that's all. Perhaps by the time Abigail grows up to know what life is, her world won't be so threatening."

"That is a wonderful thought."

"With that on your mind now go back to sleep. I will call you as soon as I can. Good night, *mon amour*."

"Good night my love." Mariah hung up and closed her eyes.

She slept past the opening of the store. Margo and Edmund were worried when she didn't come down so she looked in on Mariah. Mariah answered the apartment door still in her pajamas.

"Everything okay?" Margo asks.

"Yea, I just need to get some sleep. I had dreams all night and then Jean Paul called at four. We had a long talk."

"I don't mean to be stepping in here but are you taking care of your diabetes?"

"Yes, I am. I was up earlier and did all that. I tell you what unless something happens downstairs I'll be down a little later. How's the sale going?"

"We're steady but we can handle it. You take care of that baby. Call downstairs if you need anything."

"Thanks Margo. Oh, tell Edmund I want to see him later and I'm still counting on our dinner tonight."

"Sure thing." Margo left the room and Mariah went back to sleep. It was after three when she surfaced from upstairs.

"All right here are the totals for the sale. I've broken this down into two areas. We have the women's department and the men's department, pretty neat huh?" There were cheers from the women when Mariah announced their department so of course that set up Ben and Edmund to do their part when the men's line was announced. "Neither department can really compete against each other but guess what! The women's took in a profit of five thousand and the men's made a profit of three thousand. I don't know about you all but I think every one of you deserves to have dinner on me at the Crystal Inn at your convenience and of course with your spouses. If you choose not with your spouses I don't want to know about it." Mariah laughed as well as everyone else. "I will set up the arrangements tomorrow. I thank you all for a wonderful job and I couldn't have wished for a better tally than this. I love you all. Now go home and celebrate but not too much since we open at regular hours tomorrow. Ben you've done a great job I appreciate it."

Edmund and Mariah left the boutique around seven thirty to go to dinner. It had taken her longer to dress than she had planned. Nothing looked quite right on her. Finally she chose an evening maternity dress of pale lavender. The mini skirt consisted of layers of tulle on top with a silk underlay. The bodice of the dress was a layer of silk crossing in a low cut v style in front and back. She found after searching through her clothes that she didn't have the right bra so she decided to go without. The thought crossed her mind to find something else to wear but since she was keeping Edmund waiting so long and their reservations were for seven thirty she was going to make this dress work. What to do with her hair? She decided not to put it up this evening, it would just have to do down. She grabbed the cream silk jacket and her purse and closed the door. The look on Edmund's face when he saw her was worth the time she took. "My goddess, I don't know how you do it. Every time I look upon you, you are more beautiful than before. Shall we?"

"You're driving if you don't mind?" She handed him the keys.

"Where to?"

"You know the way. There is a little restaurant behind the Crystal Inn. I think you'll enjoy this one."

"I will enjoy any place as long as I am with you tonight."

"Mariah, come in. I have your usual table ready," Joe greeted them at the door. He seated them in a secluded corner of the room. The lights were dim and the setting was very romantic. This was the first time she had visited the restaurant since she had came back into town. She and Patrick were here that last week they were together. This was their table. She kicked herself for not requesting another table but the thought had not even crossed her mind.

"Thank you, Joe. I'd like you to meet a very good friend and colleague of mine. *Monsieur* Edmund LaRue, I would like you to meet *Monsieur* Joseph Cantrell, the owner of this fine establishment." Edmund stood up and shook hands with him.

"So you are the Frenchman who is setting this town on its heels. I am glad to meet you."

"I assure you that it is not me who is doing all you say. It is all *Mademoiselle* Mariah's efforts being the goddess that she is." Edmund smiled at her, kissed his fingers and blew it toward her.

"Don't let him kid you, Joe. Edmund here is one of the designers of my new men's line. If you haven't seen it you must come in. It's nothing this town has ever had before. I think the shirts would suite your taste."

"I will do that first chance I get. It is good to see you again. We have missed you. By the way you do look like a goddess in that dress and congratulations on the baby. Oh I have customers to see to. Order anything you want, it's on the house tonight and there will be no discussion on it either." Joe disappears through the darkness.

"He seems young to own this establishment?"

"He is, he's twenty-two. I've known him for some time now. In fact when he was seventeen I caught him trying to shoplift from the boutique. He wanted to give his grandmother a present for her birthday. She died the day after that. I couldn't press charges on him under the circumstances so I made him work off the debt in cleaning chores around here. Since then he has held down a steady job and saved enough for a down payment on this place when it sold a year ago. By the looks of things he's doing pretty well I'd say."

The restaurant was decorated in an old world Spanish motif. The waiters and waitresses were dressed in Mexican clothes and to give the place an air of authenticity there was even a roaming Mexican band.

Mariah and Edmund ate, talked and laughed the entire evening. Edmund drew a little attention to himself, as he always seemed to do when one of the female band members pulled him on to the dance floor with her for a number. He ate the moment up like a kid eating a lollipop. Mariah didn't know he knew any Mexican dances. They closed the place down at midnight. She wanted the evening to go on so she wouldn't have time by herself to think about what Patrick was doing with Amy. Was he planning on staying the night with her? In spite of her efforts in keeping her mind on she and Edmund her mind kept traveling to that forbidden place of Patrick and Amy.

As they crossed the courtyard that connected to the backside of the Inn Mariah had to sit on a park bench to get a rock out of her shoe. Edmund knelt down in front of her on the grass and removed her shoe. He noticed her feet looked even more swollen than they had earlier and was concerned about it but felt it wasn't a good idea to mention it outright to her not like this. Before he replaced her shoe she had crossed her legs and he took the opportunity to rub her bare foot.

"Edmund that feels so good."

"You feel cool, my dear. If so you can have my suit coat if yours is not enough?"

"Thank you, but I'm fine. You know I think I could sit here all night just to have you rub my feet."

There was someone coming towards them. Most of all the patrons to the restaurant had left. Mariah glances up when she heard the familiar deep voice.

Patrick and Amy were practically on top of them before she knew it. He was in mid-sentence when he saw Mariah and Edmund rubbing her foot. Patrick noticed her skirt was exceptionally high over her thigh the way she had her legs crossed in front of him. What was she doing? Seeing her sitting like that was driving him mad especially with Edmund there obviously enjoying the view. Amy noticed the look on Patrick's face, too, and then realized who he was looking at.

"Well, look who's here? Hello, Mariah," Amy greeted them. "Patrick, look who's here of all places."

Edmund replaces Mariah's shoe and as he stands up his hands travel up her legs. Patrick was starting to seethe at Edmund's actions. Mariah stood up.

"*Bonjour* Patrick, *Mademoiselle.*"

"What are you doing out so late? Shouldn't you be getting some rest?" Patrick was annoyed with Mariah and it showed. He even ignored Edmund's greeting.

"Patrick, there isn't any need to be rude. We were having a wonderful evening. I take it you two are, too? Amy dear, I would like you to meet my dear friend *Monsieur* Edmund LaRue. Edmund, this is Ms. Amy Kincade, one of my models when I do a show." Edmund kisses her hand as she extends it to shake.

"I thought so. You have that look. Haven't you done some major shows?"

"Why, yes, I have. I work mostly in New York." Amy couldn't believe her eyes and ears that this handsome man actually knew her work.

"That is where I have seen you. My partner and I often grace the city with our shows."

"So you're a designer?"

"Edmund is one of the designers of the Aristocrat men's line."

"Here is my card. If you know someone looking for a top model then please pass it on. My agent's number is on it and she'll get in touch with me wherever I am." Amy took the card out of her wallet and handed it to Edmund. He glanced at it and put it inside the breast pocket of his jacket. Patrick was tired of all this and was about to say something when Amy interrupted him.

"Mariah that dress you have on is simply it. It's a great maternity number. I really like the low neckline and the tulle. Isn't it bit chilly though since the sun went down?" Patrick did notice the dress or what little there was of it. In his opinion it shouldn't be called a maternity dress even though the skirt was designed that way.

"It is getting a little cooler isn't it? I told you you would look smashing in that outfit, didn't I? Don't you think so, Patrick?" Mariah said referring to Amy's gown.

"Huh, oh yea, she does." It threw him off when Mariah changed the subject to Amy so fast. Amy had started to snuggle up closer to him but he took a step off to the side to avoid her. She just glanced at him but kept her distance.

"How was your dinner with Becky and Charlie?"

"It was the usual dried up food and too much drink and smoke. You know the picture."

"I'm sorry."

"We were just about to get a drink in the Inn. Would you like to join us?"

"No thank you, Amy. We can't. We have a lot to do before tomorrow."

Edmund noticed Mariah was starting to sway a little and a shiver went up her even though the courtyard light was dim.

"Goddess, I think we must get you home where it is warmer and we can relax. It has been a long day for both of us and like you said still plenty to do yet." He took off his jacket and placed it around Mariah's shoulders. He also slipped his hand under her arm to help steady her without calling attention to what was happening.

"Good night to you," Edmund said to Amy and Patrick. He directed Mariah past them and out of the courtyard leaving the couple behind.

"Now why don't you tell me what is going on?" Edmund says as he helps Mariah in her car.

"What do you mean?"

"You staggered a bit. Do you need to see a doctor?"

"I did? I didn't know it and no I don't need to see a doctor. I'm fine and the baby's fine. She's been kicking me all night."

"Fine then, there isn't any business to be done tonight is there?"

"Not that I can think of why?"

"Then you just wanted an excuse to get out of that sticky situation when you said there was plenty to do yet. Is that correct?"

"I just didn't want them to think I was going home to be put to bed like a child. I know it's silly but it was all I could think of."

"My dear goddess, if you were not involved with the Count that is exactly what I would like to do pregnant or not. But you are and I choose not to be an unemployed dead man." He grinned and Mariah started to laugh just as he had hoped she would.

"Jean Paul wouldn't kill you, maybe fire you."

"One never knows what a man will do when jealousy sets in. You are carrying a label without knowing it."

"What do you mean?"

"The Count has been dead serious about you for a long time and he let it be known publicly when he introduced you to his inner circle of friends."

"How did you know that?"

"He of course wanted a new tuxedo for that occasion and mentioned briefly that he was taking you to that ball."

"I didn't know that was what he was planning. To announce me to the world?"

"It was not to the world goddess but to his world. He will do whatever it takes to love and protect you and that baby. You both are in his blood and his soul."

"It makes sense to me now. I didn't really want to go that night since I felt self-conscious, me being a "commoner" and all but he insisted. He said he needed me to go with him since he couldn't get out of it. I didn't know how to waltz until that night. I'm afraid I made a sight out of us trying to do it."

"If I know the Count the way I do, it didn't matter if you were in a wheel chair. All that matters to him is that you are with him."

"Is there a reason why you're mentioning this to me?"

"I have observed Patrick with you. He thinks he still has you in his life doesn't he?"

"I don't need to be reminded of my relationship with the Count. He's very special to me, too. He knows how I feel about him so that's all that matters. As far as Patrick is concerned he can do whatever he wants and with whom." "I'm sorry. I didn't mean to step on your beautiful toes but there is something between you and him I don't understand. It is none of my business and I assure you I won't mention it to anyone." He took her hand in his and kissed it.

"Edmund, I'm sorry, I shouldn't have snapped at you like that. Of course you don't understand. The Count knows everything about me. I have no hidden secrets. But just so you know I lived with Patrick for five years. I was with him until the time I decided to leave town. He's the father of my baby." There she said it; there was no need to go into all the details with him concerning Charlie and his involvement. The least amount Edmund knew the better it was but if she didn't try to explain he would think there was something going on other than what was with Patrick. She didn't want that, she didn't want the wrong word get back to Jean Paul. If Edmund was picking up on something then it was time to for her to settle these unresolved feelings about Patrick but she still didn't have a plan to do so. They drove back to the boutique in silence. Edmund didn't know what to say next so he didn't say anything.

He walked her up to the apartment. There he took her in his arms and kissed her on the hand.

"Goddess, please don't worry about a thing. I didn't mean to pry. Sometimes my mouth gets in the way. We are all going to be here for you, the Count and I of course if you need me in any way. I knew there was strong history with Patrick but I didn't know just how strong. This is a difficult situation you are in but it shall pass. If I can help with anything you need let me know. You promise?"

"Yes, of course, I do. I thank you for your friendship and understanding. I don't forget my true friends. Good night Edmund. Thank you for your compassion."

She watched him close the front doors and set the alarm system behind him. She then closed her office doors, locked them and turned off the lights behind her.

Edmund was already at the boutique and flitting about before eight-thirty the next morning. Mariah had seen his head together with Margo and figured something was cooking between the two of them since he was leaving town that afternoon. Little did she know what was truly going on. She came down stairs in a pale blue pantsuit and her hair was pulled up in a French knot. Edmund hurried over to her even before she got to the bottom of the stairs.

"Goddess, please go and change now. We have something very important to do."

"Yes I know. It's called working."

"Not at this moment. Now go and change into something very comfortable!" Edmund was excited. "Go!"

"Tell me what is going on?"

"I can't. You have to come with me to see it. Go!"

"Mariah go with him. I'll take care of the place till you get back besides you'll have your cell phone. Get him out of our hair this morning."

"Well Margo, you don't sound like you like our friend here."

Margo just smiled coyly at both Edmund and Mariah and walked away. Edmund looked after her and shook his head.

"Never mind her, I know better. Now go before I carry you up those stairs and change your clothes for you."

"Okay, okay I'm going."

211

Edmund drove out to the beach and found a spot where no one was using. He helped Mariah out to the sand and left her standing there while we retrieved the blanket and picnic basket he had stored in the trunk of the car. He also had managed to get her to leave her cell in the car. He turned it off and put it in the trunk.

"Edmund, I can't believe you did all this. How did you know I love picnics?"

"Margo told me you do. Besides the Count told me to get you to relax while I was here. After last night I thought I needed to do something special for you."

"Everything is okay, I promise you. I still cherish our friendship as much as ever. You shouldn't have gone to all this trouble but I'm glad you did. Thank you."

"Eat up, we have fresh fruits, cheese, French bread of course and bottled water." He held the water up in the air like it was a magical elixir.

"Strawberries this time of the year?"

"So I cheated and asked the Inn to put together a basket for me. Let's see what other goodies they have gathered for us."

They sat on the blanket and enjoyed just being together. They sat for a while watching the white caps form on the ocean and contemplated what life would be under the ocean if humans were forced to live there.

Edmund took off his shoes and socks and rolled up his pant legs. "Come on let's go for a walk."

"I don't think I want to."

"Why not? Let's be like children and walk the surf."

"I have a hard enough time putting on my shoes without not being able to tie them."

"Then I shall do that for you." He bent down on the blanket and slipped off her shoes and placed them to the side. He then rolled up her pant legs to her knees and stood up. He extended his hand out to help her get up. The baby had grown even larger since he had been in town. It was very hard not to notice her size. Finally they went back to the blanket. Edmund helped her as promised to tie her shoes. She glanced at her watch.

"Oh my gosh, Edmund it's one thirty already! We barely have enough time to make it to the airport."

"Slow down. What are they going to do, leave without me?"

"Yes. Oh. Oh how silly of me. They have to wait on us don't they?"

Together they gathered up their belongings and made their way back up to the car. Mariah allowed Edmund to drive again giving him directions to the airport. Edmund grabbed his bags from the trunk of the car and tossed her cell phone in the front seat. He found a porter, spoke to him and they walked inside arm in arm.

They found Alec and Frederick waiting in the restaurant. As soon as they had finished eating the jet was back up in the air. Mariah stood at the window waving even though she knew they couldn't see her anymore. How she wished she could be on that plane headed to Jean Paul.

"Hi, how are things going?" Mariah asks Susan when she walked in to the boutique.

"Peachy. You're wet. What have you been doing?"

"Playing in the surf. Where's Margo?"

"In the back store room, looking through some trunks that were delivered."

Mariah headed back there to see if there was a problem when she was way laid by Becky.

"Hi, you busy? Why are you wet?"

Mariah looked down at herself. She couldn't see much because of the baby so she used one of the mirrors on the floor. Her pants were a mess."

"Oh my, I just came from the beach. Edmund and I just had a wonderful time playing. Listen I need to check on something. Come and talk to me while I see about this trunk." Becky followed her into the storeroom. Margo looked up. Her face told the story.

"What is it?"

"It's been cut again. The garments are so wrinkled and look this dress hem is torn. Who ever it is and what ever they are looking for, they're not being as careful as they once were." She held the dress up for Mariah's inspection.

"I think we can fix that. Have our seamstress to shorten and re-hem this dress just enough to cover the damage. It should still flow right."

"What's going on Mariah?"

"I wish I knew, Becky. I have had several trunks now to arrive opened and damaged on the inside but this is the first time a garment has been cut. Jean Paul's trunks are being vandalized as well."

"Have you called the police?"

"Why would I do that? Jean Paul is looking in to the matter there in France. We think the problem comes from the factory. There hasn't been any damage until now to report to my insurance company, besides after the fire, I really don't want to report the little things in fear I may get cancelled."

"Mariah, they can't really do that. This is a business and there are different situations. You're covered on for a business policy."

"I will if I need to but I hope I won't. Everything else look okay?"

"Yep. I'll take these things to the cleaners to get the wrinkles pressed out. See ya in a few." Margo gathers the dresses and leaves.

"Now Becky, tell me what you need."

"I just came by to see how you are doing. I have the afternoon off since Alan took the award home last night and he's celebrating by closing the office.

"Some people have all the luck. Come on lets go upstairs. I do have something I need to talk to you about."

"You want something to drink? I have some coffee from this morning or a few diet something in the fridge. Help yourself while I change out of these things before I get asked what happened to you again." Mariah took the pale blue pantsuit off the hanger that she had worn earlier and changed in the bathroom while Becky got herself a drink and sat on the sofa.

"How was last night?" Mariah called out to her through the closed door.

"It was boring actually, like all other awards dinner. The food wasn't even good. We did miss you."

"I heard the food was bad."

"You did?"

"Yea, Edmund and I ran into Patrick and Amy last night outside the Inn. They were going for a drink and we were leaving Joe's. She was hanging all over him you know. Was she like that all evening?"

"No, I can't say that she was all the time. She did spend a lot of the time socializing with all of the eligible men, which suited Patrick just fine, I think. To tell you the truth I think he had wished he had never invited her to come. He sat at the table most of the time nursing a drink, you could tell his heart wasn't in it. Even Charlie tried to loosen him up a bit but couldn't."

"Huh. He did seem to be in a mood when we ran into them. You said he was nursing a drink all evening, then he wasn't drunk enough not to be able to go home?"

"If you're asking me if he had plans to go home alone I think the answer is yes and no he wasn't drunk when we left him. Are you worried about Amy?"

"No, don't be silly. Why should I be worried about her? And before you say anything else Patrick can see and do whomever and whatever he wants. Let's change the subject. How are you and Charlie getting along?"

"We're doing fine. Charlie is still watching himself with me, which I'm going to let go on as long as possible. I'm starting to enjoy the treatment."

"I'm glad you two could work things out," Mariah said as she sat down on the other end of the sofa.

"You said you had something to talk to me about?"

"Oh yes, I almost forgot. Would you consider being my delivery coach?"

"Me, you want me in the delivery room with you?"

"Why not? Can you handle this under the circumstances? I mean if you really don't think you can then I will understand, just tell me up front."

"It's not that."

"Then what?"

"Don't you want someone else that you know better than me? Patrick?"

"No way. He wants to be there but I don't want him there. This is going to be hardest thing I have ever done in my life outside walking away from him. The doctor is predicting Abigail is going to be a big baby. I want someone with me that will help me not hinder me with my concentration."

"Won't they do a C-section or something if that's the case?"

"I don't want that. I want natural with some good drugs of course."

"Why do you want to do it the hard way?"

"I have my reasons."

"You're still planning on leaving town."

"See how well you do know me? Just please don't mention it to anyone yet. I thought that if by some slim chance Abigail is Charlie's maybe it would help you to bond with her a little faster if you were there when she is born. Will you do it for us?"

Becky put her soft drink on the table and sat back. She studied Mariah's face for a few seconds. What she saw was a woman, a friend who needed her, who trusted her during the most precious time of her life. "If you're sure you want me then yes I would be more than happy to be your coach. Just tell me where and when the classes are and I'll be there."

Mariah scooted across the sofa and hugged her. "Oh thank you Becky. The classes start tomorrow night and go for the next month. They meet on Tuesday and Friday's at seven at the hospital."

"Alright then I'll be ready. Do you want to go together or meet?"

"How about going together but having dinner first say around five-thirty, six so we have time to eat? You can come here."

"That's fine with me. You mentioned the name Abigail? Is that what you decided to name your..our baby?" She laughed, then Mariah did too.

"Yes, her name is Abigail Angelena."

"That's unusual but I like it. Where did you come up with that?"

"Abigail is after a wonderful woman who's wisdom was given to me in the short time I knew her and I have found it has never failed me yet. She was Jean Paul's mother."

"What about Angelena? Did you just pick that up somewhere?"

"No. It's after a woman I never met but I think I would have liked her if I did. She reminds me of the type of woman I want to be. She was a humanitarian in her own way. She was Jean Paul's wife."

"You've got to be serious? You're naming your baby after his mother and wife? That's really going to bite Patrick."

"Angelena died long time ago and yes I want to honor Jean Paul and his family by doing this. What's wrong with that?"

"Why? I mean it's none of my business but are you sure you're not doing this just to get back to Patrick for hurting you the way he did?"

"That's a good thought Becky but no I'm not. You see Jean Paul's family took me in, accepted me for whom I am and what I am and accepted my baby without any questions asked. Even his brother and wife treated me like I was born into the family. I have never had that kind of acceptance since my father died. Even with my mother and brother, Sam-they didn't really have time to be a part of my life but my father did. He was the one who bought this place for me when he learned he was dying. That is why this boutique is so important to me and the love Jean Paul's family has for me and my child is as equally as important. I can't really explain it but it's a feeling I have toward Jean Paul's family that I haven't experienced for a long time and never really felt with Patrick. One of total completeness I guess is the best way I can describe it."

"Mariah, I am happy for you, for finding this whatever it is. Is this why you're planning to leave?"

"Yes, please don't say anything just yet but Jean Paul has asked me to marry him." She pulled out a black velvet box out of the safe and handed it to Becky. She opened it and her eyes popped wide open and mouth dropped.

"Oh my gosh! What is this, three carats?"

"No, actually I think its four carats. He planned one carat for every month we had known each other. You see he asked me three months ago." Becky slipped the ring out of the box and placed it on her own finger.

"And you're not saying yes to this?"

"I have said yes, but not to the date. I don't feel it's right to marry him at this point in time when my emotions are reeling around too much. I want to know I love him for him and not because of my hormones."

"Hormones or no hormones I wouldn't care. If I was in your shoes I would grab him in a minute if I loved him."

"He's willing to wait until I'm ready and until I deal with Patrick."

"Hold on! What does Patrick have to do with this except for the fact that he's probably Abigail's father?"

"What do you mean?"

"Are you thinking that Patrick's going to give you trouble over the baby? Charlie won't, you know he just wants you to be happy and if that means you marrying the Count then so be it?"

"I know."

"By the way, thank you for the ultrasound picture. Charlie couldn't wait for me to get home and show it to me. Did you know he's just about to sign on another movie?"

"He mentioned something about it to me but didn't go into detail. What's it about?"

"Don't know yet. He won't talk about it to me. Look at the time. I've got to go. I'm meeting him in a few minutes for a long weekend at the Reed."

"The Reed! That's a posh hotel. If this is the way he's sucking up to you for what he did then go for it girl and have fun."

"Let's say he's trying hard and I am enjoying every minute of it." Becky grinned. "You know the attention that Edmund and Alec paid to me ate him up. He couldn't do enough for me after we got home last Saturday night."

"Men are so insecure."

"I think we all are to some extent, don't you? I'll see you tomorrow." Becky hugged Mariah and left.

Mariah resisted her urge to make some excuse to call Patrick, to see what he had to say about the dinner last night with Amy. Part of her wanted to see why he had never told her about taking Amy and part of her reminded herself that she was the one who told him to go without her if the tickets were nonrefundable. She was secretly enjoying the fact that he seemed absolutely bored and miserable according to Becky. She wanted him as miserable as she was. Everything was his fault, his actions changed her life but now it seemed that life was stagnating and she hated it. If she could only start her life with Jean Paul, things would be better. Was she good enough to be his wife? Maybe Becky was right, everyone had insecurities of some type.

Mariah kept herself busy with work. She sent everyone home as soon as the boutique closed. She wanted the solitude and quiet of the night while she putted around the shop restocking and straightening the shelves. Just as she started to make her way upstairs the phone rang. It was the boutique's line so she ignored it and let the answering machine kick in. By the time she entered her apartment the phone was ringing.

"Hello."

"Hi, I miss you?"

"Why?"

"What do you mean why? Can't I tell you I miss you without you doubting me?"

"Patrick I don't want to play games. What do you need?"

"To see you. Do you want to get something to eat?"

"No, I have plenty here. I want to curl up with a book and relax."

"Are you mad at me?"

"Why should I be? Have you done something to make you feel guilty?"

"Not that I'm aware of. I just wanted to tell you how beautiful you looked last night when we ran into each other."

"Now you've done that. I hope you told Amy the same thing since I dressed her."

"Oh I get it, you're mad because I took Amy. I told you I was?"

"No, I'm not mad because you took Amy. I told you to go without me and no you didn't tell me. Amy did when she came in for a new outfit."

"I told you and I know I did."

"No you did not. I hope you enjoyed yourself. I know I did with Edmund." That remark cut Patrick deep. "I want to know why you decided to go out with him and not to honor our commitment?"

"First of all I told you I didn't want to go because Edmund was here and we never had a commitment. I never said I would go to that stupid dinner in the first place. Are we going to argue over this? If so I'm hanging up."

"Okay, okay. My ego was bruised when I saw you with him and especially when he had his hands all over you."

"He did not! What you saw was him being the gentleman that he is and removing a stone from my shoe. I'm having a hard enough time walking as it is. By the way you were pretty rude to him. When you're rude to my friends you're rude to me and I won't accept that. Do you understand what I'm saying to you?"

"If you want me to apologize then I'm sorry but he has irked me from the moment I laid eyes on him. I just don't like the man."

"Why? Oh, what is this? You're jealous."

"That's right I am. I can't stand seeing another man's hands on you. I want you all to myself."

"It's not going to be that way, not anymore. Look I want to go take a shower and relax. Good night." Before Patrick could say anything else she hung up on him and took the phone off the hook. If Jean Paul tried to call he would try her cell if she didn't answer the apartment line. She curled up in bed with her novel and eventually went to sleep.

CHAPTER 10

The next morning Mariah was up early, she felt refreshed since there were no dreams to plague her sleep. She met Margo coming in the door and motioned her to come upstairs for a minute. She pulled out the file and notes she had made for every shipment that came into the boutique as well as those scheduled to arrive and had arrived in New Orleans. She was starting to keep a paper trail of everything including the times the shipment was due. Jean Paul hadn't gotten back to her with any information. The last time they spoke he didn't say whatever came of the meeting between the managers at the plant. She made a note to call him soon and find out. He must be extremely busy for him not to call her last night.

"What's up?" Margo asked as she stepped in the office and found Mariah behind her desk.

"I want to show this to you." After a few minutes of explaining how she wanted the records kept she sat back with her hands over the baby. "Any questions?"

"Don't think so."

"Good. I've got a doctor's appointment in a little while so I'll be gone for probably the good part of the morning."

"Don't worry about the place. We'll do just fine without you."

"Good, I was hoping you would say that since I can't find my phone anywhere. I can't imagine what I did with it."

"Go and take care of you and your baby. We'll see you later. There's the doorbell. The troops have arrived." Margo turned and went downstairs.

Mariah poured herself another cup of coffee, took a few sips of it and made a face. The bitter taste was more than she could stomach at the moment. She poured it out in the sink and rinsed her cup out setting it in the drainer. She took a look at herself in the mirror; there was no need to change out of her jeans since she wasn't working. She ran a brush through her hair and put on some lipstick forgoing any more makeup. People would just have to take her the way she was or not at all. She found her loafers under the bed but they were pushed farther back than she thought. Mariah laid on the floor trying to reach them but couldn't. The longer she tried the madder she got. The coat hanger wouldn't even reach. Those shoes were the only ones that fit her and were completely comfortable. There was no way she was leaving without wearing those shoes.

Ben knocked on the office door but when she didn't answer he walked on in. He stopped short when he saw her on the floor.

"Boss, are you all right?" He stepped closer to see what was happening. Mariah squirmed around so she could see him.

"I'm fine, just mad at the moment. I can't reach my shoes."

"Here allow me to help you up. I'll get them for you." He extended his hand to her and gently lifted her up then he pulled the shoes out. "Are these it?"

"Thanks. I feel silly about you finding me like this."

"Don't worry about it. I guess I need to get used to it. I suspect things like this are common place when there's a baby coming."

"This and much more believe me." Mariah slipped her shoes on and stood up. "Ben please don't mention this to anyone."

"Not a word. I may be coming to you for tips on how to handle things at home with Tracy when she gets farther along?"

"Anytime. Listen, I really need to go. What did you need?"

"I was just coming in to leave you a note on some shirt sizes we need. Edmund was going to get them from me and have them shipped but I think he must have forgotten."

"Okay, write them down and leave it on my desk. I have to call France anyway." Mariah started out the door but stopped. "Ben, thanks again for the shoes." Ben just grinned at her and watched her descend the stairs.

Mariah's appointment with Sarah was delayed about an hour but she decided to wait there instead of fighting the traffic so she picked up her novel and settled in the corner of the waiting room with her feet propped up. There was no need to be concerned on who may see her since she was her only appointment this early in the morning.

Sarah walked in the waiting room in a huff. "I'm sorry Mariah, but I couldn't help it. I told that mechanic of mine the battery was going down. He didn't believe me when I told him I had a problem. Just wait till I talk to him."

Mariah got up and put her book in her purse. "It's okay. I'm not in a crunch. Take you time."

"Come on in. We can talk while I get settled. Hi Joan, how's the rest of the morning?"

"Mr. Peters rescheduled and Ms. Wallace and Timmy cancelled, said Timmy is sick."

"Good that frees me up for a while. Come on in, Mariah." Sarah held the door to the inner office open while Mariah gathered her belongings. Inside the main office Sarah poured herself a cup of coffee. "Do you want any?"

"No the taste isn't as good to me as it was."

"Do you mind if I do?"

"Not at all." Mariah sat down at the small table. Since they were more like friends and their sessions were like chats they had dispensed with the formalities of doctor and patient.

Sarah had given Mariah a lot to think about. She needed time to digest everything. It was well after eleven when she walked out of there. After her session was over they continued to talk about their upcoming holiday plans, Thanksgiving was coming fast. Mariah hadn't even thought about it. In a way she hoped that Jean Paul could come and spend the holiday with her but she didn't really want to push him to feel obligated to fly the distance sine she was thinking that by Christmas she might be back in France that is if Abigail comes on time. That was her deadline she had given herself to work through her feelings about Patrick and their relationship. She had to have things settled by then one way or the other no matter what it took. Mariah parked her car in the side lot beside the boutique. As she adjusted her seat back she noticed her cell phone on the floorboard. She remembered Edmund had put it in the trunk during their picnic. He must have placed in the seat afterwards and it fell between them. There were several calls on it since then, three from the ranch this morning and two from Jean Paul last night. Damn it, she thought how could she have been so careless. Patrick would have to wait. She wanted to hear Jean Paul's voice first.

"Hi I'm back." Mariah said walking toward the back office with Margo following her.

"I hate to throw things at you but something has happened at the ranch and they have been trying to get a hold of you. Patrick has called several times. Oh by the way your Frenchman called here shortly after you left. He said he would try you later and that he would be in meetings till this afternoon. He asked if you were all right. I told him you were and that you were at a doctor's appointment. That's okay wasn't it? He was really concerned since he couldn't reach you last night."

"I took the phone off the hook after Patrick called. I thought my cell was in my purse but I just found it in the car." Mariah sat at the desk and Margo at the side of it with a coffee cup in hand. "What did Patrick say about the ranch?"

"I didn't take the message, just that there was a problem he wanted you to know about and he wanted you to call him as soon as possible."

"Excuse me Mariah, there's a Betty on the phone for you. Line one." Susan said as she poked her head through the door.

"Betty? That's Jim's wife. It must be bad for her to call." Mariah picked up the phone and punched the line.

"Hello."

"Mariah dear, it's Betty. The men folk wanted me to try to reach you. Now don't get upset. Things are being handled here but Jezebel has hurt herself. She has a laceration on her chest and the vet has been called."

"How bad is it?" Mariah's concerned showed through. Margo frowned in response.

"I haven't ventured out there yet to see but both Jim and Patrick are out there and have been for some time."

"Oh dear. I'm on my way."

"I don't think you need to come all the way out here. Patrick just wanted you to know what was going on. That's all."

"I'm on my way."

"All right that would give us a chance to visit. I've been wanting to see you but just haven't gotten out much lately. I'll have a fresh pot of coffee on."

"That's sound good Betty. Thank for calling."

"What's up?" Margo asks as she peers around the doorway thinking she heard someone at one of the registers.

"Jezebel's hurt. I'm going out to the ranch. I have my cell. Oh I probably need my charger, no telling how long the battery will last. Call me if something comes up." She headed upstairs to get the charger.

Mariah found Betty sitting in the living room watching a game show when she entered the front door. She looked much older and frail than she remembered her to be. Maybe the chemotherapy did that to a person. "Hi Betty."

"Mariah dear, you look wonderful. I heard you were pregnant but didn't know how pregnant. Come sit down. Get off your poor feet. You can drink coffee or do you prefer something else. I'll get it for you come sit down."

Mariah did as she was told. Betty had a way of taking charge of things and just speaking her mind. Whatever she thought just came out. It didn't really bother her that Betty had made reference to her size or her poor feet. She was right by this time they were already hurting. "I tell you what. The coffee sounds good but right now I think I'd like to have some water instead. I'll get it, you don't need to wait on me."

"I know that but make this old woman feel useful." Betty hugged Mariah and brought back a glass of water for her. It felt like old times being with her, she was still filled with love, compassion and faith in spite of her illness. Mariah had always thought that Betty had the qualities that every mother should possess and hoped that she would soon fit that category. They chatted a bit longer since Mariah didn't want to hurt her feelings but what she really wanted to do was to go out to the barn and see about her horse. She finally excused herself to go out to the stable but not before she had told Betty to visit the boutique and pick something pretty out for herself."

"What are you doing here?" Patrick was in the stall with Jezebel when he caught sight of her entering the far end of the stables. His tone was one of annoyance. Jim approached her and hugged her.

"Thanks Jim, it's good to see you too unlike some people in here. You were the one to call me remember?"

"I didn't mean for you to drive all the way out here."

"Too bad, any other time you want me here. Besides I didn't come here for you, I came for Jezebel. Let me see her." Jezebel nickered at the sound of Mariah's voice. She tried to toss her head back to see her but couldn't since Jim had her tied to the corner post of the stall and Patrick had her hobbled so he could continue to hold the blood soaked compress to her chest. In spite of his efforts to apply pressure to the wound the horse was still bleeding, not as bad as before but the wound was deep.

"I want you stay back. She's spooked and we can't seem to calm her down."

"Patrick's right missy, I think you should stay back. Even I can't seem to get through to her today."

"I'm planning to go inside but I just want to see the wound." Mariah stepped to the side of the stall and gasp when she saw how much blood was on the pile of towels in the corner. "Do you have to hobble her? She's never been hobbled before, that could be what is upsetting her."

"It's the only way to keep her somewhat quiet, other wise she'll keep the bleeding going. Doc Williams said to do it until he gets here."

"So when is he planning to come?"

"I don't know what's keeping him."

"How deep is it?"

Patrick removed the towel to get a fresh one. This allowed Mariah to see what she wanted. The wound was a good eight inches long on the chest and at least an inch and a half deep into the muscle. "Oh my, how did she do it?"

"All we can figure missy is that she must have brushed up against this corner. When she busted these boards there must have been a nail in it." Jim replied while holding the lead tight around the post.

"What about tetanus?"

"She's vaccinated for that."

"Thank God for small favors." Mariah reached out her hand toward Jezebel's nose. Jezebel sniffed her hand and seemed to acknowledge her presence. "See she knows me. She'll behave with me here."

"Mariah, get your hand away from her. I'm telling you she's not her usual nasty self, she's worse right now."

The intercom that Patrick had installed from the house to the stable came on. He did it as a convenience for Mariah when they were together so if she needed something and he was outside she could page him. Betty's voice bellowed out.

"Jim, the vet is on the phone. Can you get it?"

"Here Mariah, come here and hold this. It shouldn't slip but just in case."

"Jim, I don't think that's such a good idea."

"Hodge podge, as long as she's on this side and stands back she'll be alright."

"Use the phone in the tack room."

"Can't, remember we've got to work on that line. I'll be just a minute. Betty, tell Doc Williams I'll be there in a minute." Jim called out to the intercom, which was left on. He went on up to the house leaving Mariah and Patrick out in the barn.

"I want you to go on up to the house, too. Have a chat with Betty or something."

"Patrick will you shut up. I'm here now and this is where I'm going to stay. She's my horse you know, and I love her." She did notice the horse was more jittery than normal even with her petting her.

"Yea if you would only love me like you do her," he said under his breath.

"I heard what you said. You had your chance. Stop being so nasty to me."

"I just don't want you or the baby getting hurt." He removed the towel and tried to apply a bandage the best he could while Jezebel attempted to dance around.

"Patrick, Doc will be here in fifteen minutes. He was tied up delivering a foal down at the Patterson's place. I'll be out there in a minute if that's okay?"

"I'm okay out here." Patrick was gathering up the dirty towels and throwing them over the stall. He was being cautious in moving slowly and watching intently on how Mariah was petting the horse and Jezebels response.

"I'm coming out so move over in case she jumps," he said to Mariah.

"Oh for heaven's sake she's hobbled."

"You know with horses anything is possible. That's the first lesson, remember?"

"Yes, I know that." Mariah made a face at him while she said this. "Get her feed bucket off the ground. I'll give her something to eat. Maybe that will help calm her."

Patrick picked up the bucket by the handle and heard a rattle. He dropped the bucket as fast as he picked it up. Jezebel reacted the very same moment. Mariah couldn't hold the lead even though it was wrapped around the post. Jezebel reared up and screamed out in fright. When her hooves hit the ground she stumbled and knocked Patrick against the outside wall of her stall. He hit his head and crumbled to the ground. It all came together so fast that Mariah had to have a second to comprehend what happened. She grabbed the lead and held on tighter. The only thing she could think of doing was to call out and hope Jim and Betty hadn't turned off the intercom in the house. She yelled out as loud as she could while looking for the rattlesnake.

"Mariah, I'm coming." Good, Jim had kept the intercom on, he had heard her cries for help and came running as did Betty. "What's going on?" He was out of breath when he entered the paddock.

"Patrick, he's out cold. Wait!" Jim was about to go in the stall to retrieve Patrick when she stopped him.

"What?"

"There's a rattlesnake under the feed bucket. That's why she's so agitated."

Jim reached for the pitchfork and shovel in the next stall. "Keep talking to her Mariah. Get her attention away from what I'm doing. Hold that lead tight. Betty, help her!" He also took the blanket off the next stall and threw it on Jezebel's face blocking her sight. With the pitchfork he lifts the bucket and uses the shovel blade to kill the snake in one swift movement. Jim scoops the body up and throws it over the stall toward the back of the stables. He then lifts Patrick over his shoulders and carries him out of the stall. With this done Mariah removes the blanket from Jezebel's face and loosens her grip on the lead. Betty rushes to the tack room and gets a towel from the cabinet and wets it down. She then hands it to Jim. "He's breathing." He had laid Patrick down on the paddock floor. Mariah took the wet towel from Jim and placed it on his forehead. Her hands were shaking so bad she couldn't stop them. What if he was seriously hurt? It would be all her fault. Jezebel is her horse after all. She didn't want Patrick hurt no matter what happened- she couldn't bear the thought of him being hurt that badly. He had to be okay. She said a silent prayer for him. He was developing a nasty bruise to the right temple. The cold brought Patrick around. He slowly opened his eyes. It took a minute of blinking several times to clear his vision. His head hurt terribly. He reached up to touch the cold towel and his hand covered hers. He felt her tremble and looked into her eyes and saw the love in them that was once theirs.

"What happened here?" Doc Williams saw the group sitting in the middle of the paddock. He came closer and saw Patrick hurt. "Let me see that bruise. How did this happen?" Doc was a stout black haired balding man in his middle fifties. He pulled his glasses out of his pocket. Mariah proceeded to tell the story. By the time she had finished Patrick was sitting up.

"I think you should go in town and get checked out. You could have a concussion."

"I don't need to. I've got a headache and bet I'll be sore tomorrow but I'll be fine. Just help me up."

"Jim, help me get him in the car. I'm taking him to the hospital," Mariah stated.

"You are not! Doc what about the horse?"

Doc Williams was looking over Jezebel carefully. "Well we'll have to load her in the trailer. Think she'll go?"

"Don't know. You've got to take her in?"

"Yep, that wound needs to be debrided and sutured. It's probably deeper than it looks in some places. I'd rather try to do it under anesthesia, it will be easier for her and me, too."

"Okay, we'll get her loaded one way or the other. Let me help Patrick in the house and then we'll get the horse."

"I'm fine Jim, just help with the horse before she kills someone. What happened to the snake?"

"It's dead. I flipped it over there in the corner."

"Man, I didn't even know it was there the entire time we were in and out of that stall. It could have bitten both of us."

"Jezebel knew, that's what spooked her to begin with I bet," Doc Williams entered into the conversation. "Patrick, take it easy at least until tomorrow." The vet took Jezebel's lead and unwrapped it form the post and brought her out of the stall. Patrick could see the horse was still nervous so he stepped between Jezebel and Mariah, for protection. Mariah stepped off to the side when the horse came around close enough for her to pet her. Patrick got closer and kept a watchful eye out.

"I'll see you when you get back, sweetie," Mariah said to Jezebel as she ran her hand down her withers.

"Don't worry about her. She'll be just fine. I'll call you when she can come home. Probably sometime tomorrow." Jim followed Doc Williams to the trailer. He had hooked it up earlier that morning expecting the horse's trip to the vet. Jezebel loaded without an incident and Jim drove off with her in tow.

"I told you she's a good girl. Look how easy she went in," Mariah turned to smile at Patrick.

"Yea you saw what she did to me." He touched his temple and grimaced in pain.

"But you were just as scared as she was. You both got hurt for the same reason. The only difference was she knew that snake was there and you didn't. Come on lets get you up to the house. Betty I think I'm going to need your help."

"Sure thing dear we're going to make Patrick here wish he had gone ahead to the hospital just so he won't have two women nagging at him."

"Great just what I need." He put his arm around Betty's neck and hugged her. Mariah wasn't close enough for him to touch her and her body language told him not to try.

"Who are you calling?" Patrick asked when he walked in to the kitchen fresh from the shower. By this time Jim had delivered the horse, dropped the trailer and picked up Betty and was gone. Mariah had her back to him and didn't hear him come in. She jumped when he spoke.

"You didn't have to scare me."

"Sorry. Who are you talking to? Is that my agent?"

"I'm holding for Vivian."

"Vivian! Why what's wrong?"

"Its not for me silly, it's for you. I want to talk to her about your head bashing."

"I'm fine, just got a headache." He strode over to the window and took down a bottle of aspirin and popped three or four in his mouth.

"That's going to be good, OD on that stuff then I will have a problem on my hands. Oh Vivian, thanks for answering your page. No, it's not me. It's Patrick. There was an accident. He was thrown against the stable wall by my horse. No, actually a snake spooked both of them." Mariah looked at Patrick sitting at the table and grinned. Patrick shook his head and then laid it down on his crossed arms. It was no joke he had a headache the size of Mt. Rushmore.

"No, he refused to come in and get looked at. Is there anything he should do?"

"Take it easy since he won't come in. He could have a concussion and it not show just yet."

"What do I look for?"

"Irritability.."

"So what's new on that line?" She glanced at him, with his head still on the table. Her remark blew over the top of his head without him even looking up. "I'm sorry what else?"

"He may experience lethargy, just not himself, dizziness, nausea or severe headache. He may develop a hematoma, which is a pocket of blood at the site of the injury. Also if he experiences blurred vision, any staggering or unequal pupil size may indicate there's a problem and he should get in right away."

"I think he has a headache now."

"Any other signs?"

"I don't think so."

"I imagine he'll have a headache and a lots of aches and pains by tomorrow. But if you can't get him to change his mind then all you can do is watch and wait for now. He should have someone stay with him until tomorrow morning. It would be a good idea to not let him sleep too deeply and too long at any one time. Say waking him every two hours if there's someone who can do that?"

"Really! Well I guess I can."

"Are you up to this?"

"I'll have to be, there's no one else."

"Listen, I'll be leaving here in a couple of hours so if you need me call me at home."

"Thanks, Vivian. I appreciate it."

"Don't run yourself down over this. Think about the baby."

"I will, I promise. Bye." She hangs the phone up and walks over to Patrick and places her hand on his shoulder. "Come on let's get you upstairs and in bed."

He raises his head and grins, "Sorry, not tonight honey, I've got a headache."

"Very funny. Get in bed and rest now. If you go to sleep I'll get you up every two hours."

"What the hell for? If I go to sleep I want to sleep unless you have other ideas."

"Will you stop it? Vivian said you could have a concussion. She told me what to watch for. If you have any problems, I'm just calling an ambulance that's all there is to it."

Mariah was fussing with the pillows on the bed not paying attention to what he was doing. "I want to look at your head before I go back down."

Patrick had taken off his jeans and was lifting his shirt over his head when she turned to face him. "What are you doing?"

"I'm getting comfortable. Remember I don't sleep in anything but I figure you'd be uncomfortable with me completely all natural." She felt that familiar twinge of excitement. During the five years of being only with him she still was thrilled to see him. He came up and put his arms around her. "Now what did you want to look at?"

"Your hard head."

"You're trembling. Why?"

"Am I?" She broke his bonds and pushed him down on the bed. "Sit down." Mariah moved his head from side to side looking for signs of a hematoma then at his eyes for pupil size. Everything looked good at that moment as far as she could tell.

"Well?"

"I don't see anything but I'm not a doctor either." She started to move away. Patrick took her hand and pulled her down beside her.

"You can practice being a doctor with me." He was looking directly in to her eyes. Their lips were so close and he took advantage of it. The kiss caught her off guard and she jumped up.

"And I was worried about you. You devil!"

"Actually I don't think I can do any more than that. This headache is worse than a bad hangover."

"You should know about that, too." Mariah shook her head and headed out the bedroom door. "Call me if you need anything. I'll be downstairs watching television."

The doorbell rang just as she sat down and turned on the television. She answered the door and held it open for him, "Charlie, please come on in."

"I thought that was your car. What are you doing here?"

"Patrick and Jezebel had a run in. He's upstairs in bed."

"What happened?" Mariah had told him the story as they sat in the kitchen sipping a diet soft drink. "Don't you have a class or something to do with Becky tonight?"

"Oh my, I forgot. I'll have to call her and cancel."

"No, you don't. I came to talk to him about something. Why don't I stay while you do your thing?"

"It would help me feel better about leaving. He's got to wake up every couple of hours."

"How long has he been asleep?"

"About an hour and half or so. Are you sure you don't mind?"

"It's no big deal. Like I said I need to talk to him anyway."

"I've got just enough time to make it in to town to meet Becky. Can you call her and let her know I'm on my way? Oh, when we get done I'll be back. The class shouldn't take any more than a couple of hours."

"Yea, I can call her but are you sure it's a good thing for you to come back here for the night?"

"Charlie, it was my horse that injured him. The least I can do is make sure he's all right until tomorrow morning. The injury could turn out to be serious."

"Okay I won't say another word. You know what you want to do. Now go to your class. The baby's important too."

"Thanks Charlie, I love you." Mariah and Charlie hugged each other.

"I love you, too. Get out of here and I'll call Becky."

Within seconds Mariah was out the door and down the driveway. Charlie settled down in the living room with a beer and turned the television on.

"What are you doing here?"

Charlie turned to see Patrick coming down the stairs. He instantly saw why Mariah was so concerned; the right side of his face was a bruise from his temple to his cheekbone. "Man, look at you. What a shiner."

"What? I haven't looked." He stepped over to the mirror on the wall. "Oh good. What a lovely reminder."

"By the look of things it could have been worse. How's your headache?"

"Better." Patrick looked in the kitchen as he was talking to Charlie. "Where's Mariah?"

"She and Becky had a class to do. She said something about coming back here after she's done but to tell you the truth I don't think that's wise."

"Why? And what class?"

"I don't think she needs to be taxing herself so much."

"She free to do whatever. I told her that but she's stubborn remember? What class?"

"Child birth classes or whatever you call them."

"Crud, I forgot about that. I guess that was my answer. I asked her if I could be her coach."

"Let it be. She may need some space and that's all so don't push her on it. She may still change her mind. I want to talk to you about the movie. That part I was telling you about is open. It's made for you, I'm telling you."

"Hey Charlie, oh Patrick you're up. Shouldn't you be in bed resting?" Mariah came in the house bubbling. She put her purse and jacket on the sofa and sat down across from Patrick. "Oh my word, your face is terrible. Does it hurt?" She grimaced as she reached up to touch his face. He moved away from her hand.

"Don't."

"Sorry." She withdrew her hand and got up to get something to drink. Charlie sat in his chair not saying anything but watching. "Did he give you any trouble while I was gone?" she asked as she came back in the room.

"He's always trouble don't you know that by now?" Charlie threw a pillow and hit Patrick with it. He started to throw the pillow back but stopped. "Why don't you go home and be with Becky. Stop babysitting me."

"That's a plan, man." Charlie got up and found his keys on the hall table. "Listen, you think about what I said earlier. It's a good piece of work. We'll have some fun together for a change."

"I'll make some calls. Get out of here." Patrick walked Charlie to the front door and held it open for him. "Thanks for everything."

"Sure thing buddy." Charlie patted him on the shoulder, said goodbye to Mariah and left.

"What was all that about?"

"Nothing." Patrick said as he walked in the kitchen throwing Charlie's bottle away. Mariah followed.

"I hope you didn't drink anything?"

"Do you see another bottle anywhere?"

"Man, you're in a foul mood. Are you mad because I left?"

"Why would I be? You have things to do too."

"Yes, I do. Wait a minute, Charlie told you where I was didn't he?"

"So Becky is your coach?"

"Yes, she is. I thought it might help her to bond with the baby. I'd like for her to be godmother."

"Whatever, it doesn't matter. What the hell, who am I kidding, it does matter. What about my bonding? Don't I deserve that too?"

"Patrick, we don't know if you're the father."

"I know it and I know you know it, too. Maybe not up in here.." He pointed to his head then to his heart. "..but in here, you know it, it's true."

"It's late and I think you need to sleep. Go to bed."

"Where are you going to sleep?"

"I'm not. I'm going to watch these old movies all night." She stood up after a lot of effort from taking the tapes out of the floor cabinet.

"You are not. The guest bedroom is made up."

"Sorry that's too far away. I won't hear if you need me."

"I'm fine I don't need your help."

"Good, I'm glad. Go to bed, I think we had better not say anything else to each other right now." Mariah settled on the sofa after placing the video in the machine. She kicked off her shoes and put her feet up, crossed her arms and sat there looking straight at the television. Patrick cursed under his breath, locked the front door and went upstairs. He slammed the bedroom door behind him.

It was one in the morning when he woke up. He wondered where Mariah was since he didn't hear the television anymore. Was she asleep on the sofa? Did she have a blanket? He couldn't lie there anymore wondering so he got up to find out. She wasn't in the living room or the guest bedroom. He peaked out the living room window. Her car was still in the driveway so she must be there somewhere. He searched the house and didn't find her. There was one room he hadn't looked in yet, his study, and exercise room. He cracked the door a bit and found her asleep on the chaise he had left in the corner. She had a blanket and a pillow. He didn't want to disturb her so he left the door ajar and went back to bed. How he wanted to pick her up and put her in their bed where she would be more comfortable. But he stifled the urge and went back to bed only to be awakened a couple of hours later by a phone ringing somewhere so he investigated. Standing outside the study door he heard her voice speaking softly. She was talking to Jean Paul.

Does she have to bring him in his house? He went back to bed stewing in his bitterness.

"I'm sorry we missed each other last night and this morning. No, everything with me is fine. It wasn't an O.B. appointment." Mariah told him about the birthing classes she and Becky were attending. She told him about the incident with Jezebel and the fact that she was at the ranch. She could tell he wasn't exactly happy with the fact but he didn't say much about it. What could he do about it? He was in France, wasn't he?

"I have a surprise for you, *mon amour*. We will be together this week."

"This week! You're coming? When?"

"I should be there by Thursday. Is that all right?"

"Do you have to ask? Of course, that's all right. How long will you be able to stay?"

"I'll have to leave on Tuesday but we'll have a long weekend together."

"Oh Jean Paul, I can't wait. Wait a minute you're not planning on staying on the plane are you?"

"Actually I thought your apartment. Alec will be staying in the States to visit his family, so he'll have the plane and then come back to pick me up."

"I'll get a suite at the Crystal Inn reserved. My place is too small for you."

"You mean for us, *mon amour*. I don't need a lot of room as long as you're with me."

"I want you to be able to relax while you are here. There'll be people in and out of my office through the day, we really couldn't be alone until after the boutique closes."

"Since you put it that way, whatever you want to do is fine except please put the room in my name, not the boutique's."

"I'll do it first thing in the morning. I can't wait to see you. I've missed you so much."

"Me too my love, I had better let you go for now. I will see you in a few days. *Je t'aime* Mariah."

"I love you, too, Jean Paul."

By the time Mariah woke up and dressed Patrick was in the kitchen fixing breakfast. He had a hard time getting back to sleep after the phone rang at three a.m.

"Look at you this morning. How do you feel?" She was facing his left side and didn't see the bruise on the other side of his face.

"Sore, but that's not surprising. How do you want your eggs?"

"Whatever is the easiest but I'm not very hungry yet. I should be doing that not you."

"Why? You've eaten my food before."

"That's not the point. You should take it easy today that's all." She moved around him to pour herself some coffee.

Patrick left the eggs cooking on the range and pretended to get something from the refrigerator by turning away from her. He didn't want her to see that the bruising had encompassed his entire right side of his face. It hurt like hell but he wasn't going to let her know. When she sat back down at the table with coffee in hand he handed the plate of food to her being careful not to show his face.

"Here eat."

"Where's yours?"

"All I want is coffee at the moment. I've been up since five."

"Why? You should have awakened me if you needed something?"

"I didn't and your cell woke me. I couldn't get back to sleep after that."

"Sorry, I thought I had the ringer on low. Oh my word, your face! Patrick does that hurt?" Mariah put her fork down and got an ice pack for him.

"Sit down I don't need that. It's a beauty, isn't it?"

"You're lucky not to be hurt any worse. I'm so sorry Jezebel did that to you."

"It's not her fault really, she wasn't trying to be mean this time she was just frightened. I should have taken more precautions that's all."

"I still think you should be checked out."

"I said no, I'm fine. I'm planning to work out this morning, get some of the soreness out."

"Don't over do it please."

Patrick didn't respond for a time, he sat stirring his coffee and looking out the window to the pasture.

"I know you too well. What's on your mind?" Mariah asks reading his thoughts. Patrick sighs and turns toward her.

"J.P. Does he always call you in the middle of the night?"

Mariah swallowed her coffee. Here it comes she thought. "Not always. But there is a time difference between here and there you know."

"What did he have to say?"

"We talked business."

"Did you tell him where you were?"

"Matter of fact, I did." Patrick pushed his chair away from the table and laughed.

"I bet he didn't like it. What did he say?"

"That's none of your business but he didn't say anything. I remind you that no man owns me. I do what I want to do and when I want to do it. He knows that."

"I wonder how long that will last?"

"What does that mean?"

"Nothing. I think I'll go out to the stables and let the horses out."

"Jim said he would be here to take care of them."

"All I'm going to do is let them out for crying out loud." Patrick pulled on his old boots by the back door and closed the door behind him. Mariah couldn't see but he was smiling behind his back, the thought that she told J.P. about her overnight stay astounded him. He would give just about anything to be a fly on J.P.'s wall when she told him. It had to be eating at him to know or not to know what really was happening.

Mariah took advantage of the time alone and made the call to the Inn to reserve their suite. Patrick came back in just as she was saying thank you and hung up.

"Who was that?"

"Boutique business. When is Jezebel coming back home?"

"Not sure when Jim's planning to get her. I'll go if you want me too?"

"You will not. You need to rest." The phone rang again. Mariah picked it up and handed it to Patrick. "For you."

"Talk to me. Yes, I see. When? Studio B got it. Thanks. Talk to you later."

"What's that about?"

"A movie deal. I have a six a.m. meeting scheduled on Friday. I guess I should go up Thursday night. I might be gone all day."

"You got a new script so soon. That's great. What's it about?"

"It's a remake of an old western film. Same one Charlie has his part in."

"So you two would be working together. You haven't done that before."

"Maybe, we'll see what they negotiate with me. I hate to see them now of all times?"

"Why?"

"My face is still going to be attractive by then." The phone rang again. Patrick answered and this time gave it to Mariah saying it was Margo.

"Yes Margo? He did? No not under the boutique. Tell them to book it under James Dumont. Yes that's right. She started to spell Dumont out. Yes, you have it."

Margo knew she couldn't talk at the moment and understood that Jean Paul was planning to come in town.

"Thanks, can you call the Inn now and get that settled for me? Everything okay there?" Margo assured her it was. "Good, I'm not sure when I'll be home. I'd like to be here when my baby comes home from the vet's. If not lock up. Call me if there are any more questions. Thanks again." Mariah hung up.

"Who's the James Dumont guy?" Patrick was pouring another cup of coffee as he overheard the conversation and sat down at the table.

"He's a business man, wants to see some of my stock."

"I bet! You are such a bad liar. James Dumont is none other than J.P. right?"

"Okay, yes it's him. He's coming in town next week."

"When? Maybe we can have him out."

"We? And you have him out why, just to blow him up?"

"I wouldn't do that, it's too messy. I don't want to have to clean up." Mariah gave him a snarling smile. "Seriously when is the old man coming?"

"He'll be in on Thursday and he's not old for once and for all." That meant that J.P. would be in town when he wasn't. Great, he thought to himself.

It was mid-afternoon when Jim drove up with Jezebel. Mariah was out the front door and waiting beside the trailer before Patrick was sure what was happening. Jim had already opened the trailer doors and was unloading the horse.

The wound on the horse's chest was longer than she remembered but neatly sutured except for where a drain was placed to help reduce the risk of infection setting in. Jezebel was glad to see her; she nuzzled Mariah's neck and sniffed her pocket for a carrot, which she found by the way. Mariah laughed as she handed the carrot to her. She and Patrick walked the horse back into her stall. Jim followed as soon as he unhooked the trailer. The three of them leaned against the fence and watched the horse settle back in.

Mariah had left the ranch later that afternoon when she felt Patrick was doing all right. Nothing else had been mentioned about Jean Paul and she was glad of it.

She spent the next few days organizing her schedule and keeping the boutique in shape for Jean Paul's visit. She wanted everything to be perfect for his arrival and wanted him to be proud of her for what she was doing with his line.

Patrick was in the boutique at least once a day for some kind of reason or another. He had even brought her a rose during one of his visits. Another reason was to bring her some frilly newborn dresses he had seen in one of the shops down the street. She needed to get some baby things but hadn't done it since she was still planning to leave soon after Abigail's birth. She would have to get one of those portable cribs or a bassinet to use while she was here and store it in the apartment when she left. Patrick was trying so hard to win her back by trying to get to her through the baby. She knew that so she kept herself busy even personally waiting on Charlie and Becky who had stopped by to get Becky's boss a birthday present. She wanted to have a free conscious on the time she would be taking off while Jean Paul was there.

Margo didn't appear to be bothered by it. She was just happy that Mariah was looking forward to her rendezvous with Jean Paul but she saw that Mariah's turmoil with Patrick was coming back. After each visit he paid to the boutique she seemed more and more nervous. In fact she overheard Mariah making an appointment with Dr. McKracken. She knew what Sarah McKracken did for a living since she volunteered at the hospital in the children's ward and had seen her name on the medical files. Mariah hadn't said anything to her about Sarah but hopefully she was finding some comfort talking to her. Mariah had too much on her plate to keep going the way she was. She was headed for another spiral if things didn't get under control soon. Any time she could get Mariah out of the boutique she would. She needed to have time to relax, to just be alone with her baby.

Mariah was in a meeting with Ben early Wednesday morning going over inventory and sales strategy when Margo saw him walk in. She quickly finished ringing up the customer she was waiting on and went to greet the Count.

"Count DuMoiese, it is a pleasure to see you again."

"*Mademoiselle* Williams, the pleasure is mine." He took her hand and kissed it.

"We were expecting you tomorrow. Mariah is in a meeting at the moment but I can tell her you're here."

"*Non*, please let her finish. I'm not in any hurry. I plan to be here several days."

"Good, please keep Mariah away from here as much as possible."

"That is my only desire to accomplish this week."

"She's so lucky. I'm jealous." Margo grinned at him and patted him on the back. "Come and let me show you what we have done with your designs."

As Margo and Jean Paul reviewed the new look of the boutique, the other employees gathered around to meet him and to rave on the men's line. Mariah and Ben came downstairs. She could see there were no customers in the store but what were all her employees during huddled in the men's department? She and Ben headed that way.

Jean Paul was hidden from sight when he sat down at the table and everyone gathered around him. He was speaking on how the line had developed and how he had found Edmund and Tré. Mariah stopped short. That wasn't his voice? That couldn't be his voice? Susan saw her approach and tapped her coworkers on the back. They parted and revealed him. He was sitting at the small wrought iron table, a coffee cup beside him. He looked so handsome in his black suit, gray silk shirt and burgundy tie. His hair was styled away from his face revealing the slight gray at his temples. Their eyes met at the same time, he stood up and they met halfway in between.

"Count DuMoiese, you're early." She extended her hand to him and he kissed it, and then bowed to her. A smile ran across his face as he played along with the formalities that Mariah had started.

"I am and I hope it is not an inconvenience. You see I finished my project a day early and couldn't wait to see your lovely boutique. You have out done yourself. I do like the surroundings and the furnishings if you know what I mean?"

Mariah blushed just enough for Margo and Ben to see since they were both standing beside her. Jean Paul had a twinkle in his eyes that Mariah saw.

"Ben, I would like you to meet the owner of the Aristocrat line. Count Jean Paul DuMoiese please meet, Ben Thomas, my manager of your line." Mariah recovered from the blush quickly. Ben shook hands with the Count and they talked a few minutes. The other employees went back to work one by one as customers came in. Ben was in awe to meeting the Count and couldn't wait to call Tracy and tell her.

"Now that we are alone, *mon amour*, I want you right here." Jean Paul pointed in front of him toward the carpet.

"You want me where?" Mariah closed the apartment door and walked around him playfully. "Don't you know by now that I only do what I want?"

"I know exactly what you want right now. Come here you little vixen." He caught her as she circled around him and pulled her close in front of him. His embrace engulfed her so much that she felt she had melted into his body. They were no longer two but one, one mind and one heart.

Mariah and Jean Paul were in and out of the boutique most of the day. Mariah had left several messages for Daphne to call her, which she had not done yet so they decided to hang around until they heard from her. Jean Paul was enjoying meeting the customers and talking with her staff. Martin Gray had come in to purchase some clothing and was pleased to meet Jean Paul. They sat at the table in the back of the boutique and discussed France.

Jean Paul had a way with people; he could converse on any level with anyone and he understood why Mariah needed to stay around the boutique until she heard from New Orleans so he occupied his time visiting with the customers.

Patrick had walked in without Jean Paul noticing him. Mariah was not in sight so he went upstairs. Margo had tried to catch him but couldn't and didn't want to call attention to the situation with Jean Paul so close, so she let him go on up.

He knocked on the closed office door and opened it. She was sitting behind the desk looking over some papers. "Hi, how's things going?" Mariah looked up. She had a strange look on her face he couldn't read. "Am I intruding?" Patrick took the chair in front of the desk and propped his boots on top of it.

"Ah, no not at the moment and get your feet off my desk now. What are you doing here?"

"Came to see you. I missed you. Isn't that all right?"

"Oh. Do you have any other reason? I am expecting a call from New Orleans any time now."

"I won't keep you but just wanted you to know I was thinking about you and that my plans have changed. Charlie and I are leaving tomorrow morning for my meeting. We won't be back until Saturday so how about dinner tonight?"

"Why is Charlie going?"

"The producers want to talk to him about the location shots. So what about dinner? Charlie thought it would be nice for all of us to have dinner together." Before she could answer Jean Paul entered the office.

"*Monsieur* Wainscott, thank you for the invitation to dinner but you see Mariah and I have other plans." Patrick's look of disdain was aimed at Jean Paul. He didn't get up out of the chair. Jean Paul walked around him and to the back of the desk beside Mariah. "Mariah, the call we have been waiting for is here." He reached behind Mariah and punched line two on the phone and spoke to Daphne.

"Patrick, I'm sorry this is the call I was telling you about. We really need to take this. I hope you have a safe trip. By the way your face is looking better every day."

"Oh yes, I do hope you're feeling better after your accident. That is a nasty bruise you have. You must feel lucky you were not bitten by that rattlesnake," Jean Paul stated. "Now if you don't mind we need to conduct business. It is nice to see you again. *Au revoir*." The Count's tone and manner dismissed Patrick like he was a servant and he didn't like it one bit. Jean Paul really didn't mean it when he said it was nice to see him but for Mariah's sake he wanted to appear cordial at least. Patrick was going to say something in return but stopped, it took a lot of self-control to do so.

CHAPTER 11

Mariah put the phone on the intercom system as she waved at Patrick. He sat there for a second or two then decided what was the use. He got up and headed out the door but as he did he heard part of their conversation about damaged trunks. So it wasn't a bogus call after all.

"We wanted to see how many trunks have came in damaged there? I had one last week but this time a garment was damaged, too."

"Most of them are coming in battered or the seal has been broken. The merchandise is okay. What's up with this anyway?" Daphne asks in her southern accent.

"Daphne, this is the Count. I have spoken with my assistant Claude who has been checking into this matter. It is just not the boutique's stock anymore but mine as well that is being vandalized. The problem seems to be arising from the trucking company. We have initiated a security plan. Only a few designated drivers will be allowed to do the run from Pau to Paris. The drivers will be responsible for the trunks until they get on the conveyer at the airport. Airport security will then take over and see the trunks are on the plane safely. I believe the damage is being done in France not in the States. If that doesn't correct the problem then we will change trucking companies. Please keep us posted."

"I will. We just got our fax machine working again. Sorry it took me a while to get back to you but I had car trouble this morning and then the storm took out some power lines in the area so I couldn't call until they were up and working."

"What storm?" asked Mariah.

"We had a good thunderstorm earlier today. Lightning must have struck a power line somewhere close."

"Everything else okay there?"

"Oh yea, just fine. How about there?"

"We had a much bigger profit than I had ever expected on the men's line. If we did this well here I can't wait to install it there."

"Mariah, I think you should slow down a bit and start to relax since it won't be that much longer until the baby comes."

"I think the Count is right Mariah, even though we could handle the extra work I know you would want to oversee it. Wait until the baby comes, then you can travel and get things done the way you want them. We don't really need to make any structural changes, you know we do have that extra room on the side of the shop that we can turn into a separate entrance for men only."

"That's a great idea. Start thinking about that. As soon as I can travel I'll be there and we'll get things started."

"You just don't know how to stop do you? That baby is going to take a lot of your time."

"I'm not doing this alone, you know. All of you will be working your rears off to get this line up and running. So you need to warn everyone including yourself to start getting plenty of rest now. You Cajuns can't keep up with me."

"That's what you think?" The three of them laughed.

"So Jean Paul, do you really think by installing the security measures and possibly changing hauling companies it will be that simple to correct the problem," Mariah asks after she turned off the phone system.

"I don't know. I have a feeling there is more to this than appears at the moment. If it continues then we should make a police report."

"Do you think we should be concerned now?"

"*Non,* not just yet. I can't tell you why the dress was damaged but it still could be just mishandling. The factory personnel are inspecting each trunk twice now by different people and they are signing on it when done. Now, let's see about something that is more important than the trunks."

He stands up from the side chair and helps her to her feet. While they were having the phone conversation his attention was fully on her. He was concerned about her and how much fluid she was retaining since he had seen her last. She looked so swollen; he knew she must be uncomfortable. He led her to the sofa, sat her down beside him, pulled her feet in his lap and started giving her a message, hitting all the pressure points in her feet. Mariah moaned in joy.

"Why Count where on earth did you learn how to do this?"

"I am a man of many talents, *mon amour.* You will just have to wait until little Abigail comes to find out just what talents I do truly possess."

"Is that a promise or a threat?"

"What do you think? I will enjoy showing you what you have never experienced before in your life. You will be lost to me forever, I assure you." The devilish smile on his face made Mariah's heart pump faster, she felt the excitement jump in her lower abdomen and she knew it wasn't the baby moving.

"Oh, Jean Paul, do you think it will ever be so?"

"What ever it takes, *mon amour*, I will see it happens if you truly want it."

"I do, but I just can't seem to get past.."

"Shh.. enough talk." He locked the office door behind him and came back to the sofa.

"Jean Paul, what if Margo needs something?"

"She's a big girl. She can find something on her own." He picked her up and carried her inside the apartment.

Mariah woke nestled in the arms of Jean Paul. She wanted to go back to sleep but she knew she had to get up and be downstairs before any of her crew showed up. She didn't want tongues to wag about them being together last night in the apartment. She hated to wake him but as she sat up in bed trying to clear the fog from her brain he stirred.

"Are you leaving me all ready?"

"Not on your life, but we do have to get moving."

"What time is it anyway?" Jean Paul leaned against the headboard. Mariah never tired of looking at him. She had spent a long time running her fingers through the hair on his chest, safe in his arms and at peace with her world while they watched a movie.

"Seven thirty. My staff will be arriving in forty-five minutes. I'd rather they not know where we spent the night."

"What makes the difference?"

"Just humor me will you? Tonight we shall be at the Inn and no one shall know of our secret mission," Mariah laughed.

"Whatever you say agent number one." Mariah threw a pillow at him as she tried to slip her shoes on but couldn't.

"Don't make fun of me. Damn it."

Jean Paul slipped out of bed and came around in front of her. "Allow me Cinderella." He took her shoes one by one and put them on her feet as gently as he could. Even just getting out of bed her feet were swollen. "*Mon amour*, please don't take this wrong, you are just as beautiful to me as ever, but what does your doctor say about you swelling?"

"Some women retain fluid more than others when pregnant. I guess I'm just one of those. Dr. Miles is watching me very closely since I have other health issues."

"I don't like the sound of that. Are you telling me everything?"

"Everything I know, so far so good. Come on, get ready and let's get some breakfast at the café down the street."

"Jean Paul, have you noticed that blonde hair man across the street? He's been standing on that corner for a long time."

"Maybe he's waiting on a bus?" Jean Paul continued to eat but did look up briefly. He noticed the man just seconds after they were seated in the café. The man was in his twenties, dressed as any other in jeans and leather jacket and wore wire-rimmed glasses. He leaned against a streetlight smoking a cigarette looking in their direction off and on, obviously watching the café or someone in it.

"I don't think so, all the buses have come that are going to come." Just as she had said this, the man stamped out his cigarette and walked down the street. Mariah was glad to see him go since he gave her the jitters for some reason.

"See, he was just waiting for someone who didn't show obviously. Now eat."

It was half past nine when they returned to the boutique. Margo had flagged Mariah down just as soon as they came in the door.

"Doctor Miles' office just called. They want to reschedule your appointment. Said something about the doctor having to go out of town for her mother."

"Thanks, I'll call the office. Right now I'm going upstairs for a minute. Jean Paul, are you coming?" She looked behind her at him. For some reason he was looking out the front windows.

"You go ahead, there is something that caught my eye." He headed out the door and around the corner. He thought he had seen that blonde hair man sitting on the park bench across the street. When the man realized he had been spotted he quickly disappeared around the corner and into an alley. Jean Paul had lost him. He knew there was more to this guy than some joker on the street but the question was what? There was no way he was going to scare Mariah with this but he would have to keep an eye out on things.

She thought it was odd that he would do such a thing but she really didn't have time to find out why. The baby was trying to do somersaults on her bladder at the moment. While upstairs she called Vivian's office and rescheduled for that afternoon. As soon as Mariah hung up the phone the Count entered her office.

"Where have you been?"

"I wanted to take a look at something but decided I didn't want it after all."

Mariah frowned, "I don't understand."

"Nothing to be concerned about my dear. Christmas is coming you know." He tried to pass his behavior off due to some secret gift. "Did you call the doctor's?"

"I have an appointment at four. You can check in the Inn anytime after two so if you want I can meet you there after I get finished."

"You will not. May I go with you?"

"To my O.B. appointment?"

"Oui, we can check in at the Inn afterwards."

"Sure, if you don't mind sitting in a room with a bunch of pregnant ladies looking like balloons with raging hormones."

"Sounds intriguing, *mon amour*."

"Right."

Mariah puttered around the boutique for a while and then came up with the idea of doing some shopping for the baby. The thought had crossed her mind again that she did need to do something about a crib if she didn't get anything else.

Jean Paul didn't hesitate to help her shop for one. He had picked out a beautiful white sleigh crib. It was larger than what Mariah had in mind to use but she could tell he really wanted to get it for Abigail. He mentioned that his mother's favorite winter past time was to hook the horses up and take a ride in the sleigh, snow or no snow. His father had a sleigh modified to be able to take the blades off and replace them with wheels if needed as a gift to his mother. Little Abigail deserved to have a sleigh of her own Jean Paul stated and this was just the beginning of the spoiling. They both agreed on the crib bumper set with the bright colored rainbow design. In spite of Mariah's rebuttal Jean Paul paid for everything and arranged for delivery yet that day. He wanted to help her get it set up and ready to go but first they had an appointment to make and he kept a watchful eye for the blonde man but didn't see him anymore.

Mariah stepped out of the inner office of Doctor Vivian Miles looking for Jean Paul. He wasn't in the waiting room, which was full of pregnant women, so she assumed he must be outside in the corridor. She peaked her head outside the front office door and saw him coming down the hall toward her.

"Everything okay?"

"*Oui*, just needed some fresh air. I'm sorry I concerned you. Are you finished?"

"Yes and no. Come on." She took his hand and led him through the inner doors. "There is someone I want you to meet." The sign on the door read Dr. Vivian Miles. She was standing by the entertainment center/bookcases when they entered.

"Vivian, please meet Count Jean Paul DuMoiese. Count, this is Dr. Miles."

Vivian extended her hand to shake and he in return kissed it. He noticed the wedding ring on her finger.

"*Madame*, I am enchanted to meet you."

"Count DuMoiese, I have heard a lot about you. I am honored. Please have a seat. Mariah would like to show you something." She picked up the VCR tape from the desk and placed it in the machine. "As a matter of practice we tape all the ultrasounds we do in the high risk pregnancies so we can go back and study them if we need to. This is the last one we did for Mariah and Abigail."

"I wanted you to see her." Jean Paul squeezed Mariah's hand and leaned over to her chair and kissed her.

"*Merci beaucoup, mon amour.*" Mariah could tell she had just given him the best gift she could. The look of love and pure pleasure was all over his face.

"Well now, you two watch. I'm going back to my patients. Let Annie know when you're done. See you next week. Call the numbers I gave if you need," Vivian closed the door behind her.

By the time they had arrived back at the boutique the crib had been delivered. Jean Paul immediately went to work setting it up, with the help of some tools that Ben had in his truck. Mariah placed the bumper and sheet set in it and stood back.

Jean Paul wrapped his strong arms around her and held her tight. He kissed her neck. He recognized the delicate perfume, which filled his senses, since he had bought it for her on their first shopping trip together in Paris.

"It's beautiful just like little Abigail."

"Yes, it is." She turned to face him. "Thank you for everything."

"You have nothing to thank me for. I love you and Abigail." They shared a long passionate kiss.

At the Crystal Inn they settled themselves at a corner table in the restaurant. Their salads had just arrived when Mariah saw Sarah McKracken enter the room. She excused herself from the table and greeted Sarah then brought her to their table. Jean Paul wiped his mouth with his napkin and stood up. He had one of his more expensive black suits on and looked magnificent Mariah thought. She didn't feel like dressing up but chose a casual white rayon pant suite with gold accents and gold flats.

"Count Jean Paul DuMoiese, this is a friend of mine Dr. Sarah McKracken. Dr. McKraken, this is Count DuMoiese." The Count greeted her in his usual manner with a kiss on the hand. He noticed she wore a wedding ring.

"Forgive me for asking but are you dinning alone, *Madame?*"

"Well, yes I am. My husband is working late tonight and I didn't feel like staying at home."

"Then you must join us. *Monsieur* another setting please." Jean Paul removed a chair from the next table and placed it at theirs. The waiter moved as fast as he could to accommodate the Count's request.

"He doesn't take no easily does he?" Sarah joked at Mariah and winked at Jean Paul.

"*Non,* not when I can be accompanied at dinner with two beautiful women."

After Sarah had settled herself and ordered she addressed the Count. "Mariah tells me you live in Marseille. I spent a few years in that area myself. My husband's job took us to St.-Etienne."

Mariah listened intently to their conversation about France, joining in when could but she didn't really know all the different cultures and dialects France had. Still though she enjoyed hearing Jean Paul speak with such passion about his country and his wine. During dessert she excused herself from the table. This was the time Jean Paul was hoping for.

"Doctor, since Mariah has left I know what you are to her. I am concerned about her. Is she handling everything all right on her own?"

"Count, with all respect I can't get into that with you but I can mention that the next few weeks is crucial to her. She has set a goal for herself to bring closure to her life before the baby comes. In order for her to do that she must know and feel that she has your support in whatever decision she makes and on how to achieve it."

"She knows that."

"She may know it in her head but in her heart is another story. This may be a very difficult and painful time for her. For you, too, for that matter."

"Doctor, if I read this correctly you are referring to her situation with Wainscott. I am fully aware of what she is going through. I have told her and tried to show her that I will be here for her no matter what. I have asked her to marry me several months ago. I believe that will happen, but I am not a fool. I know she must close the doors on him in order for us to be truly happy as a couple. And I know that if he turns out to be Abigail's father that door won't be locked just closed. Abigail will know him as a father but she will know myself as her father, too. I hope that I have gained enough wisdom in my years to handle this delicate situation. I feel that Mariah has enough love for me to endure this task."

"What you must do is to reassure her that whatever or however she decides to close the doors that you will stand behind her even if it means separation for you two."

Jean Paul sighed and sat back in his chair. He rested his hands in his lap. "I have already reached that conclusion but I don't think that it will come to that. You see, we are so much more than business and romantic partners, our relationship has many facets."

"I'm sure it does."

"I have asked her to be my wife and I will do whatever it takes to make her happy. My prayer is that her journey doesn't cause her so much pain that it makes her ill or harms the baby. Our life will come together I have no doubt about it."

"Count, I think you have the wisdom you spoke of earlier. You are one of a kind."

"I am just a man deeply in love with the most beautiful woman on earth."

"Are you talking about me behind my back?" Mariah stated as she approached the table.

"I am only stating how much I love you and Abigail. This much you know."

Mariah came behind his chair and hugged him. "Yes, I do know. Sarah isn't he wonderful?"

"He sure is, Mariah. He sure is." Jean Paul looked a little embarrassed. Sarah smiled and then glanced at her watch. "Oh my gosh, I'm late. I'm sorry I really do have to go." Jean Paul helped her remove her chair from the table. "Thank you for the lovely visit. Waiter, I'll have my check please."

"*Non*, it is my treat *Madame*." Jean Paul intercepted the check and handed it back to the waiter. "Please apply the check to my account. I have enjoyed our talk, Doctor. I believe Mariah has a friend as well as a doctor in you."

"*Merci beaucoup*," Sarah said. "Mariah, I will see you at our next date. Goodbye dear. Oh by the way, you are looking well."

"Its all because of this wonderful man here." She sat down next to Jean Paul and squeezed his hand.

Mariah and Jean Paul made their way to the lobby elevator outside the restaurant. When the doors opened, they entered talking and holding hands like two kids. Neither one noticed the blonde man standing outside the hotel's front door looking in.

Jean Paul was first to wake up. It was mid morning already to his dismay. He called for room service, ordered breakfast and a newspaper. When he came out of the shower Mariah was awake but still laying in bed. "Good morning, *mon amour*," he said as he dried his hair with a towel.

"Morning? It's more like noon, isn't it? It's feels so good just to lie here and do nothing. I'd like to do this all day."

"And why can't you if that is what you wish?"

"I have the boutique remember?"

"Not today. I have already called Margo and let her know you are not coming in today. She has your cell." Jean Paul crawled in bed beside her dropping his towel that draped around his waist, in the process. Mariah giggled as he took her in his arms.

"What are you thinking?"

"You know what I am thinking, *ma chérie*. He slipped her teddy over her head and they both disappeared under the covers.

The rest of the day was spent in bed eating from continuous room service and watching television. Mariah would doze intermittently in Jean Paul's arms. He would hold her for as long as she needed him too. If Doctor McKracken was right this may be the last time Mariah could really relax and feel safe until she finished her journey. She started to stir and whimper a little the next thing Jean Paul knew Mariah flew up and screamed. She was shaking and crying. He clutched her to his chest and held her stroking her soft hair.

"*Mon amour*, it is just another bad dream. Everything is all right. Shh…"

He slightly rocked her from side to side and whispered in her ear. Finally she stopped crying.

"Jean Paul, I thought you were hurt. I was running to you." He clutched her hands together and placed them over his heart.

"Mariah, listen to me. Feel this? It is my heart beating. Feel this? I am truly alive and well." Her hand in his he moved it under the covers. She remained in his arms without moving. "We are safe, you, I and Abigail." Her sobs were slowing down.

"These dreams are getting so real. I want them to stop."

"*Mon amour*, if I could stop them then I would have weeks ago. It kills me to see you suffer so. Perhaps I know the reason why you are having these dreams."

"What do you mean?"

"Perhaps they stem from your turmoil with Patrick. Perhaps it is time to close the doors."

"Maybe my dreams are from this mess. But how do I move on with my life without hurting someone? I don't have any clue on how to do that. My life is so complicated."

"*Mon amour*, there is no way you can please everybody. The main thing to remember is your goal of what will make you happy. Everyone else's wants doesn't matter."

"Your wants matter to me. You matter to me. Our life matters to me. Doesn't it to you?"

"Of course it does and you know how I feel about you, about us. But unless you can find the path to free you from the past we may be faced with more hills than what we need in our lives."

"I hear what you say but I don't want to do something stupid to hurt us."

"You won't. I will be with you no matter what you do. I love you and Abigail and I promise I will not walk out on you. You have to put the past five years behind you. That is not an easy thing to do. I know I had to do that when Angelena died. It took me a long time to move forward but I am so glad I did otherwise I wouldn't have met you."

"How did you do it? What did you do to close that door?"

Jean Paul sighed, held her closer and kissed the top of her head. "I got closer to my memories until they became me, not just something I was continuing to look at a distance. The past became one with me. When that happened I knew the answer to the big question of what if. "What if" stopped to exist. The question was what now from then on in. What was I going to do now with my life? The answers came naturally at that point."

"So what you are saying is that I should get closer to my memories?"

"Something like that."

"There's one difference..my memories are alive and well here in town with me. Yours weren't. Besides what do I do with the past, with Patrick if he turns out to be Abigail's father?"

"If that is the case then the door won't be entirely locked. You can't for Abigail's sake. She deserves to know her biological father and there will be some bond between you and him because of her, but your issues of "what if" should be resolved for you to move on."

"How do you feel about me getting closer to my past, to Patrick?"

"*Mon amour*, I will not lie to you, I am not fond of the idea. I do not like the prospects of the situation but I will not leave you to the wolves by yourself. I will be here for you now and the future just like I was a few months ago. I hope that in the end the prize will be our life together."

"Oh Jean Paul, how can I hurt you by doing this?" Jean Paul twisted in bed to face her and took her by the shoulders.

"You listen to me right now *mon amour*. You will not hurt me if you choose to do this. We will survive, our love will survive I promise you."

"You mean that don't you?"

"*Oui,* with all my heart. You can trust me, I assure you." He embraces and kisses her. She clutches to him almost afraid to let go in case he would disappear. Mariah's cell rings.

"I know I can. I have to think about things. Oh what now?" She answers it, "Hello."

"Hi, it's me. I just wanted to touch base with you on the birthing classes tonight."

"Hi Becky. You know I forgot about that. Gee, I don't know. Wait a minute." She covered the phone with her hand. "Jean Paul, its Becky. We have a childbirth class tonight at the hospital. I really should attend."

"Then do so, *ma chérie.* "

"Would you want to come?"

"*Moi?*"

"Yes, you. Please come with us. I don't want to be away from you any longer than I need to be. This is our time remember?"

"All right I shall come."

"Becky, we have a escort."

"Charlie said Jean Paul was in town that's why I thought I'd call and make sure you were still going."

"Word does get around doesn't it."

"Actually, I think Patrick told him when they were making their plans. Tell the Count I said hi and I'll see you at the hospital."

"Fine, till then," Mariah hung up.

"Are you sure you want me to come along? Are there men there?" Mariah laughed so hard she had a twinge in her side.

"My dear love, of course, there are men there. For almost every pregnant woman there is a husband, father or whatever. Becky is my coach but with you there tonight I can imagine that you are Abigail's father and the world is right with us. I do love you, you know?"

"I know that *ma chérie.*"

"Hold me, please. I need to feel your strength." Mariah scooted down in bed and in his arms. There was no need or desire to do anything else.

"All right class, before we get started I have a surprise for some lucky significant other in the room. I'm passing around this hat and in it is a piece of paper with bingo on it. That person will be the lucky one," Helen Montgomery smiled as she made her announcement. Her short brown hair framed her face giving it a rounded appearance even though her body was a size six.

"Now who has the word bingo?" Everyone looked at his or her pieces of paper. No one answered. Becky punched Jean Paul a little. He looked at his piece. It was him who had bingo. Mariah was excited. Maybe they were going to get some baby things. "Here, we have it."

"Ah, Mariah. Last week we met Becky but who is your second significant other tonight?"

"Allow me, my dear. I am James Dumont." Mariah and Becky looked at each other but didn't say anything.

"Well, Mr. Dumont, it is very nice to meet you. You are the lucky one tonight. Do you want to know why?" She went behind the desk and pulled out the vest and held it up. "You get to wear this tonight."

"What is that?" Jean Paul asks while eyeing what he thought at first was a bulletproof vest but as Helen turned it around he could see the rounded belly on it.

"This is what we call the baby belly. You see by the end of the class you are going to know how Mariah feels carrying the baby twenty-four hours a day. Come up here and let me help you put it on."

"With all respect, Ms. Montgomery but I .."

"Come on Jea..James I want to see you in it.

"For you, my dear, only for you." He got up from his chair and stood in front of the class. Helen helped him to slip the vest on and tie it in the back. She then took an instant picture of him and handed it to Mariah. She and Becky couldn't help but laugh. They passed the picture around class so everyone could see the look on Jean Paul's face. They all enjoyed it except Jean Paul. Already he could tell how difficult it was for her to move let alone sit. The belly opened his eyes on what she was actually going through carrying the baby and then with the extra baggage with Patrick on top of it, it had to be too much for her to deal with. Whatever she had to do he would hold his feelings in check.

Two hours later Jean Paul was more than ready to unload his belly. He was physically fit in every way but from what he just went through his back ached from trying to get up and down from the floor, lie comfortably and just standing. Helen slipped it off and congratulated him for being the only person to wear the belly for the entire class.

After class was over Jean Paul and Mariah convinced Becky to get a bite to eat with them before heading home. Jean Paul explained to Becky that he sometimes used the fake name of James Dumont and is careful to speak only English just so there would be fewer questions for him to have to answer in spite of his accent.

"Mr. Dumont, your tickets have arrived."

"*Merci*," Jean Paul took the package from the desk clerk.

"Ms. Remmington, you are looking as radiant as ever. I trust everything is to your satisfaction? Oh, by the way you have a message."

"Everything's fine, thank you," Mariah responded to Kent behind the desk. She took the message and looked at it. Margo wanted her to know that everything went well at the shop today. Looking up from her message "What tickets?" she asked Jean Paul on the way up to their suite.

"I have a gift for you. Tomorrow night we shall be attending the Los Angeles Philharmonic."

"Aren't they featuring someone from France? What is his name?" Mariah was tired and laid down on the bed as the Count locked the suite's door behind them.

"André Avantiér. He is a friend of mine. I made a call while you were seeing the doctor."

"You did! I heard the show was sold out months ago."

"With him it usually is. It doesn't hurt to have connections."

"Let me see that. Wow, front balcony left, box seats?"

"The box seats are reserved for guest of the performers."

"I can't wait, this is magnificent!"

"I hoped you would say that. Do you think you will feel like going?"

"I wouldn't dream of not going. You know I enjoy listening to his talent. He makes that violin practically weep." She jumped off the bed and hugged him. Their arms entangled. "You are too wonderful!" His mouth was close to hers, as he looked in her blue eyes, they kissed.

"Now you slip into that little pink number and let us relax. My back is killing me."

"Poor baby, did the belly do you in?" Mariah was speaking in the same soft baby talk voice that a mother would use for an infant.

"Let us say that was a good lesson. If every man would wear one there may be less children born. After a few hours in it nothing seems to work right or is it just my age catching up?"

"I assure you it is not your age." She slipped in the bathroom and changed.

Jean Paul was already relaxing in bed with an old 1955 movie waiting to be turned on. Mariah fell asleep half way into the movie so Jean Paul turned it off. He couldn't help but run the events of the blonde hair man through his mind again. For some reason he felt like he had met the guy before but he couldn't place him and why would he be there in Crystal River. Was he watching them or was it just a coincidence? He wasn't sure what the answers were but he had to keep his guard up for Mariah's sake. If the blonde hair man meant trouble for whatever reason he would have to be squashed like an ant and he would do exactly that if he could.

"Get up sleepy head." Mariah playfully hit Jean Paul with a pillow to wake him. He stirred and opened his sleep-laden eyes.

"What is wrong?"

"Nothing, except you're sleeping too late."

"I was not aware of the time clock this morning. What is on your mind?" He sat up in bed and adjusted the covers. Mariah was already dressed in jeans and a sweatshirt.

"Come on, get up." She took his hand and tried to pull him out of bed.

"Careful, *mon amour*, that probably isn't good for the baby. Just tell me what you have in mind?"

"I want you to meet someone special to me but we have about a half an hour drive and I really want to do this, this morning."

"Why is there such a rush?"

"Because she's stabled at the ranch and I want to get out there before Patrick comes back."

"Oh, you are talking about Jezebel?"

"Yes, now come on. I haven't seen her since she came back from the vets. I want to see how her wound is healing. If you don't get up now then I'll just have to go by myself."

"Very well." Jean Paul slipped out of bed. "Would you mind to get my khaki's out of the drawer, *s'il vous plait*." That was the closest thing he had to dressing casual.

They stopped for breakfast at the hotel's restaurant and then they were on their way to the ranch. Jezebel recognized her footsteps and started prancing around in her stall. Mariah held out a carrot she had brought with her and the horse gladly took it.

"Isn't she a beauty?"

"*Oui*, she is. She seems quiet fond of you."

"Yep, the feeling is mutual. You know Patrick and her just don't get along. At best they tolerate each other."

"I thought I heard a car pull up. I was just out in the back pasture fixing the fence. A couple of the posts fell overnight. How are you, Mariah?" Jim said as he came in through the stable doors. His clothes were covered in dirt.

"I'm fine, Jim. Jean Paul, I would like you to meet, Jim. He helps to take care of the horses."

"Excuse me for not shaking your hand however as you can see I'm afraid I'm pretty dirty." Jim tried to wipe his hands on his clothes but it really didn't work since there wasn't a clean spot to use. "I have heard about you. It's very nice to meet you, Count." Mariah and Jean Paul exchanged glances, they could only guess by whom.

"And you."

"So you're from France?"

"I am."

"It's a beautiful country. I spent a little time there while I was in the war. What part are you from?"

"South of France, a city called Marseille."

"Ah, the Gulf of Lion in the Mediterranean Sea and the oldest city in France. It was too bad the Germans tore up the city during War World II."

"*Oui,* you seem to know the area well."

"You know what I would like to see again is the Church of Notre Dame."

"The architecture of the Church of Notre Dame de la Garde is impressive isn't it? We have many beautiful historical sites that we cherish but my city is like most larger modern cities, there are high rise buildings as well." Jean Paul's voice sounded distant and disconcerting. He was watching how Mariah was brushing the horse's neck over the wooden rail and how Jezebel nuzzled her nose against Mariah's neck in response. Mariah without knowing had a smile the entire time. Jim was carefully watching, too, but not for the same reason as Jean Paul. Jezebel was still a little skittish since she had came home from the vet's but he continued to talk with Jean Paul while they leaned against the stall railings.

"I know what you mean. All those buildings get under my skin, too. I guess that's why I like working out here. So do you live in the city then?"

"*Non,* my estate is outside of Marseille, fifty acres of wooded land mostly but it is my family's estate in Bordeaux that really has my heart. I have a winery. The land and the grapes are unbelievable. They have been good to my family over the generations."

"A man of the land, I like that."

"I hate to break this up but we should be going. I don't really want to be here when Patrick comes back," Mariah said as she replaced the currycomb on the shelf at the far wall of the stable. "Jim, if you don't mind not saying anything about us being here I would appreciate it."

"Don't you worry missy, as far as I am concerned this is still your home and you have every right to be here and do what ever you want without me butting my nose into your business."

Mariah gave him a hug and kiss. "Thanks, I love you, too."

"Count, I hope you enjoy your stay here as much as I have enjoyed our talk." Jim knew who he was and what he was to Mariah even though no one spoke of his title. Patrick had blown off steam about the guy to him when he had first run into the Count. Jim decided he liked the guy anyhow and Mariah did seem to be happy to be with him. She wasn't as stressed out as she had been lately.

Jean Paul nodded, "I, too, have enjoyed our visit."

CHAPTER 12

"Don't you look handsome," Mariah said as she came out of the bathroom. Jean Paul stood in front of the mirror adjusting his tie. He had chosen Mariah's favorite black tuxedo to wear tonight. He turned toward her and a smile spread across his lips.

"I should be remarking on how beautiful you are. I don't believe I have seen that particular gown before now. I will be the envy of all the men tonight. Perhaps I shall need to go armed for your safety."

"I don't think so." The skirt of Mariah's off the shoulder mid length gown was made of yards and yards of flowing deep purple damask. The bodice hugged her like a glove and showing her off, drawing attention from the ever-increasing size of her belly. She had taken the time to French braid her hair giving her neck the appearance of being longer than what it was. She chose to wear the diamond pendant and earrings that Jean Paul had bought for her birthday before she had come back to Crystal River. She sat down on the bed to put her shoes on but before she had the chance to struggle with them Jean Paul knelt down and assisted her with the task. First her right shoe then her left, after he had placed her heel in the shoe his hands traveled up her legs. He felt her ankles, they both were still swollen, then he felt her calves, they moved over her knees and came to rest high up underneath her gown. He leaned toward her and kissed her before she could say or do anything. Her arms went around his neck to counter his weight so she wouldn't fall backwards as he pressed against her. Finally she broke the kiss off.

"As much as I like this Count DuMoiese we had better be going if we are to make the concert."

"I think I would prefer to stay here with you tonight. It will be more fun I promise you."

"Oh no you don't. I'm going to go with or without you. I have always wanted to hear *Monsieur* André Avantiér live."

"Very well, if you insist, we shall go." Jean Paul sighed. He gave Mariah a pouting look, stood up and held out his hand to her to help her up off the bed. The door closed and locked behind them.

Instead of the usher taking them to their balcony he showed them backstage. Waiting for them was André himself. Jean Paul made the introductions between André and Mariah. But what touched Mariah's heart more than anything Jean Paul had arranged for André to dedicate a love song to Mariah from him. It was their song. He hadn't forgotten.

The evening was everything Mariah had hoped it would be. Jean Paul had made it special just like he had told her he would. He wanted to give her something to hold on to after he had left her behind once again until Abigail came. He didn't want to leave her but knew that day was coming. He wanted her with him for every precious second they had. It was then he realized that he needed something to hang on too just as bad as she did. The valet brought the Mercedes to them and he helped Mariah inside. Jean Paul took the keys and started the car. Looking around at the traffic he pulled out.

"So tell me, did you enjoy the concert?"

"You know I did. I don't think I stopped smiling the whole evening. And with you, doing that sweet thing for me. I was so surprised."

"What are you talking about?"

"Having our song dedicated in public."

"Oh that, did you think I had forgotten about that? See this Frenchman never forgets."

"Isn't that suppose to be elephants never forget?"

"*Pardon.* I have been called many things but never an elephant," he laughed.

"And I would have never thought I would get to meet the great André Avantiér. He really is a gentleman. Why didn't you tell me you two have known each other for all these years?"

"You never asked. I have lots of surprises in store for you, *mademoiselle.*"

"It'll be faster if we take the bypass home, we'll miss all the downtown traffic. Turn right here."

Jean Paul could see in spite of the darkness there were a lot of hills and rocks on his left and deep slope of the ground leading to rows of trees and finally the sandy beach of the ocean to his right. The highway was full of curves so he was concentrating on the road. Mariah had leaned her head back against the seat and closed her eyes.

"Are you tired?"

"Some, but it's a good tired. You know what I mean." She opened her eyes and saw that Jean Paul was intently looking behind them in the rearview mirror. "Is something wrong?" She squirmed around in the seat to try to see; there was a car behind them.

"I'm not sure. That car tailgates then backs off. Why don't you sit straight just in case. Are you wearing your belt around the baby the way you should?"

"Yes, of course. Jean Paul you're scaring me."

"I'm sorry, *mon amour*. I'm probably being too cautious." Jean Paul glanced in the mirror just in time to see the car attempt to pass them and backed off again clipping the edge of their back bumper sending a jolt to them. Mariah looked horrified. "Hold on. I'm going to try to get away from him."

Jean Paul rolled down the window and motioned the other car to go around them as he slowed his speed. It was dark so he couldn't tell what color or the make of the car was but just as the car came up beside them the moon gave just enough light that he could see the driver was a blonde hair man. The other car sped up and crossed over in front of them in less than a second. Mariah gasped and braced for the hit. She heard Jean Paul saying *PUTAIN! CON*! He never swore in her presence before. Trying to avoid a head on collision Jean Paul quickly assessed the country side and swerved down the right side of the highway into the trees while the other car kept on going. The Mercedes hit a tree on the front left side and came to rest after hitting another but this time the tree caved in the front left door setting off the airbags and the sound of glass breaking rang in their ears. Jean Paul had managed to miss the trees on Mariah's side. He thanked God for that favor. He could tell Mariah was still in her seat when her airbag collapsed.

"Are you alright?"

"I think so. I'm shaking. I couldn't even scream. I was so scared."

"What about *le bébé*? Any pain?"

"No."

"Give me a minute to get you out." Luckily, he had left the window down, which was the only way he had to exit the car. He came around, helped Mariah out and held her.

"Why do you think they did that?"

"I don't know. He must have been under the influence of something. Do you have your cell with you?" Mariah fumbled for her purse on the floorboard and found the cell phone. She gave it to Jean Paul who called the police. "They are on their way. I want you to get checked out before we go home tonight."

"And what about you. You're bleeding." She touched the laceration he had on his left cheek.

"I am fine. It's just a cut. I hit a tree limb coming out of the car."

"Then why are you holding your left side? Let me see."

"*Mon amour*, I'm fine, but we don't want you to go in labor here."

"I think you took the worst of things. Sit down." She opened the back right door and made him sit. They could hear the sirens.

"I am glad I bought you this car. I don't believe we would have been so lucky in any other. But I am afraid this one may be totaled."

"I don't care about the car, just you."

She started looking underneath his tuxedo coat for any further signs of injury. He winced as her fingers traveled over the side of his torso.

"You two are a couple of lucky people. It took a lot of driving skills to miss all those trees. I don't know if I could have done that well," the police officer told them as he closed his report book. "We've got an all point bulletin out for the car. I'm afraid it's going to be difficult to find unless it's in another accident, we'll keep an eye out anyway. Now let's get you two to the hospital and get checked out."

Jean Paul had a minute to tell the police about his suspicions of the blonde man and his recent sightings while Mariah was being checked over by the ambulance crew. The police said they would make checks on the boutique as often as they could given the circumstances and Jean Paul was sure it didn't hurt by telling them who he actually was and what Mariah was to him. He even thought of hiring a security guard at the boutique after he left but didn't know how to approach Mariah on the subject. The one question the police asked him was did he think this was more than just drunk driving? He told the officer that he did but didn't know how much more. Who or what was the blonde hair man really after Mariah or him and why? Did it have to do with the vandalized trunks? Just like the trunks there wasn't a clear answer just yet. He had three days left to be with her until after the holidays, until after Abigail came. If he knew for sure the man was after him, he would leave immediately and lure him away from Mariah and the baby but there was no evidence to that concept at this point in time. So he was going to do the only thing he could, be with her while he could, make some calls to his security personnel and see what they could find out.

"Mariah! What are you doing here? Everything all right?"

"Hi Becky, so far so good but I'm waiting to see about Jean Paul?"

"What do you mean?" Becky was shaking her head not understanding and noticing Mariah's gown was dirty.

"I've got to sit down." The two went to the corner to talk. Mariah took the seat facing the exam room doors.

"Do you need some water or something?"

"No, I just need to know he's okay."

"Tell me what happened." Becky took Mariah's hands in hers.

"We were coming home from Los Angeles. Jean Paul took me to meet a friend of his that was playing at the Philharmonic. Anyway on the way home some idiot ran us off the road just outside of town."

"Thank God you and the baby are okay. You both are aren't you?"

"Vivian isn't here but the doctor on call is. He said we're just fine but I'm to take it easy for the next day or so and that's what I plan to do. I need to call Margo."

"Honey there will be time for that but how bad is Jean Paul hurt?"

"I don't know. He was driving and the car took the blunt of the blows on his side. His face is cut and he was holding his side. I know he's hurting but he wouldn't show it. He insisted on walking in even though the EMT's wanted a wheelchair for him. Why isn't the doctor coming out?" Mariah stood up and started pacing.

"Ms. Remmington, you can see your friend now." The gray haired man said as he touched her shoulder for reassurance.

"Doctor, how is he?"

"I'd say you two were pretty lucky to come out of the accident as well as you did. Mr. DuMoiese has some bruised ribs but that's all. You can see for yourself." The doctor nodded to the room. Mariah looked over to Becky.

"Go on in, I'll be here when you get out. You'll need a ride home won't you?"

"Thanks Becky." Mariah disappeared into the room to find Jean Paul trying to put his shirt on. "Oh my you're taped up like a mummy."

"I know and I would rather not be."

"Come on, if it's what you need." Mariah was inspecting the tape wrapped around his chest running her hands over it. "Did they put anything under this? Did they at least let you shave."

"It's my chest not my face and no it's all tape."

"OH MY! I don't think I want to be around when this comes off." She tried to hide a grin but couldn't.

"Very funny, you won't be around. I feel I'm bound like a virgin in a chastity belt."

"And how would you know what that feels like?" she laughed. "Seriously how long do you have to wear that?"

"A week or two, depending how good I am on following doctor's orders I believe."

"How about some nursing care starting right now?" Mariah reaches up and kisses him.

"Sorry to interrupt but here's your walking orders. I want both of you to go home and lie around for a couple of days. No work and no hard play. Complete bed rest, understand?"

Jean Paul looked at Mariah with a wide grin and raised his eyebrows in response to the doctor's orders. She punched him on the arm causing him to grimace and hold his ribs.

"Oh, I'm so sorry. I didn't mean to hurt you." She instantly felt bad.

"I'd say he had that coming considering the look that was on his face. You think you hurt now with those ribs just wait until tomorrow. I can tell you fooling around will be the last thing on your mind. I bruised mine a couple of years ago and I know it's no fun."

"This has been some visit. Last night I had to wear the belly all night and now this. My poor body." The doctor made a face.

"He's talking about my child birth class, he was picked to wear the vest."

"I know what you're talking about. That's an uncomfortable thing isn't it? You go home and rest now. You too, get off your feet and call your O.B. immediately if any of those things should occur with the baby."

"Thank you, Becky, for the ride. We appreciate it."

"*Oui, merci beaucoup.*" Jean Paul grunted a little when he scooted out of her car. Mariah took his arm.

"I'm glad that I was there but I am ecstatic that you two have faired as well as you have. I know Charlie will be relieved, too. They didn't come home today as expected but will be back tomorrow. Call me if you need anything."

"I will, Becky, but I think we'll be just fine."

"Forgive us if we don't call. It doesn't mean we don't cherish your friendship but the doctor gave us orders of complete bed rest and that's what I have in mind for both of us," he wrinkled his eyebrows again as he gazed at Mariah.

"Jean Paul you are such a…."

"Ah, ahh, ahhh. Don't say anymore *mon amour.*"

"Go on before you two get in a argument out here. Call me IF you need anything otherwise I'll talk to you in a couple of days." Becky drove off. On their way inside the lobby, Jean Paul couldn't help but look around to see if he could spot the blonde haired man. He had a feeling that the guy was gone at least for now. He closed and locked the door to the world behind them.

"Hi, it's me."

"What's up, we just left each other a hour ago? I'm tired and need to see to the horses."

"I just wanted to let you know that I think Mariah and the baby are okay but…"

"Wait a minute, what are you saying? Something happen?"

"Patrick calm down and let me finish. It seems Mariah and the Count were run off the road last night. Evidently the Mercedes is banged up pretty bad but they came out of it okay." Patrick sat down and let out a breath.

"Oh man. I tried reaching her a few minutes ago but couldn't. She's not answering her cell either."

"That's because she's at the Inn with him. He was driving. We should be thankful for that because if she had been alone I don't think we would have her in as good as shape as she is. It seems that she was just shaken and the baby is okay like I said but the driver's side took the brunt of the trees and impact. The Count is bruised up some but otherwise okay."

"Gee, that's too bad for him."

"Patrick don't say it, that way. Becky said Mariah told her he purposely tried to keep her side of the car from hitting any of trees. He did just that. I talked to Jake at the police station, he confirmed everything. He said he didn't know how they were able to walk away so luckily. We owe him for both Mariah and for having the good sense to buy that car. I want to go down to the yard and see it. Want to come?"

"Not right now. Where's it at?"

"The car is at Smith's. I can wait if you want to go?"

"No man, I have something else to do first, you go ahead."

"If you're planning to go over to the Inn watch your temper will you?"

"I'll talk to you later, thanks for calling." Patrick hung up the phone and headed upstairs to take a shower. The horses would just have to wait until Jim got there. He had to see for himself that she was all right even if she was with HIM.

"Welcome home. Have a nice trip?" Jim greeted Patrick as he was backing out of the driveway. Patrick stopped his black M3 BMW. It looked like rain so he decided to take the Beamer instead of the Shelby, which he had remembered was past due for an oil change and didn't want to drive it until he had that done. That car was his pride and joy.

"Sorry, I haven't done anything to the horses yet. I haven't been home long and Charlie called, said Mariah was in a car accident last night so I'm headed to see her."

"Everyone okay?"

"As far as I know. I'll let you know what I find out."

"Sure go, go." Patrick waved as he headed down the drive.

No one was behind the front desk that Patrick knew so he guessed she might be in the same suite she used all the time. He would start there. He stopped in the gift shop and picked up a mixed bouquet of flowers. Not wanting to wait for the elevator he decided to take the stairs.

Mariah and Jean Paul had just finished with their room service when the knock on the door came.

"Are you expecting somebody?"

"Not I."

"Not I said the wolf to the lamb? I guess I'll get the door."

"Wait! I'll get the door. Come over here and look beautiful in the sunlight." Patrick knocked again. Mariah gave Jean Paul a look but did what she was told. She wasn't sure if he was being silly again like he was when he told her the bed time story of the wolf and the lamb his mother would tell him and his brother when they were small or if he was dead serious. She had heard him make a call home and was discussing the accident with Claude but didn't think a lot about it until now. He cautiously opened the door to see Patrick on the other side.

"Oh, it is you. Can I help you?"

"I came to see Mariah. I know she's in there."

"Patrick, is that you? Come on in." Mariah came around the corner dressed in the light pink dressing gown Jean Paul liked. She looked so beautiful that all Patrick wanted to do was to take her in his arms and hold her, but he stopped himself.

Jean Paul held the door open for him to enter. It was then Patrick noticed the tape Jean Paul had around his chest.

"I heard about the accident. I had to see if you were all right for myself. Here these are for you." He held the flowers out to her. She took them and put them in a pitcher of water.

"Thank you, that's sweet. Come and sit down. We're fine, we're just to take it easy for a few days but that's all. I'm afraid Jean Paul took the prize for the injuries though." She went over to him and placed her hands on his shoulders. He remained sitting in the Queen Anne chair beside the sofa but did reach up to hold her hand. Patrick sat down on the sofa but as he did he was able to glance into the bedroom and saw it was unmade. He had to hold his temper and he knew it. Mariah had filled him in on details with some help from Jean Paul but he knew Charlie was correct. He did owe the Count a thank you from what they were saying.

"Now since you are here and you have pumped us, tell me about your trip." Mariah sat down on the other end of the sofa, pulled her dressing gown around her and propped her bare feet up on a pillow. "Jean Paul could you get him something to drink?" Jean Paul didn't like the fact that he was staying. He could understand why he came but he had his answers now and it was time to go.

"No, I don't need anything to drink," Patrick replied when he saw the Count made no effort to move out of his chair. Mariah saw this, too, but didn't say anything.

"Tell me about your trip. Do you have the part or not?"

"We negotiated and made the deal. We start filming in February but I have some homework to do between now and then."

"You always do. Is it being shot locally?"

"No, it'll be in the bad lands. I've never been there before. I just hope we get to see some of the country during the down time."

"What type of homework do you do for a film?" Jean Paul asked as he adjusted his position in the chair.

"I usually go and look at the site, especially since I prefer to do my own stunts if at all possible and there's going to be plenty with this one."

"So you like the thrill?"

"You might say that but I'm no fool. If I think I can't do something then it gets rewritten or I'll step aside a let someone else do it."

"Who are you trying to fool? That doesn't happen very often and you know it," Mariah chided in. Her dressing gown was sagging a bit at her shoulders revealing the low cut nightgown underneath it.

"I've been thinking about things and since I'm going to be a father I need to change a few things starting with my stunts." Jean Paul tilted his head to the side and raised an eyebrow in response to Patrick's statement but he didn't say anything. Mariah caught his look.

"I'm not discussing the baby Patrick but whatever made you rethink things I'm glad. I always thought you pushed the edge on suicide too often."

"I'm leaving again in a few days. Since we start filming after the holidays I need to check things out and see what's possible and what's not. The best thing is I get to grow my hair longer for the shoot and a beard too."

"Oh that's right it's a western of some sort isn't it?"

"Yep."

"It must be interesting for you a grown man being able to play while he works?" Jean Paul stated as curtly as he could. Patrick wrinkled his forehead at Jean Paul's remark and shook his head.

"Well, you know, they say there's a child in everyone of us that never dies. Why can't a person have some fun while they work. This world is full of people who never have fun or are caught up in some humdrum line of work with no escape. Life is too short to have a job like that. Personally, I prefer to enjoy my work and my life."

"Excuse me gentlemen, please don't get in a argument while I'm gone. Be nice. Patrick, don't take advantage of him while he's hurt." Mariah headed to the bedroom. She felt a twinge of something and wanted to check it out in the bathroom. She closed the bedroom door behind her.

"I do want to thank you for watching out for her last night. I mean keeping her from getting hurt."

"I did what I needed to do. She is my life and my love. I will protect her with every fiber of my soul if necessary." Jean Paul walked to the window and looked out to the street below. Patrick could tell by the way he was moving he was hurting. He made no attempt to put his shirt on which Patrick thought was strange but then thought back to the first time they met, the Count wasn't clothed then either. Patrick tried to ignore his comment about what he felt for Mariah but there was something else in his tone.

"By the way you say that, is there more to the story than what you two are saying?"

"I do not know what you mean, Wainscott?"

"I think you do. Is the accident more serious than what even Mariah knows?" Jean Paul shook his head and turned to face Patrick.

"I think you have what you call an over active imagination. Save it for your movies. *Excusez-moi*, I think I shall check on her."

Jean Paul knocked softly on the bedroom door. There was no answer so he went in and found the bathroom door ajar. He cautiously peered inside and found Mariah standing in front of the mirror crying. "*Mon amour,* what is wrong?" He placed his strong arms around her and gathered her close. She shook her head but didn't say anything at first. They stood facing the mirror, she clung to him, and finally he turned her to face him. Tenderly he caressed her face, wiping her tears away. "*Mon amour*, please talk to me, is something wrong with *le bébé?*"

"I think I may be starting labor. It's too early! Abigail can't come now."

"Come sit down, lets be calm. Let us call your doctor and see what she says." He handed her the phone. Dr. Vivian Miles answered her page almost immediately. Jean Paul sat on the bed beside Mariah not really knowing what to do except to be there.

"This is Doctor Miles, how can I help you?"

"Vivian, this is Mariah Remmington. I think I may be in trouble." The tears started to come again. Jean Paul rubbed her shoulders lightly.

"Tell me what's happening?"

"I just passed my "show". Isn't that the first stage of labor?"

"Any pain or bleeding?"

"No, nothing yet."

"Good, now just passing the cervical mucus doesn't always mean labor right away. I would like to see you in my office in a couple of hours. Can you make it?"

"I will be there. What if in the mean time I go in labor?"

"Then you get yourself down here to the emergency room right away. They will call me if I'm not here. Now stay calm and off your feet until you leave."

"Thank you Vivian." Mariah hung up.

"What did she say?"

"She wants to see me in her office in a couple of hours. I need to get dressed. Oh, Jean Paul is Patrick still here? I don't want him to know anything yet."

"I hope not. Hopefully he has left. I shall call down to the desk and see if the rental has arrived yet?"

"You're not supposed to drive. I'll just take a taxi."

"You will not! I am coming and I AM driving. I am not a invalid and you will not have our *bébé* in a taxi." Jean Paul was buttoning his shirt as he spoke. Mariah had started dressing when he hung up from the desk clerk. They had a rental car ready and waiting.

Patrick didn't know what to do, get mad or start to worry that it had been almost fifteen minutes since they had disappeared into the bedroom. He had just stood up and was toying with the idea of walking on in the bedroom without knocking when Jean Paul came back in the room.

"Ah, you are still here?"

"Yes, I am. I still need to finish my discussion with Mariah. Is everything okay?"

"*Oui*, she is just getting dressed. It takes her a little longer than usual with *le bébé*. She has trouble with her shoes, you know?" Patrick looked at him with a cautious stare. He didn't fully believe what the Count was saying. It was too simple of an explanation and the fact that here stood the Count in front of him fully clothed complete with a tie, the only thing he needed was a dress jacket. His solid gold cuff links were even in place. "Why don't you tell me what you need to say and I will relay it to her? There is no need for you to wait."

"Why are you trying to get rid of me?"

"It is you who has intruded our room, is it not? I think your visit is over."

"Sorry Count but you will not order me around like you do your servants. I am staying until I see Mariah and I finish what I came here to do." Patrick sat down firmly on the sofa. There was no way he was leaving. Mariah entered the room dressed in soft blue slacks and a white pearled blouse. She carried her matching blue flats.

"Could you please help me with these. I can't bend over enough to get them on." She handed the shoes to Jean Paul who was the closest to her. He helped her sit down on the sofa and gently placed the shoes on her swollen feet. Patrick couldn't help but think that her feet and ankles looked more swollen than the last time he saw her.

"Patrick, was there anything else you needed?"

"Is there something going on that you're not telling me?"

"Of course not, why do you ask?"

"Maybe for the fact that you both were in the bedroom for some time and now both of you are fully dressed and seem anxious to get rid of me. I'm not stupid." Patrick paced the floor with his hands crammed deep in his pockets eyeing Mariah and her reaction. She was playing it cool and so was Jean Paul.

"Nonsense. I just need to go to the boutique for a minute. Margo has a delivery she needs help with that's all."

"Is that so? And what about him?"

"Where she goes I go, Wainscott." Jean Paul shrugged his shoulders and took a step toward Patrick as if to challenge a rebuttal from him.

"Patrick, just please tell me what you want to say." Mariah saw the unspoken words between the men. The tension between the two of them was so thick she could cut it with a knife.

"I just wanted to let you know that I'm leaving town again this coming weekend. I'll be gone for a few days but Jim will be over every day for the horses so don't worry about Jezebel. She's healing fine." He knew this was a lame excuse for staying around but it was the best he could come up with.

"I see. Maybe I'll drop by and see her while you're gone." Mariah walked over to him to help usher him out the door that Jean Paul held open.

"Okay- then I'll see you before I leave." Patrick hugged and kissed her. He noticed the look of disdain on the Count's face and it was worth it as he left.

"Count, Mariah would like you to be with her. Could you come on in?" Vivian stood in the inner doorway to her office. He followed her to her office and sat down in the wing chair in front of her desk.

"Is she alright? Is *le bébé* alright?"

"Yes, I think so for the moment but before I get into all that I want to ask you how you are feeling?"

"*Moi?*"

"Yes, you. I understand you did quite a fine job driving the other night. In fact you took the impact of the collision. How are your ribs?"

"I am sore just like the doctor said I would be but otherwise fine thank you. I have to ask- what Mariah is experiencing now- is it the result of the accident?"

"There you are now. Please come on in and let's talk." Vivian motioned to Mariah to take the chair in front of her desk.

"I want you to tell me everything, Vivian. Is my daughter in danger?"

"Not at the moment but here's the deal. As you know, you've lost the mucus plug and that is the onset of labor. However since you have experienced no pain then the best thing that you can do for the time is to be restricted to complete bed rest."

"For how long?"

"Until the baby comes." Mariah showed no expression on her face. Jean Paul knew the next eight weeks were going to be the longest weeks in her life.

"I have a business to run. What if I go straight to bed after work?"

"I'm sorry, Mariah, but that won't due. You see the more you are up and moving around the more risk the baby has and you, too, for getting an infection. We want the baby to develop a little more so if we can keep labor from starting it is for the best."

"But…"

"There will be no buts, *mon amour*. You have always said Margo is capable of running the boutique in your absence. She did all those months you were with me, so she can again. I will see to it Doctor."

"Good. Oh by the way, Mariah that means the stairs either. I don't want you to take any chances."

"No stairs? My apartment has stairs to it. So once I'm there I have to stay?"

"Yes, unless you can stay elsewhere that is more accessible?"

"Other than the Inn but I hate to think of the next eight weeks in a hotel room."

"*Mon amour*, we'll figure something out. Right now we have to follow the doctor's orders. We have to give Abigail every chance we can, *oui*?"

"Of course we will."

Mariah hung up the phone from detailing Margo on the new chain of events. She went to the bathroom to change back into her pajamas. There was no need to stay in street clothes now that she was confined to bed. Jean Paul was already sitting in bed watching television, flipping through the channels. She crawled in beside him.

"What am I to do? How am I going to spend my time?"

"I have been thinking about that, why can't Margo bring you some paper work from time to time?"

"I have already talked to her about that. But what I was talking about is if I can't do stairs then should I even stay in the apartment? I really don't want to stay here at the Inn, but I would have room and maid service when I want it," Mariah laughed.

"I have been thinking about that, too." Jean Paul turned the television off, put his arm around her neck and pulled her close to him.

"So what did you come up with?"

"I DO NOT like the obvious answer at all but there is one place you can go where you can be comfortable and hopefully it will be without stress."

"Where?"

"Home. Your home."

"The RANCH! No, I can't do that."

"Why? You heard Wainscott say he was leaving again and then off and on for a while. Think about it. There is a downstairs bedroom, *oui*?"

"Yes there is and it does face the corral."

"There you have it. You could enjoy your horse through the window. Seriously, though there is another reason I mention this."

"I don't follow?"

"Use this time at the ranch with Wainscott away to see if you can get in touch with your past. Use it to close those doors. Use it as a way for us to become man and wife."

"Jean Paul, I can't do that? It's hard enough for me just to visit there without thinking about the past five years. I just can't do it. Besides I can't hurt you like that?"

"*Mon amour*, I won't lie to you. I don't like the thought of you there but I trust you. I know I'm playing Russian Roulette and it may be me with the gun to my head if in the long run you decide we can't be married but it is a chance I have to take. A chance you have to take. I believe you must confront those demons of the past to bury the past. I don't know of any other way to do so. Can you think of any other?"

"What about when Patrick is there? I just can't be moving around every so often."

"Like I said I trust you- Wainscott, *non*, but you, *oui*." Jean Paul gave her a long passionate kiss, his tongue exploring hers in the process. Finally she broke off for air.

"I have to think about it. Maybe I'll talk to Sarah." Mariah turned the television on and pretended to be interested but in fact her mind wouldn't shut off. What if she did move back in the ranch? It would be free and much more comfortable than the apartment or the Inn. They fell asleep in each other's arms.

The next day Mariah called Doctor Sarah McKracken's office to cancel her appointment explaining to the receptionist what was happening. A few hours later Sarah returned her call.

"You know, Mariah, the Count has a point about moving in the ranch."

"You can't mean that! Patrick and I under the same roof again?"

"It won't be like that all the time. Didn't you say he was going to be gone a lot- working or whatever?"

"Yes, he's leaving this weekend for a few days. Has everyone gone mad? How can I do this to Jean Paul?"

"Mariah dear, it was he that suggested the idea. I think he's strong enough to handle it."

"But am I? You know I'm still attracted to Patrick and I know he is to me."

"Yes, but attraction isn't everything. It's what you feel deep inside that matters," Sarah replied. "It's who your mind and your heart says you can trust and love at the same time. Besides you're in a different place with your pregnancy now. Use it to your advantage. I don't think he's going to force any issues- sexual or personal with you if he thinks the baby is at stake. And as far as you being strong enough I think you are. You can handle it and besides I'm only a phone call away. I'll be there if you need me."

Jean Paul entered the bedroom from their suite's living room. He had just concluded a call from Claude. The search for the identity of the blonde haired man was a bust and there were no new developments concerning the trunks either.

"Who called?"

"Sarah. I cancelled my appointment with her since I'm stuck in this bed." She pushed her lips into a pout. "I can't even have any fun now." Jean Paul gently climbed into bed along side of her and kissed her.

"*Mon amour*, you couldn't have fun before."

"Who says?"

"Little Abigail says so. Don't fret too much. I will make all your dreams come true when the time is right. I promise you." He kissed her again. "So tell me, what does *Madame* McKracken have to say about all this?"

"I told her about your idea." Jean Paul tilted his head to the side but let her continue. "She said she thought it would be a way to break the walls down. The question she raised was am I willing to try knowing I could be breaking us down in the process?"

"And?"

"If I do this and if Patrick agrees, I promise I will do my best to bring the past to an end. I don't want to stay in this limbo. It's not good for me and it won't be good for Abigail or you for the matter. If he agrees to my terms then I will try."

"Are you sure you want to? The more I think about this, the more I'm regretting the suggestion. I don't want you to feel that I'm pressuring you in anyway. I'd prefer you with me, safe and sound, where you can be waited on hand and foot."

"I know and I love you for it but I've needed to do this for some weeks now. I just didn't know how until now. I have to determine what is keeping me in this place. Is it my feelings for the last five years or is it the attachments in my life?"

"You know the door to your past will never be totally closed if it turns out Wainscott is Abigail's father?"

"Yes, you have said that before but perhaps the door can be closed tighter than it is now. Jean Paul, I will always have some feelings for Patrick especially if he is Abigail's father. We have discussed that all ready. My problem is identifying those feelings and putting all the other feelings I have into some simple little tied up box labeled whatever. I need to figure all this out before Abigail comes."

"Don't push yourself too hard in the process." He scooted off the bed and changed out of his black velvet robe into street clothes. Mariah watched waiting for some comment. None came and then it was too much for her.

"Where are you going? That's no fair."

"It's a surprise, *mon amour*. I'll be back soon. I do love every inch of you."

He kissed her and let his hand roam over her enlarging breast. There was no mistaking it the baby's birth was getting nearer.

Since he had left there was nothing for Mariah to do so she thought she might as well try to reach Patrick. If she was going to move in the ranch he had better know it. There was no answer at the house so she tried his cell and found it wasn't switched on.

"Hi sweet cakes, how are you?"

"What do you want, Patrick?" Margo looked up from behind Mariah's desk where she sat doing invoices. Now that Mariah was off duty her workload had increased again and she didn't want to let anything get behind. There would be no catching up.

"That's a fine hello. What are you doing up here? Where is Mariah?"

"She's not here."

"I see, so how long is the nobleman staying?"

"It's none of my business and none of yours, either." Margo didn't attempt to stop working.

Patrick strode into the apartment. Nothing out of place there, in fact it didn't even look as if she had ever been there. This gave him an eerie feeling that something wasn't the way it should be. He felt the urgency to find her and then what? He didn't know but what he did know was every minute that over stuffed Frenchman was in town she was pulling further and further away from him.

"Will you get out of there? You have nothing in there to concern yourself with." Patrick stepped back in the office and sat down on the leather sofa. Margo gave him an evil look.

"What?"

"Why don't you just leave? I have plenty of work to do and I don't need interruptions from the likes of you."

"Is she planning to come in today?"

"No…" The phone rang. Margo picked it up, she gestured to Patrick to head out the door but he didn't move. She stuck her tongue out at him and he just laughed. "Hello…Oh, hi. How are you?" Margo hadn't forgotten that Patrick was still there and listening. She had to be careful of what she said.

"So far we're fine." Mariah stroked the baby. "Listen, I need another favor but I promise this won't take any more of your time."

"Sure what?"

"If you see Patrick, tell him I need to see him as soon as possible."

"Are you sure?"

"Yes, why do you ask?"

"If you're sure? You can do that yourself." She handed the phone to him. He pointed to himself and took the phone after Margo nodded.

By the time Jean Paul returned with a feast for a king, flowers, and piles of vintage romance movies Patrick was standing at the door of their suite ready to knock.

"What do you want?" Jean Paul's voice was a low gruff of annoyance.

"For your information Mariah requested to see me, so here I am." Jean Paul placed the key card into the slot and drove the lock back. Patrick could see this took him off guard but followed the Count inside.

"Wait here." Jean Paul disappeared inside the bedroom and closed the door. After a few minutes he stepped out. "She's in here." Patrick frowned but didn't say anything, he just walked past the Count and found her sitting in bed.

"What? Have you become the lady of leisure now."

"That's not even funny. Jean Paul could you please get me a some water?" Her throat was extremely dry. Patrick noticed that she didn't even attempt to get it herself and that the Count was ready to accommodate her every need. Jean Paul handed her the water and she drank deeply spilling a little on her bed jacket. He handed her a cloth napkin and she dabbed at the spill. They all knew she was stalling. Patrick stood at the foot of the bed and watched without saying anything giving her time to gather what nerve she needed.

"Do you require anything else, *mon amour*?" He kissed her fully on the lips. Patrick's feathers started to ruffle but he soothed them down by telling himself that this was the reaction the Count wanted and expected of him. Patrick sat down on the foot of the bed and the Count in the chair beside it facing Patrick. He crossed his legs and folded his hands around her left hand. There was no doubt about it in Patrick's mind, there was a something serious going on and it concerned Mariah and the baby.

"Nothing, thank you," she said and smiled at Jean Paul.

He nodded and smiled back, "Go ahead, *mon amour*."

"Mariah, what's going on? Why do you need to see me? It's the baby isn't it? What's wrong with our daughter?"

"Perhaps Wainscott if you would stop talking so Mariah can get a word in you would have your answers quicker." Jean Paul stepped in when Patrick's voice started to rise with excitement. Patrick and Mariah both looked over at him. Jean Paul merely shrugged his shoulders.

"Patrick, why I need to speak with you concerns the baby. She's fine but there's some special circumstances that has come about."

"The accident the other night?" His heart began to race.

"Maybe, we don't know. This is so hard for me to ask and I don't even know if I'm going to be able to go through with this."

"Mariah, just ask me." He took her hands in his and waited, he saw how she was struggling to form the right sentences.

"I'm confined to bed for the next eight weeks."

"What's happened."

"I've started to dilate. If I'm on my feet there's a risk to the baby and myself and possibly early labor. Of course I don't want that so I have to do whatever I can to keep it from happening. I can't stay at the apartment because I'm not suppose to do steps and I don't want to stay here for the next eight weeks."

"Okay, I'm with you so far. So what is your plan? I assume you have one?"

"We thought that with you planning to be gone so much over the next few weeks that maybe I can use the downstairs guest room at the ranch?"

"We?"

"Yes, it was actually Jean Paul's idea since the house still has my name on it. This way I can watch the horses when they're outside."

"It is just you moving in isn't it, Mariah?" He glances at Jean Paul who showed no expression on his face.

"Of course. Jean Paul will help me move out there before he leaves town."

"And when will that be?" Patrick turned to face the Count. Jean Paul sat in the chair and didn't move. It was as if he was looking down on Patrick.

"Day after tomorrow I'm afraid. You didn't answer my question, can I use the guest bedroom or not?"

"Of course you can. The ranch is your home and I don't have to keep saying that." Patrick's heart was leaping for joy, she was coming home even if it was under these circumstances. Now if he could keep her there that was the other side of the coin.

"Thank you. If you don't mind I think I'll just take a short nap. All of this laying around is making me tired. Jean Paul can dinner wait till later?"

"Whatever you want, *mon amour*. I'm yours for the next thirty six hours."

He ushered Patrick out of their bedroom but just as he was about to leave Jean Paul took him by the arm. This was a move that Patrick hated and immediately jerked his arm out of the Count's grip. He turned to face the Count, there wasn't any more than eight inches between them.

"Don't ever do that to me again. I've refrained from any physical violence for Mariah's sake but you're pushing me too far."

"You do not intimidate me, Wainscott. I assure you I can out battle you anytime, any method."

"Is that a challenge?"

"*Non*, it is a promise and so is this. If you even harm the slightest hair on her head, if you hurt her emotionally or physically in any way whatsoever I promise I will hunt you down and hang you up by your entrails to dry and shrivel up. Do you understand me?"

"May the best man win," Patrick laughed. "And I intend to be that man, I WILL win her back."

CHAPTER 13

Patrick had spent the rest of the day in town, picking up groceries and whatever he thought Mariah might need while he was gone. He didn't like the idea of her being out at the ranch by herself and pregnant but Jim would be around for awhile each day. He knew she could get help from him if she would just ask. Maybe he could get Betty to come out, too, Patrick thought to himself as he rang the doorbell.

Becky answered dressed in her pajamas, robe and slippers holding a box of tissues.

"Oh my, you don't look so hot?"

"Thanks a lot Patrick! Did you come over here to insult me because if you did I'm in no mood to take it so go home?"

"Sorry, I didn't mean it like that. You need anything- like chicken soup or something? I have some out in the car."

"No, come on in will you." She headed in the living room. They had painted and spruced up the place a bit since the last time he was there. A woman's touch always made a house a home he thought. "I've got to sit down." Becky stretched out on the sofa wiping her nose. Patrick found the new recliner to his liking.

"I like what you've done to the place." Becky nodded. "Is Charlie around?"

"He'll be back in a minute. I sent him to the store for some ice cream."

"Ice cream?"

"Don't you have a comfort food you want when you're sick?"

"Never thought about it. Charlie didn't say anything to me about you being sick."

"I didn't tell him. I woke up with it yesterday. I hope I'll feel better by Friday when we have the baby classes."

"Better call Mariah first, I'm not sure what she's going to do about that now."

"What do you mean?"

"She's bed fast now…"

"Hi, what brings you by?" Charlie asked as he came into the room. He handed Becky the carton of ice cream and a spoon.

285

"Get the lady a bowl man, not the whole carton."

"Why? It's butter pecan and he doesn't like it, so it's all mine anyway." Becky settled down to the task of eating the ice cream and wiping her nose.

"So who is bed fast?" Charlie sat on the sofa and put his arm around Becky.

"Mariah. Evidently there's a chance that she could start early labor if she doesn't stay in bed. Something about decreasing the risk of infection to her and the baby, I don't have all the details.

"Oh my, I know how tough that's going to be for her. Is she staying at the apartment?"

"No, right now that over blown Frenchman is still in town. They're both at the Inn yet, but here is the good news. She's moving back to the ranch in a couple of days."

"She's what!"

"Yep, can you believe it? She can't do stairs so the apartment is out of the question and she doesn't want to spend the next eight weeks in a hotel room so she chose to come home. The bedroom downstairs faces the corral so she can relax and watch Jezebel."

"Speaking of that your face looks almost normal since the last time I saw you." Becky stated between mouthfuls of ice cream.

"I'm warning you buddy, don't read too much into this move. I think Jean Paul is still a very formidable person in her life. I don't think he'll just back away."

"I know he won't given the fact that he's asked her to ...." Becky suddenly realized she almost blurted out what Mariah didn't want Patrick to know just yet.

"What were you going to say, Becky?"

"Nothing, nothing of much importance. I just was commenting on... him asking her to join his style show in the spring. That's all. Excuse me I need to go upstairs for a minute." Charlie didn't believe her any more than Patrick did. The two of them looked at each other while she left the room.

"Do you know what she was referring to?"

"No man, I don't. You want something to drink?" Charlie got up to pour himself a glass of wine. Since he and Becky had tried the Count's label he had chosen not to use any other brand.

"No. I tell you now that I seem to have this chance to make things better between us, I'm going to try like hell to keep her with me after the baby comes."

"Here, try this anyway." Charlie hands him a small sample of the wine. Patrick tastes it. "Like it?"

"It's good." He wasn't concerned about the wine but the thought crossed his mind that Mariah would like it when she could drink it of course. "What kind is it?"

"It's imported from France."

"Oh, it's HIS label. Thanks a lot traitor." Patrick sat the glass on the sideboard. I had better go and get those groceries home. Look in on Mariah while I'm gone. I'm worried about her being out there alone and so close to her due date."

"Of course, and I know Becky will too. She'll be fine." He walked Patrick to his car and stood in the driveway while he drove off.

"Is he gone?" Becky asked when she saw Charlie come inside.

"Yes, what was all that about? Why did you just disappear like that?"

"I didn't want to say anything more to get myself in trouble so I left." She was putting the lid back on the ice cream and placed it in the freezer. Charlie pinned her to the kitchen cabinet.

"You're not leaving this time. I want to know what's going on."

"I can't tell you anything. I promised Mariah I wouldn't say anything to Patrick and if I told you, you would tell him."

"I don't tell him everything I know. I have a pretty good idea of what you were about to declare in there. The Count has asked her to marry him hasn't he?"

"I didn't tell you remember that. And don't you say a word to Patrick about it either. He asked her before she came back here. You should see the size of that diamond! It's bigger than Buckingham Palace."

"I knew there was a lot more to all this than what she wanted everyone to know. I won't say a word but what do you think will happen?"

"I don't know except that I know she's torn up about how things were left between she and Patrick and yet she wants to move on with her life. I think she's moving back to the ranch to help her make those decisions about her life and what directions to take with it." Charlie sat down at the table and pulled Becky to his lap.

"You really think so?" Charlie kept his arms around her waist and was quiet for a few seconds. "You know it makes sense, you may be right."

"I'll call her in a couple of days after Jean Paul leaves. Speaking of that you should have seen him at the class the other night. He had to wear that baby vest through the entire meeting. I think he would do anything for her and the baby no matter what it was."

"I get that impression too." He paused, "Would you mind being without Barbara for a few weeks?"

"Why?"

"I thought with Mariah being out at the ranch confined to bed that maybe she could use Barbara more than we can."

"That's a good idea. I can keep house and you can help with the rest of the chores."

The next couple of days Jean Paul had kept his promise to her. He had been her constant companion fulfilling her every wish. They spent their time eating, playing cards, conducting business over the phone, watching the stack of movies that he had brought in and lying in each others arms surrounded by candlelight even during the day. As a surprise to her he created a fantasy world in their suite. He brought in silk trees and placed them around the bed to give the effect they were sleeping in the jungle treetops. He pinned glow in the dark stars to the ceiling over the bed, inserted a cassette tape of jungle sounds and closed the drapes to block out the light. He even lit candles throughout the room to give it a romantic feel. Mariah loved it but she knew he was leaving in a few hours. She had sent him to the boutique to get her clothes and a few other things she didn't want to be away from for very long including the small lock box in the safe. In the meantime, she had phoned Margo and instructed her to give it to him.

They had only a few hours before he was to leave so she got up and dressed while he was gone. What was she going to do with him being gone again? How was she going to get through all of this without him so close to her? Could she stay at the ranch and was it really going to help her come to some conclusion about her life? She was terrified that she could be making a bad step here and it would cost her Jean Paul in the end. Was she testing their relationship too much?"

"You're dressed," he said as he laid her belongings on the bed. "I left your clothes in the car." He started to take the stars down and pack up the trees.

"What are you doing?" She asks while she tried to put on her shoes.

"We're not leaving these things. I'm putting them up in your room so you are reminded of me every single minute of the day and night."

"I don't need reminders of you. I could never forget you. I love you." She kissed Jean Paul as he knelt down to help her with her shoes.

"*Mon amour*, you shall be mine and very soon. Remember my words." He gently pushed her down on the bed and was over top of her locking his strong arms so he wouldn't crush her with his weight. He kissed her passionately. This would be their last few private moments for some time and he wanted every second of it to be filled with her, his senses filled with her and hers with him.

On the way out to the ranch Mariah remarked that Charlie had called earlier and said that Barbara would be very glad to come out daily and help Mariah with whatever she needed, even if Patrick was there. Jean Paul was thankful for Barbara's willingness to help and he made a mental note to pay her well for her efforts.

By the time they reached the ranch Barbara was already there to help Mariah get settled in. Jean Paul carried her two suitcases to the door and rang the bell. Patrick answered and showed them inside. He noticed the trees in the car.

"Here make yourself useful." Jean Paul handed the suitcases to Patrick and headed back out to the car. He then carried the trees in two by two and went straight into the guest room. Patrick wondered how he knew where it was. It was like the Count had been in his house before. He stood in the doorway of the bedroom with his arms crossed against his chest and watched while Jean Paul set the jungle scene up but only after he insisted on tucking Mariah in bed. She told Jean Paul where she wanted everything and he did it. Patrick couldn't stand the sight of the man any longer and ventured into the kitchen to check on the dinner he had in the oven.

Jean Paul had decided he liked Barbara right a way. She was like the hovering mother type and that was what he wanted for Mariah. He, Mariah and Barbara sat on the bed talking and even laughing occasionally when Patrick peaked in every once in a while. It was funny how he suddenly felt like an intruder in his own home, like he didn't have any right joining in the group and how he resented it all. He saw Jean Paul hand Barbara an envelope. She opened it and her mouth dropped opened.

"Oh no, I can't accept this sir."

"But you must. It is a present of my gratitude for you willingness to spend your time out here taking care of *mon amour*."

"Your what?"

"*Mon amour* means my love in French, Barbara."

"Of course, I took Spanish in my younger days. But really Charlie is paying me, instead of me working at his house; I'm going to be here doing some meaningful work. Helping you and God to get this baby here when she's due is the most important task I've had in a long time. Charlie really doesn't need me."

"And it is God's work indeed, but nonetheless take this present. Think of it as a bonus if you need to."

"You might as well accept it, Barbara. I know his mood and you won't win."

"But I don't need this much money."

Mariah took Barbara's hand in hers. "We just want to show you how much it means for you to be here with me. Now put that money away and go home for today. There is nothing you can do for me with this big guy here." She leaned over and kissed Jean Paul.

"Then if you don't mind I think I'll put some of this money to use at the homeless shelter where I volunteer."

"Not at all, after all that is a worthy cause," he said smiling.

Jean Paul's cell phone rang. "I see. All right you take care of the flight plan and I'll see you when I get there. Oh Mariah wants to speak with you." He handed the phone to her when she motioned for it.

"Hello Alec, I hope you have enjoyed your vacation with your family?"

"Yes, I have. How are you doing?"

"Too much has happened in the past few days. I'm sure the Count will explain to you but I do hate to see you take him away from me."

"I'm sorry. I don't know what to say to that."

"I know it's not your fault. It's not his but will you please take care of him and see he gets home safely?"

"You got it beautiful lady." Jean Paul brushed the tear away from her eye and he took the phone.

"Alec, I'll see you there. *Au revoir*." He disconnected the phone. "He shall be at the airport in an hour." Jean Paul turned to Barbara; "*Madame*, would you mind leaving us alone. My time is near to be off and I want to gaze upon this wonderful lady for as long as I can."

"Not all sir, I think I'll be off now myself. I'll see you tomorrow morning. Now be good young lady and stay in bed." Barbara touched Mariah's shoulder. Jean Paul stood up and kissed Barbara's hand before she left the room. Patrick walked her out to the car. He really didn't feel the need for her to be there when he was but Barbara told him that was what she was getting paid to do, and well for that matter, so that was exactly what she was going to do.

The door to Mariah's bedroom was closed when he came back in. How he wanted to kick it in and interrupt whatever was going on in there but he resisted the urge. If he did it would mean for sure that she wouldn't stay and he would loose his chance to make her happy once again. So he sat on the sofa and waited until the door opened. He heard Jean Paul tell Mariah not to worry that whatever decision she made he would still be there for her and for as long as she needed him. Patrick saw him kiss her and it wasn't just a peck on the lips either. She responded hungrily and Patrick saw that, too. He felt ashamed that he saw what was going on but he felt more ashamed that the feelings that were stirring in his gut were almost more than he could handle. He wanted to be the one kissing her and he wanted her to be kissing him back that way NOT the Count. Patrick watched as the Count tied his burgundy tie in front of the dresser mirror and then put his jacket on. The outline of the tape on his body showed briefly under his gray shirt. It served as a reminder to Patrick that if it weren't for that man perhaps Mariah and the baby, his baby wouldn't be alive today.

It was so hard leaving her behind. He paused at the bedroom door and blew her another kiss. She blew one back. This may be the last time he would see her as his if she chose her past life. The sick feeling in his gut was stronger than ever. Was he strong enough to handle this? Was he strong enough to stand firm for her?

"Take care of yourself. I want you to call me as soon as you get home. Please?"

"But of course, *mon amour*. I love you! Remember that." Jean Paul disappeared out of her sight. She heard the front door open and close without any word. She closed her eyes on the tears that were starting to fall. Her demons had to be fought if she hoped to have a life of any type. It had to come to an end now.

Patrick was waiting by Jean Paul's rental. He looked up from his boots toward the house as Jean Paul closed the front door to his home.

"At least you are kind enough to wait out here while we said our goodbyes." Jean Paul took off his jacket and tossed it in the back seat of the car. Again his taped ribs showed through his shirt. "I assume you have something to say or you wouldn't be out here." His manner was an icy one.

"Neither one of us like each other so I'm not even going to try to pretend but Charlie and I appreciate how you saved Mariah and the baby the other night," Patrick looked him in the eyes as he replied.

"She is my life and I am hers," Jean Paul's voice held a certain tone but Patrick couldn't distinguish it between possession or a warning or maybe some of both. He got in the car and started the engine. "Do you mind getting your body off of my car? My jet is waiting." Patrick straightened up from leaning on the car and dug his fisted hands deep into the pockets of his jeans. "Remember my promise, Wainscott."

"Oh, the one where you're going to hang me up to dry. Well, I have no intentions of hurting her. In fact I'm going to make her deliriously happy so much that she'll want to stay."

"We will see." Jean Paul drove away in the rented Mercedes. His heart was breaking already. He wanted to hold her so badly.

Patrick knocked softly on Mariah's door. She answered, "Come in."

"Hi, do you need anything?" He sat on edge of the bed and held her hand.

"No I'm fine."

"Dinner is almost done. Are you hungry?"

"Not really. I think I'll just take a nap before that." She slid down in bed and turned to the window. She saw Jezebel running in the corral and smiled before she closed her eyes. Patrick sighed and left the room; this was going to be hard.

Mariah screamed out. Patrick dropped the glass bowl he had in his hand, it fell to the floor and shattered. Within a second he was in her room and holding her.

"What is it?"

"The dream, it happened again. I was running and the baby was crying. Then suddenly she was gone and my whole life changed."

"Shh. Don't cry. It was just a dream. Everything is going to be okay. Our baby is going to be fine." As he held her tight he could feel her heart race. His was chasing right behind hers. They sat on the bed for quite some time just holding each other.

"Are you okay now?" Mariah nodded, the tears had stopped. "I need to clean up the kitchen floor. There's glass all over it along with the salad. Dinner will have to be without it."

"Sorry."

"Don't be silly. You couldn't help it."

Afterwards, Patrick gathered her tray up and took in the kitchen. He came back in the bedroom and found her taking her insulin. He shook his head and grimaced. "Does that hurt?"

"You get used to it. I can't wait for the day when I don't have to do this anymore."

"You need anything? I thought maybe we could sit together tonight. Watch some television or something."

"I really just want to be alone if you don't mind. I don't want to put you out and I thank you for letting me come back and for letting Jean Paul do this room."

"First of all, you are not putting me out, second this is your home, too, and as far as the room there's nothing damaged. So if it makes you happy then it's fine even though it has HIS signature all over it. I could bunk in here with you tonight just in case you need something."

"No you don't. I want you upstairs in your own room. I'll be fine."

"That's what I thought you'd say so I bought these." He pulled a pair of walkie talkies out of the night stand and handed one to her. "If you need anything just push this button and talk. I'll be here in a flash like superman."

"Thank you. Good night." She was anxious to get rid of him. Jean Paul should be calling soon she thought. Right on cue her cell rang, she was right, it was he. Patrick knew who was on the other end but he didn't say anything He just left.

"Good morning, sweetheart. How did you sleep?"

"I think that once I got to sleep that was it." She was coming out of the attached bathroom from taking a shower. The towel was wrapped tightly around her, another around her hair.

"Should you be up?"

"Sure I can bathe and I can even go to Vivian's office," she said in a manner that Patrick wasn't sure if she was kidding or serious. So he let the comment go.

"Are you ready for breakfast?"

"I'm so hungry I could eat anything you put out in front of me. But listen you don't have to cook for me."

"I'm cooking for me, I live here, too. I'll bring it in. Get back in bed before you get yourself in trouble."

Mariah dressed in her silk pajamas and went back to bed. Patrick had set up a small table at the side of the bed on which he placed his tray after delivering Mariah's to her. He had even brought in the coffee pot.

"You don't have to eat with me if you don't want."

"Well, I do and I will. You know I hate eating alone. Besides we can sit here and watch Jim work the horses just like in the kitchen. Oh, by the way, did I tell you that I made a deal with that guy from Kentucky on stud service for Cosmos Comet?"

"No you didn't mention it."

"We're expecting the mare tomorrow. I wasn't going to breed him but this Strakes guy got word of his line and offered quite a deal to use him. You know me I couldn't pass it up. His name is Brent Strakes so if he calls you know what it's about and can take a message if I'm not here."

"Sure, but doesn't the stallion usually go to the mare?"

"He's coming through the area from a show or something. The horse is with him so he's dropping her off for a week or so."

"Look, Jim's back and there's my beautiful baby Jezebel."

"Yea right." Mariah playfully hit him with a throw pillow on the side of his face. "Ouch, that hurt. What did I do to deserve that?"

"You know what. Is your face still sore from the accident in the barn?"

"It's okay. I guess I had better get these dishes out of here. Barbara should be coming soon. You know you really don't need her while I'm here. I like taking care of you."

"I know and that's why I need her here."

Mariah fell into a pattern at the ranch. She tried not to bother Barbara too much. It was really hard for her not to be self-sufficient. A lot of the time Barbara just sat with her and talked. There was not a lot for her to do since Patrick was still around. He did make a comment to Mariah that it was nice not having to eat his cooking all the time, let alone some of the housework that she took upon herself to do for them. Barbara tried to make herself disappear when Patrick and Mariah were together. She knew their history since she had kept house for Charlie for many years but she also knew that Mariah seemed troubled. She would hardly come out of her room, not even to sit on the sofa in the living room when Charlie and Becky came over or anyone else for that matter.

"Come in," Mariah answered the knock on her door.

"Hi sweetheart. How ya doing?" Charlie peered inside to see if she was dressed before he entered the room.

"It's okay, I'm dressed." She laid her book down beside her on the bed. Charlie sat down on the foot of the bed after kissing her on the cheek.

"Why don't you come out and join us. Becky's out there and wants to see you."

"She can come in here. I'd like to see her, too, but I'd rather not go out there."

"Why? Patrick says you stay in here most of the time. Didn't you tell Barbara that the doctor said you could move around a bit, as long as you don't over do it?"

"I know what Vivian said. I'm just uncomfortable intruding on his space."

"That's silly. This is your house, too."

"I'm not so sure of that Charlie. I don't know what I was thinking letting Jean Paul talk me into staying here. I really think I would have been better off staying at the apartment and making do."

"Sweetheart, this is temporary unless you want it to be something else."

"I don't know what I want. That's the problem isn't it? I guess that's why I'm here."

"Barbara taking care of you all right?"

"Yes, of course. She's a jewel and I love her but I'm afraid I'm not using her much."

"You will as soon as Patrick leaves in a couple of days. You sure you won't come on out?"

"Sorry, this is my space."

"Okay, I'll send Becky in."

"So how's the lady of leisure?"

"Come here, Becky." Mariah held her arms out for a hug and Becky gave her one then sat down in the chair by the bed.

"Listening to tapes, huh. What kind? Are they baby tapes?"

"Not exactly. Listen." Mariah put a cassette in the player and held the headphones out to Becky while turning it on. Becky took them. She heard the sounds of the jungle and smiled.

"Oh, by the way, we heard about your room. It's pretty cool and then this. It's awesome." She started to take the headphones off when Mariah fast-forwards the tape.

"Wait, not yet. Listen." Becky heard Jean Paul's voice coming through the wire. He was talking about their life together, his love for her and the baby, what Paris is like at Christmas, and how he wished he could show it to her and how he would next year and so on. Becky took off the headphones and grinned.

"Man, I don't know what to say. That's beautiful."

"I know. Look at all these. He made recordings at the end of all of the jungle tapes along with his love letter tapes, as he calls them, where it's just him talking. I didn't know he had done this until today. I've spent all day in here playing them over and over."

"You miss him, don't you?"

"Oh, Becky, I can't describe what I'm feeling about him right now. I just know that when I'm with him nothing else matters."

"Mariah, I think you love him."

"I know I love him, but.."

"No, dear, I think you are IN love with him."

"And what do I do about Patrick?"

"That's why you're here isn't it, to figure out what Patrick means to you?"

"Partly. Jean Paul thought it was a good idea and so did my doctor, but I'm not so sure. I can't even bring myself to come out of this room except to get something to eat or drink or go to the bathroom. I keep replaying that last scene between Patrick and me. You know where I found him and that woman.." Mariah dropped her eyes and closed them tightly. She didn't want to remember or see that image anymore.

"Haven't you been here since then?"

"Yea, but I never stayed. When I couldn't handle it anymore, I just left."

"Why don't you try to relax a bit and let things go as they will. There's nothing else you can do. Are you really giving this a chance to work by staying locked up in here?"

"No, I guess not." Mariah and Becky sat in silence for a few minutes. "Listen, I contacted Helen Montgomery, you know, from the birth classes. Anyway, she has videotapes that she said we could borrow and study. She says what's happening to me isn't uncommon and that's why she made these. Do you mind picking them up?"

"Sure, I'll do it over lunch tomorrow. I'll call and set up a time with you to come by so we can watch them together." There was a knock on the closed door.

"Listen, don't say anything about the tapes to Charlie. He's getting pretty close to things and I'm afraid he may slip to Patrick since they're working together now." Becky zipped her lips and smiled as the door opened and the guys came in.

"Is this a private party or what?" Patrick asked as he came through the door first.

"It was but come on in anyway," Patrick kissed her as he always did. "You need anything?"

"No, we're fine, thank you. Ouch!" Mariah rubbed her abdomen in response to the baby kicking. "She must be unhappy or something. I've gotten kicked more today than I can remember."

"She's probably like her mother- stubborn and a bad patient." Becky hit Charlie on the arm.

"Thanks a lot Charlie."

"You know I'm kidding. I wouldn't have you any other way, Mariah, you or the baby. Seriously Becky, we need to be going if we're going to make that movie." Becky went to the other room and got her jacket. She came back in and hugged Mariah and told her everything would work out like it was supposed to. She also was struck with an idea to surprise Mariah with while Patrick was gone.

Patrick came back in her room after seeing Charlie and Becky to the door. He lay down on the bed beside her, his arms folded behind his head. He didn't look at her at first but up at the ceiling.

Mariah couldn't help but notice how tight his body was, he was as tense as he could be. She removed the tapes from the bed and put them in a shoebox on the nightstand.

"Can we talk?"

"Sure, but what about?"

"Mariah, baby why are you closing yourself off in here? What can I do to make this work for you, for us?"

"I just feel better in here. This is my space and out there is yours. I don't want to bother you or your friends."

"What friends? Do you see our house filling up with people? Since when did my friends stop being your friends?" Patrick started to laugh but stopped.

"You know what I mean.."

"Baby, I love you. I do want this to work. I intend to show you how much you mean to me." He rolled over on his left side to face her. His right arm went over the baby. She kicked again. "Her timing's still good." They laughed as Mariah shifted her weight in bed. Her back was beginning to hurt.

"Listen, I was thinking since the baby is going to be coming in a few weeks, why don't I go out and get a crib. You know set up a nursery or something before I have to leave. We could convert that walk in closet over there. It's big enough for a crib, dresser and maybe a changer if you want?"

"Oh Patrick, I've got a crib all ready. It's at the apartment."

"You do? Well, how about me bringing it here?"

"It's too big. It would never fit in here," Mariah shook her head as she explained.

"Oh, well how about a smaller one. You'll need some help after she comes so we'll need one here."

"Patrick, I haven't even thought about that. I don't know what I'll do at that point." She didn't want to tell Patrick about the sleigh bed that Jean Paul had struggled with to set up. She knew it would hurt his feelings.

"Think about it baby." Jim caught their eye as he worked Jezebel outside her window. "I wanted to ask you about naming the baby. What do you think about Elizabeth Ann?"

"That's pretty but I have a name already."

"You do? What?"

"I don't want to say right now. I'm not trying to hurt you but we still don't know if you're the father or not. So don't be thinking that you have any rights until we know for sure." She shifted her weight once again. The tension in her back was building like a brick wall.

"I don't care what you say. I know she's mine, but I don't understand why you won't tell me what you want to name her?" What are you hiding?"

"Nothing, I'm just not ready to announce her name yet. This is something between a mother and child that's all," she frowned and put her hands behind her back.

"What's wrong?" Patrick rose up on one elbow causing his biceps to bulge.

"I have the most horrid backache." Patrick left the room and in a few minutes came back with warm lotion in his hand.

"Here maybe this will help. Loosen your blouse and lay on your stomach."

"Right? Are you forgetting about someone?"

"Just do the best you can. I promise I'm not after your body right now, even though I would like to be." Mariah did as she was told being careful to keep the covers close to her. The thought of the warm lotion on her back was too overwhelming. That was one thing she couldn't resist. One of the few good memories she had of her mother when she was little was them sharing lotion, her mother rubbing it in her skin and she in return did the same thing for her mother as they would laugh while doing so. In the past, Patrick had asked her so many times why she kept so much lotion around but she never really explained, finally he had stopped asking. This was a memory she didn't want to share, perhaps if she did the magical bond that hung so precariously on a thread of mother and daughter would be lost forever leaving more of an empty feeling than what was already there.

She was almost asleep when Patrick finished his back massage, his hands under her pajama top. As he stroked her back his fingers went up and down her sides. He tried consciously to keep his hands away from the swell of her breasts; the lotion had made her skin slick and soft. He couldn't keep the thoughts of caressing her out of his mind. Her eyes were partially closed but her lips were parted. She turned over on her back careful to keep the covers over her, still very relaxed and it showed in her eyes. The massage had helped the ache. It was too much for him. He leaned over and kissed her. Her lips tasted sweet and full. He wanted her so much. It was more than her body that he craved, it was her mind and her heart. She was once his and he knew how much of a fool he was for ruining it all. It took her a minute to come to her senses but before she had the chance to stop him, he was off of her and looking down at her. "Darling, I love you. You're home now." He left the room not trusting himself to stay any longer even though he knew they couldn't make love, not now, not until after their daughter was born. He headed upstairs to take a cold shower. Mariah fastened her pajama top and lay in bed trying to control the tears that fell on her pillow. What was she doing here anyway? She thought as she cried herself to sleep.

Barbara found Mariah still sleeping when she got to the ranch. She was cooking breakfast when Patrick came running down the stairs and through the kitchen. He stopped to grab a piece of toast she was buttering and kissed her on the cheek.

"Good morning to you, too. What is all this about?"

"I'm off on an adventure. I'll be back soon.. I hope."

"What do you have in mind?"

"It's a surprise for Mariah." He bolted out the back door without closing it. Barbara went over to the door, closed it and shook her head as she did so.

Mariah was dressed and sitting on the sofa in the living room watching television with Barbara when Patrick came home.

"Afternoon I should say. I'm glad to see you out here." He kissed her as he flew by and headed into her room. There was a rustle of noise and furniture scrapping on the floor. Mariah and Barbara looked at each other. Patrick carried in covered box after covered box. Then he came back through with tools in hand. After a couple of hours he came out excited and took Mariah by the hands. He picked her up in one swift movement and carried her inside the bedroom. Barbara followed. The look on Mariah's face told him what he was hoping for. She liked what she saw. In the corner of the room stood a bassinette and a changing station/dresser unit. He was careful not to destroy what Jean Paul had set up because he knew it would just upset her. That he didn't want. It would only serve as another barrier between them. He would get to her through the baby if she wouldn't let him into her heart right now. It was an avenue even if he didn't like it.

"Oh Patrick, I love it! You didn't have to do this. I told you I'm set up at the apartment." Mariah scooted off the bed and ran her fingers down the satin and tulle bassinette with the pink blanket set inside.

"That's there baby, you're here now. I'm sure it's not as fancy as what he bought you but.."

"Patrick this is fine. She won't get lost in the size of it." She wondered how he knew Jean Paul had bought the crib but she tried to let it go. "Thank you." Patrick came up behind her and put his arms around her. She turns and kisses him on the cheek. "What's in the boxes in the corner?"

"Open them." Barbara bent down and placed the six boxes on the bed. Mariah found baby clothes and supplies in each one. "You spent too much money." There were undershirts, sleepers, booties, diapers, receiving blankets, waterproof sheets for the bassinette and frilly dresses with socks and shoes to match.

"No I haven't, I'm just not sure what you'll need. I told the sales lady to fix me up with whatever it took to get started and then I thought we'll go shopping as soon as the doctor says you can for whatever else you need."

Mariah could see this wasn't going to be easy. She was touched that he had done all this not really knowing if Abigail was his or not. She would try to make more of an effort to stay out of her room. If she could just keep her mind from wondering upstairs to their bedroom, his bedroom now. If she could try to put the past behind her and keep her focus on today, she could perhaps complete her task.

She didn't have any idea of what tomorrow was going to bring but today she had to keep her sights on having a healthy baby.

"Trouble?" Patrick asked as he came in through the kitchen and set his work gloves down on the coffee table. Mariah hung up the phone. Barbara wasn't anywhere to be seen.

"Get those dirty gloves off that table! That's solid cherry, that muck will ruin the polish."

"Sorry." Patrick removed the gloves and stuck them in his back pocket of his tight fitting jeans. Mariah made a face in response. Now all that stable muck would be in the laundry. "Is there a problem with the boutique or something?"

"Nothing that you can fix. She's handling everything fine and the new men's line is exceeding what I thought it would, but I have some trunks missing again. I should have had the shipment two days ago. Do you mind if I call New Orleans on your phone? My cell is down," Mariah asked as she brushed the top of the coffee table off.

302

"Why do you do that? Call whomever you need, I wish you wouldn't act like you're a guest in your own home." His irritation showed through his voice even though he tried not to show it. There was more to it than that and he knew it. He immediately was sorry he had said those words. The thought of her calling the Count on his phone didn't set well. "Where's Barbara?"

"I sent her home. She had a headache and I really don't need anything right now. She made pot roast, it's in the slow cooker so we don't have to do anything until it's done."

"That's what smells so good. I'm going to miss her when she's gone. Maybe we should think about a housekeeper and cook?" he said as he came back in from the kitchen with a glass of water in hand smiling even though he was still irritated with himself. He sat down in the chair across from her.

"Do you mind to change your clothes if you're going to stay in? I don't want the stable muck in here."

"I'm going back outside, I'm starting on those holes in the yard. It's going to rain and I want to get as much done as I can since I'm leaving tomorrow. Are you sure you're going to be okay while I'm gone?"

"I have Barbara don't I?" She was reaching for the phone. That was Patrick's cue to leave her alone. He sat down next to her and caught her off guard as she looked up. Their lips touched. The kiss was brief but delivered the message he wanted to send. The warm unexpected look on her face was worth the chance he took.

"It's good to have you back home even if you are nagging at me already." He brushed the sofa and chair off with his hand and pulled the gloves out of his pocket. As he headed out the door he heard her asking for Daphne.

Two hours later she was still on the phone. She couldn't be talking to Daphne all this time. Mariah wasn't in the living room so he followed the sound of her voice, which led him to her room. The door was open and he walked on in. She glanced up from taking notes on the pad in front of her and almost dropped her cell phone, which was attached to the jack on the wall giving her minimal movement. "Yes, Claude, I understand. I agree that should be the next step." I don't care who you use. Jean Paul and you know the trucking industry better than I. Maybe this will stop now. *Merci beaucoup. Oui*, I will take care. *Au revoir*."

"What's up?" He asks as she put away her notes.

"I have to talk to Margo and Daphne again." He left and returned with the portable phone in hand.

"Here use this. Who is Claude?"

"He's Jean Paul's assistant. He's working on our shipping problems."

"You didn't talk to OLD J.P. himself?"

"No, I did not. He's in Paris with meetings at the moment."

"I see, so what is going on?" Patrick continued to lean against the dresser that he had moved next to the bed. Mariah sat on the bed stacking up her notes in a pile. She wondered why his tone changed after she mentioned that Jean Paul wasn't reachable.

"All my trunks, my entire shipment to both boutiques are missing. Two trunks here and four to New Orleans."

"What does what's his name say?"

"It's Claude and he says Jean Paul's trunks to some of his destinations were included. It's the whole shipment out of the factory that's gone. The trucking company says they delivered my trunks to the airport and followed procedures so they don't know what happened after that."

"Has this happened in the past?"

"Yea, but not this bad. I've been getting damaged trunks in here and the New Orleans' store off and on but none unaccountable."

"So what's the good Count going to do about it? This can't be good on business for either one of you. Mind you, I really don't care about his business, but you've worked too hard to get what you have. I hate to see this drag it down."

"Jean Paul doesn't know about this last development but he has given Claude the responsibility to do whatever he needs to correct this mess while he is away."

"Does he trust this guy that much? I don't think that's so wise when it comes to business. How do we know this Claude isn't the one causing the problem?"

"Patrick, how can you say that about someone you don't know? I know Claude and I assure you he is not like that. He's been in service with Jean Paul for years and years. I would trust him with my life I had to."

"Huh. It was just a thought. So what is he doing to find the trunks?"

"He's got a tracer on them and is notifying the trucking company that they are being replaced. I suppose if the trunks aren't found then the company will have to pay for them through their insurance or something. I need to call Daphne and let her know what's going on. Do me a favor." She held out her fisted hand and opened it into Patrick's when he put it under hers. "Put my jewelry in the box behind you." Patrick opened the small heart shaped box and placed her watch and ruby ring inside. It was the same ruby ring he had given her their first Christmas together. He didn't notice the diamond ring she had forgotten she had placed inside. She had the diamond out of her lock box trying it on and wondering what it would be like to be married to Jean Paul.

The morning came before Mariah was ready. She woke up with the sounds of rain on her windowpane. She got up, washed her face, and looked out the window. The horses were still inside the stable. She doubted that Jim would be over early today since the rain had come. He could only work inside the barn and it didn't take that long to refresh the stalls. The phone rang and she started to get it but she heard Patrick answer. He was up already, probably in the kitchen was her guess. She stuck her swollen feet in her slippers and padded off. He waved at her as she entered the room and poured herself some coffee. Cup in hand, she sat at the table listening to the conversation about the breeding. After a while Patrick hung up.

"Good morning beautiful lady."

"Is Mr. Strakes coming today?"

"No, it'll be tomorrow. I need to talk to Jim so he can handle things."

"What time are you leaving today?"

"Anxious to get rid of me? How many people are you planning to have over for that wild strip party you're planning?"

"Shut up. Can't we have a decent conversation without you entering sex into it?"

"Nope. Never. You know me. I need to be off by five. The plane leaves at six fifteen I think. What do you need?"

"Nothing. I just wondered. Be careful since this is Halloween, you know?"

"The trickery will be down here, not up in the air."

"Don't be so sure. Just be careful."

"Of course. You sound like you actually care?

"I mean about practicing any stunts. You know how I feel about that."

"I promise I'm not doing any this time. I'll be back in a couple of days or so. Is Barbara coming over for the night?"

"Yea, she'll be here." Her cell phone rang. "That's my phone. It's in the bedroom."

"What is this the Grand Central Station?" Patrick ran to get it. "Yes she's here, just a minute." He handed it to her. She gave him a questioning look and he shrugged his shoulders.

"Hello."

"Hello Ms. Remmington, this is Sheriff Tobias. I'm sorry to bother you. I hope you are feeling better since the accident."

"Hello Sheriff. I'm fine. What is this about?" Patrick sat down at the table beside her listening intently.

"I've tried reaching Count DuMoiese since yesterday but haven't been able to. I was hoping perhaps you could help me reach him?"

"Sheriff, the Count is in France, actually he's in Paris for meetings currently."

"I see, I wasn't sure when he was leaving. Then there is no way I can reach him?"

"Is this about the accident?"

"Yes ma'am. I have some pictures I wanted him to look at, see if we can get a positive I. D. on that drunk driver. So far we haven't been able to locate the car. Do you think you could make an I.D.?"

"I'm sorry Sheriff but there's no way I can. I didn't see anything or anybody but the trees. It all happened so fast."

"I understand. Listen, I know you're out at the ranch.."

"How did you know that?"

"Uh, the Count contacted me before he left and told me. If you need anything just call 911, we'll be there in a flash."

"Why would I need you? Is there something you're not telling me?"

"No ma'am. Many babies been born in the back of a squad car, you know."

"Well, not this baby. Listen, I can give you the Count's fax number if that would help? His assistant could forward things to him at that point."

"Sure would. Sorry to bother you ma'am." Mariah recited the number to him and turned off the phone.

"So?"

"That was Sheriff Tobias, he's faxing pictures to Jean Paul for an I.D. on the drunk driver."

"I'm was wondering what the police were doing to follow up on the accident. I hope they catch that guy."

"I hope so, too. I hate to think that somebody else may suffer due to his drinking. You know Jean Paul's working very hard to create stiffer laws on drug and alcohol abuse especially driving under the influence of either. That's why he's in Paris now. We all should be more involved in that aspect."

Patrick got up nodding his head in agreement and poured what was left of his coffee in the sink. "Breakfast is in the oven. Forgive me for not eating with you, but I really need to finish the yard before I leave."

"It's raining!"

"So, it rains a lot. All little boys like to play in the mud." He kisses her and heads out the door. Patrick couldn't get the Sheriff's call out of his mind. He continued to toss it back and forth while he worked. He thought he had seen more patrol cars out this way than what was usual. He wondered if the two events had anything to do with each other.

Barbara answered the back door while Mariah was sleeping. Becky, Margo, Betty, and all of the female staff at the boutique quietly stepped in and began to set up decoration around the kitchen. Just as they placed the last pinned diaper forming a bowl holding chocolate candy on the bar, Mariah walked in rubbing her eyes, clearing the sleep out of them.

"SURPRISE!" They all yelled out scaring her to death. Mariah jumped.

"What the.. oh my gosh." She took in the decorations. "Is this what I think it is?"

"Yep, now sit down." Margo put a chair under Mariah and Becky gently helped her down into it. She then got another chair and raised Mariah's feet in the seat of it. "Now are you comfortable?" Mariah nodded. "Good, now let's party." The girls whopped and settled themselves around the kitchen. Barbara poured drinks for everyone and joined the party.

"I can't believe you all did this for me. Thank you for all the wonderful baby gifts. Can I keep the chocolate diaper?"

"I think you're going to have a lot of those chocolate diapers but if you want it here." Becky took the pins out, emptied the chocolate out of it and placed it on the rest of the baby gifts.

"Look girls, I have the ultimate present for this party." Becky whipped out the tapes from class. "Lets give it a watch huh?"

"Wait a minute. What's that?" Mariah ask wondering if it was some hunk tape knowing her friends.

"Come on." Everyone followed Becky in the living room while she placed the taped in the VCR. Margo and Betty settled beside Mariah on the sofa after Mariah placed her feet on a pillow laying on the coffee table.

"Oh my word! Becky, this is the childbirth class. I don't think I want to see this right now."

"Sorry. There are enough mothers in this room they can tell us if it's all true and if not, what does work instead."

"Oh my! That looks painful."

"Honey, labor's just a bad case of gas." Mariah looked at Betty as she patted Mariah's knees. Everyone started laughing at the look Mariah gave Betty. Betty just smiled back.

It was after nine o'clock when Becky had left. She stayed to go over the tapes a little more with Mariah and wrote down any questions they had so Helen could answer them when Mariah called her. Mariah was tired but she still got excited when she looked over the baby stash lying on the end of the sofa. There was nothing else she would need for the baby now. Abigail had more clothes than what she did.

The next two days went by fast. Mariah was getting tired of having someone around her all the time. She wanted her space. If it wasn't Barbara, then it was Becky or some other well-meaning friend stopping by. She barely had time to think for herself through the day but at night when Barbara was upstairs Mariah's thoughts would catch up with her. She missed Jean Paul, but she knew she had to give this living arrangement a chance. She resisted the urges to call Jean Paul at every whim. They had discussed it before he left and this is how they decided to conduct things. They would talk but it wouldn't be every day, thus the tapes he had made. Even if he couldn't hear her voice she could his. The only way she knew he knew about the shipments was that Claude called her and told her what was happening. She mentioned the pictures and Claude acknowledged the Count received them. Part of her was beginning to think Jean Paul was being cruel to her by not calling her but part of her knew why. He wanted to help her make a decision without any pressure.

She felt as if things were closing in on her. She needed her space so badly that she sent Barbara in town for some watermelon. She knew that was one thing Barbara didn't stock on the shelf. When all was quiet she turned her mind on the task of what to do about her life. She studied how she felt about Jean Paul, she studied her feelings she had being back in her home and her feelings about Patrick. Next came her feelings of their past life, their past five years, and the last day she had spent in this house. Her mind kept heading upstairs. She knew she wasn't supposed to maneuver stairs but she couldn't help it. Suddenly she found herself half way up. She stopped feeling a twinge but when the pain left she continued on up. She entered their room and stood in the doorway looking around. There were no traces of what it looked like or whom it held months before. She sat on the bed running her fingers over the bedspread. Tears were coming down her cheeks fast and hard and she couldn't hold them back nor did she. This was the first real time that she allowed her feelings of being betrayed to flow out unrestrained. Her body shook with rage, sadness, and emptiness of all the years past. Maybe this cleansing is what she needed after all. She cuddled the pillow close to her and lay on the bed crying. Her thoughts went in a million places, they left Patrick and whomever the woman was, to her father and his love for her, to her mother and their relationship, to her brother who she didn't understand, and back to Patrick and the love that they shared before she had lost their child and to that love that started to fall apart after the miscarriage. She blamed herself for not being stronger, for not being able to hold the glue to their relationship. Her thoughts traveled to the many holidays she and Patrick shared in this house. Eventually she fell asleep on his bed. This is where Barbara found her still asleep.

CHAPTER 14

"Hello Barbara." His voice was low and right behind her. She stood at the sink washing some coffee cups. He startled her and she dropped the cup back into the dishwater splashing water on the counter.

"Now look at what you made me do." She wiped the water up with the dishtowel he handed her. "I didn't hear you come in. How was your trip?"

"Okay, where's Mariah?" He stole a cookie from the plate on the table.

"She's resting. Poor child needs to sleep."

"Why? What's going on?" The concern was all over Patrick's face as Barbara turned to look at him.

"She's not been sleeping well. Now I know that's normal in this stage of pregnancies, but she's pushing herself too hard. Every day she's been on that phone doing business or whatever she's doing. She's supposed to be in bed most of the time but I find her up and walking around like there's something amiss. I'm starting to get a little worried about her. Why yesterday I found her upstairs when I came back from the store."

"Upstairs! Damn it! What is she doing?" He put down his coffee cup hard on the table sloshing the coffee over the rim of the cup. He reached for the stack of napkins in front of him.

"I don't want to speak out of turn but she's trying to work something out. So don't get all boiled up about things just yet. This is a difficult time for her, it always is when the baby's this close to coming and the last few weeks are worse for patience in any pregnancy. A woman gets really tired of carrying that extra weight at this stage. I know all about that I've had four children myself."

"I didn't know that. In any case she knows better than to try those stairs. That's why she's here and you're here to help her." He strode through the living room to her bedroom. The door was closed, but he opened it anyway. She was snug in bed with the covers pulled up to her neck. She looked like a child that her parents had tucked in bed he thought. He would let her sleep for now then they would have a talk.

Jim was still tending to the horses when he stepped in the stable.

"Hi, is that the mare?"

"Well, look who's brought the cat home. She's a beauty isn't she? No wonder Mr. Strakes wants to breed her. I think we've got the job done."

"Congratulations, Grandpa," Patrick slapped him on the back. "Have you talked to Mariah lately?"

"I did yesterday. She seemed fine, why?"

"I'm just worried about her that's all."

"She's just probably having a hard time being confined and all. You know she was never one to sit back and do nothing. Give her time." Jim picked up the empty pail and took it inside the tack room leaving Patrick to gaze at the new mare in the stall before him.

Patrick was sitting on the sofa in the dark with his feet on the coffee table watching television. He was dressed in a short sleeve tee shirt and sweatpants.

"Barbara, why do you have the lights off?" Mariah asked as she came in the room yawning. She flipped the table light on that sat next to the sofa. "Oh Jezopete! You scared me. I thought Barbara was here. When did you get home?" Patrick looked at her and blinked. She wore a yellow lace camisole with matching satin shorts.

"This evening. You were sleeping so I didn't wake you. You feel okay?"

"Fine after I recover from seeing you. Where's Barbara?" She sat down on the sofa next to him and pulled his feet off the coffee table.

"I sent her home. Your knight in shinning armor is here to take care of the castle and his woman." Patrick said in a gruff voice.

"Yea right."

"By the way you look wonderful in that..whatever you call it. But aren't you even a little chilly?"

"No, I've had hot flashes all day."

"Yea, right."

"You want something to eat? I can fix whatever."

"Not right now. I ate and took my meds before I fell asleep. I think I'll get some water. Excuse me." Mariah came back in the living room with a tall glass of water in hand. "How was your trip?" She asks sitting back down on the sofa.

"Tell you what, let's get you back to bed and we'll talk in there."

"Why?"

"I just think you've been out of bed enough. Weren't the orders bed rest and off your feet?"

"I'm okay.."

"You or the baby won't be if you keep disobeying orders. When is your next O.B. appointment?" Patrick led her in the bedroom, put her in bed, and covered her up.

"Tomorrow morning. I hope she'll tell me I can have a normal life again."

"Don't bet on it. I'll take you."

"Listen, I want to talk to you about that. I'm going to call the rental company and arrange for a car to be sent out here. I'm paying for it so don't even think about it."

"You can't drive."

"I can, she didn't tell me not to if I had to. What if something came up and there was an emergency. I would just feel better having a car. You're not going to be around and I don't want to impose on my friends any more than I have to."

"But everyone would be more than happy to help you out, you know that."

"I'm not going to do it. I've made up my mind. Oh, by the way, I'm paying you back for the baby stuff, too."

"No you're not paying me back. I'll concede on the car situation since I see I'm not going to win but you have to promise you won't use it just to go on joy rides. It's for emergencies only."

"Right. Now tell me what about your trip?"

Patrick sat on top of the covers next to her. He placed his arm around her neck. She picked up the scent of her favorite aftershave mingled with his shampoo. For an instant she felt as if she was truly home, but just for an instant. "Didn't do much this trip. Just got the feel of the place and the tour guide took us around to the old haunts, told us the stories of the people and places that's all. I go back in a couple of weeks this time to start reviewing the stunts. The coordinator couldn't make it this trip. Oh, by the way, we're supposed to be doing this on one of the tightest budgets I've seen for a long time."

"Think it can be done?"

"I don't know, we'll see won't we. I'm not getting what I usually do but what the heck it ought to be fun. Who cares if I don't win an Oscar- it's not about that for me even though it would be nice." He shrugged his shoulders and shifted his weight more on the bed.

"Hand me the remote. It's over there on the dresser." He glanced over his shoulder and went to the dresser and noticed the tapes beside it.

"What's this?" He picked them up and as he did so, he accidentally knocked her little jewelry box to the floor but he continued to read the label. "Natural Childbirth, part one and two."

"Those are tapes from my class. Becky brought them over since we can't attend in person."

"Let's watch them." He bent over to retrieve her belongs off the floor when he noticed the diamond ring. It was the size of the Hoover Dam. He held it up to the light. "What is this? How big is it anyway?" Mariah scrambled out of bed and took it away from him.

"Give that to me. It's mine."

"Obviously and I can only guess who it's from, the good OLD Count. Is this an engagement ring?" The last words almost stuck in his throat. He felt as if his heart and head were spinning out of control. She couldn't have said yes, she was there with him now; she was home in their house with him, not Jean Paul. That had to mean something. God that had to mean something, he thought.

She placed the ring back in the box he had set on the dresser. How could she have been so stupid not to put it back in the lock box? She had forgotten all about having it out the other day and that upset her, too. "I'm not going to discuss it with you."

"Then, it is an engagement ring? Were you even going to tell me?" He was angry and it showed in spite of him trying to tone the anger down. He couldn't look at her so he turned his glare out the window.

"When and if there would be something to tell. I haven't said yes, yet. He proposed to me before I came back to town."

"You let Charlie and I propose to you, too. Do you think we're some fools off the boat or what?" He stuffed his fist in his other hand.

"No Patrick, I don't think that. Charlie's proposal was sweet but that was all it was. Don't you see I still have to be sure what I want. It doesn't matter what anyone else wants. It's my life and my daughter's that we're talking about. I don't really need a man in my life. I can do just fine without one if I had to."

"OUR daughter needs her FATHER and that's ME!"

"We don't know that now, do we? Many children grow up in divorced homes or without even knowing their fathers."

"They're either in jail or doing drugs. My daughter's not going to fit in that category."

"Now you look here!" She waved a finger in front of his face. She was mad and there was no turning back now. "I'm not going to let that happen. A mother who loves her very much will raise her. I never said she wouldn't know her biological father for the man he is, but I never promised anything else." She felt dizzy. Her hand went to her temple, it was throbbing all of a sudden. Patrick could see she paled. He caught her as she fell backwards toward the bed.

"Mariah, here lie still." It was his voice that kept her from passing out. She concentrated on the deep tone of it. He brought her a wet cloth from the bathroom and placed it on her forehead. She held it in place.

"Better?" She nodded in response.

"I'm sorry, baby. I didn't mean to get you upset. It's just a shock. Don't you see how much I love you and our child. I can't bear the thought of you being with anyone else." He bent over and kissed her on mouth then lay beside her on the bed. He wanted her and even though the response wasn't as drastic as she had given before he could still sense some hunger there. He was sure she still loved him. After a few minutes of letting her calm down and him, too, he sat up on the bed but continued to look at the wall.

"Mariah, is that what you're doing here? Looking for answers on what to do with your life? Is that why you were upstairs in our bedroom?"

Mariah removed the cold cloth from her head and struggled to sit up. The baby had shifted her weight and it wasn't easy for her to get up.

Patrick held out a hand to her but she refused. "Please Patrick just go." She wondered how he knew. For all she remembered Barbara wasn't home when she went upstairs and just as she sat down on the sofa Barbara was coming in the door with the food.

He got up from the bed and paced the room. "Mariah, you know I love you and I think you still love me. Why else would you really come back to town after all these months? Why are you fighting this so hard? Baby you're home now. Make it permanent, please. If it's this house and what happened then we could sell it, we'll find a new place where we make new memories, better memories. We don't need this place if it's going to keep us apart. We were meant to be together and now our child confirms it and our love."

"It's not the house, Patrick."

"Ah ha! So you do love me."

"I didn't say that."

"But you didn't refute either, now did you? Therefore, I think I'm right, you do love me but you just don't know what to do about it. Right?"

"Patrick, some part of me will probably always love you…" He sat down next to her on the bed and took her in his arms.

"You said you love me."

"There's a difference between being attracted to a person and being able to actually live with that person. Don't you see, I made mistakes in our relationship, too. I put a stress on it when I had the miscarriage. I wouldn't let you inside my pain. I made you suffer by doing that. I've only realized it since I've been back here. I've been thinking a lot and I can't move forward without putting all the pain… what I have caused and what you have caused behind me. I'm not sure I can do that and I'm not sure I can stay. Like I said, I caused a lot of our trouble in the beginning. I know now, that after my miscarriage I closed up. I'm sorry for that."

"Since we talking about this, baby, no matter what I tried I couldn't get near you, I mean emotionally. I felt like you were dying and taking me with you. I was grieving, too, for our child. Sure we still functioned as a couple. We made love but there for a few months it was like you weren't there. Then you did a 360-degree turn around. You became needy. That was never you. You went from one extreme to the next and I didn't know how to handle it. I got scared like I've explained before. That's when I betrayed you. Don't you see, if I could have tried to help you a little more then none of this would have happen. I should have been more understanding. It was me who brought things to a climax."

"A bad choice of words, don't you think?" Mariah's head whipped around to look him in the eyes. There was no laughter in them.

"Sorry, I didn't mean..you know, what I mean. Our life would be different today if I had taken the time to help you."

"MY life is totally different now. I'm not the same woman I was."

"I know, you've told me that from the beginning and I'm okay with that. I still love you and I believe we can work this out. For the sake of our daughter we have to try. I'll show you how much you both mean to me, even if I'm not her father. I know it's not going to be peaches and cream all the time but what relationship is?"

"I don't know, Patrick. Can you live knowing that her father may be your best friend? Every time you look at her will you see a betrayal?"

"You didn't betray me, it was me who did you and that is the cross I have to bear. Can't you even consider staying? My proposal still stands. I'm ready to have you as my wife now and forever."

"Patrick, I don't know. I don't want any pressure on the matter. Don't you see all I can do right now is get through one day at a time? There are other people to consider, not just you."

"J.P.?"

"As I have said before, yes, Jean Paul. He is a good man. He loves me and Ab.. and I love him."

"Wait a minute, you were going to call the baby by name. What is it?" He had heard her say she loved Jean Paul but chose to ignore it.

"I'm not sure, yet, so I don't want to say." Mariah was in hopes of stalling. She wasn't ready for him to know just yet. He would give her problems over that, too.

"Huh." He knew she was stalling. "Then let's name her together."

"I'm not discussing that anymore. I want to sleep. Please leave me alone."

After a minute or two standing in front of the window gazing out, he turned to speak but saw she had turned on her side and was sleeping so he left softly closing the door. Mariah opened her eyes as the door closed. She didn't know how else to get rid of him. She got up, searched the room for her cell phone, and dialed the number.

"Bonjour."

"Bonjour. I hope I'm not calling at a bad time. Can you talk?"

"Mon amour, I'm in between meetings. How I have missed you."

"I know the feeling. I know we said we would keep the calls down but I had to hear your voice. I had to be reminded that you're still on this earth." Jean Paul looked around in the hall that he was standing in. There seemed to be no private place he could go. Then he spotted a door and peaked inside. It was a janitor storeroom so he stepped inside. "Are you there?"

"Pardon, I wanted to find someplace quiet so we could talk. *Ma chérie,* I am here waiting for you. How are things going?"

"I think I've made some advancements. It's tough being here and part of me hates you for convincing me on the idea but that same part of me knows I needed the shove."

"It distresses me to hear you speak that way. I don't want you to have ill feelings."

"You know, I love you. I just want to get all this over with and get back to my life and the way I want to live it. Is that so much to ask?"

"Not at all *ma chérie*. Remember *je t'aime*. How are things with *le bébé*?"

"Everything's the same. I go back to the doctor tomorrow?"

"How are things with Wainscott?"

"He just got back today. We've had a talk but I feel more confused than ever."

"Is he creating problems?"

"He wants to be a full time father. He wants us to be together again."

"Of course, I expected that from him. What did you say?"

"I told him that Abigail would know whoever her father is, but that I can't make any decisions yet. I told him that I love you."

"What was his reaction?"

"He ignored me. He pressured me until I admitted that I care about him but I tried to explain its different now. I've done a lot of soul searching these past few days. I know now that I wasn't the only victim in our relationship. After I miscarried I didn't behave very well. I closed down for a while and then he said I went to being needy, too needy."

"Mariah, you were grieving for the loss of your child. Any mother worth her salt would do that. There are no two reactions that are the same. I remember being told that when Angelena and I lost our son. It is pure hell, there is nothing you can do to stop death from coming when its time."

"Yes, but Patrick was grieving, too, and I didn't want to see it. It was more of a reminder than what I wanted."

"You weren't ready to handle anyone else's grief."

"Maybe. What I'm afraid of is am I going to react the same way any time something bad happens in my life?"

"*Ma chérie*, listen to me, you are a stronger woman now. Did you react that way when your father died?"

"No."

"There is your answer. You can get through whatever comes your way. I know that and I think you know that deep down. Besides, you have me to lean on if you need it. My love for you will never die. I will always be by your side if you let me."

"Oh Jean Paul.." Her voice was soft. He had to strain to hear her. The bell rang announcing the commencement of the meetings.

"*Mon amour*. I have to go but keep the faith and the goal. *Je t'aime* and that will not change. We will talk soon. *Au revoir*."

"*Au revoir*." He clicked the phone off before she could ask him about the trucking situation. She guessed she would have to call Claude for those answers.

She then immediately called Sarah. Talking to Jean Paul helped some but it wasn't the quick fix she was hoping for. He did reassure her on his feelings for her. Sarah picked up and they spent the next hour and half on the phone. By the time she hung up the house was quiet. Patrick must have gone on up to bed. She crawled up in bed with her journal and started writing. Upon Sarah's suggestion she had started a journal for her thoughts and feelings concerning the baby and her pregnancy.

The next couple of weeks found Mariah, Barbara, and Patrick falling in to a pattern of every day living. Becky and Charlie would come over to visit her about every other day. Then Margo would take the time to come out to the ranch and keep her updated on business and any good gossip that may brighten her day.

She was seeing Vivian one to two times a week now. Once for the baby and once for her blood pressure which was elevating off and on. The baby was still growing and predicted to be big. Vivian was talking more and more about a possible cesarean section and scheduling a date for the middle of December. Mariah and Patrick disagreed on that. She didn't want surgery but he thought it would be great to schedule the birth so he could be around when the baby came. He wanted to be in the delivery room, but she wanted Becky with her.

"I'll call you when I get there." Patrick hugged Mariah as she stood in the doorway of the kitchen watching him get a drink of water. He was dressed in jeans, dress shirt, and the new hounds tooth sport coat she had convinced him to buy from her boutique. He approached her and took her in his arms seeing the look on her face. "Listen, please don't worry about me. I promise I'm not going to do any stunts that could remotely get me killed. This is a dry run remember?"

"That's what you say."

"I'll be back before Thanksgiving. We'll celebrate together I promise." He leaned her back and kissed her fully on the mouth. She felt his strong arms supporting her back and the extra weight of the baby. "Will you promise to be good and get some rest? Please stay in bed. We only have four and half weeks left to go."

"Yea, I know, it's not soon enough for me."

Jim came in the back door. "You ready to go?"

"Just a minute. I've got to get my bag." Patrick released Mariah and went upstairs.

"Where's Barbara?" asks Jim.

"She'll be here soon. Something about a pipe bursting."

"If she needs anything tell her to call me. I'd be more than happy to help her."

"Thanks, Jim, I will. She'll appreciate it. Listen, you be careful on the highway. You know the police never identified the man who ran us off the road. He could still be out there trying to kill people."

"Don't you worry missy. We'll be fine. I'll get him to the airport safe and sound and be back in no time. You'll be okay, right?"

"Sure."

"Here I am," Patrick said coming in the room. "Now young lady get yourself to bed. I love you." He kissed her again then he and Jim walked out leaving the kitchen door ajar. She closed it and locked it. Barbara had her own key.

Mariah heard her cell phone ring, she ran the best she could to get it. Out of breath, she answered.

"Hello."

"*Bonjour, mon amour.*"

"Jean Paul! I am so glad to hear from you. I have tried to call several times but couldn't get through. Where are you?"

"I'm at the vineyard. I finished my meetings and decided to come here for a bit. There is work here I want to get done, so I plan to stay a few weeks. I have given the contractors three weeks at the most to get it done and not a day longer."

"What are you doing?"

"It is a surprise. I can't tell you."

"Be that way," she said pouting. "You will see I promise," Jean Paul laughed knowing she wasn't really serious about her hurt feelings.

"How did your meetings go?" She knew she wasn't getting anywhere with the pouting so she decided to let it drop.

"We got the legislature to agree. The laws needed to be tougher and now we have it. This is going to cut down on the border problems tremendously."

"I'm so proud of what you helped to do."

"I'm glad it's over even if it was for a good cause. I have good news on the home front."

"What, tell me please?" Her voice was full of excitement.

"Guy and Katelin are renewing their vows on Thanksgiving. If you remember that is their wedding day. I am best man again."

"Oh, I'm so glad things worked out for them. What happened to that woman who was causing problems for them?"

"She finally admitted that Guy was not her child's father. She was using the chance to extort money from him. She is now facing charges herself but not by Guy's actions. He doesn't have the heart to send her to jail because she's pregnant."

"She deserves something out of the deal."

"Perhaps. Oh and I'm rather surprised as well..Guy has taken off running the vineyard business. He has a natural eye for the grapes and seems to be a fast learner."

"Good, I'm so glad, now maybe you can take some time off and enjoy life for a change."

"I will when I see you again. I would like to plan a trip to see you around your due date if that is all right with you?"

"Is it all right?!" Of course it is. I want to see you, too. I understand about Thanksgiving. You need to be there for your brother. I'm glad you two are close. I don't even know where mine is. But please don't worry about me. I'm not going to be doing anything other than eat, and gain more weight. Can we talk that day?"

"It is for *le bébé*, remember? I will call you, I promise."

"You'd better. Oh the doctor wants to schedule a section. The baby is getting bigger and bigger."

"You need to keep me posted. I definitely want to be there to welcome Abigail in the world."

"Jean Paul, I love you."

"*Je t'aime*. How are things there?"

"Patrick is gone again. He'll be back around Thanksgiving."

"*Non*, what I mean is there still a lot of pressure from him about staying together?"

"I think he just assumes so but I haven't told him anything to make him believe that."

"Just remember that you have to do what is right for you. It doesn't really matter what he wants or for that matter what I want."

"I know, that's what Sarah says, too. I can't wait to see you. Just think in a few weeks Abigail will be here. Oh did I tell you that I had a baby shower. I have everything a mother could need I think."

"I'm glad your friends did that for you."

Their conversation lasted another hour. They discussed how much help Barbara was and her thoughts on starting the men's line in the New Orleans' store. They also discussed the trunk shipments and the new truck line handling it. The missing trunks had finally showed up in a warehouse in Paris. It was assumed the previous trucking line had accidentally delivered it since they were making other deliveries at the same warehouse. The garments weren't harmed just rustled about but the outside of the trunks were beaten up and the seal of the lid was broken again.

She also said how she's been reading and playing the cassette tape of André Avantiér's music he had bought for Abigail. Mariah even mentioned that when she played the tape the baby seemed more active, like she was dancing or something. She also told him she had rented a car just since the insurance company had totaled hers. She had placed the money in her account to use after she was able to drive. Maybe he could help her get another car as soon as she delivered. He agreed he would. She felt better when they hung up. She felt like they were back on track again. The next few weeks settled into a routine of just she and Barbara. Southern California had seen its share of rain in the past few days and Mariah was tired of the dull gray skies. She wanted sunshine; she wanted to see the horses out playing. She wanted to be free from her confines but the end was getting closer. She wanted to be able to sleep. She had two more dreams since Patrick had left. They were all the same as before, she was running away from something but what she didn't know. Jean Paul had called several times in the past two weeks. Neither one could stand not talking to each other longer than two or three days. Their pact of no communication while she was figuring things out had to be broken. In spite of things her mind was getting clearer. If she stayed here with Patrick it would be hard for her to handle her career, to help promote her designs. She had already filled four sketchpads with new designs these past few weeks. Patrick wouldn't understand about her picking up and flying to France or anywhere else she needed to be with the baby. He would expect them to be home with him. She determined she wanted more than just managing the boutique here in Crystal River; there was the boutique in New Orleans that needed to be looked after. She felt she could be a good mother and still work, after all, many women did just that. Why not her? Maybe that was the real reason she left Crystal River to begin with- to find a more exciting life than what she had there.

Becky and Charlie had stopped by a few days ago and explained that he had received a call from the producer and they wanted him on location for a few days. Since Becky had some vacation days she had to use up before the end of the year she was going with him. They planned to be gone a week or so, but Becky assured Mariah that she would be home in plenty of time for the baby. Mariah wished them a Happy Thanksgiving and sent them on their way. Becky had plenty of time before her duties in the delivery room had to begin.

"Good morning Mariah." Barbara said as she came in through the door carrying bags of groceries. "I hope I got everything for dinner tomorrow. Have you heard from Patrick yet?"

"Not yet, I guess he'll call." Mariah said looking up from her drawings as she lay on the couch with her back propped up with pillows.

"I'm fixing the entire dinner today, so all we have to do tomorrow is warm it up. Just think no extra dishes to do tomorrow."

"Sounds like a plan to me. Listen, I really thank you for doing this. I know you have your own family you want to be with."

"It's not a problem. My kids aren't coming in until the day after tomorrow. We'll have our Thanksgiving then."

A few hours later the house was filled with the smell of roasting turkey. Barbara had been in the kitchen for most of the day. Mariah heard the phone ring but she was too busy to answer it. Barbara brought the portable in the living room and handed it to her.

"Hello."

"Hi, baby. I just wanted to let you know I'm coming in tomorrow afternoon at three. I waited too long to get the return flight so I had to take what was left."

"That's fine. You wouldn't believe what Barbara is doing right this minute."

"What?"

"She's cooking dinner for tomorrow. The complete traditional meal including pumpkin pie. It's going to play havoc with my diet and insulin but I don't care. I'm going to eat tomorrow even if I pay for it the next day."

"Did you ask the doctor what's okay?"

"Don't worry, I talked to her."

"Just wait till I get there to eat, can you do that?"

"Of course. I'm not going to have dinner without you. Thanksgiving's no fun by yourself. I'm sending Barbara home early tomorrow. She's having her family over the next day."

"I don't know if that's a good idea. I don't like you being there by yourself."

"Please, I'm a big girl. Everything will be fine. Now what about Becky and Charlie?"

"They just arrived this afternoon. She's really excited to see the area."

"Good, I hope they enjoy it. You know the weatherman's predicting a lot of rain again tomorrow. It's done nothing but rain for the past three days. Speaking of that, I hate to say this, but I really need to hang up. I have to go to the bathroom again. The baby's on my bladder again. Can we talk tomorrow?"

"Sure. I'll see you tomorrow. Love you."

"Be careful coming home." Mariah hung up, went to the bathroom and then back to work.

"Barbara, it's me. Listen, I would feel better if you didn't come over today. The weather is so bad. It's done nothing but rain all night and it doesn't look like it's going to stop."

"But I'm not afraid of the rain. I hate to leave you there by yourself."

"Really I'll be fine. Patrick's coming in at three. He should be here by four at the latest. I promise I'll be good and stay in bed or on the couch until he gets here. I'll even let him warm dinner up."

"Are you sure about this?"

"Yes, I am. Enjoy your time off. Happy Thanksgiving."

"Happy Thanksgiving to you too. Call me if you need anything, I'll be right out."

"Don't worry about me. I'm just going to wait here for Jean Paul to call. His brother and sister-in-law are renewing their marriage vows today."

"Well then give him my regards and I'll talk to you in a couple of days unless you need something."

"I will and I won't. Enjoy your family and again thanks for everything?"

"Anytime." Barbara hung up.

There was a knock on the back door then Jim came in through the kitchen "There you are. I was just letting you know I was out in the stable. Thought I'd get the horses done so Patrick wouldn't have to do them when he gets in. It won't take long. Where's Barbara?"

"I just told her to stay home. The weather's so bad I don't want her driving over here and having a problem. Besides, I don't need anything. Dinner is cooked and waiting for Patrick and I'm going to lie here, draw, and get fatter by the minute." She laughed at her own words.

"I'll be back in when I'm done. Go easy today, please missy."

Mariah fell asleep on the sofa; it was the rumble of distant thunder that woke her. She glanced at the grandfather clock in the corner of the room. It said one thirty but looking out the window the morning gave the impression of late evening. The rain had not let up. She went to the kitchen wondering if Jim was still out there but found his note on the table. He said he found her sleeping and didn't want to disturb her but if she needed anything between then and when Patrick got back to call. She heard the wind pick up and then there was a bang. Looking out the back door she saw the main stable door flapping in the wind. She knew the sound would scare the horses as the wind and storm got worse. She had no choice but to put her coat and boots on and latch the door. As she prepared to go, she felt a major pain. She doubled over until the pain left. It was probably another Braxton-Hicks she thought to herself, except this one was a little stronger than what she had been feeling. Heading out the door the wind whipped around her. She felt the rain strike her face. Before she closed the door she peaked in at the horses and made sure every one was still in their stall. Satisfied, she closed and latched to door behind her and headed up to the house. Suddenly she found herself on the ground. She had fallen in one of the potholes that Patrick was filling in before he left. She was immediately frightened when she felt another sharp pain in her abdomen. What was she thinking coming out here? What had she done to her baby?" Getting up on her hands and knees and crawling to the stone seat a few feet away from her she hauled herself up to a standing position. So far so good but lightning flashed across the sky. Now she had to get in the house. Carefully she managed to do that but as she just got inside the back door the sound of lightning hitting something close startled her. She had another sharp pain. This time the warm water that ran down her leg wasn't the rain. She had to call 911 to help. If she remembered the tapes right, she was in labor. She dialed 911 but the line was dead. The lights in the house flickered intermittently and then went off. "Great! This is just great!" she mumbled to herself. She fumbled for the candles and matches in the kitchen drawer. She found them and lit the candles. She had to stay calm. She had to think of what to do next for her sake as well as Abigail's. Her cell phone, where was it? She went to the bedroom and couldn't find it right away. She had another pain. Contractions weren't supposed to come this fast, she was supposed to have plenty time in between them to get to the hospital. Why wasn't this going like the tapes? There under the bed was the phone, but it was dead. She had forgotten to recharge the batteries. Why hadn't Jean Paul tried to call? Of course he couldn't get through if the lines were dead. The nearest neighbors were the Dealers and their ranch was two miles down the road over the creek. She couldn't panic. Maybe this was the Braxton-Hicks after all. She could only hope and pray.

CHAPTER 15

She was cold by this time and knew she had to get out of her wet clothes. She found her sweats and put them on with her robe and socks. Maybe the contractions were because she was so chilled, the thought ran through her mind. The baby wasn't due for another two weeks but didn't she hear in class that sometimes they came early. Panic started to swell up inside her again but she took a hold of it and tried to calm down. She remembered hearing stories when she was in New Orleans of slave women working in the cotton fields in the south giving birth right there and then going back to work immediately. She didn't know if any of that was really true but if it was and if those women did it then by golly she could do it alone if she had to do. Didn't her instructor say that most of the time Mother Nature takes the upper hand anyway? She had to be able to think straight. Feeling a little warmer she placed a towel around her wet hair. The lights were still off and the storm was raging outside. She went in the living room and turned on the gas fireplace for an extra heat source. As she sat down on the floor she felt another contraction. This one was five minutes since the last one and stronger than before. She wrapped a blanket around her and sat by the fireplace. The lights flickered on for a few seconds then went off again. She sat there trying to think of everything she and Becky had seen on the tapes. But she couldn't, her thinking was jumbled at this point in her head no matter how she tried to keep a clear head. If she only had recharged her phone she would have taken Sheriff Tobias up on his offer for a ride to the hospital. She had the thought that maybe she could drive the rental down to the main highway and there she could flag down a motorist to get her to the hospital but quickly nixed that idea. It was too dangerous. The radio in the kitchen, Patrick just put new batteries in it, maybe she could get some news of the weather from it. She slowly crawled over to the sofa and pulled herself up. Because of the weight of the baby she couldn't just stand up anymore.

In the kitchen she turned the radio on and then it hit, one major contraction. She grabbed her abdomen and cried out. The radio fell on the floor. She definitely was in labor. This time she couldn't keep the panic down. She sat on the floor crying. She wanted Jean Paul but then decided anyone else would do, just as long as she wasn't alone. The back door creaked open just a bit; the wind must have jarred it because she thought she had closed it when she came back in.

"Who's there?"

Maybe it was Patrick but in the darkened room she saw no person coming around the corner toward her but what she saw was a puppy. It's fur was wet and muddy from the storm but it entered the room and came straight toward her.

The yellow lab pup couldn't have been much over 6 months old. By the way she looked she could tell the pup had been forging on her own for some time. She looked thin and as Mariah ran her fingers down her spine she felt every bone possible. She nudged her face and licked her. She was grateful that the dog was friendly. The pup lay down quietly beside her as close as she could. She had the feeling that she needed the companionship as much as she did right then. She had the crazy thought that the dog knew that she was in trouble. The thought crossed her mind maybe the dog was her answer to her prayer- of not being alone through this. Her tears were slowing down.

The contractions came again and stronger. She found herself yelling. The dog just moved closer to her and lay there licking her hand. Patrick came in the front door just as she screamed. He dropped his keys on the floor, tried turning on the lights, which didn't work. He ran in her bedroom she wasn't there. He looked in the kitchen, but didn't see her from where he was standing so he was heading upstairs. His heart and respiration were out of control with excitement.

"Mariah! Where are you?"

"Patrick!" She yelled. Her voice came from the kitchen. He found her huddled in the corner by the pantry. He took note of the dog.

"Oh for love of God! What's happened? He tried to push the dog away not knowing if it was friendly or not. But the pup growled. He took the dishtowel from the counter beside them and threw it on the dog's face and scooted it away from Mariah.

"Stop! She's friendly. Don't hurt her, I actually want her here." Patrick looked at her blankly. "She just walked in and laid down beside me. I think she's lost."

"Never mind that, what about you?" But before he could get the full question out of his mouth she screamed again grabbing her abdomen. It was clear that she was in labor.

"Oh God, you're not in labor are you?" Mariah tried to control her breathing and took some deep breaths before answering.

"It looks like that Jack! Get me to the hospital now!"

"Baby, I can't do that. The creek is out. I had to go around it to Larry's house on foot and borrow his four-wheeler. Luckily the Dealers were home."

"I'm not having this baby here!"

"You're wet and cold. Let's get you by the fire." He picked her up as gently as he could. The extra weight she had gained and the fact that he had winched his back again on the set didn't help, but he wasn't going to say anything about that.

"What are you doing wet anyhow?" he asked as he put her on the sofa.

"The wind blew the stable door open, it was scaring the horses so I closed it."

"You did what!? Mariah, you knew better than to go out there. You could have gotten yourself hurt." His tone was impatient with her, she knew he was mad and she deserved his furry.

Mariah didn't want to think of what she could have done to the baby when she fell. She wanted to talk to Vivian. "I don't need a lecture right now. I want your cell to call the doctor. There's got to be some way of getting me to the hospital." There was another contraction. She grabbed her abdomen, bit her lip, and moaned very loudly. Her back was really beginning to hurt. Patrick searched his coat pocket for the cell, and found it.

He dialed the hospital. The nurse at the emergency room desk answered. He asked for Dr. Vivian Miles and was told that she had to be paged since she was in another area of the hospital. Could the doctor return the call?

"Hell no she can't return the call, I need to speak to her now."

"I'll try to page her," the nurse said before the line went blank then he heard some song from the 70's on the line. After a few minutes, Vivian's voice traveled through the line.

"Hello, this is Dr. Miles, may I help you?"

"Doc, it's Patrick Wainscott. We need your help."

"Patrick, what is it? Is it Mariah?"

"Yea, she's in labor and I mean labor! I just got home and found her. The creek is flooded so we can't drive across. I'm afraid we're stuck here unless the helicopter can fly."

"Sorry, we just received the word that the life flights are cancelled until the storm calms down. It's too dangerous to be out there in this storm. There are flash flood warnings out all over the place. Can I talk to Mariah?"

"We're on my cell. The phone lines are out as well as the lights here." He handed the phone to Mariah. She took it.

"Hi."

"Hi sweetie. How are you doing?"

"I'm not sure right now. I'm in labor. Isn't it too early?"

"You're only two weeks early. Many babies are born at this stage and do fine. Yours will, too, now listen to me. You have to stay calm, we don't need your blood pressure up over this, understand?"

"I do."

"How's your sugar today?"

"It was normal."

"Okay, now tell me what's going on with your labor, start from this morning."

"When I got up I was okay but I did have a couple of Braxton- Hicks I thought. I was tired so I fell back to sleep for a while. When I woke up the storm was coming and the wind blew the stable door open so I went outside and closed it. Coming back to the house I fell in a pothole and.." Even in the dim light she could see the anger on Patrick's face as he looked quickly at her and swore under his breath. She looked away and tried to ignore him, anyway there wasn't anything they could do about it now.

"Mariah, what happen when you fell?"

"I had a sharp pain and then my water broke."

"Did you see any blood?"

"No, I don't think so. I was wet already but no I'm sure I would have noticed that." Panic started to rise in her voice again.

"Mariah, keep calm now. I'm sure you would have noticed it, too. I agree with you. That's good. Now how far apart are the contractions?" Vivian tried to reassure her.

Right on cue another contraction hit Mariah like a lead balloon. She couldn't help but give a half yell, half moan. Mariah started rocking back and forth, the pain in her back was worse. "My back hurts as bad as the contractions."

"You're having back labor. Mariah, ride the pain out with your breathing exercises, remember them?"

"No, I don't. My back is killing me." She was starting to cry again. Patrick took her hand and squeezed it with his right hand while his left arm went around her shoulders.

"How far apart are the contractions?" Vivian asks again trying to be patient with her but she really needed the information. Mariah didn't answer. Patrick took the phone.

"It's me, she's hurting."

"I know. How far apart are the contractions?"

"About seven, eight minutes it looks like to me on most, sometimes it goes for five."

"Okay, it looks like you're going to have to help deliver this baby. Are you up to it?"

"Do I have a choice?"

"No. Have you ever done anything like this before?"

"Not with people, I have with horses. Is it the same thing?" Patrick was watching Mariah, she glanced up at him when she heard the word horses.

"I'm not a vet, but I would think the process is the same. Where is she at now?"

"On the sofa."

"Okay, get her to bed and try to make her comfortable. I'm afraid she may be having some back labor, in which case she's going to have a lot of pain through her back. Here's what you do for that.."

After a few minutes of discussion, Vivian wanted to speak to Mariah again. Patrick left the room and took down the shower curtain and placed it on the bed. He then covered it with a clean blanket and propped a bunch of pillows up for her to lean against so she could be in the semi-sitting position the doctor recommended. Towels, he took all the towels he could find out of the linen closet and placed them on the foot of the bed. He came back in the living room, Mariah was still on the phone.

"I understand what needs to be done but I don't like it." Another contraction hit before she could say anything else. This time she did the breathing technique Vivian went through with her. After the pain subsided she held out her hand for help to get up. Mariah gave the phone back to Patrick and started to walk to the bedroom.

"I've got things set up."

"Good, give her a minute, she's getting herself ready, and now one thing I forgot. Do you have a plastic ruler?"

"Probably."

"Get it and wash it, you're going to need to check her dilation for me. Here's how you do that."

"I got it."

"Patrick!" Patrick practically took two strides and he was in the bedroom. She was doubled over in the bathroom again. He dropped the phone and helped her to the bed. He then covered her with a sheet to provide some privacy and then looked for the phone.

"Vivian, I'm back."

"What happened?"

"She had another contraction. I've got her in bed now. Listen I have a head set somewhere…this is getting to difficult. Can you call me back in a few so I can get the set? My cell number is…"

Patrick had just finished his task when the phone rang. "Yea.. we're at four inches."

"Okay that's the same as ten centimeters, it's full dilation. This stage could last another hour or so… Oh, listen I'm being paged in the E.R. I really need to answer that but I think you guys will be okay for a little bit. I'll call you as soon as I get done with whatever it is. Keep her doing the breathing technique. If you start having anything different than what you have had, then call me immediately. Understand?"

"Yes. Okay, talk to you soon. Thanks." He disconnected the phone.

"Why did you do that? She can't leave us now."

"She had something to do in the E.R. She's going to call us back. Listen, Mariah, we can do this. She says we have a little while before the baby is born, but we're in stage two, you're fully dilated."

"What is this we crap? It's me lying on the bed, spread eagle, and in the most intense pain I've ever been in, in my entire life."

"If it'll make you feel better go ahead and call me the worst names you can think of. Isn't that what you women do at this point?" He flashed her a big smile and kissed her on the cheek. She glared at him, grabbed herself again, and yelled.

"Baby, do the breathing. Do what I do. Come on, focus on this." He started doing the sounds of he's and ho's while drawing in air and exhaling it. She did as she was told. They spent the next half hour breathing together. Mariah learned to breath with the whole abdomen and tried hard not to get tense when the pain was too much. She rested between contractions. Patrick wiped her forehead with a cool cloth and even rubbed lotion in her feet in between contractions. Patrick checked the baby's progress with each contraction. He was about the call Vivian when the phone rang. It was she.

"Hi, how are things going?"

"I was just about to call you. The contractions are really close and she wanting to push."

"Okay, do you see any bulging at the same time a contraction hits?"

"Yea, that just started. Now what?"

"When she has the next contraction see if you notice the baby's crown, the top of the baby's head."

"Wait a minute, she's having another one." Mariah screamed in between her he's and ho's." Patrick positioned himself, he did see the baby's head. She was coming. "Vivian, I see the head! I see the head!"

"Good, so far so good. The only thing I'm afraid of is the size of the baby. She's going to be big. Normally we do an episiotomy but that's not an option now. Expect some vaginal tearing. It's not going to be pretty so have some clean cloths ready and try to pack the area to help stop the bleeding. Whatever you do don't let her know what's happening. It'll probably scare her. Keep your expressions the same. Also as soon as you can grasp the baby's head gently rotate it so the face is sideways. As you do this see if you can clear the mouth and nose from any substance. Understand?"

"Damn it, I want to push! I'm going to push! I can't handle this anymore!" She yelled at the top of her lungs as the contraction hit.

"Keep her breathing but let her push. Let's have this baby!" Let me talk to her." He put the headset on for her and went back down to the foot of the bed.

"Mariah, are you ready to have this baby?"

"I want to get this done now! I've got to push!"

"Go ahead sweetie, push. You can do it." Mariah did just that, she pushed for all her life but had to stop to catch a breath. The lights in the house came back on. Patrick thanked God for small favors mentally.

"Come on Mariah, you can do it. Just a little more, she's coming, I see her..harder…push, push, and push!"

"Oh God, help me! Something doesn't feel right. Is the baby okay?"

Everything hurt with her and she couldn't stop the tears. She felt like she was on fire. Mariah screamed at the same time. The baby's head was half out.

Patrick felt sick to his stomach seeing someone he loves going through this much pain and suffering. The tearing was bad he thought, but couldn't do anything to stop it so he concentrated on the end goal and helped her the best he could. "The baby's almost here. Mariah, you need to push and push now. We need to get the baby's head out. Now come on you can do it,"

Patrick's voice was soft and soothing. She took reassurance in his tone. He was so calm and that was helping to keep her calm as much as possible. Mariah concentrated on pushing and breathing again. The burning and pain stopped. The contraction came again and she started pushing as hard as she could. She could feel the baby. She was getting tired and was about to give up when he yelled.

"Stop! Don't push! Wait a minute."

"What's wrong?" Mariah felt a chill to her heart, she had started crying again. Something was wrong with the baby. Patrick didn't answer her, he was busy freeing the tightly wrapped umbilical cord from the baby's arm, which was a shade of blue but quickly went to pink afterwards. He let a sigh of relief. "It's okay, she's okay. The cord's free. Now push!"

"Are you sure she's okay?" Mariah spoke in between sobs. She couldn't see anything to make sure he was telling her everything. Then another contraction hit and she started pushing with everything she had.

"Come on baby, you can do it. You can do it…"

Mariah took a deep breath, gritted her teeth, and yelled through them. She bore down hard. The effort rewarded Patrick with a baby that fell in his arms.

"We did it! Vivian can you hear me? We did it! She's a girl." He knew he had to clear the mouth and nose, he had to get that done now he thought to himself to keep his emotions in check until he knew the baby was okay. As soon as he wiped the membranes out of the way the baby took her first breath in the outside world. Her cries were music to both Mariah's and his ears. He grabbed a towel and wrapped the baby in it so she didn't get too cool.

"I hear that wonderful sound. Congratulations Mama," Vivian said to Mariah who was still wearing the head set.

"Vivian, she's crying." Mariah was crying. She looked at Patrick who was crying, too.

"I know sweetie, I hear her. Listen you have a few more minutes of pushing yet. Mariah listened and did what she was told to do and then with the job accomplished she rested. Patrick took the head set and was instructed on how to cut the umbilical cord. The task done, he thanked the doctor and hung up. Now all they could do was wait. He found himself crying in joy and relief that everything was over and well. He couldn't believe what they had just accomplished. With shaking hands he then placed the baby in Mariah's arms.

Mariah thought she was the most beautiful baby she had ever seen with her full head of black hair and Mariah's nose but she had her father's eyes. Abigail's fair complexion copied Mariah's. Patrick thought she looked like him the instant he laid eyes on her. He had to be right, she had to be his and he knew the DNA test would confirm that.

"We did it sweetheart. Vivian's sending help as soon as she can get it here. We're okay, everything is okay. I love you so much." He gave her a long kiss.

"I love you too," Mariah said as she stroked and talked to Abigail who was puckering up.

Patrick then saw to Mariah's needs, remade the bed and lay down beside her and Abigail. He was tired but didn't dare sleep. Instead he watched Mariah and the baby doze. The feelings in his heart were unbelievable. He knew there would be no other woman for him. She was remarkable! And seeing his daughter born was a feeling that he couldn't describe. He thanked God the birth went as well as it did and everyone was fine as far as he could tell. About an hour later he heard the distant rumble of the helicopter.

"Hi sweetie, how are you doing?" Dr. Vivian Miles asked as she walked through the door of Mariah's hospital room. Deloris was getting her settled in bed. Patrick was sitting beside the window.

"Well, I thought you had left a hour ago?" Deloris said looking up from smoothing the covers and smiled.

"I had to wait till my favorite patient and her new baby arrived. I just saw her. She's beautiful. She's got all ten fingers and toes too."

"She is beautiful isn't she?" Mariah's fingers entwined Vivian's as she took Mariah's hand.

"If you need anything just buzz the desk. See ya." Deloris left the room.

"I think she's got the bluest eyes I've ever seen. Hello Patrick, I'm sorry I didn't mean to ignore you." Patrick nodded at her before she turned back to Mariah. "I'm just happy everything turned out like it did. I was in the O.R. when you came in. Any pain with the stitches?"

"No."

"Have you heard how the baby's doing?" Patrick stood up and approached the bed.

"She's fine, I heard she weighs in at nine pounds and six ounces and a whopping twenty-one inches long. Didn't I tell you she was going to be big? I bet if you carried her another two weeks she would have been close to being ten pounds. All the newborn tests are fine and she's really alert."

"Can I see her soon?"

"Of course sweetie, but I suggest you let the nursery keep her tonight so you can get a some sleep. You look pretty wiped out." Vivian squeezed her hand tenderly.

"I think that's a good idea," Patrick added.

"You ought to get some rest, too. Can you get back home yet?" Vivian looked at Patrick.

"I haven't heard but seeing the amount of rain we've had I know it'll be tomorrow before we can cross the creek."

"Why don't I see if we have an extra bed downstairs in family services where you can bunk in for tonight?"

"I thought about staying here actually."

"Sorry, you both need to sleep and I think you'll both do better separated than together. Besides Mariah doesn't really need you here tonight. Tomorrow is a different day and if Mama's rested I'll let them bring the baby in to room in the morning"

"Alright, I'll go downstairs. Anyway I'll be able to be back up here early enough to see the baby first thing."

"I'll ask Deloris to call downstairs and see what they can do for you. I'd like to talk to Mariah for a minute."

"Everything okay?" Patrick had a fleeting moment of concern.

"Of course, after everything you two have been through I'd tell you if it wasn't. What a Thanksgiving gift huh?" Vivian smiled as she reassured him.

"Good night, baby. I love you. I'm so proud of what you've done."

"I'd say you had a part in things, too."

"Just like horses, just like horses." He grinned at both Mariah and Vivian and kissed Mariah good night.

"Oh you!" Mariah picked up the pillow that was lying on her stomach and threw it at him hitting the door instead. He continued to smile as he left the room. The truth in the matter was he was tired both emotionally and physically. He waited outside in the hall for Vivian to see about his room.

"Is Abigail okay?"

"Yes dear, she's fine. I have these birth certificate papers for you to fill out. We'll need these back tomorrow. If you both do well tomorrow then I'll let you guys go home day after." She handed the papers to Mariah who took them and read them over.

"Do you have the time to help me with these now? I want to get her name entered legally before something happens." Vivian looked at her curiously.

"Sure I'm free." She pulled the chair up to the bedside table to assist.

Mariah started filling out the papers. She entered "Abigail Angelena Remmington." What address could she give? Since she was staying at the apartment when she came to town they agreed she could use that address. It took another twenty minutes to complete the paperwork. Abigail's social security number would be mailed to the boutique. Margo could forward it to wherever she was at the time.

"Oh there's one more thing. Do you still want the paternity test?"

"I guess so. It's doesn't matter to me but it does to Patrick and Charlie."

"You know who she looks like, don't you?"

"Yes, I do. I've seen baby pictures of him and she's almost identical."

"Let me suggest something. Why don't we do both tests at once."

"Charlie isn't in town but he'll be back in a few days. Can it wait that long?"

"Sure, when he comes in, tell him to go to the lab and leave a sample. I'll leave an open order for him. Patrick can give his sample at any time and we have the baby's sample already. Will that work?"

"I don't see why not."

"Good. You know what, I'd get the guys to pay for the test if I were you, after all it is they who want it." Mariah nodded.

"You're right. I was wondering what to do about that."

"Well sweetie, I ought to be going home now. I'm glad it all worked out. Oh listen, I was going to talk to you tomorrow about something but I might as well do it now. It's not uncommon for a woman to have a back-to-back pregnancy so decide what you want to do. We'll talk about it on your next visit. It's easier the first few months to get pregnant again after delivering. The nurse will go over release instructions tomorrow with you. Good night. Get some sleep. Believe me you'll need it when you get home with that precious baby." Vivian picked up the paperwork and put it in her folder.

"Thanks Vivian." Vivian smiled and turned off the light as she left the room. Mariah drifted off immediately.

Before Patrick turned in for the night he called Margo and told her the news, she said she would spread the word. Then he tried Charlie and Becky but their cells were off.

Mariah woke to the cries of Abigail coming in her room in one of those plastic bassinettes all hospitals uses.

"Hi Abigail. Come to mommy." She sat up in bed and held her arms out. The nurse placed the baby in her arms. Abigail looked up at her, stopped crying and nudged her face in Mariah's shoulder.

"I think she's hungry mommy," the nurse stated. She advised Mariah what to do and Mariah knew she had to be a fast learner. Abigail wasn't going to wait. Her cries were starting to tune up again. She placed a pillow in front of her and carefully laid Abigail on top. The nurse helped her to position the baby, but it took only a minute for Abigail to figure things out. She had breakfast ready and waiting. Right after Abigail had finished nursing Mariah's phone rang. She positioned the baby on the side of her and picked up the phone.

"Hello."

"*Bonjour, mon amour.*"

"Jean Paul! Oh my gosh. You've heard?"

"Yes I have. Congratulations, mama. How are you and Abigail?"

"We're fine, just fine. I've got her with me. Here maybe she'll make a noise or something." Mariah held the phone down toward Abigail. She looked at it and made a squeaking sound. Mariah could hear Jean Paul talking to her.

"Did you hear her? She tried to talk back to you."

"I did. Is she well?"

"She's wonderful. I'll probably be going home tomorrow. Oh, by the way, it's official, her name is Abigail Angelena Remmington. She's got a head full of black hair and blue eyes but the best part she has my nose."

"I know she's beautiful just like her *mère*."

"I don't know how beautiful her mother is right now," Mariah laughed. "How did you find out about us?"

"When I couldn't reach you at the ranch, I called Margo last night. She said Wainscott had just called her to tell her of the news. I waited to call until today because it was late and I didn't want to disturb your sleep. What I hear you had a scary time of things between the labor and the storm?"

"It was at first. You know I should have never gone outside to get that stupid barn door but I did."

"The main thing is that both of you are alright."

"Did you hear what her weight and length is?"

"I did, *mon amour*. That is what I was talking about. Giving birth to a child that large isn't easy to do."

"I don't think I could have done it if Patrick hadn't been there. He kept me going when I wanted to give up."

"I see, well now, how can I top that? I can get my calendar clear for a day or so. Would you like that?"

"Would I! I'm not able to travel just yet, but as soon as the doctor releases me all together.." The nurse came in to check on the baby. Seeing how Abigail was sleeping she smiled and left. "The nurse just came in but she's gone now. Anyway when do you think you can come?"

"What about if I leave within the next hour or two. Is that soon enough? I'll be in town by late tonight if the weather is good."

"Are you serious about coming today?"

"*Oui*, of course. Is there a problem?"

"No, not at all. I'll call the Inn and get a suite for you."

"Please, *non*. I will sleep on the plane if it is too late to see you and Abigail. I do have comfortable quarters you know?"

"Are you sure?"

"*Oui.* I would travel the ends of the earth to get to you if I needed to. *Je t'aime, mon amour.* And I can't wait to see you both."

"I can't wait either and wait a minute you know what she just told me? She said she couldn't wait to meet you; that your voice sounded so dashing and wonderful. I think she likes Frenchmen." Jean Paul laughed.

"I don't want to hang up but if I'm going to get there by tonight I had better be off, there are still a few things I need to do first. I have Alec already waiting for me."

"You do! Then you had better get busy. I want to see you as soon as you can get here. Jean Paul.."

"*Oui?*"

"Be careful."

"Of course, *ma chérie*, of course. *Je t'aime. Au revoir.*"

"I love you, too. *Au revoir.*"

Mariah was thrilled to learn he was coming, even if it was a brief visit. She hung up the phone and looked up, Patrick was standing just beyond the curtain watching her.

"How long have you been standing there?"

"Long enough." He dug his hands deeper in his front pockets. "So old man J.P. is coming, huh?"

"That's pretty ugly of you. You just don't like him because of his feelings for me. I bet if I wasn't in the picture you two would like each other."

"We don't exactly share the same life styles, now do we?"

"I don't think I've ever seen you have trouble getting along with people even with different backgrounds. I don't think you're even trying to." Abigail squirmed a little in her sleep and Mariah spoke softly to her.

"So when's the guy coming in?" Abigail opened her eyes and started to cry. Patrick walked over and picked her up. He started talking to her and she stopped.

"He'll be in sometime tonight. He wants to meet Abigail."

"Abigail? Is that the name you picked out?" He had heard the name but where? In his opinion it was an old fashion name and not heard a lot of now days and wasn't real fond of it.

"Yes, it is."

"Can we at least pick out a middle name together or do you have that, too?"

340

"I've already signed the legal name to the birth certificate."

"You have! When did you do that?"

"Last night. They brought it in after you left. It's done and so is the paperwork for her social security number."

"So give it up. What's my daughter's full name? Don't I have the right to know that much?"

"We don't know if she's yours yet, now do we? If you don't get out of that ugly mood I won't tell you another thing."

"Okay, I'm sorry. Please tell me her name. What am I supposed to do call her, hey girl, for the rest of her life?"

Mariah smiled but secretly hoped that he had not done any homework on Jean Paul or his family. She didn't want any trouble over her choice of names.

"Abigail Angelena.. that's a little unusual." Patrick heard the name Angelena and it all came back to him. She named HIS daughter after Jean Paul's family!

"You named her after his dead mother and his dead wife? How could you do that?"

"Let me explain, why don't you." Mariah knew she might have to so she was prepared. You see when I went to France for the first time I met his family. It didn't matter to them who I was and that I was carrying another man's child. It was like I belonged somewhere finally."

"Okay, so you met them but.."

"Let me finish please. The Countess was like no other woman I have ever met. Immediately, it felt like I had known her all my life and in just a few days she knew more about me than my own mother did. She treated me like a daughter. I became rather fond of her and it hurt me tremendously to lose such a friend. Jean Paul's whole family is just that way, they were very accepting toward me and the pregnancy and what I do for a living. You see for once in a very long time I felt like I had a family who loves me and wanted to have me around. And Angelena, well, I didn't get the chance to meet her but what I know about her, she was a remarkable woman also. She died shortly after their son passed on. She had trouble dealing with that but what mother wouldn't. I know I couldn't handle it if something had happened to Abigail. Maybe that was what my dreams were about.. I was afraid something might happen with Abigail. Anyway, Angelena was more than just Jean Paul's wife; she was a wonderful person who cared about people. If I can bring up

Abigail with the same moralities and compassion that her name sakes held then my mission here on earth would be fulfilled."

"I think you should have discussed it with me before you signed anything," he sighed and the look on his face wasn't a happy one. Mariah was waiting for more from him but was surprised when it didn't come. "I guess there's nothing I can do about it now. If you can live with it, little girl, I guess I can, too." Patrick held Abigail up to his shoulder and gently patted her back. I love you anyway." He kissed her as he gave her back to Mariah. "Did Vivian say anything about when you may get to come home?"

"Yea, probably tomorrow."

"Good, that'll give me a chance to get the place cleaned up for you two. We left such a mess, you know. Barbara wants to come over and help but I told her no. I halfway expect she'll be there anyway."

"About me coming home.. I'm not so sure I'll do that."

"Why? You're going to need help and you know it."

"With Jean Paul coming in, I think it'll be best if I don't bring him to the ranch, that's all."

"Fine then don't, but what does that have to do with you and Abigail?"

"You still don't get it do you? I want to see him while he's in town. I want the three of us to spend it together."

"Oh, now I see, you want to shack up with him while he's here but after he's gone then what back to the ranch with me? Last night you said you loved me. Doesn't what we went through together mean anything to you? I suffered as much as you did. Forgive me, but what the hell do I have to do to get you to say I love you to me and mean it?" He walked over to the window and stared out. Yes his ego was hurt, he thought she had meant it when she said those words.

"Patrick, I do love you, but I can't explain it exactly.. what you and I have is different from what Jean Paul and I have. I know we owe you a lot. If it wasn't for you I'm not sure Abigail or myself would have made it. When I was ready to give up you pushed me on. You and that dog showed up when I needed the support the most. By the way what happened to her?"

"So I'm put in the same classification as the dog, huh?"

"Don't get your feelings hurt over it, you know what I mean."

"I left her in the kitchen remember? I forgot all about her after we got here last night. Damn, she probably has eaten a hole through the cabinets or strung the trash all over the place by now."

"Whatever you do don't give her any of the Thanksgiving dinner. It'll make her sick. Look, the puppy has obviously been lost for sometime judging by appearance so I'd like to keep her if I could? I mean would you mind? What would a little dog like that do anyway?"

"Little dog? That dog will be growing up faster than this little girl will be." Patrick saw the look on Mariah's face and couldn't help himself. Jim would just have to feed another animal while he's gone. "Okay, okay. I'll keep her providing she doesn't bother the horses."

"Thank you, now Abigail will have her own little puppy to play with." Mariah stuck her face closer to Abigail's and rubbed her little face with her hair.

"Does that mean you'll be coming back to the ranch?"

"You said yourself, I'll need some help at first. Barbara can come over and help. After all, Jean Paul did pay her rather well on top of what Charlie has done." Mariah paused for a minute. "So you understand about us being with Jean Paul?"

"No I don't, but I guess that really doesn't matter does it." He walked over and picked Abigail up and held her close. This little girl was the one that mattered. He knew he was in love with her and he would stop the world if he had to for her happiness. "I think if you're okay I'll go on home for a couple of hours and start cleaning up the place." He gave Abigail back to Mariah and kissed them both. "I love my two girls even if they don't love me back just yet. I'll see you both later." The truth in the matter was he had to get out of there. He wanted to scream, to kick, and to destroy something. He had to get home. How dare that over confident TITLE horn in on his territory. Couldn't he just leave them be? But he knew in his heart that if it were he, he would do the same thing.

Patrick went immediately upstairs to the gym and spent the next two hours working out. He pushed himself to the limits especially since he had hurt his back trying to do a stunt. The house cleaning would just have to wait. He was just stepping out of the shower when the phone rang. Wrapping a towel around his waist and bolting across the bedroom, almost knocking the phone off the table as he answered it, thinking it may be Mariah.

"Yea."

"Hey buddy, it's me. Did you try to call me?"

"Hang on a minute." He put the receiver down and grabbed a robe. "You caught me getting out of the shower. Yea, I did earlier." He sat down on the bed.

"What's up? You just left here yesterday."

"Got some news for you. I got home just in time for the baby to be born."

"You what? Whose baby? Wait a minute you mean our baby?"

"Fool, how many other women do you know that's pregnant?" Patrick laughed. "Yes, Mariah had the baby last night."

"She wasn't due yet. What happened? Are they alright?"

"Both mother and daughter are fine. The baby weighed in at nine pounds six ounces and twenty-one inches long. We had a pretty good storm here yesterday; well evidently she went outside to get the barn door and fell. I'm not sure if she was already in labor prior to that or if that's what started it, anyway when I finally got home I found her almost ready to deliver."

"I can't believe that you got there just in time again, but I'm glad you were able to get her to the hospital in time."

"That's just the thing, I couldn't. The creek was out and there was no way to get across except through the woods on the Dealer's four-wheeler. There was no time to spare. We delivered here at home and then later the hospital sent the life flight chopper to get us when the storm let up."

"Oh my! I don't know what to say. You're sure they're okay?"

"Yea, the baby was nursing well this morning when I left. I came home to clean the house. She'll be getting out tomorrow."

"Will she be at the ranch then?"

"I don't think so at first anyway. That overstuffed Count is coming in tonight. She flat out told me she wants to spend time with him while he's here."

"Don't give your feelings away just yet. I don't think it'll help."

"I know but here's the clincher- she named the baby after HIS family! Try Abigail Angelena. Abigail after his dead mother and Angelena after his dead wife. What do you think of that?" There was a moment of silence before Charlie answered.

"Well, it's not up to us is it?" Charlie sighed while he spoke. He knew it was probably the naming that was upsetting his friend more than anything else but nothing could be done about it. Mariah did have the right to name the baby anything she wanted to. He would see if Becky knew any reasons for it since they were getting closer.

"Hey, Becky's punching me in the side. She wants to know what color hair and eyes?"

"Abigail has a full head of black hair and the prettiest blue eyes you've ever seen." Patrick heard him repeat it to Becky.

"We can't wait to see her and Mariah, too. Please give them our love and we'll be home in a few days. Listen, I'm being called. Got to go but before I do just a reminder, you can handle the situation with the Count. Don't let her know things are getting under your skin."

"I don't need that advice. I know better than that."

"Becky says she'll call Mariah when we get back to the hotel. There's my second call, got to go. Bye." The line went dead.

Barbara came just like he had thought she would and helped. Everything in the house smelled of disinfectant. It was almost overwhelming so he opened the kitchen window to air it out. As soon as he did the pup heard it and started barking. Jim had brought over his old doghouse and placed it in the back yard between the house and the stable. They attached the tie out to the doghouse until they could make a pen for the dog. She had to learn to leave the horses alone. Biting after their legs was big fun, one that may cause a major hurt someday.

There was one errand Patrick wanted to make before going to the hospital. He stopped by the store to get more diapers. Somehow he didn't think five packages were enough to keep on hand and he wanted to make sure she had everything she could possibly need with him having to leave again in a few days.

"Hi, how are my girls this afternoon?" Patrick entered the hospital room finding Mariah nursing the baby again. She was sitting in the bedside chair and had a receiving blanket draped over her shoulder giving her privacy for unexpected visitors. He kissed Mariah and sat on the edge of the bed watching them. He was just amazed at what he felt every time he looked at the baby. She was making little suckling noises while kicking her feet in enjoyment.

"Hi, Abigail is busy at the moment and can't receive visitors. I swear she's a chow hound."

"That's good isn't it? On my way over here I picked up three cases of diapers for you."

"Three cases! Why so many?"

"I wanted you to have enough while I'm gone."

"Thank you but I hope she doesn't go through that many diapers that fast. Besides I do have cloth diapers, too, if I need them."

"I know, but I don't want you to have to wash them out if you don't have to."

"That's sweet but you know there are still mothers around who don't use disposable diapers. We'll do just fine thank you."

Abigail had unlatched herself so Patrick took her and tried to burp her. He tried and tried, patting her back every way he could think of. Mariah took her and that was all she needed, Abigail exploded with a loud burp. They both laughed. Patrick stayed at the hospital until after visiting hours were over. Jean Paul had not arrived yet, so he decided to go on home. Deloris wouldn't let him stay the night and he knew she wouldn't let Jean Paul in to see Mariah either, no matter who he was. He kissed Mariah and the baby good night, told them he loved them both and would be there early tomorrow morning to find out about the going home arrangements. They actually had a nice relaxing afternoon, both spending the crucial bonding time they needed with Abigail and each other. As he left, he had the feeling they were closer now than what they had been a week ago but he knew they still had a ways to go. He also knew the wild card in this triangle was still Jean Paul.

Nine o'clock, visiting hours started and with it Jean Paul was waiting in the lobby to go upstairs and see Mariah and Abigail. He could hardly contain himself. He had two-dozen white roses and the Christening gown he had worn as an infant in hand. Katelin was going through some trunks that Abigail had carefully packed away and found the gown still in excellent condition. She had bought a tiny fabric bonnet that came close to matching the design in the gown and a lovely lace blanket for the baby. He was in the elevator as soon as the intercom voice announced visiting hours. Knocking on Mariah's door, he entered when he heard her voice.

"Good morning, *mon amour*."

Mariah was pacing the floor with the baby. She turned around and the smile on her face grew. "Come over here and meet this little girl. I'm so glad to see you. I was getting worried."

"We shall talk in a minute but right now there are urgent matters to deal with." He kissed Mariah hello then drew his attention to the baby. Mariah adjusted her so he could see her better. He took her from Mariah's arms, which surprised her and held the baby close. His voice was deep but soft as he spoke to her and she listened to him. Abigail's eyes went wide but she didn't cry, she couldn't take her eyes off of him nor he off of her. Mariah had the eerie feeling that they knew each other all ready. "She is the most beautiful *bébé* I have ever seen. I knew she would be, look at her mother." Mariah flashed him a smile.

"I think she likes you. Look how she's watching you." Jean Paul cradled the baby up against him with one arm and drew Mariah closer to him with the other. He kissed Mariah once again; their lips lingered together. Abigail kicked her feet and made a baby sound. They both looked down at her, Jean Paul adjusted his hold on her but he couldn't take his eyes off the baby.

"Her eyes have the souls of the past and the future generations in them."

"Oh look, she almost smiled at you. Oh by the way, are those roses for me?"

"*Pardon.* I forgot about everything when I saw the two of you. *Oui,* they are and you know it." Mariah went over and picked them up from the bed and smelled their sweet aroma. She then glanced at the box he had carried in and laid beside the roses but before she could open it Patrick walked in without knocking. "Am I breaking something up?"

"*Bonjour.* I am admiring this beautiful *bébé*."

"For once we agree on something. She is isn't she? When did you get in?"

"Late last night, I had unexpected business before I left." He sat down in the rocking chair with the baby and started talking to her. Patrick wanted to take the child from him but held the urge back to act on his desires.

"So how long are you staying?"

"Patrick!" Mariah said with a scowl on her face.

"What? I didn't mean anything by it. I'm trying to make small talk here." Patrick leaned against the heating unit in front of the window.

"That is quite all right, *mon amour*. My plans are for a day. You see I have a very important project starting the day after next. I have to be present so everything gets done the way I want it."

"I see, so that means you'll be leaving tomorrow?" Patrick's mood was insistent for an answer.

"*Oui*, tomorrow afternoon. I have to give Alec time to rest even if I do occasionally fly the plane myself."

"I never knew that! You have your pilot's license?" Mariah sat down on the bed facing Jean Paul and Patrick.

"But of course, *mon amour*. If something ever happened to Alec in flight what would I do then, especially if Frederick wasn't with us?"

"I never thought of that. I always assumed you didn't know how."

"*Mon amour*, there isn't a lot that I don't know how to do. I just find you more attractive than the control panel." There was a grin on Jean Paul's face as he raised both eyebrows at the same time. Mariah smiled and Patrick caught the unspoken words between them. Mariah blushed a little in response.

Dr. Miles walked in. "Good morning everybody. I have some good news. Mariah, are you ready to go home?"

"You mean I can go any time?"

"Yep, I've already signed the release papers for both you and Abigail, so when you can get packed up you're out of here. I want to see you in my office next week, okay?" Mariah nodded and took the piece of paper she held in her hand. "Here is a list of dos and don'ts for yourself. I expect these to be followed to the tee and not like what you did by going outside and falling in the potholes. Understand?"

"Yes ma'am," Mariah answered meekly. "I learned my lesson." The men looked at her but didn't say a word. Jean Paul wasn't exactly sure what they were talking about but he would find out. Vivian stayed and talked to each of them for a while including the baby. Mariah started packing her things even before Vivian had left. She was ready to get out of there.

"What are your plans?" Patrick asked through a fake smile. Jean Paul still held the baby but didn't say anything. He was waiting for Mariah.

"I thought I'd stay at the apartment for today. You know, let the guys at the boutique see the baby and give me a chance to get caught up with things there. I've been away and even though Margo has done a super job keeping me posted, it's not the same as hands on. Jean Paul, could you take us there?"

"If that is what you want. I have a car."

"Oh, by the way, old man, how are your ribs?" Patrick asks trying not to put emphasis on OLD man but his disappointment showed that she didn't want to go back to the ranch just yet. He couldn't help it.

"Thank you for asking, but I assure you there is no need for concern, my body is in perfect working condition. I am a new man in every way." Jean Paul's reference was not lost. He grinned at Mariah as he replied and Patrick caught it. She smiled back at him. Patrick and Mariah both knew what he meant and why he said it. Patrick couldn't lose his grip on things. He had to ignore the statement. He had to even though he was seething inside. The thought of that man having his hands on her was driving him mad. He didn't trust himself any longer and knew he had better leave before he totally lost it.

"Huh, I'll guess I'll be going. Mariah if you need anything call me please. Do you have any baby supplies at the apartment?"

"Yes, I do. I should have everything I need but thank you anyway. Listen would you tell Barbara I'll be back out there later? Jean Paul can drop me off when he gets ready to leave."

"Sure." Patrick kissed Mariah but she turned her head in time so that he had to kiss her cheek instead. "Call me."

"I will, I promise."

Patrick turned and started to leave.

"Wainscott, by the way, thank you for taking care of Mariah and Abigail through the labor." Patrick nodded and walked out shocked to hear those words from a man he despised.

CHAPTER 16

It was noon when Mariah, Jean Paul and Abigail entered the boutique. Margo looked up from sorting the sweaters on the shelf when she saw them. Within seconds, the rest of the staff and some of the customers in the store had surrounded them. Jean Paul adjusted Abigail so everyone could see her. It took a few minutes for the commotion to calm down. Abigail was wide eyed but didn't once cry. Enough was enough, Jean Paul felt it probably wasn't good to have some many people around Abigail so he excused them asking Margo to spread the word Mariah was not to be disturbed the rest of the day and they went upstairs. As soon as he laid the baby in her crib and took off her little shoes she was asleep. He covered her with a receiving blanket. Mariah put the roses on the table by the window and walked over to the crib. Jean Paul placed his arms around her waist and drew her closer to him. They stood together watching Abigail sleep.

"She looks so tiny in that big bed."

"But she isn't that small and in no time that bed will not be big enough. She looks just like I had imagined her to be when I saw that bed. I am very glad we got it for her."

"Me, too." Mariah walked over to her bed and picked up the Christening outfit that Jean Paul had brought with him. "Did I say thank you for this gorgeous gift?"

"Many times, *ma chérie*. I will be sure to tell Katelin you liked the idea."

"Please do, I'll send her a note, too. I've been meaning to call her but you know how things have been."

"She understands but she misses your talks. She told me so." Jean Paul sat on the bed watching her wrap the outfit in the tissue paper and place it back in the box. He noticed Mariah look tired but also knew she wouldn't give in to it.

"Come here, *mon amour*, sit down beside me. Abigail will be fine. Let us relax while we can." Mariah kicked off her shoes and crawled on top of the bed beside him but just as she did he got up and walked in the bathroom.

"Well now, that's fine and dandy. I sit down and you get up."

351

"You stay where you are," he called from the inside the bathroom. She heard the water run and then he came out with a bottle of lotion in his hand.

"What are you doing?" She gave a little nervous laugh when he sat down beside her. His face was close to hers, their eyes met, and their lips touched briefly at first then again but this time the kiss was a long sensuous, passionate one. He sat back from her, his eyes wide with desire but knew this was not the time, not yet, but soon. His hands massaged her feet, then her legs and as he did he ever so slightly moved the hem of her skirt higher out of his way until it was less than half way up her thigh.

"Jean Paul, I can't-I mean not yet," her voice was soft but uncontrolled. She was shaking inside. He had such an effect on her she thought.

"Shh, it's all right. Just relax while you can. Abigail won't sleep very long." He reached under her skirt and found the garters that held her stockings in place.

The memory of when Mariah was just starting to show and couldn't find a pair of pantyhose to fit her figure right, in her exasperation she declared that she would only wear stockings from that point on. In his opinion, a woman in stockings was definitely sexier than one in pantyhose. One by one, he unfastened them until he was able to free her from the silky threads. Gently he moved them off one leg and then the other. With her legs bare, he stroked the lotion in her skin starting with her toes, massaging every one, and working on up her leg, her knee and higher, his fingers needing and caressing her skin. The warmth of the lotion was so relaxing that she started to doze off to sleep. Jean Paul covered her with an extra blanket. He checked on Abigail who was still fast asleep. He closed the curtain to block out most of the daylight, took his shirt off, and lay down beside Mariah holding her. He was lucky to have her in his life and he thanked God everyday for her and now he had something else to be thankful for- Abigail. He fell asleep only to be awakened by the cries of a newborn babe. Mariah stirred but he gently covered her back up, Mariah closed her eyes again but heard Jean Paul picking Abigail up and seeing to her. After he changed her diaper and she wouldn't stop crying he knew that what the baby wanted he couldn't give. By this time Mariah was awake and ready to nurse.

"Bring her to me." Jean Paul was holding Abigail in his arms and turned around. "I'm sorry, but you can't do what I can." She placed a pillow on her lap. He gave her the baby and immediately Abigail nuzzled Mariah. Jean

Paul lay down quietly beside them on the bed and watched as Abigail had her fill. He smiled feeling content. This was what life was about. A family. The look on Mariah's face told him that she felt the same way.

Eight o'clock in the morning found Jean Paul on the phone to Sheriff Tobias. Mariah woke hearing his voice inside her office; the door between the rooms was almost shut. She checked Abigail who was sleeping in her crib; she was ready to enter the office when she heard something change in his voice. She stopped short and listened.

"I see, do you think that could be the case here?" Jean Paul's back was to her so she couldn't read his face but his tone was serious. "Fine, if you come up with anything you have all of my numbers. *Merci*, Sheriff." He hung up the phone. The door squeaked and he turned to see Mariah standing in the doorway, with her old terrycloth robe around her and her hair tussled from sleeping. The sight of her looking so beautiful made him ache for her. She could have been in a gunnysack for all he cared. Motherhood agreed with her.

"*Mon amour*, did I wake you?" He embraced her and then slightly tilted her face upward. He kissed her. Mariah took note that he was fully dressed minus his suit jacket thus revealing a slightly crooked tie.

"No, you didn't. You're dressed, are you going somewhere?"

"*Non*, just ready for what the day may bring. Word will surely get out that you and Abigail are here. You may have friends to come by, *oui*?"

"Maybe but .. wait a minute.. you were talking to Lee Tobias. Why?" She backed away from him and gave him a suspicious look.

"I was just following up on the accident and the portraits he had sent me." Mariah had noticed that he had made a pot of coffee, the machine was making the usual gurgling sounds as it finished brewing the black liquid. By the way the aroma hit her she knew it he had made it extra strong. He did that sometimes when he was tired. The night had been hard on both of them.

"What did he have to say?" She poured them both a cup and handed one to him. She took a sip and the bitterness hit her taste buds hard, she coughed. She was right. It was stronger than his usual pot.

"Are you alright?" He placed his cup on the sideboard without drinking. Mariah shook her head while regaining her throat.

353

"Yea, it's just hot and strong. Tell me what Sheriff Tobias said, please."

"They are putting the accident on the shelf. None of the portraits I saw were of the man. They have come up empty so far and I don't like it! He needs to be found for your protection." The last part slipped out in his anger. Mariah was watching him very closely.

"What do you mean for my protection?" She placed her cup beside his and stood in front of him. He didn't answer. She shook a pointed finger at him. "Count DuMoiese, if you don't tell me what you mean by that remark I'll...I'll"

"You'll do what, *ma chérie*? Flog me? Or perhaps you are just practicing for the time when you will need the skill for Abigail?" His voice was soft and the amused look on his face didn't help Mariah to keep her stern look.

"Don't you patronize me. What did you mean?" He knew he couldn't joke his way out of this. By this time he had come up with an answer.

"I just meant that while the mystery man was out there, you, Abigail, and everyone else aren't safe. I will do everything in my power to see that you two are."

She put her arms around his waist and kissed him. His arms around her holding her tight, she could feel him pressed against her. The tension was there again; it gnawed at both of them.

"I know you would."

As Mariah was clearing the lunch dishes from the table Jean Paul's cell phone rang. He pushed back his chair and went over to the bed to get the phone lying on his jacket.

"*Bonjour*. This is he." Mariah standing at the sink took note that he had changed from English to French in the course of the conversation. He had left the room and went into her office again. Why was he doing that? The question played over and over again. She dropped the dishcloth on the counter and followed him. He disconnected the phone just as she entered the room. That made the second time today it had happened and she was beginning not to like it.

"What about the trunks?" inquired Mariah. He turned around and placed the phone in his pant's pocket.

"The missing trunks have been found in Italy. They are destroyed but at least we know where they are."

"Italy? I don't understand why they keep showing up there? Who found them?"

"The police. They came across an abandoned truck on a back road. Upon investigation, they found the trunks inside with the garments. So they made a few calls and found Tré. It was he that called. The police have the trunks, they want someone to identify them for insurance purposes. I want to see to this myself. Do you understand?"

"So that means that you have to leave earlier than we planned?"

"*Oui.* I want to get to the bottom of this as fast as I can."

"I understand, but I don't like this. Something isn't right here."

"There is nothing for you to worry about *ma chérie* everything will turn out just fine. Now do you mind getting whatever you need together so I can get you two back to the ranch."

"I only need to pack the baby's bag. I'll be ready in a few minutes." She went to dress Abigail for the trip and as she did she heard Jean Paul telling Alec to change their flight plan.

Patrick had to do something to keep busy. His mind was on Mariah, the baby and the Count of course. He had cleaned the house again even though it wasn't dirty and then went out to the stable and started working on the tack. Jim had kept up with the chores, even the tack, but he had rubbed down most of the leather anyway. Someone was coming up the drive, tack in hand he walked out the stable and he was surprised to see the Mercedes pull up in his driveway so early in the day. Mariah saw him first standing in the paddock doorway. He was dressed in tight fitting jeans with his shirt sleeves were rolled up over his biceps. Before he could put the tack down and get to the car the Count had helped Mariah and Abigail into the house. Patrick didn't like the freedom the Count felt with HIS house but couldn't say much since Mariah still owned half of it. He entered through the back door and found them in Mariah's bedroom.

Abigail was in the bassinette watching the mobile that he had picked up after she was born as a surprise to Mariah. Mariah and the Count almost whispering to each other stood with their backs to him.

Patrick stood in the doorway with his arms crossed, he cleared his throat. "Can anyone join this party?" Mariah turned around.

"Come on in, Patrick. Abigail likes the toy. Come and see." She motioned for him to approach. He didn't need the gesture as he was already there practically.

Patrick stayed behind with Abigail when Mariah walked Jean Paul out to his car. He missed seeing his daughter last night, all ready that little girl had his heartstrings in her tiny hands.

"I am so surprised you were actually civil to Jean Paul," Mariah said as she came through the front door. Patrick had the baby in his arms and was rocking her. He looked up at her remark.

"I'm not always undisciplined. I kept my tongue for Abigail's sake."

"I thank you for that." She sat down on the sofa and crossed her legs.

"How was last night?"

"What?"

"I mean with the baby?"

"Oh, it was long. I think when you get her to sleep I'm going to do the same, too. I have a feeling that I'm going need to sleep when I can."

"When did she nurse last?"

"Just before we came."

"Then she should be okay for awhile. Go on to bed, I'll take care of her."

The next three days found a pattern in living for the three of them. Patrick shared the night duty as much as he could and for that Mariah was once again thankful. Charlie and Becky hadn't been able to come home yet since Charlie had come down with the flu and that delayed what he was doing on the set. They promised to be home next weekend to see the baby. Patrick also got a call from the producers who wanted him back on location the same weekend. He tried to get out of going back so soon but couldn't. Barbara had been coming over everyday to help with things so he knew she would be there for Mariah. He would have to take advantage of that so he could prepare for Christmas, which was right around the corner.

Mariah wanted the tree out of the attic so she could put it up for Abigail. She might as well stay at the ranch since he was going to be gone for a few weeks. It just made sense since the place was bigger for her and Abigail.

She was going back to work in a couple of days and planned to take the baby with her so she had to prepare for that. Jean Paul had called and told her the trunks were being investigated but no news yet. She had the house all dressed out for Christmas by the time Charlie and Becky came home.

"Well look at you, you're skinny." Charlie kissed Mariah on the cheek as he walked by her to let Becky in the door.

"Right, not hardly. You know nothing goes back like it did after a pregnancy when you're thirty."

"Still, you look good. How are you?" Becky hugged Mariah after she closed the front door.

"Come on in."

"Wow, look at this place. You've really out done yourself on the decorations this year."

"Never mind that, Charlie.. I mean the place looks nice but I want to see Abigail. Where is she?" Becky was looking around the corner into the kitchen as she said this.

"Here." Patrick came in the living room holding her. He had just dressed her in a red and white lace and ruffle dress complete with a red lace headband, white socks and red shoes. Charlie and Becky went over to see her. Becky automatically took her and started to love on her. She held the baby up to see Charlie who carefully took the baby's hand. Abigail looked at him and smiled. Charlie saw the resemblance to Patrick and felt a twinge of disappointment. He was secretly hoping that this precious little girl was his. Becky and he had come to terms over the situation and were ready to do what needed to be done if it was true that Abigail was his. Even if she wasn't, they were still godparents of a beautiful little girl.

The next day Charlie arranged to have lunch with Mariah alone. She brought the baby since she thought she would stop by the boutique on the way back to the ranch and see what was going on there. Sitting over cappuccinos Mariah noticed that Charlie didn't act like himself.

"I wish you would just tell me what is on your mind. Have we not known each other long enough to be able to do that?"

"I can't hide anything from you can I?"

"Then don't try, talk to me." Abigail kicked her feet and cooed. Both their eyes went to her immediately and the baby smiled at the attention.

"She knows what she wants doesn't she?"

"Yes, she does."

"Patrick is really good with her isn't he?"

"Yes, he seems to be. Why does that bother you?"

"I've decided not to pursue the paternity test." Charlie saw Mariah's mouth drop open.

"Why? I thought it was important for you to know."

"Look at her, Mariah. I see you in her, but I see more Patrick. She has his coloring and hair."

"But didn't your mother have black hair?"

"Yes, she did but like I said, look at her. Can you tell me that she reminds you of me more than him?" Mariah sat there looking at him not knowing what to say next. He was hurting and she knew it. She reached out for his hand and entwined her fingers in his.

"Charlie, you were wanting her to be yours weren't you?" Charlie didn't say anything. "She can still be, you know, that's why I wanted you to be godfather to her. She needs you in her life and I do, too. Nothing's changed."

"It feels like it has."

"You think you know who her father is, but we really don't now do we? I'm not any closer to that answer just by looking at her. Are you sure you don't want the test?"

"I don't see any point in it. I'm disappointed enough as it is."

"Does Becky know how you feel?"

"I think she does even though I haven't mentioned it to her."

"Well if you're sure about this, we can have the test done at anytime."

"I'm still going to love that little girl like she's mine and you, too." Mariah leaned over to Charlie and hugged him.

"I love you, too."

Upon hearing Charlie's refusal for a paternity test, Patrick didn't see any reason to proceed with one either. He was solid in his heart and his mind that Abigail was his. He had firmly believed that for weeks before her birth and now to look at her only confirmed it. He was going to drop the subject just as Charlie was doing. He had other things to think about since he was leaving for location the day after tomorrow.

Mariah and Abigail were going back to the doctor for their check ups. He wasn't worried about them but he did wish that Mariah wasn't so damn independent. She had started driving the rental car long before she was supposed to. She had even started talking to Daphne about adding the Count's line to the Louisiana boutique. Her goal was to have it installed by Christmas but since that was just a couple of weeks away she had set a new goal of the New Year. Daphne had told her the renovations to the boutique were almost done. Mariah had not wasted time in drawing up plans and faxing them to Daphne who then in turn would fax more back to her. Patrick felt like she was working too hard and needed to be at home with the baby but so far she seemed to be handling things. Abigail was starting to sleep all night long now and had even accepted the bottle if Mariah couldn't nurse. She had invested in a pump and had learned how to correctly freeze her milk giving her a little more freedom if she needed it. She still preferred letting Abigail nurse her directly but there were times that she was too sore to let her.

Patrick had to be in town so he thought he would see if she was still at Vivian's office. He was entering the door when she was coming out.

"What are you doing here?" she asked as she struggled to catch the door with one hand and hold the baby's carrier in the other. Patrick took the door and held it open for her.

"I was in town and wondered if you were done? Are you?"

"What do you think?" She was heading out the front lobby doors to the car parked outside.

"So tell me, what did Vivian say?" He stopped Mariah from going any farther on the sidewalk.

"She said we're fine. The baby looks good. Now, if you don't mind, I need to get back to the boutique."

"Oh come on, do you have to? How about lunch?"

"Patrick, you know I'm doing the renovations, those take a lot of time and details."

"I know, but I'm leaving tomorrow for a couple of weeks and we need to talk."

Mariah knew that was true, she had been trying to avoid doing that but it was time she stopped waffling on what to do.

"Can we talk tonight? I'm really busy today."

"Why don't you let me have the baby today while you're working? There's plenty of milk in the freezer."

"I want her with me. You know I'm set up for her upstairs and I do have those monitors, too. I think it's for the best that she stays with me. Do you understand?"

"Do I have a choice in the matter?" Mariah picked up on the disappointment in his voice and sighed. Patrick had buckled the baby in the car seat and was holding the door open for Mariah.

"I'll tell you what, maybe I can get home a little early this afternoon." He took note that she referred to the ranch as home again. This was the first time he had heard her actually say the word, perhaps this was an indication of what she was planning to do he thought to himself. He kissed her as she brushed by him to get in the car.

"I'll take what I can get. Be careful driving and call me if you need anything."

Mariah still had Margo doing a lot of the management duties but she wanted to go over the shipment records for both boutiques again. Maybe she had missed something. Maybe somewhere in all the paperwork was a clue as to why those trunks ended up in Italy. The phone buzzed and scared her so badly that she practically jumped out of her chair.

"Yes."

"Mariah, the Count is on line two."

"Thanks Margo." She switched the line over. "I was wondering when I was going to hear from you again. Where are you?"

"I'm still in Italy. I wanted to give you an update. The trunks were actually like the police said. They and the contents were destroyed. The police feel that someone was looking for another type of shipment. They have dusted the trunks for fingerprints but so far they haven't come up with anything."

"What about the truck, any fingerprints there?"

"*Non*, it's clean as far as they can tell. Who ever took the trunks knew what they were doing. Oh the van was a rental but the information that was given to the company was false. The business name used for the rental doesn't exist."

"Why would any one do this?"

"I don't know. The clerk at the rental company is looking at mug shots today. The garments are useless at this point. The police want to keep them as evidence."

"What kind of loss do we have?"

"I'd say ten thousand or so between both of us. The trunks were from your line and mine. I've already reported it to the insurance."

"You know, I've been sitting here pouring over all the shipment invoices for the past three months and there is nothing I can pick up on that even gives the scent of Italy." The baby woke from her nap and started making little crying sounds. "Wait a minute, I need to check on Abigail.." Mariah put the phone down and went in the other room. Abigail was wide-awake and ready to be with her mommy. Mariah picked her up and carried her to her office. She had her in her lap when she switched the phone to speaker. "Sorry but I have someone here that wants to talk to you."

"Abigail, how are you today? Are you training mommy well?"

Mariah laughed. "She sure is but you know what she actually slept through most of last night. I wish you could see her, she's looking all around for you."

"I wish I could see her mother, too. Are things at the ranch passable?"

"Yea, they're fine. Patrick wants to help with Abigail but Barbara is still coming over. Oh there's a new development though."

"What?"

"Charlie has decided not to do the paternity test. He saw her and decided that Abigail looks too much like Patrick. I think he's disappointed."

"*Monsieur* Osswell is a good solid man. His feet are planted firmly in the soil."

"Yea, I agree."

"Is that sound what I think it is?" He heard the suckling sounds of Abigail.

"That's all I get done. Vivian said put her on a four hour schedule but I'm having trouble doing that. I don't want her to be hungry."

"You saw the doctor today?"

"Just for a check-up and before you ask, we're both fine." At first Mariah thought they had been cut off since Jean Paul didn't respond. "Hello," she stated.

"I'm here, *mon amour* but I have to go. There is something I need to see about. We will talk soon. *Je t'aime*." He didn't wait for her to answer back but just hung up. That was odd, it wasn't like him to just hang up on her, she thought as she placed the phone down.

Jean Paul was still at the police station while he made the call to Mariah. He looked at the photo the officer had placed in front of him. His mouth went dry and the ache in his gut was almost overwhelming.

Mariah walked in the back door with the baby to be greeted by Ginger, the pup that had found her way to Mariah that day when Abigail was born. Patrick had given her a bath and she was prancing around in the kitchen. "Hi Ginger, look at you." Mariah placed Abigail's carrier on the table away from the reach of the dog. Patrick came in without a shirt on and holding a towel.

"That dog heard your car and got away from me." He grabbed for Ginger but she sidestepped him and he landed on the floor. Mariah had to laugh at the site.

"Well don't just stand there, grab that beast." Mariah called the dog over to her as he got up. She handed the dog to him to finish drying but only after Ginger had kissed her a million times.

"Where's Barbara?"

"I told her not to come out today. You've been in town all day and there was no need. Besides Charlie and Becky could probably use her." He dried the dog off and put it outside. "I don't know why I bother, look at her she's rolling in the dirt again." He sighed and walked over to Abigail. "How was your day little lady? Daddy missed you." He unfastened her and picked her up.

"I wish you wouldn't do that?"

"What?"

"Use the "daddy" word. We don't know that for sure. It'll only confuse her."

"You may not want to accept it but I know she's mine and for the record she can't understand anything yet so there's not any confusing." Patrick shook his head at her statement. He was getting tired of repeating those words. Mariah saw his mood had changed so she decided to change the subject.

362

"What's for dinner?"

"I have a pot roast in the oven. It'll be done in about an hour."

"Good then I have time to take a bath. Do you mind watching Abigail?"

"You don't even have to ask, silly mommy. Yes, she's a silly mommy, isn't she?" Patrick held the baby close as he talked to her, she grinned back.

An hour later Patrick had the baby asleep and the table set. Dinner was ready but Mariah still hadn't come out of the bathroom. He wondered if she had fallen asleep in the hot tub. He heard the radio on but no other sounds so he knocked on the door. No answer, he waited a minute longer than opened the door. Mariah was just stepping out of the tub. The brief moment he caught sight of her told him she was getting her body back after the pregnancy. He wanted to take her in his arms right then and there but before he could make a move she grabbed a towel and wrapped it around her tightly.

"What are you doing?" He knew she was put out with him for intruding on her space.

"Sorry, I knocked, but you didn't answer. I thought you might be asleep but then I got worried, okay?" He closed the door. From the other side he said, "Dinner is ready and the baby's asleep."

Mariah walked in the kitchen in a pale blue jumpsuit and socks. Her wet hair was up in a towel. "This looks good." She eyed the table, salad, pot roast, and vegetables.

"Sit down. You want tea or water?"

"Tea's fine, thank you," she said rather coldly.

"Again, I'm sorry for walking in on you but I did knock." He handed the glass he had just poured to her.

"Forget it, just please knock louder next time." They ate in silence most of the time making small talk whenever one of them thought of something to say. She mentioned about the missing trunks showing up in Italy. Mariah wanted to avoid the pending conversation she knew was coming and Patrick didn't know how to start it. Together they cleaned the kitchen up. Abigail was still asleep and Mariah almost had her mind made up to wake her so she would sleep through the night. But Patrick stopped her from leaving the kitchen; he took her arm as she passed by him.

"Here, sit down a minute please." He motioned to the table. She did as he asked as she knew there was no avoiding it now.

"What's on your mind?" she tried to keep her voice uplifted in spite of the impending doom she felt.

"This isn't easy for me but we need to talk about us." Here it was, the subject was on the table now.

"Patrick, please I don't think this is the time to do this. Abigail is going to be awake soon." She tried to get up but he held her hand fast across the table.

"What time would be good for this conversation, you tell me?"

"All right, you've got a point. Why don't you start?"

"Mariah, you know I love you and that gorgeous little girl in there. You have to know I love having you back home again, that's what makes this so hard. I don't want to say the wrong thing but I need to know where we stand. Will you make our living arrangements permanent?"

"I'm, I mean, I'm not sure.." She darted her eyes away from him.

"Look at me!" He took her chin in his hand and tilted her head so she had to look at him. "Look me in my eyes and tell me what you see."

"I see a man who's wanting everything in the world and expecting it."

"Okay, maybe so, but that isn't bad. Do you see the man you fell in love with? The man who has shared the last five years of your life with you, the good and the bad. Can you sit there and tell me that you don't love me? Look at me and tell me." Mariah lowered her eyes again, she didn't want to do this right now. She couldn't tell him. A single tear fell from her eye.

"I knew it! You can't look at me and say those words. You do love me."

"All right, yes I do love you but it's a different…Oh are you satisfied now? You have what you wanted me to say, what more do you want of me?"

"I want you. I want all three of us to be the family that we are. We need each other. Abigail needs her father, she needs me."

"She needs her mother more at the moment. You can't give her what I can."

"I can give her a life here, a good solid life, one with roots. Marry me Mariah?"

"I can't Patrick. I'm sorry."

"You can't or won't? Is it because of HIM?"

"I've told you that I love him. He's very important to me, to us."

"Only in your mind? He's nothing to Abigail? Don't you see that?" Mariah saw his patience was becoming taxed but hers was beginning to thin too.

"You don't know what you're talking about! He is a good man but I won't justify what I feel for him to you, not now, not with your attitude." She got up from the table and walked to the back door. Ginger was lying in her doghouse but raised her head when she saw Mariah at the door. Patrick followed her.

"So you won't marry me because of what he can give you. What if things fall through then what kind of life can you give our daughter?"

"It's not the material things Jean Paul gives me. Don't you ever criticize me again! I may not be rich, but I'm doing all right. I CAN support MY daughter very well thank you." Her face was full of rage when she turned to face him.

"Sure if you continue to travel. You have to promote your designs don't you? What kind of life is that going to be for a baby growing up?"

"I can give her a good life, believe it or not, without you! And yes, I plan to travel whether I'm here or not. I do have another boutique to handle remember? You're going to have to accept that. And another thing Jean Paul and I do have a working relationship as well. If it wasn't for his connections I would never have made that designers list. I happen to like that life. It's what I've always wanted. I will be traveling and I will be taking MY daughter. You can't stop me."

"What about the needs of our daughter? How can you talk this way?" She squirmed past Patrick and went back to the far side of the table.

"What about my needs?" Patrick sat down across from her.

"Sweetheart, I can take care of you both if you would just let me. I love you."

"But I don't want that. Don't you see?" The tears were falling again.

"I guess that's my answer isn't it?" Patrick suddenly hit the table with his hand and got up. Mariah jumped in her chair. He walked to the window and pressed his hands on the counter.

"Patrick, I don't want to hurt you. I haven't even been released from the doctor, yet. I still have a week or so for that. You know I can't go anywhere until then."

"So what then?"

"I don't know what I'm going to do, yet. Don't you think I know I'm not being fair to you or to Jean Paul or even to myself. I have to bring this triangle to an end somehow and I don't want to hurt anyone in the process. I'm just having trouble figuring things out." Patrick turned toward Mariah who was sitting at the table with her head in her hands.

"And when are you going to do that?" he asked her dryly folding his arms across his chest.

"Maybe we had better stay at the apartment. We'll leave first thing in the morning."

"Stop it! That's the most idiotic thing I have heard from you. I'm leaving tomorrow remember, so you can stay here."

"I don't know, I don't know what I was thinking staying here. I should have listened to my head and stayed at the apartment."

"Mariah, listen to me, I didn't want things to happen like this. Please stay here at least until I get back." Abigail started to whimper.

"I don't know about staying, I'll have to sleep on it tonight?" She regained some of her composure and walked out of the room to see to Abigail and then went to bed.

It was noon before Mariah and Abigail left the bedroom for the day. Mariah had spent most of the night tossing and turning. She had gotten up before Patrick and raided the kitchen for breakfast and returned to her room. She had heard him outside her door a couple of times but made no attempt to open it to him. Now the time came for him to leave for the airport and he was knocking again.

"Mariah, I'm going to have to be leaving in a few minutes. Can I please see you and Abigail?" She opened the door with Abigail in her arms. Patrick took her immediately. He was good with her and she seemed to bring out the best in him. She couldn't deny that.

"I wanted to let you know, that while you're gone I'll stay here. We'll talk more when you get back. I'll have some answers by then, I promise."

"Thank you and I am sorry for last light. I hope you slept better than me." He kissed her on the cheek.

"Mum. You have a safe trip."

"You be sure to get Barbara over here to help out. Do you think you'll be okay at night?" Patrick gave Abigail back to Mariah and picked up his bag by the door.

"I don't know why not. I'm a big girl now remember?" Mariah secured Abigail in her swing and turned it on.

"I know that's the whole problem." She was standing right behind him at the front door. He couldn't stop himself he took her in his arms and held her tight against him. She felt him and he felt her next to him. His hand traveled down the small of her back. She pulled away from him before he could go any further.

"Patrick, you can't do…" He took her face in his hands, her shoulder length blonde hair fell around them and he looked deeply into her blue eyes.

"Baby, we've been through so much. Don't turn away from what we have. Give us another chance. I promise I'll try to understand about your career, why you want more than the boutique here. I should be back a couple of days before Christmas. We'll spend the holiday together, right?"

"I said we would didn't I? That's all I can say for right now. You had better go. It's getting late and you'll miss your plane." Patrick glanced at the clock. He had a half hour to get to the airport and go through the security stations. She was right he had to leave now. He kissed her again but this time he gave her a kiss she wouldn't forget too easily.

The next three days Mariah spent towing Abigail into the boutique. She had taken the bassinette apart and was using the basket part in the shop converting the small office downstairs into a make shift nursery. Becky showed up at lunch with sandwiches in hand.

"Hey, Mariah. I took the liberty of bringing this for us. I thought we might have lunch together." She held up the brown bag.

"That's so sweet. Come on back here. I have someone who wants to see her godmother. It's been too long." Mariah took Becky's arm in hers and guided her back to the office. They ate while Becky played with Abigail.

"How's things between you and Charlie now?"

"You know he's really committed to us. I think he learned a lesson with all this. In fact he wants us to go to Las Vegas over Christmas since the set's going to be closed for the holidays."

"Can you get the time off from the office?"

"Yea, it's closed between Christmas and New Years, since the courts are closed down, too." Becky continued to play with Abigail who was eating up the attention. "What about you and Patrick? What's going on there?"

"I'm not sure. We had a rather nasty fight last night. He tried to get a commitment out of me."

"And?"

"And I can't give that to him, Becky. My life is totally different and not just with Abigail. I have come to realize that I want the glamour, the pizzazz of the designer world. Don't get me wrong, I love my boutiques, but I just don't want to stay in one place anymore. I finally have a chance of having my dream of being a world known designer. I can't do that if I'm stationary. I want more out of life for myself and Abigail."

"And you would take Abigail with you? What does Patrick say about that? You told him right?"

"Yea and he reacted just like I predicted he would. He brought Jean Paul into it and took it personally."

"But isn't Jean Paul a big part of it?"

"No, he's just a part, but not all. He gives me the freedom to run my business the way I feel it needs to be run. He only gives advice when I ask him for it, but Patrick tries to make my business his no matter what it is. He tries to run my life. I've just come to that conclusion, he did that before and he'll do it again if I let him. Everything I did all those years was mostly what he wanted me to do."

"I don't think he knows he's doing that? I think he wants to do whatever he can to make your life easier now and in the process make you happy."

"But don't you see, Becky, he can't do that. It's only me that can make me happy in the end. Not Patrick, not you or Charlie or Jean Paul for that matter, only me."

"All I can say, Mariah, is you do exactly that. You make yourself happy first. You and Abigail deserve it."

"Then you don't think badly of me for wanting my dream and taking Abigail along for the ride?"

"Of course not. You'll do right by her, Charlie and I both know that. Oh, by the way, Charlie may be rethinking his decision on the paternity test. I just wanted to warn you."

"He's thinking about doing it? What changed his mind?"

"I think he just has to know for sure one way or another, no doubts for the future, you know."

"Are you two getting really serious?" Becky nodded her head and shared a wide grin with Mariah.

"I think he's going to pop the question soon. We've been talking about having a family some day."

Sheriff Tobias hung up the phone. It had been almost a week since he had received the faxed photo from Italy. There were no signs of the man in town and his men were being meticulous with the investigation since he had to answer to the Count. He promised he would keep up the patrols around the boutique and the ranch without Mariah knowing. He agreed with the Count that at this point there was still no need of alarming her. The police didn't really have anything solid to go on except that a blonde haired man fitting the photo was seen in the vicinity of the abandoned truck in Italy. The Count had reported that he was ninety-five percent sure the photo that was sent over was the drunk driver that had run he and Mariah off the road. Sheriff Tobias was in close contact with the police in Italy but the man had disappeared. The man had done some time a few years back for burglary, other scams pointed to him but nothing could be pinned directly on him. He was a sly one, this man with several identities.

Charlie had called Mariah to set up a luncheon. He wanted to see her and the baby before he went back to the set for a week. Christmas was just two weeks away and he wanted to be in Las Vegas for it- just Becky and him. Once the shooting of the movie really got underway there would be no break until it was done. The producers anticipated it might take longer than usual since they were trying to get the history just right and that meant he would be apart from Becky for an extended time. He spotted Mariah and the baby, sitting in a back booth of the café.

"Hey sweetheart, don't you look pretty today." He kissed Mariah as he slid into the booth. She had placed her hair in a French knot, which showed off her pearl earrings. "Is that a new design?" He was referring to the deep violet dress that crisscrossed on the bodice that she wore.

"No, actually I just don't wear it very often. It's not my label."

369

"Well, it looks good on you, anyway. Can I hold her?" He held his hands out for the baby. As Mariah gave Abigail to him he started talking to her. She laughed out loud. "When did she start doing that?"

"Yesterday. I heard her true voice for the first time." Mariah was beaming with pleasure. "Do you want to order first or do you want to talk? I assume that you have something on your mind."

"Yea, I do. Do you have the time to talk first?"

"For you, I have all the time in the world. Let's have it."

"I wanted to let you know I'm taking Becky to Las Vegas in a few days. I hope you don't get mad but I planning to elope with her. I thought if she wants we can have a ceremony here with friends and family later."

"Get mad! Well actually, I am disappointed not to be there but as long as I get pictures I'll be satisfied. Just promise me you'll do it with style and not by some Elvis impersonator as the minister. You owe Becky that much."

"I promise the wedding will be done tastefully." Charlie laughed at the thought of them standing in front of Elvis repeating their vows.

"You know you just may have a surprise in store too."

"What do you mean?"

"Nothing, but Becky will let you know I'm sure when the times right." Mariah grinned."

"What do you know?" Charlie gave her a side look.

"I'm not telling. Now to change the subject, is that all you wanted to see me about?"

"No, actually I wanted to discuss having the paternity test done. Is it still all right with you to do it?"

"Sure, but what changed your mind?"

"I just have to know one way or another. I'm pretty sure of what the results will be but I have to have it settled. If I don't, there will always be a part of me wondering. Do you understand?"

"Charlie it's okay, I do understand. I'll call Vivian so she can set things up. I guess I should take some of Patrick's hair from his brush in so it can be run at the same time, huh?" Charlie nodded and proceeded to play with Abigail. Having Abigail in his life made him realize what he was missing by not settling down with Becky and having a family of their own. The thought had played in his head ever since he had held Abigail for the first time. It was another hour before he escorted Mariah and Abigail to her rental car. It was time to pick up the rings from the jeweler. Then he would stop by the lab and give whatever sample they wanted for the test.

Margo was holding up the phone when Mariah and Abigail stepped in the boutique. She was hoping it was Jean Paul and the look on Margo's face confirmed it was. He had made it a ritual to call her everyday in the middle of the day, that way he wouldn't wake Abigail at night. Even before they had finished their conversation Margo came in the back office. Mariah looked at her questioningly since Margo tried not to disturb her while she was talking to Jean Paul.

"Not to interrupt you but hang on a minute, Margo just came in," Mariah told Jean Paul and put the receiver on her shoulder.

"What is it?"

"Sorry, Mariah, but I think you should talk with Daphne. She's on line one."

"Jean Paul, let me call you back in a few minutes. Something is up in New Orleans."

"I'll be waiting, *ma chérie*." She switched the phone over.

"What's up, Daphne?"

"Mariah, I wanted to let you know all twelve trunks have come in damaged. The locks are off and the seals are broken and the lining is slashed up. Some of the garments are damaged, too. This is the worst I've seen."

"Oh boy, have you talked to Ted in the baggage department at the airport?"

"Yea, he said when the trunks got off the plane they were in that condition. He said he took the liberty of looking inside them and that's why he called us to pick them up. He didn't want the delivery truck to do so. Do we have any idea of what's going on, yet?"

"Jean Paul just got back from Italy, remember the missing trunks, they surfaced there and were destroyed, too. I was just talking to him. Listen, I've been thinking about flying out there anyway. You know, to see about the construction, but we'll see if we can come up with anything else on the trunks as well. I'll be there by tomorrow. Oh, do you think you could have a crib set up for me at the boutique and at my apartment?"

"Yea, sure, but can Abigail fly so young?"

"I don't see why not. We're both fine. Listen, I need to make some other calls..oh, call the insurance company and tell them about the trunks."

"I have and they'll send an adjuster out to take pictures. In the mean time I've stored them in the back just the way they are. Everyone knows to leave them alone."

"Good. Talk to you soon. Bye." Mariah hung up the phone and looked at Margo who was sitting in the chair in front of her. "Guess you'll be holding the fort down here all alone again. I hope you don't mind?"

"You know I don't." The phone rang again. Mariah answered it.

"Remmington's. Hello Ms. Barnes, what can I do for you?"

"Ms. Remmington, I'm calling to let you know that shipment we ordered came in damaged today." The look on Mariah's face was horrid. Cleo Barnes owned a very large department store chain on the east coast. It had taken Mariah six months to sell her line to the lady and now this was happening. She couldn't believe it. This was the worst thing that could. This could break her success if word got out that the Remmington shipments were not to be counted on.

"Ms. Barnes, I assure you I will rectify the situation today. I will have another shipment sent to you immediately. I am so sorry this happened. I'm not sure why but my boutique in New Orleans just had the same thing happen to them. I'm all ready investigating that incident."

"Very well. I guess things like this can happen once in a while. I'll over look it this time, but I suggest you get yourself a new shipment manager." Mariah heard the line go dead. She then placed the receiver on the hook.

"Oh Margo, what is going on? This is getting serious now."

They sat there looking at each other trying to brainstorm the reason why. Finally she picked up the phone, she had to make some arrangements. Thankfully the baby was still sleeping peacefully in the other room.

"*Bonjour* Jean Paul."

"Everything all right *mon amour*?"

"No, its not. All of the shipment to New Orleans came in damaged, the trunk locks and seals broken and the garments were vandalized as well. Then on top of that, the first shipment to one of the biggest department stores chains on the east coast came in damaged as well."

"I see…" Jean Paul didn't say anything else at first. He was taking it all in.

"Are you there?" Mariah sounded distraught.

"*Oui*, give me the name and address of the store and I will see that the problem is taken care of."

"I need the plane. I want to go to New Orleans," she said after giving Cleo Barnes information to him.

"Why?"

"Two things, I want to see about the construction progress and the shipment that came today. The insurance is sending an adjuster."

"*Mon amour*, I think it would serve you better to stay where you are?"

"Why? Oh, are you using the plane?"

"No, of course not, you know you can use her anytime. That is not it."

"Then what is it?"

"I'm just concerned for you and Abigail of course." He knew he couldn't tell her the whole truth but she was being stubborn at the moment. If he refused the plane she would just find another flight even if she didn't like going commercial.

"Very well. The plane will be there tomorrow. I will have Alec call you when he is within two hours away. Will that work?"

"That's fine. Thank you."

"After he delivers you to New Orleans then he can take the trunks to *Madame* Barnes. He'll probably visit his family while he is waiting for your return flight."

"Whatever. Oh that's a good idea about flying the trunks to Cleo. I'll be ready and waiting in the morning. Thanks."

"*Mon amour*, just be careful."

"We will be, after all, I am flying on your plane. That's as safe as it gets. I will talk to you after I get there okay?" she said missing his point all together.

"Till then, give Abigail my love and kisses and to you, too."

One phone call down and the next to be made she thought. This was going to be the hardest of all seeing how Patrick had made his feelings known about her traveling with the baby.

She wouldn't call his cell in case he was working. She would call the hotel and leave a message, that's what she would do. It would be the easiest, that way they wouldn't get in an argument over her decision. She dialed the number and a man's voice came on the other end.

"Hi, could I leave a message for room 1312 please?"

"I believe the occupant is in. I'll connect you." Before Mariah could stop the clerk she heard the phone ringing. A woman picked up. She didn't recognize the voice.

"I'm sorry I must have the wrong room. I was looking for Patrick."

"Patrick Wainscott?"

"Yes."

"Honey you have his room or should I say have his old room. He's staying down the hall in 1316, Rochelle Rainsfield's room." There was silence. "Hello? Hello?" the woman repeated and then hung up the phone. Mariah stood there dumbfounded. What was he doing in Rochelle's room? She had met the vixen once before and didn't like her then and sure as hell had more reason not to like her now. Rochelle who at forty-five was a woman of five foot six and an almost skinny body. Her long dyed red hair looked as if she had scalped a child, it didn't fit a woman of her age. She was known to have slept with most of her leading men. Even a few had become her husbands for a short time. She had a way of getting control of their assets and then leaving them empty handed in the dust she left behind. Why hadn't Patrick told her that she was in the movie too? Why hadn't Charlie confided in her? She sat behind her desk with her hands folded in her lap, a look of resolve on her face. That settles any question she had ever had about getting back together with Patrick she thought. No wonder he was spending so much time on location. His so called promise that he had been faithful to her since that ONE mistake was a pack of lies. No wonder he had left her physically alone- almost alone- these past few weeks when she was stuck at the ranch. She had thought she had finally gotten through to him that she needed space. She knew the truth now. She was not going to be able to trust him again. She was right to leave the last time just like she was doing now. This time she wasn't going to look back.

CHAPTER 17

Mariah woke before Abigail, since she couldn't sleep much. Her dreams were jumbled bouncing from people with hideous painted faces laughing at her to fields covered with flowers and sitting in the middle of it was Abigail and herself playing, then suddenly her dreams changed to her running away from whoever, whatever once again. The danger was real once more and she woke with a start, cold sweat poured down her forehead. It had been weeks since she had the dream, none since Abigail was born. Why now, she thought? Maybe it did have to do with her feelings about Patrick? Maybe her hormones were still screwed up? She was due to see Sarah in a couple of days again so she picked up the phone and left a message on her office machine saying she was going to New Orleans and would call her later. She then unpacked and packed again what she had packed the evening before. She was on edge and not sure she was remembering everything but she made sure she was packing Jean Paul's Christening outfit and Katelin's gifts. If she didn't pack everything for herself then it was no big deal. She had access to all the clothes she needed at the boutique. Finally sure that she was ready to go she carried the two suitcases out to the car and placed them in the trunk. Now all she had to do was to get the baby dressed, fed and wait for Alec to call. She had called the car rental company and arranged to leave her car at their desk at the airport. Next she called Margo one last time. The horror of the dream and Rochelle Rainsfield lingered in her mind. She tried to close her thoughts down as Margo answered.

"Hi, I just wanted to say thanks for everything. I know you'll do a good job at the shop for me."

"You sound like you're not coming back. Is there more to the story than I know?"

"I'll be back but I just don't know when. You know how to reach me if there's a problem right?"

"Of course. Mariah you sound funny. What's up?"

"Let's just say I should have known better than to almost fall in the same trap again. This time I really learned my lesson."

"Uh oh. What did Patrick do?"

"Did I say anything about him?"

"You don't have to."

"All I can say is that some people never change no matter much they try. Listen if anyone comes in to find out about me, just tell them I'm still in New Orleans and will call when I have time. I'm having a messenger deliver a letter to Becky explaining business came up in New Orleans and I had to take care of it immediately. That's the story I'm using. I just don't want Patrick to come looking for me."

"That's the truth and don't worry I won't say anything as to where you are if HE should come in."

"Thanks. All he knows is the area where my apartment is, not the exact address. My phone isn't even listed there so it may be hard for him to find me. Oh, if Charlie or Becky comes in asking questions be careful, they may be asking for Patrick. You never know."

"Mariah, is all this secrecy really needed?"

"I'll talk to everybody when I'm ready. I just can't deal with Patrick right now. I'll call them in a few days. And tell the staff to keep up the good work. I'm proud of them. They only need to know that I'm in New Orleans on boutique business."

"You don't have to say anything else. I had all ready come to that conclusion. Will you do something for me?"

"What?"

"Will you please be careful you sound so upset."

"I'm fine. Listen, I hear another call coming in. Maybe it's Alec. We'll be in touch, I promise. Oh I'm asking Becky and Charlie to bring the rest of my things and the baby's things over to the apartment. I've got to get that call."

"No problem. You and Abigail take care. I'll miss you and good luck getting to the bottom of things."

"See ya, you take care till I see you again." Mariah punched the call-waiting button. It was Alec; he was just about there. She had time to get to the airport and turn in the car.

Abigail was sitting in her swing playfully smiling. Mariah picked her up and held her tight. "I hope you never feel the pain as Mommy does in your life time. I know I can't always protect you but if there is anyway I can, I promise you I will," she said to Abigail. She placed her purse in the diaper bag and hung it on her shoulder. Keys in her one hand and the baby in her other arm she locked the front door behind her.

She went out to the stable and said goodbye to Jezebel once a gain. The tears started to come. She wished she could somehow take the horse with her but vowed that one day soon she would have her with her. Jezebel took the carrot out of her hand and Mariah placed the note she had left for Jim on the nail by Jezebel's stall. She knew he would take care of the horse for her but if he saw there was a problem keeping Jezebel at the ranch then she wanted him to board the horse elsewhere and send the bill to the boutique where Margo would forward it to her.

"Hi Mr. Wainscott, feeling better I hope?" The little teenage star struck set-extra looked at Patrick through her big brown eyes in hopes he might notice her for some future part in a film.

"Yes, thank you. Is there any fresh coffee around?"

"I'll get you some right away. Black isn't it?"

"How did you know that.. it is Jill right?"

"It's my job to know about everyone's likes and dislikes and, yes, it is Jill, Jill Meyers." She was pleased to know he had noticed her name badge the other day before he had fallen ill to the flu. She had accidentally left the badge on her dresser this morning. "I'll get that coffee." With that she disappeared. Patrick took a chair away from the commotion just to sit and get acquainted with the progress of things since he had been out of the stream of things for two days. Charlie had warned him of the nasty virus going around the set but he didn't think to have a flu shot before leaving Crystal River. Then there was the hotel mix up where they had over booked the rooms due to some convention in the area and the movie crew had to double up. Thankful Rochelle's room had been paid for in advance so the hotel couldn't move her and since she was gone for a few days he had decided to move in so as not to contaminate anyone else with the virus. He would have to call Mariah later and see how things were going with the baby but right now he had work to catch up on.

377

Becky and Charlie were surprised to learn that Mariah had left town without personally saying goodbye but according to Margo she didn't have much choice since urgent business came up in New Orleans. They were disturbed by her request to help move her things out of the ranch back to the apartment but did as she asked. They both had the feeling that the split was permanent for Mariah and wondered if it was a mutual agreement between she and Patrick. Margo wasn't saying anything and until they heard from Mariah or Patrick they couldn't be sure of anything. Charlie had tried to call Mariah in Louisiana but every time was told she was out of the boutique and would be given the message. Her cell phone wasn't working either. Something was up and he knew it. The more time and distance that came, the more upset he got with Patrick. He intended to have a talk with him the minute he set foot back in Crystal River, meanwhile he and Becky would continue to call Mariah.

Alec had delivered Mariah and Abigail safely to New Orleans and was on his way back from seeing Mrs. Cleo Barnes.

"Afternoon, Mariah. I just wanted to let you know Mrs. Barnes is one happy customer. I paid extra attention to her personally to help smooth out any rough patches and she ate it up."

"You didn't have to do that, but I do thank you. She's happy now, huh?"

"Very much so and I was glad to be of service. How are you doing there?"

"We're doing well. The insurance adjuster is finally coming at three today. We have searched the paperwork and made calls and can't come up with a reason as to why this is happening to our trunks."

"Have you spoken to the Count yet?"

"Yes, this morning, but there's nothing new."

"Are you planning to stay there for a few days or do you want to go back to California soon?"

"No, I'm staying put for awhile. If you're thinking about visiting your family for a few days then go ahead. I'll call you if I need you, but I don't think I will."

"*Mademoiselle*, I am at your call twenty-four hours a day. I will be an hour away from you if you need anything. Are you sure you don't mind my detour? It is my sister's birthday today and I would like to surprise her."

"Then go for it, man. Enjoy and give my love to your family."

"You have my number, correct?"

"Yes, of course I do, don't worry. Go on and have fun. I'll talk to you later."

"Very good, *au revoir.*"

"*Au revoir* Alec." She no sooner hung up than Daphne entered her office.

"Mariah, I hate to bother you but that Charlie person is on the phone again. He says he has to talk to you."

Mariah sighed and placed Abigail in the crib beside her desk. "Very well what line?"

"One." Daphne played with Abigail for a second then left the room to give her boss some privacy.

"Hello Charlie, now before you go off on me I have a very good excuse for not seeing you before I left."

"Slow down! Where have you been? We've tried calling you for the past two days. Did you know your cell isn't working?"

"No, I didn't. I'll check on that immediately. I've been so busy here and I do apologize that I worried you, but everything is okay."

"What happened?"

"You did get my letter, didn't you?"

"Becky got it."

"Then it's just like I said, I had some damaged trunks come in here and the insurance needed me to be here to inspect them, and then there was another shipment that was screwed up on the east coast I had to deal with, too. And as you know I'm putting in Jean Paul's line here and wanted to oversee that so I decided to kill several birds with one stone you might say."

"Is there anything more to the story than that?"

"What do you mean?"

"What about moving your things out of the ranch? I spoke with Jim and he told me about your note to him. What happened between you and Patrick?"

"Nothing happened. I just decided it was time to leave there. It just didn't feel like my home anymore, that's all. Did you guys get my things?"

"Yea, they're all at the apartment. Oh, by the way, Becky felt sorry for Ginger so we took her home with us. I hope you don't mind until you get home? When are you and Abigail coming home?"

"I'm not sure yet. There's still a lot to do here and I need to see about the trunks. And thanks for taking care of the dog for me. She's house-broken."

"How is Abigail?"

"She's fine. She took the flight well. We're okay, please don't worry."

"Where are you staying?"

"At my apartment of course. Charlie we're fine and we have everything we need." She didn't want the conversation to go on but knew she had to convince him everything was okay.

"Honey, I don't have your apartment's number or address there. What is it if I need to get a hold of you?"

"Charlie, listen, I can't talk anymore, the insurance adjuster just walked in. I'll call you later. Give my love to Becky." She hung up the phone before he had the chance to question her once again. She wished the adjuster would get there, she had been hanging around in case he came early and was tired doing so. She had trouble keeping her mind on the remodeling downstairs since her thoughts were trailing back to her phone conversation with whoever she was concerning Patrick. All she knew was she didn't want him around her ever again. He had lied about caring for her and Abigail. If he had, he would never had been with Rochelle Rainsfield and who knows how many other women in the past.

"This is quite curious, Miss Remmington. I have never seen this type of damage done in shipment in all my twenty years at State Insurance. This is most queer," the short pudgy middle age man stated as he looked over the damaged trunks through thick glasses. His appearance gave Mariah the feeling that he had been up all night since his gray suit was wrinkled. He continued to look through the garments inside the trunks. "Did you call the police on this?" Harvey Simmons inquired.

"Why should I have?"

"Anytime we have this type of damage, it's best to get a police report. Let's do it now. I'll wait and take a copy of it with me for the claim."

"What do you think is taking them so long to come out?" Daphne asked as she placed her gaze on the back storeroom door.

"I don't know but I'm going to find out. Will you listen for Abigail?"

"Sure thing, Mariah."

Mariah entered the storeroom to find the police officer and the adjuster discussing things in low tones. "Gentlemen, can I ask what you two are discussing?"

"Ma'am, I started dusting for prints and then I found this." The officer pulled back part of the satin lining on one of the trunks to expose a trace of white powder clinging to the underneath side of it. It was hardly noticeable to Mariah.

"So? I don't understand?"

"Ms. Remmington, does the factory use any type of powder in making these garments or is there a use for it in anyway?"

"No, not that I'm aware of. Why?"

"Let me ask this, are these trunks used by anyone else other than your shipments?"

"Well yes, they're used by my associate as well."

"What happens to them when they reach their destination?"

"I store them and when I have enough to go they're usually flown back to France, but it may take a while to recycle them since that only happens every few months. What happens elsewhere is up to the destination manager. I suppose they're tossed away or reused at whatever they want. Why?"

"Who else handles the trunks?"

"The trunks are packed at the factory and then moved by truck to the Paris airport, shipped here by plane to their destinations. My customers are responsible for movement from the airport to their shops at that point. They all have their own pickup service of some kind or another. Again I ask why? Mariah noticed Harvey Simmons looked troubled. The officer kept a stone cold look on his face.

"I'm sending a man over with a field kit to test this. We'll know more at that time."

"What about finger prints?"

"Who ever did this must have been wearing gloves. I only came up with the prints of Mr. Simmons here, you, and your store personnel, of course. Ms. Remmington, where are you staying? I understand you have a boutique in Crystal River California, right?"

"Yea, that's right, but I have an apartment outside of town…" Mariah proceeded to tell the officer her address and she mentioned that there had been several other instances of delayed or damaged shipments in the past few months for her and for the Count as well and what he had done to stop the problem.

"We'll be contacting this Count I'm sure."

It was an hour and half later when Mariah got her partial answer to the question that was plaguing her for so many weeks. The officers walked out of the storeroom with a grim look on their faces. Mariah, Daphne, and Harvey were sitting in the back office drinking a cup of coffee while waiting for the test results the officers were conducting. Abigail was on Mariah's lap when they approached the office door.

"Ms. Remmington, sorry to intrude, but I think you have a major problem here." One of the officers said, the other started talking to Abigail for a second then stepped back as if to go back to work. Mariah looked quickly over to Daphne and then to Harvey and back to the officer.

"What- what type of a problem?"

"The trunks have tested positive for traces of cocaine or meth."

"Cocaine, meth? No, there has to be some mistake here. I don't know anything about that. This can't be right? My trunks can't have this in it. I mean our trunks- Jean Paul has taken stands on stricter drug laws. I've got to call him immediately."

"Ma'am we'll be contacting him on this. There will be an investigation I'm sure. We're taking what samples we can to the lab for a "large test.""

"What's that?" Daphne asked looking as white as Mariah did.

"It'll tell us for sure what this is and the content of it. I would advise you to stay around for any other questions we may have." The officer looked directly at Mariah but tried to soften his words. "I'm not actually sure what is going on here and who is to blame, but we have some of the finest drug enforcement officers in the country. If someone is using your shipments to smuggle this in then we'll find them. We need you to stay in town for the investigation. At this point we can't be sure of anybody. Anyone could be behind this."

"Officer, I assure you, this is a total surprise to me and I know it will be to the Count."

"We'll get down to the bottom of all this but in the mean time stay close. Here is my number. Something comes up call me immediately. We'll be in touch when the test results are in." The officers left, leaving Mariah, Daphne, and Harvey Simmons standing looking at each other.

It was Mariah's fifth time in an hour trying to put a call in to France without any luck. She even tried Jean Paul's cell number. He evidently had the phone off. She resorted to sending him a fax stating very little except to call her immediately, hopefully, he would get it if she couldn't reach him through the phone.

Ten o'clock in the evening Mariah's doorbell rang. So far there was no change in being able reach Jean Paul. The operator said the over seas lines were having difficulties. She answered the door still dressed in her work clothes. Matt and Chris stood in her doorway holding a large dish of something.

"Good evening, love. We know it's late but saw your light," Matt greeted her and pushed past her to the kitchen where he sat the dish on the table.

"Yes, you see, we just came from one of those posh parties," Chris interceded and sat down on the sofa after helping himself to a small glass of the Count's white wine he kept in the cabinet.

"Well, actually, I catered the party you see. So I had this magnificent casserole left and thought you might like it. It's one of my newest recipes. Lamb and rice in a full bodied red wine sauce." Mariah didn't say anything to them and turned away in hopes they wouldn't see her eyes. Since putting Abigail to sleep she had done nothing but cry, first out of dismay, then out of anger. She still couldn't believe someone was using her and Jean Paul's shipments to move drugs in the States. Why her? Why him? Of all the shipments that come in the States why theirs? She didn't understand any of it. All she knew was that she wanted to talk to Jean Paul.

Matt picked up immediately on her distress. "Mariah love, what's the matter? You can tell us. We want to help?" He stepped in front of her and hugged her. Chris came over and embraced the two of them.

"There a group hug is better than a single hug." He kissed her on the cheek. "Now tell us and see if we can help?"

"Thank you guys, but there isn't anything anyone can do at the moment. I'm not to talk to anyone about this but I can't get a hold of Jean Paul and

I need to tell someone. The police found traces of drugs in the trunks that carry my shipments in the States."

"They what? Surely not!" Matt's reaction was very loud and Mariah had to stand back.

"Surely they don't suspect our little Mariah do they? What did they say?" Chris was more coherent in spite of him having more to drink at the party.

"The police haven't said anything except for me to stay close. I can't believe this." Mariah shook her head and pulled a tissue from the box she had put on the end table.

"Have you called the Count? He needs to know."

"I've tried, but can't get through." She sat down on the sofa and pulled her legs under her. She started shaking and couldn't stop.

"Lovey, you're cold. Here wrap yourself with this." Chris placed the heavy throw around her shoulders and sat down beside her. Matt sat on the other side holding her hand.

It was three am when Mariah heard something hit the outside of her front door. She had fallen asleep on the couch after Matt and Chris had left around midnight. She turned on the porch light and looked out the peephole. There was no one around that she could see. From the window she saw no one on the street below so she cautiously opened up the front door and peeked out. At first she stood there in disbelief and horror. She took a step outside to get a better look. There on her door was a red substance, it had been delivered in a balloon which upon impact splattered the contents all over the door and the outside of her apartment. She touched it to see if it was paint, maybe some kid's idea of a joke but the substance was sticky. Then the scent came to her when the wind changed, it was blood. Oh my God she thought, please help me. Help me to keep Abigail safe she prayed. Then she saw the note lying on the porch. She picked it up and hurried inside locking the door behind her. She knew the back door and windows were all locked, but ran around the apartment checking them anyway. All secure in her mind, she went back to the note. As she read the words, it was like she was in some dream state. "You may be next. Call off the dogs." She put the incident with the trunks and this together. Whoever was doing the smuggling knew the police were involved now. What was she to do? The thought had come to her to call the police but what if they knew she would do it? What if they were waiting, for her if not tonight, then tomorrow? She had to keep Abigail safe. That was the most important thing to do for the moment but she didn't know how to do it. She was afraid to call the police now. Just then her phone rang, she practically jumped out of her skin. She stood there facing the phone but couldn't move. It could be them, she thought to herself. She waited for the machine to pick up and then she heard Jean Paul's voice. She ran across the room and almost fell trying to get it before he hung up and she succeeded.

"Jean Paul, I need you," she was breathless and there was urgency in her voice.

"*Mon amour*, what is the trouble? If I worried you, I am sorry. The storm here has knocked out the phone lines to Marseille."

"Jean Paul, our trunks are carrying drugs. The police are testing for cocaine and meth…" She began to relay the story to him piece by piece including what just happened at the apartment.

"Here is what I want you to do. Listen very carefully to me. I want you to pack whatever you can in Abigail's diaper bag, nothing more than the essentials for the baby and yourself. You'll have everything you need when you get here. Use only what cash you have, no credit cards, nothing traceable. Be ready to meet Alec. Get to the airport as soon as you can. I'll call him to get to you immediately. You're coming home. Do you understand?"

Mariah couldn't think of anything else but to get what she had to have for Abigail and get out of there. She wanted to be the farthest she could from this place. She scribbled a note to Daphne to let her know what was going on then decided against it. She tore it up in tiny pieces and threw it away in the trash under the sink. She then bagged the trash and set it by the door. If she was to leave she wasn't going to leave it there to gather bugs or to smell. She had no idea of when she would return. She would call Daphne as soon as she could, but she hated doing this to her, leaving her to deal with this mess at the store but she couldn't think about that now. All she could think about was to get Abigail out of danger. What she was about to do wasn't for her sake but for Abigail's even if it meant answering for whatever she had to with the police. She'd deal with that later.

Mariah didn't have to wait long for Alec, he was there just like he said he would be. She had taken several turns and twists on roads that eventually lead her to the airport. If she were being followed she would have noticed it but as far as she could tell there were no cars behind her doing so. She had left her car keys with a note instructing as to where to find the car, inside the drop envelope the rental company provided outside their door of the office. They already had her business credit card number and were instructed to use it for any unpaid fees. She sat back and tried to relax for the first time since this afternoon when all this began with the insurance adjuster and police. She looked at Abigail peacefully sleeping on the bed beside her. How she wished she could sleep like that not knowing what was really going on around her. That precious little girl had become everything to her and it was her duty to protect her in any way she had to. Soon she would be with Jean Paul and it struck her just how much she really wanted to be with him not just now but for the rest of her life. Her place was with him. She sat up on the bed, opened her purse, and took out the little pouch that held his diamond ring. She placed it on her left hand and smiled. This was it. She had finally made her decision and the relief that she felt overwhelmed her so much that she started to cry again but this time not in fear or confusion but for pure and simple joy. Together they would get through this. They would be a family. She lay back down beside Abigail and held her tiny body next to her, it suddenly hit her- her dreams- the one about her running away from danger with Abigail. Her life at this moment was her dream. It had been a warning to her, which was why it kept reoccurring- someone had been trying to warn her of this moment. Suddenly her father's face flashed in her mind. Maybe it was her father who was trying to get a message to her. Could he really be watching out for she and Abigail? Was it possible or was that idea just a dream, too? The thoughts went through her head so fast she couldn't stop them.

CHAPTER 18

Jean Paul stood at the edge of his runway located on the other side of the Japanese Gardens and the mazes of ten-foot tall hedges, which blocked the sight of his private airport. He was scanning the sky when he saw the jet. At first, it was just a glimmer but as it descended he knew it was Mariah and Abigail coming home.

Moments after landing, he was inside the plane holding Mariah. Abigail was still sleeping so he had the chance to embrace Mariah and to kiss her. He had no idea that she had spent much of the flight crying. She had grabbed her make up before leaving the apartment and applied a new face but he could feel the weariness in her body.

"Come, *mon amour*, let's get you in the house and warmed up with some tea."

"Jean Paul, we have to talk. It can't wait."

"Yes it can, and it will, until you get some nourishment." He wrapped the baby in her blanket. By this time Alec had joined them inside the cabin. "Alec, please help Mariah down the stairs. I believe she is feeling a bit weak." He started down the stairs with the baby.

"Yes sir, it'll be my pleasure." Alec took Mariah's arm and steadied her as she descended the stairs. The Count was right, he noticed she was shaking. The concern he felt for her was real. He wasn't sure what was going on, what made the Count's voice over the phone so frantic, but he knew the urgency and didn't ask any more questions. Alec had learned a long time ago the Count would confide in him if wanted to, otherwise, don't ask questions.

He would see Mariah inside then go back for the baby's bag. That was all Mariah had brought other than her purse, which was strange, too, but yet he knew she still had a lot of her personal things at the estate. Maybe it was just easier for her to travel this way he thought.

"Come upstairs, *mon amour*. I have prepared the nursery for Abigail," Jean Paul said as they entered the back door. Inside Claude, Annette-the cook, and Margarette, who is the head housekeeper, but whom Jean Paul had promoted to Abigail's nanny, greeted Mariah. They had plenty of other staff to help with the house chores. Mariah greeted all of them; it was good to see them again.

Annette handed her a cup of hot tea as Mariah passed by which she took gratefully and smiled. Annette tipped her head slightly and smiled back.

"Margarette, please come with us." The three of them headed up the stairs. Margarette was a petite slim woman in her early sixties; her long gray hair was knotted up on her head and her blue eyes sparkled from behind her glasses.

Standing inside the nursery, Mariah couldn't believe her eyes. Jean Paul had taken the small library that connected to his room and made it into Abigail's nursery so she could be close. He had decorated the room in the same rainbow theme as she had back in Crystal River. He had even found the same gorgeous sleigh bed they had bought together along with the dresser and changing table to match. The walls were painted a pale blue with a mural of a rainbow extending from one side of the room to the other.

"Do you like?" he asked searching her face for approval.

"Oh Jean Paul, this is so beautiful. You did all this for Abigail! Where did you put your study?"

"I never used that room so I combined it with the main library downstairs." Jean Paul held Abigail up so she could see her new room.

"*Mademoiselle*, I think she likes it. Look, she's smiling." Margarette played with Abigail's hands. "May I take her?" Mariah nodded.

"Of course." Jean Paul handed Abigail to her.

"Mariah I have engaged Margarette as Abigail's nanny. I hope that is all right with you. Let them get to know each other."

"A nanny? I never even thought of a nanny. I like the idea of taking care of her myself," Mariah said after Jean Paul had taken her arm and led her inside his private quarters out of Margarette's earshot. She sat on the bed and laid back. Jean Paul closed the door and turned off the intercom on the wall.

"But *ma chérie*, you won't be losing any of those duties. There may be times when Abigail will need a nanny for one reason or the other. Or perhaps, you will want to rest for a few hours with Margarette's help. She is very good with children. Actually she helped Katelin and Guy with their family so she is very well qualified." Mariah sat up.

"I'm sure she is. Okay, as long as I don't have to give up my rights."

"*Non*, but I assure you, there will be times when you and I are together that you will be glad to have a nanny." He smiled as wide as he could and his left eyebrow lifted. "This time is for us?"

"There is only one thing, where is Margarette's room? She'll have to be fairly close. Not in the nursery I hope?"

"*Non*, her room is across the hall down two doors. There is an intercom in the nursery that is connected to her room and to ours. Each intercom can be turned off at will except for Abigail's of course. The staff or Margarette can not hear what goes on behind closed doors."

"What is this about "OUR ROOM?" Mariah's look on her face was stern.

"I…I assumed you would want to.. I can move my things into the next room if you prefer?" The confusion in his tone was apparent. He didn't quite understand.

Mariah threw a pillow at Jean Paul and hit him in the head. "You silly man. You did all this for us. You flew us to safety and now you think I'm kicking you out of your rooms. I don't think so, but I got you didn't I?" Mariah laughed out and Jean Paul looked sheepish. Then he approached her and gently pushed Mariah down on the king sized bed. He was leaning over top of her.

"Now who has whom?"

"Jean Paul, we need to talk first. I have to tell you everything," she spoke in between his kisses and pushed him off of her.

"All right- let us discuss what has happened." He accepted her seriousness with a sigh.

Mariah had recounted everything to him. The news was still appalling to Jean Paul. This sort of thing was actually what he had been fighting against those weeks in Paris.

"I assure you, whoever is doing this will be punished. We know how things are happening, and now we need to know whom and why. This we will know but in the mean time you and Abigail are safe here with me. Please *mon amour*, I know this is stressful, but don't cry." He kissed her tears away and together they lay in each other's arms. Mariah snuggled up against his body, she felt his muscles surround her and for the first time in a long time she felt like she was truly home. The love that erupted out of her heart took

389

her by surprise and she knew what she wanted. She sat up and quickly took his ring off her finger. Until now he hadn't noticed she wore it.

"What are you doing?"

"This." She held out her fist, Jean Paul placed his open hand underneath hers. He had a frown on his face but Mariah's held a grin. She dropped the diamond ring in his hand. He sat on the bed looking her in the eyes.

"What does this mean?" he asks.

"Silly man, what do you think? I'm here, this is where I belong, and this is where Abigail belongs."

"*Mon amour*, are you saying?" His heart was in his throat. Suddenly he couldn't remember ever being this nervous.

"Why don't you ask me and see what my answer is?" she said teasingly. Jean Paul slid off the bed, knelt down on one knee in front of her, took her hand and kissed it. She was making him propose once again. He cleared the lump out of his throat before he could speak again.

"*Mon amour*, I love you and you love me. You are the most beautiful creature I have ever seen, and in here, too.." He pointed to his heart. "You changed my life the moment I laid eyes on you that day in New Orleans. You and Abigail are the most important thing on earth to me. I would give up everything I have for you. *Veux-tu m'epouser?*"

"On one condition, don't give up everything. There is one personal thing I desire of you- all of you." She grinned. "Yes, I will marry you."

Jean Paul placed the ring on her finger. She scooted back on the bed. He stood up and sat on the bed beside her. He took her in his arms and kissed her deeply, his mouth pressing hard against hers, his tongue eagerly searching hers. Their breathing came hard and raspy. He started stroking her neck, her shoulders and then her breast. Mariah winched a little and pulled away.

"What is it?"

"It's okay, I'm just tender since Abigail hasn't nursed for a while but that isn't it."

"Again what is it then?"

"It's just that we've waited so long, I really want to wait until we're married. Does that sound silly?"

"Ah… we are not teenagers, *oui*? I can accept that, if that is what you want. I am nothing but a gentleman. Answer me one question?"

"What?"

"How long do you expect to keep this hot blooded Frenchman waiting? I can't do this much longer, I assure you."

"I want to be your wife as soon as possible but I don't know the law here?"

"Is tomorrow soon enough?"

"Are you serious? Tomorrow?" The smile spread across her mouth and her eyes sparkled.

"I'll make a call." Just then they heard Abigail cry, she was hungry and Mariah's body responded, she felt the wetness against her clothes.

"You make that call. I will be back." She left the room leaving Jean Paul holding the phone.

It was almost an hour later when Jean Paul entered the nursery. He found Mariah rocking Abigail and singing to her softly. Mariah smiled at Jean Paul who pulled up the footstool beside her. He held her hand under Abigail and said *"Mon amour*, it's set. We shall be married tomorrow. I have certain connections, I have friends in high places. The Pope will be here at noon tomorrow."

"The POPE?" Her eyes got wide.

"Oui. He is in town and I was planning a meeting with my old friend anyway, so I just asked him if he would perform the ceremony? Is that all right?"

"Yes, of course. I didn't know you knew him?

"I have known him for many years. I assume you brought your medical records and I have mine. I just completed a physical. That should be enough for the license. Anyway, who could refuse the Pope?"

"Luckily, I brought both our medical records. I can't believe I'm getting married tomorrow. Oh my gosh, I have so much to do. Do you think we could call Guy and Katelin as witnesses?"

"I have already done that. They are on their way and should arrive tonight. Oh there is one more person I invited. I hope you don't mind?"

"No of course not, who?" Jean Paul took the baby and handed her to Margarette who entered the room after knocking.

"Madame, if you please watch over little Abigail while her mother and I talk about our wedding tomorrow." He extended his hand out to help Mariah out of the rocking chair. Margarette responded with a smile.

"Congratulations to both of you. I hoped for several months now that this day would come. Mariah, you have been good for him." She hugged Mariah and then the Count. "If I can do more than help with the baby, please don't hesitate to ask. Welcome to our family."

"Thank you Margarette. You know I have felt like you all have been my family for a long time. We're just making it legal finally."

"Come, *mon amour*, we need to discuss one more thing." Jean Paul took her hand and led her downstairs to the library. There he closed and locked the door behind them. Mariah stood leaning against his desk.

"You never told me who the other guest is? You look so serious. What is it?"

"I have invited *le Premier Minister.*"

"The Prime Minister? My, you do have connections. You know the Prime Minister, too?"

"Actually Guy knows him better than I do."

"I'm going to be really nervous just with the wedding but to actually meet these people. What if I drool or something, I'm going to embarrass you and myself."

"You can always blame it on Abigail," he laughed and took her in his arms and kissed her. "Seriously, I must confess, I asked Guy to use his connection for us. I have spoken with my lawyer concerning this trunk business. I already offer you and Abigail protection here with my security but now with us getting married you will have the legal protection of being the Countess…"

"The Countess! Oh my, I never thought of that… I'm to be a Countess.."

"Of course, since the title of Count was given to me by my father and his father and so on."

"I'll try to do the title proud, I promise."

"You will just be yourself. But as I was saying we need to give that same legal protection to Abigail. She needs to have dual citizenship."

"Won't she have that when we marry?"

"*Non*, she will only if I adopt her. That is my dream and hope that you will allow me to do that?" Mariah's hand went up to her mouth and she sat down in the chair beside her.

"You want to adopt her?" She sat in silence for a few seconds staring at the expensive Italian carpet in front of her. "What about Patrick?"

"What about Patrick?"

"You know what! Charlie wanted a paternity test after all, so I had one done for both of them before I left for New Orleans and now all this mess blew up. What if Patrick's the father, which you and I know he probably is? Won't I have to say I don't know who her father is?"

"Do you have those results yet?" Jean Paul sat down behind his desk stroking his chin with his right hand. He couldn't read her thoughts so he searched her face for help.

"No, the lab said it would take a week to get back."

"Then if you allow the adoption tomorrow right after the wedding, you can say legally that at this point in time you do not know the identity of her father. Would that not be the truth?"

"It would."

"Do you have any objections to the adoption? The Prime Minister can take care of the matter for us." His voice was soft and hesitant.

It all became clear to Mariah now. If there was true danger concerning the drugs then they would need every ounce of protection they could get. After all, she did come here for his help but also for his love, which she knew, she could count on unlike Patrick's. She wanted a better life for herself and for Abigail, better than she felt they would have with Patrick. "No, Jean Paul, I don't have any objections, this just took me by surprise. Everything is happening so fast. Abigail deserves to have a father like you. You are the most caring, unselfish man I have ever known. But you know we will have to deal with Patrick at some point?"

"*Oui*, I already have my lawyers on the situation. They are drawing up adoption papers as we speak. After we do this, we will draw up a generous visitation agreement concerning Patrick. Will that be okay? We will need to discuss what you want concerning the matter." Mariah sighed, she knew he was right she had to do this, somehow she was going to have to make Patrick see the urgency here. "We will be in this together, we will talk to him together." Jean Paul read her thoughts

"Are you sure you want to bring all my baggage into your house?"

"*Mon amour,* your baggage is my baggage and has been for several months now." He stood her up and kissed her. "Tomorrow night, is our night. Keep that in your thoughts, not the nasty trunk business, not Patrick, just us, just our little family."

"Just think we'll be married by Christmas. What do you want by the way?"

"*Mon amour*, I just want you," he whispered breathlessly in her ear. The feeling in his groin told him he couldn't wait much longer. He pulled her so close to him that she thought she would explode in his tight grip. He kissed her again, sending chills down her spine, she wanted him too, regretting her decision to wait until their wedding night, but she had to do it.

"You had better let me go if you want to get married tomorrow. I have so many things to do between now and then."

"*Non* you don't. We have a full staff to help. I have already taken the liberty on some of the arrangements."

"You have, what arrangements?"

"I have asked Claude to order the flowers. I know that roses are your favorite. I wish this was summer and the rose garden would be in full bloom but this is not, so hothouse roses you will have anyway. Annette is very talented in wedding cakes. She had done several for friends of the family so her feelings would be hurt if we asked someone else to do it for us."

"Of course, that's fine with me. You have been a busy boy haven't you?"

"BOY! I assure you *Mademoiselle* Remington, there is no boy in this room. I will prove that to you tomorrow night. In the mean time, I will have your things moved to the room across from the nursery for tonight and mine down the hall. I warn you to be sure and lock your door." He grinned as he released her from his arms.

"Why are you moving out of your own quarters?"

"By tomorrow night the room will be new, it will be refreshed to pick up the essences of us." Mariah tilted her head not quite understanding what he was saying but she had other things to think about. She had to call Tré or Edmund and get a dress and she knew just the one she wanted.

"Oh I just thought of something, since everyone is going to be here for the wedding, could we have Abigail's christening after our ceremony? I promised Charlie and Becky that they could be Godparents but since we're here do you think Guy and Katelin could be her French Godparents, sort of back up?"

"How many children can say they were christened by the Pope. I think he would love to do it. I'll call him and ask and I think that Guy and Katelin would be honored to be Godparents. We can always have another service to include Charlie and Becky, I know they are very important to you."

"I wonder if they're married, yet. He was taking her to Las Vegas to surprise her."

"How romantic!" Jean Paul said frowning as he picked up the phone.

"Well, in a way it is, just the elopement is exciting. I sort of feel like that's what we're doing."

"I hope our wedding is much more than that. I want it to be everything you have ever dreamed of. You deserve that much." He dialed the phone. Mariah stood behind Jean Paul and wrapped her arms around his neck.

"It will be even if we're married in paper sacks and in the pouring rain."

Jean Paul laughed as he reached up and took her hands in his and kissed each one. "IT WON'T BE LIKE THAT! I thought we'd use the family's chapel. It would be safer with this drug business going on. We'll have all the security we'll need especially since the Pope is coming." He was interrupted when the line was answered on the other end. Mariah blew him a kiss and left the room. It had been a while since she had looked in on Abigail and Margarette. She knew in her heart there wasn't a need but she couldn't help it, she missed her baby every minute when they weren't together.

"Margarette, how's she doing?" She was rocking Abigail in the nursery when she walked in.

"She's an angel. We're getting along just fine and I want to assure you that tomorrow night I will be ready and happy to take care of her. Tomorrow night is your special night. You just be sure you have enough milk in the freezer for us."

"I know you two will be fine but I miss her."

"You're a mother true and true. But tomorrow night you need to be a bride not a mother. Is there anything I can do for you?"

"Well, there is something. I was going to ask you does your niece still do hair?"

"*Oui*, do you need her to help tomorrow?"

"I thought I might do something different. Do you think she has the time in the morning?"

"I will see she has the time. I'll call her right away and get her here first thing."

"Thank you." Margarette laid the baby in the crib and covered her up. She left to make the call.

Mariah sat in the nursery reflecting on the past week. She was at the ranch just a few days ago trying to recapture something that didn't exist anymore. She knew that now, if only she had known that before- before she had wasted so much time between she and Jean Paul. She had given Patrick a second chance and he blew it. Now she was moving on. That was the last thought in her mind until a knock on the door woke her from a deep sleep.

"Come in."

"Excuse me, *mademoiselle*, but I am to tell you dinner will be ready in a half hour. And may I say congratulations. I am happy that you and the Count have decided to marry. It has been the opinion of everyone in the household that you two should be together." He spoke English to her instead of his customary French.

"Thank you Claude." Mariah stood up, smiled and smoothed her skirt. She glanced at Abigail who was still sleeping. She hoped Claude wouldn't see her blush.

"I also wanted to say Countess that I am at your service as I am the Count's." He bowed his head as he placed both hands behind his back.

"Claude, please, I can't fill the shoes of a Countess. I'm no different than I was the last time I was here. Please call me by my name, not Countess."

"I'll make a deal with you, during formal affairs I will use your title with the respect you deserve and when we are casual then I will address you with your name or *Madame*. Will that do?"

Seeing how she wasn't going to win in this conversation she hugged Claude and he in return slightly hugged her not wanting to step on the Count's toes. "We'll be down in time for dinner. I'll just freshen up first."

"Very well and again congratulations. It's nice to have a child in this house again." He closed the door behind him.

Mariah chose a soft green skirt and beige blouse for dinner. There wasn't much in her closet but that situation was being rectified. Tré and Edmund both were coming at nine with her wedding dress and other items to fill her closet. She placed her hair up in a French knot since she hadn't washed it yet. She hadn't had time since she arrived. After refreshing her makeup, she dressed Abigail in a frilly pink dress, socks, shoes and a headband to match. She was just about to go downstairs when Jean Paul knocked at her door and came in without waiting for a reply. He embraced her and kissed her taking her breath away.

"Are you ready for dinner, *ma chérie*?" He seemed relaxed and dressed in black trousers and a gray shirt with the two top buttons open. He wore no tie.

"I'm afraid I don't have much to chose from in my closet so I thought I'd dress Abigail up instead." She held her up and Abigail cooed when she saw him.

"You look beautiful in anything you wear and anything you don't wear for that fact." He kissed her and took the baby. "How is my little girl tonight?" Jean Paul kissed her, too. "Come *ma chérie*, lets dine."

Jean Paul seemed like himself during dinner, playing with Abigail and joking with his brother and sister in law- Guy and Katelin who had arrived in the middle of dinner. Their children were being brought out tomorrow by their nanny. Katelin thought it might be easier to help Mariah with whatever she needed if they didn't distract her tonight.

After dinner Guy and Jean Paul retired to the library and Katelin and Mariah went up to the nursery with Abigail. Around ten Guy came to collect his wife.

Mariah sat in her bedroom listening for Abigail who was sleeping peacefully but the silence got to her. She knocked on Margarette's door and asked her if she would listen for Abigail. She had to do something. She tried Jean Paul's quarters- the door was locked just like he said it would be. She went to his room down the hall but found no one. Where was he at this time of night? It was past eleven thirty. The library? Could he still be there? She tied her robe even tighter around her and headed for the library. She knocked on the door.

"*Entrez*," his voice was low and quiet but she heard him through the heavy wooden double doors.

"Jean Paul? Is everything all right?" He was sitting behind his desk with his head in his hands. He looked up at her.

"*Mon amour*, I thought you were asleep." He ran his hand through his hair. His action reminded her of what Patrick did every once in a while. She quickly brushed the thought out of her mind. "What can I do for you?" He stepped from behind the desk, kissed her and held her in his arms.

"I couldn't sleep. I missed you. Something's on your mind, will you please tell me what it is?" She was starting to get worried, his expression and manner hadn't changed. He was very serious.

"I do not know what you ask?"

"We've always been truthful with each other. I know you and I know there's something going on. Please tell me. Is it the drug business?"

"Ah, partially. It does concern me greatly."

"Okay, but we can deal with this together can't we?" She sat down in the wing chair by the tall double windows at the side of his desk. He stood up and walked to the other side of the room and poured himself a glass of wine.

"Would you like some?"

"No thank you. Will you please sit down and talk to me? I have to ask you- are you having second thoughts, I mean about the wedding?" Mariah felt her gut tighten up, she didn't want to hear his answer. She knew that had to be it.

Jean Paul gulped the wine and set his glass down hard. He turned to her, she thought for a second she saw anger on his face, but if she had, it had disappeared as quickly as it came on.

"*Mon amour*, don't ever doubt my love for you." He had her in his arms so fast she had to catch her breath.

"I'm sorry if I hurt your feelings but you're starting to scare me. Talk to me please." He walked over to gaze out the window, his fist gripping the drapes.

"All right, we do need to talk. There is something that's bothering me. Since you have been here and excluding our conversation concerning Abigail's adoption you have not mentioned Wainscott's name. Why?"

"Why should I? He's not concerned in any of this."

"It was critical for you to close those doors back home, did you do that?"

"Yes, I did. I wouldn't be marrying you tomorrow if I hadn't." She tried to keep her voice steady but she didn't dare approach him. He would see her shake.

"How were you able to do so?"

"Let's say that I wised up. If I knew four months ago what I finally realized last week I would never have left. I'm sorry I screwed us up."

"What did he do to you?" Jean Paul looked her straight in the eyes when he asked. She was a little uncomfortable; his hands were on her shoulders.

"I don't know what you mean?"

"Wainscott must have done something to make you discouraged with Crystal River. There was more to you leaving than boutique business. If he hurt you...so help me... what did he do?"

"It's not important. He's not important. I know now he doesn't have any bearing on my life anymore. He was just being him. Since Abigail came my priorities have changed. It's not important any more that I'm there, Margo knows her job." She tried to steady her nerves and approached him. She took his arm and turned him around to face her. "Jean Paul, listen to me. I love you and this is where I need to be and it's not because of the trunks. It's true, I do feel safer here with you, but I LOVE YOU! You asked me not to doubt your love well I'm asking you to do the same. Don't doubt my love for you. We were meant to be together. I know that now and again I'm sorry I didn't see it before. I need you! I don't know what I'd do if I didn't have you."

"I just want you to be sure." He took her in his arms and held her tight.

"I promise you when we're old- you're in a wheelchair at the age of one hundred and I'm seventy-two I won't be out looking for a younger man. You're all the man I'll ever need." She kissed him and he responded with his mouth and body pressed hard against hers.

"Mariah, my niece is here to do your hair. Are you ready for her?" Margarette asked as she peaked her head in the bedroom door.

"Please send her in."

Katelin came in with Mariah's gown and hung it up on the closet door. "This is so beautiful. I can't wait to see it on, but right now I need to get ready then I'll help you. Okay?"

"Go ahead. My hair may take a little while."

Jean Paul knocked at her bedroom door. He was on his way downstairs to greet their guest but he wanted to see Mariah first. The door opened with Katelin standing on the other side.

"What do you want?" she said in a very dry voice and spoke totally in French.

"What are you, Mariah's pit bull?" he grinned when he responded in French, too, but was disappointed that Mariah wasn't alone. He heard her laugh in the background.

"You can just go on downstairs. She doesn't want to see you."

"What do you mean? Oh, she's not superstitious. I must see her."

"No, you're not. Go on now or do I have to call your own security? You are not going to see her until the wedding." She closed the door. He heard the lock hit home. Jean Paul shook his head and started knocking harder on the door.

"Mariah! Open this door. I need to see you." he called out through it.

"Jean Paul, you may be my bother-in-law but I swear I'll call security. Go away." He heard more giggles from behind the door.

"No, I want to see Mariah."

"What do you want?" her voice came through the door.

"Mariah, please open up." She opened the door a crack, but still stood on the other side of it. He tried to open it farther but couldn't. All of the women must be standing on the other side counteracting his movement. He moved to the side in hopes that he could catch a glimpse of her but couldn't.

"Okay, now I've done that so tell me what's so important."

"I just wanted to tell you how much I love you. You have me acting and feeling like a schoolboy today. And I wanted to tell you I may not wait until tonight."

"Just like his brother. It must be hereditary," Katelin spoke out loud so he could hear her.

"Oh *non*, it's just a man for you. His brains are in his pants most of the time. Honey, I know what I'm talking about. I've been married three times," Margarette spoke out and laughed.

"Margarette! I'm not employing you to talk about me this way!" He tried to sound angry but couldn't and it showed.

"Shh. I love you, too. For a minute I had this silly thought that you might want to cancel things."

"*Mon amour*, you have me for eternity like it or not. Here, I wanted to see this on you, but I guess I'll have to wait." He handed a large velvet box through the crack of the door. She took it and gasped when she opened it. Inside was the most superb three-strand diamond necklace she had ever seen.

"Quickly get the chair!" Jean Paul heard Margarette say as the door closed abruptly in his face.

"What is it? What's happening?" He was almost frantic.

"She's fine Jean Paul, just overwhelmed by your gift. Any woman would be. Your brother never gave me a gift like that. You need to talk to him. Now go, leave us or this wedding will never be on time."

"*Excusez-moi*, Count, there is a telephone call for you," Claude said as he approached them from the staircase landing.

"I'll take it in the library. Find my brother. I want to see him right away."

"*Oui.*"

The two men disappeared down the stairs. Claude went one way and the Count went the other. Mariah wondered what was going on but she had other things to worry about. Like getting in her dress since she had the baby.

She stood in the view of the full-length mirror and was immediately impressed. She looked like she hoped she would. The dress fit her like a glove and with her new hairstyle she couldn't believe her own eyes. Maybe this look was from her new hair? She didn't really know but it captivated her. She never really thought of her self as sophisticated but now she looked the part.

"You are beautiful in that gown. We may need more security just for your protection when Jean Paul sees you in that," Katelin laughed as she slowly turned Mariah around. Mariah blushed a little, she couldn't say anything but stood there looking at herself in the mirror. The full-length gown of winter white satin had a sleeveless tight fitting bodice with a straight fitting skirt that featured an ample slit trimmed in white mink, going up one side and ending half way up her thigh. She ran her fingers down the plunging neckline of white mink. The mink hid the point of the neckline, which ended at her waist. She put on the matching matador style jacket also trimmed in mink. She was going to nix the jacket but after hearing the Pope was going to be there she thought better of it. She would reveal the gown after he left. She put her three inch heels on which consisted of a series of straps. Margarette handed her a blue pearled garter.

After that, she placed the diamond necklace around Mariah's throat that Jean Paul had just given her. Mariah then placed the matching elbow length gloves on to complete her ensemble.

Edmund and Tré knocked at the door. Margarette let them in. "You are beautiful," they said almost in unison. "We wanted to come by and again give our love to you before we go to the chapel," Edmund said as Tré gently turned Mariah around to get the full effect of the gown. "Absolutely magnificent," Tré stated and kissed her cheek.

She stood in the front foyer of the chapel. Katelin was in front of her. Claude came in with their bouquets. Katelin's was of white roses so it would match anything she chose. Her full-length gown was of burgundy organza. It had a low neckline, too, but a full skirt. Mariah had told her to wear what she wanted since nothing was planned anyway. Mariah held a dozen white roses that had been dipped in gold sparkle. She smiled when she saw them; they were the same as he had sent to her on the day of her style show.

The music began to play. She hadn't even thought about the music. Jean Paul was unbelievable. Claude opened the double doors that separated the foyer from the rest of the chapel. Mariah was standing off to the side but when she saw he had fully dressed the chapel in gold roses, ivy, tiny lights and lit candles at the alter, tears came to her eyes. She had to blink several times to stop them from ruining her make-up. Katelin walked up to the door and started down the isle slowly giving Mariah a chance to get in position.

Mariah moved up then stopped. She had a fleeting wish that she could share all this with Charlie but dismissed it quickly. Claude took her arm.

"*Mademoiselle*, I am to tell you that due to unforeseen circumstances the Pope cannot be here today, however he has sent his top Cardinal in his place. Now if you would allow me to walk you down the isle. I do not feel worthy in the shadow of your beauty, but I would very much like to welcome you formally into our family. By the way, your hair becomes you if I may be so forward." He kissed her hand lightly careful not to soil her glove.

"*Merci*, Claude. I would very much appreciate your arm. I really don't think I can do this by myself without falling from nerves." She took his arm and together they proceeded down the aisle. The entire staff was there of course and she heard Abigail's laughter. Then she saw the Cardinal in his formal robes and then the Prime Minister who was there just like Jean Paul said. Guy was standing up front and then as if by magic she saw Jean Paul. There he was in his black tails looking as dashing as ever. She saw his eyes and his smile widen as she got near. She felt his look travel down her body, the look she had hoped for. She didn't have her body back all together so soon after the baby and even though he said otherwise she still wasn't sure what his reaction to her would be.

The Cardinal began the ceremony. She felt she was in a dream up until she heard Jean Paul's voice vowing to honor, cherish, and love only her until the end of eternity. She thought to herself that he had changed the vows. She had to listen carefully not to miss something. She liked that word- eternity- instead of the traditional line- until death. The rest of the vows were the traditional ones.

Mariah felt her knees go weak when Jean Paul slipped the gold band on her left finger. Encased in the solid gold were ten perfect diamonds. She knew instantly one for each month they had known each other.

Jean Paul steadied her and smiled. He wiped a tear from her cheek with his finger and kissed her. She placed his matching band on his finger.

"*Pardon* Count, but in this ceremony the groom waits to kiss the bride at the end," the Cardinal jested and a few of the guests laughed as well.

"*Excusez-moi*, but she is too beautiful to wait. I cannot help myself.. continue please," Jean Paul spoke softly but the chapel seemed to echo his words.

Abigail's christening took place immediately after the wedding as planned. The family and staff were invited to stay for the private ceremony. When all of the guests had left the chapel for the reception in the main house, the Count and new Countess stayed for the matter of the adoption of Abigail with the Prime Minister. The Cardinal stood as a witness. There was no going back now for Mariah. What was done was done. Both the Cardinal and the Prime Minister went ahead to the house after Jean Paul had asked for forgiveness for being rude to his guest but wanted a moment alone with his bride. They smile at each other and left.

"Jean Paul that was terribly bad."

"I know but I can't wait any longer. I need you."

"Not here! I.." He took her in his arms and kissed her hard on the mouth his tongue caressing hers. "You have to wait just a little longer. We have guest to see," she said breathlessly.

"I don't care about them. I want to see you in that gown. He took off her jacket. His eyes immediately followed the neckline down her breast.

"What is this? Mink? How seductive, *mon amour*." He fingered the fur lovingly and then caressed her inside. She pulled his hand away.

"Ah, ah, ah, you have to wait remember?"

"What is this?" He tugged open the slit of her skirt to reveal her thigh. His hand traveled past the mink and on up. Again she slapped his hand.

"Now what did I tell you? I can see I'm going to have to train you after all to listen to me," she said teasingly.

"*Mon amour*, right now you could lead me over a waterfall and I would gladly go."

"Then come on. We have a daughter to see."

"Wait!" He took her arm as she started to turn and leave. "I haven't told you that I think your hair is becoming even though I like running my fingers through it. That was the first thing I noticed when I saw you in the chapel. Why did you cut it?"

Her new style was more sophisticated. The length was shortened by a few inches but the lower body of her hair was layered and angled framing her face. Her hair was parted and flipped over to the left side of her face creating bangs that slightly covered her left eye. The style also called for her ears to be cut out thus creating fringes in front of them. This was much different than her thick all one length style.

"I wanted new beginnings on everything. I'm glad you like it, besides it'll be easier for me to take care of since it's Abigail who needs my time now."

Mariah's feet were hurting when she saw the Prime Minister, who had stayed to visit with Guy, out the door with Jean Paul. Margarette had taken Abigail upstairs but to a bedroom on the east wing of the house where some of the resident staff lived including Claude and Alec giving the new Countess and Count some privacy. Guy and Katelin had plans to go to the opera and wouldn't be back until late. They had insisted taking rooms on the east wing of the house also. That meant the entire west wing would belong to Jean Paul and Mariah for the night.

The rest of the staff was just about to finish cleaning up. She had the thought of helping them as they closed the heavy front doors behind the cold and the darkness. Jean Paul locked the doors but by the time he had done this she had sat down in the Henry VIII chair in the foyer and was trying to unlace her shoes.

He stopped her hands and pulled her up from the chair and in one scoop he had her in his arms and was carrying her up the stairs effortlessly. He kicked their bedroom door open and placed her gently on the bed. Mariah looked around. The whole room was transformed into something out of the French palace. The twelve-foot ceiling had delicate golden woodcarvings on it with a huge crystal chandelier centered in the room. Off to the side sat the carved antique walnut four-poster bed complete with a canopy of navy satin trimmed in gold braid and navy drapes hung on all four-corner post. The massive intricate carved armoire filled almost one whole wall with the dresser and mirror on the other. The ladies vanity and mirror set sat by the stone fireplace for warmth in the wintertime. The walls were covered in expensive navy, gold and white wallpaper. The drapes on the four large windows were of fine gold satin that matched the bedspread. The room had the space to handle the dark color without it looking smaller than what it was. It was filled with roses and lit candelabras bathing the room in subtle light. It was very different than his old décor. It was obvious that he too had wanted new beginnings as well. He locked the door and stood in front of her. She was sitting on the bed at this point.

"This is wonderful…" she started to say referring to the room but he placed a finger to her lips and helped her to her feet.

"*Non mon amour*, YOU'RE wonderful. He kissed her as he held her tight. She felt his need and his urgency. She felt her own. This is what she had been waiting for and she knew it. Her heart was racing.

"Jean Paul, how about blowing out the candles. I'd like to have darkness." He stood back from her for a minute and gave her a look with a raised eyebrow.

"*Mon amour*, there is no need to be shy or nervous. Not now after all this time we have known each other."

"I just.."

"Childbirth has not changed your body. You are still as beautiful to me as the day I met you. I want the light to see you and you need the light to see how I look at you." They were so in tune with each other that he had read her thought and feelings.

He stood behind her bathed in the candlelight, their reflections in the cheval mirror. His arms around her waist, "*Mon amour*, watch and feel." He kissed the back of her neck moving her hair out of the way. His mouth went down her shoulder, one and then the other, so very slowly. His fingers unlatched her necklace and he placed in on the table beside them. He continued to stand behind her. His hands stroked her cheek, his fingers touching her lips, she parted them and playfully bit at them. She saw him grin in the mirror. His finger stroked her shoulders and then her neck. She was embarrassed at first to watch but then found she was indeed lost in the scene. He seductively played with the mink on her neckline and his hand found its way inside the bodice of the gown while holding her tightly against him so she could feel how full of life he was. He found the gown's zipper hidden on the side and gently led it all the way down. It fell to the floor.

"You are so beautiful. Do you feel it?" Mariah slightly nodded she was beginning to feel that way. The shyness was leaving. The candlelight cast shadows around the room and on them but still there was enough light and he was pleased with the effect in the mirror. Still holding her against him he reached in front of her and unfastened her lace bra freeing her of her confines. He gently caressed both of her breasts at the same time. She arched her back and moaned. She felt the tingling sensation of lactation. His hands left that part of her just in time. They traveled down her body crisscrossing around to her back and then to her abdomen again. His hands slid effortless inside her lace panties, embracing her, all of her, his fingers expertly finding their mark. He teased the garment off of her all the while exploring her. She moaned, her body feeling hot with desire. He then unfastened her silk stockings and took them off one leg and then the other. Her garter belt fell away along with her blue pearl garter Margarette had given her. "Do you feel the beauty?" She nodded once again mesmerized. "The beauty is inside you as well as out. It always has been and it always will be no matter what." He knelt down in front of her and kissed her.

"Oh Jean Paul I can't stand this." She pulled him up and as he did so he kissed her body. She slipped off his tuxedo coat, then his tie and his shirt. She stroked his chest running her hands through his thick hair. She kissed him, her mouth searching his, then his throat, and his chest. He kicked off his shoes and socks while her hands unfastened his cummerbund and let it fall to the floor with the rest of their clothes. She took off his belt and helped his pants to fall, her hands coming to rest on him. She had touched him before but this time everything was different. There was so much electricity and excitement between them that neither one of them was going to be satisfied very easily. Their breath was fast and sporadic. His mouth was on hers when he picked her up and laid her on the bed throwing the bedspread to the floor with his free hand in one swift movement.

His body poised over top of her, her arms around his neck, he kissed her ears and neck. "*Je t'aime.* I will never give you a regret for marrying me *mon amour.*"

"I know you won't and I promise you the same."

"One thought before we go any further. Is it all right for you to be doing this so soon after the birth?"

"I'm fine and we're NOT going to stop now. I'm so happy I can't begin to tell you." He smiled and kissed her again and again.

"Shh. Don't tell me, show me." He cupped her heavy breast in his hands and began to kiss them. To his surprise she started to lactate. They both laughed but then he took her fully in his mouth and suckled. She tasted sweet, it was no wonder Abigail was growing so well. She moaned. The pure strength of him tugging and pulling at her sent shivers down her spine and such an ache that engulfed her body. The stirrings in her abdomen grew stronger. She felt like her other breast was going to explode with pressure, she was letting down. He sensed her discomfort and relieved it. He looked into her face with a twinkle in his eye. "Is that better?" Mariah nodded unable to speak. She could feel him against her. His skin was hot. He was ready but was she? She wanted him. It was never like this with Patrick and he was the only one she had ever been with except for Charlie that one time. What if her inexperience with men wasn't enough for him? His hands traveled down her sides, across her abdomen and her hips. He teased her inner thighs. She couldn't stand it anymore and she opened for him. He raised her hips and took her. She stiffened and moaned softly. The pain shot through her and he sensed it and stopped.

"What is it? You said you're all right?" He was angry for not being gentler and for being lied to. He tried to move but she wouldn't let him go. She grinned.

"Shh, I'm all right. Don't stop, not now. Don't stop. It feels like the first time but only better, much, much better. This IS my first time. I want you like I have not wanted anyone before. Take me, now, you feel so good." She was breathless and kissing him. Her heart was racing and he was throbbing. He was about to lose his mind if he didn't have her right then. He raised her again, she grasped the headboard and he plunged deeper and deeper being tenderer at first and then fiercer, her appetite for him grew with each time until they both climaxed together. Their first time was sweeter than he could have ever imagined and for the first time she could remember she felt totally loved; body, mind and soul. The rest of the night was spent in repeats between short naps and nourishing their bodies with strawberries and whipped cream and glasses of wine that Annette had left for them outside their door after they disappeared in their quarters. It was dawn when they both fell asleep in each other's arms.

CHAPTER 19

Mariah woke first, she glanced at the alarm clock, it was after noon all ready and she was hungry. She knew Abigail would be, too, and in spite of the activities last night she did miss holding her little girl. She opened the closet, pulled out one her new dresses and then she heard a rustle outside the door. She put on her robe and opened it expecting to see Margarette with Abigail but instead there was a tray. She carried it inside and set in on the dresser. She read the note that accompanied it. "Mariah, thought you may need some sustenance after last night. It does run in the family. Enjoy and don't worry about Abigail. She's eaten twice already and playing with her cousins. Love Katelin and Guy." Mariah smiled and peaked inside the silver dome. She found waffles with fruit and heavy cream, bacon, eggs, orange juice, and coffee. If she ate like that all the time she would gain back her baby fat.

She crawled up on the bed and knelt beside her husband. She started to stroke his back and then his chest. He woke and blinked a couple of times.

"Morning *mon chér*, are you hungry?"

"It is true. You're not a dream."

"*Pardon*! I'm not your dream come true? How that hurts me," she grinned and kissed him. He wrapped his arms around her and pulled her on top of him. "If you were a dream I couldn't do this to you.." She laughed as he untied the belt to her robe and their love showed all over again. It was another two hours before they stepped in the shower.

Mariah was on the arm of Jean Paul when they entered the informal dinning room and found Guy, Katelin, and Margarette with Abigail. She was taking a bottle but dropped it when she saw her mommy. She held out her little hands for her. Guy set down his glass of wine and grinned.

"See, I told you *ma chérie*, they would come out for air sometime. There was no need to worry they were dead. One doesn't die from constant love making, at least I haven't yet." Katelin blushed and hit her husband on the shoulder.

"You brother, are younger than I. This woman nearly killed me for waiting so long. What else could I do, I had to make up for lost time."

This time it was Mariah who hit her husband on the arm. Mariah gave an embarrassed look and took her attention to Abigail.

"There's my little girl. How I missed you." Mariah kissed and hugged her. Jean Paul stood beside her and took the baby in his arms.

"Correction, *mon amour*, our little girl. I missed you, too."

Everyone was sitting around the table sharing coffee, wine, and cheese when Claude entered the room. He was in mid sentence when he saw the Count and Countess included in the group.

"*Madame,* Count, welcome back to us." Mariah smiled.

"Come Claude, sit and share some wine with us," Jean Paul stated as he poured a glass in front of him for Claude.

"No thank you. I do have some urgent business that must be attended to right away. Perhaps your brother can take care of this for you?"

"Be happy too, what is it Claude?"

"*Monsieur,* if I could speak to you in the library." Claude had a serious look on his face, one that Jean Paul couldn't dismiss.

"*Pardon,* I think I need to see to this too. Claude join me." The three men left the room leaving the ladies looking at each other. The joy that was in the room had left almost instantly when Claude entered. They felt it and so did Abigail, she started to get to a bit fussy. Mariah put all of her attention in Abigail but she had the feeling it had to do with someone trying to frame her for drug smuggling.

She walked by the closed library doors in hopes she could hear what was going on. If it had to do with her she wanted to know about it. She took a deep breath, stood straight up and knocked and Claude answered.

"*Madame*, what can I do for you?" Mariah brushed past him and went straight into the room and squared off with her husband. The other men kept a cool look on their faces wondering what was about to happen. It was clear that something was upsetting her.

"What is it, *mon amour*?"

"Don't what is it me! I want to know what's going on. All this secrecy is about the drug business or me or both. I demand to be filled in completely. My boutiques are involved with this. My reputation is involved with this. I am not a child and won't be handled like one!" Jean Paul walked over to her and tried to put his arms around her but she pulled back.

"Ah oh, looks like their first fight already?" Guy ducked as she picked up a heavy ashtray on the drum table beside her and threw it at him missing her mark completely. "Look out, we have a wild cat in the family," he laughed but stopped when Jean Paul threw him a look that could have killed. Inside he was somewhat amused, too. He had never seen this side of her and knew he must have gone to far in trying to protect her these past few days. She had a point. She deserved to know what was going on.

"Guy, if you can keep your mouth shut then you can stay, otherwise go! *Ma chérie*, sit and we will fill you in. You are right in needing to know. I was hoping not to have to spoil our honeymoon for a couple of days that is all."

Back in Las Vegas, Charlie and Becky were attending a style show. Becky wanted to scoop the competition for Mariah. She insisted Charlie tag along. Their wedding yesterday was all that she wanted, it was simple and yet he had managed to make it elegant. He had proposed the day before but it took him that long to find the right church. She had surprised him with the dress that Mariah and her had picked out and he knew that in spite of his efforts to keep his plans a secret he obviously couldn't. The church was on a small knoll and the architecture was gorgeous. After Charlie speaking with the minister in length he agreed to marry them the next day. He wanted more of a traditional ceremony than what Las Vegas usually offered and there was no way he was going to have Becky stand in line to get married.

At the reception after the show, they were milling about the patrons when Becky overheard a man talking about a kidnapping involving a woman and an infant. She stepped closer and heard it occurred in the New Orleans area.

"Excuse me sir, but I overheard you. Did the news release any names yet as to the identity of the woman and child?" Her body went cold at the thought.

"Why yes, you haven't heard? It's one of our own. Mariah Remmington and her new little baby." Becky dropped the glass she was holding spilling it on Charlie's pant legs. Charlie looked stunned at what she had done but all she could do was shake her head no and put her hand to her mouth.

"Are you all right? You act as if you know her?" The tall black haired man in the dark suit asked her. Charlie took the radio receiver out of his ear, he had been listening to the ball game the entire time the show was going on. No wonder he had sat there and didn't complain to Becky about a waste in time.

"What's wrong, Beck?" tears starting to flow down her cheeks.

"It's Mariah! She and Abigail are missing," was all she could get out before the man announced a news brief was coming on the television the designers had on. They stood in silence, Charlie supporting Becky who was still shaking. His gut was aching, too. The reporter told how the drugs were found in the trunk and tested positive for pure cocaine and how her neighbors had reported the blood smeared on the outside of her door and apartment.

The reporter continued about how the police had found her front door unlocked and all of her personal items inside including her cell phone. There were traces of some the baby's things left behind but not much. He also announced that a mutilated chicken had been found down the street and the blood tested positive for it and not human blood. Police were still investigating and no other information was available.

"We have to call. We have to," Becky kept saying, shaking her head no.

"Come on we'll go back to the hotel." He led her out of the party and back to the hotel. Sitting on the bed she held her head.

"Charlie, she's not involved in the drug smuggling. I know she's not and neither is Jean Paul." Charlie poured her glass of water and handed it to her.

"I know that. The police must know that. Baby, I want to go down there."

"I'll pack. I'm going with you but first I'm calling my firm. They know someone in New Orleans. We may need them."

"God I hope not. Wait a minute what about Patrick? Do you think he knows?"

"If he does, why didn't he call us?"

"I'll try to reach him. He may be on his way home by now. You call the firm."

Charlie rung the set and was informed that Patrick had left early this morning. He checked his watch. It was a three-hour trip and he should have made it in by now so he dialed the ranch.

The phone was ringing when Patrick came in the door. He had tried to reach Mariah for the last twenty-four hours to tell her he was coming home a day early. They had finished early for the holidays even though everyone was becoming ill from the flu. It had taken a lot out of him those two days. He had guessed she had been throwing herself in her work at the boutique.

Margo had told him that Mariah was busy taking care of some urgent business but that she was all right. That was yesterday and that was part of the reason why he decided to leave the location early. That had to be her calling."

"Hello baby, where are you? I've been trying to reach you."

"Patrick, its me. I hope Mariah is there, is she?"

"No, I don't think so. I just got in from location. I've been trying to reach her but Margo said she's taking care of something urgent that came up with the shop. She told me she's okay when I spoke to her yesterday. We just keep missing each other, why?"

"Pat, I don't think so. It's got to be true."

"What?" Patrick laid the bag of Christmas presents on the floor by the sofa and struggled to take off his coat with his free hand. He then checked the mail and saw there was a letter from the hospital's lab. Probably a bill he thought but stuffed it in his coat pocket for some reason instead of laying it on the desk with the other mail.

"Buddy, I don't know how to say this but Mariah and the baby are in trouble, serious trouble. She moved out of the ranch. You didn't know?" Patrick went to her room and found no personal items. "I'll explain that later on, right now she's in the biggest trouble of her life. It's on the news again. Turn on the television."

Patrick did so and sat down on the sofa. He and Charlie didn't speak until the newscast was over. "Oh my God! She's no more a drug smuggler than I am. I knew she was having shipping problems, but this.."

"What I hear is that the police really aren't looking at her as the smuggler and now she's missing with the baby."

"Wait a minute, they didn't say that here. She's missing!"

"Yea, this is serious. Becky and I are on our way to New Orleans as soon as we can get a flight."

"I'll go by the boutique and get Margo to confess everything she knows. I'll meet you and Becky. Keep your cell on so I can call you as soon as I have any information ."

"He called Jim and let him know he was heading down to New Orleans. They talked for a few minutes about Mariah's situation and what he knew of her moving out of the ranch. He then went by to see Margo. She was undoubtedly upset about the situation and told him everything she knew up to the point when Mariah received the call from Daphne about the damaged trunks coming in and the insurance inspectors coming. From that point on she hadn't heard from Mariah herself but Daphne was keeping her abreast of the situation there. The police were suspecting foul play in her disappearance since her apartment was hit with the blood and not that she was ever a suspect in the actual smuggling part of things. She told Patrick that the police located her rental car at the airport but if someone wanted to cover their steps and make it look like she took off on her free will that was one way of doing it. There were no answers just yet to any of the questions and the police weren't ruling any possibilities out.

Sheriff Tobias had heard the news release, too, and had made a call to New Orleans, perhaps he had news that may help them. The Count had made sure the investigation on the accident wasn't forgotten all those weeks and now he was sure it was all tied in to this new chain of events. He hung up the phone after talking extensively to the detective in Louisiana. The FBI was involved in this now considering the investigation could spill over into France and probably would in a very short time.

On the plane Patrick reached in his pocket to call Charlie and tell him what police station to meet at but instead he found the hospital's letter. He opened it and his mouth dropped as he read it to himself. It was the paternity test results. She had it done after all without telling him. Abigail was his daughter and this proved he was right all along. His heart was filled with mixed emotions- happiness and joy in knowing he was her father without any doubts but also with sheer dread and terror at the same time. What had happened to her and Mariah? Were they even alive? He tried to push the thoughts out of his head. He wasn't going to allow himself to think like that, not now, not ever. He would find her and bring she and Abigail home safely. He would do whatever it took to get her there. Christmas Eve was tomorrow. He had to find her and the baby.

Jean Paul had told Mariah everything that was going on including the mug shots of the blonde hair man and his police record. It was he that ran them off the road that night. Claude filled in some new details as Jean Paul went along trying to give her the news as gently as he could. Guy sat in the corner of the room watching but not intervening. He noticed that a couple of times Mariah's color blanched out in response to what was happening so he got up, poured her a glass of wine. She took it without saying thank you and drank a sip. It burned her throat. He felt a strong tug on his heart for her; this was supposed to be their honeymoon, some honeymoon. She had already been through so much in this past year and now this. He would do whatever he could to help she and his brother get through this ordeal. He knew the drug smuggling could lead to something more sinister and he said a silent prayer that it did not. His dealings with people like this in the past weren't good and thank God those days were over. Not that he ever smuggled or even did drugs, but he knew certain people who claimed to be on that side of the law. That happened long before he had met Katelin and that part of his life was his own, no one knew and no one would know. He stopped the associations, with difficulty, of course since they were threatening him if he ever told what he knew. After all these years, he still felt confident that this mess didn't have anything to do with him. He was no threat to any one, any news he possessed had to have expired long ago.

"*Mon amour*, I have put in a call to the New Orleans police. We must let them know that you and our daughter are alive and well so they can concentrate on the real matter of who is using our trunks."

"Charlie I have to call him. He's bound to hear about all this by now."

"I can't allow that right now, *mon amour*." The look on her face shot through him. "Please let me explain. You see when news gets out that you are well these people may come looking for us."

"You mean me, not us?"

"*Non,* I mean us. My trunks are involved, too. I had my some of mine tested. They showed positive to the same drug. Whoever this is, whatever this is, it's much grander than I would have ever imagined. And to think I lobbied to stop all this." He stopped pacing the floor and sat down behind his desk. She went to him and put her arms around his neck. He held her there. No one spoke.

"*Excusez-moi*, if I may bring a thought here," said Claude. He continued, "I have given this situation a lot of meditation. I think it would be wiser for you and the Countess to reside at the family's estate outside Bordeaux."

"Why?" Guy asks.

"Here it is too public, security may be hard to maintain but at the vineyard it is more secluded. The main house is not in plain sight as we are here. You could still be able to continue your honeymoon there. Calls have been coming in from well-wishers since word got out that you were married yesterday. When all of the other news breaks as I am sure it will you will be glad to be there and not here. I will hold things down here and keep in touch as we have always done, but I think it's imperative that you two leave immediately for the vineyard. There is another practical side to all this, you would be closer to the factory if you were required to go there for whatever reason." Mariah pulled away from her husband. The frown on his face told her he didn't really like either solution. He was not a runner and never would be but Claude had a point. He had to do whatever he had to for Mariah and Abigail's sake.

"I don't like it either brother but Claude has a point. We know you stand and face off your adversaries but this time bide your time and see what happens. Go to the vineyard and have what peace you two can find at least for a few more days. I'll stay here and help, try to make things look as natural as we can but I think I will send Katelin and the children to visit her mother for a while."

"You men talk like this is war? I'm sure the police can handle this," Mariah stated.

"*Mon amour*, this could be war, war against my family and it will stop," Jean Paul finally released his anger and pounded his desk top, which startled everyone in the room except for Claude. He knew his employer was building up to it in spite of all of his calm and control. After all, he was feeling the same.

"All right, we shall leave as soon as we get packed. Call Alec and tell him of our plans."

"I'll alert the vineyard of your arrival," Guy said as he picked up the second phone as Claude was already on the phone to Alec with the first line.

"Come, *mon amour*, lets get things ready. Margarette will need time to pack too."

"She'll be coming?"

"Of course, she and Abigail are inseparable since last night. We will need her for the same duties."

"Even now you're thinking of sex?" she was astounded as she spoke softly.

"Countess there is no such thing as sex with you. It is my duty as your husband to satisfy all your requirements. Making love to you is the most productive thing we can do at the moment," he whispered in her ear and she smiled. Guy caught the action out of the corner of his eye as he continued with his call and shook his head. The DuMoiese men were all alike.

The staff was ready and waiting for the Count and Countess DuMoiese to arrive. They greeted them on the front porch of the family home. Mariah had seen the estate once before but now it all looked different to her. Maybe it was because she was a part of it now.

"Come, *mon amour*, it is late. Tomorrow we will deal with whatever comes. Raul, please show *Madame* Margarette to her rooms. Are things set up for the baby?"

"*Oui*, just like you requested."

Jean Paul nodded and led Mariah up the stairs and to the right. Raul, Margarette, and Abigail followed. The rest of the staff brought the luggage up behind them. The house was smaller than the one in Marseille but after all this one had been in the family for generations. It still had all the original woodwork and some of the antiques in place to this day. His staff worked hard keeping it looking good. They took the master bedroom suite at the far end of the hallway and Margarette took one of the other six down the hall from them. Tonight Abigail would bunk in with her parents as instructed by the Count.

They settled the baby down in her crib and she went off to sleep. Mariah was very glad to have their daughter with them.

Becky and Charlie were sitting in the police station waiting for Patrick when he arrived.

"Sorry, but my flight was delayed," he said as he pulled off his coat dropping the lab's letter out of its pocket. Becky bent over and picked it up.

"Here you dropped this." She started to hand it to him.

"Give it to him. I guess now is as good as time as any to drop my bomb. It's not going to get any better I'm afraid," Patrick said to Charlie. Charlie took the envelope and read the return address. It was addressed to Mariah but he opened it and read the letter. Charlie sighed and folded the letter back into the envelope.

"Here you might need this." He handed the letter back to Patrick.

"Sorry. I didn't know she was doing this."

"We did, I asked her to."

"What? Oh Charlie, was that the paternity test? Abigail belongs to you?" She turned to Patrick and he nodded his head.

"Charlie, I'm sorry. I know this must hurt."

"I'm sorry I acted the way I did when she first came back to town. You know about the fight and all."

"Forget it. I knew in my heart that it was unlikely that the baby was mine but I had to know for sure one way or the other. Let's see if the captain is ready for us and take care of what really matters."

They sat in the captain's office and added whatever they could to help find Mariah and the baby. The detective on the case handed them the note that Mariah had left concerning her car and asked them to verify it was her handwriting which all of them agreed upon. Patrick was asked to add anything he knew about the car accident that she and the Count were involved in. Patrick looked at Charlie who shrugged his shoulders. The detective added Sheriff Tobias had called with the information. He mentioned the Count was extremely upset when he I.D. a mug shot of the "drunk driver" who was the same man he had seen around the boutique and finding out the man listed as "John Portland" had a police record on top of things. The front desk clerk knocked at the door and then entered.

"Sorry Chief, but there's a call I know you want to take. Line three."

"Excuse me, a minute. Why don't you take these people out there for something to drink. The coffee isn't that good around here but it won't kill you I promise." Patrick, Charlie, and Becky left the inner office.

"Have a seat, Bill." The gray haired captain pointed to a chair. Detective Bill Morgan had known the man on the other side of the desk. They had gone through the academy together. Captain Steve Curtiss was a fair man and he wasn't jumping to any conclusions just yet on this drug case. Anyone else may have accused Mariah Remmington of being part of the smuggling team.

"Hello, this is Captain Curtiss. What can I do to help you?"

"*Bonjour*, Captain. My name is *Monsieur* Guy DuMoiese. I'm calling from Marseille, France on the behalf on my brother Count Jean Paul DuMoiese." The Captain switched the phone to speaker.

"Yes, *Monsieur*. I have heard of your brother the Count?" Bill and Steve exchanged glances. If the Count had heard of his fiancé's disappearance it could mean trouble if they didn't find her right away.

"We just received word on what is going on there. We, my brother and I want to assure you that Mariah and her child are well. She is here with us." Steve slowly shook his head.

"What do you mean, there with you?"

"That is exactly what I mean. When she found the blood on her apartment she was terrified for herself and for her infant daughter. She flew here at once."

"We knew nothing of her being listed as a missing person until this morning. We at once began making calls to get through to your office but the international lines don't always cooperate with our desires."

"Is she there now?"

"*Non, pardon* but she is not. She and my brother are on their way to the family's estate for privacy. I assure you Captain that both she and little Abigail are fine, shook up, but fine. The Count is investigating things here on his end as well."

"Then you don't have any problems if I contact your law enforcement agency."

"*Non*, not at all. You see the Count has already done that himself. As I said, he is investigating things here as well. It is all of our family's belief that whoever is doing this drug smuggling and terrorizing *Mademoiselle* Remmington should be punished severely.." He referred to her as being single without thinking. It would take him a few days to remember to call her the Countess or even *Madame*.

"Very well, I'll make the call then. Whom do I ask for?"

"*Pardon*, I do not know but I'm sure they will direct you." The phone line went dead.

419

Steve Curtiss tried redial but didn't get anywhere. "Damn it."

"You think this is real?"

"At this point, Bill, anything is better than what we've got now. Call the FBI and let them know. This is probably a lot bigger than even we suspected." Bill nodded and started to open the door.

"What about those guys?"

"I'll talk to them but it's going to be very little until we know our facts. Call the police in France and see what they say."

Bill motioned for the others to enter the office. Captain Curtiss tipped his chair as he leaned back in it and waited for his guest to be seated.

"Sorry for the interruption but I just received a call concerning your friend." The three of them looked at him, Patrick sitting on the edge of his chair.

"Well- are you going to tell us?"

"Mr. Wainscott, it would serve you better to be more patient. I need to ask you all a few more questions. Does any of you know a Mr. Guy DuMoiese?" He read the name off of the paper in front of him. Charlie and Becky shook their heads. Patrick repeated the name, then it flashed in his head that was the Count's brother. He knew that through his friend the private investigator.

"Yea, I do. I believe that is the Count's brother."

"Yes, it is. And you know this how?"

Patrick told what he knew about the Count and his family and then asked a few questions of his own without getting answers. It was clear to all three of them that the Count had something to do with Mariah's disappearance.

Charlie told Becky to go on home and he was going to France with Patrick. There was no way he would let his best friend walk into something like this alone. He had also promised Mariah he would always be there for her and that's what he intended to do.

The first flight out to Paris was at eight a.m. the next morning. Charlie felt guilty leaving Becky alone for their first Christmas as man and wife but she assured him it was okay and that she couldn't have a nice holiday not knowing about Mariah anyway. Patrick congratulated them on their marriage and kissed Becky before she boarded her plane back to California.

It was Charlie's idea to find Mariah's apartment before it got any darker. They wanted to see for themselves what went on. The taxi pulled up to what appeared to be an expensive brick apartment house. There were six apartments on the ground floor and six above. It was obvious which one was hers. The police tape was still around the door and the blood stains were dried on the brick. Patrick paid the taxi fare and the two of them walked up the outside stairs to her apartment. Two men coming out of a downstairs apartment approached them.

"Can we help you?" Matt, a tall thin brown haired man with a moustache asked Patrick. Charlie and Patrick glanced at them. The other black haired man was shorter and stockier but there was a certain flair about him that struck both Patrick and Charlie as odd.

"Maybe. What do you know about this?" Patrick asked.

"It's just awful, isn't it. We are just so upset about all of this and to think we spoke with her that same night she disappeared. And that sweet little girl, oh my. Dear Chris, please I can't talk about this anymore." Matt disappeared toward the car, tears welling up in his eyes. He covered them with his hand as he turned to leave.

"Don't mind him, we've both been upset about this. You see we know the lady who lives here very well. My name is Chris and that's Matt. We live in the building."

"Mariah told me about you two. I'm Patrick Wainscott and this is Charlie Osswell. We're.."

"I know who you two are. She spoke a lot about both of you. You're the one that broke her heart." Patrick took a quick breath and wanted to punch him but refrained. Charlie took a step closer to Patrick in case he did just that. "I didn't mean it that way, its just she's had so much to cope with and now this happens just when things were looking up. I haven't heard anything new on the news reports.. Have they found her yet?"

"No, not yet, but I'm sure we will."

"I hope so and I do hope she and the baby are okay." Matt blew the car horn. Chris turned around and waved at him. "Nice talking to you. If you do see her please tell her as soon as they let us we'll have this place clean as a whistle and that we love her."

After Chris was out of earshot Charlie asked, "Are they what I think they are?"

"Yep, they are. And he doesn't know how close he came to eating that remark."

"I'm glad you didn't. We don't need more trouble on top of what we have."

Mariah was nursing Abigail when Jean Paul woke up. "Good morning husband." He turned on his side to watch them. The sheet fell away from his chest and she had the urge to run her fingers through his hair just to reassure her that he was here and was making everything okay again.

"Save some for me, *mon amour*." He grinned and she smiled back.

"Not this time. Abigail needs all she can get. I'm afraid the strain is keeping me from lactating properly. I can't seem to relax enough."

"You didn't get much sleep did you."

"Some. Ouch!" she grimaced again. "I can't do this right now. Abigail was impatient with her, too." Jean Paul slid out of bed. He didn't try to put any clothes on but took the baby from her and tried to sooth her. After a few minutes they decided it wasn't working and Abigail started to cry. Then Mariah started to cry too. Jean Paul placed the baby in the crib and found his clothes. He called downstairs and found Margarette there, he asked her to come and see to Abigail. The baby needs a bottle he told her. Her knock on the door came before Mariah even had the chance to get dressed. Jean Paul gave her a robe and opened the door. Margarette tried to reassure Mariah that this happens sometimes but for right not she would take care of Abigail and to get some more rest.

"Come, *mon amour* I know what you need." He slipped out of his clothes and put on his robe. He took her hand and led her out of the room.

"Wait! I don't have anything on under this robe."

"Nor do I."

"Where we are going? What about the staff, they'll see us?" He ignored her protest and led her to the indoor pool but insisted that she close her eyes before they entered.

"Listen, what do you hear?" He asked as he unlocked the door and led her in.

"Birds, I hear birds. And what is that? It's a warm breeze just like a beach on a hot day. That's sand under my feet." She opened her eyes and the smile spread across her lips. She gazed around and couldn't believe what she saw. He had built a romantic traditional nineteenth century style glass conservatory around the swimming pool and transformed it into a tropical paradise. Tall palm trees stood in every corner along with other foliage scattered around to give the effect of a tropical shore. Standing beside the palm trees were four parrots in very large cages talking and squawking. The indoor pool is separated from the conservatory by huge carved columns extending up into open space and a small latticework fence between each one. The pool then connected to the outside pool through a huge glass solar window that went all the way down to the bottom of the pool controlling either one to be used at the desired temperature. It has a door in the middle of it for easy access to the outside. He explained that he was overseeing this renovation over Thanksgiving as a present for her. Taking her hand he pulled her farther inside the room and locked the door behind them. She was in his arms before he even had time to turn from the door. He freed her from her robe and she did the same for him. He carried her in the water and there they made love under the fourteen-foot waterfall. They swam and drank Champaign in between making love.

When they were totally exhausted they laid on a blanket she had placed on the warm sand. "This is wonderful! You've beaten my bedroom back at the ranch." He smiled at her and kissed her hand. "You know I don't know if I've told you but those tapes you made got me through all that. I'm just so sorry that I didn't see how much I love you. I've wasted so much time with you."

"*Non, mon amour*, you did what you had to do. No more regrets, it is done and I did what I had to do; my patience has won you. You are my friend, my business partner, my lover, and my life."

"But still I was pretty stupid not see what we have."

"*Mon amour*, that gives me great distress. I don't ever want to hear you call yourself that again. You are not stupid as you say. You are the most resourceful person I have ever known. You are very intelligent and I am sure you would have figured out what I have known for a long time sooner or later. I'm just glad it was sooner even though I would have waited many life times for you." He leaned over and gave her a passionate kiss, her hands began to explore his muscularity. She knew every part of him but the excitement would always be there for her. He moaned, "Countess, do you know what you are asking for when you touch me like that?"

"Why Count, I wouldn't be doing this if I didn't." She kissed his chest and pulled him on top of her, she opened to let him inside once again. They spent the rest of the morning in the pool, from there she spied a doorway that was shielded with live green ivy draping down.

"What's that?" She pointed to it.

"That's the bathhouse. Come let us explore."

"The bathhouse, get real?" She laughed but allowed herself to be pulled from the warm water.

Inside the room, they found a recessed large tiled open shower stocked with various shampoos and lotions. Jean Paul helped her down the six steps to the shower so she wouldn't slip. He tested the warm water before he pulled her in the stream. There he started grooming her, washing her hair, scrubbing her back and stroking her body with the soap's lather. She repeated the same for him.

What they felt for each other showed in their intimacy. Even without making love they were making love. She wrapped a towel around her and headed up the step only for Jean Paul to stop her. He grabbed her ankle and she turned her head to look at him behind her. He had that look again.

"Where do you think you are going?"

"To get my robe aren't we done here?" she couldn't help but laugh.

"*Non*, I don't think so."

His hands traveled up her legs and he jerked off her towel exposing her skin to the blast of warm air from the vent above them. It blew her hair around her face. She lost her balance when her towel was jerked away and landed on the stairs with her hands and arms underneath her for support. Jean Paul felt his body respond to seeing her. He could tell she was all right but didn't wait to ask her. He came up behind her and his hands found her full breast. Her round bottom was against his lower abdomen. She moaned at his touch, one hand teased each breast while the other stroked and teased her below. She felt her heart quicken and the need was growing inside her again. She felt his chest against her back as he moved adjusting his weight on the steps. She was above him and he was under her. He moaned as she moved backwards against him, she felt his hardness against her. The desire hit her hard. She had never experienced anything like this- the desire, the insatiable sexual need for a man, for her husband. This was so different than what she had ever experienced with Patrick. She was meant to be with Jean Paul and there was no doubt in her mind. His breath was rapid and she felt him throb. His skin was hot against hers. The vent blew hot air down upon them again and she couldn't stand his touch anymore.

"Count, I want you now," she said almost breathless. She spread herself and felt his fingers explore her softness. His voice was husky, "Countess as you desire." She braced herself and then he entered, hot, full and throbbing. She moaned and moved with him. She enveloped him; they were made for each other. Her fingers grasping the carpet on the stairs trying to give leverage for her position. Her milk was starting to come but she didn't care. Her words of yes echoed in his ears. He took her there on the stairs to heights that she only imagined existed. It was more than he had dared to dream about, too. The climax was like fireworks going off in his head. For a brief moment before the wedding he had the thought what if he couldn't live up to her desire. After all, he was in his late fifties but then he dismissed that thought. He was not an old man but a man in his prime and his sexual desires were very much intact and in good working condition.

They lay in each other's arms once again on the warm sand, not speaking, just enjoying the feel of each other. Their bodies entwined as close as could be and still as one.

"I love you more than you will ever know," she said before she drifted off to sleep. He stroked her hair and hugged her closer.

"*Je t'aime*, I love you, too, Countess." His words drifted through her as she closed her eyes.

CHAPTER 20

The plane's stewardess asked them to fasten their seat belts for the landing. Patrick handed her his glass and she smiled. It was late on Christmas Eve and this wasn't how he had planned the evening. He was supposed to be home with Mariah and his daughter getting ready for her first visit from Santa, instead he and Charlie were on this crowded plane landing in Paris. They were lucky enough to get the last two seats when the cancellation came in. He glanced at Charlie reading a hunting magazine.

Inside the terminal, the loudspeaker went on and a female voice spoke French. Charlie took out his French handbook that he had bought at New Orleans International Airport and was trying to decipher what she had said. Patrick was about to ask a passerby if he spoke English and to translate until the same voice repeated in English that their connecting flight had been grounded. No other flights were available until the next morning. The two men looked at each other and Charlie threw the handbook up in the air. Coming down it almost hit an old woman who gave him a dirty look. He tried to apologize but she kept on walking thinking he was an idiot. Patrick couldn't help but laugh.

After a lot of effort they pulled away from the airport in a rental car. They would be in Marseille by morning. They had no idea of where to go after that but surely someone could give them directions. The Count's home had to be well known.

"Stop! This must be the drive," Patrick told Charlie as he rounded a corner. It seemed like they had driven out of the town and back into town five times trying to find the address. Charlie pulled the car off the main road on to the drive and sat there looking around.

"I don't see a house. Are you sure this is the place?"

"Look, according to the map that gas attendant made it matches. See the brick wall behind the shrubs. Didn't he say something about iron gates?"

"I don't know what he said. It fits though. Mariah said he likes his privacy. How more private can you get when you don't see the house."

"Just drive, will you."

About a mile up the drive stood a guardhouse. Two men in suits came out but it was apparent they both had guns hidden under their jackets.

427

"What do we have here?" Charlie said as he pulled the car to a stop and the two guards approached.

The guards split up and covered both sides of the car. They looked inside to check things out. The one at Charlie's window spoke to him.

"I'm sorry we don't speak French. Do you speak English?"

"You need to turn around. You are on private property."

"We are looking for Count DuMoiese's home. Can you tell us if this is it?"

"Give us some I.D." The guard had a stern look on his face and held out his hand. Charlie and Patrick gave him the I.Ds. "Stay inside the car," he ordered and left for the guardhouse to make a call.

"Gee some welcome, huh?" Charlie said looking at Patrick.

"What's the big idea, just because he has some title?"

"Well, yes, and given what is going on, don't you think that has something to do with all of this?"

Patrick sat in the car feeling more impatient than ever. The other guard stood by watching them closely.

"Look, he's got cameras all over the place. They knew we were coming the second we pulled in the drive. Those shrubs must be hiding the security system."

"Man, I don't like this. It feels like an armed camp around here." It was a good ten minutes before the guard came back. He handed them the driver's license and passports and said something in French to the other guard who smiled.

"Gentlemen would you please step out of the car?" Charlie and Patrick looked at each other but did as asked. The two guards searched the car and what luggage they had. Patrick was about to say something when Charlie squeezed his shoulder. Luckily the guards were still busy and didn't see it. "I am sorry for the inconvenience however we must be sure of who enters the grounds. *Monsieur* DuMoiese has given permission for you to go on up. By the way, Merry Christmas."

They got back in the car and looked at each other again. Patrick shook his head unbelieving what just happened. It was like something out of a movie. It took them another ten minutes to cover the grounds that consisted of woods and a stable off in the distance.

So the old man liked horses, Patrick thought to himself. Then suddenly the woods gave way to a well-tailored front lawn. It was sectioned off between three large water fountains, the far sides of the lawn were covered in rose gardens and surrounding the largest fountain located in the middle was a Japanese garden complete with stone seats scattered around. The drive circled around to the right of the gardens and then they saw it- the mansion.

"Holy shit!" Patrick exclaimed as he took in the sight. "He lives in this place." Charlie stopped the car and placed both arms on the steering wheel.

"This isn't a home, it's bigger than a fricking cruise ship."

The French Provincial mansion was of white brick and sported the black angled roof covering the three floors of windows. The east and west wings of the mansion were separated by a large circular middle section encasing the front door. All together the mansion and the grounds made a spectacular sight there was no doubt about that. The driveway flowed into a brick drive that led up to the front door. Parked in rows like tin soldiers showing off were a number of cars including a 1955 Bentley Continental, a 1949 J2 Allard, a new Jaguar, and an HJ Mulliner convertible Rolls Royce.

"You had better go on up, they're probably watching and laughing."

"You think all those cars are his?"

"I don't know but there is some money in them. Look at that convertible." Patrick replied wishing he had the time to examine them more closely.

As they pulled to a stop by the front door a tall man in a gray suit came out to greet them. He didn't speak but nodded and held the front door open for them. Charlie went in first, then Patrick. The whole house as far as they could see was decorated for Christmas, a large tree sat over to the right of the foyer.

The front foyer opened up into a huge area of space. Right in the middle of that space was another fountain and high above the water was a crystal chandelier. The light from the wall of windows on the far backside of the room danced on the crystal chandelier, which reflected the color spectrum in the water. Patrick was noting everything he possibly could just in case he needed it. There is a wide staircase behind the fountain and wrapping off in the directions of each wing. Intricate ornate iron railings giving the appearance of being made in the 1800's guard the stairs. The entire floor was Italian Marble, Charlie noticed as he looked around. Huge mirrors hung in every corner and recesses of the room. Gilt moldings caressed the wood paneling and the ceilings.

"Nice place," Charlie said to the man who didn't speak. He assumed he didn't know English.

"We call it home. *Monsieur* DuMoiese will be with you in a moment. Your coats.." He held out his hands to relieve them of their belongings.

A voice came booming from their left, they both turned to see a black haired man with in navy trousers, a light blue shirt, and navy tie approaching them. "Gentlemen. Welcome to my home." He extended his hand out to both of them. "Please forgive me for not greeting you myself but I was delayed with a call. You must be *Monsieur* Charles Osswell and you are *Monsieur* Patrick Wainscott. Please come in and sit. You have come to share in our Christmas festivities, oui? Oh *pardon*, I am *Monsieur* Guy DuMoiese." His resemblance to the Count was obvious but a few years younger.

"No actually, we came on another type of business," Patrick stated.

"We'd like to see the Count. Is he here?" Charlie added.

"*Non*, I am truly sorry but he is not at the moment. Perhaps I can help you. Please come to the library. We shall talk."

A second man showed up behind them out of nowhere it seemed. He's tall, around thirty-five to forty and also had on a black suit. His complexion was lighter than Guy's and his hair was a dark brown. But there was the black suit again. Patrick had the thought, what was it about the black suits? Did no one own any other color than that?

Guy led the way to the library while Claude brought up the rear. He closed the door behind them.

"Gentlemen, please have a seat." Guy picked up the phone and buzzed the kitchen. "Annette, please bring a tray of coffee and some your crescents to the library. We have guests, *Merci*." He hung up the phone and walked to the bar to pour him a glass of wine. Claude stood at the door. "Forgive me, perhaps you may like some of our fine wine instead?" He turned to Charlie and Patrick. Patrick was eyeing him and he knew it, but the Charlie fellow seemed more relaxed.

"No thank you, the coffee is fine. You see we've driven from Paris since the flights were down last night." Charlie glanced at Claude who didn't move a muscle but just stood watching.

"This is *Monsieur* Claude St.Clair. He is an invaluable asset to our home." A knock came at the door and Claude opened it letting Annette, who was wearing the typical black and white outfit but had on a Christmas apron, in with the tray. She placed in on the bar.

"Sir, will there be two more for Christmas dinner?" she asked in French.

"Gentlemen, will you please join us for Christmas dinner? We have plans to eat after the parade." Charlie and Patrick looked at each other. "The family can not have our guests going without dinner on such a fine day. It wouldn't be right." Patrick was about to say no but Guy spoke to Annette in French. "I told her to expect you." Annette left the men to themselves.

"We know this must be an inconvenient time to meet with us since this is a holiday and you have plans and have other guests to attend to."

"Ah, you must be speaking of the automobiles outside. You see my brother has a fancy for cars. They are his toys along with his gun collection. I prefer the horses which has gotten me in trouble on occasion." He laughed a little and Patrick caught the smirk on Claude's face as well.

"The Count likes to show off some of his collection in the parade every year. It's never the same car twice." Patrick wasn't that impressed; he had other things to be concerned about. "My wife and the children will go to the parade with the rest of the staff when they arrive. So you see your intrusion is no intrusion." Guy handed them each a cup of coffee and placed the tray of crescents and condiments before them.

"I also want to appologize for the strict security at the front gate. But as you are aware, the days of laxity are over for the entire world. One can not be too careful concerning his family."

"I don't mean to be rude, but we came on business," Patrick said.

"And *Monsieur* Wainscott, that business concerns my brother?"

"Actually it concerns Mariah. We came to see her."

"Mariah? W hat makes you believe she is here?"

"We were at the police station when you called yesterday. Even though they didn't say anything it wasn't too hard to figure out that the Count, possibly even you know where she is. I have to see her and my daughter."

"Your daughter?" The look on Guy's face told Charlie and Patrick he knew nothing of her paternity.

"Yes, Abigail is my daughter. Mariah took the baby and went to New Orleans without telling me and then I find out they're both missing. So you can see why I need to talk to her."

"She is not here either but I assure you the last I have heard she is well and so is little Abigail. Such a sweet child. She is named after my mother; the family thought that was very touching. The old lady would have liked that." Patrick opened his mouth to say something but Charlie stepped in seeing his eyes flash.

"We can't go back without seeing Mariah. We know about the drugs and we want to help her."

"Do you mind if we call each other by our first names? Charles, we all want to help. This is a dreadful misfortune for both my family and yours, however all we can do at the moment is to let the police handle things. I do not believe anyone including Mariah is being charged with any crime. All precautions are being taken for her safety as well as *le bebe's*. You saw some of those precautions at the gate."

"I take it she and the Count are together?"

"*Oui*."

"When do you expect them back?"

"I am not sure. I do not keep my brother's schedule. Claude can you give that answer?" Guy looked at Claude who was still standing by the door with his arms behind his back.

"*Non*, I have not heard from him since yesterday, *Monsieur*."

"Perhaps if you stay with us today, they may arrive. After all, it is Christmas," Guy stated while puffing on a cigar, his body in a relaxed position behind the desk. It was certain to both Patrick and Charlie they weren't going to get any information out of him or the man at the door. "Besides, I do not believe you will be able to find a hotel room in the city on this holiday. We have plenty of room." Guy had learned a long time ago to keep your enemies close and he wasn't sure what these two men had on their mind. Jean Paul had briefed him in the previous days of whom they were to Mariah and even the thought of possibly Patrick Wainscott coming to find her but not Charles Osswell, the coolest between the two of them. He had to watch this one. Hot heads tend to show their hands too quickly and that is how he saw Patrick.

The door burst open and four children all with dark hair came running in yelling "Papa!" with their arms out. They continued to speak French to Guy. He stepped out from behind the desk and laid his cigar in the ashtray and hugged each child.

Behind them a woman entered the room holding a toddler in her arms. She saw the two Americans. "*Pardon*, I couldn't keep them from coming in." She spoke in French. Guy went to greet her with a kiss. He spoke to her and she smiled.

"Welcome to our home," she said with as much grace and sincerity as she could muster up. She didn't want anything else spoiling the happiness that Mariah and Jean Paul had finally found and these two men could do just that.

"This is my lovely wife, Katelin and these are our children obviously. *Ma chérie*, would you please take the children and have the staff prepare two rooms on our wing. It would be inhospitable to isolate our friends on the other side of the house."

"*Oui*, of course." She nodded and spoke to the children who bowed their heads and murmured "*Pardon*" as they left.

"Come Patrick, Charles, let us celebrate this holiday together. Claude, please see that their luggage is taken upstairs. I'm sure they want to rest up. Later I will show you the grounds and then perhaps show you our lovely city if there is time."

On their way upstairs they passed the portrait of Countess Abigail DuMoiese and beside her portrait was an empty space showing markings that another portrait had hung there. Katelin had thought it best to take Angelina's down. She had plans to commission a wedding portrait of the Count and Countess for its place. The painter had captured the grace Abigail had possessed. Charlie and Patrick had remarked on it on their way past. Each had separate rooms complete with their own bath. They were next to each other on one end of the hall and Guy's room on the other with the children. Patrick walked in Charlie's room and sat on the bed. It was just as spacious and airy as his with a king size bed in the center of the room. Charlie was on the phone with Becky giving her an update on things.

"This is not going to be easy, you know. Do you really think they'll be coming back today?" Patrick asked when Charlie had put away his cell phone.

"That thought crossed my mind, too. I don't know but we can't assume the worse just yet. He says she's okay, until we have other evidence we have to believe that."

It was becoming clearer to both of them that all this was a stall tactic. At the last minute before they were to be given a tour of the town Claude announced that Guy had a call he had to deal with. So Guy stayed behind while Claude himself handled the tour. He drove the Rolls Royce without a care and told about the town. It is the second largest city after Paris. They saw the canal linking with the Rhone River. He even took them to see the site of the 16th century Chateau d'If, that was mentioned in The Count of Monte Cristo and the 19th century Church of Notre Dame de la Garde. Charlie was getting into the history of the town, but not Patrick, he was starting to brood, he wanted to see Mariah and Abigail, not the town.

By the time they returned back to the estate, dinner was ready. Going into the dining room, Patrick and Charlie were taken back. It was decorated in a truly eighteenth century Louis XIV Regence style. Sconces adorned all four walls. Allegorical paintings decorated the white and gold walls and ceilings. Another huge crystal chandelier hung over the massive table. In two of the corners stood a Louis XV bureau plat and a Boulle marquetry chest complimenting the dining table and chairs. Heavy fringed dark green and gold drapes hung at the four windows of the room. They shared the traditional Turkey dinner. Christmas music played and while the staff placed the dinner on the table, they, too, sat and shared the meal. This was customary for the family since no one was really considered the hired help but a part of the extended family on holidays. The kids laughed and joked. It seemed like a normal family gathering. Charlie missed Becky and Patrick wanted Mariah and Abigail, but neither one could do anything about it at the moment. Every time one of them tried to mention Mariah's name, the subject was changed. Finally, later in the evening, Guy and Claude returned to the great room where the immediate family had gathered announcing that the Count and Mariah would be arriving tomorrow instead. Katelin looked surprised, both Charlie and Patrick had caught it. They had no choice but wait and see what happens.

The three of them had spent a joyous but quiet Christmas together. Jean Paul and Margarette had spoiled the baby and her with too many gifts. He had bought her a full length, three hundred thousand dollar silver mink coat. She started crying when she saw it. "Why do you cry? You don't like it?"

"Jean Paul, I love it, its beautiful but I don't have anything that precious to give to you." He took her in his arms and kissed her.

"Yes you do, *mon amour*. You are more priceless than that little piece." He picked her up and carried her down the hall leaving Abigail and Margarette playing in the middle of the floor.

The plan was for Guy to stall until tomorrow and then to tell Charlie and Patrick that the two of them had decided to go on an extended holiday somewhere warm. It was his hope that the men would then decide to go back home. They would only complicate things if they hung around. The investigation was moving along but it wasn't fast enough for the Count. Between the police and his security everyone was being looked at secretly, from the factory to both trucking companies. It took time to do this properly but it didn't help the uneasiness he felt concerning the situation. It nagged on him enough to immediately change his will the same time Patrick's visitation papers were drawn up. He saw no need to worry Mariah about it and instructed it to be kept secret until it was needed and hopefully it would be a long time coming. He had no plans of leaving this earth now that he had her and a daughter in his life.

He woke up with Mariah shoving him. "What?" he asks turning on to his back to find her leaning over top of him.

"You were dreaming?"

"Mum, *pardon*, I didn't mean to wake you." He pulled her down on top of him. "But now that I'm awake and you are, too." He smiled and she shook her head no.

"Don't you ever get tired?" grinning as she said the words.

"I haven't heard any complaints from you, Countess. It seems like you have just as much energy to burn as I do."

Slowly the dream started to come back to him, Angelina was standing in front of him in a haze of gray holding a baby out to him. Behind them was the most beautiful rainbow a person had ever seen. It was then when Mariah had awakened him and the dream was lost. He hadn't had a dream with her in years. Why now and what did it mean?

Patrick had found one of young stable hands working alone so he took the opportunity to try to pump him for information about the Count. They started talking about the horses and led the conversation to the family's wine and vineyard. It was what he needed! The boy had mentioned the family's estate in Bordeaux. It was a lead that they needed to check out. He was on his way to the main house when Charlie and Guy found them.

"I see you were visiting our stables. Charles told me you have horses yourself."

"Buddy, the Count just called. It seems that Mariah wanted to go to the Bahamas. They spent Christmas there."

"Did you talk with her?"

"No, but I heard the Count on the phone. He said she was busy with the baby."

"I see. Did they say where in the Bahamas?"

"*Non*, sorry he did not and I didn't think to ask. *Monsieur* Wainscott, I wouldn't worry about Mariah or *le bébé*. They both are in good hands and very well protected." Guy saw the look on Patrick's face. "I'm sure when all this nasty business blows over then she will be in touch with you but for right now she needs to remain "missing". The note that was left at the apartment was not a joke, I assure you."

"What note?" Charlie asked looking at Patrick.

"Your police didn't tell you? Whoever splattered the blood on her door left a threatening note. That is why she left like she did and that is why she must remain missing until all this is cleared up. No one must know where she is."

"Then she may not even be in the Bahamas. She could be any where?" Patrick looked Guy straight in the eyes and he returned the same look. Guy's expression showed no answers.

"Look, I'm not condemning the way she left but why didn't she call me. I would have left the set to get to her," Patrick stated as he paced around his room.

"The truth is you couldn't have helped her as fast as he did. You know that." Charlie doodled on a piece of paper lying in front of him. He was sitting at the desk making notes. "You know we're at a dead end."

"Not yet, I got one of the stable hands to talk before you guys came. He told me where the vineyard is. I think we ought to check out the FAMILY'S vineyard. It sounds like its secluded enough to offer whatever the Count thinks he's doing."

"He's doing what he thinks he has to."

"What I want to know is what makes him better than the police in protecting her."

"Would you be satisfied if the police were their only protection?" Patrick was silent for a minute.

"Here's what we're going to do…"

"Thank you for your hospitality," Patrick managed shaking hands with Guy and then with Claude who was standing beside him. Charlie did the same. They drove away in the darkness under the pretense of leaving France empty handed.

Claude made the comment that he didn't believe they were leaving and they should call the Count in the morning and update him. Guy shook his head in agreement. He sighed as they went inside. It was late and he was tired. He headed upstairs. News of her disappearance hit the airwaves all over France and it stirred an incredible interest in both Mariah's and the Count's clothing line. Everyone wanted his or her garments. Guy had messages from both Tré and Edmund trying to find his brother. This he would deal with tomorrow as well.

Patrick headed toward Paris in case Guy had them followed but then cut cross country and back tracked. They stopped for the night in Pe'rigueux, a place outside Bordeaux, knowing it would give them time to locate the estate. Patrick knew they were close in finding her. He tossed and turned the rest of the night keeping Charlie awake, too.

The wide streets of northern Bordeaux gave way to the older section of town with narrow, crooked streets. The town boasted many buildings constructed in the 15th-century architectural style. Charlie found this to his liking and made a mental note to bring Becky back on vacation some time just to look at the history. She would love the architectural designs of not just the homes and businesses but the churches, the Cathedral of Saint Andre', the Church of Saint Croix and the Church of Saint Seurin. The farther they drove out of town the more they noticed the acres and acres of vineyards. It was hard to tell when one ended and one began.

"Where do you think this place is?" Charlie took a drink of his coffee. He needed more than this to clear his head. His brain wasn't working well since Patrick had kept him up all night.

"I don't know but I guess we should turn around and find someone who can help us; otherwise we could be driving to nowhere and never find it." He pulled the car onto a gravel drive and was just about to back up when a white sedan blocked him from doing so. Two men got out and approached them.

"Don't look now, but we have company."

Charlie placed his coffee cup on the floor of the car and looked around. "Pinch me if this doesn't look familiar. I think we may be in trouble."

"For what? This is a public road isn't it?"

"The hell if I know." The man on the driver's side knocked on Patrick's window. He rolled it down. The man spoke French to them and Patrick tried to communicate that they didn't speak English. The man motioned them out of the car which they did. Patrick and Charlie handed them their identification but the men glanced at them and gave them back not concerned about it. The man standing beside Charlie radioed someone and the other man started searching Patrick.

"What the.."

"Shh. I don't know about you but I bet these guys are packing. Go along with it if you want to see that daughter of yours again," Charlie said quietly but then it was his turn to be searched. The guards were satisfied they had no weapons on them but they turned their attentions to the car at that point. After finding no weapons there, the guards motioned Patrick and Charlie back in their car but they took the car keys.

"Well this is a fine mess we're in. What do we do now?" Patrick asked.

"I think all that we can do is wait and see what happens."

Jean Paul woke to his pager vibrating. He had given orders to security that at anytime during the night he was needed he should be contacted by the pager so as not to wake the Countess. He glanced at the clocked. It was seven in the morning. Mariah was still sleeping and so was Abigail. He put his robe on and went downstairs to use the phone. On his way up he knocked softly on Margarette's door. It took her a few minutes to answer and he apologized for the early hour but he needed her to be sure that Mariah and Abigail stayed upstairs until he saw it was safe to come down. She saw the concern in his face but didn't ask any more questions. She understood enough.

He dressed quietly and pulled a SIG Sauer Pistol out of a lock box he kept in the top of his armoire. He checked the magazine for shells and loaded it. The click was loud enough that Mariah stirred but went back to sleep instantly. He placed the gun in his shoulder holster, his wallet with his license to carry in his back pocket, and then grabbed his coat. He had

TORMENTED DREAMS

business to check out. On his way out he ordered security to do a full lock down on the house.

"How long are we going to sit here? It's been forty-five minutes all ready. I think we should get out and try to talk to these guys?"

"Patrick, I think we should stay put." It was a matter of seconds when a black Lamborghini pulled up in front of them.

"Well, well, we have more company. Look at that Lamborghini!"

"Yea, look who's getting out. How did we do this?" Patrick said.

They saw the Count place the gun in his belt underneath his coat as he got out of the car. He was ready for anything. His senses were keen as he approached their car.

"Is he packing, too?" Charlie asks.

"I think so. What has Mariah gotten herself into?" They sat in the car watching the Count talk with the guards, he glanced at them and then went back to their conversation. The guards nodded and walked up to their car. They motioned Patrick and Charlie out once again and toward them. The Count recognized them and dismissed the guards. Patrick was handed the keys to the car before the guards left to continue their patrols.

"*Monsieur* Osswell, *Monsieur* Wainscott." He held out his hand to shake. "*Pardon* for the actions of my security but they are doing what they are paid to do. How did you find my estate?"

"It was pure luck, believe it or not. This is yours? It doesn't look like an estate. There are no signs."

"My cameras have you driving on my property for the last hour and a half. I have thirty thousand square acres of prime grape territory. Most of it belongs to the vineyard to the north of here. Somehow you found the rear of my property. I do not want to stand here and converse with you, Wainscott. I suggest we take this to the house. Follow me."

Charlie and Patrick stood in the same spot and watched the Count pull off his coat. He took the pistol out of his belt, dislodged the magazine, and stored the gun in his shoulder holster. The Count turned the Lamborghini around on the blacktop road and started back up the hill in front of them. "You think he'd use that?" Patrick asked out of concern for Mariah and the baby. Charlie nodded yes.

The French Chateau built in the early 1600's, was all stone and fashioned much out of the same architectural style as what the city held. Trees, a stable, and several gardens surrounded the 12,000-square-foot residence but

439

it still wasn't as large as the mansion in Marseille (even though it held only two floors). On each end of the house were tall stone round turrets with shiny copper tops. The front entrance was enclosed in a stone archway with wisteria growing up the sides. The front courtyard also held a fountain and gardens. Everything was understated; this was definitely a country family home. The Count had parked the Lamborghini to the right of the house in the automobile court. Waiting for his quest, the Count and another man were standing side by side on the front steps. The Count clenched his fist behind his back, his body tense and ready. He was definitely not happy with this new aspect of things. Patrick pulled the car beside the Lamborghini.

"Come gentleman." He spoke French to the man beside him. "Please give your keys, my driver will move your car to the garage." He saw no need to introduce his staff just yet." Dogs were barking somewhere in the background.

The house was spacious inside with a cherry wooden staircase off to the left side of the living room. The entire house was filled with the original detailed carved cherry woodwork. The main focal point in the room was a huge fireplace. Charlie noticed all the doorways were arched including the tops of the doors. The Count ushered the men in his study without resending the lock down order and closed the door. "Now, what can I do for you two? Please sit. Would you like something to drink?" His tone was dry and obviously not happy. He took a key out of his pocket and pulled open the top drawer of his desk, in it he placed the pistol and magazine and locked it back in place. He then stoked a fire in the fireplace. It was damp outside and it had given him a chill. He poured a glass of wine and drank it.

"Do you always carry and drink?" Patrick asked.

"Rest assured I am in FULL control." There was no doubt in the minds of his guest, the Count meant more than he was actually saying. "A man has a right to protect what is his. Don't you agree? I don't mean to be rude, but I am a busy man. You have come here for a reason. What is it?" The Count continued to stand by the fire soaking up the heat with glass in hand.

"We would like to see Mariah," Charlie spoke trying to cushion the tension that was developing in the air between Patrick and the Count. The Count looked at them with a raised eyebrow.

"And you think she is here?"

"We believe she is. Your brother said you two were in the Bahamas and yet we find you here, therefore given the security around here, she must be."

"We're concerned about her and the baby. The news is reporting that she is missing. This is the most obvious place for her to be." Charlie sat on the sofa.

"I see. And what if she is still in the tropics and I had to come back for business."

"Count, we're no fools. The security is tighter here than at your other house. For heavens sakes, we were frisked."

"Ah, my guards did that!" He was laughing as he said this. "They were being thorough. I must commend them."

Patrick squinted his eyes; he saw the Count was enjoying this game. Damn him he thought to himself.

"Count, we really need to see Mariah and Abigail for ourselves. That's all we ask." Charlie stood up and walked to the window. Out in the far yard he saw a couple of guards milling around the trees with a dog. He turned to face the Count. "All this drug stuff has got to be scaring her. She needs to know we are with her and that we love her. She's like my sister, you know that."

"*Oui*, Charlie, I do and I am not insensitive to your need, but she is sleeping at the moment and I do not want her awakened. She needs her rest."

"Is she ill?" Patrick asked.

"*Non*, not yet and it is my intention to keep it that way. She has not been sleeping well."

The telephone buzzed on the desk. Jean Paul picked it up. "*Oui..*" He spoke French to Mariah on the other end. She wanted to know what was going on and was coming downstairs. He stopped her from hanging up and told her he would be up in a minute but to keep Abigail upstairs for the moment. Charlie and Patrick were talking in the background.

"Those voices.. they're not Charlie's and Patrick's are they?" she asked.

"*Oui*."

"Oh no. They're come here because of me, right?"

"They want to see you. What do you want, *ma chérie*?"

441

"I'd like to see Charlie, but I'm not ready to deal with Patrick yet. Can you send Charlie up please?"

"If that is what you wish. Do you need time?"

"No, it's okay… I love you Jean Paul."

"And I you." He hung up the phone. "Charlie, Mariah is awake. She would like to see you. She is on the second floor. The door is to the left and at the end."

"Thank you, Count," Charlie replied. Both Patrick and Charlie got up.

"Wait Wainscott, she said just your friend. NOT YOU."

"I don't understand. Why doesn't she want to see me? What kind of brainwashing have you done to her?"

Jean Paul laughed, "It was not I who did the brainwashing. You will stay. I want to speak to you alone." There was something in his voice that Patrick couldn't pick up on. Charlie patted him on the shoulder.

"Listen buddy, I'll talk to her and see what's up." Charlie nodded at the Count and went on upstairs.

Patrick turned to square off with the Count. Now was his chance and he was going to make it clear he wasn't going to be bullied by an old guy like him, title or no title. "Okay, you have something to say, so say it."

"You will not be hurting Mariah any longer. What did you do to her at the ranch to hurt her? She will not speak of it to me?"

"I don't know what you're talking about. I've been gone for the past couple of weeks on location. It was only when I got home and found she had moved out and then missing that I knew anything was wrong." The Count was in his face by this time and he didn't like it. "I need to talk to her." He started leave and Jean Paul stepped in front of him.

"Not until the Countess says so. Do you hear me?" The words echoed in his ears. He was visibly shaken.

"What do you mean the Countess? She didn't MARRY YOU?"

"*Oui*, almost a week ago."

"No this isn't true, it can't be." He walked to the window and then turned back to the Count. "You had to say or do something to get her to marry you. She loves me."

"*Pardon*, Wainscott, but it was she that asked me to marry her. And I assure you that was the best thing I have done in my life for a long time. We were made for each other in EVERY way. All of our DESIRES match completely."

"Oh come on. Do you really think that I believe that. I know her much better than you do. I was with her for five years. We should be together now, not you."

"*Oui*, you did but you never touched her in the way I have. Our wedding night was spectacular, the virginity was definitely there."

"You mean to tell me that before then, you two never slept together? I've seen you together in the hotel, remember. I hate to burst your bubble, but she wasn't a virgin when you met. She was pregnant with my child."

"Ah, that is true, but as you don't see, eleven months of celibacy gives a woman back her virginity even she said so. Place me as old fashion, but a gentleman should never endanger the one he loves and an unborn child just to calm his needs even though it has been a distress all those months not to feel her in that way."

"I'm not playing these head games. I want to see her and Abigail, now." Patrick was angry and it showed. The count held steadfast. It was too much for Patrick to contain himself, he threw a blow that hit Jean Paul across the chin. It caught him off guard and he was angry for not seeing it coming. His face hurt, but before Patrick could do anything else Jean Paul had his wrist in his hand in one quick movement.

The Count's eyes went dark with furry and between clenched teeth he spoke, "You will have this one but the next time you try to lay a hand on me or anyone else in my family, I assure you, you will pull back a bloody stump. Do you understand me!? You will NOT see her until she says so and you will NOT hurt her ever again. There is one more thing to discuss." He released Patrick's wrist, the circulation was cut off briefly and his hand was a faded color of blue.

The Count took papers out of the desk drawer and handed them to Patrick. "Now if you can behave like a gentleman in my home we will discuss this. The Countess wanted to tell you herself, but given what I just saw I think I made the right choice of doing it myself for her safety."

That made Patrick simmer even more, him thinking he could hurt Mariah. "What is this?" He read the papers and threw them on the desk. "She allowed you to adopt Abigail? You can't do that! She is my daughter and I do not relinquish my paternal rights. I have papers to prove what I claim." Patrick took the paternity test out of his pocket and threw them on the desk. Jean Paul didn't bother to pick them up which made Patrick even madder. "I'll fight this, you know."

443

"There is nothing you can do, Wainscott. At the time the adoption was finalized she did not know the test results. We only suspected that you were Abigail's biological father. The law was not broken. Look at the signature on the adoption." Jean Paul shook his head as he spoke and remained cool. He knew he staggered Patrick and felt a little sorry for him, but just for a moment. Patrick picked up the papers and read them. It was signed and sealed by both the Prime Minister and the Pope's office as witness, he knew even if he tried to fight, the Count could keep this tied up in a lengthy court battle for no telling how long. He threw the papers in the trashcan.

"Am I just to walk away now? Is that what you expect? I'm sorry but I can't and I won't do that. That little girl may have your mother's name but she has my blood."

"*Non*, it is not our wish for you to walk away. Abigail should be able to visit you. I have taken the liberty of drawing up a very fair visitation schedule for you. I am more than sure you will admit to that, in return, Mariah asks nothing of you except to be able to live her life as she wants and with Abigail, of course. I do not see why this can't be so." He handed the new set of papers to Patrick. He read them.

"I have to talk to her. She can stop this."

"You don't see anything yet do you? I love Abigail just like she is mine. I will protect her like I do her mother. With the adoption, she now has duel citizenship and has more protection around her than imaginable. She, Mariah, and any other children we have are the heirs to my estate and title, with that, certain perks go along- the protection of my security, which you have felt first hand, but the protection my title and family can give as well as my country. This all had to be done in urgency."

Some of what the Count was saying made sense but a headache was coming on. He didn't even ask for a drink but helped himself to a glass of wine. He wished there was something stronger. "I'm not signing anything."

She stood in the doorway in a white dressing gown and slippers. When she saw Charlie turn the corner from the staircase she met him halfway. Charlie noticed she looked a little drawn. "God thank you," he whispered as she went into his arms. "Look at you, beautiful. I like your hair." He hugged her and kissed her on the cheek. "What have you gotten yourself into woman?"

"Shh. Let's go in here to talk." She pulled him inside her bedroom.

"Wow, look at this room."

"This is only half of it. Why are you here?" She flopped herself on the king size poster bed drawing her legs under the dressing gown. The sight brought back a memory of when she and Charlie were kids. It flashed for a brief instant in his head.

"Why do you think? It's all over the news about your disappearance and the drugs. Did you really think I wouldn't come?"

"I'm sorry to have worried you but there wasn't anything else I could do. I had to for Abigail's sake. I was afraid to go anywhere but here. You do see that?"

"You should have called me. Becky and I were sick with worry. I have to tell her."

"No! You can't, I have to stay gone. No one must know, too much is at stake."

"We'll get you out of the drug stuff somehow, I promise. Patrick is here and wants to help."

"I can't see him. I'm not ready."

"Why? What happened between you two?"

"A lot has happened, Charlie. My life is never going to be the same again and I am so happy about that." A knock came at the door. Mariah opened it and an older woman brought Abigail in. Mariah thanked her and took the baby. "Look Abigail, its Uncle Charlie." She gave the baby to Charlie who made over her. Mariah sat back down on the bed. "Charlie, I need your help but not in the way you came for. Jean Paul is handling that."

"What?"

"You have to talk to Patrick. You have to get him to see reason with all this. Last week I married Jean Paul. See!" She held out her hand for his inspection of her wedding rings.

"Oh my!" he sighed. "Is this what you really want?"

"Yes, Charlie, I do more than anything else. I'm just sorry it took me so long to figure it out. This is where I belong and with Jean Paul. My life was good with him before but marriage to him is beyond my wildest dreams. I have NEVER felt so loved and so completely happy in all, of my life. Even his family accepts me without questions. I can't explain it, it's like there is a reason why things happened like they did. This was the reason why my relationship fell apart with Patrick. It was over between us when I walked in on him the first time. I should have been smart enough to see it." She sat on the bed with her eyes down. Charlie raised her face up.

"Again, are you sure about this?"

"He loves me Charlie and I love him with all my being. Jean Paul is a good man. When you get to know him better, you'll see. Oh, Abigail has won his heart. She's his."

"No, Mariah, she's Patrick's. The lab sent the test results to the ranch after you left. She's Patrick's." Mariah had the baby now. She shook her head no.

"Charlie, Jean Paul adopted her after the wedding last week. She will hold the title of Countess some day."

Charlie drew in a breath. He didn't expect this and she was right, Patrick would go ape mad when he learned of the adoption.

"There's one more thing you should know. We had Abigail christened here with Guy and Katelin but I'm planning another ceremony at home with you and Becky as her other Godparents. Please don't be mad."

"Sweetheart, that's okay, whatever you want. I'm not mad and I'm sure Becky won't be either. We'll be ready to do our part, just let us know. You two being safe is what's important. Now getting back to other- I know something happened between you and Patrick at the ranch. What was it?"

"I don't know why I thought he would change. I was trying to forgive him and was almost there. It was he who helped me through Abigail's birth. That man who did that was the old Patrick but he didn't last long. I called the hotel one day to tell him about me going to New Orleans but some woman answered his phone. She said he had moved in with Rochelle Rainsfield. He had given up his room."

"You mean she said he was staying in Rochelle's room with her?" Mariah shook her head yes. "Did you ask him about it?"

"Why? To be humiliated again, I don't think so. I didn't even bother trying to call anymore. He showed me his true colors. That's when I left and asked you to move my stuff."

"I can't believe he did that. The last I knew Rochelle was leaving the set for an extended holiday somewhere before production started." Charlie sat on the bed beside her with his arms around her and the baby. "You know, I talked to him on the plane and he said didn't seem to know why you moved out. He doesn't know you called."

"That doesn't matter now does it?" she sighed and placed Abigail on the bed to play with her toy.

"You wanted to hurt him like he had you, didn't you? That's why you married the Count and allowed the adoption," Charlie spoke softly more thinking out loud than actually making a statement to Mariah.

"Some might see it as that but that's not it. Jean Paul has given more to me than Patrick has and I don't mean material things. I have my confidence back as a woman, as a lover, and now as a mother. This is where I need to be. I know it in my heart and that's what counts." They talked another hour or so and Charlie told her about his wedding to Becky. Finally, the door opened and the Count walked in.

"Everything all right in here?" He smiled at his wife who embraced him at the door. She kissed him in front of Charlie.

"Everything is fine. Congratulations Count, welcome to our family." Charlie extended his hand out. Jean Paul accepted and smiled, but was surprised when Charlie embraced him for a moment. "I can see that you are taking very good care of her and for that I thank you. Is there anything I can do to help?"

"*Oui*, keep your friend under control or I will." He rubbed his chin, it still hurt. He had to give credit for a good right hook to the man. "*Mon amour*, I just took a call from the police, they want to come and speak with us later this afternoon."

"Jean Paul, your chin, it's bruised. Did Patrick hit you?" She was mad and there was no stopping her. She turned on her heels and flew downstairs before the two men could stop her. She flew past the staff in her dressing gown and slammed the library door behind her. Patrick looked surprised as she did so. He was standing at the fireplace with a glass of scotch in his hand contemplating his next move. She was on top of him before he knew it and slapped him in the face spilling his glass on the expensive piece of woven carpet that covered the middle of the floor. "What the hell! Why did you do that?" He stepped back from her. His face stung and he had more than his share to deal with already. His anger was loose but he kept it contained. He still loved her even though she was another man's wife now.

Jean Paul had given the baby back to Margarette and he and Charlie went downstairs not knowing was going on.

Outside the closed doors they heard Mariah's voice. Jean Paul was about to enter when Charlie stopped him.

"I think we need to let them work this out. There's some unfinished business between them. He won't hurt her." Jean Paul knew he was right but he didn't want Mariah to face Patrick alone.

"Don't you ever do that again! You have no right coming in my home and striking my husband. You have no right coming here period."

"Don't you tell me that! I came looking for you and MY daughter because you two are in trouble only to find out that your married and MY daughter is now the daughter of another man, too. You had no right to do that!"

"So you know. Good it saves me the time and trouble to tell you. I'm sure you've been told everything so don't you even think about taking Abigail away from me. It will never happen! We will see to it, so help me God!" The venom poured out of her mouth and she couldn't stop it.

"Come on, Count, I think she can take care of herself by the sound of things. Let's give them some privacy. Let me share some things about your wife. And if things start to break then I'll be the first in, I assure you," he said after seeing Jean Paul's face. Jean Paul knew she had a temper after the episode at the mansion but he didn't expect this out of her. Guy was right, he did have a wild cat on his hands after all.

"Why did you move out?" Patrick asked after she had calmed down.

"Why do you think? I wasn't going to be anywhere near you after your stint with Rochelle." She gave him a sour smile. "I hope you enjoy yourself with her."

"Rochelle? Rochelle Rainsfield? What does she have to do with anything?"

"Your affair had everything to do with it and I'm glad I finally wised up. I now have everything I never knew I was missing because of you two."

"What affair?"

"Don't play dumb with me. I called the hotel; some woman answered your phone. She said you moved in with Rochelle and gave her your room."

"I did not! Wait a minute- I used Rochelle's room when I had the flu for two days and wanted to die. The hotel was over booked and her room was paid for in advance so they couldn't change it. She wasn't there. Damn it! I didn't want to contaminate anyone else with the bug."

"You've had a few days to work on that one haven't you? I don't believe it."

"You know, suddenly I don't care. If you're so quick to jump to that conclusion without even finding out the truth then why should I bother explaining things to you." He pushed the chair out of his way.

"Good because it doesn't matter anymore now does it? I have a good life with a man who cherishes me and my daughter."

"You call this a good life? You're like a bird in a gilded cage. You can't even come and go as you like."

"Yes, I can, and it's not always going to be like this. It's just all this mess."

"Then come home with me. You'll be safe there."

"I'm not going anyway and I or Abigail won't be safe until these smugglers are caught. There is nowhere we can go but here. You need to go on home. I don't want you here."

"Sorry, I won't do that, not as long as you or MY daughter is in danger."

"Patrick, you don't get it, do you? Let me spell it out for you. I am married to a wonderful man, whom I love more than I knew possible. He loves Abigail. We have a life here. He loves us tremendously. I am where I belong and so is Abigail."

"We'll see about that."

"Don't you even think about taking Abigail away from us! It's too late. Didn't you see the signatures on the paper? There is no court here to argue with that." She stood face to face with him, anger flashing in her eyes as she pointed a finger at him. "You even try to do something, so help me I will.."

"Do you think I'm afraid of all this? I'm not, but you're the one that said I was planning to take Abigail. I don't plan on losing my daughter to anyone. Do you think that little of me to take a baby from her mother? I love you, I have always loved you, and heaven help me always will, I guess, even if you are married to some over stuffed old man." Patrick took a step closer to her and grabbed both sides of her face with his hands. He kissed her hard and she tried to push him off but didn't budge. She brought her knee up and struck him in the groin but because there wasn't a lot of distance between them it wasn't a hard strike, just enough to cause him to let go of her. He stumbled backwards. His elbow hit the bookcase knocking a crystal vase to the floor where it shattered.

Jean Paul and Charlie looked at each other for a second. "I told you so," Charlie stated as he jumped up behind Jean Paul to see what was going on. Jean Paul was first in the room. Mariah was standing in front of the desk and Patrick was in front of the bookcase doubled over by the door. He also knew she had picked up the heavy ashtray off the desk and was hurling it toward them. Jean Paul caught it in mid air before it put a hole in the door. He caught Mariah's hand as she was reaching for something else to throw.

"*Ma chérie*, is this the way a Countess acts?" He grinned as he said it. She threw a look his way. His arms were around her waist. Her dressing gown flared open revealing her nightgown. She tried to break free of her husband's grip but couldn't.

Patrick stood up. "What in the hell did I ever see in you?" He stormed out of the room and out the front door. Charlie stood there and was grinning, too.

"What did I tell you? She's got fire when she gets lit." Charlie went after Patrick.

Jean Paul closed the door, he knew part of the staff had to have heard what was going on. "I see we should lock up the valuables from now on. Calm down and tell me what happened in here?" He asked as he released her.

"Nothing, I couldn't handle."

"Obviously. Did he strike you?"

"No, he tried to kiss me. Why did God make a MAN anyway?" she muttered out loud. She was still mad and had to get out of there. She went upstairs to change. Jean Paul contacted security to alert them Charlie and Patrick were on the grounds. He didn't need any problems on that concern.

"Where are you going?" he asked Mariah as she pushed past him. She was still angry and it showed.

"I'm going for a ride. I want to be alone," she said on her way downstairs. Jean Paul shook his head. He had never seen her this riled up and didn't like it one bit. He phoned security to arrange for two men to meet her at the stables immediately and accompany her on the ride. He had business to tend to.

It was an hour before Patrick and Charlie came in from their walk. He had cooled off and did see why she had done the things she had. He had to accept that he had lost Mariah forever but he didn't have to lose Abigail. He wanted to see her. The Count saw them walking up the drive and summoned Margarette to the living room with Abigail to wait for them. He knew that Patrick wanted to see her and hadn't done so. The news had been dropped about the adoption and the shock was over he hoped. But he was not going to take any chances, Margarette was instructed to remain with the baby no matter where they went in the house. If there was trouble she was to push the pager he had given her.

It was still another hour before he was notified that Mariah was back at the stable. He checked on Patrick and Charlie who were enjoying Abigail and then headed out the door. He sent the security on their way when he reached the stable door.

"I hope you're feeling better. You shouldn't ride the horses that hard, you know." She glanced up at him but didn't say a word. She was sweaty and cool from the ride but she didn't care. Jean Paul sat down on the hay beside her and put his arm around her. "Are you ready to tell me what happened earlier between you and Wainscott?"

"Nothing, I just told him what's what. I told him I was sorry I had ever met him and how much I love you. We argued and I gave him my knee. You know that felt good, I've wanted to do that for so long but didn't have the nerve."

"I am glad it was him and not me," he laughed. "If the Countess makes it a habit to do things like this we must work on her finesse in doing so. But I promise, I will not be the practice dummy." She hit him on the shoulder in a playful way. He pushed her back in the hay and lay on top of her. The back of his hand was caressing her face. She closed her eyes as his fingers traced her lips. She licked them and playfully bit at his fingertips. Mariah could feel her husband's response.

"Jean Paul we can't do anything here. We're in the stable. Anyone could walk in."

"Don't worry about that. We have security but they have instructions to leave us alone. As long as you don't throw anything at me that makes a noise they will not bother us."

"I'm sorry about that. I just lost control. How much was the vase worth?"

"A couple of thou maybe. It doesn't matter if it put Wainscott in his place."

"I don't want to hear his name. As I told him, this is where I want to be, this is where I need to be with my husband, my one true love." He kissed her and unzipped her blouse. He took the blanket hanging on the hook and covered them over. She laughed as they struggled under the blanket.

Abigail went down for a nap and Charlie went to make a call to Becky. He wanted to tell her they were fine and not to worry. But he knew he couldn't say much about Mariah and the baby, not yet. It had to be that way. Maybe she would read between the lines. The Count had told them to feel free to make themselves at home at least for today.

Patrick headed for the stables. Maybe he would find some comfort there with the horses, territory he knew about. He saw security standing outside the stable at a distance but didn't think any thing about it since they were all over the place. He started to enter the stable's back door but stopped. Mariah's voice came drifting toward him. It was a soft moan, he thought she sounded like she was in pain. Then before he could find her he heard the Count's voice. "*Ma chérie*, you are just as sweet as the first time." He moaned and his voice had a husky sound to it. Patrick didn't have to see them to know what was going on. He felt sick to his stomach. They didn't even have the decency to go behind locked doors. A few months ago he knew she would never had even considered what she was doing now. He turned and left with their sounds burning in his ears. He took off running. His jeans cutting in his legs and his boots were not made for running but the physical discomfort he felt didn't match what he felt mentally.

The library was filled with the three officers, Jean Paul, Mariah, Patrick and Charlie. The Count and Mariah sat together behind the desk with everyone either on the oversized leather sofa or in the wing chairs. Patrick was trying to concentrate on the meeting but his thoughts kept reverting to the stable scene.

"Countess, let's get down to business straight away. We do not intend to arrest you on any drug charges, as we believe, that you did not know what was going on. You stepped on someone's toes when your insurance company called the police. And that someone is a lot bigger than we thought at first. We suspect that the problem originates from here in France, not the U.S." Mariah was holding her breath afraid of what was going on. Jean Paul felt her relax next to him. "We've had a break on the case," FBI agent Marc Willington spoke.

"What is that?" Jean Paul asked.

"An informant has come forward and identified someone who was blowing off steam in one of the local taverns. We don't have a name, but it seems he's a dockworker of yours who has been promised riches in return for helping the smugglers. We want to search the factory in Pau and see what we come up with," Detective Christian Lemouré from Bordeaux said.

"But of course, I do have to tell you my men have already done that. They found nothing."

"We will be using the dogs, of course. They can find even the minute traces of cocaine."

"I need to contact my manager there? My employees need to be told. Perhaps, I should close it down for the day."

"No Count, that's not a good idea," Detective Bill Morgan interrupted. He had been asked to accompany by the FBI to help in the investigation since he had been in on it from the very start.

"Here is what we want to happen. You will give a press release on the situation stating that you are cooperating fully and production will continue on both garment lines. That Miss Remm.. excuse me *Madame*, that together you two are concerned about this and will search every avenue to punish the smugglers." Agent Marc Willington handed Jean Paul and Mariah a prewritten press release to look over. They read it and Jean Paul threw it on the desk.

"*Non*, this will not happen!" his voice bellowed out. Patrick's thoughts snapped back to the present. What just happened he thought to himself?

"*Pardon*, Count?" Detective Lemouré asked puzzled at the Count's reaction.

"I will not put my wife in danger by doing this. I brought her here to keep her from danger and now you want to throw her to the wolves! His anger was so strong that he was shaking.

"Count, we can understand how you feel but the press release can be taped here on your grounds and sent to the stations. She would never have to leave this place, besides between your security and the extra we'll be adding, this place will be locked up like Fort Knox. We need to have them make a move. This stalemate could go on for a long time," Detective Willington added.

"There's something else to consider here gentlemen, if the mastermind behind this ring really wanted the Countess here, I truly believe she would have been hit and not the apartment. She wouldn't have known what had happened to her if that was the case. All that was a scare tactic, possibly to ward off any future police calls."

The men sat in silence. Mariah was studying things in her mind. It was she that spoke first. "Jean Paul, I don't mean this the way it's going to sound but you have never run from a fight before. You have always stood fast and proud. The way I see it, that's what we have to do now. I don't want to live the rest of my life looking over my shoulder or Abigail's. I like the seclusion here with you but I don't want all the extra guards. I want things like they were before all this happened and I want these people caught and punished. Let's do it for Abigail and for all the other Abigail's born today. I know dissolving this one ring won't do much to stop the problem but it's a start. I'm ready to do my part."

Charlie had remained silent through all of this but he couldn't do so now. "Mariah, you can't be serious! You're putting yourself in danger. What about Abigail? She needs you, remember?"

"Charlie, I know that. I'm doing this for her and her future."

"Mariah please, you can't do this." Patrick's tone was quiet but forceful.

"*Pardon*, but my mind is made up. Jean Paul, will you help me do this for our daughter?" She looked at him, he sat there looking in her eyes and shaking his head. He didn't want to but knew that she was right. It had to be done. He had to be sure his security was top notch to cover any lapses the local police had good as they were. She and Abigail had to be safe at all times! He wouldn't lose another family.

Patrick and Charlie refused to go back home considering what was about to happen. It had been decided that they were to take Abigail along with Margarette and two police officers back to the residence in Marseille. There they would stay with Abigail until things were safe for her to come back to Mariah. Guy had told his brother he would ensure Abigail's safety and the Americans would not take her back to the States with them. All this would happen as soon as the press release came out which was scheduled in a day or two. The police wanted the tape shown the after the surprise visit to the factory enabling everyone to get back to the vineyard safely.

The tape showed both Mariah and Jean Paul sitting beside each other holding hands. Jean Paul stated "their innocence in the entire matter and their disgust toward the ring. They were cooperating fully with the police and had confidence that the ring would be dissolved quickly thus making the streets of France a little safer for the children. As far as Mariah's disappearance, she had left for a planned trip and wasn't at the apartment at the time of the incident. It had all been a misunderstanding." The tape was ready. The police were ready to visit the factory and so was Jean Paul. He was going no matter what. Patrick was insisting on going, so Charlie thought it was best that he tagged along to help keep Patrick's temper in check.. There were more security and plainclothes police all around the grounds and in the house as well. Mariah and Abigail would be safe with them gone.

"We've got something here!" The trained German shepherd was on the scent of something. He was excited and scratching at a locker. Detective Christian Lemouré ordered the locker open by the manager. Edmund and Tré were standing by. They were shocked to think that their designs were being treated this way even though all the publicity for both garment lines were getting was increasing the demand for them. They had production working overtime and still behind on orders. Jean Paul had asked them to take more of a role in production for the time being until all this ended.

The locker was opened finally and sure enough inside was a baggie with a very small amount of a white substance in it. The field test turned blue. "Gentlemen, I do believe we have cocaine here. Take this for analysis.

Mark it urgent," Detective Lamouré said. This was his territory and no FBI or States cop was going to tell him how to do his job.

"Who does this locker belong to and where is he?"

"I wish I knew. Peter Abbott hasn't been here for a week now. He didn't even bother to call in and say he was quitting. It's strange isn't it? I mean him just going off and leaving his locker that way," the manager said looking at Jean Paul, Patrick, and Charlie who were standing together off to the side.

Detective Lamouré was called on his radio to meet an informant along the Gironde River bank and that it was urgent. When Detective Morgan asked to come along, Lamouré motion for him to hurry. They left Detective Willington to handle the factory situation alone but what they did not know was that the tape of Mariah and Jean Paul had been released prematurely and at that moment thousands were watching the television.

"So they think they are going to stop me!" I am bigger than what they think I am." The woman was in her middle forties. She carried a medium build and possessed a fairly plain face except for a few wrinkles around her eyes. Her red hair was cropped short and tapered. She took her glasses off the top of her head and put them on. She had been one of the top madams in the area in her younger years making her money off of her "girls". Later, she invested in other "profit making endeavors" and presented herself as a banker. This position had opened several doors for her she thought would never exist. She enjoyed her extravagant life and had no intentions of giving it up. She worked too hard to have it taken away from her. She noticed the couple before her holding hands. She noticed Jean Paul's left hand as he scratched his temple, he wore a gold band with a diamond centered in the middle of it on his ring finger. The woman glanced quickly to Mariah, Jean Paul had lifted his right hand off of hers for a second. It was long enough to see that she also wore a set of rings on her left hand. It wasn't long enough to see what they were but she had the feeling she knew. This was her time now. She was tired of games and she wanted him to pay. He had put a crimp in her operation long enough. She made a call.

"*Bonjour*, did you see it? So let them. There is nothing to connect me to anything." She paused as she listened. "I see, where is he now?" she sighed. "You fool! There are better way to dispose of unwanted goods than that." She listened. "You had better hope he's not found. As far as this other matter goes, I think we need to put some more emotion in the bank. You know what I mean. Do what ever. What do I care how? Just as long as my investments give me back some capital gains and I don't mean just money. All this unfortunate business is costing me. If I can't ship, then you don't get paid. End this now. Understand?" She hung up and sat down on her sofa with a glass of Champaign in her hand and laughed.

Edmund approached Jean Paul, Charlie and Patrick who were standing inside the factory's main doors waiting for the detective to finish.

"Count, your press release sounded good. By the way, did I tell you your wedding was spectacular? Mariah is one beautiful bride and that dress she designed ..."

"Wait, did you say press release?" Patrick asked turning to Edmund and then to Jean Paul and Charlie. Jean Paul caught Edmund's words, too.

Patrick yelled for the Detective but before he knew it Jean Paul and Charlie were out the door and heading across the street to his Rolls. Patrick told Willington what had happened and he had radioed his men back at the estate. He headed out the door with Willington but stopped short on the sidewalk. The sight that was enfolding in front of his eyes was like a dream- Jean Paul crossing the street with Charlie at his heels. A car was barreling down at top speed toward them. Charlie looked to his right and saw the white sedan. He rushed forward and pushed Jean Paul out of the way sending him lunging behind the Rolls. The car struck Charlie who bounced off the hood and landed to the side of the street. His head thudded as he hit the hard concrete.

Patrick was first to reach Charlie and then the detective. Willington called for an ambulance. Jean Paul had cut his temple on the car's chrome as he went down on the pavement behind it. He wiped the blood off the side of his face with his hand.

"Don't move him," Willington ordered to Patrick. "The ambulance will be here in a minute."

"Is he?" Jean Paul asked while assessing the area.

"No, he's breathing," Detective Willington said. "Did you see who was driving?" he asked Jean Paul.

"I did. The guy had blonde hair. He wasn't after Charlie, he was after YOU." Jean Paul didn't know if it was Patrick's look he gave him or if it

457

was his words that gave him the chills. They heard the sirens coming. Jean Paul stood up from kneeling beside Charlie.

"Wainscott, you go to the hospital with your friend. Detective, tell them to contact me for the expenses, what ever it takes. I'll be in touch!" He was getting in the Rolls.

"Where the hell do you think you're going?" Patrick yelled as the Count was pulling away.

"To protect my wife." He drove away.

At the riverbank Detective Christian Lamouré stood above the body that was floating face down. "Are you sure this is the guy that was bragging at the tavern the other night?" he asks his informant.

"*Oui*, it is the man." Lamouré slipped him a few bills. He knew the guy would use it for booze and that's what kept him giving information to the police. It was a way of supporting his drinking habit.

The body was of a young man in his middle twenties. His wallet held the drivers license of a Peter Abbott. This was not a robbery. This was cold-blooded murder and probably a result from his involvement with the drug ring itself. "Some way to get rich," Detective Lamouré told his "friend" and walked away leaving the scene to the other officers.

CHAPTER 21

"Mariah, Mariah!" His voice bellowed throughout the entire house. Several servants came running. Mariah was upstairs nursing Abigail when she heard her husband call. She gave the baby to Margarette who had become accustomed to visiting with Mariah when she nursed. The two women had bonded quite nicely. Mariah straightened herself and stood at the top of the staircase. The servants immediately disappeared hearing her voice. They were not ones to eavesdrop.

"I'm here, Jean Paul. What is it?" She was halfway down the stairs when he met her and embraced her. His heart was pounding and he was out of breath. He kissed her hard. She saw his cut.

"Thank God you're all right?" he said as he kissed her again. She pulled back.

"What happened to you? You're bleeding, come let's get you cleaned up. You might even need stitches on that one." She took his hand and tried to lead him upstairs to the bathroom so she could treat his wound but he stopped her.

"Come, *mon amour*, we have to talk." He led her into the study and closed the door. She stood in front of him, her arms crossed in front of her and had a bewilder look on her face.

"You're starting to scare me, Jean Paul. This is serious isn't it?"

"Someone released our statements to the press."

"It wasn't supposed to go out for another two days. We were to have time to get Abigail to your brother. Who and Why?"

"We can't do that now. It's too dangerous for her to leave here and if I knew who did this insane act I'd flog him until he died."

"Jean Paul, did something happen while you were at the factory? Wait a minute, where's Charlie and Patrick? They went with you." She was truly frightened now and sat down in the chair by the desk. "Something happened, tell me what it is now!"

"The police found traces of cocaine in an employee's locker, but it seems that the man hasn't showed up for work for a few days. Edmund told us he had seen the press release." Jean Paul stepped in front of her and put his arms around her as she stood up. "Charlie and I were crossing the street to get to you when out of nowhere a car came. Charlie saw it before I did and pushed me out of the way. He was struck."

"No, no it can't be," Mariah started shaking and sobbing.

"Mariah, he is still alive. I don't know his injuries but I will find out."

"Where's Patrick?"

"Wainscott is at the hospital with Charlie as we speak."

"I want to see Charlie." She tried to free herself of his arms but he kept her from doing so.

"*Non*, it is not safe to go at this moment."

"He's hurt, he's like a brother to me. I have to go." Her tears were falling and her voice quivered but she wasn't out of control.

"*Mon amour*, it's not that simple. Wainscott saw the driver. He described the driver as the same one who ran us off the road. Don't you see our accident was not an accident and neither was this time. I was the target." Mariah looked at him blankly then it all registered. She shook her head in disbelief.

"This can't be true! Was the apartment vandalized because of you, too?"

"Possibly, perhaps whoever did it thought I was there and not you." He held her and neither spoke for a time. "I will call the hospital and find out what is going on. We will get steady reports, but you cannot leave this house until it is safe. Understand me?" Mariah nodded her head. Right now all she wanted was news on Charlie. Someone had to tell Becky she thought.

"Keep me posted every half an hour as to what is happening there. *Oui*, I'll be home. *Merci*." Jean Paul hung up the phone and turned to Mariah who was pouring herself a glass of wine. She had to have something to steady her nerves. Too much was happening too fast. He watched her since she seldom drank but didn't stop her. "That was Taylor. I called security to send a man to the hospital as a precaution. He reports that Charlie has a concussion and a fractured leg. It looks like he was lucky but will be laid up for a while. They don't want to do surgery for the fracture until tomorrow. The concussion is the main priority right now."

"Is he awake yet?"

"*Non*, not yet. Taylor will be calling every half an hour with an update."

"Is Patrick okay?"

"He is with Taylor. I assume so.

"Someone needs to call Becky." She got up to do so.

"Wait, *mon amour*. Let's wait until we know he's awake. She will feel better with the news." Mariah and Jean Paul went up to their bedroom and closed the door. Margarette saw them enter the bedroom so she went downstairs with Abigail. They both looked haggard.

Patrick didn't come back to the estate all night. He stayed with Charlie until he woke the next morning.

"Where am I?" Charlie said as his focused on Patrick asleep in the chair in his hospital room. Patrick recounted the events and assured Charlie that Jean Paul was okay. He then took out his cell phone and placed a call to Becky for his friend.

"Mariah, where are you?" Jean Paul sat up in bed trying to figure out where his wife had gone.

"I'm in here. I'll be out in just a minute." She had taken the phone call concerning Charlie's improvement and had even spoken to him at that time. Her spirits were much higher than what they were the night before. She felt like celebrating this morning since Charlie was going to be all right. She had a plan to relieve the stress they had been under and in spite of what was going on she wanted to show her husband how much he meant to her. It would have been her husband hit by the car if it hadn't been for Charlie. She stood in the bedroom door with her hands on each side of the door facing raised above her head. His eyes slowly traveled down her body.

The outfit she wore consisted of black leather elbow length gloves. The black leather and rhinestone under wire bra and thong barely covered her. His eyes moved to her matching garter belt which held the black fishnet stockings and completing the attire on her feet was a pair of black leather straps with a six-inch stiletto heel. A smile spread across Jean Paul's lips, his eyes wide with amusement and anticipation. His mouth went dry and the pounding ache in his groins grew with every second he watched her. She moved toward him as if floating. She placed the toe of her shoe on the bed beside him, forcing him to look at her leg. He stroked it tenderly.

"What is this all about?" he asked almost in a whisper, his senses going wild.

"This is my anniversary present to you. With everything going on the past few days neither one of us thought about it. We need to usher in the New Year in the right way. So relax Count, I'm in charge of things now." She took the point of her shoe and pushed him down on the bed. He laid there watching her with a smile. She had grown in the past week from being shy about herself to this. What had he created? He didn't care as long as she was his and only his.

They still weren't downstairs at noon when Patrick and Michael had arrived home from the hospital. Charlie was out of surgery and his leg would heal without problems but the doctors said it would be a few days before he would go home. So it was settled, the Count would have houseguests a little while longer whether he liked it or not. He assumed the Count would be out doing whatever a Count did and Mariah resting since she wasn't down yet either. He wanted to see how she was doing and was about to knock on her bedroom door when he heard their voices. Not again, he thought. They were almost to the point of being perverted. He didn't know this Mariah at all.

The police visited the estate and told of finding Peter Abbott's body in the river. It was their theory this particular drug ring had something personal to work out with the Count's family, and perhaps they didn't care who got hurt in the process. Even their residence in Marseille wasn't safe now. Abigail had to stay where she was- a trip was out of the question for the time being. Everyone had to take special precautions, including Patrick like it or not. Anytime he went to the hospital or anywhere else on the grounds he was to take a bodyguard, which he thought was ridiculous but agreed that he would. He was more concerned about Mariah and Abigail than anyone else in the house. They were his first worry; he had to do what he could to help protect them. After all, he still loved them both very much.

The Count and Countess had become accustomed to staying in their bedroom until noon each day. After Abigail nursed and visited with them Margarette would take her downstairs to spend some time with everyone else in the house. It was then that Patrick got to spend his time with her and he loved it. The staff was even getting more relaxed around him. He had no idea of stealing Abigail away from this security. Even he had to admit things were probably safer here than anywhere else as long as she stayed on the estate.

A couple of days later Charlie had called the estate to have some of his shaving things brought over. He could actually sit up in bed now without getting a wave of nausea and the room spinning out of control. Patrick had decided to take the items to him. He had been cooped up long enough with the Count even though the highlight of his days were spending time with his daughter and with Mariah when she wasn't trying to avoid him. With everything going on they had forgotten about him signing the visitation papers and he wasn't going to remind them of it. He left with Mason, the Count's main chauffer, and a security guard to go to the hospital.

The police wanted to go back to the factory and see if there was anything they missed in Peter's locker. They had proof that Peter Abbott and John Portland "the blonde haired man" had known each other and had occasionally been seen together. Abbott was dead, but the question remained, where was Portland? Was he plotting to run someone else down in the family? Jean Paul met them; he wanted first hand knowledge of what was going on. The house was secure and he felt safe that everyone would be all right until he got back. He reminded Mariah how much he loves her and how happy he was to have her in his life. He had even taken to writing love poems for her on small pieces of paper and placing them where she would find them unexpectedly the next day. The poems were all over the house; in places he knew only she would look. This made her happy each time she found one.

It was around four o'clock when the phone rang. Raul, their butler entered the living room where Mariah and Margarette were watching the baby play.

"*Pardon*, Countess there is a call from the hospital for the Count." Mariah looked at him and then to Margarette.

"Do you want me to take it, *Madame*?" Michael, who has been the Count's security chief for years, asked getting up from the chair in the corner of the room. He had been dozing off and on but was alert now. Things had been quiet until now.

"No thank you, Michael I'll take it. It's probably *Monsieur* Osswell."

"*Bonjour*," she said.

"*Bonjour*. This is Doctor Timothé. We have been given your number as a contact person. I regret to deliver the news to you that *Monsieur* Osswell is not doing well at this time. He has had a set back and wants to speak with the Count right away. Please advise him that it is urgent that he gets here before it is too late." The man's voice faded as he hung up without giving Mariah a chance to respond. Her hand was shaking as she tried to replace the receiver on the hook. Tears were starting to fall.

"*Madame*, what is it?" Michael asked. Mariah shook her head.

"Michael have Algernon bring the car around. I'm going to the hospital. *Monsieur* Osswell is dying."

"*Non, Madame*, I can't allow you to go. This is dangerous."

"Now you listen to me. I am going with or without you even if I have to drive myself. I want the car NOW!"

"*Madame*, I must call the Count and let him know."

"Fine! The doctor said he wants to see him. He's not here and I need to be with him. He can't die on me, he just can't. He's like my brother." She rang Jean Paul's cell.

"*Bonjour*." He answered promptly.

"Jean Paul, the hospital just called, Charlie's taken a turn for the worst. He's dying and requesting you. I'm on my way, so meet me. Love you." She hung up the phone before he had the chance to respond. He wondered why he hadn't been called himself by the hospital or by his security still there. Then it came to him. He yelled "*Non*." All three Detectives were with him. They looked at him. He called Taylor at the hospital who answered the phone laughing.

"*Oui*."

"It is I. What is going on there? Is Osswell dying?" The Count's voice was impatient.

"*Non, Monsieur* Wainscott and I are with him as we speak. *Monsieur* Osswell is not dying." Patrick and Charlie stopped laughing. They both went white at the same time. Taylor listened to the Count repeat what Mariah had told him. He gave the order for Mariah to be protected at all costs.

"Count, that goes without saying. I will die for her if need be." Taylor closed the phone and disappeared out of the room. Patrick followed him for the details and Charlie threw his plastic water glass across the room out of frustration. He was stuck there in the hospital while something was going down concerning Mariah.

Patrick and Taylor went down to the main entrance of the hospital. They alerted hospital security on what was going on and Taylor arranged for one of them to be posted outside Charlie's door until they got back.

The detectives radioed for backup at the hospital. The Count drove his Lamborghini to the factory without any security. He took the SIG Sauer out of the glove compartment and placed it in his belt before he exited the car to meet Patrick and Taylor outside the hospital. He had been in contact with the estate and learned that Michael, Mariah, and Algernon had left over a half an hour ago. Algernon had taken the silver Mercedes. No one had seen them since they left the estate. Jean Paul was frantic. The detectives put a APB out on the car and its occupants. There was a citywide search-taking place and so far no one was finding his family.

Jean Paul was in the hospital's chapel. He was still full of rage, rage at Mariah who disobeyed his orders to stay safe at home no matter what, rage at the people who were doing this, rage at the whole world. Patrick handed him a cup of coffee. He saw the pistol outline under the Count's sweater and knew this time for sure; the Count could use it if he had to and without regret if he needed to. This man could be capable of anything but for now all they could do was wait. Wait for what? After a couple of hours it was clear that his wife was not going to show up at the hospital. The police wanted them go back to the estate and wait for whatever ransom note or communication from the kidnappers that may come. Patrick went up and spoke with Charlie who was about to come unglued. He couldn't move- he couldn't do anything to help find her. He understood that the kidnappers used him as part of their scheme to get to her, to the Count, and he hated that.

Jean Paul had locked himself in the shooting gallery in the basement. He placed his earphones on and singled out a key on his key chain to the tall steel cabinet.

Patrick followed him and knocked on the door. He answered hoping it to be word that Mariah was back and the car had mechanical problems instead of what was really happening.

"What do you want?" The Count turned his back on Patrick and pulled out a Barretta from the cabinet.

"What the hell!" Patrick peered inside the cabinet. The Count had an expensive collection of guns, including an original musket from the French Revolutionary War, a 16 GA Belgin made Browning shotgun, the Barretta shotgun he had in his hand, and a another SIG Sauer Pistol which happened to be his favorite of all. The expense of the gun was worth the accuracy it gave.

"Do you shoot, Wainscott?"

"No, I never have. I don't like having guns around. But just because I don't have any doesn't mean that I don't know an expensive collection when I see it. Do you really think this is necessary?"

"If you believe that, then you are a bigger fool than I thought you were. There are some things in life that are necessary, whether you like them or not. If you are going to stay then you had better put on a pair of those." He pointed to the bookcase that held more headphones. "If not, then you had better go." His shotgun was ready and he sent a target on the pulley to the other side of the room. He pulled the hammer, the gun rang, and the shell hit its mark- the heart of the paper man. The count didn't even flinch when the gun dislodged. Satisfied, he pulled out each gun one at a time, cleaned it, readied it, and fired it. Time and time again hitting the heart of each man. He did all this in silence. Patrick felt the chill in the air and it wasn't from any draft. This man that Mariah had married meant business there was no doubt about it. The Count turned to Patrick.

"Here." He handed him the SIG out of his collection.

"What's this for?"

"You're going to learn to shoot."

"I don't.."

"Wainscott, you don't like me and I don't care for you, but if you care anything about my wife or little Abigail you will learn to shoot before you leave this room. You just might have to." His voice had become as cold as the room. "Their life may depend on it, yours, too, for that matter."

"That's what the police is for, isn't it? We're not living in the 1800's, you know?"

"Sometimes things happen faster than one expects. Now, you either learn to shoot or leave me to prepare. I will do what I have to, to protect my wife and my daughter." He turned back to the shooting range and began to fire. Patrick found himself putting on the earphones and picked up the SIG that he had laid down on the ledge in front of him. Jean Paul laid down his own gun and started the lesson. His contempt for the people responsible for all this was apparent. And he would see they would pay for a very long time. He was a man on a mission. He would find his wife alive and their family would be reunited once again. It was all over the news and the television that this time it was true that Countess Mariah DuMoiese was kidnapped along with her chauffer and her bodyguard. There were no other details available. Becky gasped as she sat at the breakfast table drinking her coffee. She was just about to call Charlie when the report came over the airwaves. Somehow all this entwined her family now. How many more innocent people were going to be dragged down in it?

The silver Mercedes had stopped for traffic. They had just cleared the estate's back property ten minutes before when a blue sedan at a high rate of speed crashed into the left side of the car taking the three occupants by surprise. Algernon was dead at the scene. Michael saw the car a fraction of a second before it hit them. The plan was to push Mariah out of her passenger door and he was to follow and get back to the house on foot but for now he wanted her on the other side of the car for cover. She must be in shock he thought to himself. She's too calm. She was crouching on the ground behind their car. "Countess, I'll get you back home, I promise." Michael pulled his weapon out and took aim. He pulled the hammer back and fired killing one of the attackers. Just as he took aim, he was hit. Damn it, he thought as he fell to the ground unconscious. Mariah watched in horror. She couldn't tell if he was still alive but she knew she had to do something now, it was up to her. She reached for Michael's gun but a shoe kicked it out of her way. She looked up. A blonde haired man was towering over her and sneering.

"Well, well, who do we have here? No wonder that was too easy. This calls for a different plan." He pulled Mariah up by her arm. She tried to fight him but he was too strong. Before she could try to knee him something struck her head and she slumped over. He carried her to a car that was hidden just beyond the tree line. C.J. wouldn't be happy about this but he couldn't leave witnesses and he wasn't one to kill a woman in cold blood especially one this nice to look at.

The call came from the police; children walking their dogs had come across the scene and called the police. The driver was dead apparently from the crash but Michael was in very poor condition and was being transported to the hospital at that time. Michael had told the children to tell the police "Portland" before he lapsed into unconsciousness again. Jean Paul placed the phone on the table and stood by the window, his hands fisted in each other. "I shall kill you myself, Portland, if it is the last thing that I do." His voice was low and chilly but Patrick heard what he said since he was standing close to him. The other staff members had left the room sensing that the Count needed time to himself. They were all concerned and hoped for the best but this call showed even them that it was far more serious then even they imagined. After a few minutes, Patrick was able to get Jean Paul to recount the call.

"What the hell do we do now?" Patrick said quietly. Somewhere upstairs Abigail was crying and other than that sound the entire house was stone quiet. Jean Paul had to see Abigail. As soon as the Count had disappeared upstairs, Raul, the butler, asked Patrick what the call was about. Raul said the Lord's Prayer to himself as he left the room to tell the rest of the staff.

Mariah woke, her head hurting, she touched the knot that had developed on the side of her head. She looked around. She was in some sort of a warehouse. She was lying on a make shift bed that consisted of flat cardboard boxes and a torn blanket. She was alone for the time being. She tried the door even though she knew it would be useless. The bars on the window were steadfast. Looking down she could tell she was on the third floor of the building but none of the other warehouses looked familiar to her. Except for one thing, the smell of the place. She tried to pinpoint that smell but couldn't, her head hurt too much to think about it anymore. She lay down on the blanket and almost started to cry. Her resolve set in at that moment. No, she wouldn't do that! It was all her fault that she was in this situation. Jean Paul had told her not to leave the house, but then they didn't expect to be tricked that Charlie was dying either. Oh God, how she hoped that was a trick. What was it that her kidnapper said before he hit her with something? "That was too easy- or something like that." Jean Paul was right; maybe they were after him instead of her. How she wished she were with him right now. She would be strong and do what she needed to do to keep alive until her husband could find her. He would find her. She knew he would. It was just a matter of time. She reached inside her coat pocket to see if she had anything at all to help herself. She found something soft and pulled it out. She had sometime or another stuffed one of Abigail's little receiving blankets in the deep pocket. She clung to it and couldn't help but lose control at the sight of it. Her little girl needed her and she needed Abigail. She would get through this and hold her in her arms again. One consolation was that at least she didn't take Abigail with her. She was safe at home. Then her thoughts went to Algernon, poor Algernon. She said a prayer for his soul and then she remembered Michael falling to the ground. What happened to Michael? Was he dead because of her, too? She wept, there was no other way of releasing what she felt at the moment. Then she slept.

Mariah woke to feeling the point of a shoe in her side. She looked up and blinked. The blonde haired man spoke French to her. She didn't respond. He spoke again.

"I know you speak both French and English, woman. It doesn't matter to me if you talk or not. There's food if you so chose."

He pointed to the table at the other end of the room. Keeping his Ruger pointed at her he leaned against the wall. She sat up. The dirty tray held a plate of cold bacon, biscuits, and water. Her appetite didn't exist. She sat upright on the cardboard bed folding her legs underneath her long skirt for warmth. The blanket didn't offer a lot of comfort since it held several holes.

"Let me get a few things straight right now. You behave yourself then you'll get to go home. If you don't then I suppose you won't. I don't have a say in what goes on in all of this. I just do what I'm told but that doesn't mean that I won't use this if I need to. Look what happened to your friends. Understand?" Mariah nodded.

"How long are you going to keep me here?"

The man laughed. "You expect me to know that? How ever long it takes. Now eat, Countess." The look on Mariah's face was horror. He knew who she was.

"You know who I am?" she spoke softly. "What do I call you?"

"It was unexpected to have you as our guest. I am sorry the hotel room isn't better for such a lady as you," he laughed again. "To you *Madame*, my name is Fly."

"Fly? Why Fly?"

"I never stay in one place for any length of time." He used the same tone as the doctor on the phone.

"It was you that made the call about my friend dying. How did you know about that? Was the call a fake?"

"I have known about you for a long time. And yes it was a prank." It all clicked at that point in Mariah's head.

"My god, it was you that ran us off the road in California, it was you that hit Charlie the other day." Her hand went to her mouth her anger flashed. "You bastard!" She sprung at him thrashing at him with her hands. He sidestepped and laughed as she hit the wall hurting herself.

"So you do have some spunk after all. This just might be fun." He grabbed her arm behind her back and sat her in the folding chair. He then tied her feet and her arms to it while she was kicking at him. "I do truly hate to have to do this to such a beautiful woman but if we are to get along then you have to find some manners. This behavior doesn't become a Countess." She spat in his face and glared at him. He took his linen handkerchief out of his pocket and wiped his face. He then stuffed it in her mouth just enough to keep her quiet. "There we wouldn't want you to get dehydrated now would we? You may have all your spit back." His phone rang. He answered it as he walked out of the room and locked the door behind him. She could hear his voice on the other side. He was talking to someone by the name of CG. Who was CG?

Detectives Willington and Morgan were still at the estate. They had pretty much planted themselves firmly in the soil there. Detective Lamouré and his locals were tracking leads most of the time. So far, no one had come up with anything. There hadn't even been a call for ransom yet. It was like she had vanished in thin air for the last twenty-four hours. Everyone knew that if a call didn't come soon, it probably wasn't going to.

Jean Paul and the police visited the hospital. Michael was finally able to have visitors. His injures were serious but he was making progress. The bullet grazed off his vest and penetrated just underneath it.

"I tried to protect her. I am sorry I failed Count?"

"You did your best, Michael. I am grateful for that." Jean Paul took Michael's hand careful of the I.V. hooked to him.

"I knew better than to let her go. I made her call you and told her we would wait until you checked things out but when Algernon pulled the car up she bolted out the door. I had to follow her. She didn't give any time to get backup. I tried calling from the car. Why didn't they come?"

"Security said they didn't hear from you after you left. Michael no one blames you. You did your job. When Mariah gets something in her head there is no stopping her," Patrick added. Jean Paul glanced at him but didn't say anything. The past few hours the two men were forced to accept each other. Everyone had to work together to get her back safely and they knew it.

"Did they tell you? It was John Portland who took her." The Count nodded his head.

"Isn't that the guy who ran us down?" Everyone looked toward the door; Charlie was sitting in a wheelchair.

"Look at you. Getting out and around all ready," Patrick said as he held the door for the nurse to wheel him in to the room.

"Never mind that. I want to be filled in on what's going on," Charlie said as he settled himself beside Michael's bed.

Mariah sat looking out the window. There had been no one in sight all day. No one she could have banged at the window in hopes to catch their attention. It was getting dark and since her captor had left she had no contact with anyone. She was thankful that he had untied her before he left and was glad he had since she was feeling uneasy when he looked at her.

It was another twenty-four hours before she saw him. He had brought her more food and water, only this time he had given her some hot coffee and a decent blanket. The night had gotten colder than he thought it would. CG was upset that they had the Countess, at first, then seemed to enjoy the thought of her being captive. The main goal was to bring the Count for a meeting but the woman got in the way. The plan was altered to demand monetary compensation for the inconveniences that had been made due to the Count's involvement in the new drug laws that was cutting into the traffic and his involvement personally with the trunks. The factory was definitely off limits for CG for the time being.

"Morning Countess, how do we feel today?" He tossed her the blanket and she wrapped herself in it. She had been sleeping in her coat but she was still chilled. The boxes offered no reprieve from the cold floor.

"What do I owe for this coffee?" She drank deeply letting the hot liquid burn her throat.

"We must have you in top form." He grabbed her by the hair and tugged slightly. "I must say you don't look too bad this morning." He was watching her breathe. He pulled a small comb out of his pants pocket and started to comb her hair. She tried to move away from his touch but he grabbed her hair and pulled her back to him. Her pulse had quickened and so did her respiration out of fear. "You're going to talk to your family today. But you won't say anything to give them a clue of where you are. If you do, that precious little baby of yours won't be around for her next birthday. Understand?" He had seen her lactate yesterday even though she tried to hide it. She would have to have a baby didn't she, he thought as he started to leave her in the cold warehouse? He had the door open, now was her time to make a move.

"How dare you make a threat on her life. So help me! You hurt her and I will kill you, myself." She flung at him, he turned, slammed the door before she could get past and pushed her down on the floor with his hand brushing against her chest. That was all her body needed and she couldn't stop it. He cursed and threw the blanket on top of her.

"As much as I would like to partake at the moment, cover yourself before I change my mind." He picked her up by the arm and threw her on the makeshift bed where she landed with a thud. He was on top of her, his knee in her lap while he tied her hands behind her back. He shifted his weight and faced her. His face was so very close to hers. She could smell the cigarettes on his breath and he could smell the aroma of her shampoo. Having her restrained he made the call to the estate. The phone rang and Jean Paul answered right away. The steel barrel of the gun was cold against her chest. She felt its tip through her blouse.

"*Oui*," he stated as he switched the phone to speaker. Everyone in the room was dead silent but the police were trying to get a fix on the caller's location.

Fly had placed a device on the phone to filter out his true voice. "We have her."

"I want her back, now! If you have hurt her, I will personally kill you, myself."

"Count, I will make this short and sweet. I know you have a tracer on the line. The Countess is all right at the moment, but she won't be if you do not do what we tell you. We want two million dollars for her release. That is what you have cost us by your laws. You see, it is you that has caused this in more ways than one. You have the money ready by noon tomorrow and perhaps you will be with your wife, if all goes well."

"Wait, I want to speak to her. How do I know you haven't already killed her?" The chills went down his spine and Patrick's, too.

"*Mon amour*." It was Mariah's voice. She sounded tired and weak. It was all she had the time to say before Fly took the phone away.

"Details will follow." He hung up.

Jean Paul cursed when the police said the call wasn't long enough to get a trace on it. Patrick took out the front door in the rain. He didn't care; he just started running until he couldn't any longer. The running gave an outlet for him, everywhere he went in the house he couldn't help but wonder how THEY had spent time together in whatever room he was in- the pool, the gym- he couldn't even go in the stables anymore. He knew the security was watching him and he was angry with them. They should have been watching her better. In spite of the Count's efforts to keep her safe as he boasted, he couldn't do it and now she was paying for whatever mistakes he had made in the past and present. As he sat under a tree in the rain, it struck him that really, all this was still his fault. If he hadn't had that stupid affair, she would never have left him to find the Count and none of this would have had to happen. He put his head in his hands and for the first time released all of his emotions at once.

"Very good, Countess"

"Why didn't you let me ask about my baby? I need to know she's okay?" She tried to squirm out from underneath his weight but couldn't. "Untie my hands now!" she demanded.

"My your anger does flare, doesn't it?" The end site of his gun ripped her blouse and cut her shoulder in the process as she tried to move from him. Blood trickled through the fabric. "Now look at what you did. You stupid woman! My gun could have gone off." He grabbed Abigail's blanket and used it to wipe the blood. He had orders not to hurt her until CG came to look at her later today. He felt his pulse quicken as he touched her. She flinched but held still. His gun was in his other hand. She hadn't thought about that prospect. The bleeding had stopped but he still held his hand to her skin. His face was close to hers. "I would like to be the one to curb that anger from you. I have always wanted to tangle with a mother grizzly bear." His fingers touched her cheek and found them soft. He looked at her eyes, there was no fear in them like most women would have, only contempt for him and it turned him on. But he could tell she wasn't like most women.

Jean Paul and the police were still conversing over the phone call. The kidnappers wanted two million dollars. He didn't care how much the ransom was if it would bring her back to him, but it would take him a few hours to have that kind of money available. That was only a drop to what his true worth was. He had just gotten off the phone with Guy when Patrick walked in drenched. One of the maids saw him and grabbed a throw off of the sofa and placed it around him. He went upstairs to change his clothes.

Jean Paul knew how he felt but couldn't show it. There were too many people around and Mariah needed him. He felt her strength and hoped that if she could feel his she would remain so.

There was nothing to be done until the money arrived and the next call made. He went upstairs and sat in the nursery alone with Abigail. Patrick walked by the door and saw the two of them playing. It still bothered him that he was getting so close to his daughter but he had discovered the Count wasn't as bad as he thought originally. It was apparent that he loved Mariah and Abigail greatly. The thought came to him in an instant that there are a lot of children who aren't loved by their parents as much as Mariah. Jean Paul and he loved Abigail. She was a lucky child to have that in her life. He would leave them alone for a while even though he wanted to spend time with her as well.

Fly had tied Mariah back in the chair but not as tight as he had done in the past. He let a red haired woman inside the room. His gun in his hand was ready if need be. By his demeanor Mariah knew this must be his boss. The woman dressed in a knee high leather boots, fur coat, and hat crossed the room. She walked around Mariah sizing her up. The woman took off her hat and laid it down on the table by the door. She unbuttoned the coat to reveal an expensive navy suit and silk scarf underneath. She kept her gloves on so as not to leave any fingerprints.

"She's not the woman I imagined," CG announced and laughed. "Are you sure this is Countess DuMoiese?" The woman turned to Fly.

"*Madame*, ask her yourself."

"Are you?" The woman smiled at Mariah. "Look at yourself, your hair, your makeup?"

Mariah tilted her face to look up at her. The sun shown brightly in the one window the room had and obscured her sight to some degree. "Those things don't matter to me. I know who I am and that's all that matters."

"My, you still have some pride, huh. What was it that attracted the Count to you anyway? Couldn't have been your sense of style. For a so called fashion designer you have no style."

"You are a pathetic woman! Who do you think you are speaking to me like that! You seem to think you are so much better than me but in truth you sound like a bitter woman. You're lower than the fungus that grows under a stone! You sell drugs to children and you don't even care, that's why I AM better than you."

The red haired woman struck Mariah across the face with her gloved hand. Mariah's head snapped back but she held fast. Her face ached but she was not going to lower her eyes for this scum. Fly grimaced when he saw the strike but didn't move to stop anything. If he did she would most likely take out her 25 gauge and shoot him. He wanted to stay alive to enjoy his share of the money.

"What I want to know is why were my trunks going to Italy? Why are you doing this?"

CG laughed, "I have my reasons. I want the Count to pay for everything he has done. Some of my biggest customers are in Italy. The Count's connections to Italy helped tremendously to get it across the border until as of late. Now I have to be more careful, business is not as usual."

"What did he do, cut into your business? Made it harder for you to push? I don't see other drug lords kidnapping innocent women? Why this? Why?" Mariah's tone was forceful. She gathered all her strength to stand up to this woman. She could feel Jean Paul with her.

"It's much more than the smuggling, you see it's personal." The woman turned to Fly. Tomorrow morning call with the details, I want the drop the next day. Let's prolong his agony a little while longer. Then do whatever you want with her. You see it doesn't matter to me. I wanted him." She picked up her belongings and left.

When Fly was sure of her departure, he untied Mariah and inspected her face. It was still red but no bruising had set in. She removed his hands from her face and turned away. The rain had stopped and the sun was trying to come out.

"I still don't understand why she's doing this." It was more of a thought than a question but she spoke it out loud.

"Isn't it clear. She's a woman scorned by a man."

Mariah sat on her cardboard bed and wrapped herself in the blanket that he had brought to her. Maybe she could get in good with Fly, get him to trust her a little more, maybe she could use it to her advantage and escape this place. She sat there thinking as he closed and locked the door behind her. He would be back before the day turned to night. She only had a few hours to think about things. She had to make a move soon. Then it hit her again. The man Fly referred to could it be Jean Paul? Was that the "personal reason" she spoke of?

She started looking around the room, she had to find anything to help her but there wasn't much to work with. She would do anything she had to, to stay alive, to keep Abigail safe. Her daughter and Jean Paul needed her and that became her driving force. She felt uncomfortable around Fly, he was becoming more and more friendlier to her in ways that she didn't want so maybe her earlier idea wasn't as good as she had thought. If he had something else in mind for her then she would have to deal with it when it came. She had to stay alive for her family no matter what happened to her in the mean time.

Mariah had found a warped floorboard in the corner of the room. She worked at with her bare hands trying to pry it up, there was just enough room for her to wriggle it around on the loose nail. Slowly it gave. The door lock turned and she knew someone was coming in. Quickly she placed some empty boxes over the top of it and sat down on her bed.

"So I see you are in the same spot as when I left you. Here, I brought you some ointment for your face." Fly tossed the small tube her way.

"Thank you."

"Eat while it's hot, it's going to be getting colder tonight." He glanced at her torn blouse when the blanket fell away from her as she stood up. The cut looked red and sore. He was careful to keep his gun out of her reach but he touched the wound. It was hot and infected by the look of it. She flinched and moved back then stood to face him.

"What do you want of me?"

"Dear Countess, you don't want to ask me that question." He moved around her and stopped. She felt the gun barrel in her back but didn't move. He wrapped his arm around her waist. His breath was hot on her neck. "You see I am just like any other man." Fly pushed her away and she fell on the floor. "Use that on your shoulder," he said referring to the ointment. He wasn't an insensitive man and this woman bothered him a lot. She was different from the women he had known but he still had a job to do. Why did she have to get in the way? She was complicating things for him. He took a sip of his coffee and watched her as she did what she was told. He couldn't take his eyes off of her. They sat in silence once more, just sharing space. Finally, he had had enough, he got up and took the chair with him. His orders were to stay there until he had a call from CG on how to handle the details of the drop. What then he didn't know but he was going to wait in the hallway. He didn't trust himself with her anymore. The feelings that were stirring inside hadn't surfaced for a long time, not since his stint in a Spanish prison for rape. The woman was a date and she consented but she told the police that he raped her. Maybe he was too rough with her but in his mind that was all. She wanted it just like he did but he was convicted of the crime and did four years for it. That was before he had met CG and her girls. One thing led to another and thus a job that paid well for doing her errands.

The next day Fly made the call to Jean Paul. Told him to drop the money on the bank of Bay Biscay in Biarritz and alone. No one else or she was dead."

"Biarritz, is that where my wife is?"

"You just don't know, do you?"

"I want my wife returned when I pay the money."

"*Pardon*, you still don't get it do you? You're not calling the shots on this matter. You do as I say or you won't see your wife alive."

"Wait, I want to speak to her again."

"The Countess is not here. I don't have time to play these games with you."

"You listen to me scum. If I don't speak to my wife I will not be there with the money. I will have to assume that she is already gone from my life. And if that is the case you shall die for it by my hands." Jean Paul's voice was cold. He had to talk to her and he was desperately trying to keep the line open for the tracer to work

"It's a cell number. It didn't work."

The phone rang again. Jean Paul answered.

"Jean Paul, take care of Abigail for me. I love you." The line went dead again before he had the chance to respond to her. "Mariah, *Je t'aime*," he said to himself.

Patrick found Jean Paul in the basement again putting an extra round in the pockets of his jeans. He then took out his bulletproof vest and put it on. The gun went in its holster.

"The police want me to stay in case there's a call."

"That's probably for the best. I'm doing this alone." He walked past Patrick, went upstairs and out the front door.

It was windy and cold when Jean Paul stood at the bank. There was the tree with the trunk that branched off into a V. He wedged the money inside the trunk and backed off. No one seemed to be around but he couldn't be sure of anything, since even the police were well hidden. The police had come much earlier to settle in for cover but in hopes that the kidnappers would come to scout the area out. Three o'clock came and went there was no sign of the kidnappers. The money was still there. Then above him on the bridge a car horn was blaring. He looked up just in time to see Mariah in the back seat of a brown sedan. She raised her hand to wave and then was gone.

"Damn it!" he said. He threw the rock he was playing with toward the car not even coming close to hitting it. His cell rang. "You fool, you just tied the noose around your neck. You tricked me!" His words were full of anger.

"Wait Count, it's me. A woman just called. Said to leave the area NOW or Mariah is dead. She's not there is she?" Patrick's pulse was racing.

"She was." He hung up and ran to his Lamborghini. He headed the car toward the direction the kidnappers took Mariah. Detectives Willington and Morgan instructed Detective Lamouré and his men as to what was happening. Fly had delivered Mariah back to warehouse and removed her blindfold and the restraints around her wrist, and left without saying a word. She checked her coat pocket for the small mirror she had found in the back seat of the car. Perhaps she could use it somehow.

It was only after darkness fell that the money was picked up. With the cover of night, Fly whisked in, picked up the money, and left without making a sound. He had two million dollars in his hands for a few minutes and it felt good. The thought had crossed his mind to just disappear with it but he quickly nixed it knowing that with CG's connections, she would find him and kill no matter where he went.

Jean Paul hadn't slept much since all this began. He couldn't bring himself to lie down on their bed. Everywhere he looked he saw her, saw her love for the family, for him, their love still lingering in the air. The staff heard him walking the house all hours of the night. Raul had made the comment to Patrick that he had done the same thing for weeks after Angelina had died. He was barely eating and the staff was concerned about him. Patrick felt the same but he'd taken up running on the estate several times a day if he needed to, to keep his feelings in check. He hated calling Charlie to give an update on what had happened last night but he knew he had to. During the call, Charlie had mentioned that the doctor was going to send him home tomorrow, home would be the estate for the time being. There was no way he would go back to California without knowing Mariah was safe even though he couldn't do anything to help. Patrick looked out the window of the study as he spoke with Charlie. It was early and the sun was starting to come up. Jean Paul walked in the room, dressed in a cream turtleneck and jeans. He looked as if he was ready to go out.

"Anything up?"

"*Non*. It is the same damn thing of waiting." He poured himself a drink and sat down behind the desk. He started doodling at first then wrote a love letter to Mariah while Patrick finished his call to Charlie. Jean Paul told him he would send someone to bring Charlie to the estate tomorrow.

Guy walked in the study without knocking, "I thought I would find you in here." Jean Paul looked up and a grin spread across his face. He greeted his brother with an embrace.

"It is good to see you. Why are you here? Claude did not say anything about you coming when I spoke to him earlier. What has happened?" He was very concerned suddenly.

"Everything is fine at home- well as fine as it can be. The family and staff are very concerned about the Countess, they all want to let you know they are praying for a safe return. You and Mariah have all of their love, mine included. Claude is of course his efficient self. He is doing an excellent job handling things but he didn't say anything because I just made my mind up to come. I felt I needed to be here for you today. I heard what happened last night. Is there anything I can do? Any word?" Guy poured himself a drink and sat down on the sofa.

"Brother, make all this go away." He shook his head no. "Why now when we are finally happy? When we are finally together as it should be?"

"I don't know, Jean Paul. I don't know." Guy was watching Patrick who was still looking out the window. His back was to the brothers.

"You look like you haven't slept for a while. What good is that going to do for Mariah when she comes home to you if you're ill?"

Patrick heard Guy tell his brother. He felt like he was intruding and he didn't want to think about her coming back to HIM but it would be better than not doing so. At least, he would know where she was. He left to see if Abigail was awake yet.

Mariah was looking out the window when she saw a bag lady going through the trash in the alley between the warehouses. This was the first person she had seen in the alley since her capture. She tried knocking on the window but the lady didn't hear her. She took the mirror and tried flashing the sun's rays on it toward the woman. She looked up at Mariah. It worked! Mariah was extremely happy. The woman started to walk away. "No! Don't go away. Please don't go away." Mariah grabbed Abigail's blanket and tied her note she had written inside it. Fly had given her a piece of paper and pencil to write a note for her daughter in case she didn't come out of this alive. He knew the note would not ever be delivered but if doing it helped her to cope then why not. He knew she really didn't have a chance of coming out of this alive. Not in CG's mood, which was getting nastier by the minute concerning the situation. Such a waste of a good woman he thought at the time. He had taken the pencil with him when he left but he didn't bother to read the note.

She had placed her name and the estate's address in the middle of the letter. She raised the loose floorboard and wedged it between the bars of the window. With a lot of effort, the board broke a small hole in the window. The bag lady looked up. There coming down toward her was an object. She picked it up and unfolded the blanket. She read the note and tucked it away. That was a pretty classy address and perhaps she could get some real money from this. But what she couldn't understand was why someone would be in that old warehouse anyway. It had been condemned a long time ago.

Jean Paul saw Guy to the door. He had a meeting set up at the vineyard concerning quality control since supervision by the government was strictly enforced in the production of wine. He had to see everything was in order in case of an audit but mostly for something to do while the family waited. Before he left Guy embraced his brother.

Jean Paul spoke quietly in his ear, "I love you too. You have always been there for me. Thank you."

Guy released his hold on his brother, looked him in the eyes and smiled, "You have been there for me big brother. Keep in touch." Guy took his hat off the rack and descended the steps.

Jean Paul then went upstairs to see Abigail. He found Patrick still there playing with her. He sat on the floor with them. Patrick gave Abigail to him and he took her. "*Merci*" He sat there rocking her side to side and sung a song to her in French. His voice was deep and rich and the baby listened intently as if understanding every word he said. He did love Abigail and it showed more and more or perhaps he was just letting his guard down around Patrick a little more each day.

There was a commotion downstairs. Jean Paul and Patrick looked at each other. Jean Paul hugged Abigail and kissed her one more time before he handed her to Margarette who was sitting in the rocker in the corner. He even kissed Margarette and thanked her for watching Abigail so well. Margarette stood in the hallway with the baby in her hands looking after the men. That was strange, she thought to herself.

481

The detectives were called to the back property of the estate. A woman had been spotted walking around the edge of a clearing of trees on Jean Paul's land. But when she saw the dogs and the security personal she got scared. By the time security arrived at the area the woman had disappeared but had dropped Abigail's blanket on the ground with the note still attached. Detective Bill Morgan read the note and handed it to Detective Marc Willington.

"Look at this, Marc."

"Oh shit, you know what this sounds like?"

"Yea, a damn goodbye letter." He dropped the letter out of the blanket revealing the blood stains in the center of the blanket. "Damn it. Come on?" Detective Willington took off running toward the car with Detective Morgan right behind him.

They came barreling in the front door. Detective Willington yelled, "Any word yet?"

"No."

"I'll call Lamouré," Detective Bill Morgan said as he was dialing the extra phone line.

"What is going on down here?" Jean Paul asked as he came down the stairs at a half run. He stopped short when he saw Abigail's blanket and the blood stains. He was sick to his stomach. Patrick caught him as he staggered on the stairs. Willington handed Jean Paul the letter.

"Do you recognize the writing?"

"*Oui,* it's my wife's." Jean Paul read the letter and buried his face in the blanket. He noticed the blanket had a smell. What was that smell? Then it came to him- the paper mills in Pau. He told the men that he wanted to be left alone and went down to the basement. Patrick followed him shaking. He couldn't believe what just happened, she couldn't be gone. He wouldn't believe it. The detectives were having the bloodstains on the blanket analyzed. They tried to assure the Count this wasn't necessarily a sign that she was dead. That maybe somehow she was able to get the letter out to them. Willington said he was not giving up yet not until she was found. He gave the order for a complete ground search for the woman. No stone would be left unturned. The woman knew where she was.

Patrick found Jean Paul in his gun cabinet. "This isn't the time to be playing with guns."

"This is the perfect time to play with guns. I'm going out." He took his SIG Sauer out of the cabinet, loaded it and placed it in his shoulder holster. He then took the bulletproof vest off of the rack.

"Where the hell do you think you're going?" Patrick was concerned about what he was doing and his frame of mind.

"To find Mariah. She's still alive and I know where she is." He headed out of the room and out the walkout entrance to the basement. His leather jacket in hand.

"Where?"

"She's at one of the old paper warehouses in Pau."

"Wait, we have to tell the police."

"I don't have time. You do it, junior! This is my battle and mine alone. I will bring her home myself."

Patrick headed upstairs yelling for Willington. He told him everything he knew and ran out the front door when he saw the Lamborghini rounding the driveway in front of the house. He ran out in front of the car causing Jean Paul to slide on the concrete. He slowed down just enough to allow Patrick to jump in the car while it was moving

"Get the hell out!"

"No way! Do you think I'm going to sit back while all this goes down? I think not. Like it or not I'm in this mess and I owe it to Mariah to help her, too." The Count looked at him and then drove away. The police were getting in their cars when Jean Paul was already down the road. Willington and Morgan knew they had to stop the Lamborghini before it was too late. They issued an APB on the car. The detectives knew Jean Paul was just tired and upset enough not to be thinking straight. He had to be stopped- they had enough to worry about with getting the Countess back home alive but now they had to deal with the Count as well. This day was getting worse by the second.

There were a total of ten warehouses located beside the paper mill. She could be in any of them. The Lamborghini took all the back roads the Count could find to avoid the police. He knew they were probably trying to find him but he reached the mill area first. Jean Paul slid the car to a stop. Patrick started to get out.

"Wait, Wainscott." Patrick looked at him. The Count tossed him the bulletproof vest.

"What?" The Count shook his head in disbelief at Patrick's question.

"Put that on. I don't need a dead American on my hands, too. How would I explain that to Abigail when she gets older? I hope you learned your lessons well." He pulled the other SIG out of the glove compartment and handed it to Patrick.

"I don't know about this."

"Look, you can either stand out here and whine about things to the police or come inside with me. Either way I am not waiting. She's in one of these buildings and time may be running out for her."

Patrick put the vest on and Jean Paul went through some basic information about the gun as a reminder to Patrick. Together they headed into the first warehouse.

Fly was untying her from the chair after CG had left. The Countess was particularly nasty with his boss this time around. Standing outside the door, Mariah heard her give the order to dispose of the Countess, that she was tired of this game. What better way to hurt the Count than make him a widower again? She left the room with Mariah spitting after her. That was all she could do being tied up. Fly really didn't want to carry the order out. He had to think. He entered the room. He untied Mariah's hands and feet. She knew she had to catch him off guard. She had to turn his mind away from the conversation that just took place. She did the only thing she could think of. She had to escape somehow or she would be dead by tonight.

"Fly?"

"What?"

"Why do you work for her? She's one ugly person and her disposition is nasty. I know you can do better than work for her." Mariah was rubbing her hands and wrist to get the circulation back into them. She sighed heavily but continued. She rubbed her shoulder where the cut was, pretending that it hurt even though the ointment was healing the wound. She went over to her cardboard bed and pretended to faint. Fly rushed over and caught her before she hit the floor. He still had his gun in his hand. She was hoping that he would lay it down. When he realized that she was pretending, he bounced her against the wall. He was angry now for what she had done. She was forcing him to do something he didn't want to do. He had been trying to think of some way not to carry out CG's orders but now he knew the Countess couldn't be trusted. If he let her live she would be the death of him. He would have to kill her. CG was right, not to leave any witnesses. But first he wanted something else from her. He pressed his weight against her pinning her so she couldn't move in either direction. His right hand had both of her wrists above her head and in the other hand his gun.

"Countess, you have gone too far. I can't help you now even if I wanted." He pulled her the rest of the way down on the floor. "I can give you your last few minutes filled with pleasure." He knelt down on top of her still with her wrists in his hand and ran his gun up the inside of her thigh under her skirt that he had moved partially out of the way. The cold steel bit into her skin. She gasped just once and stifled the cry she was about to make. She would not let him have the satisfaction of hearing her cry. The gun caught her panties. She felt the delicate lace give way. She couldn't stop the "Oh, no you don't." It exploded out of her mouth before she knew it. He had plans to rape her before killing her. If she were about to die she would do it fighting. She reached for the floorboard she had hidden under her blankets. She swung it and the nail on the end of the board caught Fly between his temple and his eye sending blood everywhere and on to Mariah. The weight of his body shifted but he kept his grip on the gun even though he eased up on his grip on Mariah's other hand. He was still on top of her when the door burst open.

Jean Paul and Patrick searched the first floor of the third warehouse, which was mostly empty floor space and one small room and found nothing. They were on the second floor catwalk when they thought they had heard voices. Quietly they found the stairs to the third floor. That floor consisted of rooms probably used for offices at one time. They heard a scuffle in the last room over top of the distant sirens. Patrick was grateful that the police were coming and he hoped they hurried. Jean Paul motioned Patrick to go to the other side of the door. When they were positioned, Jean Paul kicked the door in and went in with Patrick at his heels. There was no turning back now. Fly looked up, saw Jean Paul and took aim. The gun blast rang in

Mariah's ears, she was still on the floor when Fly fell. The bullet caught him in his forehead. Mariah felt his blood splatter her. Jean Paul had gotten off his round first. Mariah ran to him crying.

"Shh. It's all over. Did that bastard hurt you?" He assessed her torn blouse, the cut on her shoulder and the fact of Fly's position over top of her and the disarray of her clothing.

"No, you came just in time. He was going to rape..." He kissed her, held her and told her he loved her.

For once in his life Patrick felt rage with what he saw. He came to the realization fast that if Jean Paul hadn't shot that bastard he would have. Patrick stepped over and Mariah hugged him. He kissed her, too, but was careful not to kiss her as he really wanted to.

"Is Abigail okay?"

"*Oui*, she is fine, she misses her *mère*. Lets get you out of here."

They turned only to find the door blocked by CG holding a gun on them. "Well, isn't this touching? *Bonjour,* Jean Paul. We meet again."

"Colette Gisgardé," said Jean Paul.

"That's correct. You do remember me. I am so surprised. I thought I didn't mean anything to you. Drop the gun," she nodded to Patrick. Then she saw Fly lying in a pool of blood. "Too bad, John Portland was a good employee and in bed, too," she said still keeping her attention and her gun on the trio. Colette turned back to Patrick, "I said drop it!" He looked at Jean Paul for an instant, there was no expression on his face so he did as he was told. Jean Paul hiding his gun behind his back. He had a hold of Mariah's sleeve and slowly inched her behind him.

"Do you really think you can protect her? You haven't done so well these past few days have you?"

"You've done this? Why?"

"Because you have cost my operation a lot over the past months- I can't move my shipments like I used to and because of the way you threw me over."

"You're smuggling the drugs?" Patrick was stunned that a woman could be in charge of that kind of operation.

"Smart man."

"Colette, this doesn't have to happen this way."

"You're wrong me dear friend, you see, I loved you more than anyone and you threw all that away. You didn't even give US a chance. You could have had even more than you do now, which by the way is nothing."

"Colette, we were never an US. You wanted something more serious. I didn't. It's been over two years! I'm sorry if I hurt you but at the time you didn't seem too upset. You were in the business then? How could I have not known? Give yourself up. The police are on their way as we speak."

She laughed as she pointed her gun at them. "What do you have behind your back? Drop it now!" Jean Paul knew he had to make a move she was so close to firing. She took aim. He pushed Mariah out of the way, brought his SIG up and shots rang out. Colette dropped to the floor in a pool of blood. It was apparent that she was dead. Mariah ran to Jean Paul who stood still. Things seemed to happen in slow motion in Patrick's brain. Jean Paul dropped his gun and put his arms around Mariah and kissed her.

"*Je t'aime.*"

"I love you, too. I love you, too," Mariah felt him slowly go down. She couldn't hold him. Patrick saw what was happening and caught him before he fell revealing a large red spot on the front of his sweater.

"OH GOD, NO! Jean Paul!" Mariah placed her hands over the area. His breathing was ragged.

"Mariah, I am sorry for all this. This is my fault. I knew her long before we meet. She wanted more than I did. She only wanted what I could give her and I didn't want to give. I did not know what she was doing. I did not see her very long."

"Shhh. Don't talk. The police are coming. We'll get you to the hospital. You're going to be fine." Mariah was crying and kissing him. "Stay with me, please I need you, Abigail needs you."

Patrick could tell things weren't good. He was bleeding out too fast. Jean Paul stared straight ahead of him, his eyes widened a little.

"What do you want of me?" he asked softly. Mariah and Patrick looked at each other.

"What did you say?" Mariah was cradling his head in her lap.

"Wainscott." Patrick moved in front of him.

"I'm here."

"She is still in danger. Get her out of here."

"NO! I won't go without you. I'm taking you to the hospital. I won't leave you."

"Wainscott, it is up to you now." He turned his eyes to Mariah. "*Mon amour*, I will always be with you. Remember our wedding vows. Being married to you has been more than words can express. The children need you." He spaced out again. Mariah looked at him.

"Jean Paul, what children, you mean Abigail?"

"Don't you see them?" he asks, pointing to the air just to Patrick's right. Mariah looked but there was nothing there. She couldn't see the image of Angelina and his mother standing beside them.

"Who?"

"I understand but she is stubborn." Jean Paul was talking to the air again. Mariah and Patrick looked around and then at each other confused. It was obvious he was seeing something but no one else could. Patrick thought he must have been hallucinating due to the pain. Jean Paul grimaced and turned his attention back to his wife.

"Mariah you must promise me something. Tell Abigail about her heritage. *Mère* is proud of her and so is Angelina. Our Abigail has two guardian angels to watch over her and I will be yours. We will be together but not yet. The children are more important." Patrick moved over to the side.

"Abigail will know her father and his family. You WILL watch her grow up. Jean Paul, please don't leave me. I need you! She needs you!"

"I will be with you until eternity ends. Hold me closer, let me feel your softness." She held him as tight as she could, tears rolling down her face uncontrollably. He looked at her and said, "*Je t'aime*. You have made my life complete." She gave him a long kiss.

"And mine, too." She felt his body ease and she pulled him even closer to her. The sound that came out of her was not human. She screamed "NO! DON"T LEAVE ME," as she sat there rocking him back and forth. Her words echoed through the vast space.

Damn it, Patrick thought and he cursed under his breath, his opinion of the Count had softened a bit since this whole deal went down. He knew there was nothing left for them to do there. He still heard the Count's words "to get her out of there, she's in danger" and that's what he was going to do. All of this had taken place in a matter of a few short minutes. The police pulled up outside. He tried to pull Mariah off of the Count but she wouldn't let go.

"Come on, there's nothing we can do for him now. We'll come back and get him, I promise. We have to get downstairs to the police. Come on, damn it, we've got to go." He forced her to lay down the Count's body. He picked up their guns and put them in his waistband. They were out the door and halfway down the staircase when a man's voice rang out.

"Stop it right there." They stopped and started to turn around. "Put your guns down NOW or I'll shoot." Patrick didn't move, he tried to keep Mariah close to him. "I said throw down your weapons." The man clicked his gun.

"All right," Patrick did as he was told. With his back to the gun he had no idea of where it was pointed at, at him or Mariah but he wasn't going to take a chance on it. Where were the police? They must have started searching in the first warehouse.

"Good, now move!" The man had both Mariah and Patrick captive. He was afraid to make a move with Mariah so close. The man took them back upstairs and into another room and shoved them both toward the far wall. Mariah was racking her brain. She knew that voice but who was it?

"Countess, it's regrettable that you came into all this, but there isn't anything we can do about that. Colette had her say evidently, and now I must finish her work. Turn around Countess I want to look at the woman who irritated my wife so much. Keep your hands up, both of you. I want only her to turn around."

Mariah didn't want to but that voice was too close to her. She had to know. She turned slowly and the expression on both her and the gunman was astonishment.

"Sam!"

"Oh Shit!" Her brother couldn't believe his eyes. "This can't be true. Not you?" Patrick turned around slowly. Did he hear her right? Did she call her brother's name?"

"It is you!" Patrick said in disbelief. Sam laughed.

"And it's you," referring to Patrick.

Sam's hand wavered a tad. He shook his head. "Now what am I going to do?"

"What happened to you? How did you get mixed up with all this?" Mariah put her hands down and took a step toward him.

"Why? I had to do something to make money didn't I? Dad spent everything he had on that dress shop of yours. I got nothing remember. So I got into the import, export business."

"I would have helped you if I knew where you were, but you left. I didn't know where you were."

"Sam, put the gun down. The police are already here. It's just a matter of minutes before they find us." Patrick took a step closer. Sam pointed the gun at Patrick and he stood still.

"Sam, why did you go along with this? We're family. We're flesh and blood."

"Colette was my family. You see, I enjoy a rather nice life style due to her efforts." Sam started laughing, "Now it's all mine. I thank you for that."

"Why, Sam?"

"Why not, I have everything I have ever wanted in my life. You? How did you get involved? Colette told me that she had the Countess locked up?"

"I am the Countess." The weight of it all bared down on her, her anger flashed at him. "You and your wife killed my husband! He was the best thing that ever happened to me." Her words cut Patrick but he had to concentrate on what was important here, their lives.

"Hum, sorry sis, but that's business. Now you know how I feel- I mean felt about poor Colette."

"I don't know you. You're just as vindictive and cold blooded as your asinine wife. I'm glad Jean Paul killed her. She deserved to die. Do you know how many people you've hurt? How many children?" Her voice carried through the warehouse. When she felt she was pushed to her limits she started yelling and throwing things and she was at that point.

"Everyone is someone's child," Sam replied smugly.

She started to lunge toward him and Sam pointed his gun at her. Patrick grabbed her and pulled her down just in time. The bullet just missed her. She sat on the floor stunned that her brother would do such a thing. Patrick stood up. He had to do something.

"Sam, I know we've not always seen eye to eye on things, but for God's sake don't do this. Too many people have been hurt in this. Don't make matters worse. Give yourself up, we'll do what we can to help."

"It's too late for that," Sam laughed. "No one can help me or you two now. Turn around both of you." Patrick's heart started to race. He was going to shoot them in their back. Sam didn't even have the guts to watch them die. The Count had the foresight to make him wear the vest but Mariah didn't have one. She was unprotected. He owed it to the Count to protect her if he could. He gave his life for her.

"Sam don't do this. She's the mother of your niece."

Sam's eyes darted from Patrick to Mariah. "Is that so? I have a niece. Well, well, I would have thought the Count didn't have anything left in him to father a child at his age." He thought for a second. "I can't do anything about it. This work is done. Turn around NOW." Patrick and Mariah turned around. He grabbed her and pushed down in front of him. He didn't mean to push her so hard but she hit her head on the floor. Somewhere behind them a door opened and a gun went off at the same time. Mariah was either out of it or scared to move. Patrick stood still waiting for the impact but didn't receive one.

"*Monsieur* Wainscott, are you all right?" Detective Lamoure's voice rang out.

Patrick looked around, the room was filled with police. He glanced at Sam lying on the cold floor. The bullet penetrated his right temple. He opted to kill himself instead of them. Patrick turned back to where Mariah was. Detective Lamoure' was helping her to sit up. Detectives Willington and Morgan were working the scene.

"Countess. It's all over. You're safe."

"Sam? Patrick?" Patrick knelt down in front of her.

"Baby, it's okay."

"Are you hit?"

"No, he committed suicide." Her eyes darted from the detective, to Patrick, to Sam, where a police officer was covering his face.

"I know this guy, it looks like we've finally got both Samuel Ruemont and his wife Colette Gisgardé. They've evaded us well, until now."

"If they were married, why the different last names?" another officer asked as he took notes.

"They were the head of a multimillion dollar drug operation. It was harder to track them if they had different identities," Detective Willington stated as he approached them. The other police office got up, shook his head and started to mark the floor.

"Detective, his real name was Samuel Remmington. He was her brother," Patrick interceded. Lamouré gave Patrick a look of question.

"Countess, is that correct?" he asked.

Mariah shook her head, "*Non*, this man is not my brother. I don't know him and never did." She stood up, started to the door and stopped keeping her back to the scene. She suddenly realized that her hands and clothes were smeared with her husband's blood, the blood that he shed for her. She wept but not for her brother, but for husband and the life they would never share. Mariah couldn't think about what they were saying concerning her brother. Her thoughts were about her husband. "Jean Paul, I love you," she said to herself as she walked through the door.

Patrick and Detective Lamouré looked at each other. There was nothing either one could do to stop her pain. Patrick was steadying her as she swayed a little.

Detective Lamouré accompanied them to the waiting ambulance. Then he went back to the scene, he would see to it that even in death the Count would be given the respect he deserved. He could at least do that much for his friend of many years and for the Countess. It was upon Jean Paul's request that he had been assigned to the case. The Count had called him when all hell broke lose concerning the trunks. If only he had been able to save all three of them. His heart was full of sadness.

CHAPTER 22

The estate in Marseille was full of people. At the top of the staircase hung the wedding portrait that Katelin had done of Mariah and Jean Paul holding little Abigail. It occupied the empty space beside Countess Abigail's portrait. Upon hearing of Jean Paul's the death, his friend the Pope had sent the Cardinal that had presided over their marriage to conduct his funeral and entombment in the family's chapel and mausoleum. The same chapel they were married in a little more than two weeks ago. How life had changed in the past few weeks for Mariah. Mariah sat in the corner of their bedroom with Abigail on her lap. She reflected on her joys with Jean Paul and all the stupid time she wasted trying to figure things out, their wonderful time they spent together as man and wife and now to her life without him. She had spent time downstairs with people she didn't know but was amazed how many lives her husband had touched. They all offered her consolation but no one could bring Jean Paul back to her. Guy and Katelin showed their concern for her but she didn't want to be watched. She didn't want anyone around her but Jean Paul and Abigail. She still felt his presence, his love. Her dream last night when he came to her was so vivid, so real. She woke up expecting him to be lying beside her. Her hand explored his side of the bed. Oddly there was an indentation on his side but the sheets weren't warm. She cried and cried and now she was crying again. A knock came on the door.

"Please go away. I'm not taking any visitors." The door opened anyway. Patrick and Charlie stood in the entrance.

"Hi. Can we come in?" Mariah looked up but didn't say anything. They walked in, Charlie on a cane since his leg was in a cast. Patrick got a chair for him and put it beside Mariah and the baby. He leaned against the wall. His eyes assessed the room. HIS room and hers, he felt like he shouldn't be in here giving his feelings for Mariah but he couldn't leave her alone up there. He had to see her. She had kept her distance from everyone since they had arrived home from the warehouse. Guy, Katelin, and Margarette were the only ones that she would talk to. Charlie took her hand and nodded to Patrick to take the baby. She let Abigail go to him and she started sobbing as Charlie put his arms around her. Becky entered the room and knelt beside them and embraced Mariah. Patrick left the room with Abigail. It was too much for him to see her hurting this way. She really did love HIM!

A few days later the family gathered in Jean Paul's library. Patrick, Charlie, Becky, Edmund and Tré were there for support for Mariah but sat in the back of the room. Jean Paul's will was being read. He had left the winery to his brother, Guy. He also stated that if he chose to leave the winery or the family business that he would have to turn it all over to Mariah first. Nothing could be sold unless all was in agreement. He stated in his will, that if the winery was managed right it would more than take care of Guy and his family's needs and more left over. He had faith that his brother could handle such a task and the land would stay in the family for more generations.

He left the main estate in Marseille to Mariah. She also had full control over the factory and both of their design lines. There would be no changes for Tré or Edmund in production except they were to consult with Mariah instead of him. Mariah and their children, Abigail included, inherited his entire estate leaving them very wealthy.

A week later Mariah, Abigail, Guy, and Katelin stood on their private runway. The jet was ready. Alec and Frederick were waiting for their passengers.

"Are you sure you won't come home with us?" Becky asked Mariah as she played with Abigail. Charlie and Patrick are standing beside her thanking Guy and Katelin for the hospitality. Patrick asked them to please watch over Mariah and Abigail, and if she needed anything to call him. They understood.

"I can't. This is my home."

"You have two homes." Charlie hugged Mariah.

"But don't you see, Charlie, he's still here. This is our home. This is where we belong." Becky understood what she was saying and nodded.

"Please don't forget sweetheart, we love you. You can come home anytime you want." Mariah just smiled. She kissed them both and they walked toward the plane. Patrick stayed behind. Guy and Katelin headed back to the estate.

"Baby, come home with us."

"No, Patrick, I need to be here."

"I'm concerned about you."

"There's no need, Patrick. Jean Paul is still here. I feel him everywhere. You know you owe him, too."

"I know baby, I know. He was a good man. He loved you and Abigail very much."

"I found these." She held out the last letter Jean Paul had written to her. "I think he wanted to keep reminding me of his love." She started to cry again. "I think he knew I would need it to get through this." Patrick hugged her. "I also found a set of tapes for Abigail but for some reason he referred to her as our children. He told her how much he loved her and what joy she had brought to his life. Did you know he even sang to her on them? He had a wonderful voice." Patrick shook his head.

"Please baby, come with me. Things will be better if you don't have all these reminders around. I love you."

"No! Abigail and I are staying. This is where we belong." She wiped the tears from her face and stood tall. "I never had the chance to say thank you for saving my life. You and Jean Paul had your differences but in some ways were just alike. Have a safe flight." She smiled a bittersweet smile, she turned, and started up the brick walk toward the gardens and the estate. Patrick sighed. His heart was breaking, too. He had lost her and he knew it.

Charlie had come up behind him and patted him on the back. "Come on buddy, we can't change her mind at this point. She needs to grieve in her own way. We can't do anything for her but be there if she calls. Katelin and Guy assure me they'll look after them." Patrick nodded. A single tear fell as he walked away. Charlie was right, there was nothing else he could do.

///////////////////////////

Mariah, Abigail, and the baby were sitting by the window watching the waves crash against the rocks. Avondale, New England was a small peaceful town situated on the coastline. It gave the solitude and break that Mariah needed from the hustle and bustle of carrying on her and Jean Paul's work to promote better lifestyles around the world, as well as their design adventures. Edmund and Tré had continued to carry on Jean Paul's line and for the second time in a row she had made the top ten designer's list.

Mariah stayed in the three-bedroom cottage most of the time for the past three weeks. This was a place that she had never shared with Jean Paul and she missed not having his things around for comfort. On the coffee table sat their wedding photographs, Abigail had gotten them out the night before and wanted to look at them. Mariah spent most of her time tending to the children and conducting what boutique business that had to be done. She had asked Michael to serve in the capacity of her bodyguard after his wounds had healed and Margarette still as a nanny accompanied her everywhere she went. She was afraid to be alone, mostly for the children's safety but maybe for herself, too. She wouldn't allow those thoughts to creep inside her mind very far but the kidnapping and Jean Paul's death was something she was trying to deal with. Dr. Sarah McKracken had given her name of a friend who was practicing in Marseille to help her through the rough times.

Katelin, carrying a tray of lemonade in the room, sat it down on the table. She handed a glass to Mariah. Margarette stayed in the kitchen allowing Katelin to visit with her sister-in-law in private.

"The ocean is pretty today, isn't it?" Katelin said as she sat down by the window.

"Hum, there's strength in those waves. I just wish it wasn't so cold, we'd go for a walk," Mariah spoke softly still gazing out the window.

"If you want to go, I'll be more than glad to watch the kids. I'll tell Michael." Katelin started to get up. Michael, hearing his name mentioned, came in to the living room from the kitchen. He stood in the doorway waiting, ready to give assistance.

"No, what kind of hostess would I be if I did that." She took Katelin's hand and held it. She sat down on the hassock beside her.

"Mariah, I know this past year has been a hard one. It's been full of joys and sorrows. I have something to say to you. I feel we've gotten really close this past year so I'm taking the liberty to talk to you like this."

"Katelin, you know how I feel about you. You're the sister I never had. You, Guy, and the kids are the family I never had. I thought we could talk about anything together."

"I'm glad to hear you say that. You know how we feel about you and of course the children. So here it is, please don't get mad but we are concerned about something."

"What?"

"We- Guy and I have been thinking."

"Jean Paul would want you to be happy honey. He would want his children to be happy." Mariah gave her a frown.

"Dear Katelin, you know we're okay. Have I told you? He knew we were having a child. He told me before he died at the warehouse. He said I had to go on for the children. I didn't know what he was talking about. I thought he meant keeping the world's children safe from drugs."

"I know honey, you've told me. And you've done well with your efforts for the cause and all the others you've entered into on behalf of Jean Paul. You've continued in Jean Paul's footsteps well. But that's not what I'm talking about. Mariah, again, we love you and the kids. Our lives would have a great hole in it if we didn't have you so please try to understand why I'm talking to you like this. Guy thought it may be better if we talked about it woman to woman," Katelin continued. "Michael, my dear, please leave us." He nodded and went outside.

"What? Please, just say what's on your mind." Mariah asked shaking her head from side to side.

Katelin put Abigail in her playpen and lay Jean Paul Noel in his carrier. He looks just like his father, everything about Noel was his father the Count. Katelin still couldn't get over the resemblance. She took both of Mariah's hands in hers. "Honey, Jean Paul would have wanted you to be happy. You're not and its time that changes. I know you've poured yourself into work and the kids but you need to do something for yourself now. You're doing a wonderful job with the kids but you need to start living again. Don't grieve any more. Jean Paul wouldn't want this for you." Mariah looked at her and frowned.

"I have been living."

"No, you haven't. Have you even seen your friends since you've been back?"

"No."

"Have you even spoken to them?"

"No, I just want to be.."

"Mariah you can't just "BE" anymore. I've called *Monsieur* and *Madame* Osswell. They know you're back. You have to fight back, fight back for the life that filled you. That is what attracted Jean Paul to you. You know he told me that soon after he met you. He loved the fire in you. You're not a woman without a spine. He told me he felt like you gave him his life back when you two met. You did give him so much- now show him the gift he gave you, your life full of love and happiness.

Noel started crying, Mariah got up to see to him. "Margarette, please come and get the baby," Katelin called out. Margarette took the children into their bedroom. She had been listening to their conversation and was crying herself. She prayed that Katelin would get through to Mariah. Jean Paul's death had taken something out of her and Margarette wondered if it would ever be found again.

"Katelin, I think he gave me more than I did to him but I thank you for your concern. Really I am fine. I just need a little vacation with the kids. You know I still feel him around me even after all this time, even here. I do have plans for my future. I do. I have a full plate to contend to, you know that."

"I know but do those plans include happiness?"

"Of course, they do. I'm the Countess." Mariah smiled.

"Honey, see you're friends. Contact *Monsieur* Wainscott. He called for you last week, you remember? Start living again. You owe it to Jean Paul. He gave his life for you to LIVE, not just exist! And that's what you're doing. You're NOT living. I don't want to be harsh but we can't seem to get through to you any other way. We love you, Mariah. You are one of us and always will be. You have to move on, you have to trust the people you love again. Did you really have a brother all those years, personally, I don't think so, but you have a family with us. We want you to live again, live for Jean Paul. Get your life back before you can't." Katelin's words struck a nerve in Mariah. She stood up and took a deep breath.

"Michael, stay with the children. I want to be alone." She took her jacket off the hook by the door and slammed the door behind her. She had to go for a walk to cool off. How dare her to say that to her. That was cold and callus.

An hour and half later Mariah walked in the back door of the cottage, cold and wet from the ocean's mist. Michael was starting to get worried about her and had just put his coat on to search for her. "Are you alright Countess?" he asked as she entered the kitchen. Mariah smiled and touched his shoulder in thanks as she brushed past him to hang her jacket on the hook. He took it from her and hung it up.

Margarette had put on a large kettle of vegetable soup. The aroma filled the air. Her mood was better at least. She came through the kitchen door expecting to find Katelin, Margarette, and the kids in the living room playing but instead she found Charlie and Becky.

"Hi, sweetheart," Charlie greeted her. He held her tight. Becky came up and joined the two of them.

"Oh my gosh! I can't believe you two are here." She hugged Becky then back away. "Are you pregnant? When are you due?" Mariah was happy for them.

"In April," Becky replied smiling and hugging her friend.

"Why didn't you tell me?"

"Forgive us, but we wanted to wait before we told anyone, you know the old jinx thing," Charlie said as Mariah gave him a hug, too.

"I'm so happy for you guys. Come sit down, let's talk."

Katelin and Margarette excused themselves as they went to the bedroom and closed the door giving Mariah time alone with her friends. Michael decided to go outside for a smoke.

"What brings you guys here?"

"Abigail's birthday is soon. Do you think we'd let that go by without doing something for her?"

"No sir, we brought presents, we brought cake, ice cream, hats, and blow things- whatever they're called. We got it all!" Becky proudly stated.

Katelin headed back to Bordeaux, France the next day. She had reminded Mariah that their home was her home. She and both the children were part of their family no matter where she was. She was, after all, the Countess and nothing would change that fact. Mariah told her she would be back home, that she still had business to do in France but for now she needed this solitude. Katelin kissed her goodbye and got in the taxi that was waiting to take her to the airport where Alec and Frederick were waiting. She could only hope that Becky and Charlie could reach Mariah, where she and Guy couldn't.

Sitting at the kitchen table with the children playing beside them, Mariah and Becky were talking. Charlie had gone for a walk along the coast.

"He is so precious. I just can't get over his looks."

"I know, Becky. There are times he looks at me and I swear Jean Paul is looking at me through his eyes"

"Maybe he is," Becky replied and was quiet for a few seconds. "I do have a question. If his name is Jean Paul why do you call him Noel? Where did that come from?"

"Noel- it's an old French-Latin name that's used unisexually now, it means Christmas. He was conceived at Christmas. He was Jean Paul's present to me." Becky smiled and held Mariah's hand. Her lip quivered but she didn't cry.

"You know everyone missed not having your style show this year."

"Maybe next year, Claude and Margo couldn't arrange it with Edmund and Tré in time and I didn't want to leave France because of the baby. It seemed something was always getting in the way."

"Why don't you come back to Crystal River, you can see how the boutique is doing?"

"I don't know. How is every body there?"

"Fine, Margo is still plugging away."

Mariah nodded. "The reports that I get shows both boutiques are doing well. Edmund and Tré do a good job keeping me posted on their end of things. I talk to Margo and Daphne once a week unless something comes up."

"I get the feeling you're asking about someone else at home? What you mean is how's Patrick doing?" Mariah didn't say anything.

"Sweetie, its okay to say his name. Jean Paul wouldn't mind. It was he that told him to take care of you, remember? I think in the end they had some kind of understanding by what Patrick has said off and on." Mariah raised her eyes from Noel to Becky.

"What do you mean?"

"I think Patrick was given an insight to Jean Paul and knows what you two had and I think he accepts it now."

"REALLY?"

Becky nodded yes, "You know he's still living at the ranch. Nothing has changed. Jezebel is still there waiting for you. I know he's glad that everything went fine with Noel's birth. He was really concerned about the pregnancy, given Abigail's, but he knew you were in good hands with Dr. Rantoul. We all were. He told us that he was disappointed you were in Paris on business when he went over to see Abigail last summer. That he didn't get to see you."

"I heard somewhere that he was serious about Amy, that they're getting married."

"No, not at all. You know how those tabloids are. He was seeing Amy there for a while but it wasn't that serious, at least not on his part. She's the one that mentioned they were dating to the press and you know the rest- how things get twisted up so easily. Now she's with some big attorney in Los Angeles. Don't get me wrong- he's dating off and on but nobody special and definitely not on a steady basis. He spends most of his time at the ranch when he's not gone for a film of course. He's changed, too. He's more reserved than he used to be. Call him. I know he wants to see Abigail. Wait a minute." She left the table and brought back two wrapped packages and handed them to Mariah.

"What's this?"

"Open them."

Mariah read the tag on the larger package. It was for Abigail's birthday. She opened it and pulled out a huge teddy bear. It was as big as Abigail. The tag on the little package was a late birthday present to her. She opened it and smiled. Inside was a music box of two glass angels holding an infant and a small child- the angels were of a man and of a woman- she knew instantly it signified Jean Paul and his mother-Abigail, as guardian angels over little Abigail and Noel.

The scene played in her head where Patrick would have taken Sam's bullet for her. She had been wrong about being able to trust Patrick ever again but things were different now. When Jean Paul died in her arms, she went over that cliff of normality. It was her children that held her together.

Mariah did a lot of soul searching after Katelin, Charlie, and Becky's visit. They were all right about what her life had become. She had stopped living. She had lost herself somehow but was she ready to find that woman again? To be the woman that Jean Paul fell in love with again? Was she brave enough to try?

She, Abigail, and Noel was sitting in a field of cornflowers. The wind was blowing softly and Abigail was toddling around trying to catch the blossoms as they danced. She held Noel in her arms. The sun was warm on Mariah's face as she had a sense that suddenly they were not alone. Where was Michael she thought? Then she thought she caught a whiff of HIS favorite cologne that he wore. It couldn't be. There wasn't any way it could be possible or was it? She turned to her right and there she saw Jean Paul sitting quietly beside her. She sat there not saying or doing anything but just looking in amazement at him. He smiled and his voice rang out in her head. "*Mon amour*."

"Jean Paul? Is it really you?"

"*Oui*, it is. I have tried to reach you many times but until now you were not receptive. My time is short."

"I have missed you so much." She started to reach for him but he moved away. She pulled her hand back and frowned.

"*Mon amour*, you have to listen to what I say. I am disappointed with you."

"*Moi*? What have I done?" His thoughts almost crushed her and tears were starting to well up in her eyes. "Have I not carried on your work, our work, as we would have together? Have I disappointed you as a mother? Look at our children, they are well and happy." Abigail was still playing and Noel was sleeping in her arms.

"*Mon amour*, you have done well with the duties of being a Countess and the demands of your career and as the mother of our children just like I knew you would. I was there with you when Noel was born as I have been many other times. It is not that I speak of, it is your personal life."

"I don't understand? Please don't hurt me like this."

"*Mon amour*, I am not trying to hurt you. I could not do that. Listen to me, feel my love surge through your body." Mariah did feel him, feel his love as it engulfed her. Noel moved slightly in her arms and smiled in his sleep. She had the impression he felt it, too, as she looked down at him. "You are a vibrant woman, one who deserves to be loved fully, one who deserves to give love to another. Your heart is full of that love but you won't allow yourself to do so."

"I do love my family."

"I am talking about the love that only two people share, that intimate love."

"I don't want that. I love only you."

"We will have our time again, but not until you see my grandchildren. Our children will do well because of you. Time is but a fleeting moment where I am. We will share again but until then, do not isolate yourself like this. Do not mourn me like this. Celebrate what we had on earth. Celebrate our children and their children. Honor me this way, not the way you have. Trust your friends, trust your family again, and trust HIM." For a brief second she thought she saw Patrick in Jean Paul's face. She blinked and the image was gone. "They all love you."

"I know that."

"GO HOME, Mariah! You cannot avoid him. Do not be afraid. He is not that man you knew. I will always be with you no matter where you go or who you are with. Your soul is tied to mine. Open yourself up to the love of the universe, feel the continuation of my love for you and the children and take comfort in it but open your heart to the love that is there waiting for you and the children. GO HOME. Be happy until we live together again. I will be with you and our children until eternity, but be complete now. I must go." He blew her a kiss.

"No, please don't."

"I must- but remember this not as a dream but my eternal love. BE HAPPY. *Je t'aime.*" Mariah blinked and he was gone. She reached to the spot where he was sitting and felt a tingle in her fingertips. His love still filled her mind, body and soul, he was really there, and she knew it. Abigail came running up to her laughing and holding a cornflower in her hands. Mariah woke with the sun coming in the window striking her face. It was morning already.

Three weeks later Mariah stepped out of the taxi with both children in hand. The jet was late getting in; it was after midnight. She dropped Michael and Margarette at their rooms at the Crystal Inn before she left town. The taxi driver helped her up to the door with her baby bag, seeing how both children were asleep in her arms. He rang the bell a couple of times and stepped back setting the baby bag on the porch.

Patrick came downstairs bare chested and miffed that someone was at his door at this time of night. Ginger was padding down the stairs at his heels wagging her tail. He was tying his sweatpants at the waist when he opened the door, his eyes wide with disbelief and happiness as she said hello and walked inside with the children. He brought the baby bag in and closed the door behind them.

ABOUT THE AUTHOR

Rita lives in Indiana with her husband and two children. She is formally trained as a Veterinary Technician.

In the summer of 2002, she became inspired to write *TORMENTED DREAMS* due to an actual dream she experienced. Some may say *TORMENTED DREAMS* was divinely inspired and the growth one experiences in her book is both spiritually and emotional. The storyline poured forth feeding upon itself. She had not felt this type of inspiration before- the urgency for *TORMENTED DREAMS* to be born.

Her style in this contemporary romance suspense is totally captivating, and the character's life's easily become yours. She gives you the sense of "immediacy".

Rita has discovered an untapped talent that lay dormant until this point.

Printed in the United States
17226LVS00003B/37